MW00652173

Edited by Mike Myers

By

Rob J. Hayes

Once mighty, twice broken, cursed hunter of the dead.
Both beyond and seeking, in service to the grave. A battle
even by time forgotten.

What words can mean no words can say. A vow before god
unbroken.
Stained by sin with ink run red, a purpose much thicker
than water.

A reflected face reveals the mirror's truth, shattered into
nothing but edges.
Familial ties, a mother's love, vengeance for all those beyond
saving.

All embers die leaving ashen remains, yet dead sparks can be
rekindled.
A heart passed on, no flesh to bind. Before gods and
monsters waiting.

Once killed, twice lost, a remnant beyond harness or
taming.
With vengeance for skin and purpose for soul, a fleeting
memory of all that was taken.

Prologue

The school burned. Konihashi, the Fifth Sage Under Heaven, paced through halls thick with flames and smoke. There was no saving his beloved academy now. The fires had spread too fast, unnaturally so. His students screamed of terrifying figures in the courtyard, his fellow teachers of a serpent wreathed in black fire. The Onryo had come for him. Everything was his fault, and he had to stop it.

The Fifth Sage Under Heaven stepped from the flames of his burning school and out into the frigid night air. Snow and ash fell black and white into the courtyard, covering the ground with grey sludge underfoot. Across the slushy ground and falling snow, just a dozen paces away, the Onryo waited for him. There were four of them, each one a monster.

"He's so ancient," said an immense woman, crouched on her haunches and straining at the confines of her hanfu. Two segmented spider legs reached over her shoulders, each one plucking at the air like the strings of an invisible koto. She smiled at him, and Konihashi saw serrated fangs glistening behind ruby lips. "The old ones always taste of dust and lemons."

The tall man beside her groaned. "Must you always prattle on about eating?" He had a perfumed beauty at odds with the surrounding wreckage and wore a woman's kimono. His long hair floated around his head and shoulders as though he were underwater, each braid tipped with a vicious metal barb.

"Quiet!" said a hideously ugly man squatting on his haunches. Flames flew like spittle from his mouth when he spoke, and he leered at Konihashi with goggling eyes. He was bald and short even in platformed wooden clogs, and his round belly poked out of his robe. Flames drooled from the corner of his mouth like saliva, melting the snow at his feet and scorching the ground black. "This is the sagey-sage we're here to find." He glanced sideways at the last figure.

The last onryo wore a white robe and said nothing. Dark smoke from the burning academy surged along the snow toward them, pooling beneath their robe and billowing out from their sleeves. Their hood was up and there was nothing within but an empty void.

"Where is your master?" Konihashi said. If he was to fight the Onryo, he would fight them all at once. He would defeat them once and for all, make them pay for their atrocities.

Konihashi took a few steps toward them. His years hung heavy on him, and his body ached from a fatigue only ancient bones could know. His kimono was stained with soot and scorched by fire, his walking stick blackened by the flames. Despite his age, his qi roared within him like an inferno that made the burning academy seem a dying ember.

The white-robed figure glided closer on a blanket of smoke. Golden swirls of winds and cloud patterning crawled along the robe. "Tell us where to find the final prison, Sage." A woman's voice scratched from the darkness of the hood.

"Never!" He was the only one left who knew the location of the final prison. The Century Blade was dead. The Gilded Crone was gone. The Ticking Clock was worse than dead. If the Fifth Sage Under Heaven was to join them, so be it. He'd guard the secret to the grave, just as they all had.

The fat woman chuckled, her massive body shaking, and two more spider legs stretched out from behind her, tugging at fine strands of silk. "I can make him talk," she said.

The beautiful man sighed. "Please no, Xifeng. You always leave such a dreadful mess."

The squat man stood up to his full, inconsiderable height, leering at the white-robed woman. "*He* put you in charge of this mission, Crow." Flames spat from his mouth with each word. "How do you want to play this?"

Smoke billowed out from the woman, creeping around the

courtyard, winding between her companion's legs, staining the snow a dirty grey. "Not all of your students escaped, Sage," she said. One of the smoky tendrils dragged a struggling boy from behind them. A young Cochtan lad, Dorje. Ash and soot blackened his uniform. His hands, feet, and mouth were bound by thick strands of silken webbing. The tentacle of smoke lifted him up by his wrists, dangling him before the robed woman, and then threw him at Xifeng's swollen feet. "Tell me where to find the prison or my sister will devour the boy."

Konihashi sighed. They left him no choice. He knew the Onryo would come for him, but he had hoped they would leave the students out of it. It was a foolish old man's hope. He had condemned them all. "Look at me, Dorje." The boy's tear-filled eyes met the Sage's; there was nothing but wild, animal fear in them. "I am sorry."

Konihashi raised his hand and flicked a falling snowflake with his finger. The flake flashed toward Dorje and vanished, piercing his chest and heart as surely as an arrow. The boy tensed and then relaxed, a red stain already seeping into the slush beneath him. Konihashi hated it, but he had no choice. The boy's life was nothing compared to the havoc the Onryo would unleash upon the world if he didn't stop them.

"Aww, that was mean," Xifeng said sulkily, dark spider eyes staring at Konihashi. "They taste so much sweeter when alive." Her spider legs were already pawing at Dorje's body, silken strands shining in the flickering fire light as she wrapped a cocoon around his corpse.

Konihashi took another step forward, feet crunching the snow beneath him. He stood up to his full height and felt his old bones crack with the strain, his muscles aching with the effort. They thought him weak because he was old. Thought him infirm because he stooped. They would soon learn the Fifth Sage Under Heaven was still a force unrivalled. "I will never give up the prison. Not to monsters like you." He let his qi flow. Snow and ash blasted away, swirling around him, caught in the invisible currents of his power.

Dark wings fluttered above Konihashi, and something heavy thumped to the ground behind him. He glanced over his shoulder and grimaced. The master of the Onryo had come for him.

Chapter 1

Haruto pushed open the tavern door to a motley collection of hostile stares, exaggerated shivers, and one bearded bear of a man frozen with his drink halfway to his mouth. He took a single step inside the tavern and kicked the caked snow from his sandals. He eyed each of the patrons, hand on his katana. They were all men, some wearing kimonos, others still in their work aprons. The owner fretted over a clay cup, wiping at it with all the vigour of a newly wedded couple. Snow drifted in behind Haruto, settling on the floor.

"Out the way, old man," Guang growled, shoving Haruto in the back and sending him stumbling into the tavern. "It's colder than a snowman's shoulder out there."

Guang Meng bustled inside and slammed the door behind him, then shook the snow from his heavy fur cloak and hung it on a hook next to the door. The tableau broken, the tavern lurched back into life. Conversations resumed and the two newcomers were all but forgotten. Guang had a wonderful habit of putting folk at ease, even without trying.

They found an empty table in the corner, as close to the fire as they could manage, and Haruto knelt before it. He took his five ritual staffs from the holster on his back and leaned them against the wall behind him. Then he slid his katana, saya and all, from his belt and laid it on the floor next to him. Always within reach. A shintei should never be without their sword, not that he was a shintei anymore. Hadn't been for so long he'd almost forgotten the rituals. Guang all but collapsed on a pillow by the table and then set to lounging. He stretched his legs out and rubbed his cracking knees.

"Have I mentioned I hate Ipia?" Guang asked quietly as he

struggled to get comfortable. He was a small man who wore his age like a ratty old cloak, loved well enough to keep, though it stank of mildew and was held together by a few threads and a handful of hope.

"Once or twice," Haruto said, smiling. "Today at least. You've been quite reserved for a change."

"Would chairs be such an imposition?" Guang said as he brushed ice out of his patchy beard. He'd long since lost his hair, but he loved his failing attempt at a beard. He claimed it kept his face warm, even as he complained about the cold.

"If we had chairs, you wouldn't be able to reach the table," Haruto offered unhelpfully.

Guang grunted and wriggled about on the pillow, folding one leg under him, then trying the other. "Cabbage!" he swore. "At least give us a bigger cushion."

"I hate that vow of yours," Haruto said. He ran a hand through his long hair, shaking out the snow that clung there. He shivered as a chunk of ice slivered down his back.

"I don't give a turnip what you hate, old man," Guang said and chuckled.

The owner arrived and bowed to them. A tall man with a cherubic face and kind eyes, he glanced at the ritual staffs against the wall and his eyebrows jumped like a bean on a drum. "What can I get you?"

"We'll start with two bottles of wine," Guang said, finding himself some cheer amongst the grump.

"Three bottles," Haruto corrected his friend. "We'll have company soon enough."

"She's here?" Guang asked, glancing about the tavern. "I don't see her, old man." The owner glanced at the two of them in turn, a question forming on his lips.

Haruto shrugged. "Some food too, whatever you call the house special." He waved a hand in Guang's direction.

Guang fished inside his purse, pulled out five lien, and handed it to the owner with a wink. "I keep the money or the old man will lose it."

"Old man?" the owner asked, glancing between them once more. He gestured at Haruto. "He does not look old, but you..." He fell silent when he saw Guang's glare. "Apologies." The owner bowed low.

Haruto pulled out a little wooden imperial seal from the sleeve of his kimono and held it up. "And if you could hang this in front of the bar while I'm here, I would be grateful."

The owner's eyes lit up like a sunrise. "We have work for you, Master Onmyoji. Wait right here and I'll fetch your food." The man dropped into another respectful bow, then grabbed the seal, and shuffled away.

"Work work work," Guang mused. "What I wouldn't give for a day off."

Haruto scoffed. "One of us has to earn some lien."

"Hah! I'll have you know I'm heavily sought after in Hosa."

"No, you're not."

"Powerful men send me gifts to have me pen their histories."

Haruto rolled his eyes. They'd repeated this conversation every other day since they left Ban Ping. "They really don't."

"Women swoon over my words."

"Not for a good twenty years."

Guang narrowed his eyes at Haruto. "*With hurtful words, the dagger drives deep. But the ice does crack, and beneath, the water runs clear.*"

Haruto chuckled. "You are a terrible poet."

Guang scratched a hand through his beard and nodded. "I admit, it wasn't my best."

The owner brought them three bottles of wine and some cups. Haruto poured a cup for himself and set another aside. After a while, a small tortoise crept out of the kitchen, plodding toward the table. It stopped next to Guang, stared up at the ageing poet, and pawed at the table with one stumpy foot.

Guang glanced at the tortoise. "Do it yourself."

The tortoise made another laboured attempt to raise a foot high enough to mount the table, failed, and looked at Guang once more. Then it opened its mouth and whistled.

With a sigh, Guang whisked the tortoise from the floor, flipped it over and placed it on the table, shell side down. The tortoise flailed at the air with its legs.

"That's a little mean," Haruto said.

Guang scoffed. "She can right herself if she wants to. Just likes to play at being helpless." He leaned down to stare at the little beast, reached out a finger and poked it, setting it spinning around.

With an audible pop, a dark ball of fuzzy hair the size of a kitten leapt free of the tortoise. She looked like a giant dust bunny with wide eyes and thin, hairy legs. She paraded around the table while the tortoise waved its legs about in the air. Shiki was a playful little spirit who loved to possess animals, but she rarely gave much thought to the position she was leaving them in when she gave up the possession. She stared at Guang with wide, glimmering eyes, she pushed a spindly arm out of her furry body and shook it at him, chirruping softly.

"What's she saying?" the old poet asked.

Haruto smiled. "She says you're an ignorant brute."

Guang flipped the tortoise onto its feet, then set it down on the floor. "I shouldn't have bothered asking." The tortoise turned and walked back toward the kitchen.

Shiki gave up her tirade and waddled over to the third cup of wine. Her thin legs never seemed strong enough to hold her weight, and she always seemed so ungainly in her natural form. It was probably why she often possessed animals instead. She sat down on the table in front of the cup of wine, her legs vanishing as if they had never existed, and lifted the cup in unsteady black paws. A wide mouth opened up within the depths of her fur and she swallowed down the wine in one gurgling gulp. She licked her lips, then her mouth vanished as if it had never been there. She'd been Haruto's companion spirit for as long as he cared to remember, but her antics still never failed to make him smile.

"Delightful," Guang said.

Haruto shrugged.

"No no no," the owner said when he arrived carrying two

bowls of what appeared to be steaming broth. "No... uh, animals? They frighten my tortoise."

Shiki glanced up at the owner, blinked at him, and then looked at Haruto and fluted.

"Shiki isn't an animal," Haruto said. It seemed he had this same conversation with every tavern owner in Hosa, Ipia, and Nash. Well, maybe not Nash, but then they didn't even care if you brought a horse into the tavern with you. "She's a spirit."

The tavern owner gawked for a moment, his eyes flicking to Shiki and then again to the ritual staffs against the wall. "A yokai? That's worse."

"She's not a yokai," Haruto argued. "She's a companion spirit. *My* companion spirit."

Guang scoffed. "Yokai cause trouble. She causes trouble. What's the difference?" Shiki glared at him.

"You're not helping, Guang."

The tavern owner stood there red-faced, holding their food hostage.

"Shiki," Haruto said, nodding at her. She stood, twirled around on the spot, leapt up onto Haruto's shoulder, and stared at the owner for a long moment, blinked and vanished. Haruto could still feel her little hairy tail tickling the back of his neck. He'd pay for it later. Shiki hated going invisible.

"I thought your kind kill yokai?" the owner said as he placed the bowls on the table.

Haruto winced. "I'm an onmyoji," he said. "We don't *kill* spirits. Well, we do, but only evil spirits. Yokai mostly. Shiki is not a yokai."

Guang slurped his wine and wiped his face with his shirt sleeve. "I have written a few poems about his deeds. Perhaps *The Battle of Two Bridges*? How did it go? *Two bridges crossed the river Shou, yet only one could you see. The other led to parts unknown--*"

"Guang," Haruto said, shaking his head. Apart from being a terrible poem, it painted neither of them in a bright light.

The tavern owner frowned and then waved another of his

patrons over. A squat fellow with a messy scraggle of hair and an apron so stained with old blood it belonged on a battlefield stood from a crowded table and approached.

"Nobu." The owner gestured to Haruto. "Tell them."

"You sure?" the man in the apron asked.

The owner nodded. "He's an onmyoji, even has the empress's seal." He pointed to the wooden charm Haruto had asked him to hang on the bar.

Nobu glanced at the charm, then at the ritual staffs, and finally at Haruto. "Have you heard of the Wailing Woman?"

Guang chuckled and took another sip of wine. "Have we heard of the Wailing Woman?" He crossed his legs, put his hands on his knees and leaned over the table. He was going to tell a story. "Have you?"

Long ago, before Hosa's ten warring kings and before Cochtan's infernal Blood Engines, the world was a more peaceful place. Hara Chinami, a young woman with eyes like a hawk and hands steady as a buried rock, loved to paint and produced some of the finest works of art Ipia has ever seen. So revered was her skill that Ise Katsuo, the Emperor of Ipia, despite her humble birth, wished to bestow upon her the honour of painting him. To render him immortal with her brush. But Hara looked upon the emperor, and her piercing gaze saw beneath the surface of the man, for that was her true technique – not her skill with the mixing of paints, nor her flourish with the brush, but to see the truth of things. She refused Emperor Ise, declaring that she only painted scenery. Valleys so beautiful none could look upon them without tears, a river so lifelike it swept viewers away upon currents of brush strokes.

Emperor Ise was not pleased. After all, he was the emperor

and nobody refused the emperor. He came to her again the next day and demanded she immortalise him in her vision, make a painting of him so vivid that all who see it would weep. Again she refused, for Hara was strong like the konara trees of Mount Soka, and she was not easily intimidated, not even by the emperor. He was not the first powerful man to make demands of her.

Enraged, Emperor Ise sent soldiers to Hara's house. They dragged poor Hara Chinami away in chains, burned down her home and all her paintings. Inside the palace grounds stood a well long since dried to dust and mud, and into its black depths they threw Hara. Ise Katsuo placed a cover over the well so no light shone down. Until Hara agreed to paint him as only her skill could render, she would see no light, no colour, none of the beauty of nature that so inspired her. She would make art of him, even if he had to break her first.

Hara wept. She had tried to spare the emperor the pain of looking upon his true self, for that was what her brush would reveal. But in refusing him, she had revealed him all the same.

Come the tenth day of Hara Chinami's incarceration, Emperor Ise pulled back the well cover and stared down upon her. She begged him to free her, and he demanded she paint him. Of course, she refused, knowing that to do so would only stoke his ire. For when men like Emperor Ise Katsuo are forced to look upon their genuine selves, they always place the blame for what they see on others. Ise ordered the cover replaced and left Hara to the darkness.

On the fiftieth day of her incarceration, long past Hara's counting, the emperor came to her once more. Again, he demanded she paint him. Again, she refused. She believed he would set her free. For despite the monster she saw in him, she would not do as he asked, and he would see she would not be broken.

Hara was wrong. Emperor Ise replaced the cover and went in search of another artist of equal skill to paint him.

Three years passed and three hundred artists failed to paint

Emperor Ise in the glory he knew he deserved. Compared to the divine skill of Hara Chinami, all others were amateurs. He went to the well, certain that after three years of darkness and isolation, Hara would have no choice but to agree to his demands. But when he pulled back the well cover and stared down into the darkness, it was empty. He sent men into the depths to search for Hara, but they found no sign of her, no tunnel out, no remains. No trace of the woman at all.

That night, a terrible wailing woke everyone in the castle. It came from the walls, from the floor. It rose from the foundations and echoed all the way up to the stars. None could find the source of the ghastly screams, but everyone knew the voice. All had heard Hara crying down in the well. For three years, all had heard the artist's screams.

The next morning, soldiers opened up the emperor's rooms to find them empty. He had vanished. Hanging above the emperor's bed was a new painting. Ise Katsuo's likeness painted in shades of red. The canvas reeked of blood.

No one ever saw Hara Chinami or Ise Katsuo again. But Ise Katsuo is forever remembered as the Crimson Emperor. And now and then in the dead of night, if you listen hard, you can still hear Hara's chilling wail echoing from the well.

The entire tavern had fallen silent to listen to Guang's rendition of the *Wailing Woman*, and a few of the men looked terrified.

Most village stories of nearby yokai were nothing but fiction, but Haruto had to wonder if perhaps there was some truth to this one. Though he had lost count of the inconsistencies in Guang's tale, he had learned over the many years they had been together to let the poet tell tales his own way. There was no better way to drive up the price of dealing with a yokai than to attach a ghastly story to its history.

"It can't be Hara Chinami," the cherubic tavern owner said.

"There is a well at the academy," said a man with a bulbous nose covered in a web of red veins.

"She only wails at night," said a rakish man with a hair lip. "We've all heard her."

"So I was right?" Nobu said, wringing his hands together. Haruto took him for the town magistrate, despite his bloodstained apron, dishevelled hair, and the substantial bags under his eyes. Suchi did not appear the most prosperous of places, and in remote towns the magistrates often held other jobs. "It's a yokai? A vengeful spirit on account of the academy burning down?"

Guang heaved himself to his feet, knees popping. "Heiwa Academy burned down?" he asked, grabbing Nobu's arm.

Nobu tried to pull his arm free, but Guang held on tight. "Uh, yes. Two weeks ago. The students and teachers have all disappeared, and no one will go search for them with the Wailing Woman haunting the ruins."

Shiki whistled in Haruto's ear. There *was* a yokai close by, she told him. One steeped in pain, driven mad by a desire for revenge. The vengeful spirits of the dead came back in many forms, and it was his job to send them on their way.

"There's the matter of payment," Haruto said. "Onmyoji do not work for free. One hundred lien, and I will deal with this yokai of yours."

Nobu coughed and gaped at Haruto. "A hundred lien?" He glanced at the other patrons for support. Most of them looked away. "We couldn't possibly manage that. You must understand, Master Onmyoji, that much of Suchi's income came through the academy. Without it, we are struggling to pay many of the artisans who moved here. I could scrape together fifty lien."

Haruto pulled his pipe from his kimono and set about packing the small bowl with loose leaf. The pipe had a long, plain wooden stem, and the bowl was copper and bell shaped. It was not the best pipe he'd ever owned, but he had a regrettable habit of losing them. He flicked a glance at Guang.

Guang cleared his throat. "Hara Chinami is an exceptionally dangerous yokai," the old poet said, not missing a beat. "The older they are, the more dangerous they are, as I'm sure you wise fellows know. And if much of your income came from Heiwa, well, I assume you would want the area cleared of danger sooner rather than later so you can petition Empress Ise Ryoko to rebuild. We are not uncaring, but there's the danger to consider. And the law states that onmyoji do not work for free. That is Imperial law."

The magistrate looked to the baby-faced tavern owner who gave him a brief nod. "Sixty lien is the absolute most we can afford."

Haruto finished packing the bowl and tucked the stem in his mouth. Shiki reappeared with a pop and leapt into the lantern on the wall behind Haruto, possessing the flame. She floated over to them, eyes wide as a full moon and mischievous inside the flames, and lit the leaf in the bowl. Haruto puffed a few times to get it burning and nodded. Shiki popped back into her spirit form, her flames guttering out, and scrabbled up Haruto's kimono to sit on his shoulder. "Sixty lien will do just fine," he said around a mouthful of smoke. "We'll deal with your yokai as soon as I've finished my soup."

Chapter 2

The charred bones of Heiwa Academy stretched up before them. In the dim gloom of night, the cracked beams and blackened timbers looked like dark claws tearing their way out of the earth and reaching for the clouds blanketing the sky. Two smaller buildings still stood, but the inferno had gutted the main structure of Heiwa, burnt away floor and walls and roof. What was left had collapsed in on itself, staining the snow black with ash.

The destruction was profound. The place must have been huge, a bustling cacophony of children doing... whatever it was children did. It had been so long, Haruto couldn't even remember his childhood. He was certain he had suffered many beatings at the hands of his older brother, but it was a subject not even a historian would recall. How many had died the night of the fire? And which of them had risen again as a yokai?

Haruto's foot landed on something hard buried beneath the snow. He brushed the dusting away to find a bronze sign with *Heiwa Academy* embossed on it. Its corner was bent like it had been ripped off the low wall surrounding the academy grounds. Shiki whistled quietly from her perch on Haruto's shoulder. The little spirit was right. The fire had not done this. This had been an act of violence.

Guang was uncharacteristically quiet. He huddled tight in his fur-lined cloak, its hood pulled up over his liver-spotted head, frost dusting his patchy, grey beard; and stared at the burnt-out husk of the school. There was a tightness to the man Haruto had not seen before. A bow string drawn to the point of no return. Either it would snap, or deliver terrible violence. Haruto could allow neither.

"It's about time you tell me why we came here," he said to his friend.

Guang shuddered and looked at him without comprehension. Then he shivered and looked away, into the burned bones of the school. "Heiwa was founded by the Fifth Sage Under Heaven after he left the Century Blade's service. It is... *was* a school dedicated to teaching children who had dangerous techniques. Children who had nowhere else to go. Or sometimes children whose parents had enough money to secure them the very best education." Guang shook his head. "Every teacher here was a master, every student a hero in the making. Who could do such a thing? Why would they do it?"

A piercing wail split the quiet of the night, echoed around the ruined school, and promised blood.

Shiki let out a tremulous whistle, the coarse fur on her back rising and turning dark blue. She dropped behind Haruto's shoulder, clung to his kimono and hid there. "Such a cowardly little spirit," Haruto said as he reached over his shoulder and picked her up by the scruff, depositing her on his shoulder again. She stared about with eyes so wide they were nothing but pupil, and whistled into Haruto's ear.

"You're sure?" Haruto asked.

"What did she say, old man?"

Haruto sighed and stepped past the low stone wall into the academy grounds. "That we're in for a fight."

"You are," Guang scoffed, some of his usual humour creeping back into his voice.

"Well, yes, of course. You're welcome to watch and write an epic poem of my victory."

"Do I need to remind you of the Basan of Toroto village?"

"I'd rather you didn't."

Guang barked a laugh, though it sounded strained. "It damn near ripped your arm off and beat you with the wet end."

Haruto thought about arguing, but Guang wasn't wrong. "I still beat it though."

Guang grunted. "Only because you confused it by not

dying."

"What was it that old philosopher used to say? A win is a win?"

"*Victory is worth any cost. Defeat is a coin with no value*," Guang said.

"I was close," Haruto said, his feet crunching in the loose snow.

Another wail severed the night, a cry of pain and fear and grief all rolled into one, expelled with such force even Haruto's steps faltered. This was no lesser yokai. It was young but powerful. Its aura was a writhing mass of confusion, trying to lure them in with compassion, a human desire to comfort its insatiable grief, but also trying to repel them with a terror that petrified.

"How did you know of this place?" Haruto asked once the scream had died down. He could fight the aura, years of training to resist it hardened him against the alien emotions it pressed upon him. But Guang was a poet, not an onmyoji, and the best way to keep him focused away from the aura was to keep him talking.

Guang let out a wordless grumble. It was the noise he always made when trying to collect his thoughts. "My son taught here," he said as they came across the first of the bodies buried in the snow.

Haruto knelt in the snow by the body. "Shiki."

Shiki drew in a deep breath, inflating to thrice her normal size, then exhaled it all in one gust of air that blew the snow from the corpse. She finished with a satisfied chirrup. Two little arms pushed out of her furry body, rubbed together for a job well done, then vanished again. It was a young man in a school uniform frozen solid, his skin was white as the snow, his eyes wide, mouth gaping. The snow beneath him was stained red, a blossom of crimson around his chest. He wore a necklace of cogs, springs, and bolts, so Haruto guessed he was from the Cochtan empire far far to the north. His hands were bound by silken rope. Thin strands of something white trailed from his clothes, and when Haruto touched them they snapped, brittle in the cold.

"I haven't seen my son in years," Guang continued, his tongue loosened. "He was angry with me for giving up the sword. Always thought I should be the one here teaching, instead of--" He let out a bitter laugh. "*--wasting my life writing lies about a worthless charlatan.*"

Haruto laughed, and then stopped suddenly. "Wait, am I the worthless charlatan?"

Guang just stared at him.

Haruto turned away. "Call me a charlatan? How many lives has *he* saved?" He stopped and wagged a cold finger at his old friend. He was about to insult the man's son, but realised he might also be buried in the snow somewhere.

Guang patted Haruto on the shoulder. "I know. I know. It wasn't *you* he was angry at, old man."

Closer to the schoolhouse, the earth was cratered, buildings blasted apart. Dozens of weapons scattered about appeared to be formed from ice. The yokai screamed again, and Shiki squeaked and fled into the folds of Haruto's kimono. Her fur itched his skin, but whenever he tried to reach for her, she evaded his hand. Spirits would do what they pleased, and Shiki had ever been a sneaky one.

They found more bodies on the snow-covered path around the main building. Some appeared to be students, and some were more likely teachers. They were burned, stabbed, ripped apart. Many had died with weapons in hand, but sharpened steel had done them as little good as whatever techniques the academy taught them. It was a massacre.

Towards the rear of the main academy building, they spotted the yokai stumbling through the burnt wreckage, digging through the debris with its black talons. The patchy moonlight shone off its dark skin. Its hair was a mess of charred stubble. It wore the remains of a ragged black hakama over its legs and was naked from the waist up. Its back was covered in little wounds, some of them still bleeding. Spidery black veins radiated out from a couple of puncture wounds on the yokai's neck. It was not the Wailing Woman, not Hara Chinami. She was just a story told to frighten. This creature was real, a vengeful spirit formed from one of the teachers or students of Heiwa when it burned. Haruto watched as the yokai pulled something out of the ruin, a frozen arm. The vengeful spirit let out another wail, all pain and so powerful it whipped the falling snow it into a frenzy. Haruto winced and turned to find Guang staring in horror at the vengeful spirit.

"Is it him?" Haruto asked. "Your son?"

Guang was trembling. He nodded once, then turned away. A great sob shook him, and the old poet shrunk in on himself.

"I'm sorry, Guang," Haruto said. He placed a hand on his friend's shoulder and Guang collapsed to his knees in the snow, shaking.

The yokai turned and stalked further into the ruin of broken beams, charred walls, ash and snow. It raked at the debris with its claws as if looking for something. They caught sight of him properly then. He was tall and slight. He had been strong in life, but in death he was a wraith, covered in small wounds, blood oozing in dark rivulets. His eyes were black, no trace of any colour, and his lips were a ruin of cuts and jagged teeth that jutted from his gums. He was an hasshaku now, a yokai who would abduct children, feed on their blood. Guang's son had been a teacher, protecting and training children, but his violent death had perverted everything he had been in life. He was now a young, powerful yokai, formed not of one death, but of the collected tragedy of all the students and teachers who had died at Heiwa.

Guang sniffed as he climbed back to his feet. He wiped his eyes with the back of an ink-stained hand. "Can you..." He trailed off into silence. Guang had been travelling with Haruto for almost fifteen years now. He had seen enough yokai to know what could and couldn't be done for them. "I have no right to ask, but can you help him move on?"

Haruto squeezed his friend's shoulder. "Nor do you need to ask," he said. There were many ways to deal with yokai, some more peaceful than others, some kinder than others. "What was his name?"

Guang sniffed again. "Tian Meng." His voice broke on the name.

Haruto drew the fire staff from the holster on his back, four feet of metal with an iron circle about the size of his fist at its head containing a small orange flame that burned with no fuel. Without another word, he stepped forward into the ruin of Heiwa and clambered over the debris towards Guang's son.

"Shit!" A charred beam snapped beneath Haruto's feet and sent him careening down the snow-strewn debris. Something stabbed him in the leg and it was fiery agony. He rolled to a stinging heap, covered in soot and lying at the feet of the very yokai he was hunting.

The hasshaku stared down at him with those hateful black eyes. He flexed his talons; saliva drooled from his haphazard fangs. A hasshaku was born of grief, from watching a family member, or perhaps a student, die before they themselves passed away.

"Not my finest entrance." Haruto struggled to his feet and brushed the snow and ash from his kimono. A splinter of charred wood was sticking out of his left thigh, though calling it a splinter was much like calling a horse a pony. He wrapped a hand around the shard and wrenched it free in a spray of blood and a pain that made him want to vomit. To make matters worse, he'd dropped the fire staff.

The hasshaku didn't give him a chance to recover. It shrieked and leapt at Haruto, clawed hands reaching for him. Haruto flung himself to the side, crashing into a pile of ashen beams and sending up a plume of soot and snow. Then he rolled to his feet just in time to see the hasshaku leap at him again. He ducked a slashing talon, but the next strike shredded his coat and kimono and the flesh beneath it. Shiki squealed and crawled further down his kimono.

Haruto staggered back, clutching at his chest, feeling fresh blood leaking out of the wound, staining his tattered clothing. He reached for his katana by instinct, but stopped, his hand brushing the tsuka. He couldn't just kill this yokai. He had to put it to rest. To set it free. He knelt and dug in the charred ruins for his fire staff, and saw it lying in the rubble behind the hasshaku. The yokai drew in a breath, bellowed an ear-piercing scream, and then charged Haruto.

The yokai was too fast and nimble, and Haruto was already staggering from pain. He flung himself at the spirit, and they collided, crashing to the ashen ground. Haruto felt talons dig into his side. He rolled away and lurched back to his feet, staggered forward and snatched the fire staff from the ruins.

"Alright," he growled through gritted teeth as he turned to face the hasshaku once more. "Now we do this properly." In order to trap the yokai, he needed to place the staffs in the perfect order and pattern. Five staffs in the shape of a five-pointed star. Each one needed to draw blood before he placed it.

The hasshaku cried out and rushed at him, talons flashing in the moonlight. Haruto whipped the butt of the staff out, knocking away the clutching talons, spun around and slammed the head of the staff against the yokai's face hard enough to draw blood and send it careening away.

"There's one," Haruto said as he thrust the staff down into the ground. "Fire." The little flame in the staff's head burst into a miniature inferno, engulfing the staff.

He reached over his shoulder and drew the earth staff. In the circle at the head floated a small rock. He stepped to the side, twirling the staff in his hands, eyes locked on the hasshaku as it recovered and turned to face him.

"You're in pain, I know," Haruto said.

The hasshaku snatched up a hand full of ash and flung it at Haruto. Haruto sidestepped the flying debris and swung the staff just as the yokai reached for him. He smashed the head of the staff into the spirit's wounded chest, whirled it around and bashed into its face, drawing dark, oily blood again. Then he planted the staff in the ground. "Earth." The ground rushed up around the staff, encasing it in soil and stone.

Haruto reached for the metal staff, the one with a chunk of

iron ore suspended in the circle. The hasshaku lunged and grabbed hold of the staff in Haruto's hands. They wrestled for it, stumbling back and forth over the debris. The yokai screamed in Haruto's face. His ears popped, and his head felt like a kunai was whirling around inside of it, but still he held on to the staff, desperately pulling against the yokai as it lurched toward him, its monstrous teeth snapping just in front of his face. With one big heave, Haruto fell backwards, pulling the staff and the hasshaku with him. His back hit the ground, a dozen shards of wooden debris driving into his flesh, and he kicked up, throwing the yokai over him to crash down just a hand span away. He flipped from his back to his feet, turned and lashed out with the staff, cracking the yokai across the face once more. Then planted the third staff in the ground. "Metal." Charred nails, discarded knives, and a whole host of small bits of metal were drawn to the staff, sticking to its length.

The water staff held a floating globe of liquid inside the circle. Haruto backed away from the hasshaku as it thrashed and clambered to its feet.

"I won't go easy on you anymore," he snarled at the yokai as it crouched down, ready to attack. The problem with yokai like this was they didn't tire, and no bodily injury would stop them. Killing the body would only send them looking for a new, recently dead host. They had to be properly put to rest.

The hasshaku came again; this time Haruto stepped in to meet it, delivering a flurry of blows with the staff, each one staggering the spirit and spraying blood across the snow. He planted the staff in the ground. "Water." The globe of water at the head of the staff expanded, drops running down the metal length and freezing into the snow on the ground.

Haruto drew the final staff, the one with a chunk of bark in the circle.

The hasshaku stumbled toward him, shaking its head, spitting blood. Haruto darted in, twirled the staff around, smashed it into the hasshaku's temple, sending it rolling onto the snow and ash in the centre of the other four staffs. "Wood," he said. He took a step back and drove the staff into the ground, so exhausted he almost missed. Roots wormed their way out of the dead wood of the nearby beams, coiling around the staff and climbing up it.

Haruto stumbled backwards and collapsed onto a scorched wooden beam, groaning and wincing in pain. "That will hold you for a few minutes," he said. He drew in a deep breath and sighed it out. He looked down at his stinging arm and pulled a bent nail from an oozing wound.

The hasshaku rose slowly to its feet and charged him, slamming itself into the invisible barrier created by the five ritual staffs, bouncing back and crashing down to ashen debris and snow. It scrambled up again and ran away from Haruto, only to hit the barrier once more and fall flat on its back. Haruto sat on the charred beam and watched the yokai bounce off the barrier several times until it eventually stopped trying to escape and reached for the earth staff. Sparks flared and it pulled its talons away, howling in pain.

It knew it was trapped. Yokai like this weren't stupid. There was little of the original human left in them, that much was true, but little was not nothing. Somewhere deep down inside all yokai, was the human they had once been. The hasshaku were a type of mononoke, a pitiful type of yokai. Haruto chided himself for the thought. No, not pitiful. Tragic. They deserved compassion, not pity.

The hasshaku stalked about its invisible cage, snarling like a beast, the hundred wounds on its chest and back and arms dripping foul ichor. The black veins in its neck pulsed. Wisps of silk clung to its shoulders and trailed in shreds from its hakama. Haruto watched and steeled himself for what was to come. For what he had to do.

Shiki climbed up out of his shredded kimono and perched on his shoulder. She chirruped at him like a bird. Eyes wide and white as cooked rice.

"I'm preparing," Haruto said.

Shiki chirruped.

"Yes, of course I'm procrastinating," Haruto said, throwing

up his arms. "Do you want to do it?"

Shiki chirruped.

"Didn't think so." Haruto sighed, rocked forward, and shot to his feet. "Best get to it before the blessings wear off."

He approached the barrier. "Omoretsu," he said, invoking the name of his shinigami patron. "In your name, I act. In your stead, I serve. With your blessings, I bring peace to the dead."

Haruto drew in a deep breath. "This is going to hurt." He stepped through the barrier into the hasshaku's cage.

The yokai rushed him, and Haruto stepped weaponless into its charge. It hit him like a gale, talons digging into his flesh, tearing into his chest. It screamed at him so loud he felt blood leak from his ears. He clenched his jaw, growled, pressed one hand to the hasshaku's forehead and the other over its heart. Then he shouted into the spirit's face, "I name you Tian Meng!"

The hasshaku faltered, retracted its talons from Haruto's flesh and lowered its arms to its sides. Still it screamed at him, its mouth impossibly wide, ruined lips bleeding, serrated teeth flexing out at his face.

"I name you Tian Meng," Haruto repeated, hissing the words through the pain. "Son of Guang Meng. Teacher at Heiwa Academy." He coughed and tasted blood. "I name you Tian Meng, aggrieved, wronged, murdered." He drew in a breath and screamed once more into the wailing spirit's maw. "I name you Tian Meng!"

The scream died away as the hasshaku's mouth slowly closed. It staggered back a step, and Haruto collapsed to one knee before the hasshaku. His kimono in tatters, soaked in his blood. He felt ill from the pain, but he forced himself back to his feet to face the yokai. The hasshaku's eyes slowly cleared, the black voids becoming human once more, deep brown like Guang's.

Tian slowly raised his hands in front of him and stared at his black-taloned fingers. He reached up and prodded his mangled mouth, the hideous teeth that erupted from his gums. He looked down at the bleeding wounds all over his chest, the wounds that had killed him. Then he looked up at Haruto.

"I know," Haruto said. He stepped forward and put a hand over Tian's heart again. "It hurts, I know. The desire for vengeance is a burning whip driving you to violence. Let it go. I will carry it. I will take your pain, carry the burden of your grief. Give it to me, Tian, and I will carry your vengeance to its source. Let it go and let me carry it for you. Please, let me give you this peace."

Tian reeled. His eyes clouded over with darkness again for just a moment; then they cleared, and he opened his mouth to speak. His malformed teeth carved into his cracked lips, and his wounded tongue flicked over them, washing them in blood, but he managed to speak just one word. "Onryo."

Haruto felt the anger flooding him, sweeping him away, drowning him. The need for vengeance was so strong it eclipsed thought and reason, so great it made the sky small and the sun cold. He swallowed it down and felt it settle in his gut and around his heart. One more pain he would carry.

He was on his knees, though he did not remember falling. With a grunt, he stood and faced Tian. "I will carry it for you," Haruto said. "And you can rest. In Omoretsu's name, be at peace, Tian Meng." The hasshaku bowed its head a little.

Haruto drew his katana and held it out to his side. "Shiki." The spirit leapt from his shoulder into the sword with a pop, and the blade turned a deep crimson. "Rest." Haruto gripped Shiki in both hands and plunged her into Tian's heart.

Chapter 3

The dazzling light of a new morning was just cresting the eastern horizon when Haruto finally staggered from the burnt-out husk of Heiwa Academy. He was carrying Tian's body, and had torn off a scrap of his kimono and placed it over the man's head. He didn't want Guang to see his son's face twisted into the monstrous mask of a hasshaku. The old poet was waiting, his coat pulled tight around him, a small fire crackling, beating back the snow and the cold. He said nothing as Haruto approached, but his eyes were red and puffy.

Haruto laid the body on the snow next to the fire, and stumbled forward to collapse in front of the flames. Shiki wobbled on his shoulder, her fuzzy dark hair tickling his cheek. She whistled and leapt into the fire with a pop, possessing the flames. Haruto wished he could feel her joy at such a simple act, but right now all he knew was Tian's rage and grief. The riot of emotion inside him made him raw, and he promised himself not to snap at the grieving father. They sat in silence for a few minutes, neither of them wanting to be the first to speak.

"Looks like it hurt," Guang said. He took a plank of scavenged wood from the ground next to him and poked it toward the flames. Shiki's eyes went wide within the fire, and flames reached out, snatching the plank from Guang's hands.

Haruto laughed. "I'm going to need a new kimono." He picked at the ragged, bloodstained linen. It was barely clinging to one shoulder, uneven and shredded, and crusted with blood. And it was starting to smell.

The old poet cracked a grin at that. "You go through them faster than a courtesan."

"I'll wager they have more fun about it."

They fell into an awkward silence until Guang asked, "How are the injuries?"

Haruto shrugged. "What injuries?" He pulled aside the ragged remains of his kimono to show smooth skin, unmarred by wound. Dried blood was the only evidence of battle left behind. "They healed quickly. The yokai wasn't old enough to curse the wounds. Few are."

Neither said anything more, and Haruto started searching for his pipe. He patted down his kimono, checked the ground around the fire, but did not find it. Then he looked up to the sky. "Damn you, Natsuko," he cursed the God of Lost Items. "That's the fourth one this year."

Guang smiled and started rifling through his pack. "Lost another one?" He pulled out a pipe, turned it over in his hands and then handed it to Haruto. "I was saving this one, but well... I guess I was saving it for now."

It was a thing of beauty. White wood, carved from a single bough. The stem was much shorter than Haruto usually liked, but the bowl was carved with a dragon claw clutching it. He ran his finger over each scale and talon. Such an exquisite pipe, it was almost a shame to use. Almost.

"This must have cost me a fortune," Haruto said as he set about packing it with loose leaf.

Guang laughed. "Your money was well spent, I assure you."

Guang sat in silence while Haruto smoked. Neither of them wanted to start the conversation, but they both knew it had to happen. Haruto glanced at Guang to find him staring into the flames, Shiki's white eyes staring back at him. The old poet looked up and Haruto quickly looked away, stared at a patch of snow. When he looked back, Guang was still staring. They both laughed, but it was forced.

"Alright, let's stop dancing about it, old man," Guang said. "Did you do it?"

"Yes," Haruto said, puffing on his new pipe. "Tian is free. I took his burden from him and sent him to Omoretsu."

Guang grumbled a bit, digging his finger absently in the

cold dirt, and then said, "Good. Good." He stood and walked around the fire. When he reached Tian's corpse, he bent over it and groaned. Hundreds of little puncture wounds puckered its chest, each one frozen with blood. Black veins crawled across his neck and shoulder and up his cheek. Guang's shoulders trembled and tears fell from his cheeks, splashing apart on Tian's chest. Haruto turned away and puffed on his pipe.

"Vengeance, was it?" Guang asked, his voice tight.

Haruto threw another broken plank on the fire and watched Shiki leap onto it, savaging it like a wolf with a fresh kill. "Yes."

"How long do you have?"

This was the part Haruto didn't want to talk about. He had taken Tian's burden and sent the man on to Omoretsu. He had set Tian free, but he had not moved Tian on. If Haruto could fulfil Tian's vengeance in time, Omoretsu would shepherd him on and he would be reborn into a new life. If Haruto did not fulfil the vengeance in time, it would draw Tian back to earth and to Haruto. Tian would possess Haruto and either kick him out of his own body or consume his spirit, neither of which would be pleasant, and both would be quite fatal. "Hard to say," Haruto said. "A few weeks, probably. He was young. Powerful, but young."

"Come on then. Out with it," Guang snapped. "Who did it? Who are we hunting? Who killed my son?"

"We're not," Haruto said. "I took his burden, Guang. It's mine now. You don't have--"

"Shut up!" Guang reached out a hand and paused just before touching Tian. "He was my son, old man. My son! Whoever they are, they took my son from me. Don't you dare tell me this vengeance isn't mine as well. Don't you dare tell me I can't help carry my son's burden. Don't. You. Dare!" He glanced over his shoulder, furious eyes red with a rage and grief.

Haruto puffed on his pipe. Shiki waddled out of the fire in her spirit form, crawled into Haruto's lap. She closed her eyes and was asleep in moments. Guang was right, of course. Haruto had hoped to spare his old friend the burden of his son's ghost. Well, not actual ghost – they were rarer than yokai and occasionally more dangerous. But Guang knew what it meant for Haruto to take on a yokai's burden, its unfinished business. Haruto couldn't rest. Rage and grief that wasn't his own would plague him. And that part of the burden he could not share.

Guang returned to the fire and sat down, his knees popping. "So, who is it?"

Haruto mulled it over while he dragged on his pipe. "Onryo," he said, repeating Tian's single word.

"Huh? I know that word. That's... uh... a type of yokai."

"The rarest," Haruto said. Onryo were also often the most powerful, but he decided to leave that bit out. "It was all Tian said. Onryo."

"All of them?"

Haruto sighed. "I hope not." That would be a burden of vengeance beyond him, beyond anyone.

When the sun reached its zenith, they buried Tian's body. Digging into frozen ground was tough work, but worth it. His soul was at rest for now, Haruto had seen to that, but Guang needed to bury his son. He needed to say goodbye. It was late morning by the time they finally staggered from the academy grounds, exhausted and sweaty despite the frigid winter chill. Haruto wondered if Empress Ise Ryoko would bother rebuilding the school, or if she would let it and Suchi village fade away like so many others in recent years. Her war with Emperor Ido Tanaka might have moved from outwardly violent to clandestine plots, but it still ate up a vast amount of her resources, and rebuilding the academy would be expensive. Either way, it was not his problem.

They found another body just a stone's throw from the gate as they were leaving. It was an old man, pale and frozen. He had several wounds: stabs, burns, and some that looked suspiciously like bite marks. Whoever he was, his end had been violent. They didn't stop to bury him.

Guang was the first back through the doorway of the tavern,

rubbing his hands against the cold. The snow had picked up, and the chill bit through their fur coats. Haruto barely felt it, but he had grown up in Sky Hollow, which made Suchi seem like a tropical paradise. There was no one else in the tavern; most likely the townsfolk were still about their jobs. He followed the old poet in and placed his inert ritual staffs against the wall. Then he collapsed in front of the table nearest the door and slouched in a way that his old masters had tried to beat out of him more times than he cared to remember.

"Wine and food and all that," Guang said as he huddled in front of the hearth, pushing his hands towards the flames.

The cherub-faced tavern owner hurried over. "Is it done?"

Haruto didn't bother to answer. He slouched even further until he was lying on the floor with his eyes closed.

Rest did not come.

Something light and furry batted him in the face. Haruto opened his eyes to find Shiki sitting on his chest, gently slapping him with a hairy arm. He groaned and sat, picked the spirit up by the scruff and placed her on the nearby table. "Beast!" he said accusingly. She giggled.

"Is it done?" the tavern owned asked again.

"Of course it is!" Haruto snapped. "I've dealt with your damned yokai. Now fetch us some food."

The man quickly and quietly retreated to the back of his tavern. Haruto hoped he would get about the business of feeding them, and fast. He found Guang staring at him, a calculating look in his eyes.

"I'll apologise when he comes back," Haruto said and lay back down.

Again rest did not come. He dozed for a short time, but it brought no respite. Terrifying, formless images filled his mind.

After they'd eaten, Nobu, the village magistrate returned. Haruto was feeling a little more himself after a good meal, but the anger still churned just below the surface like a geyser waiting to erupt. Yet it wasn't his anger. It was Tian's. It was the rage of a vengeful spirit swirling inside his chest, clawing at him from the inside to get out, heedless of who it hurt.

Nobu dropped a large purse on the table and bowed low on his hands and knees. He had apparently been up to Heiwa and confirmed the wailing had stopped and there was no sign of Hara Chinami anywhere. Haruto decided there was no point correcting the fool.

"Do you have any spare kimonos?" Haruto asked. "I seem to have somewhat ruined this one."

The magistrate bowed again. "We have some men of your size in the village. I will have one brought to you immediately, Master Onmyoji."

He supposed a second-hand kimono was better than nothing. He only hoped the previous owner didn't have lice. "What about a temple? Does Suchi have one?"

"Of course," Nobu said. "Just down the main road and to the left there is a temple to the stars. It's small." He spread his hands in apology.

Haruto rolled his eyes. "I need a real temple. To the gods."

Nobu grimaced. "Taka has a shrine to Natsuko in his home."

That wasn't good enough. He needed a proper temple to re-bless his ritual staffs or they would be useless next time he encountered a yokai. He sighed and pinched the bridge of his nose.

"Where's the nearest temple of the gods?" Guang asked. He was slouching at the table with Haruto now, looking much better after his meal. Colour had returned to his cheeks and some of his usual good humour flavoured his voice.

Nobu bowed once more. "Minazuri is a few days to the south. I believe it has a temple."

The tavern owner grunted in agreement.

Haruto tapped a finger on the table. Shiki had been dozing, curled up in a fluffy ball, but she uncurled at the sound and pounced on his hand, delicately savaging his fingers. "Did anyone see any strangers about town around the time Heiwa burned down?" Haruto asked.

The tavern owner opened his mouth, but Nobu glared him

into silence.

"Out with it," Haruto snapped. He didn't like the edge creeping into his voice.

Nobu sighed. "The widow Mezu said she saw robed figures on the road south, but she is prone to... false visions."

"Minazuri it is then," Haruto said as he played with Shiki, flipping her onto her back. Little legs and arms pushed out of her furry little body and she slapped at his fingers. South felt right somehow; Tian's vengeance was drawing him that way. They were on the hunt for the onryo.

Chapter 4

The first sign of Minazuri were deep tracks in the snow, trodden often enough the ice was packed hard as stone underfoot. They had been travelling for three days, heading south from Suchi, and the snow and the cold were relentless demons and Guang was in hell. It was the only plausible explanation: hell had frozen over and they had wandered into it like the fools they were. Haruto claimed it was the altitude, that they had been hiking steadily uphill. It made sense, Guang had to admit, but his hell theory was far more poetic.

"*Through blankets of white.*
Time loses sense, meaning lost.
The road diverges."

"That's your worst one yet," Haruto said as he slogged through the sheeting snow.

"Too cold to think," Guang said through chattering teeth. "Makes words hard."

Occasional breaks in the snowfall and clouds gave them glimpses of deep valleys surrounding them, frozen lakes and forests bleached of all but the most determined colours. Frost clung to his beard, worked its way inside his coat, and snow caked his clothes. It was all made worse because Haruto looked like he didn't feel it at all. He wore only a kimono, blue with white stars, and a winter cloak, and he didn't so much as shiver. He claimed it was because he grew up nearby, in a place where the snow never stopped falling even in the height of summer, but Guang didn't believe him. Even the people that lived here bundled up against the cold. Haruto just didn't feel it. Perhaps he felt nothing.

"*A man so broken, his curse untold. He seeks not*

redemption, no way to atone." Guang smiled and decided to commit that one to memory. It was too cold to write it down, and his ink was likely frozen solid. He wasn't sure if the poem was about Haruto or himself, but then it didn't really matter.

The tracks in the snow became furrows made deep by wheels. And then, out of nowhere, high walls and an open gate loomed in the snowy air before them. A couple of bored-looking guards stared down at them from the wall walk. Beyond the gate, the snow was thinner and Guang saw at least two people hard at work shovelling it off the main street.

The guards called out, asking their business. Haruto held up the wooden seal that declared him an onmyoji sanctioned by the emperor. They were technically in the empress' territory, but it was all Ipia. Besides, no one wanted to anger an onmyoji regardless of who sanctioned them, lest they call mischievous spirits down upon them.

It was early afternoon, and the town was a buzz with people carrying baskets of food or bundles of sticks. A woman walked past leading a gaggle of children who were far more interested in catching snowflakes on their tongues than paying attention to their chaperon. A couple of soldiers wearing leather scale breastplates and helms stood about chatting around a brazier, their breath misting in the air between them. They wore heavy furs over their armour and carried spears, but paid little attention to what was happening around them. The town stretched on all around them, squat wooden houses pressed against two-story inns and warehouses with sharply slanted tile roofs. It was clearly many times the size of Suchi, possibly even larger than Kaichi, Guang's old home back in Hosa. It seemed impossible that a town whose primary resource was snow could rival one that had green fields on all sides and a flowing river instead of a frozen one.

"How does this place survive with nothing but snow all around?" Guang asked as they walked.

Haruto chuckled. "It's only like this in the heart of winter. For half of the year it's completely thawed out... Almost completely. The valleys on either side are forested and provide lumber and furs, and the lakes fish. There are even fields on the south eastern side of the mountain where they grow vegetables and rice. Or at least there were. I assume they're still there." He shrugged.

Shiki was riding in the fold of Haruto's kimono. She spotted a black cat down an alleyway next to a butchers and whistled excitedly. Guang had no idea what the little spirit was saying, but Haruto shook his head. A moment later, Shiki leapt from his kimono and tumbled across the snow like a hairball caught on a breeze. She raced into the alleyway and Guang heard the cat shriek.

Guang grumbled and followed Haruto through the bustling streets, dodging around a man who was struggling to force his donkey to move. "A nice warm tavern would be good."

"Temple first," Haruto said. "The tavern can come after."

Guang grumbled again. "As long as the tavern has baths. And hot food. And a bed. I hate sleeping in the wild."

"And how will you pay for all that?"

Guang stepped around an old woman who hurried past them, a basket of fish on her back. By the smell of it, the fish were freshly caught, and he wondered how the townsfolk were fishing in such a frozen hellscape. He hurried to catch up with Haruto and damned him for his longer stride. "You have sixty lien from the last job. That's more than enough."

"Thirty lien," Haruto corrected him, shooting a sorry smile over his shoulder.

"What happened to the other thirty?" Guang didn't really need to ask, he already knew.

Haruto shrugged snow from his shoulders. "I guess I lost it back in Suchi."

Guang groaned. "No wonder we're broke. You are far too kind for someone so old."

At least the temple was warm. Guang hustled inside and barely remembered to take off his boots before running over to one of the braziers and all but hugging the flames to his chest. He wasn't cut out for the cold; it seemed to get inside his joints and make them ache. His knees felt like a pestle and mortar grinding together with every step even on the warmest of days. The shrine attendant gave him a knowing smile and then went to see Haruto.

"May I direct you to a particular shrine," she asked. She was a tall woman wearing a black-and-white kimono, and her hair was short enough to tuck behind her ears. A mole on her cheek made her look like she was crying.

Haruto reached inside his kimono and retrieved the seal that identified him as an onmyoji. "I brought my own. I just need space."

The attendant glanced at the staffs holstered to Haruto's back and bowed quickly. "Of course, Master Onmyoji. We have an empty shrine just this way. We don't get many onmyoji here. Actually, I think you're the first in... uh, a long time. Are you hunting a particular spirit?" She chatted excitedly with Haruto while Guang glanced about the temple. It was a manic cluster of shrines set out on tiered levels. On the ground floor were shrines to the tianjun, the lord of heaven; then the god of war, the god of weather, and the god of life. A visitor could walk to the side and mount a few steps to reach the next level up, where shrines to the god of gambling, the god of fire, the god of wrath, and a dozen other smaller shrines were suspended on wooden boards. Guang counted no less than six tiers, and it was quite possible they extended further back into the recess of the temple. There were also stairs leading up to the next floor of the pagoda, and he wondered how many of them had similar nests of shrines. Some temples were dedicated to individual gods and some were to the stars, and occasionally they came across one like this that was dedicated to half the pantheon. But Haruto would not find the shrine he needed no matter how many gods the temple worshipped. He prayed to an obscure shinigami, a lord of death, a reaper. And so he carried the shrine with him.

Guang detached himself from the brazier, feeling a little warmer but no less chilled, and went searching for his own deity. Champa, God of Laughter, had a small shrine on the fourth tier. There was no effigy, only a small nameplate and an alcove for gifts. Someone had placed a crude drawing of a horse kicking a man in the crotch inside the alcove, and Guang chuckled at it, which he supposed was the point.

He knelt in front of the shrine. "It's been a while, Lord Champa," he said. "Not much cause for laughter lately, I suppose. Look after my son, if you can. Tian. That's his name. Don't let any of those shinigami do anything weird to him. He was a good boy. A good man. Didn't like me much, but maybe that's something you can laugh about together." He fell silent as he ran out of words and tried to find it within himself to make an offering. "I still have my vows." He fished in his satchel and laid the four scrolls out in front of the shrine. "Keeping them all, just like I... well, vowed."

Haruto knelt on the prayer mat in front of the empty shrine. Most of the larger temples had them, in case visitors came to worship the more obscure deities. He laid his ritual staffs on the floor before him. A small, black cat sauntered in, sat down next to him, and started cleaning its paws. He glanced down at it. It looked up at him, flattened its ears, and let out a lazy meow.

"Get out of it," Haruto said.

With an audible pop, Shiki leapt out of the cat and rolled on the floor, trembling with laughter, looking a lot like an overgrown dust bunny with eyes, and a grinning mouth. The cat bolted.

The temple attendant gasped. "A yokai!"

"Not a yokai," Haruto said. "Her name is Shiki. She's my companion spirit. And a little pain in my arse."

Shiki cocked her fuzzy head at the attendant and stretched out her arms yawning dramatically, then she clambered up onto the shrine and sat before the little doors. Her arms vanished back into her body.

"I'm going to have to call on him," Haruto said.

Shiki narrowed her eyes and shook, her dark hair turning a slick shade of green. Despite being given to Haruto by Omoretsu, she really did not like the shinigami. Haruto didn't blame her.

From somewhere deeper inside the temple, a man let out an

uproarious bellow of laughter. Guang making an offering to Champa. Haruto pulled his katana from his belt and laid it down beside his ritual staffs. At the end of the hilt, attached to the kashira by a bit of string wound around the hilt, was a small charm. It was a little wooden statue of an old man, a squat figure with a grotesque and wrinkled face, a bulging belly, and bare feet. Haruto unwound the string and pulled free the charm.

"You may want to leave," he said to the attendant. "It's unwise to gain the attention of a lord of death."

The attendant bowed low and hurried away.

Haruto set the charm on the shrine next to Shiki. It had an odd way of staring at him, almost as though its eyes were real and followed him, unnerving in their scrutiny. "Omoretsu," Haruto said.

The light in the temple dimmed, the braziers dying down to embers, the candles flickering out. An acrid smell like burning juniper filled the air. A new laugh echoed around the falling gloom, at once an ancient croak and a child's giggle. Haruto felt a presence over his shoulder, staring down at him. His patron shinigami always did like to make an entrance.

"Hello Haruto," said the voice of a child. Haruto glanced over his shoulder to find a young boy staring at him. He wore black funeral clothes, a crimson scarf, and had eyes as pale as snow. No matter how many times Haruto met with Omoretsu, that stare unnerved him more than any of the thousand monsters he had slain. "Thank you for sending that hasshaku my way. It was delicious."

Omoretsu approached and knelt beside Haruto. He was colder than the winter wind. It seeped from him, sapping the warmth from the world. Haruto shivered.

"His name is Tian," Haruto said. "I took his burden to free him. He's not yours to play with, kami."

Omoretsu laughed, a sound like snakes slithering across sand. "Not until you fulfil his dying desire, Haruto," said the boy's voice. "You know the rules. You have taken his burden, but it is still *his* burden. And until you carry out his vengeance..."

Omoretsu turned those pale eyes on Haruto once more and his voice deepened into the menacing croak of something truly ancient. "He is mine!" He laughed and turned his voice back into a boy's. "As are you."

The shinigami was right, of course. Haruto might have told Guang his son was free to join the afterlife, but it wasn't true. He was trapped, a plaything for the shinigami until Haruto fulfilled his burden. But that was not something Guang needed to know. Better he thought his son was waiting in some sort of divine paradise.

Omoretsu reached forward and stroked Shiki. The little spirit shivered, her hair standing on end, and let out a frightened whistle. Omoretsu hissed and Shiki reluctantly shuffled into the shinigami's lap. A reminder that although Shiki was Haruto's companion spirit, his guide and his friend, she was also Omoretsu's creature.

"So, my cursed onmyoji, why am I here?" Omoretsu asked, his voice high and playful.

Haruto waved a hand toward the ritual staffs. "They need blessing."

The shinigami scoffed, but just like that the five elements reappeared within their respective staffs. Fire, earth, metal, water, and wood. Five ritual staffs blessed by a lord of death.

"Is that all?" Omoretsu asked, a hint of menace in his voice.

"No. What do you know of the onryo?"

Omoretsu was silent a moment while an icy breeze stirred the candle flames. Shiki grumbled and leapt from Omoretsu's lap, scrabbling onto Haruto and burrowing inside his kimono.

The shinigami stood. "The onryo do not serve any shinigami. They are free to do what they will."

"Do you know where they are?" Haruto asked. He glanced over his shoulder to find the boy staring at him with a face like an ocean storm.

"Close," he snarled. "There are two nearby." He turned away from Haruto. "I wonder, will your curse protect you from them?" And then he was gone, along with the darkness and cold and the scent of burning juniper.

Haruto sighed and shook his head. "My curse," he said bitterly. "It's your bloody curse!"

Chapter 5

They found the largest inn in Minazuri and set up shop. Which is to say Haruto handed his imperial seal to the owner who promptly hung it outside, and word spread faster than weevils through rice. By the end of the day, Guang had two scrolls full of potential jobs. Reports of yokai had been on the rise for the past ten years because spirits had been returning to the world like an unchecked plague. Of course, most people couldn't tell the difference between a hasshaku and an otoroshi, so they classed them all as yokai and begged the nearest onmyoji to eradicate them. Most onmyoji were happy to oblige as long as they were offered lien.

Night had long since fallen, bringing a welcome lull in people claiming to have been wronged by vengeful spirits. The inn was packed full of travellers and townsfolk who just needed to unwind with a bottle or two of sake. The inn was furnished with both Ipian tables low to the ground, and also higher ones with chairs for Hosan visitors. At Guang's vociferous insistence, they were sitting at a Hosan style table.

"Alright, let's go through them," Haruto said. He puffed out smoke in a ring and Shiki cooed and leapt from his shoulder, scattering the smoke.

"Will it help us find the onryo?" Guang asked as he unrolled a scroll and used an empty wine bottle to pin it to the table.

"It might," Haruto said. "The onryo are strange. Spirits might be drawn to them as dust is drawn to an eddying wind."

"That's almost poetic," Guang said with a grin.

Haruto shrugged. "Perhaps I should give up my staffs and become a wandering poet. I hear it's quite easy, especially if you find someone useful to mooch off."

Guang nodded sagely. "True true. Though you have to be careful. It's far too easy to fall in with an artless melon who thinks an emerald is green." He sipped at a cup of wine, fished a pair of antiquated spectacles from his pack and perched them on his nose. The left lens was cracked in three places, and the wire had been bent and re-bent so many times it looked like a jagged mountain trail. "I envy your curse," he grumbled as he squinted at the scroll before him. "Reports of fires burning on the graves of the recently deceased at Yokashi Cemetery." He glanced up.

Haruto considered the possibility. Spirits certainly, but no yokai. Maybe a hakanohi. They were harmless spirits feeding off the residual memories of the dead. Once they had collected a sufficient store of those memories, they returned to heaven on their own to add those memories to the Library of Nothing. He waved a hand in the air. "Next." Shiki mimicked his gesture and squeaked.

Guang grunted and squinted at the scroll again. "Fisherman working the frozen lake have reported seeing something large and serpent-like swimming beneath the ice. One fellow said he caught a proper glimpse through the hole he cut, and it was white and had a child's face. Sounds promising."

"Sounds like a ningen." Haruto scratched at his chin as he considered. "They form from a child who drowned in freezing water. They try to pull others down to their deaths. Probably nothing to do with the onryo, but if there's a reward..."

Guang shook his head. "Nothing yet. It's only sightings. You know how these things work – until someone dies or it gobbles up all the fish, no one is going to pay us for getting rid of a rumour."

Haruto blew smoke out his nose. Shiki formed a mouth and blew at drifting patterns.

Guang read out a few more of the spirit sightings he had collected, none of which seemed likely to be yokai, much less onryo.

"A woman reported seeing red hands hanging from a tree up near Tyoto village." Guang groaned. "Have these people never seen a tree hanging onto its leaves in winter?"

"Wait," Haruto said. "What else?"

"Huh?"

"Were there any other reports from Tyoto?"

Guang stared down the scroll through his spectacles, then pulled out the second scroll and started down that one too. "A man working the frozen lakes claimed a beautiful woman lured him to a tree and pulled him down to sleep. His wife wasn't pleased and said it was a fool's dream or a dalliance." Guang chuckled. "Given the size of her arms, I hope for his sake it was a dream. I've seen smiths with less muscle."

Haruto glanced down at Shiki to find the little spirit staring at him, no longer playing with the smoke. She often preferred to possess animals while visiting inns, probably because people fed cats and swung heavy objects at spirits, but she was in her natural form, her coarse hair a little red at the tips. "Akateko sometimes take the form of women lounging beneath red-leafed trees. They're soul suckers, pulling the unwary down and draining them of their qi. Most people wake a few hours later, weak and exhausted, but also pleasantly numb." Haruto rubbed some of the tiredness from his eyes. "Anything else from Tyoto?"

"One man said the local villagers have been complaining of a small, hairy man stealing fruit," Guang said. "Sounds a bit like that, um, otoroshi we dealt with last year. The one who sat atop the shrine at Sechan and threw snails at us. Annoying little onion!" He continued scanning the scroll. "A woman lost a child a few months before it was due, and there've been complaints about a baby's crying coming from her house." He groaned. "I don't like the sound of that, old man."

"Nobody does. That's why they are complaining," Haruto said with a smile. Guang did not look up.

"I've got three more reports of things coming from Tyoto. Ghost lights along paths at night. A one-eyed woman no one seemed to know. And an old villager, found dead. His left arm was skinned, but the rest of him was fine."

Haruto waved the owner of the inn over. He was a tall man with a thin horseshoe of hair around his head, and sounded like he talked through his nose.

"More wine, Master Onmyoji?" the owner said with a bow.

"No," Haruto said.

"Yes," Guang said.

"Fine. Yes. But first. What can you tell me about Tyoto?"

The owner smoothed down his moustache and puckered his lips, making a show of thinking. "Not much. It's a half day further up the mountain. Not much up there but a few trees and some goats. Rocks. Streams trickle down into the lake, but they're as frozen as it is right now."

"What about the village?" Haruto pressed.

"Goat farmers and ice fishers mostly. A hundred people, maybe less. The old crone."

"Old crone?"

The owner sniffed. "Wise woman, or so she claims. Some folk trek up there to ask about things, but the scholars say she's crazy as a bat in a bucket."

He waved the man away and grinned at Guang. "Tyoto it is."

The next morning they set out for Tyoto. The snow fall had eased off a bit, fat flakes drifting down in languid waltzes rather than thrown at them in a frenzied fury. Guang still clutched his cloak tight, shivered and grumbled. But the sun shone through the clouds, lifting Haruto's spirits a little. Shiki played in the snow. She'd possessed a fluffy brown tanuki and was pouncing on snow drifts, tunnelling down and leaping up in a different place, covered in snow and ice. The little spirit was a bundle of unbridled joy at times.

They found the tree not far from the village, the first buildings visible just a little way up the slope. Afternoon was well underway by then, and the sun had dipped behind grey clouds, casting the world in funereal shadow. The tree was small with a dark brown trunk and red leaves, shaped like a child's hands. Beneath it lazed a woman in a white kimono. She had dark hair cascading down her back and framing her face, ruby red lips, and was singing a soft lullaby.

"Looks like a nice place to rest," Guang said, already taking a step off the packed-snow path.

Haruto held a hand up in front of him, but Guang didn't seem to notice. He pushed past it, dragging through the snow, eyes fixed on the woman and the soft patch of snow beside her. Her voice rose in a haunting melody.

"*Come sit with me. Come lie with me.*

Take from me your comfort, and I will take from you your woes."

Haruto hurried forward and grabbed Guang by the shoulder. The old poet shrugged free and lurched forward another step. The woman's smile was welcoming as a warm bed, but there was something predatory about her oil-dark eyes. Her voice rose and fell like a gusting wind.

"*I see your pain, your need, your torpor.*

I know you feel it too.

Come sit with me. Come lie with me.

Let us ease each other's woes."

Haruto could not lie – she made a compelling argument. He was half tempted to see what she could do for his own malaise. But he already knew the truth of it: only those under her spell enjoyed her pleasures. He stepped in front of Guang. "I'm sorry, old friend." He put a hand on the poet's chest, a leg behind him, and pushed. Guang tripped backwards and hit the icy ground in a plume of snow. He stared up at Haruto, his eyes glazed over and distant. Then he blinked and he was back.

Guang thrashed about, snow flying everywhere as he struggled to get back to his feet. Haruto was certain he heard the old poet's knees pop as he helped his friend up. "You chuckling onion, what was that for?"

"You were about to have all your qi sucked out, you old fool," Haruto said.

"Who are you calling old?" Guang grumbled. He had a fair point. "I was just... uh... What was I doing?"

Haruto stepped aside and gestured a hand toward the

woman. She had stopped singing now. She stood beneath the red-handed leaves of her tree and stared at them, her head cocked to the side, her smile promising unearthly warmth and comfort.

"Huh," Guang said. "She's stunning."

Haruto chuckled. "Sings like a goddess too." He took a few more steps toward the woman and saw her stance stiffen. She was holding a red leaf in each hand. There was a shimmering disturbance in the air around the tree. Haruto barely even noticed it himself, and he was trained to do just that. Under the scattered leaves and twisting, naked branches of that tree was her domain, and if he walked there, he might never walk out again. Shiki popped up out of the snow at his feet and barked a warning before leaping free of the tanuki and scrabbling onto Haruto's back and up his kimono to sit on his shoulder. The tanuki stared at Haruto a moment, barked and bounded away.

"You're older than I am," Haruto said. The woman continued to stare at him. She wanted him to step inside her realm, to meet with her. Not to rest or to take comfort, but to meet in battle. And what a glorious battle it would be. A fight the poets would write about for generations to come. She would sing the song of his defeat, and he would worship her for it.

"Oi!" Guang snapped, punching Haruto hard on the arm. "Now which one of us is being a carrot-faced fool?"

Haruto looked down to find his foot raised, poised just above the edge of her domain. She watched him, head cocked to the side, a coy smile on her blood-red lips. Haruto staggered back.

"Come on." Guang tugged Haruto's arm, pulling him away. "No one's paying us to deal with her, and Tyoto is just up ahead. I can see the buildings from here."

They trudged along, following the foot-packed path through the snow. Haruto glanced over his shoulder. The woman shrugged dramatically and returned to sit down against her tree. Guang was right. No one was paying for them to get rid of her. Not yet anyway.

Chapter 6

Tyoto was no more than a couple of dozen buildings clustered around a small, frozen lake. It was high on the mountain, and the wind bit through Guang's furs like teeth. Some buildings had a distinct lean to them that proved the wind sometimes blew strong as rampaging herd of buffalo. The roofs were slanted and thick with snow. Words drifted through Guang's mind, the first stirrings of a poem.

"*A place of marvels.*
Bleached white so peaceful, remote.
Foul presence lingers."

Haruto grimaced at Guang and shook his head.

"Yeah, definitely not my best. Are they here? The onryo?"

Shiki growled.

"What did she say?" Guang asked.

Haruto sniffed the frigid air. "She said your poem is awful. Where is everyone?" They stood at the village outskirts, the sun was still above the peak of the mountain, but there was no one in sight. A lazy trail of grey smoke rose from the furthest building, dwindling on the breeze.

Guang saw a discarded fishing line out on the lake, the end still dangling down into a hole cut in the ice. As he watched, the line jerked and then was pulled down through the hole. "A nap with a nice lady under a tree doesn't seem so bad anymore," he said with a forced laugh.

A gust blew over them. Shiki sniffed the air a few times, then scurried inside Haruto's kimono and whined. "She smells blood on the air," Haruto said. "Stay behind me, Guang."

"No argument from me, old man." Nevertheless, he wasn't about to walk into danger without some way to protect himself.

He unshouldered his pack, pulled out a long length of paper and his brush and ink pot. The ink was frozen solid. "Shiki, get over here and give me some heat, will you?" The spirit squeaked and remained hidden in Haruto's kimono. The little creature never responded to anyone but Haruto.

Haruto crept forward ahead of Guang. The snow was deep here, and the tracks through it looked fresh. His feet sunk deep into the powdery white, but some other tracks almost looked like someone had glided across the snow, barely touching it. Haruto drew his fire staff and held it ready. They trudged to the nearest building, a crouched hovel leaning over the path, and mounted the porch, their footsteps thunderous on the old wooden boards. Haruto pressed his ear to the door. Guang edged over to the shuttered window and tried to peer through the cracks. Nothing but darkness within.

Haruto tried the door. It was not locked. He pulled it open quickly. He made a disgusted noise and backed away. Guang hurried to the door to look. A body lay on the floor, a woman dressed in thick furs, her eyes frozen open in terror. Guang inched inside the building and squatted by the body. His knees popped like firecrackers, but it was nothing. Or at least it would be nothing compared to the pain when he stood up. Growing old in Hosa was one thing – it was nice and warm. But being old in Ipia was another matter entirely. The cold seeped inside and made little daggers in all his joints.

The woman was frozen solid, her skin pale and frosty. Guang didn't see any wounds on her, but whatever killed her had terrified her first. Guang used a wooden chest against the wall to push himself up, his knees creaking like rusty gates. He walked around the little house, into the bedroom and the storage room. There was no one else. The poor woman had died alone and frightened out of her wits.

He made his way back outside, finding Haruto checking the next building along the path. One glance inside seemed to be all the onmyoji needed. He closed the door behind him, stepped down into the snow, and started up the slope to the furthest building, the one with the smoke wisping from it. It sat on slight rise, the ice-capped top of the mountain rising far behind it.

Guang struggled after his friend. "Is it the onryo?"

Haruto twirled the fire staff in his hands. "It's close. Shiki feels its presence."

"These people have been dead a while, old man."

As they approached the last house, its door opened and two women stepped out to meet them. One was an older lady with a firm jaw and long black and silver hair, tightly braided. She wore a leather jerkin with some faded green scales sewn on it, and carried a polearm with a long blade and a solid pommel. The other was a young woman of maybe sixteen years, with onyx eyes and black hair chopped messily at her shoulders. She wore a black hakama and a haori to match, both patterned with yellow birds. The older woman held up her polearm in front of the younger and whispered something to her.

Haruto froze in the centre of the path, his staff held ready. Guang caught up to him and gave his old friend a quick nudge. "Is that them? The onryo?"

Shiki scurried up onto Haruto's shoulder and babbled something into his ear, hairy little arms pushing out of her fur and gesturing wildly at the two women. Haruto cocked his head to listen, then shrugged. "The young one is an onryo. The old woman is a... old woman."

Guang grumbled. It was not unknown for yokai to travel with humans. Sometimes the people knew what they were, and other times they didn't. Haruto claimed the onryo were special, though Guang was more than a little frustrated that his friend wouldn't say how.

"Do you want to take this one?" Haruto said as he pulled his katana from his belt and held it out.

Guang looked down at the sword and felt his gut curdle. Haruto knew he couldn't touch the damned thing. It had been fifteen years since he had held a weapon, and he certainly wasn't about to start now, not even to avenge the death of his son. "Not even funny, old man," Guang said flatly. "I'll keep the old lady busy."

Haruto smiled at him, then shoved the katana back through his belt. "She has a bloody great naginata and your ink is dry."

"I'll think of something."

"Don't die!" Haruto said lightly.

"On that we agree, old man." Guang stepped away, leaving Haruto and circling around to come at them from a different angle.

The old woman stepped down into the snow. "We didn't kill these people," she said, a slight rasp in her voice.

Haruto took a couple of steps forward, reached inside his kimono and pulled out his imperial seal. He threw it into the snow at the onryo's feet.

The old woman looked down at the seal, and her eyes widened. "Get behind me, Kira."

"No!" the onryo said. She leapt down from the porch next to the old woman and stood atop the snow as though she weighed nothing. "I can fight too." She had a polished dagger in her hand that reflected the dying light of the day.

"This isn't a game, Kira," the old woman snapped. "He's an onmyoji."

A flicker of something like doubt passed across the onryo's face, but it vanished, leaving only savage determination in its place. "Good!"

The onryo twisted her hand so the light flashed from her little dagger. Haruto turned sharply, swinging his staff behind him, but there was nothing there. The onryo then threw her dagger at him. It thudded into Haruto's shoulder, sending him stumbling.

"I got him!" the onryo shouted giddily. She jumped up and clapped her hands.

"Focus, Kira," said the old woman.

"Oh, of course. Sorry." The onryo wiped the smile off her face and furrowed her brow.

Haruto grunted as he reached up to pull the dagger out of his shoulder. It shattered in his hand, a thousand little mirrored shards twinkling all around him. The onryo ran across the snow, another little dagger already in her hand. The old woman cried out for her to stop to no avail. She struggled through the knee-deep snow behind the onryo, spinning her polearm and preparing to strike.

The onryo closed the distance quickly and struck at Haruto's chest. He blocked it with his staff. She stabbed at his left arm and he let it through, crying out in pain, but swinging his staff with his right and slamming the onryo in the face. She tumbled into a deep snow drift beneath the awning of a nearby house. "Fire!" He snarled as he planted the first ritual staff in the frozen earth and drew the second.

"Haruto!" Guang shouted as the old woman closed on him.

Haruto turned just in time to deflect the woman's polearm. They both planted their feet in knee-deep snow and traded blows. Staff and polearm spun in a dizzying blur that Guang's old eyes couldn't quite keep up with. Then it was clear the old woman had the upper hand. She might be grey and wrinkled and probably ached as much as Guang did, but she was good. She whipped her polearm up in a flurry of snow and batted Haruto's staff aside. While he tried to regain his balance, she drew back onto one leg, using her other as a counterbalance, leaned forward, and thrust the bladed tip of her weapon in his side and left it there.

Haruto cried out, a red stain blossoming quickly on his kimono. "Alright, that's enough," Haruto growled. He grabbed the blade sticking into his side and pushed it out, clenching his teeth and hissing.

The old woman stepped back, confident the fight was over. The onryo was on her feet again, a mirrored dagger in each hand.

Haruto launched into motion, leaping into the air and kicking the old woman square in the chest with his left foot, spinning in mid air and kicking her in the head with his right. She flew through the air and landed heavily in the snow near Guang's feet. She groaned and stirred but was slow to rise.

The onryo's eyes went wide, and she started forward. "Yan..."

Haruto shouted over the girl, "Guang, keep the woman busy.

I'll deal with the onryo." He turned to the girl as she crept toward him. "That's a fun little trick, pushing qi into your feet to spread your weight so you don't sink into the snow." He grinned and jumped up onto the snow. "In the name of Tian, I will kill you, onryo."

The girl's face crumpled. She tilted her head and looked him up and down. "Huh?"

Guang had no more time to watch. The old woman grabbed the polearm from the snow and was pushing herself to her feet again. She was puffing steam from her mouth, but didn't look too badly injured.

"I will be your opponent," Guang said with a confidence he didn't feel.

The old woman narrowed her eyes at him, then started toward Haruto once more. He was trading lightning fast blows with the Onryo, staff and daggers whirling so fast Guang had to look away or be mesmerised.

"Hey!" Guang growled as he started after the woman. "Don't you ignore me." The old woman swung her polearm at his throat, and he leaned away just in time to avoid becoming a bloody mess in the snow.

"Don't get in my way, you old fool."

"Who are you calling old, hag?" Guang snarled. He pulled a length of paper from his pack, and bit down hard on his thumb, tasting blood. His ink pot might be frozen solid, but he had other ways to use his technique. The old woman stopped, glancing between him and the battle, then decided Guang clearly needed killing first. She shuffled through the snow toward him, spinning her polearm, and thrust.

Chapter 7

Guang had just enough time to bleed a single word on the paper. *Shield*. The paper solidified into a rectangle as wide as his body and half as tall with a couple of handles on the back side of it, the word he had written emblazoned proudly between them in deep red. Guang stepped toward the woman, gripping the shield in both hands. She swung the polearm at him and he blocked it, staggering back from the force.

Guang recovered his footing and dared a peek over the top of shield. The old woman frowned at him. He smiled back at her. "You didn't see that coming, did you? How about we just agree we're far too old to fight and sit this one out? I'll write a poem to commemorate your ferocity instead."

The old woman glanced back at Haruto and the onryo. Haruto had planted the staff of earth in the ground, and they were circling each other, trading attacks. Somewhat maddeningly, Guang thought, they were both grinning.

The old woman growled and advanced on Guang, levelling a spinning slash at his shield, forcing him back. It felt like a hammer blow on his shield, and the blade scraped away at the paper. The old woman was trying to carve through his defence, but if she realised she was better off striking at Guang, he was probably dead. He gave ground again, keeping his eye on the blade. He didn't need to attack. He couldn't. He knew he was no match for the woman's skill, but it was more than that. He had vowed never to wield a weapon again. A shield didn't really count, but that might change if he tried to hit her with it. All Guang had to do was keep her occupied until Haruto had finished the yokai.

The woman dipped into a crouch, one leg out before her, her

polearm reversed, then she uncoiled, thrusting the butt of her weapon against Guang's shield, knocking him from his feet and sending him sliding away on his back. She stood staring at him, wincing at some pain.

Guang groaned. It had been years and more since he had been involved in anything like a battle. He stayed clear of them for a good few reasons these days, and only one of those was how much they hurt. He rolled onto his hands and knees and saw blood leaking from his thumb, trailing a thin river on the snow beneath him. He tried to get to his feet, slipped, landed hard on one knee, and cried out. He wasn't on snow anymore – this was ice. She had knocked him onto the frozen lake. A dozen paces behind him was the discarded fishing line, a little stool sitting beside it. Guang was sorely temped to call a surrender and test out the comfort of that stool. He wanted no more of the fight, that was certain.

The old woman started forward and slid to a stop on the ice. She took a moment to steady herself, then smiled and started sliding toward Guang across the ice.

"How about we call it a draw?" Guang said, backing away from her. The ice groaned beneath him, and he really hoped he was only imagining the insidious cracking sounds coming from somewhere below him.

"If I have to kill you to help Kira, then I will," the old woman said. "I will not let you take her." She frowned, wrinkles turning into ocean-deep lines. "She's all I have left."

Guang risked a glance at Haruto as he continued backing away. The staff of water was in the ground now, but Guang was so far away he couldn't even hear the battle anymore, and the snow drifting about was doing a good job of obscuring them from view.

"Then she shouldn't have killed my son," Guang said. The words didn't taste right in his mouth. The ice groaned again beneath him.

"I told you, we didn't kill these people."

"I don't care about them," Guang snarled. It was true. He

knew he should care, but compared to the loss of his son, they meant nothing. "I'm talking about my son, Tian."

The old woman slid to a stop just within striking distance. The fishing stool was beside Guang now, and the ice was keening and crepitating with every step. He clutched his paper shield, waiting for the strike.

"Tian Meng?" the old woman asked. "You're Tian's father?"

Guang lowered his shield to stare at the woman. "Yes. You didn't kill him, did you?" And finally the words sounded right.

A shadow passed beneath Guang so fast he thought he imagined it.

"Tian was my friend," the old woman said. "We taught together at Heiwa." Her frown lifted and she gasped. "You think Kira destroyed Heiwa? No. She was a student there."

Guang cursed himself for a fool. They had to stop Haruto before he cleansed the wrong yokai. He looked past the old woman, but the snow was picking up again, and Haruto was lost to the blizzard and Guang's poor eyesight. The ice creaked again and a jagged white line raced between Guang's feet, cracking like thunder. A shadow whipped under the surface between him and the old woman.

"Ah cabbage!" Guang cursed.

The ice split and a white serpent erupted from the depths, breaking through and sending chunks of frozen lake flying.

The cracks spread along the ice like forking lightning, and the lake split into a thousand drifting patches of ice, each one twisting, turning, floating, tilting. Some sank away into the darkness of the water and others further split into small chunks. Guang teetered on his own raft of ice, desperately trying to keep his balance. The serpent reared above him, white as frozen flesh, a crest of spines along its back. It had a human face, a chubby, snarling child's visage with fangs instead of teeth and giant fish eyes. Two little pudgy human arms poked out from beneath its head, childish fingers flexing open and closed, open and closed.

The serpent lunged at Guang, and he thrust his shield at it. The beast slammed its head into the hardened paper, smashing him down onto his back on his little ice patch. Freezing water rushed over him, soaking his clothes. Fangs gnashed against the paper shield. Guang growled, gripped it with both hands, tried to hold on as the serpent pushed him toward the water. Two pallid hands grabbed hold of the shield and wrenched, trying to rip it from his grasp, but Guang held on as the serpent reared up and tossed him across the broken ice like a child's doll. He crashed onto another patch of ice and wheezed the air out of lungs. The ice was already tilting, threatening to tip him into the water, and he knew if he fell in, he would be dragged down and never see the surface again. His legs slid into the icy cold, scrambling, kicking, sinking. He heard a thump.

The old woman leapt onto the ice chunk next to his. It was bigger and flat. She balanced herself, then thrust the butt of her polearm at him. He flinched and closed his eyes and... nothing. He opened one eye to look. She was holding out the polearm for him. He grabbed hold of it, still clutching his paper shield with his other hand, and she tugged and pulled him up out of the water and onto her own patch of ice. It rocked and teetered, tilting one way then the other.

"Don't move!" she shouted.

"Wasn't planning on it!" he said.

They clung there, on their frozen pontoon as it gently came to rest.

"Thank you!" Guang said.

"You're... welcome." The old woman puffed and panted, squinting at the serpent.

The serpent shrieked and pulled back under the surface, sending ripples along the water that rocked the shattered icescape.

The old woman placed her feet wide apart and glanced about, trying to see the serpent beneath the surface of the water. "By the stars, what is that thing?"

Guang struggled to remember. "What did Haruto call it? A ningen, I think. A type of yokai created when a child drowns in icy water."

"How do we kill it?"

Guang grumbled, holding his paper shield close. So far he had kept the water away from the blood, but if his inscription was damaged his shield would become nothing but expensive arse wipe. "No idea. Haruto is the onmyoji. I'm just a poet."

The old woman narrowed her eyes a moment, then looked away. "Will cutting it work?"

Guang shook his head. "Only one way to find out. I'll do my best to block it, you take care of the stabbing and slashing and such."

A ripple wobbled the ice patch again. Guang and the old woman jumped away from each other just as the serpent erupted from the depths once more, splitting the patch of ice apart and flinging frozen shards in every direction. Guang landed on a small berg and the woman on another, the ningen between them. It peered through icy fish eyes at Guang, then swung its head toward the old woman and floated toward her. It was smarter than Guang thought it should be.

"Come on, old knees. Time to be nimble," Guang shouted at himself and leapt onto another patch of ice, sprinted across it and onto another and then another.

The ningen lunged at the old woman, and she stepped onto an adjacent chunk of ice. Childlike, pale hands latched onto the iceberg she had been standing on and flung it away, smashing it into pieces. The old woman slid to a stop, and Guang leapt onto the same patch of berg and held his shield up in front of them.

The serpent twisted about and lunged at him. Guang swung his shield, batting away its open mouth. He planted his feet as best he could on the slippery wet ice and braced himself as the serpent lunged again. Its twisted childish face crashed against the hardened paper, pale hands flailing, clawing at him. The old woman thrust her polearm over Guang's shoulder. The blade skidded across the creature's white scales and sliced in between them in a spray of steaming ichor. The ningen howled and thrashed, pulled back and disappeared under the black water.

The old woman struggled to catch her breath. "That seemed to work."

Guang glanced about. He'd gotten turned around and, in the blowing snow, no longer knew which way led back to the village. "We need to get back to Haruto and your girl," he said. "Unless you have some fabulous technique that can kill this onion in one, it's just going to harry us to death, and I for one am too old for this."

"Do you have any fire?" the old woman asked.

Something rocked the ice they were standing on.

"I have a flint," Guang said, reaching inside his coat pocket and pulling it out. It was damp and wouldn't create anything more than a spark.

"It'll do." The old woman snatched it from him just as the serpent leapt out of the water, arcing towards them, its entire body clearing the floating ice. Guang swung his shield and thumped its head, knocking its descent aside. It plunged into the water next to their ice, the entire length of its pallid body scraping against his shield and nearly capsizing their raft. "I need a minute."

"I'll give you as long as I can."

The serpent rose again next to them, spraying icy water over Guang. It slapped at his shield with its hands and then lunged at the old woman. He stepped in and thrust the shield at its face. The impact shuddered through the shield and up his arms, but the serpent backed away. Its fangs gnashed against the paper, its arms scrabbled at the edges. Water dripped down the inside of the paper shield, running a damning track towards the blood inscription. "Hurry!" Guang shouted.

Guang's knees wobbled, and pain shot up his legs. He really wasn't cut out for fighting anymore. When did poetry become so dangerous? He glanced over his shoulder at the old woman. She had sheathed her polearm over her back and held the flint in her hands. She struck once to no effect, then again and the spark fizzled out instantly. "Damnit, Yanmei, you old fool," she snarled at herself. "Be faster."

"Yes!" Guang said as his left knee buckled and he dropped to kneel on the ice. "Please do."

The old woman struck the flint again and it sparked, flared

up, and her arm burst into roaring fire. It looked like it hurt. She drew a deep, wheezing breath. In her eyes, Guang saw something terrible – a look of acceptance, of resignation. He had seen it before many times. It was the look people got when they realised they were going to die and they welcomed it.

"Bellow's Breath," the old woman snarled, drawing another breath, sucking the fire from her arm into her chest. She held it for a moment, stared at Guang in wide-eyed panic; he realised he was in the way and flung himself down on his shield on the wet ice. The old woman blew out an inferno into the ningen's snarling face.

Scaled, sallow flesh sloughed from serpent's head and lower jaw. Its hands were burned to flailing stumps, and its eyes melted in its face. It screeched in agony, thrashed about and then dropped back into the water with such violence that the ice Guang and the woman were standing on rocked and bucked.

The old woman breathed out the last of the flames and collapsed, falling onto Guang. She was breathing in starts, unable to catch her breath, and clutching at her chest. She was in pain, agony by the looks of it, and her eyes were wild, darting about and finally met his own.

"I don't fancy waiting about to see if you killed it," Guang said. He started to his feet and realised his shield beneath him was a bed of soggy pulp. Well, it had served. He clambered up despite the rusty nails stabbing through his knees, and threw one of the old woman's arms over his shoulder. Together they jumped onto the next iceberg, and then the next. Eventually they reached the shore and stepped onto the loosely packed snow. The village was just up the gentle slope from the edge of the lake, and Haruto and the old woman's girl were still fighting.

As Guang struggled up the slope with the old woman, Haruto slapped the girl across the face with the wood staff, planted it in the ground and shouted, "Wood!" Haruto stepped back from the completed barrier. "It's over, onryo."

Chapter 8

Haruto drew his katana and held it out to his side. "Shiki," he said. Nothing happened. He cleared his throat and tried again. "Shiki!" The spirit chittered from within his kimono, but refused to come out.

The onryo got to her feet inside the barrier created by the ritual staffs. It wouldn't last forever, and he needed to kill her while it was active or she wouldn't be truly destroyed. Without the power of the staffs, she wouldn't be sent to Omoretsu. An uncleansed yokai could always find a way back from heaven to earth.

Those mirrored knives of hers were a problem. Whenever he looked at them he saw illusions, monsters behind him about to attack, Guang being slaughtered by the old woman, a hundred images of the onryo surrounding him. They were all lies, images in the reflections and nothing more. Of course, it wasn't easy to fight her when he couldn't look at her weapons.

Haruto pulled his kimono open a little and the cold seeped in. "Shiki, you little sod, get out here." The spirit chittered, staring up at him but did not move.

"What are you doing?" the onryo asked. She took a step closer, peering at him, a curious half-smile tugging at her lips.

"Damn it!" Haruto let go of his kimono and clutched his katana in both hands. It would be harder to kill the yokai without his spirit blade, but not impossible. "In the name of Omoretsu, I..."

"No!" the onryo wailed. "No no no no no no." She dropped her knives and ran, passing between two ritual staffs and completely ignoring the barrier. She slid to a stop at the edge of the frozen lake. Guang was there, half carrying the old woman.

She was wheezing, clutching at her chest with her free hand. Her other hand was a raw, weeping mess of angry flesh and oozing sores. Her lips were cracked and charred. "No no no," the onryo said as she pulled the old woman from Guang's arms and helped her sit down in the snow. "Yanmei, you didn't! You can't do that anymore."

Haruto poked at the nearest of his staffs. The metal staff. It was firmly planted in the ground, and the barrier was active, its soft hum an electric thrill like the moment before a first kiss, but the onryo had passed through it. He left the staffs in the ground and walked to the edge of the lake. "What happened?" he asked.

Guang had his coat pulled close and was shivering, his face pale. "That, uh, ningen thing," the old poet said through chattering teeth. "Serpent. Attacked us. She set it on fire."

"You can't," the onryo cried into the woman's blackened face. "The Sage said that technique is killing you, Yanmei. You can't use it anymore. Please. You can't. You can't. You..."

The old woman gave the onryo a wan smile through her blistered lips and raised her a trembling hand to the onryo's face. "Didn't have much choice. The serpent was trying to kill us."

"You should have fed it the old man and ran."

"Hey!" Guang said.

"I taught you better than that, Kira," the old woman said.

The onryo sulked for a moment, then turned to Guang and bowed deeply. "I'm sorry."

Haruto glanced back at the ritual staffs, still buried in the snow. The girl was a yokai. She was onryo, Shiki confirmed it. But something was wrong. She had passed through the barrier with ease, and here she was showing concern over this old woman, perhaps her grandmother. And apologising to Guang for insulting him.

"Did we kill it?" Guang asked. "The ningen."

Haruto shook his head. "With fire, you just hurt it. It will rest at the bottom of the lake until it recovers. If it hasn't fed on anyone, it might not have the energy and will probably fade and return to heaven. If it has fed, it will rise again eventually, healed." He turned to the old woman and the onryo. The girl had positioned herself between them. "I think we need to talk."

"Inside," Guang said, shivering. "Around a fire."

"The Crone lives in the last building," the old woman said as the onryo helped her to her feet. "She brews a wonderful pot of tea."

The Crone's hut was just big enough for them to kneel around the table in the centre of its front room. Guang hustled toward the fire and hunched in front of it, extended his shivering hands almost into the flames. His lips were a pale blue and water dripped from his clothes onto the floor. Haruto hated that his friend had almost died battling a yokai, and he hadn't been there to protect him. He promised himself not to let it happen again.

"Oh, you're back," the Crone said as she shuffled out from a small kitchen at the back of the little house. She was ancient, wrinkled like a prune, and her white hair looked as brittle as straw. She walked with a cane, tapping before each step, and wore a strangely vacant, beatific smile. "I am so happy. And this must be your husband, Yanmei," she said, pointing the cane at Guang. She shuffled over to the fire and placed a hand on his shoulder. Guang startled, staring at the Crone with wild eyes. "Your daughter is such a good girl."

The onryo grinned at that. "Shall I help you with the tea, grandmother?"

"Such a good girl!" She shuffled back to the kitchen and fussed about. The onryo sprang up to help, running a hand through her messy mop of hair to shake the snow out.

Haruto watched the Crone move about through the doorway. He recognised her, but couldn't quite dredge up the memory. She had been much younger. Full of life.

"Your mother?" Guang asked from the hearth.

Yanmei shook her head. Despite her injuries, her laboured breathing and scorched hand and lips, her back was straight as she knelt, and her eyes were sharp. It quickly became clear she would not volunteer anything.

"You say you're not responsible for the deaths in the village here, nor the academy fire, but why should I believe that?" Haruto asked. "You are harbouring an onryo." Tian's anger still bubbled over inside him like a river broken its banks, but it was not directed at the girl.

Yanmei tilted her head just slightly toward the hearth. "And you're an onmyoji travelling with the bandit Blood Dancer. If we are weighing sin, I would wager Kira sits above us all on those scales."

Haruto glanced at Guang, and the poet shook his head sadly. "She has a point, old man."

"How far do we have to go before no one recognises you?" Haruto asked.

The old poet turned from the fire and chuckled. "Further than the stars? You can't buy notoriety like mine." All the mirth seemed to leech out of him then. "And if you could, you would ask for a refund."

"Even my father thought you were a rabid dog who needed putting down," Yanmei said, her voice tight.

Guang nodded. "Can't argue. Who's your father?"

"Flaming Fist," Yanmei said. It was a name people remembered with almost as much venom as Blood Dancer. Flaming Fist was a legendary bandit who had burned his way across half of Hosa back when the first Emperor of Ten Kings was uniting the empire. He was renowned for his technique of setting his own hands on fire. Well, that and all the murdering and pillaging.

"Ahh." Guang grunted and turned back to the fire. "Cabbage!"

"Not going to apologise for the death of my brother?" Yanmei asked.

Guang just stared into the flames. "Wouldn't mean anything if I did."

Yanmei snorted and turned back to Haruto just as the onryo and the Crone appeared from the kitchen. The onryo breezed about, oblivious to the tension in the room. She placed a tray with a teapot and five cups on the table.

"Such a good girl," the Crone said, sitting and patting the onryo's hand with her own gnarled claw.

Shiki squeaked, probably smelling the tea. She scurried around Haruto's midsection and clawed her way up to sit on his shoulder.

The onryo gasped. "It... it... it's so cute!" She hurried around the table to stand next to Haruto, as if they hadn't been trying to kill each other minutes ago. Shiki switched shoulders, stared at the girl and then reached out spindly limb to touch the girl's prodding finger. She chirruped happily, leapt onto the girl's arm, scurried up onto her shoulder and cavorted about. The onryo giggled and twirled about with the spirit on her shoulder.

"Traitor," Haruto grumbled, but the spirit didn't seem to care.

Guang was looking over his shoulder from the fire. "Huh. I thought the little beast only liked you, old man."

Yanmei sighed as Shiki and the onryo danced about in a cacophony of laughing and chirping. "Kira," she said, not sharply but sternly. "These men are here to kill you. This is a situation that requires gravity."

The onryo froze and Shiki with her. Then she moved to the table and sat down in a chair next to Yanmei. "Sorry," she mumbled. Then she poked Shiki with a finger and smiled as the spirit tensed dramatically and toppled from her shoulder, playing dead.

The Crone startled. "Well, where did you come from, little one?" She stood slowly and shuffled back toward the kitchen. "I bet you'd like a fish. I have some around here somewhere." Shiki warbled and leapt from the table to follow the Crone.

"I guess one of us needs to start," Haruto said. "An onryo destroyed Heiwa Academy and killed Guang's son, Tian Meng. We came here searching for the culprit, following the trail of spirits that always seems to be left in the wake of onryo – a village full of dead people." He waved a hand towards the girl. "She appears. You know the rest. But what I really want to know is how you walked past the spirit barrier?"

The girl grinned and shrugged. "Spirit barrier? Do you mean those staffs you kept hitting me with? Maybe you set it up wrong?"

"I did not."

Yanmei reached for the tea pot and poured four cups. "Kira was not responsible for Heiwa. She was a student there and has been for almost ten years. I was a teacher." She paused, sipped at her tea, regardless of the thick plumes of steam still rising from it.

"Yanmei! You mustn't," the girl said.

Yanmei startled and placed the cup back on table. "I'm sorry. I didn't mean to."

"If you keep using your technique, it will kill you." There were tears in the girl's eyes. "You can't leave me. I can't lose you. I'm not..." Her tears spilled over on her cheeks and she started breathing hard. Haruto heard a sound like glass cracking.

Yanmei reached over and squeezed the girl's hand. "I'm not going anywhere, Mirai," she said calmly. "See, I'm letting it cool."

The onryo nodded and wiped her eyes. When she looked up again, she was smiling.

"It was not just one onryo that destroyed Heiwa," Yanmei continued, still holding the girl's hand. "There were five of them. They came at night, set fires, slaughtered the students and teachers. I was only able to save Kira." She sighed and looked over toward Guang sitting at the hearth. "Tian was with us for a while, but he went back in to find others. I'm sorry he didn't make it out."

Guang grumbled but didn't turn from the flames. "The stupid onion always wanted to be a hero. Said he would make up for all the pain I caused." There was a sadness to the old poet's voice that Haruto was not used to hearing. He felt a rage boil up inside him, an anger so hot all the snow on the mountain would melt before its fury. He grit his teeth, swallowed it down, knowing it wasn't his. It was Tian's anger. The rage of a yokai passed on to him and demanding vengeance. He glanced at the girl. She was Onryo. He could feel her energy; it was undoubtedly a spirit's qi, but Tian's anger was not directed at her. Yanmei was telling the truth, this girl, Kira, was not the onryo they were hunting.

The Crone shuffled into the room again, preceded by the tap of her cane. Shiki followed, proudly displaying a fish in her spindly arms as if she'd caught it herself. The Crone knelt next to Kira, and the girl poured her a cup of tea.

"How did you come to be here, then?" Haruto asked. "Are you hunting them too?"

Yanmei shook her head. "The Sage..."

"Konihashi?" the Crone asked. "Is he coming? Oh, I would dearly like to see him again. Did you know we once..." she trailed off, frowning, her eyes roving about as if searching for something she couldn't quite find.

"He's not coming," Yanmei said. "Konihashi isn't coming." She patted the Crone's gnarled hand and then looked up at Haruto again. "I was preparing to leave Heiwa. My technique is hurting me. I can't stop the fires from burning me anymore. Konihashi was known as the Fifth Sage Under Heaven. He knew many techniques, but he was not a healer."

The Crone nodded and a smile crept onto her face.

"He told Yanmei to seek the Fourth Sage Under Heaven," Kira said. She sipped her tea and pulled a face like it tasted of lemon. "He's supposed to fix her."

Yanmei sighed and shook her head. "He said the Crone in Tyoto might know where to look. I was planning to go alone, sneak out in the middle of the night."

Kira scoffed. "You are *not* leaving without me." She and Yanmei stared at each other, both setting their jaws in a similar looks of determination.

Eventually Yanmei looked away and continued telling them what happened. "Then the onryo attacked and burned Heiwa to the ground. We came here to find the Crone, but the onryo had already been here too. The village was their doing, not ours." She picked up her cup and blew steam from the tea.

Haruto felt something was still missing. He groaned. He hated mysteries and thought he was old enough that none were left to him. But life was never that simple no matter how long it lasted. "Who is she?" he asked, nodding at the Crone. "Who are you, that the onryo came and left you alive?"

The ancient woman smiled a gummy grin at him.

"She's the Gilded Crone," Guang said. He stood and limped over to the table.

Generations ago, long before Hosa's unification and even before war consumed the four nations, the Nash empire was a bountiful place. Horses roamed the plains in great herds and the Nash people moved with them. They were nomadic by nature, travelling across the vast nation in a hundred different clans. It was a time of prosperity, decreed so by the gods themselves, and the great Nash vhargan, lord of all the clans, decided some of his people should settle in one place. He wished to emulate the success of Ipia and Hosa by founding great cities for his people and a capital unlike any the world had yet seen. And so he chose a spot, close to the ocean for fishing and easy trade, but also within sight of the plains so none of his people would forget where they came from. There he built his magnificent city from the dust, and he called it Drakhan.

But there are people in this world who do not listen to the gods. They were not bound by the laws of harvest decreed by the tianjun, the lord of heaven, and they saw this great city the Nash had built as a ripe fruit for plucking. We call them the Seafolk. They are a savage race, tall and fair and brutal. They care for just three things: battle, their ships, and the taking of slaves. With their sights set on Drakhan, they sailed ashore at night in their thousands and laid waste to the city.

Men and women and children died in the fires the Seafolk set, to the axes and spears they wielded. The Nash were herded in droves onto the ships of the Seafolk, never to be seen again. None could stop them. None were prepared. Warriors of Nash, trained all their lives for battle, were cut down as easily as children. They were horse riders, after all, best suited to combat from the saddle. In the packed streets of their new city, their greatest advantage was rendered impotent.

Eventually the Seafolk struck so deep into the heart of Drakhan that they came across the Stables of Ever. A vast building the Nash vhargan had ordered built to breed the mightiest of his horses, beasts like no other. The Seafolk saw this as a bounty, for their own lands have no horses, no beasts of burden of any kind save slaves. What a bounty they could bring back: not mere slaves, but something far more valuable.

But there, standing before the Seafolk horde, was a single woman. She was tall and lithe, as many of the Nash are. Her skin shone like gold and her hair was dark as coal. The Seafolk laughed. A single woman against a horde? They came at her in ones and twos and she slew them. They came at her in tens and twenties and she cut them down. They came at her as an uncountable horde and she laid them waste.

Eventually, one of the Seafolk gods stepped forward to meet her. For their deities do not watch from heaven, but walk among them. He was a giant of a man with arms that rippled with muscle and a belt that bristled with steel. He attacked with all his might and fury and all his weapons. But his blades grew dull, their edges blunt, even as he swung at her. His armour rusted and crumbled from his body at her touch, and before long, he stood before her naked. He snatched up the weapons of his fallen people, but they too fell to ruin. Yet the woman's weapons only grew in strength and number, for everything she touched gained a glowing golden edge as sharp as starlight.

They clashed again and again, and she dealt him such wounds that she proved even gods may fall before mortal might. Those of his people who survived her wrath dragged him away, a god beaten and bloody, a crippled ruin of divinity. The woman did not give chase. She returned to her vigil and watched over the Stables of Ever as had been her duty all along.

When the Nash vhargan arrived to find his glorious city a smoking desolation, he was distraught, inconsolable. Until he entered his stables. He found her there, this woman of gold, the sole survivor of the first Nash city. And his grief was tempered by the sight of his horses, the one thing that survived the worst raid the Seafolk ever launched.

No one knew the woman's name and she would not give it. The vhargan begged and demanded and threatened and pleaded, and still she kept her identity to herself. And so he named her the Gilded Crone, eternal stable master, slayer of foreign gods, the greatest hero of the Nash.

The Crone cackled as Guang finished his story. She sipped at her tea and stared into its ripples through glassy eyes.

"That would make her... ancient," Haruto said.

Guang scoffed. "You're one to talk, old man."

Haruto ignored him. "Why would the Fifth Sage send..."

"Konihashi?" the Crone asked. "Is he coming?"

Yanmei shook her head and patted the Crone's hand.

"Oh," the Crone said sadly. "I would dearly love to see my old friend again."

"Why would the onryo come here to find her?" Haruto asked as he drummed his fingers on the table. "Are they looking for all the Sages?"

"I don't know," Yanmei said. "And I don't think she does either. Age has stolen from her what a long lifetime of enemies could not."

"What happened here, Crone?" Haruto asked. "How did the

people in Tyoto die?"

The Crone squinted at him. "The villagers? I..." She frowned and stared at her tea a moment, then her face relaxed again. Eventually she smiled and looked up at Yanmei. "It seems all my children are coming to visit me these days." She seemed to think Yanmei was her daughter. "Your brother came by the other day. He... kept asking about a prison. I think maybe he was in some sort of trouble. On and on about the prison. He was very demanding and wouldn't touch his tea, kept saying it was too cold. I told him, the only prison I know of is Sky Hollow, and then he left. Never drank his tea. That's probably why he's grown so ugly. Tea gives us smooth skin and kind eyes." She finished by sipping her tea.

Guang was staring at him now. "Sky Hollow," the old poet said as if Haruto hadn't heard. Haruto sullenly refused to meet his friend's gaze.

"It sounds exciting," Kira said. "What is it?"

Yanmei poured herself another cup of tea. "The fortress where Ipian shintei warriors are trained. It's said nobody but the shintei know where it is."

Haruto pushed his tea cup around a bit and refused to meet anyone's eyes.

Guang scratched his beard and stared at Haruto. "Old man?"

Haruto said nothing.

"He knows where it is," Guang said.

Haruto shot his friend an icy stare.

"You can evil eye me all you like, old man. You're the one carrying Tian's burden."

Shiki let out a plaintive squeak.

"Don't you start," Haruto snapped at the spirit, hating the anger in his voice. "Yes, I know where Sky Hollow is."

Yanmei smiled. "Then we set off in the morning."

"Huh?" Haruto shook his head. "I never said I would take you."

"We get to see a fortress?" the onryo asked, clapping her hands. "After ten years of being cooped up at the academy, I'm thinking its destruction was the best thing to happen to me." She frowned. "That's wrong, isn't it?"

Yanmei nodded. "Many people died, including your friends."

The girl scoffed. "Friends. As if I had any." She was silent for a few seconds then shook her head and slapped her cheeks. "I should be sad? I should grieve for them."

Again Yanmei gave that slight nod.

"Even though they hated me?"

Yanmei reached out and squeezed the girl's hand.

There was something wrong with the girl. She seemed to need Yanmei to tell her how a person should feel. Haruto pushed it to the back of his mind to figure out later. If they wanted to follow him to Sky Hollow, so be it. The shintei may take oaths never to reveal its location to outsiders, but those oaths didn't bind him. And keeping the girl close seemed a good idea. He might need to send her to meet Omoretsu before she hurt anyone.

"We'll leave tomorrow then," Haruto agreed. "If you don't mind us staying for the night, Crone?"

"Oh, wonderful. A couple of young men like you? I have plenty of jobs need doing."

Guang chuckled, then shrugged when Haruto looked at him. "What? She called you young."

Chapter 9

Everyone was asleep when Haruto crept out of the Gilded Crone's house. It was the dead of night, and though the snow had stopped falling, it was colder than a monk's disapproval in Tyoto. Haruto rarely felt the bite of a chill, but even he pulled his newly ruined kimono a little tighter and wished he had a coat as thick as Guang's. His cloak might keep the snow off, but it did little against the cold. He drifted through the village more ghostly than any of its previous inhabitants, who lay dead in their homes, murdered by onryo searching for – something. A prison? A sage? Something in Sky Hollow. Yet there was nothing there but shintei, and yokai or not, one would have to be insane to assault the place.

He collected his imperial seal and his ritual staffs by moonlight. He still wasn't sure if something had gone wrong with Omoretsu's blessing on them, or if it was something to do with the girl. Onryo were rare and powerful, and he had to admit, in all his long years, she was the first he had encountered. If the staffs were not enough to hold one of the onryo, he would need to find something else to bind the spirits who destroyed Heiwa and killed Tian.

Haruto retraced his steps down the mountain path and left Tyoto village behind. He wasn't going far and he needed to do this while the others were asleep. They wouldn't understand.

He stopped when the tree came into sight. Its colours were muted in the moonlight, its red leaves a ruddy brown, but there was still no mistaking the figure lounging beneath its canopy. Even though the clouds covered the sky in an immutable grey blanket, the yokai and her tree were lit as if in brightest moonlight.

In the worst Guang impression he could muster, he told himself to "Stop hesitating, old man."

He heard a warning whistle. Shiki faded into existence, shuffling along in the snow behind him in her natural form, snow clinging to her bristly hair. She sat down beside Haruto, stared up at him accusingly, and whistled again.

"I know it's dangerous but I can't just leave her here."

Shiki leapt up on his leg and scrabbled up to his shoulder. Her hair had a yellow tint and scratched at the stubble on his cheek.

"I'll be fine. You can go back if you're scared."

Shiki harrumphed and faded away. She was still close, though, watching over him in case he needed her. He wouldn't. He wouldn't need a spirit blade for this yokai.

As he approached, the yokai looked up at him. The leaves above her rustled though there was no breeze, and she flowed gracefully to her feet. Haruto stopped at the threshold of her domain. The snow was different underneath the tree, a light sprinkling untouched by the wind. It was her realm.

"Akateko," Haruto said by way of greeting.

"Master Onmyoji," the akateko said with a mocking bow that exposed enough pale cleavage a man could get lost and never find his way out. Haruto tore his eyes away. She licked her lips and cocked her head just a little to the side as she regarded him. A few stray strands of dark hair fell loose and gave her a tousled look. "Would you like me to sing for you? Come. Come sit with me and let my voice soothe your worries away."

This was how the akateko worked. Seduction, a beautiful man or woman offering to give you whatever you need if you just sit with them for a while. They eased your worries, soothed your aches, warmed your soul. And all the while they drained your qi to sustain their own lives. Not enough to kill, though they could if they wanted, but enough to make you feel diminished for a time. Even with all his training and his years of experience, Haruto felt the pull of her and yearned to give in.

"You can't stay here, akateko."

"I had a name once," the akateko said, staring up into the red leaves and running a slender hand along her winter-pale cheek. One delicate finger caught against her ruby lip and tugged at it a little. "I don't remember it any more. I've been calling myself Snow recently. It's fitting, don't you think?" She bit her lower lip and stared at Haruto then. Her eyes were large, enticing, demanding, yearning, and dark as the void between the stars. "Do you have a name, Master Onmyoji?"

"Haruto," he said without thinking.

"Haruto." She played with his name on her tongue, devouring the taste of it. She was still staring at him and he couldn't look away, didn't want to look away. He knew it was a technique, the akateko's seduction, but he didn't care. "Haruto," she purred again, a frown crinkling her brow, making her even more irresistible. "No. You have another name."

Shiki popped into existence in front of Haruto and hissed at the akateko, her fur standing on end. Haruto shook himself free of the yokai's technique. The akateko snarled at Shiki, teeth bared and fingernails extending into claws.

"Enough!" Haruto said, hearing the exhaustion in his own voice. He needed to sleep, and knew he couldn't. Sleep was never easy for him, not since he'd made his deal with Omoretsu so long ago. Now that he was carrying Tian's burden, rest was even harder to come by. He reached down and plucked Shiki from the snow and put her back on his shoulder. She growled and waved an arm at the yokai threateningly. For her part, the akateko stepped back to lounge against the tree, running a hand down the fold of her kimono, hinting at untold delights. "You can't stay here, akateko. Sorry, Snow."

The yokai moaned and smiled at him again. "Why not?" She pouted. "I like it here. The cold suits me. The colours are wonderful for my complexion. And the foolish men who stop by are delicious. Who knew such frigid conditions might produce such burning qi?" She drew in a deep breath and let it out as a ragged sigh of pleasure.

"Because all the people of Tyoto are dead," Haruto said.

She shrugged, her kimono slipping easily from one shoulder. "That wasn't me." She smiled and slowly dragged her kimono up.

"The people of Minazuri won't care, Snow. Or won't believe it. As soon as they learn the people here are dead, they will blame you. This goes beyond seducing old men away from their wives for a few hours. They will blame you and they will hire an onmyoji to kill you."

"Is it a fight you want then, Master Onmyoji?" the akateko asked. She stepped away from her tree again, and dipped into a battle ready crouch, eyes twinkling with desire. Her fingernails stretched into talons again, and the snow around her feet stirred, whipped into motion by her qi.

"No!" Haruto snapped. "I'm not trying to fight you. I'm trying to save you."

Shiki squeaked. The akateko stood from her crouch, a look of utter confusion on her face. All attempts at seduction drained away, and she blinked at him, a smile pulling at one corner of her mouth. "Why? You're an onmyoji. You hunt my kind."

Haruto shrugged. "Because you don't hurt anyone. Not really. You take some of their qi, leave them feeling drained for a day or two. In return, they find a few hours of peace. You give them something they're missing. They probably don't even realise they need it, but you give it to them. I've been doing this long enough to know that not all yokai are evil, just as not all people are good. If you stay here, they will hire someone to kill you. It won't be me, but someone will come. Not all onmyoji are as discerning as I am."

"Let them," Snow said, her voice husky. "I'll bring them to my bosom and drain them dry."

"And then another will come. And another after that." Haruto shook his head. "The lost things are returning to the world, Snow. Spirits, techniques long forgotten. The onmyoji won't stand for it. They'll purge you all over again."

She smiled wide, teeth sharpening into fangs. "You do not know how right you are." Then she leaned back against her tree once again and stretched her arms up to play with the leaves, arching her back. Haruto struggled not to stare at her cleavage, and the gaze she sent his way said she knew it. "Fine, fine. I will leave."

"Thank you, Snow." Haruto bowed. "I don't wish to see a spirit as grand as you vanish from the world."

"Grand, am I?" She bit her lip again. "I will leave in the morning." She stepped away from the tree and approached the limits of her realm, close enough for Haruto to reach out and touch her. Then she opened her arms to him. "Would you like me to sing for you now, Master Onmyoji? Would you like me to help you rest?"

Haruto nodded, his shoulders slumped, and he stepped across the threshold.

Chapter 10

They were on the road again, heading back down the mountain trail toward Minazuri, and Kira was near giddy. She skipped across the snow, using the simple technique the Fifth Sage had taught her, and occasionally letting the technique go to tumble into a large drift of powder. Now that she thought about it, she was in fact giddy with the experience of being out and about, exploring the world with Yanmei once more.

She'd liked Heiwa well enough. The teachers had been interesting, though Kira had always struggled with lessons. It was all sitting still and learning, and she wasn't good at that. Far too often she was chastised for staring off into space, daydreaming, not paying enough attention because she'd seen a bug crawling across the floor. It was infinitely more interesting than which king had claimed which throne when.

Then there were the other students. Most of them had ignored her, which had been better than those who didn't. Some called her names, threw things at her, played cruel pranks, and speared her with harsh laughter. She had always struggled to fit in at Heiwa. The other students were all human, after all, and she was... well... not. She was stronger than them, different. They often joked and she didn't get it. When she was younger, she had tried to join in and play with the other students, but something had come out of her and... there had been injuries. No one had died, but she had hurt people and that was not good. Yanmei had been very... not angry. Not even disappointed. But she had been something. Something Kira couldn't quite figure out. People were strange and complex.

Also, ten years cooped up in the academy after eighty years trapped in a mirror had been frustrating on top of boring. Not that she remembered her time trapped in the mirror. Only vague images of darkness and music, nightmares of monsters and pain. But that was all over now. She was free, and seeing the world with Yanmei.

"You look tired," Kira said to Haruto as he slogged his way through snow. He had wandered off the trail and was knee deep, his eyes distant and glazed over. The little spirit sitting on his shoulder waved at her with a furry black arm. Kira waved back. It was so cute she wanted to hug it. And why shouldn't she? Kira reached out a hand towards the spirit.

"Hey!" Haruto snapped, stumbling in the snow and then purposefully walking away from her. The spirit on his shoulder whistled in his ear. "What do you know?" the onmyoji told it.

"Kira," Yanmei said firmly.

"I wasn't trying to hurt him," Kira said, shaking her head. "I just... wanted..." She fell silent. People really were complex. Many of them didn't like touching or sharing their things. Boundaries, Yanmei called them. Boundaries were important for humans. She thought that was something she should remember. She had been human once. But it was all just vague flashes in her mind likes dreams fading the moment she tried to remember them. "Sorry."

They walked in silence for a while. The onmyoji kept glancing at her and moving away slightly, so Kira danced across the snow and walked on the other side of him. The old poet was a little further back and Yanmei behind him. Kira had been hoping for more talk and laughter, maybe some interesting stories of places she'd never seen before. She'd been hoping adults wouldn't act like the children at Heiwa, that they might treat her differently.

At least the snow had stopped. It was still thick on the ground, obscuring everything, but now Kira could see down into the valley and the white-capped trees looked fascinating. She'd heard all sorts of stories about forests and things hiding in them. Sometimes from the teachers during the more interesting lessons and sometimes from the other students as she hid from them and eavesdropped on their conversations. They would always fall silent whenever they saw her.

"So you know all about spirits?" Kira asked the onmyoji after a while. The silence grated on her, always had. It reminded her too much of the mirror and those were memories she was glad were fuzzy.

Haruto glanced at her and shrugged. "It's my job."

"Onmyoji," Kira said, happy he had actually replied. "Spirit hunter."

"No," he said grumpily. "I don't hunt spirits. I... treat with them."

"Hmm." Kira danced ahead a few steps and turned around, walking backwards on top of the snow. "Yanmei always said the onmyoji hunted and killed spirits like me."

"Well then, Yanmei is just as ignorant as the rest of the world."

"No she isn't!" Kira narrowed her eyes at the man and wondered if she could find a reflection for him to look at. Then she could teach him a lesson for insulting Yanmei.

The onmyoji looked at her, and the little spirit on his shoulder whistled again. "Really?" he asked it tiredly. He looked exhausted. Dark bags hung under his eyes, and his every step seemed weary and plodding. Kira had slept like the dead, which was a term she always found hilarious considering she *was* dead. Or had been dead. She wasn't entirely sure how it all worked, but she had definitely died at some point even if she couldn't remember it.

"We onmyoji aren't spirit hunters. We're occultists. We do track down yokai, but we don't kill them. We can't kill them, not really. We talk to them, find out what they want, and send them on their way. At least, that's what we're meant to be."

Kira considered this for a moment. She let the technique fade from her feet and sank down into the snow to walk beside the onmyoji. "You weren't trying to talk to *me* yesterday. You kept hitting me with those staffs, which hurt by the way."

"Sorry."

She ran a hand through her hair, dislodging some ice that had crept in. "It's alright. I stabbed you first. Not that you seemed to care much. Hey, why aren't you dead?"

The old poet chuckled. "Yeah, why aren't you dead, old man?"

Haruto shot him a venomous glare over his shoulder. "I can't die. But that doesn't mean being stabbed doesn't hurt."

That answer gave Kira even more questions. "Sorry then, about stabbing you. But why can't you die?" She thought everyone could die given enough prodding with sharp things. That was certainly what she had been taught back at Heiwa. Although the Sage had always seemed beyond death... until he wasn't.

"How old are you?" Yanmei asked as she caught them up. "You say you can't die and Blood Dancer keeps calling you 'old man'."

"I would appreciate it if you called me Guang," the poet said. "Or pretty much anything else other than... that name."

Kira was dying to ask him why he was called Blood Dancer and why he hated the name, but she also really wanted to know why Haruto couldn't die. People were fascinating.

"So how old are you, Haruto?" Yanmei repeated.

Haruto shrugged. "Old enough to be a parable."

Kira thought about that, but didn't know what he meant.

They crested a small hill and Minazuri came into view below them. A great wooden welt sheltered from the worst of the weather at the base of two mountains, filled with houses and people, and so many other things Kira had never seen before. High wooden walls surrounded the town, and people swarmed over them like ants. Kira and Yanmei had skirted the city on their way to Tyoto. She hadn't been allowed in, but she had wanted to see it. She wanted to know what it felt like to be surrounded by so many people and spirits. It looked exciting.

"Something's wrong," Haruto said.

"Eh?" Guang grunted. He was squinting.

Yanmei shielded her eyes with a hand, but her eyesight had

been getting worse for a couple of years now. She tried to hide it, but Kira had noticed. She missed things and had trouble reading, especially small lettering.

"There are spirits everywhere," Haruto said, an edge of something in his voice that Kira couldn't quite place. She looked to Yanmei for the guidance she usually gave, but she was focused on the city.

"Is that not normal?" Kira asked. She had spotted them right away: two little monkeys clinging to the walls. They were vivid orange with black spots along their sides, a line of cobalt-blue fur down their backs and fleshy wings between their front and back legs. They were gnawing at the walls, chewing on the wood and spitting it out. A fur clad guard swung a spear at one of the little beasts, but it passed straight through it. The little spirit laughed and spat a wadded chunk of wood at the man. Kira giggled at the antics.

Above the city, a dark cloud hung in an otherwise clear blue sky. As the cloud roiled and shifted, Kira thought she caught glimpses of a laughing face. Up on top of the wall, people were desperately trying to light lanterns against the gloomy shadow cast by the cloud, but every time a wick lit, a ghostly woman appeared and blew it out. All around was chaos, people shouting and chasing spirits that ran and played and mocked them. It all looked like a lot of fun.

"I've never seen spirits act so brazenly before," Haruto said. Shiki chirruped and scuttled about his shoulders. She was clearly agitated, and Kira could almost understand what she was saying.

"Something to do with the onryo?" Guang asked. He glanced at Kira. "I mean, the other onryo." She smiled at him, and he shook his head at her.

"Only one way to find out," Haruto said and doubled his pace down the trail toward the city.

When they reached the walls, they quickly found themselves surrounded by city guards, who looked none too pleased to see them. Most of the guards carried spears or swords, a few of which were even levelled at them. Yanmei remained calm, so Kira decided it was best to imitate her. She always had a much better grasp of how to act than Kira. It took a human to really understand other humans.

"You!" screamed a woman from up on the wall. She had a chubby, bright red face like a tomato had grown eyes and hair and was quite angry about it. She stabbed a finger at Haruto. Then she disappeared from the wall and a handful of seconds later stormed out of the gate with two armed guards at her back. "You did this!" she shouted at Haruto.

The onmyoji held up his hands. "I don't even know what *this* is."

"Oh, yes you do." The angry tomato stopped in front of Haruto and poked a finger at his chest. Kira half expected him to grab her finger and snap it, but he just stood and weathered the assault.

The guards closed in, and Kira felt her chest tighten and started looking for an escape. This was just like when Minato and his gang found her alone at Heiwa. More than once, they chased her down and surrounded her. They called her inhuman, spat on her, threatened to beat her with sticks and wooden practice swords. She flicked her wrist and grabbed hold of the dagger that appeared in her hand. Then she heard a soft icy snap like a crack splitting across glass and felt something shift inside.

The chubby woman got right up in Haruto's face and screeched, "Am I supposed to believe it's a coincidence that an onmyoji shows up and finds no paying work and just leaves. Then these... these yokai just start showing up ... EVERYWHERE! My city is besieged. And not two days later, here you are again. You did this! You sent the yokai against us so we would have no choice but to pay you. You... you charlatan."

"I assure you, I have nothing to do with it," Haruto said. "We've been up at Tyoto. All the villagers there..."

"Don't change the subject. I've dealt with your kind before. Tricksters who would pretend at being onmyoji but are really in league with the yokai. Let me see your imperial seal."

Haruto sighed and reached into his ruined kimono. "These

aren't yokai. They're just spirits. Well, most of them are just spirits."

"Huh?" The woman snatched the seal from his hand and stared at it. "Spirits, yokai, same damned thing. A nuisance at best and dangerous at worst. They should all be destroyed." Kira wondered if that meant her as well, and realised of course it did. "Whose seal is this? Emperor Ise Aketo? Our Empress is Ise Ryoko."

"Ipia currently has two royal lines," Guang said.

"You think I don't know that?" The woman waved the wooden seal at him, staring at the poet as though he were mud traipsed in by an unwanted boot. "I am the magistrate of Minazuri. I *know* the royal lines, both of them, better than you. This is Empress Ise Ryoko's territory, not Emperor Ido Tanaka's. And I've never heard of an Ise Aketo. This--" she waved Haruto's imperial seal in the air. "--is fake!" She gripped in both hands and made to snap it, but Haruto shot a hand out and pulled it away from her. Kira wondered what was on the piece of wood that made it so important.

The guards readied their weapons. They even held them just like Minato and his gang did.

Kira raised her knife and tilted it until the guard opposite her glanced down into its mirrored blade. In the reflection, a great shadowy bear with two heads, teeth like swords and claws gleaming with fire rose behind him. His eyes went wide and he screamed. He spun around, tripping over his own feet as he stabbed out and almost impaled the surprised soldier behind him. Kira tensed, shifting her grip to stab the knife into his neck. She heard more glass cracking, felt a tingle race along the skin of her arm. Then a hand on her shoulder was pulling her back. Yanmei.

"No, Kira!" Yanmei shouted.

"But..." Kira looked around. More guards were tromping toward them, all armed and threatening, closing in on them like darkness around a dying flame. It was just like Minato and Heiwa all over again. The sound of glass cracking filled her ears. She looked down at her arm, saw a crack in her skin along the back of her hand. She shivered, heard a mirror shattering all around her, shards of mirrored glass fell from her, scattering in the snow. The crack along her hand was gone. She looked up to find Yanmei staring into her eyes, intense and worried. "But they're attacking us, aren't they?" Kira asked.

Yanmei held her by her shoulders and bent just a little so they were face to face. Kira looked into her eyes and then away, ashamed. She knew that look. She'd done something wrong again. Yanmei's face was wrinkled and severe, the grey streaks in her hair harsh against the black. Yet there was something else in her eyes too, a desperation Kira was not used to seeing, as though something had changed. Maybe something to do with Heiwa burning down. She didn't understand.

"They were attacking us. I thought... I had to defend us. Defend you," Kira said. She was babbling. She always babbled when she got confused like this. All the tutors at the academy thought she was simple because of it. They talked over her like she would never understand them. Regardless of how hard she tried in their boring classes, or how strong she was in martial training, they all thought her stupid and slow. All of them except Yanmei. Well, maybe Yanmei and the Sage, but he was dead. They were all dead now. All the tutors and the students. Her mind was racing, a hundred thoughts assaulting her at once, refusing to slow down.

"Kira Mirai, look at me," Yanmei was saying. But Kira looked everywhere else, down at the snow, at the guards brandishing spears behind them, up at the white clouds circling the mountain above and the dark cloud hanging over the city. "Look at me." Her voice was calm, not angry. Yanmei was never angry, not with her at least. She wasn't even disappointed. Just that strange... something that Kira couldn't understand. She glanced at Yanmei, just a quick look to appease her, but she got caught in the depth of her eyes. They were paler than they had been, losing their colour just like her hair.

Kira didn't know how long Yanmei held her there, but it was long enough that her mind stopped babbling at her and a pleasant calmness settled on her like a heavy blanket.

"They're not attacking us," Yanmei said. She glanced over her shoulder, raised her voice and gave it a hard edge. "Are you?"

The chubby woman stared at her, hands on hips. "I haven't decided yet."

Haruto stepped forward, and a spear poked him in the chest, the snow-covered guard on the other end of it, almost trembling with fear. He was the one Kira had shown the monster to. Haruto slowly pushed the spear aside. "Let me see what I can do about your spirit problem."

The chubby woman seemed to consider that for a moment, her cheeks puffing with each steaming breath. "Fine! But we're not paying you a single lien. This is all your fault... somehow."

Haruto merely shrugged.

"And you'll be under guard." She signalled to the armed guards around her. "Keep an eye on them, and don't let any of them wander off."

Yanmei gave Kira's arm one more squeeze, then stepped up next to the onmyoji. "I guess we're together for a little longer then."

The dark cloud boiling above Minazuri rumbled, and to Kira it sounded an awful lot like mocking laughter.

Chapter 11

Minazuri was under siege. Haruto had been an onmyoji for more years than the average fool could count, and he had never seen spirits gather like this. They scampered across the rooftops, played in the snow and tormented the people living there. Some were simple mischievous little things: furi and inugami, possessed animals cavorting about just pleased to be back on earth for a while. Others like the jinmenken and kyokotsu were more dangerous and malicious.

As the guards escorted them through the city, Haruto began to suspect there was more than just the presence of an onryo drawing the spirits to Minazuri. They were everywhere. Some of the townsfolk had locked up their homes, desperate to keep the spirits out. Others were forming bands of roaming militia and arming themselves, trying to succeed where the guards failed. They too would fail. Some spirits could be killed by mortal weapons, but only the body would die. The spirit would simply find a new host. They needed to be cleansed and sent back to heaven in a proper ritual.

Kira danced around, and her manic energy made Haruto nervous. Whatever had afflicted her earlier had faded; she bounced around from one side of the street to the other, staring into windows, delighted at what she saw. Occasionally, she stopped and talked to the spirits, even the ones who could not or would not talk back. She spent a good thirty seconds having a one-sided conversation with a parasol that flapped and flew about on its own until an old woman chased the kasa-obake away with a broom. Kira giggled as she watched the spirit float away. The guards tried to keep her in line, but whenever they met her eyes, they staggered away, terrified by whatever they saw there. Haruto was still not sure what she was exactly: an onryo but able to move past his ritual barrier? A yokai but more human than any he had ever known? Could he really just leave her to wander the world? She was dangerous, that much was obvious, but Yanmei seemed to be able to control her.

"*Mired in chaos.*
A tempest of evil spirits."

Guang tapped his chin as he considered the last line. "*My friend, the saviour?*"

"Awful," Haruto said.

Guang nodded sadly. "It was. I'm sorry for that one."

"Where would you even start with all this?" Yanmei asked as a small dog-like inugami with ten legs charged past, the severed hind leg of a horse clutched in its slavering maw. Blood trailed through the snow behind it, and three men behind that, each one carrying an old sword or spear that probably couldn't cut a straw-stuffed mattress.

One of the men chasing the inugami stopped in front of Haruto. "Master Onmyoji?" he asked, and without waiting for an answer, shouted, "The onmyoji has returned!" He dropped to his hands and knees in the blood-stained snow and bowed his bald head. "Please, Master Onmyoji, help us. These yokai have already killed two of my horses." The other two men dropped to their knees next to the bald fellow and bowed.

"We're sorry for any insult we gave you, master," said the youngest of the three, barely a boy with only a dusting of hair on his jutting chin.

The guards escorting Haruto and his companions looked uncomfortable. Almost as uncomfortable as Haruto felt.

"Take them back and we'll pay you, I promise," said the baldy, still on his knees.

Guang grumbled and nudged Haruto with his elbow. "They really think this is all your doing."

Haruto turned and glared at the old poet. "It's not!"

"Well, I know that," Guang agreed. "But you do come across as a little sullen."

"There's a difference between 'a little sullen' and summoning a horde of spirits to plague a town."

Guang held up his hands in defeat and stepped back, grinning.

Yanmei reached down and helped the oldest of the three petitioners, a bent-backed ancient, to his feet. "The onmyoji is here to help," she assured him. "He has agreed to rid the town of your problem."

"For free!" said one of the guards, a woman with a jutting chin and a beard only slightly less wispy than Guang's.

Haruto just sighed and stepped past the whole display. They could think it was all his fault if they wanted. He was no stranger to being hated or feared. Ahead of him, a building exploded, debris scattered across the snowy street. People screamed, some shouldered out of their homes carrying children or belongings and ran towards Haruto. Others stood around, trying to understand what had happened. None of them could see it. Not even Haruto could see anything more than a shimmering blur, but he saw the footsteps. Hundreds of little hoofed depressions in the snow. A woman ran for the destroyed building, maybe she knew people inside. Haruto called out, but it was too late. The invisible creature lunged, snatched her up in its jaws and ripped the woman in half in a torrent of blood that gushed over the creature, briefly making the monstrous centipede visible.

Soldiers gasped in horror. The gap-toothed woman, too brave for her own good, stepped up beside Haruto, spear held at the ready.

"Amazing! What is that?" Kira asked.

Yanmei glanced at her. "Someone just died, Kira."

"Oh," the young onryo lowered her voice. "Sorry. What is it?"

"An omukade," Haruto said, stepping past the line of guards. "This one *is* a yokai. Stand back."

"Right you are," Guang said. "All yours, old man."

The omukade coiled and sprung forward into another building, smashing it apart with its armoured head. A man screamed, and the omukade pulled back, wrapped its invisible body about the poor fellow and crushed him, spattering itself with gore. A woman behind them wailed and fell to her knees in the snow.

Haruto drew his katana. "Shiki." The spirit leapt into the sword, turning the blade crimson. Haruto crouched and tensed as the omukade turned its bloody head toward him.

It uncoiled and charged. Haruto launched into a sprint to meet it. Its huge head snapped at him. Haruto swayed away from the crushing mandibles and stabbed Shiki into the monster's exoskeleton. The blade slid through its plated armour with ease, and he dragged open a huge wound in its side.

The omukade slowed to a stop, swivelling its blood-smeared head and gnashed its massive fangs. Haruto dropped into a crouch and prepared to thrust his blade into it again, but the spirit's legs gave out and it collapsed into a steaming heap. It would fade soon, its connection to earth severed. In minutes, it would be nothing but memories and the pain of those grieving for its victims. He hadn't sent it to Omoretsu, but he had killed it with Shiki, so it would flee back to heaven rather than hang around on earth looking for another body to possess. He wiped Shiki in the snow to clean off the ichor.

"That was amazing!" Kira shouted, skidding to a halt on the snow next to Haruto. She stared at the omukade, so excited she was almost vibrating. "I thought it had you when it lunged, but you just slid out of the way."

He glanced at the girl. "You could see it?"

"Of course," Kira said. "Couldn't you?"

Yanmei and Guang walked up to join them. The old poet was red faced and kept his distance from the carcass of the omukade, but he also looked excited. "Once I find the words, this is going to make such a poem."

Yanmei was more reserved. She had her naginata drawn and held at the ready. "Can we help?"

Haruto shook his head. "Not unless you're hiding a companion spirit in that weapon." He stepped past the fading body of the omukade and stared up at the sky and the dark cloud hanging there. "I need to find the source of all this. Omukade never come to cities. They prefer crevices and caves where they can wait and ambush the unwary. Something is drawing the spirits to Minazuri, and unless I find it and stop it, they will keep coming."

The guards were creeping along now, wary of the dead yokai and the bodies it had left, but determined to keep Haruto and the others in sight. Haruto was somewhat surprised they were more scared of the city magistrate than they were of an invisible man-eating centipede.

"What's next then?" Guang asked.

Haruto pointed Shiki up at the sky. "I'm going to return light to the city." He smiled and stepped forward. "I name you akashita," he shouted at the cloud. Lightning crackled along the dark folds, and for just a moment a distorted face appeared, huge and angry. Then the cloud starting roiling and bulging, and a funnel of darkness reached down and touched the ground.

The cloud pulsed and bubbled as it pushed more and more of its mass down onto the ground. It swamped the street in inky darkness, devouring the giant omukade carcass. Windows in the nearby homes shattered from the pressure, doors were blown from their hinges, and the ground shook. A giant figure strode forth from the cloud. Guang wished he had his ink to hand, for this was a monster worth committing to paper. It was human shaped but larger, taller than the two-story wooden hovels that lined the street. Its body was roiling cloud, the shape of a man but like it was struggling to escape. Its clawed hands trailed along the ground, tearing furrows in the dirt. Its face was half man and half beast with a bulging hairy chin, a flat nose, and huge eyes almost entirely white save for tiny dark pupils. It flicked its fat red tongue over serrated teeth and lightning crackled from deep within.

"Crap," Haruto said. Shiki popped from his blade and scampered up the sleeve of his kimono. He reached over his shoulder for his fire staff.

"Any chance this is the source of this spirit infestation?" Guang asked.

His old friend turned to look at him; the long suffering expression on his face was all the answer he needed.

Guang scratched at his patchy beard. "Right then."

"It's a yokai," Haruto said. "A powerful one, but it couldn't have drawn all the other spirits here."

"I can help," Kira said. She was grinning and bouncing with excitement.

"No!" Haruto spun his fire staff in his hand. "You'll only get in the way. Everyone, stay back."

Kira stopped bouncing and sulked, balled her hands into fists. Yanmei placed a hand on the girl's shoulder. "It's dangerous, Kira."

The girl sighed, looking like a puppy with its favourite bone taken away. "So am I."

"You ready?" Haruto asked. Shiki let out a quavering whistle. "Yeah, me either." And with that, he ran at the akashita, staff already twirling for the first strike.

The akashita swung a clawed hand down at Haruto, and Haruto dodged sideways. He swung his staff at the akashita's leg, and it passed straight through it, barely swirling the dark cloudy limb. Haruto's momentum sent him stumbling forward. The akashita slammed a hand into Haruto's side, throwing him against a nearby building, his staff holster ripped off against the wooden wall as he hit it. Guang winced as the old man hit the snowy cobbles, rolled to a stop. He rose quickly, but it was clear he was wounded. His back was bloody, his cloak in tatters, barely clinging to his neck, and his kimono was torn open completely from the waist up. Haruto planted the first staff in the ground and shouted, "Fire." Then he snatched up the Earth staff and dashed forward, strips of his cloak and kimono fluttering behind him.

These were the worst moments for Guang, watching his friend fight yokai and knowing he was useless to help. He knew Haruto wouldn't die, knew that he couldn't. Guang had seen proof of it many times, but he also knew every wound hurt. And there was always the chance, no matter how slim, that Haruto's immortality could fail him. The mysteries of the gods and spirits were beyond Guang's knowledge, and who knew when and why the shinigami would take away Haruto's curse?

Haruto swept the Earth staff through the akashita's arm, stirring its cloudy form, then plunged the staff into the ground and called out, "Earth." He reached up for the next, but it wasn't on his back. He'd left the others lying in the snow when the holster ripped. In his moment of confusion, the yokai kicked out its massive clawed foot, knocked Haruto off his feet and pinned him to the ground. Haruto cried out, but it was cut off, the air driven from his lungs. Thunder rumbled from the dark clouds above and lightning rippled across the creature's chest and face.

A fire flared to life next to Guang, and Yanmei ran past him, the blade of her naginata ablaze.

"Yanmei, no!" Kira shouted, starting forward herself, mirrored daggers flashing in her hands.

"Stay there, Kira," Yanmei shouted, not looking back. She sliced at the akashita's legs as she ran past it. Her blade passed through the yokai, but the fires beat back the cloud, the dark vapour hissing and steaming from the heat. She twirled the weapon about and slashed at the foot pinning Haruto to the ground. It wavered and Haruto rolled away, jumped up to stand side by side with Yanmei.

Kira stamped her feet in the snow. "She's not supposed to use her technique. It's dangerous for her."

Guang looked at her and scratched his beard. "I think you'll find parents will risk any amount of danger to protect their child."

Kira glanced at him, her jaw clenched and brow furrowed, then she looked away. "I don't need protecting. She should just let me help." Guang thought he heard glass cracking.

Age, the relentless hunter, was sapping Yanmei's strength. She was struggling, breathing heavily, slowing down. Haruto planted the Metal staff, rolled away from the yokai and snatched the Water staff from the snow. Yanmei had the akashita's attention now, her flaming naginata seemed to be more dangerous to the spirit than Haruto's staffs.

"It's hard to sit back and do nothing," Guang sighed. "But sometimes, that's the best help we can offer." He glanced down at Kira, but the girl was gone. "Oh cabbage!"

Haruto thrust his Water staff, the head punching into the cloud for just a moment, and then drew it out and jammed it into the ground. "Water." He looked about for the final staff.

"Here," Kira shouted. She had circled the battle and was standing next to the building over the last of Haruto's ritual staffs. She bent down to pick it up.

"No!" Haruto roared. But it was too late.

Kira picked up the staff from the snow. The wooden core at the centre of the staff's head crumbled to ash. She stared at in confusion, failing to notice the akashita spinning toward her. It bent down and roared at her. Lightning spewed from its sharp-toothed mouth and blasted the girl through the window of the building behind her, sending shards of glass crashing over her.

Yanmei screamed. Flames rushed down the pole of her naginata and up her arms. She leapt at the yokai, slashing chunks of dark cloud from its chest and abdomen in great billows of hissing steam. The akashita reeled from the attack. Yanmei continued to tear into it, her anger expressed in rage and flames.

"*Wreathed in flame...*" Guang mused. "Beautiful." The poem just burned to be written.

Haruto found the Wood staff in the snow where Kira had dropped it, but it was useless. The wooden core was gone and Omoretsu's blessing with it. "Shiki," Haruto called loudly. With the top half of Haruto's kimono torn off, the spirit had been clinging to his legs. She scurried up his side and leapt into his katana. The blade turned a menacing red once more. He stood still a moment. His hair had come loose of its braid and the gashes in his back and side had almost fully healed. He cut a heroic figure. Guang wrestled with the words to capture the scene.

"Akashita," Haruto screamed into the dark whirling cloud. The yokai stumbled away from Yanmei's flaming blade and reached a clawed hand to the sky, its cloudy form already swirling up to rejoin the clouds above. "No you don't!" Haruto shouted. "In Omoretsu's name, I sever you from this body!" He took two steps and leapt into the air. Twisting away from a clawing hand, he slashed out once with Shiki and then landed in the snow on the other side of the akashita. The yokai's head hit the ground just behind him and dissipated, its body and the dark cloud above slowly evaporating into nothing.

Chapter 12

Yanmei dropped her naginata and thrust her burning hands into the snow to put out the flames. Her face was twisted in agony, teeth clenched, tears sizzling and evaporating as they rolled down her cheeks. "Kira, are you alright?" she shouted, voice quavering with panic.

Haruto sheathed his katana and bent over, hands on his knees, glad to catch his breath. Shiki popped from the blade and waddled through the snow to the building Kira had crashed through. She leapt up, clinging to the broken door frame and stared through the shattered window. She squeaked excitedly. "Kira's fine," Haruto said bitterly as he staggered over to where his Fire staff was planted. The blessing was gone. "Just regretting some of her choices."

Yanmei pulled her trembling, blistered hands from the snow and stumbled toward the building just as Kira pulled herself from the wreckage and clambered over the broken door back into the street. Yanmei wrapped her arms around the girl and pulled her into an embrace. Shiki scrambled up Kira's singed kimono and joined in, hugging Kira's neck.

"That went well, old man," Guang said. "One cleansed akashita and all you lost was another kimono." Guang picked a scrap of fabric from Haruto's hair. The old poet was smiling far too much, but then he hadn't just been knocked about by a giant cloud. Still, he wasn't altogether wrong; it could have gone much worse. But the yokai wasn't cleansed. Haruto had killed the body, but he hadn't sent it to Omoretsu. Eventually it would find its way back to earth. But that was a problem for another day. There were still plenty of other yokai in the town that needed dealing with.

Haruto glanced down at himself and shrugged. His haori

was in tatters, most of it shredded or burned to ash, but his hakama was mostly intact, though covered in blood. With nothing covering his chest, he realised he was actually a little cold. "The Wood staff is done for," he said. "And those are a real hassle to replace."

Guang nodded. "I remember."

Haruto sighed and patted at his chest, then glanced about at the wreckage in the street. "And the pipe."

"Another one?" Guang frowned. "I can't keep buying you new pipes in every lettuce-stinking town."

Haruto rolled his eyes. "It's my money you're spending."

Guang harrumphed. "I provide an invaluable service to earn my share."

"Of course you do," Haruto said, clapping his friend on the shoulder. "It's well known every onmyoji needs a starving poet to support. If not for you, who would carry my staffs in these trying times?" He tore a thin strip from the hem of his hakama and wrapped it about his staffs before tying them together and thrusting them into Guang's arms. "See. Almost as good as pack mule, and a similar stench too."

"I'm here to immortalise you in words, not smell nice, old man."

Haruto laughed at that. "I'm already immortal. What use have I of your words. Also, pack mules don't complain, so shhh."

"I'll show you a pack mule." Guang kicked Haruto in the shin.

"Ow!" Haruto feigned pain and made a show of hopping on one leg over to Yanmei and the girl.

"You're not healing the burns," the girl said, clutching Yanmei's cracked and weeping hands. Shiki scurried down Kira's arms and stared at Yanmei's wounds.

"I'm fine." Yanmei winced and tried to pull her shaking hands away, but Kira held on.

Yanmei had been a great help, but Kira... The damned girl had just gotten in the way. "I told you to stay back and let me handle things," Haruto snapped.

Kira wouldn't meet his angry glare. She let go of Yanmei's hands and found an interesting patch of snow to look at. "I was just trying to help."

"Well, thanks to your *help*, an akashita is now free to find a new body and cause chaos elsewhere. *And* I have to replace my Wood staff."

"I didn't know it would break."

Shiki climbed up onto Kira's shoulder and squeaked.

Yanmei stared at Haruto, her jaw set like granite and her hands trembling. "And what about me? Was my help unwelcome too."

"You're damn right it was," Haruto said, knowing he was lying. "When I say stay back, I mean it. I'm immortal, you're not." He saw her open her mouth to argue, but he cut her off, pointing at Kira. "And *you*, do not touch my staffs." With that, he turned and strode toward the centre of the town.

"You're touching them," he heard Kira say to Guang. She was right, of course. She couldn't have known what would happen. It wasn't her fault that the staffs were already attuned to the akashita and she was another yokai. Nevertheless, Haruto was angry. It bubbled up inside him, demanding to be let out, coating everything he said with resentment. He didn't like it. Didn't like how it felt.

Shiki waddled through the dusty street and stared up at Haruto and whistled.

"Follow his anger?" Haruto snapped. "What does that even mean, Shiki?" Another whistle. Shiki leapt onto his hakama and scrabbled up to his waist. He plucked her by the scruff and placed her on his shoulder as he strode on. "That makes sense."

Shiki was right. Haruto was feeling Tian's anger, his vengeance calling out from the heavens to will Haruto into action. To find his murderer and fulfil his burden.

Haruto slowed to a stop in the middle of the street, closed his eyes, and took a deep breath. The clamour in the city was making it hard to concentrate. Children screaming, men crying, spirits wrecking homes, starting fires, taunting people. He blocked it all out. The wind was howling through the streets, whipping up snow and stealing breath. He blocked that out too. The spirits' energies pressed in all around them. Some were playful things, visiting the mortal realm to cause some trouble and spend some time on earth. They didn't matter. Others were yokai, drawn to Minazuri by... something. An imbalance in the city.

Shiki chittered in his ear. He was going about it the wrong way. He had to assume whatever was causing this siege of spirits was connected to the onryo. If he wanted to find them, he needed to follow Tian's direction. He knelt down in the snowy street and closed his eyes, steadied his breathing, and felt for the anger. He found a pulsing orb of tension resting in his gut, twisting his insides tight and small, a heat that flared whenever he felt for it, a pressure that built in his limbs until only violence could release it. Tian's anger, nestled inside him, coiled around his spirit, tearing at the threads of his soul.

Haruto stood and opened his eyes. From the side of the street, a soldier with a cleft lip, cradling one arm, was yelling something at him. Haruto ignored the fool and followed the anger, quickening his pace to a jog. The anger grew hotter in his chest, tightening its claws around his heart and lungs, a deep ache in his guts. All too suddenly, a tall pagoda rose above the shambles of the city, the temple where he'd met Omoretsu just the day before. Haruto knew he had arrived, had found the source of Tian's anger.

"Cabbage, old man," Guang shouted. "Slow down." The old poet arrived panting, with Yanmei and Kira a step behind. A few of the guards hurried behind them. Guang doubled over, hands on his knees, gulping the cold air. Yanmei was out of breath as well. Kira looked as if she could run all day, but her bubbly excitement had vanished and a dark look clung to her like a cloak. Haruto wondered if he was looking at the yokai or the girl.

The area around the temple was vacant and relatively quiet. Haruto caught the odd glimpse of a spirit, but none ventured too close to the temple, and there were no people. The noise and chaos of the rest of the city rose between the buildings and from the alleyways, but on the temple grounds everything was still and silent.

"Out of sight, Shiki," Haruto said. The spirit narrowed her eyes, whistled, and faded away. Haruto could still feel her clinging to his shoulder. "Everyone else, stay out here." He stared at Kira for a long moment, and she stared back without flinching.

"This the source of it all then?" Guang asked between breaths.

Haruto nodded, felt his hands fidgeting nervously. "Yes. And you don't want to go in there."

The old poet laughed. "How am I supposed to write an epic poem about your heroic deeds if you never let me watch?"

Haruto shrugged. "Make it up. All the good poets do."

Yanmei reached a blistered, trembling hand to draw her naginata. "I can help."

Haruto shook his head and grit his teeth as the anger surged inside him. "One more time – I'm immortal. You're one strong gust of wind from death's door. Whatever is in there, you'll only get in my way."

The old warrior sighed, but she didn't argue.

Haruto pulled open the creaking temple door and stepped into the gloom beyond. The braziers that had been burning the last time he had been here had all gone out, and the space was shrouded in darkness. He brushed cobwebs out of the way as he walked toward the tiered altars, the wispy strands sticking to his face. Something scuttled across the floor.

The shrines were menacing shapes in the gloom, fading into the blackness of the far reaches of the temple. Cobwebs were draped over everything, strung between the shrines, running up the walls, clogging up the braziers, dangling from the high ceiling in thin strands that waved with his passing and tried to cling to him. He looked up and saw lumps of webbing not far from the ceiling, giant cocoons dangling from webs as thick as rope, dozens of them. Suddenly he knew exactly what he was dealing with.

"Shit," he whispered. Then he heard a woman's laughter, soft and melodic like glass beads tinkling into a marble bowl.

Haruto drew his katana from its saya, holding the blade ready to his side. He stepped lightly around the main floor of the temple, glancing into the shadowy recesses. It was too dark to see much of anything. The temple was a huge cavernous space surrounding the cramped shrines.

Something tugged on his blade. Dozens of thin strands of webbing had stuck to it, clinging to the metal.

An obese woman landed on her feet on the floor in front of him, nearly bursting from her hanfu, yet she moved with undeniable grace. Four hideous segmented legs rose over her shoulders and around her bulk, and her hair was a wiry, oily mass that sprouted from her head in a hundred different angles. She waddled toward Haruto. Her eyes were two black orbs, not a bit of humanity in them.

"Hello, little fly," she said, her mouth full of furry, glistening fangs. She stabbed two spidery legs at Haruto. One punched into his shoulder and the other into his side. He howled in pain. He tugged his katana, but the weapon was stuck in a thick web. He backed away from the yokai, clutching at his wounds, his katana hanging in the air between them. Webbing stuck to his back, his arms and legs, and he stumbled backwards into an enormous cobweb.

With a throaty chuckle, the woman crouched on her spider legs and then sprang up into the darkness. Haruto tried to tug himself free of the webs, but more sticky threads fell on him, some thin as hairs, others thick and glistening in the dim light. Within a few moments, he was covered and bound, unable to move. At least the pain from the wounds was fading, his immortality already healing them. He'd often wondered just how far that immortality went. If the yokai cocooned him, how long would he survive all wrapped up like a fly? Forever? That did not sound like a fun way to spend eternity.

Haruto flailed his arms and legs against the web, but the spider's silk was too strong and there was too much of it.

Suddenly he was wrenched off his feet and up towards the ceiling, ten feet, twenty feet. The temple floor vanished beneath him. Up near the rafters, the strands of web were thicker, arcing from one wall to another. He counted eight of the cocoons as he rose and had a feeling each one held a person inside. When he finally stopped rising, the yokai sat opposite him, nestled in a hanging throne of silk.

"It's been so long since I last saw an onmyoji," the woman said, her voice a rasping lisp. "My name is Xifeng, little fly. What's yours?"

Haruto glanced about, looking for anything to help him escape. There was nothing, of course. He was bound, hands against his chest, held up only by the very webbing that restrained him. Tian's anger boiled in his chest, an icy rage that threatened to swallow all reason. Haruto wanted to thrash, to scream, to choke the life from the onryo with his bare hands, but he couldn't move. He gritted his teeth and swallowed down the anger.

"You're a jorogumo, aren't you?" he asked. His old master always used to say: 'If you can't fight your way out, talk your way out. And if you can't do that either, start praying'.

"Yes!" the yokai said, clapping her flabby human hands together. The spider legs resting over her shoulders plucked at the air, always moving.

He'd never met a jorogumo before, but he knew their ilk. They were people who had died of spider bites. Those with strong will and unfinished business, often those who were murdered. A venomous spider introduced to a person's bedding while they slept. A victim lured into a nest of the little beasts and left to die. But this was no ordinary jorogumo, she had become an onryo somehow: half yokai and half human. This was a danger like none he had ever faced before.

"Do you know what I did to the last onmyoji, little fly?" the jorogumo asked, leaning forward eagerly in her silk throne. Spider legs tapping at the air and she grinned, showing him fangs sharp as knives behind her lips.

Haruto shrugged. Or at least he tried to. The webbing made

it impossible. "You ate him, didn't you?"

Her face cracked into a savage smile, the fangs behind her lips quivering in excitement. Again he wondered about his immortality. He doubted he could survive being eaten and wasn't sure he'd want to.

Haruto struggled, thrashing about, kicking his feet, pushing his elbows against the thick web. It was pointless. He couldn't move at all. The jorogumo watched him struggle, her dark eyes shining.

Haruto's heart was thunder in his ears. Sweat dripped from his forehead, stinging his eyes. Struggling was getting him nowhere; he had to think. He remembered what the Crone had said – the onryo were looking for something, a prison. "You were at Heiwa?" Haruto asked. "Did you kill Tian?"

The jorogumo leaned back in her silken throne, her spider legs twitching over her shoulders. "Who?"

"A teacher at the academy you destroyed." Haruto felt the anger surging back like a fire inside of him. "He had bite marks. Stabs wounds. Strands of silk hanging from his clothing."

"I killed many at the school," the jorogumo said, tilting her head slightly. She didn't blink. Her eyes were dark orbs, voids of light. "Teachers. Students. But the Master wouldn't let me eat."

"Master?" Haruto said. "Who is your master?" If it was a god or another shinigami, one in opposition to Omoretsu? That would explain how she could desecrate the temple and get away with it.

The yokai didn't answer, just stared at him in silence, her spider eyes giving nothing away.

"What do you want with Sky Hollow?" Haruto asked, trying a different angle.

"Tricky little fly, aren't you," the jorogumo said. "How do you know about the third prison? Who have you been talking to you?" She grimaced and something dark and glistening dribbled from the corner of her lips. "I bet it was Shin. He does love the sound of his own voice."

Haruto knew Sky Hollow, had trained there for over a

decade, and he had never heard of a prison there. But it had been more than a century since he had last seen the place.

"No matter," the jorogumo said, her smile stretching her lips once more, fangs glistening with venom. "You die now, little fly." She scuttled across the webbing to him.

When she was barely an arm's length away, Haruto heard a soft crackling sound above them. The jorogumo must have heard it too. They both looked up toward the ceiling. He heard the sound once more, then shards of glass rained down on them. Some fell straight down towards the floor, others bounced from webbing and stuck into the long strands of silk. Haruto looked at them sparkling in the dim light and realised they weren't glass at all, but shards of mirror, each one reflecting an image of the temple on fire.

The jorogumo flailed about and shrieked, "Fire. Fire!" She stabbed with her legs, shaking webbing all around, and swung her head around. But there was no fire.

"What is this trickery?" she snarled.

A dagger flew out of the darkness above and hit the jorogumo in the face, sank deep into her left eye. The jorogumo screeched, her spider legs curling about her as she fell backwards and toppled into the darkness below.

"I told you to wait outside," Haruto growled.

Kira dropped down and landed lightly on a thick strand of webbing, barely even shaking it. She held her arms out and walked along it like a tightrope. "Is that your way of saying 'thank you for saving me from the big spider'?" she asked. She stopped walking along the thread and bent down to stare at Haruto. "Or possibly, 'please free me from my sticky prison'?" She flicked her hand, a new dagger appearing in her grasp, and sawed through a few strands of the web encasing Haruto.

"I didn't need rescuing," Haruto grumbled. "I had her talking. Never interrupt an enemy when they're talking. You never know what they might reveal."

Kira straightened up and crossed her arms. "So should I leave? Let her come back and eat you?"

"It's a bit late for that."

A scream tore through the temple, echoing around the walls. The jorogumo pulled herself up on a line of silk. "My eye!" she howled. "How could you? HOW COULD YOU?"

Kira staggered back from the yokai and stumbled. She glanced down, and Haruto could see her foot was stuck in the web. He sighed. The jorogumo scuttled up, her front spider legs poised to strike, but she stopped when she saw the girl. "Sister? What are you doing with him?"

"Huh?" Kira said.

The jorogumo glanced at Haruto with her good eye. She had removed the dagger from the other, which was oozing gore. Then she turned her head toward Kira, hissed loudly and leapt up, jumping from web to web before crashing through an open window near the top of the temple.

Haruto stared up into the darkness, trying to make sense of it all.

"Did she just run away?" Kira asked.

Haruto managed to wriggle one of his hands free of his sticky prison, then started tearing at the webbing binding him. It was strong stuff, clinging to him tenaciously, but it seemed weaker than it had when the onryo was close. He wondered if perhaps her presence and her qi had been strengthening the strands. Eventually he tore enough of the webbing away and dropped, plummeting to the floor. The landing sent a shock through his legs, and he felt something snap. Pain lanced through his thigh. He cried out, limping about until his immortality healed the damage.

Kira screamed from up above. Haruto looked up to see her hanging by her foot from the web she'd been standing on. She reached up and sliced through it with her dagger, but it stuck to her foot and she swung down awkwardly, bouncing from one sticky thread to another, until she had wrapped herself up. She came to a halt just a few feet from the floor, swinging back-and-forth upside down, and just as encased in webbing as he had been. "Um, help?"

Haruto sighed. "Is that your way of saying 'please free me from my sticky prison'?" He pushed her cocoon, sending her swinging and spinning about.

"Hey! Stop that!" she hollered. "I was only trying to help."

"And?"

"And, um, I'm sorry if I got in the way?"

Shiki appeared on Haruto's shoulder, then leapt onto Kira's cocoon, whistling as she scampered down to hang upside down from Kira's shoulder.

"Yes, I'm stuck," Kira said.

Haruto ignored them and picked his way through the hanging strands of silk to look for his katana. He found it still suspended in mid air by the webbing. He grabbed the hilt and twisted, started sawing through the strands.

Shiki squeaked again.

Kira sighed. "I thought if I rushed in and helped, he'd realise I'm not useless. And Yanmei would accept that I don't need to be protected all the time."

Shiki whistled a short, plaintive melody.

"Yes," Kira said. "I did mess up."

Haruto stopped sawing at the webbing and stared at them. "Wait. You understand her?"

Shiki squeaked, still riding upside down on Kira's shoulder as she swung and spun in her cocoon.

"Not you. Kira, you can understand Shiki?"

Kira nodded, her short black hair waving a few feet above the dusty floor.

Haruto finished sawing his katana loose and walked over to squat in front of Kira. "Why did the jorogumo call you sister?" he asked, placing the tip of his katana against Kira's cocoon, stopping her from spinning. He could kill her with a single thrust, end her before she became dangerous.

"I don't know," she said. "I've never even seen her before today. Was she one of the onryo?"

Haruto considered the girl for a moment. He couldn't decide if she was telling the truth.

Shiki dropped from Kira's cocoon to the floor and turned to face Haruto, her eyes narrowed, hairy little arms crossed. She let out a low trumpet.

"You trust her?" Haruto asked the spirit.

Shiki nodded, arms still crossed and eyes narrowed.

Haruto stood and groaned. He ran a hand through his unbound hair as he considered. The little spirit had always been a good judge of character. It was, after all, she that convinced Haruto to save Guang all those years ago. He pointed his katana at Shiki. "In you go." Shiki whistled happily and leapt into the sword, turning the blade crimson. Haruto considered Kira as she hung there in the webbing, pouting. He'd probably never get a better chance to kill her. To rid the world of an especially dangerous yokai.

"Try not to move." Haruto levelled his katana, and Shiki cut through the webbing like flames through snow.

Kira tumbled from the cocoon and sprawled awkwardly on the temple floor. She sat up quickly and rubbed her head. "Sorry about..." She stopped, sighed, then scrambled onto her hands and knees and bowed her head to the floor. "I really was trying to help."

Haruto tried to think of some advice. Guang would know what to say. Some old philosophical mumbo jumbo passed down through the ages, or a poem about some great hero with a moral at its core. Unfortunately, he was not Guang. "Just, don't get in the way next time," he said and turned away. He walked over to a vaguely human-size cocoon stuck to the wall in the corner of the room.

"Next time?" Kira said.

Haruto groaned, realising his mistake. He'd never be rid of the girl now. He carefully slid Shiki into the cocoon and sliced it open. Rotted flesh and gore-stuck bones tumbled to the floor. The smell hit Haruto like a gut punch, and he staggered away from the cocoon. He knew then there would be no survivors. All those cocooned were dead.

"That is disgusting," Kira said, holding a sleeve of her

kimono over her nose. "What is that smell?"

"Death," Haruto said.

Shiki popped out of the katana and paraded about, a little arm over her eyes as if she were holding a nose. Of course, in her current form she didn't have a nose, but the little act made Kira laugh.

"Time to go," Haruto said. The temple had been desecrated, and he had no wish to be around if a god showed up looking for someone to punish.

Chapter 13

Crow drifted about the room, caressing the items she found with her vines of smoke. They were in Lord Izuchi's manor, not half a day from Minazuri. The Master had come here to wait for all the others to gather, and Lord Izuchi had been gracious enough to allow them to stay. At least, he had been after his son had been taken away and held hostage. Humans would suffer through a great deal for their children, it seemed. It was almost as if they didn't realise they could just make more.

Lady Izuchi stood trembling by the shoji that divided the main room. These were her chambers. But she kept her mouth shut like a good little captive and stood ready to wait on Crow, should she need it. But Crow needed nothing. There was plenty she wanted, plenty she'd never have. But need? She couldn't remember the last time she needed anything. Had she ever *needed* anything? Perhaps when she was human, when she was alive.

She reached out a smoky tendril and wrapped it around a small, bone-handled hairbrush. Some dark strands of hair were still weaved around its prongs. She lifted the hair brush to get a better look. Not that she had eyes, or even a face beneath her hood, but she was most comfortable mimicking human mannerisms. She carefully unwound one hair from the brush and put it inside her white robe to study later. She heard Lady Izuchi gasp, but ignored her. Crow remembered having hair once. Or did she? She couldn't remember her name, her face, her life, but she knew she had been a human once. Some things stirred images, feelings, though not quite memories. She placed the hairbrush back on the little table. It was black with soot now, the residue from her smoke, but then so was everything Crow touched.

She pulled her tentacles of smoke back inside her white robe and continued drifting about the room, leaving a trail of soot on the polished wood floor. So many little items in Lady Izuchi's rooms stirred those not quite memories in her. Crow wondered if she once had a room like this. Maybe she had been a lady. Maybe she had owned perfume and powder, hair brushes and beautiful dresses. Maybe she had looked into a mirror and saw a face staring back at her instead of a churning cloud of sooty smoke. She stopped in front of Lady Izuchi's mirror and stared at that smoke now. A swirling, drifting mass of nothing.

"Come here," Crow said sharply.

Lady Izuchi hesitated for a moment, then caught her breath and stepped toward Crow, keeping as much distance as possible, leaning away from her, but not daring to disobey. Crow moved back a little so Lady Izuchi stood before the mirror. "Stand there and let me look at you."

Lady Izuchi stifled a sob. She was pretty, beautiful even. Her powder was artfully applied to accentuate her cheeks and lips. She had a few lines, age just beginning to lay waste to her smooth features. Crow studied every line and curve and contour. The shape of her eyes, the length of her nose, the tiny scar on her chin. All the features that made up Lady Izuchi's perfectly beautiful face. And then Crow formed the smoke inside her own hood to mimic them.

Lady Izuchi recoiled, gasped, covered her mouth with her hand as she came face to face with herself written in sooty smoke. Crow could feel it, too. She had a face again. She had a nose and could almost remember smells, like the cherry blossom perfume the lady was probably wearing. She had eyes and could pretend she was using them to see. She had a mouth and stretched it into a smile.

Lady Izuchi suddenly squawked and stumbled backwards, tripped over a cushion and scrabbled away across the floor. Crow turned to the mirror to see what she had become, but it was already too late. One cheek sagged and bulged and then burst, billowing out smoke. Her nose simply fell away, hitting the floor in a puff of soot. Her eyes eddied and split into more eyes. And then it was gone entirely, leaving her with dark smoky nothing inside her hood. Because it wasn't *her* face. She could mimic another while she stared at it, but it would never stick because it wasn't hers. Such an exercise in futility that had been. It always was. No matter how many times she searched for her own face, it always ended the same way. Crow drifted from the room, ignoring Lady Izuchi crouched in the corner.

Lord Izuchi had his own dojo in his compound, as many rich lords did, and that was where Crow hoped to find the Master. It was only a short float across the snow. She slid open the dojo door with a sooty tendril, and floated inside. The Master was kneeling in the centre of the room, his feathers draped over his shoulders like a cloak, his tengai hat, a large bucket-shaped thing of dried bamboo, on the floor beside him. Lord Izuchi stood in the corner, waiting on the Master just as his wife had on Crow. Amongst the humans, he was a powerful man. Not just rich, but a warrior famed for his skill with the sword. He went by the name Ice Heart and had apparently accomplished many heroic deeds. But here, he was nothing. His money meant nothing. His strength and skill meant nothing. His name meant nothing. His was just another life waiting to be taken by the onryo. It was a lesson the Master loved teaching to those who thought themselves strong.

"Still searching, Crow?" the Master asked, his voice like the crackle of old parchment. His motley of black and white feathers rippled as he spoke.

"Always," Crow said, drifting a little further into the dojo and closing the door behind her. Lord Izuchi glanced at the soot she left behind, but quickly looked away and said nothing. She would cover everything he owned in her soot before she left. Let him have a bare taste of her torment.

The Master shrugged. "Lady Izuchi's face was not to your liking?"

Crow seethed a little inside, dark smoke billowing out from beneath her robe, rising around her like a nest of thrashing snakes. "It was not my face."

"My wife..." Lord Izuchi said, panic making his voice

quaver.

Crow turned toward him, and he paled. "Is fine."

"You didn't kill her?" the Master asked.

Crow drifted toward the wall, where a dozen ancestral swords belonging to Izuchis long dead were mounted. "What purpose would that serve?" she asked. "The woman has done nothing wrong. She just has the wrong face." Crow trailed a smoky vine over the wall of swords, staining the wooden wall with her soot. One sword was missing from the display. A katana belonging to an Izuchi shintei, if the nameplate was correct. The Master had it, lying on the floor in front of him, the blade still sheathed in its saya.

The dojo door opened again, and Shin stood there, one eyebrow quirked as he stared down at Crow's trail of soot. His lip curled in distaste, and he stepped around the trail. His barbed hair floated around him in long, thick braids, each a prehensile weapon he could control at will. He wore a new kimono, a woman's dress, blue as a summer sky and patterned with white triangles. He belted it too low, leaving it hanging open to expose his chest and one elegant shoulder. Such a proud creature, obsessed with his own appearance. Crow envied him. Not for his beauty, but simply because he knew his own face.

"Xifeng has returned," Shin said haughtily. He stepped aside and grimaced as their sister squeezed her bulk through the door.

Xifeng was hurt. Her spider legs were wrapped around her protectively, and one eye was an oozing, ruined mess. Another spidery eye was forming above it, punching through her skin. She was one of the oldest of them and one of the most changed. Except for Crow herself, none of them were more inhuman.

"There is an onmyoji," Xifeng said as she ambled into the dojo. She was always clumsy on her human legs, but fast and agile on her spider legs.

"Where have you been, Xifeng?" the Master rasped.

"The city," Xifeng replied. She stopped behind the Master and unfurled her spider legs to the floor to support her bulk. Crow saw Lord Izuchi recoil in disgust; she couldn't blame him. The other onryo said there was always a smell around Xifeng. Shin described it as worn, sweaty small-clothes tossed into a corner and left to fester. Crow wished she could smell it.

"Why?" asked the Master. The weight of the word settled on the room like a tombstone.

Xifeng opened her mouth to reply. Crow could see her fangs rubbing together; the rasping sound stirred some almost memories that made her... uncomfortable? Curious? She wasn't sure.

"I--" Xifeng shifted nervously, the tips of her spider legs scrabbling on the wooden floor. "I thought a little chaos would cover our tracks."

The Master stared at Xifeng over his feathered shoulders. His face was a mass of folds and wrinkles, his nose a long hook, and his eyes were a swirling dissonance of colours. Xifeng backed up a couple of steps.

"You wanted to feed," the Master said slowly, filling each word with menace. "You wanted to make the humans suffer. And now you have summoned an onmyoji to hunt us."

Xifeng shuffled about, spider legs scratching the fine wood floor. She looked to Crow for support, but Crow wasn't having it. At last she said, "It was only one. He was weak. I-I almost killed him, but then another onryo showed up. She did this." Xifeng pointed at her ruined eye. "She hurt me!"

"A new sister?" Shin asked. "Oh, I would love to find a... clean one for once."

Xifeng turned and hissed at Shin. His hair rose about his head like a nest of kraits ready to strike.

"We're running out of time," the Master said, turning back to his contemplation of the katana he had taken from the wall. He reached down and drew it from its saya. "If one onmyoji has found us, others may follow. We cannot wait for Zen to return. Shin, you and Crow will go to Sky Hollow right away. Find the third prison and release the prisoner."

Shin gazed sidelong at Crow. "Does she have to come with me? She's so messy."

"Would you prefer Xifeng?" asked the Master.

"No," he said it so slowly the word long outstayed its welcome.

"Xifeng," the Master continued, "you and I will find the final prison."

Xifeng let out a low grumble. Something black and viscous dripped from her lips. "How?"

"By paying Empress Ise Ryoko a visit." The Master glanced at Lord Izuchi. "You have heard too much." With a flick of his wrist, he sent the katana flying. It struck the lord in the chest, pinning him to the wall of the dojo. He gaped at the Master, blood frothing from his mouth, and pawed at the sword in his chest as if his body hadn't yet realised it was dead. Then his arms dropped, his knees buckled, and he crumbled to the floor like a puppet with its strings cut.

The Master stood slowly, his feathers ruffling as they draped around him to the floor. He picked up his tengai hat and lowered over his head, covering him from the shoulders up in tan wicker. Nothing could be seen of his face but a glimpse of green-gold eyes, swirling like water circling the drain. He turned to Xifeng. "Have your fun, sister. Kill them all. The entire household."

Chapter 14

The onmyoji spent almost the entire day dispatching the most dangerous of the yokai in Minazuri, though he refused to cleanse any of the spirits that he deemed playful rather than violent. Kira followed him, taking great interest. She was fascinated by it, by the world being revealed to her. She could only learn so much from books and stories, and life at Heiwa Academy had offered nothing else. She'd known almost nothing about spirits, despite being one... or at least part spirit. She wasn't really sure on the details yet, but she hoped to find some time to ask the onmyoji. He seemed to know everything about spirits, no matter what sort they encountered. He didn't let her fight the yokai though, telling her firmly to stay back each time, and after her failure in the temple, she wasn't willing to disobey him again.

Yanmei lagged behind. She was clearly in pain. Her technique was killing her. Every time she used it, the fire hurt her more and the wounds took longer to heal. Kira had been there when the Fifth Sage told her to stop using it. Yanmei was strong, he had said, but fire was not a force to be contained. It was destruction made manifest. It burned until there was nothing left. They needed to find the Fourth Sage Under Heaven to heal Yanmei. Until then Kira would just have to make certain Yanmei did not use her technique, no matter what happened. She would protect Yanmei at all costs.

The old poet laboured on beside Yanmei, alternating complaints about the cold and his knees. Kira liked him, partly because he was the only one not angry at her for trying to save Haruto's life. She didn't understand that either. She had thought Yanmei would be happy she tried to help, proud even. But instead Yanmei was all disappointed stares and reprimands. And every time Haruto encountered another yokai he looked right at her and told her to stay, like she was a poorly trained puppy. Then he went off and got himself beaten up for a bit. He should have been covered in wounds, but they healed so quickly.

By the time night fell, she was standing on the porch of an inn with the onmyoji, who was sitting on the step, barely awake. His eyelids kept drooping, and his head falling forward. Then he would wake with a start and grumble something under his breath. Kira wasn't really sure why she was there with him, save he was angry with her and she wanted to make it up to him.

Guang reappeared with a new kimono folded over his arm, a dull yellow with autumn leaves sewn into it. He draped the haori over Haruto's shoulders rather than disturb him, and the onmyoji didn't even stir. Then the old poet vanished again to find them something to eat.

"What?" Haruto asked peevishly. He didn't even look up, just sat slumped over on the porch. People were moving about the street in front of the inn, some tending to the wounded or fighting fires, others just trying to go about their lives despite the spirit invasion. The guards were there too, four of them watching over Haruto just as the magistrate ordered. "You're hanging about, staring at me. Why?"

Kira sat down next to Haruto. She hadn't even thought he'd noticed her. "What's an onryo?" she asked.

He lifted his head a little and glanced at her out of the corner of his eye. Then he sighed. "You are."

Kira fiddled with her hakama, twisting the dark fabric around between her fingers. It seemed she wouldn't get a straight answer after all. She felt it was important though, knowing what she was.

"You really don't know what you are?" he asked her. Then he lifted his head to look at Yanmei as she ran a whetstone down the edge of her naginata blade. Shiki stood in the street in front of Yanmei, her little hairy body crusted with snow, staring in fascination and cooing softly at the way Yanmei moved the blade against the stone.

"She's an ungaikyo," Yanmei said. "I rescued her from a mirror about a decade ago."

Haruto narrowed his eyes and stared at her. "An ungaikyo is a yokai created when someone is murdered while looking into a mirror." He looked at Kira as if that should mean something, but it didn't. She had some vague impressions of her life before being trapped in the mirror. Before she was murdered, she supposed. Then a fuzzy period of being inside the mirror, mostly feelings of loneliness and anger, and then the ten years since Yanmei freed her.

She remembered her time at Heiwa with Yanmei. Clinging to her trousers as she was introduced to the other students. Kira had been so scared she followed Yanmei to her rooms rather than sleep in the dormitory with the other students. For two weeks she slept curled up in Yanmei's bed, nestled against her. Eventually the Sage had put a stop to that, ordering Kira to the dormitory. The bullying had started that same night.

Even after being banned from Yanmei's rooms, Kira had followed her about. She used to watch Yanmei train with her naginata, mesmerised by the way she spun the weapon in her hands and moved through the snowy grass of the academy courtyard, flowing so gracefully from one form to another. One time, Kira snuck away from a lesson on politics or history or something equally boring and found Yanmei practicing. She'd watched for a while and then sneaked off to find a broom. When she returned, she joined Yanmei in the snow and tried to replicate her movements. She failed, possessing none of the necessary grace. But Yanmei hadn't chided her for skipping class, nor did she mock her for failing. She simply slowed down, moving through the forms deliberately and occasionally correcting Kira's posture or the way she held the broom handle. Kira remembered nothing from her time before Yanmei, nothing of her old life, nor her time imprisoned inside the mirror, but even if she could remember it all, she was certain that time spent training with Yanmei would be her favourite memory of all.

Shiki waddled over to Haruto, climbed into his lap, and

closed her eyes. Within moments, she was snoring softly.

"Onryo are yokai who have reclaimed something of their humanity," Haruto said eventually. "Sometimes by staying around after getting their revenge, and sometimes by another method."

"What other method?" Kira asked.

Haruto sighed and turned his tired eyes on her. "I don't know." He held up a hand to quiet her before she aimed another question at him. She had dozens of the little buggers lining up in the back of her mind just begging to be asked. "I only know what my old master taught me when I was training to be an onmyoji, and he didn't know much. Everyone knew of the onryo, that they existed, but nobody had ever seen one. Or at least, none of the onmyoji had ever seen one and lived to talk about it." He gently scratched at Shiki's fur. "Onryo are sort of half yokai and half human. I was taught that it makes them stronger and..."

"Why?" Kira asked. "Or how?" She needed to know, felt it was important to understand herself.

Haruto glanced at her, then lowered his eyes and sighed. "I think it's to do with qi. People generate their own qi. It sustains us, gives us strength. For a spirit to exist on earth, it also needs qi. But spirits can't generate their own, at least not here on earth.

"When most spirits come here, they can exist only as long as their qi lasts, then they fade away and return to heaven. Some, like the inugami, feed off mischief. It provides them the energy they need to stay here. Others, like yokai, steel qi from people. Some by frightening them, others by killing them. It is rarely a willing transfer. And then there are companion spirits like this little fur ball." He tapped Shiki on the head and she stopped snoring, opened her eyes, then tried to playfully bite his finger. "She feeds off my qi. As long as I'm alive, she has the energy she needs to stay here on earth. And when I finally..."

Shiki stopped savaging his finger and squeaked.

"True," Haruto said. "*If* I finally die, she'll fade and return to heaven."

Kira frowned. The tutors at Heiwa had often tried to teach her about qi, but she had never really understood what they were talking about.

"How are the onryo different?" Yanmei asked, still running her naginata's blade down the whetstone.

Haruto shrugged. "Onryo generate their own qi, just like a human. They don't need to feed off people. It means they are almost always unbound to any shinigami or gods. And as I'm sure you are already aware, they have some strange techniques."

"Like the spider lady?" Kira asked. "Um, Xifeng. She said her name was Xifeng."

Haruto nodded. "She was a jorogumo. Or at least she was once. Killed by spiders, almost certainly in a nefarious manner. Usually the jorogumo take the form of a giant spider with a human face, their original face, on their abdomen. Or a spider body and a human torso. But this one has regained some of her humanity and... well, you saw what she has become."

Kira shuddered. She didn't like the spider lady one bit. All maggot-white flesh and segmented legs, and those bottomless black eyes... She felt a sudden chill and hugged herself. "Does that mean I was different too? When I was an ungaikyo?"

Haruto shrugged and looked past Kira at Yanmei, as if she had the answer. Yanmei's hands faltered, the blade falling still against the whetstone. "You would have to ask someone who saw you before you were freed from the mirror," Haruto said.

"Was I different?" Kira asked again. All she really remembered of her time in the mirror was that it seemed like forever and it felt like being trapped. Mostly she remembered the anger, despair, and loneliness. And occasionally some hope mixed with... She couldn't remember. It all just slipped away from her whenever she tried, swallowed up by something inside. Something waiting inside. A black pit that yawned and devoured everything.

Yanmei looked at her sadly then away, her blade moving along the whetstone once more. "It doesn't matter."

Kira felt an itch on her neck like an insect crawling across her skin. She heard glass cracking, and the far away sound of a song so quiet she couldn't even make out the melody.

"You!" The chubby magistrate stormed up the road toward them, a host of armed guards at her back. Kira heard the glass cracking again, felt the tickle crawl up her cheek. She grinned. It was about time she got to play. With a flick of her wrists she had mirrored knives in her hands. She angled them towards the approaching soldiers and made them see new monsters rearing out of the wrecked buildings, talons bloody and reaching for them. A couple of the soldiers broke ranks and swung their spears at nothing.

"Kira, no!" Yanmei said. She rushed to her feet and stepped in front of Kira, blocking her view.

"But they mean us harm," Kira said. She didn't understand. They were armed and clearly aggressive. It was better to attack them first.

"We do not attack people for no reason," Yanmei said. "Ever. Look at me, Mirai."

Kira glanced at Yanmei, at the urgency on her face, and she shattered, mirrored shards falling around her clinking on the floor of the porch. She'd wanted to attack them, but the itch that had been creeping across her skin had vanished. She lowered her gaze and shattered her daggers, letting the pieces fall to the snow with the rest of her shards. She sighed and a weary exhaustion made her limbs feel like they were made of rock. "I'm sorry. I don't understand."

"This is their home," Yanmei said softly, laying a trembling hand against Kira's cheek. "And they are scared."

"Of me?"

"Yes," Yanmei said. "They don't understand you, and you're so much stronger than they are." It felt just like back at Heiwa. Yanmei always said the other students were scared, that was why they called her names, and they would stop once they got to know her. They never did though.

The chubby magistrate stormed up to them, and Kira fought the urge to show her true anger in the windows of the inn behind her. They weren't as good as mirrors, but any reflection would do.

"What is the meaning of this, onmyoji?" the magistrate

asked Haruto. Her hands were balled into fists, and she was trembling with rage.

Haruto didn't get up. He raised his head to look at the woman but said nothing.

"You said you would deal with the spirit problem," the magistrate shouted at him.

"I said I'd deal with the yokai," Haruto said quietly.

"There are still monsters all over my city."

Haruto shrugged. "Spirits. Not yokai. Not monsters. Just spirits."

"So get rid of them!"

"I don't do that." Haruto somehow remained calm despite the chubby woman yelling in his face. Kira was certain she'd have stabbed her by now, or maybe just showed her something so terrifying she peed herself. That would probably be more fun. "The spirits are here because a yokai made the temple its home. The gods don't like that sort of thing. If you want the spirits to leave, you'll need to cleanse the temple."

"So do it," the magistrate shrieked.

Haruto spread his hands. "I'm an onmyoji. You need a monk. And a lot of incense probably. I suggest airing the place out for a few days too."

The old poet hurried up the street, puffing from the effort. "What's going on here?" he asked, slowing to a stop to stand protectively over Haruto.

"The usual." Haruto shared a tired smile with his friend. "I'm being blamed for all the ills of the world."

"I want you out of my city," the magistrate yelled.

Guang raised his hands in a manner he probably thought quite calming. "Hey now. We did what you--"

"My city is still infested with yokai."

"Spirits," Guang said. "We got rid of the yokai. Right, old man?"

Haruto stood slowly, swaying on his feet, and put a hand on Guang's shoulder to steady himself. Then he walked off the inn porch straight past the magistrate onto the street.

"That's right!" the chubby woman sneered. "Leave now. All of you." She swept a hand at them, clearly including Yanmei and Kira.

Kira stepped forward, hands bunched into fists, but Yanmei took her by the arm and steered her away. She almost fought. Yanmei was tired and her strength was failing. But she wouldn't fight, not against Yanmei. Kira knew she struggled to understand people and situations. Yanmei always knew what was best.

"You will find no welcome in Minazuri. Leave and never come back," the magistrate shouted. A few of the guards joined in, jeering at them. Some locals had gathered, too, and were shouting for them to leave, the magistrate whipping them all into a frenzy.

Kira clenched her jaw and looked around for some reflections to use against them.

"It's not their fault," Yanmei said quietly, her hand still wrapped around Kira's arm. "They're just scared."

"But we helped them!" Kira said. She really didn't understand. Why were these people yelling at them when all they had done was help them?

"It doesn't matter," Yanmei said. "They need someone to be angry at, and the magistrate has made us the target. Either we leave now, or we will end up fighting the entire town."

"So? We can win!"

Yanmei shook her head sadly. She dragged Kira to catch up with Haruto in the street.

"It's five days to Sky Hollow," he said without looking at them. "We'll find a warmer welcome with the shintei." He lowered his voice to a whisper. "I hope."

They stopped to wait for the old poet, who still stood staring at the chubby woman.

"*Snow covered beauty,*
covers old rot, filth and bile.
Eyes open to truth."

With that, Guang tramped through the snow after them.

"That was your best one yet, Guang," Haruto said when the

poet caught them up.

Above them, the walls of Minazuri swarmed with guards and spirits. Behind them, the people of the city gathered, throwing insults and even a few stones, though none of the latter struck home.

"Hmmm," the poet grumbled. "Shame the subject isn't worth remembering."

Chapter 15

It was a tough few days after Minazuri. Yanmei and Kira had little in the way of supplies, and Haruto and Guang had less. But they made it work. Haruto ate less than the others and didn't seem to feel the cold. Yanmei knew the feeling well. The fire she carried inside never truly went out, and it helped chase away much of the chill. But the winter was a harsh one; the snow never stopped falling. When the drifts became hip deep, even she shivered and pulled her cloak tighter.

Haruto led the way. He was the only one of them who knew where to find Sky Hollow. Yanmei still wasn't sure why they were going to the hidden fortress of the shintei, but the Crone had called it a prison. Yanmei and Kira were searching for the Fourth Sage Under Heaven, but they did not know where to look, and if the onmyoji was searching for justice for Tian and Heiwa, then that was a worthy enough cause to follow. So many of Yanmei's friends and students had died at the academy. She carried a guilt inside she couldn't give voice to. When the fires started and the screams echoed through the halls, she had only one thought: save Kira. She should have gone back for more. She should have tried to save more.

Kira spent much of her time up front with Haruto, dancing atop the snow or playing with the little spirit, Shiki. She'd always had such an infectious energy about her. Many of the children at Heiwa had shunned her out of fear, but Kira had never let it quash her spirit.

"You're smiling," the old bandit shouted over the howling wind as he paced alongside her. "I know that smile." They were walking along a wide mountain trail with a sheer cliff face on their right and nothing but grey sky and deadly drop on their left.

It was treacherous footing with so much snow on the path.

Yanmei scowled at him. "Do you, Blood Dancer?" They had been heading up a slight hill for a while now, and her legs ached from the strain.

"I wish you would stop calling me that. It's been... thirty years."

"You think that's long enough for your crimes to be forgiven?" Yanmei couldn't help but needle the man. Bandits were a blight upon the world. They were monsters, as much as any yokai. Perhaps even more so. Yokai were only doing what was in their nature, pursuing vengeance against an unkind world. Bandits had the chance to do better, be better. The choice to not murder and take, and leave only ruin behind.

"Forgiven?" Blood Dancer chuckled bitterly. "Cabbage! No. Never that. I was hoping for *forgotten* though. You know what it's like, you lived the life."

Yanmei shook her head and paused as the wind whipped a flurry of snow into her face. "I was born to it. Raised in it. I never chose it." Her father had been Flaming Fist, one of the most notorious bandits the Hosan Empire had ever seen. Men flocked to him, drawn by his strength, his indomitable will, and his technique: setting his hands on fire in battle. But really, they were drawn to the excuse he gave them to be less than human, to be beasts who sought violence and blood and ill-gotten wealth. Her father was an evil man who infected all those around him with his evil.

"You never left him though, did you?" Blood Dancer shouted into the teeth of the wind.

"I tried," Yanmei mumbled.

"What?" Blood Dancer shouted.

"I tried!" she shouted. "Every time I ran, he tracked me down and dragged me back."

"When you were younger, sure." Blood Dancer ran his pale, wrinkled hand through his messy, snow-caked beard. "That excuse might fool some people, but how long did you stay with him even after you had grown stronger than him?"

"He was my father," Yanmei said. It was a weak excuse.

The old bandit blew into his hands and rubbed them together. "At least Tian left when he realised what I was."

He was right. When she was much younger, still a girl, she had tried to run away. She had been in love with one of her father's bandits, Zhihao, and they'd tried to run. But her father found her. Every time she ran he found her. When she hid at an inn, he slaughtered everyone inside as an example. When she begged refuge from a town, he laid siege to it, burned it down, and dragged her back to camp. There was no hiding from him, no escaping him. After Zhihao disappeared, Yanmei stopped trying to run away. Even after she had become stronger than her father, she didn't run. She made excuses for him: He wasn't as bad as some other warlords; he had rules, principles. He never sacked a roadside tavern or killed farmers. He gave money to orphanages. But even that was all lies. Flaming Fist never sacked a roadside tavern or killed farmers because it was better business to steal from them and let them live. He gave money to orphanages so he could visit them, take the most promising children and train them to be bandits. Yanmei had always known the truth. She was as bad as any of the bandits she hated. She was as bad as her father.

"I've spent the past fifteen years trying to make up for all the evil he made me do," she argued, aware she was trying to convince herself more than him. They were the same arguments she had been using for years no matter how tired and false they sounded. "The types of children he took to be bandits, I took to Heiwa."

The old bandit tripped over a rock under the snow and fell forward, plunging his hands into the snow to steady himself. "Ach, turnip!"

"Can you say the same, Blood Dancer?" Yanmei snarled. "Have you even tried to make amends?"

"Nope," he said. He straightened up, rubbed his legs and struggled on. "Some people can't be redeemed. The things they've done... the things I've done... I don't deserve forgiveness. I'm not asking and nobody would offer it. So what's left for old bandits like me? Turn myself in? They might execute me. Or they might not even care anymore. My crimes are older than most of the heroes wandering the empires these days. They might throw me in some gaol and forget about me. Either way, it serves no one. Instead, I follow Haruto, help him bring some good into the world. Help him stay true. It's not about redemption or atonement. It's just better than the alternative."

"And the money an onmyoji earns?" Yanmei asked.

Blood Dancer laughed at that. Kira, still pacing up ahead with Haruto, turned and grinned, and Yanmei forced herself to smile back.

"Money, sure," Blood Dancer said. "Do you see us swimming in lien? That old fool undercharges and then always seems to *lose* half of the pay. I can't count the number of tavern owners who have paid us a handful of lien to rid them of some yokai only to find a pouch of coins sitting on the table after we've left. Back there at Minazuri, did you see him ask for any lien?"

Yanmei hadn't really considered that. It was common knowledge an onmyoji never worked for free. Imperial law required that they be paid for their services. "What about your cut of the profits?"

Blood Dancer scooped up a handful of snow and rubbed it on his cheeks to wash away the sweat. "I spend a little on supplies. Someone has to keep us fed. The rest I spend on him because he sure as cabbage won't spend any on himself. That onion goes through kimonos and pipes like you wouldn't believe."

Yanmei stared at the old bandit and wondered if maybe she had misjudged him. Blood Dancer had killed her brother, but that was a lifetime ago now, and Daizen was always a psychopathic little brat who took after their father too much and delighted in tormenting his younger sister.

"What?" Blood Dancer said without looking at her. "Out with it."

Yanmei ground her teeth together so hard she heard them creak like trees in the wind. "I was just thinking about my brother."

"Oh." The old bandit pushed back his hood and wiped a papery thin hand across his bald pate. "I'm not sorry for his death."

"Neither am I," Yanmei said. Blood Dancer arched his snow-flecked eyebrows at her, and she replied with a savage smile. "Daizen was ten years older than me, you know. As a child, I used to idolise him almost as much as I did my father. I followed him around the camp, copied the way he walked and the way he spoke. I listened to his every word like it was wisdom of the ages.

"In return for my veneration, Daizen hated me. Not a day went by when I didn't catch a fist for standing too close. If I tripped, he kicked me. Once he broke my finger because I tried to hold his hand. I was scared of something – I don't even remember what – and I wanted the comfort of my older brother. He screamed that I burned him, then twisted my finger so hard it snapped." Yanmei swallowed hard. She hadn't thought about Daizen for a long time, and was quickly realising the pain still ran deep. "If any of the other bandits tried to help me, he'd threaten them. If they laughed along with him, he'd give them gifts. It didn't take long before they all chose to hate me."

Blood Dancer shook his head, ashen face staring into the swirling blizzard. "Didn't your father stop him?"

Yanmei scoffed and wiped a tear from her eye. "Daizen was smart about it. He stopped whenever our father was near, suddenly becoming the caring, dutiful brother. My injuries were explained away as the clumsiness of an uncoordinated little girl."

"And you never said anything because that isn't how things were done."

Yanmei found she wasn't finished. The words, like a loosed arrow, needed to complete their flight. "He was my brother. I felt a bond with him. And our father's torture was far worse. He burned me." She hid the scars, even now, but she was covered in them. Her arms, chest, legs, back. "He burned me again and again, and every time, he would tell me it was to protect me, to make me stronger, to awaken his infernal bloodline technique within me. And the absolute worst bit about it... it worked." She glanced at Blood Dancer, couldn't take the compassion she saw there, and quickly looked away.

They slogged on, ever uphill through knee deep snow. Yanmei was tempted to use her technique, melt the snow ahead of them to make the going easier as she had done so many times before, but the Fifth Sage had warned her it would kill her. Better to keep her technique and her qi quiet until they found the Fourth Sage.

The wind eased a little, making the going less tough, but with less snow blowing in her face, it was harder to ignore the old bandit's sympathetic stare. To change the subject, she forced some civility into her voice and asked, "Why did you quit?"

"Banditry?"

"Yes." Yanmei scooped up a handful of snow to rub on her cheeks, but it melted too quickly in her hands. "Even my father never knew what happened to you. Blood Dancer just disappeared one day. Some of your bandits joined Flaming Fist, others went their own way. What happened?"

The old bandit pulled his cloak a little tighter. "You're probably looking for some grand, romantic reason, hmm?" He laughed. "No, I didn't find love or have some great epiphany. It was Tian. I came home one day, covered in blood, I guess." Blood Dancer stopped talking a moment, his eyes distant, a pained look on his face. Then he continued, "He looked at me as if I was a stranger, some gore-smeared maniac come to do him and his mother harm." He shook his head. "I didn't want my boy looking at me like that. But the damage was done. He never looked at me like a father again. Always guarded, wary, edged with fear. Even the last few times I saw him, when he was a grown man, strong enough to kick my old arse from here to Cochtan, he still looked at me with that fear in his eyes."

They walked in silence for a while. Yanmei had vented her pain, though she felt no better for it. There was more, of course. There was always more. One thing she had long since learned was that childhood trauma was never truly dealt with. No matter how much of it she accepted, there was always more waiting like a gang of thugs down a dark alley.

Blood Dancer kept opening his mouth to say something, then closing it again. Whatever he wanted to say, he couldn't find the words, and Yanmei had no wish to prompt him.

They trudged on through the mountain path, keeping the cliff face close on their left. The wind picked up, blasting snow at them, the clouds above obscuring all but a faint light from the sun. A shadowy, snow-capped peak appeared ahead of them, looming in the distance past the swirling snow. Yanmei had thought they were already high up, but the mountain that rose ahead of them reached up to the heavens. Haruto stopped and waved back at them. The little ball of fluffy, dark hair he called his companion spirit leapt from his shoulder to Kira's. Then Kira giggled, scooped up a couple of handfuls of snow and dumped it on Haruto's head while he wasn't looking. Kira danced away across the snow, laughing, the spirit whistling happily on her shoulder.

"Dragon's Peak," Haruto shouted over the wind, clumps of snow falling from his head, sliding down his cloak. "Up there is Sky Hollow." He thumbed over his shoulder.

"How far?" Yanmei asked. She, Haruto, and Blood Dancer huddled close, their bodies cutting out the wind so they could hear each other better.

"Two more days to the sheltered plateau," Haruto said. He extended his hands toward Yanmei, warming them off her natural heat. Even with a firm grip on her technique, she ran hotter than most people. "Sky Hollow is near the top. Damned near impossible to find unless you know it's there."

The wind seemed to pick up again, howling around them and pelting them with snow. Kira rejoined them, frowning and hugging herself. She slipped in beside Yanmei and hugged her. She might have just been doing it for warmth, but Yanmei's spirits soared all the same. She draped her arm across Kira's shoulders and realised that soon she wouldn't be able to do it anymore. They were already almost of a height.

Blood Dancer blew into his hands again. "At least tell me the trail up the rest of the mountain is sheltered?"

Haruto smiled. "It's not. If anything, the snow will be thicker."

They all groaned except Kira, who was still giggling with Shiki.

"There is another way up," Haruto said, "assuming it has been maintained. It's shorter, a day maybe, but we might get half way up and find it has iced over. Then we'll have no choice but to turn back."

"But it's sheltered?" Blood Dancer asked.

Haruto shrugged snow from his shoulders. "Mostly."

"It gets my vote, old man."

Yanmei nodded, and as soon as she had, Kira joined in.

"I know it's a bit late to ask," Blood Dancer hollered, brushing snow from his face, "but are you sure the shintei are going to be happy to see you, old man?"

"Of course. I mean... probably."

The old bandit didn't look convinced.

"Hopefully," Haruto shouted into the storm. "They never forbade me from coming back. Not expressly."

"What did you do?" Yanmei shouted. She could barely hear herself in the wind.

Haruto glanced at her, then at Blood Dancer. Then he turned and started walking again. "This way. We need to reach the steps by nightfall."

Chapter 16

Crow drifted over the snow, leaving a dark smear of soot behind her. Shin walked a stride ahead of her, his feet barely touching the surface of the frozen mountain path. Now and then Crow caught him murmuring something about how gorgeous it was. Whenever he glanced back at her, he sneered at the trail she left as though she somehow ruined the beauty simply by existing.

She wondered how he didn't feel the cold. Crow had no body and no sense of temperature or smell or taste; she wondered how it felt to be cold or hot. To feel the snow crunch beneath her toes, the wind on her face. She could see it flapping her robe, but couldn't feel it. She could see and hear, and touch with her smoke, but she mostly relied on a general sense of things around her, knowing where everything was without sight, hearing without ears. But Shin had a body. He wore his kimono so loose that the snow and wind swirled inside it. The belt had long since come undone and flapped about him in the wind. His long, barbed braids floated around his head, defying the roaring wind, and he wore no shoes, preferring to glide over the snowy ground in his bare feet.

She leaned forward against the wind and floated a little faster, catching Shin up and drifting along beside him. He glanced at her, arched an eyebrow and shook his head, then turned back into the swirling blizzard.

Crow used to struggle to keep the wind from snatching away her smoke, blowing her apart and carrying her off wherever it would, but the Master had given her the robe to contain her, an anchor to hold on to even as the roar of the world tried to tear her asunder. For the truth was, it didn't matter if there was wind or not: the world, the mortal realm, didn't want her here, and she had to hold on to her anchor to stop it from having its way. That was why she envied Shin, and Xifeng, and all the others, yokai and humans alike. They had bodies. They did not know how hard it was to simply exist without one.

"Do you remember how you died?" Crow asked Shin as she floated along beside him.

"What?" Shin drawled. He had a way of speaking that drew out each word, as if he savoured the taste of its genius. "Of course I do." He smiled, daggers hiding behind silk. "You still don't remember?"

Crow shook her hood. It was a close approximation to a human shaking their head, but without a body she couldn't quite get it right. "I don't remember my life, or my death. I don't even remember my time as a yokai, before I became an onryo. I..." She almost said more, then remembered who she was talking to. Shin could not be trusted. They were siblings, true, all the onryo were, but Crow didn't doubt Shin would use whatever she told him against her at the first opportunity. When she said no more, he sighed dramatically and turned back to the blizzard and the climb.

After a drawn-out moment of silence, he said, "I was a courtesan once, when I was human."

"A courtesan? A prostitute?"

"If you wish to attach such a crude definition to it, then yes," Shin said. He smiled, his lips forming a perfect crescent moon. "I lived in Wu province in Hosa. In a grand parlour with my own rooms and wardrobes. Three separate wardrobes filled with the most wonderful clothes. Every cut and colour I dreamed of. Men would come from far and wide to see me. They called me beautiful and showered me with lavish gifts. Perfumes and paints, clothes and rings, mirrors and brushes. Trinkets and baubles all. They liked to call it courting, wooing, seduction." His smile faded quickly. "In the end they paid the mistress and took me to bed, and then they left. Rich men, powerful men, men from all around." He trailed off, his pale eyes distant.

"But the most powerful of my... *suitors*, didn't come to the parlour. He sent for me. It wouldn't do to be seen visiting the parlour, though a visit from a young man might be explained away for any number of reasons. So he sent a servant for me. He was a prince of Shin province, I was told, a rich and powerful man. Would you believe it? I did. I was a fool." He paused. Crow saw the muscles in his jaw bulge as he clenched his teeth. Then he continued, "They ambushed me on the road, beat my bodyguard unconscious and dragged me away. They were men, just men like any others. Nothing special about them save the hate they carried in their hearts." Shin paused then. When he spoke again, his voice was cold and detached. "They punched me and kicked me, called me 'unclean', 'wrong'. They wrapped a rope around my wrists, tied it to a horse and dragged me along the ground, all the while shouting at me, calling me a 'disease'. They claimed they were doing the world a service, saving their children from my evil, even as they pinned my arms and shoved my head into the lake. I watched my hair float about me, my blood swirling into the murk, as they held me and punched me, stripped me and drowned me."

Crow said nothing, feeling her smoke roil inside her robe. Anger. She could still feel something then. It churned inside her, a tempest screaming for violence.

"Are you surprised, sister?" Shin said. Crow realised he was staring at her again, his lips curved into an even more perfect crescent moon, but this time it was full of sharp teeth. "We are, after all, yokai. Vengeful spirits. Did you think I had died peacefully? We all died horribly, before our times, murdered, our dreams left unfulfilled." He turned away from her once more. "And we all know who is to blame for it. Mortals. Humans. Such pitiful creatures. But how beautifully they die!"

They passed through the blizzard, eventually climbing above it, and reached the plateau, high on the mountain, nothing below them now but swirling grey cloud and the odd patchy glimpse of the white world below. What lay before them was a rocky expanse that looked like a peak of the mountain had been flattened by a great force. Perhaps a god had come here and stepped upon the mountain, crushing it down before venturing off oblivious to the wonder they had created. And as humans always did, they capitalised on this benign act of divinity and colonised the spot like worms rushing up to the surface after a heavy rainfall.

In this case, the worms had built a small village, squat stone buildings dotting the plateau, an open square between them, men and women moving through training katas with their swords. Some of the warriors looked like veterans, but most were young, barely more than children. Beyond the buildings and the plateau rose the mouth a great cave, and stretching all the way across that maw were the walls of Sky Hollow. A legendary fortress sunk deep into the mountain's heart. It was said the fortress of Sky Hollow was unassailable, and that the greatest warriors in all of Ipia were trained there. The mighty shintei.

"Oh look, a greeting party," Shin said with an annoyingly light laugh. Four men and two women were approaching, dozens more behind them.

The two onryo stopped and awaited the warriors' greeting.

"How did you find this place?" asked one shintei, a stout, muscular woman. Like the others, she wore a loose hakama over her legs and a belted haori over her chest. A saya tucked into her belt promised a sharp katana within. Her hand hovered over its hilt, and the others stood behind her close and ready.

Shin stepped forward, clasping his hands together before him. "We are but simple travellers," he said with all the sincerity of a hawk telling a mouse it was just watching. He took another step forward, his hair floating around his head like a writhing halo. "We happened upon this spot by chance alone and would appreciate a place to rest for the day. Perhaps behind those magnificent walls of yours. Oh, they do look so very high and safe. I'm sure no one has ever broken in." He grinned devilishly.

"Stop and turn around, or I will be forced to strike," the shintei said. She flowed into a ready crouch, hand on hilt. She glared at Shin, her eyes so intense Crow thought he might catch fire. She wasn't a pretty woman, her jaw too prominent and her nose bent to the side. But those eyes were deeper than sin.

Beneath her hood, Crow moulded her smoke to the woman's features. Not pretty, but so very striking. The features slipped away even as she moulded them, and she was glad no one could see into the darkness of her hood.

"A duel, is it?" Shin said, taking another step forward. "How wonderful. "Which of us will draw first, do you think? Which of us is faster?" He took another step and settled into a perfect mimicry of the woman's fighting stance, resting lightly on the balls of his feet, his legs wide apart, one further forward than the other. His hands hovered at his waist, over a katana that was not there.

Shin and the shintei stood there in perfect stillness, watching each other. His hair floated about him in a hundred barbed braids, and the shintei's eyes flicked to them briefly before moving back to Shin's face. He smiled. The shintei drew, moving with the speed of a striking cobra. Her katana never even cleared its saya. Shin took one step, and a dozen of his braids shot forward, piercing the shintei along her arms, chest, and neck.

The shintei wavered for a moment, swaying as the concept of being dead caught up with her body. Shin didn't give it a chance. "Wonderful!" he said. He rose from his crouch, placed one hand on the woman's neck and the other on her chin, and tore her head off. Blood washed over the snow, splattered the rocks, and the body crumbled to the ground. He tossed the head into the snow at the feet of the other shintei.

The other five shintei stared down at the bloody head for barely a moment. Crow might have respected them for that; but there was no point in respecting the dead. Then they rushed Shin as one. The younger ones, who had been training in the courtyard, also started toward them. Such bravery was commendable, though they were all about to die.

"Yes! More!" Shin cooed as he rushed to meet the shintei. They surrounded him, and Shin stepped willingly into their circle.

A shintei with a sloping forehead rushed in first. He slid to a stop two paces from Shin, slashed with his sword, then stepped back turning the move into a feint. Behind Shin, two more shintei, a gangly woman with one eye and a man with a cross of scars on his cheek, darted in. Shin laughed as he lurched forward after Sloping Forehead. His hair darted in, five braids wrapping around the shintei's sword arm, barbed tips driving into flesh. Shin spun away from the shintei, his hair constricting. He ripped Sloping Forehead's arm from the socket, tossed the bloody limb at Gangly and One Eye, and then tottered at them, already drunk on blood lust.

Crow saw Shin changing as the battle rage took him. His arms, legs, and chest all swelling with muscle to grotesque size. His skin stretching and straining, barely able to contain the brute he was becoming.

"A challenge," Shin roared. "A challenge. Someone please challenge me." He slipped past Gangly's thrust, grabbed her arm in his giant hands, snapped it at the elbow. She opened her mouth to scream but Shin punched her hard enough her head snapped back, face a ruin, neck broken. One Eye and another man with a chest so hairy it tufted up around his neck, rushed in while Shin's back was turned. One Eye thrust high and Hairy Chest slashed low. Shin's hair shot out, blocking both swords as though they had struck stone.

A fifth shintei, a woman all grey hair and wrinkles, leapt over the toppling body of Gangly, her sword stroke striking down on Shin's head with the fury of a lightning bolt. Shin caught her mid-air, his now giant hands wrapping around the old shintei's. He crushed her hands against her sword hilt, mangling her fingers into pulping ruins. She screamed, Shin laughed. Braids of Shin's hair darted out, piercing the old shintei's chest over and over. Five wounds, a dozen, twenty, fifty, each strike so fast even Crow could barely see it. Blood spattered Shin's face and he roared with laughter. He dropped the ruin of a corpse and turned as One Eye and Hairy Chest struck at him again, one from each side. Shin parried One Eye's strike with a single braid of hair, grabbed his head in one hand and squeezed, crushing his skull with ease. Hairy Chest's thrust found a gap in Shin's writhing guard of barbed hair, and sliced into his straining kimono and the skin beneath. Shin tittered like a girl, his gore-streaked face manic. He backhanded Hairy Chest across the face hard enough to knock all sense from the man, then grabbed him by his hairy chest, lifted him into the air and slammed him down onto the ground once, twice, again and again.

Crow sighed and turned away. She drifted past the slaughter as more of the young shintei ran screaming to throw their deaths at Shin's feet. "And you call me messy," she said bitterly. She left a trail of smoke behind her, but Shin showered the plateau with spilt blood, torn flesh, and shattered bone. And all the while he changed, growing larger, and laughed in ecstasy.

One of the younger trainees, a boy with a bald head and only one ear, darted off toward the walls of the great fortress, no doubt trying to warn the shintei inside. Shin was too engrossed in the massacre he was creating to notice. With a flutter of her robe, Crow dashed after the boy, flying like a wraith, leaving a trail of smoke behind her. She soared past the shintei running to join the fight, weaving between them too quickly for them to strike at her. She flew between the outbuildings and over a low wall, so close to one of the trainees she left soot on his clothes.

The boy fleeing her was a mere hundred paces from the fortress when Crow caught him. She wrapped a smoky tentacle around his legs, pulling him to a halt, then another around his arms, pinning them to his side. She clung to him, enveloping him in her smoke. He opened his mouth to scream, and she forced a plume of smoke down his throat, pulling the air out even as she filled his lungs with acrid fumes. Crow let his body fall onto the rocky ground, his pale flesh stained black by her soot.

After a while, Shin joined her, his hulking form shaking the ground with each step. He was dripping gore and every single one of the shintei behind him was a bloody mess. She glanced up at him and found him grinning madly at the fortress before them. He was huge like this, a titanic monstrosity.

"Do you think they know yet?" he asked, his voice still soft and melodic as though it couldn't fathom that his body had changed.

Of course they knew. Crow had killed her prey silently, but Shin had made enough noise to wake the dead. The thought would have brought a smile to Crow's lips if she had any.

"They say the gates of Sky Hollow are unbreakable," Crow said, looking up at Shin towering above her. "Care to test it?"

"Oh yes. Oh yes!" He took off at a sprint towards the gates. If the shintei didn't already realise they were under attack, they soon would. And Shin would serve as a useful distraction. He would have his fun and perhaps there would be something left afterwards, but Crow doubted it.

Crow flew towards the walls, then up, and darted inside a slim window. Now that she was inside Sky Hollow, and she had a prison to find.

Chapter 17

The steps were on the sheltered side of the mountain where the snow was lighter, but the full force of the wind blasted them with every breath it had. The steps snaked up an almost sheer cliff face. Sometimes they sunk into the mountain itself, either taking advantage of natural caves or cut from the rock by hand. The steps had been carved a thousand years ago. Since then, the snow and wind and time itself had been doing a bloody good job of trying to smooth them away. Ages ago, two people could climb them side by side, but now it was almost impossible for even one person to cling to the cliff face in some places.

Every year, all the shintei trainees were sent onto the mountainside to clear the steps of ice and take hammer and chisel to them where needed to make the route a little safer. In Haruto's day, there had also been a rope running through iron rings hammered into the side of the mountain all the way up, but though the rings were still there, encased in frozen rock, the rope had long since been lost. When he thought about it, the steps didn't look like they had been tended to for a while, and he wondered if the tradition of making the trail safer had been lost to time.

They camped in a small cave near the base of the steps, grateful to be out of the snow. Haruto remembered the cave well. He and Toro had stayed there one night after chipping ice from the steps. The sun had set while they were still working, and there had not been time to ascend the mountain. The little cave hadn't changed much, despite the passage of so many years. It smelled of musk and old animal droppings. There was a small clay pot in one corner, cracked open, the contents long since dried up.

Guang set a struggling fire and melted some snow in a pot,

then added a few of their remaining ingredients. A thin stew, but at least it was something. Guang was staring into the pot when he suddenly started shouting about bats. Haruto and Yanmei both looked up to the cave ceiling, Yanmei half to her feet, but there was nothing there. Kira laughed, and Yanmei was quick to tell the girl off.

Haruto stared at the girl. There was something wrong with Kira, something beyond her not being entirely human. She had a vicious streak to her, but seemed contrite enough whenever Yanmei called her out. She seemed not to realise when she was doing something hurtful. Perhaps it was just the casual cruelty of all children. Certainly Haruto had been no shining example of morality when he was younger, but with Kira it seemed like something vicious. But Shiki liked her and Haruto counted that as a good sign. The little spirit didn't like anyone much, or at least she did a good job of hiding it.

Come morning, they were moving again. Using the first rays of light to start their climb up the steps. It was relatively easy going at first, but by mid-morning their pace slowed. The steps were worn and fragile, some crumbling and others thick with slippery ice. Even Kira climbed cautiously, pressing herself against the face of the cliff. Each time the wind picked up to a menacing howl, they all clung to the icy rock like barnacles on a boat, lest they be thrown to a plummeting death. Well, Haruto guessed he might survive the fall, but he didn't like the idea of spending his immortal eternity in pieces beneath bottomless snow drifts below them.

"Whose idea was this?" Guang shouted over the wind as they rested in the shallow shelter of a cave dug out of the cliff face for climbers to rest.

"Yours," Haruto shouted back. "Vengeance for Tian."

In Haruto's time, the cave would have been stocked with supplies, but that was another thing the shintei had let slide. From the mouth of the cave, they could see out over the Singsen valley and the lake beyond, where despite the freezing cold, several fishing boats floated. The lake was fed by underground hot springs, and even in the heart of a winter as vicious as a tiger, it never froze. It was said to be deeper than the tallest mountain and held enough water to drown all of Ipia should the waters ever escape.

"Cabbage!" Guang shouted. "The boy was always a little turnip, let's go find a tavern instead."

Haruto sighed and leaned back against the rough stone wall, shifting about to scratch an itch halfway up his back. "I really wish you would just tear up that stupid vow."

Kira sat on the stone floor of the cave, shivering and hugging her knees. "What vow?"

"My fourth vow," Guang said. "Never to swear. And I can't tear it up. I'll never make it to heaven if I forsake even one vow."

Haruto groaned. They'd had this argument before. "But it's idiotic. Not swearing doesn't make you a better person. It just makes you a sanctimonious tit. Besides, you do swear. The words you use aren't important. It's the intent that matters. Substituting vegetables for swearwords doesn't mean you're not cursing."

"You're wrong," Guang shouted, even though the wind had momentarily subsided. "On both counts. I know this because I have conclusive proof."

"What proof?"

"You are a carrot-faced onion!" Guang grinned. "See? Proof. If you were right, my vow would have prevented me from saying that."

Haruto shrugged rather than concede the point.

"And it does make me a better person," Guang continued. "It's not about the vow in this case, but what it signifies. It's proof I'm trying to be better. And that makes me better."

"That's all it takes to be good?" Kira asked. "To want to be good?"

Yanmei shook her head. Of all of them, she was the only one who didn't look cold. Just sitting next to her, Haruto could feel her heat like sitting next to a cooling hearth. "Wanting it is a start," Yanmei said. "You also have to act. To try. Otherwise, it's nothing more than an empty promise."

Kira frowned and shuffled closer to Yanmei. "You're using your technique."

Yanmei smiled at the girl. "It's cold."

Haruto hugged his arms against his chest, yet the wind, which had picked up to strident yowl again, still found all the gaps in his kimono. Shiki wriggled a little deeper, shifting around to the small of his back, her fur making him itch. "Sky Hollow is surprisingly warm," he shouted. "The shintei dug deep to funnel heat from the mountain. And there's a bath."

Guang grumbled.

"What is a shintei?" Kira asked. She was wide eyed and shivering, her hands clutched together like pale claws, but she was smiling despite it all.

"An order of warriors," Haruto said. "The most elite Ipia has ever trained. They are taught to be one with the sword and swear themselves to honour and the path of oaths."

"Path of oaths?"

It seemed the girl never ran dry of damned questions. "When a shintei takes an oath to do something, they give a lock of their hair to the recipient of the oath. When the shintei has completed the task, the recipient burns the hair to tell the gods and the stars that they have fulfilled their oath. When a shintei dies, their successes and failures are weighed. If they have led a good and virtuous life, fulfilling their oaths, they are reborn into the next generation. If they have not, they are cast back to earth as a demon. A tengu."

"That sounds exciting," Kira said, clapping. "I want to take an oath."

Haruto looked at the onryo. She seemed so earnest at times, and so malicious at others, but for now she appeared to be excited about the prospect. "Oaths and vows should never be taken lightly. There is power in a promise that goes beyond the words. They bind our souls to a purpose, and failure can rend a person in two as surely as any blade."

"But what if it's the right thing to do?"

Haruto glimpsed Yanmei smiling as she peered down at the

child. "Then that might be an oath worth taking. But you need to make sure it's the right thing to do." Far too often, the right thing was actually the wrong thing in a pretty dress.

They rested a few more minutes and then continued their climb.

Just as the sun was beginning to dip below the horizon, they came upon a section of the cliff that had cracked loose and tumbled away, taking about ten steps with it. It didn't seem like much; the other side of the gap was so close. Not much at all, and yet also everything.

Haruto stood on the precipice, staring into the abyss. "We have to turn back," he shouted into the gale. There was no climbing around it. The gap extended up to the peak and down into the clouds.

"I can make it," Kira said, squeezing past Guang and almost shoving him off the steps. She stepped up beside Haruto, pressed between him and the cliff face. "I can make it," she said more confidently this time. She crouched, ready to leap.

Haruto gripped her arm and pulled her away from the edge. She glared at him, and a mirrored dagger flashed in her hand. He let go of her arm slowly. "None of us are jumping across. Look." He slowly extended an arm over the gap. The wind blew his kimono sleeve this way and that in a frantic flapping. "The wind will take you the moment you jump and that'll be the last we see of you."

Kira pouted, and the mirrored dagger in her hand shattered, twinkling shards scattering in the wind.

Haruto turned around to face Yanmei and Guang. "We turn back, take the main pass up to Sky Hollow."

"Three more days?" Guang asked. "I'll freeze solid, old man."

Yanmei shook her head, her hair whipping about in the wind. "We don't have enough supplies. In this weather, we'll starve before we reach the shintei."

Guang grumbled something about his knees as he pulled his satchel around and started fishing inside. "Once again it falls to the poet to rescue you. Honestly, you glorious warriors should be ashamed of yourselves. It's not all about stabbing people and battling monsters. Here." He pulled out his ink pot and handed it to Yanmei. She took it with a questioning look. "Warm that up for me."

Yanmei chuckled. "Two old bandits. One vowing only to battle with words. And the other reduced to a portable camp fire."

Guang seemed to think about that a moment. Then he laughed, too. "Best use for us." He took a roll of paper from his sling and held it tightly against the whipping wind as he squeezed past Yanmei and told Kira to get out of the way. She edged back to stand with Yanmei, and he shimmied up to stand next to Haruto and stare out over the drop. "Have I mentioned that I hate heights?"

Haruto smiled and put a hand on Guang's shoulder, steadying the old poet in case the wind took a turn. "I'll add it to the list," he said.

"You shouldn't be using your technique," Kira shouted as Yanmei warmed the ink.

"I don't have a choice." Yanmei leaned against the girl for support. Haruto thought she looked tired, old, worn thin. Her battle against the cold was taking a toll on her. She handed the ink pot back to Guang and flattened herself against the cliff face next to Kira.

"Thank you," Guang said. He took a steadying breath, then whipped the roll of paper out in front of him. The wind took it immediately, whipping it about and trying to tear it from Guang's hands, but the old poet held on tightly and his brush flowed across the parchment. He wrote a single word, *BRIDGE*, and the paper flattened out and became rigid even against the howling wind. The far end touched down on the stairs opposite them, and he quickly placed his end down and stood on it to keep it secure.

"Easy," Guang said as he put the stopper back on his ink pot. He wrapped his brush in oiled cloth, and slid them both into his pack.

Haruto grinned. "If it is so 'easy', then why are you

sweating?"

Guang shot him a look. "It's too warm up here, of course. Have I mentioned that I hate the heat."

"Are we supposed to walk across that?" Kira asked. "It's paper."

Guang smiled. "I'm sure our brave onmyoji, hero of numerous glorious epic poems, would like to go first."

Haruto shrugged. "It's your bridge. After you." He knelt down on the paper to secure it for Guang to cross.

"Cabbage, old man. I knew you'd say that." Guang turned to stare at Kira. "If it can hold my saggy arse, it can hold you." He stepped out onto the paper bridge.

The wind buffeted him, catching in his clothes and cloak, trying to rip him this way and that. He quickly sank down onto his hands and knees, his complaints whipped away by the wind, and crawled forward, hand over hand. His progress was painfully slow. When finally he reached the other side, he scrambled off the bridge, backed against the cliff face, and rested there for a few seconds, eyes screwed shut, trying to catch his breath. Eventually the old poet scrambled around and clutched the other end of the bridge. "Next," he said, barely audible in the wind.

Kira leapt forward and dashed past Haruto.

"Be careful!" Yanmei shouted.

The girl scampered onto the bridge and the wind hit her, slammed her back. Her feet slid sideways on the paper. She teetered on the edge for a moment, arms flailing, then quickly dropped to her hands and knees. She crawled the rest of the way in silence, and when she reached the far side and turned around, her face was pale as milk, her messy hair slick with sweat.

"Showing off almost got your girl killed," Haruto said as Yanmei stepped past him.

She lowered herself to her hands and knees before she even got to the paper bridge and glanced back at Haruto. "She's trying to impress you." And with that, she started crawling across the bridge. Even in the buffeting gale, the shimmer of a heat haze surrounded Yanmei. He wondered if she could stop it, or if the technique was part of her, like his immortality. She reached the other side, stood, and quickly wrapped her arms around Kira. They hugged each other.

Then it was Haruto's turn. He let go of the bridge and looked up. "Have you got it?" he shouted.

"I've got it," Guang said, gripping the other side of the bridge tight and frowning in concentration.

"Are you sure?"

"I'm sure, old man."

"Because I know how your hands shake these days."

"Just get a move on, you annoying onion."

Haruto laughed as he crawled onto the paper bridge. "That's still the most ridiculous vow I've ever heard of." The bridge bounced more than Haruto had hoped, since one end was no longer secure.

Guang stared hard at his hands gripping onto his side. "Squash you, old man. They're my vows, and I can better myself however I choose."

The bridge bucked beneath Haruto and he glanced back to see the unsecured end creeping perilously close to the edge. He looked down, which was a very bad idea. The world spiralled away below him, the clouds a churning mass of grey over dizzying patches of snow and stone. He felt nauseas. His hands were frozen to the bridge, unwilling to move. It would be a mighty fall. Even *if* his immortality kept him alive, he would be pink paste. The pain would be beyond anything he had ever felt. He shook his head, desperately trying to clear the thoughts away.

"Hurry up, old man!"

The bridge bucked again. Haruto pushed to his feet and leapt forwards just as the wind caught the flat side of the bridge and tore it from Guang's grip, flinging it out into the void. Haruto crashed on the rock steps and scrabbled for anything to stop him from plummeting into the whirling clouds below. Hands clutched his arms, and he looked up to see Guang leaning over him, red faced and grunting from the strain. Sweat dripped from his nose onto Haruto's forehead.

"Pull me up!" Haruto shouted as he scrabbled his feet against the stone, the wind swirling around him mercilessly.

"Does it look like I'm brewing tea?" Guang grunted.

"Pull harder!" Haruto shouted. Shiki squealed from inside his kimono, scrabbled up onto his shoulder, took one look around, and buried herself back inside his clothes.

Yanmei's wrinkled face appeared above him, and she extended a hand. Haruto let go of the rock with one hand and grabbed it, then grabbed hold of Guang with the other hand. He scrabbled, scraped, his feet flying out over the void, as the two old bandits pulled him up, scraping his chest against the stone step and finally flopping onto them. They all lay back in a tangle of sweaty limbs and trembling fear.

Kira stood a few steps above them, watching, hopping from foot to foot in anxious worry. When the others got to their feet, she let out a sigh of relief, rushed down, and wrapped her arms around each of them in turn. As soon as she let go and backed away, Guang did the same, holding Haruto in a tight embrace. Haruto wrapped his own arms around the poet, and they stood there, leaning against the cliff face for a few moments, breathing steam into each other's face and smiling.

Eventually they pulled apart, and Haruto nodded his thanks to Yanmei as well. "There's not much further to go," he shouted over the wind, hearing the tremor in his own voice. "We should be there by nightfall." He was trembling and sick with residual fear lying heavy in his gut. He couldn't show it; he had to be the strong one, the immortal one. But he couldn't shake the feeling the mountain didn't want him to return to Sky Hollow. It had good reason.

Chapter 18

They were all near frozen by the time they reached the top of the steps. They turned sharply into a tunnel dug straight into the cliff face, away from the yawning drop and the relentless wind. Kira heard it howling outside the cave mouth, a ravenous beast robbed of its prey. There was barely a breath of a breeze inside and the air was warmer, rising from the ground. Still, they were all shivering except Yanmei.

"Is this mountain a volcano?" Yanmei asked, placing a palm flat on the rocky cave floor. Kira copied her, earning a smile, but she felt nothing but cold rock.

"No," Haruto said. He was hunting around the walls, looking for something.

"The stone is warm," Yanmei said. "There's a heat source buried somewhere below."

Haruto shrugged. "Sky Hollow has always been warmer than it has any right to be." He turned from the wall to look at her. "But not this warm. Shiki, give us some light."

The little spirit scrabbled from his robes and gave an annoyed squeak. Kira laughed.

"I know you're not a torch," Haruto said. "More of a grumpy lantern really."

Shiki squeaked again.

"Please," Kira said.

Shiki turned and stared at Kira with those eyes that were far too large for her little fluffball body. Then she opened her mouth wide and drew in a deep breath, inflating herself to almost twice her normal size and growing bright as she did so, until she let out an audible pop and burst into a fierce orange, like a bright flame that didn't flicker. No warmth came from the little spirit, but she shone enough light for Kira to see around the cave. She floated from Haruto's shoulder, stunty legs pawing the air as if she was trying to swim.

"Thank you," Kira said with a bow to the spirit. She turned and glanced at Yanmei, who smiled at her, and was relieved she had done the right thing for once.

Guang let out a whistle as he walked toward the back of the cave, staring at the walls lit by Shiki's light. The cave opened up into a long corridor with a high ceiling and walls covered in script, then disappeared into the gloom further into the mountain. "How far does this go?" the poet asked.

"Far," Haruto said. "Up and down and all over. The fortress itself is above, on a sheltered plateau, but Sky Hollow is the size of a small town." He shook his head. "It's all winding passages and cavernous rooms. I cannot tell you how many times I got lost in this giant ant hive of a fort. I remember when the whole place was filled with people. We were packed in here like buns in a steamer. The masters led classes hundreds strong." He smiled wistfully. "One time Toro and I painted a sheet of canvas as rubble. It was terrible really, but in the dim hallways it almost looked real, especially to a trainee in a blind hurry. We went to master Shiba's class early and hung the canvas over the entry corridor. When the rest of the class finally showed up, they thought the corridor was blocked and had to find another way round. The whole class was late, everyone except Toro and I. Master Shiba hated tardiness and ordered the entire class to run down and up the steps." He stopped and sighed, then shook his head. "There should be some torches around here somewhere."

Yanmei peered at a section of lettering on the wall next to Kira. "What's all the writing on the walls? I can't read it."

"They're written in old Ipian," Guang said as he joined her. "Not used much anymore. Most people only speak and read Hosan these days. Everyone just accepts it as the most common tongue. But a few hundred years ago the Ipians spoke Ipian and the Nash spoke... grunts and farts mostly, I think."

"They're warnings," Haruto said. "Stories of shintei who lost their way or broke their oaths. Part of a long tradition of scribing the order's greatest failures on the walls. They put them all leading towards the stairs because the trainees had to come this way regularly, so they would constantly be reminded of the failings of others, and how not to be a shintei. Here we are." He found a sconce on the wall with a few old torches lying cold and forgotten. He took them all and spent a few moments lighting them with Guang's flint, then handed one to Guang and one to Yanmei. He did not give one to Kira, as if he didn't trust her with fire somehow. She wanted to say something to the onmyoji, but stopped when Shiki popped back to her normal size, her light fading as she plummeted to the floor. She tugged on Kira's kimono with one squat arm. Kira picked the little spirit up, and she scurried up to sit on her shoulder.

"Hey, old man." Guang pointed to some script on the wall. "You seen this one?"

Haruto joined the old poet at the wall and groaned.

"What is it?" Kira asked. She joined them and stood on her toes to look over Guang's shoulder. The words on the wall almost made sense to her. It was as if she had once known what they meant, but had forgotten.

Guang chuckled and glanced at Haruto.

"Where is everyone?" Haruto asked, turning from the wall and striding away. "There should be people here. Trainees, shintei, masters. We should at least be able to hear them by now."

Guang didn't move from the wall, so Kira stayed there too, still peering over his shoulder, thinking maybe the words would eventually make sense. Yanmei joined them. She looked tired after the climb, her face drawn in long wrinkles. Kira gave her a hug, the only comfort she could think of, and Yanmei smiled and hugged her back.

Haruto stopped walking and looked back at them.

Guang raised his eyebrows.

Haruto shrugged. "Fine. But you already know it so you can tell it as we walk."

A long time ago, hundreds of years, there was a young man who went by the name of Nightsong. He was just fourteen, yet he already earned himself the title hero. A prodigy with the sword, he clashed with local bandits time and again, each time turning them back from his hometown. The people loved him. So it was no surprise that when he came of age his parents sent him to Sky Hollow to train as a shintei. For in Ipia there is no greater honour for a family than to give a child to the shintei.

Already a renowned warrior, Nightsong was destined for greatness. Such was the level of skill he showed that the emperor of Ipia came to Sky Hollow to see him train. This was unprecedented, and a great celebration was thrown with feasting and contests of blade and of poetry. Emperor Ise watched Nightsong defeat his fellow initiates in duel after duel. None could stand against him, and the Emperor had eyes for no other.

One of the initiates pitted against Nightsong was a raven-haired young man named Toshinaka Heiru. He had been at Sky Hollow for longer than Nightsong. He trained harder, put himself through gruelling regimes to make himself stronger. None of the initiates worked as hard as Toshinaka, and none fought so fiercely. Yet Nightsong beat him with ease. Three times Toshinaka attacked Nightsong in their duel, and three times Nightsong delivered a blow that would have been fatal in a real fight. Toshinaka wished to fight on, but the shintei masters dragged him away. In Nightsong's long shadow he was soon forgotten.

So impressed was Emperor Ise that before Nightsong was even confirmed as a shintei warrior he was given land and holdings. The Emperor even married him to a distant cousin, Iso Izumi, attaching Nightsong, and any deeds he would achieve in life, to the throne. Never before had such an honour been extended to someone of such humble birth... and never was such a risk taken again.

Years after the emperor's visit, Nightsong was confirmed as a shintei warrior. Oaths were taken, swords forged. The shintei order, already famous, grew in popularity, and Sky Hollow received more recruits than ever. Young men wanted what Nightsong showed them all was possible: strength, power, riches, recognition, even royalty.

Nightsong took few oaths and never failed to complete them. They called him unbeatable, a warrior without equal, the greatest shintei ever. But – and of course there is a but – he only fought the battles he chose because he was certain he could win. He took no risks, preferring to bathe in the luxury of his fame.

Now, remember Toshinaka Heiru. His life could not have been more different from Nightsong's. He was granted no privilege, given no special honours. He struggled for every victory, even against his fellow trainees. In a time of heroes, he was all but forgotten. He was eventually confirmed a shintei, though he was not picked for greatness. But he had something Nightsong did not, a burning drive to succeed, to grow stronger, to achieve.

After he left Sky Hollow, Toshinaka wandered Ipia, taking every fight he could find. Victories were scarce. In Hitsu, he fought a tavern brawl against not one but many bandit thugs to protect the owner. He knocked down two, but the others jumped him, and Toshinaka fell to the floor amidst a torrent of falling fists. The owner of the tavern received a similar beating, and Toshinaka's lock of hair went unburnt, his oath failed.

Outside Akaro, Toshinaka fought a duel against the bandit warlord Mournful Spear. He was outmatched from the start, but he had given his oath and the people of Akaro were relying upon him. Toshinaka took a wound so grievous the stars called for his return to them, and only his own stubborn will kept him alive. The people of Akaro suffered from his failure and cursed his name, and another of Toshinaka's oaths went unfulfilled.

On the Burning Peaks, where the sunrise sets the rocks on

fire, he was knocked unconscious by Serpent Jun. In Sanso town he alone stood against the assassin Shadow Lark and received a poisoned knife in his back for his effort. The lord he had promised to protect was murdered as Toshinaka watched, paralysed. Yokonora village burned to ground after Toshinaka failed to protect it. Covered in blood, he watched the fire consume the village, leaving only smoking bodies behind. More oaths unfulfilled. More hair unburnt.

But Toshinaka never stopped fighting. He took every oath he could swear. Fought every battle he could find. Duelled anyone with a blade and a name worth knowing. He never stopped.

Years later, Toshinaka saw the fame and wealth that Nightsong had gathered and found hate inside of him. Hate for a man who was so skilled, yet had done so little with it. A man lauded as being unbeatable, yet never tested. Toshinaka found he had always hated Nightsong, and with every defeat suffered, every wound taken, and every oath failed the hate grew.

Now, once every fifty years Ipia held its traditional grand tournament, the Proving of Champions. The eventual winner can name one reward of their choosing, within reason of course, and the emperor would grant it. Nightsong did not take part. He had no need to prove himself; everyone knew his skill was unmatchable, a warrior without equal. But others lined up in their hundreds, and one among them stood out. A giant of man with a pointed chin, a nose like a parrot's beak, who wore his oily black hair loose rather than in a warrior's braid. The years had changed Toshinaka, and none who knew him at Sky Hollow recognised him now.

The tournament competition was ferocious, and many heroes lost their lives. Yet Toshinaka walked through it unscathed. His many defeats had truly made him stronger. No sooner had his last opponent fallen than Toshinaka strode forward and demanded his reward from the emperor – a duel against Ipia's greatest hero, a duel against Nightsong for no other reason than to prove who was better. The emperor agreed it was within reason and ordered Nightsong to the field.

The two warriors fought. Two shintei trained at Sky Hollow who could not have lived more different lives. They clashed again and again, katanas sparking in the moonlight, and each time Nightsong was thrown back. Toshinaka was relentless, battering Nightsong with greater strength, greater skill, and the experience of one who has fought and lost and fought again. Nightsong had grown nothing but lazy, and Toshinaka destroyed him in front of the Emperor and all of Ipia.

As Nightsong lay beaten and bloody upon the arena floor, his family and friends all around, the Emperor of Ipia asked how it was possible. How had such a champion been beaten in his prime? Not just beaten but dismantled so utterly by a man who should have been tired from so many previous battles. Could the masters of Sky Hollow have chosen the wrong man?

Toshinaka thrust his blade into the ground next to Nightsong's head. Then he turned and strode away. He never explained his hatred for Nightsong, nor how he was able to beat a man who had once been so much stronger than he, who was supposed to be stronger than everyone. But the shintei who were watching knew.

Nightsong lost because he chose to fight only against those he knew he could beat. He learned only to win, not to fight.

"How did I do, old man?" Guang asked.

Haruto shrugged. "You laid it on a little thick."

"Poetic licence."

Kira wanted more. The walls they walked by were covered in similar writing, and she wondered how many other fascinating stories were hidden here.

"Besides," Haruto continued, his voice sharp as a blade.

"Every time I hear the Tale of Nightsong, the rest of the story is missing. It's always framed as a warning against resting on one's laurels and letting oneself grow lazy. Nightsong always plays the fool while Toshinaka is the hard-working hero." He scoffed. "Tell the rest of it. Tell how Nightsong just wanted to live a peaceful life away from the violence of constant fighting. Tell how Toshinaka made him an enemy, a focus of his anger at his own inadequacy. Tell them. Tell them how Toshinaka couldn't let his hatred go. How beating some humility into Nightsong wasn't enough. Tell them how Nightsong returned home after recovering, only to find his house a smoking ruin and his wife murdered." Haruto stopped walking for a moment and slammed his hand against the wall. "They always leave out that part of the story of Nightsong and Toshinaka."

Haruto sounded hurt, sad. Kira wanted to help him somehow, but neither Yanmei nor Guang said anything and they probably knew better. They understood people better than she did. And yet, he was in pain, and she couldn't just let him suffer. Yanmei said being good was about helping others even if they didn't realise they needed it.

Kira sped up a little to walk next to Haruto. She waited until he looked at her, then smiled. "Sorry about your wife."

"I suppose I made that obvious," he said. His pain seemed to slip away. He flashed her an empty smile. "I wish the story of Nightsong ended like it did on the wall, but there's more. So much more."

They all fell silent then, and Kira reached for something else to say. "At least you can remember it," she said eventually, already suspecting it was the wrong thing. "I don't really remember anything from before Yanmei rescued me from the mirror. I think there was... I think I hurt people."

Haruto scoffed. "Be glad you don't remember. You were a yokai, a monster. A vengeful spirit that existed only to bring pain to others."

Kira didn't feel like a monster. Even in her vague memories from the mirror, fuzzy as they were, she never felt like a monster.

She didn't want to be a monster. She felt Yanmei's hand on her shoulder and realised she had slowed, letting Haruto pace ahead of her.

"He didn't mean it," Yanmei said softly, pulling Kira into a walking embrace. Though it had felt so natural when Kira was smaller, it felt a little awkward now that they were almost of a height. "Some people can only deal with hurt by passing it on to others. That doesn't make it right, but for some it's all they know how to do. He didn't mean to hurt you, he was just trying to deal with his own pain."

"What can I do?" Kira asked.

Yanmei was silent for a moment. Kira relaxed into her embrace, enjoying the familiar, intense warmth of her. "You have to decide if they mean it or not. If they mean to pass on the hurt, there's nothing you can do. If they don't mean to, the best you can do is give them time and be there for them when they need you."

Kira sighed. "Being good sounds hard. Is being bad easier?"

Yanmei bit her lip. She always did that when Kira posed her a tough question. "No. Not easier. Just a different set of problems."

"There's a dojo just ahead," Haruto said over his shoulder. "We should be able to cut through it and find the stairs up to the fort, assuming there isn't a class being taught."

Guang paced ahead to walk next to him. "Does it seem a little too quiet to you, old man?"

Kira saw Haruto nod, but he said nothing.

When they reached the dojo, the reason Sky Hollow was so quiet became apparent. Bodies were strewn across the floor. Some were mostly intact, others were torn flesh and spattered blood as though they had been ripped apart, gore soaking into the packed straw. Weapons lay about too, no doubt hastily pulled from the wooden racks around the walls of the dojo. By the looks of it, they did no good. Kira had never seen such butchery. Many of the dead were young, probably close to her age. It was just like Heiwa. Students and masters all fighting together and dying together, their blood mingling in streams, running down the uneven floor to pool against the far wall.

Haruto stalked silently between the bodies, looking down on each one as if committing what was left of their faces to memory. Guang skirted the carnage, keeping close to the walls, never venturing near the spreading blood.

Yanmei knelt by a mostly intact corpse. "There is still warmth here. It's fading, but... this happened only recently. A few hours ago at most."

Haruto stared back at her. There was a grim set to his face Kira had not seen before. The flickering fire from his torch turned his features into sharp shadows. "Then they're still here," he growled. Kira recognized the rage inside him, the hatred, the suffocating need for vengeance. It touched something inside of her and she heard the icy snap of glass cracking, felt an itch travel up her chest.

The onmyoji spat on the floor and sprinted from the dojo.

Chapter 19

Crow rushed in between the two shintei. They slashed at her passing, but their blades passed harmlessly through her trailing smoke. She reached out and snuffed the torches as she passed, and the room fell to utter darkness. The two shintei closed ranks, each instinctively knowing where the other was. They were well used to fighting together, relying upon each other. Even in the dark they were disciplined. Crow respected that. Not that it would matter.

A side effect of only seeing the world in black and white was that she needed very little light to see. She did not even understand how she saw with no eyes, but the world was painted in myriad shades of grey. Even in the deepest, darkest caverns she saw everything painted in grey hues.

"You will never reach the prison, demon!" one of the shintei spat at her. A man with sagging skin and a drooping moustache, his hands were steady on his katana.

For a while now, Crow had drifted through the lower levels of the warren that was Sky Hollow. She heard Shin far above her, revelling in his rampage, and wondered if he would leave any of the shintei alive. Probably not. Once Shin got going, there was simply no stopping him. He was the strongest of them all, physically at least, and his power grew with his bloodlust, which would be insatiable by now. No doubt he would lament and curse the mess he made once he calmed down, but for now he'd hunt down every living soul in Sky Hollow. Crow preferred not to kill. She had avoided most of the shintei, hiding as they passed her. A benefit of being made of smoke was that she could drift along the ceiling as easily as the floor.

Whether they meant to or not, the shintei had just confirmed that Crow was in the right place. The two of them had been guarding a large wooden door. She let them flounder about in the dark while she investigated. The door was locked. Sturdy. Secured into the surrounding stone. She probed it, sending a wisp of smoke drifting in between the seams and through the lock, around the edges. Then she gripped the edge of the door, tore it from the rock and flung it aside.

"Stop!" screamed the saggy-skinned shintei. He shuffled forward and slashed, but Crow was already gliding away from him into the great cavernous space beyond.

It was vast and empty save for a large circle of metal, embossed with fanciful designs of clouds and fire and trees, secured firmly in the far rocky wall.

"Get that torch re-lit," said the saggy-skinned shintei still floundering near the broken door behind her.

Crow crossed the room to stare at the circle of metal. It was built into the wall of the cavern, almost like a carved relief, symbols all over it in a language she didn't understand. It took up almost the entire wall, a mess of gears and pistons and intricate carvings. The Master had told her to expect something like this. It was a Cochtan engine. The Cochtans were a people without techniques, without qi, but what they lacked in spirit they made up for with ingenuity. From flying thopters to Blood Engines that made a person stronger and faster. Their devices had many uses including, apparently, locking away titans.

Crow puffed smoke along the engine's surface, exploring it as intimately as a lover's touch. By the time she was done she knew its every nook and cranny. There was no obvious lock, but there were two holes at opposite ends of the device, each extending a short way into the device and containing numerous sharp objects.

Behind her, the shintei lit their torches and barrelled into the cavern. "No further, demon!" shouted the saggy-skinned shintei.

Crow turned and drifted back toward the shintei. "Do you know what lies beyond this wall?" she asked. "Do you know what you guard?"

The old shintei placed his torch in a wall sconce and took his katana in both hands. "The shintei of Sky Hollow vowed to the Fifth Sage Under Heaven to guard this prison. There is no greater task."

"Yes, I understand. But do you know why?" The world was full of people performing tasks they didn't understand. They were all fools. They did not know what they guarded or why it was here.

The two shintei split up and circled Crow to attack her from two sides, an old man with a drooping moustache on one side, a young fool with a sneer on his pretty face on the other. She let them think they had a chance.

"This door is a Cochtan engine. How should I open it?" Crow said as they closed on her, talking more to herself. "Did you know Cochtan engines run on blood? I, unfortunately, do not have any blood. Thank you for volunteering yours."

They attacked, and Crow would have grinned if she had a mouth to do it. She couldn't kill them, not yet. She needed them alive.

Haruto rushed up the stairs past cooling corpses and little rivers running red. It was the onryo. It had to be. Maybe not the spider – there were no webs or cocoons and the bodies were torn apart – but an onryo was in Sky Hollow. Tian's thirst for vengeance burned inside his chest. He heard the others' footsteps behind him, their voices calling out. He ignored them.

A shout from up ahead, a battle cry echoing through the desecrated halls. Then a scream of agony.

Haruto burst into the temple hall, panting from the headlong flight. It was as he remembered it: a high ceiling and five stone pillars, each representing one of the five great constellations. Lanterns on the walls lit the entire space in flickering yellow light, and a hole in the roof let in a ray of light that lit the dais at the far end. Upon the dais was a shrine to the tianjun, the lord of heaven. In his time, the tianjun had been Mira, the god of harvest, but she was dead now and the god of missed opportunities sat the

Jade Throne. Benches and bodies were scattered all about. Dozens of shintei, old and young, lay slaughtered here in a place that should have been holy.

Standing amidst the carnage was a man, tall and lithe, his clothing all but torn away from the loose hakama that clung to his waist. His skin was pale as chalk and he was covered in blood. His hair floated about his head in a hundred thick braids, each as long as a whip, coiling and writhing like serpents. Despite the skill and techniques of the shintei that lay in pieces on the floor, he did not appear have a single wound. He held the body of young woman in the air. She looked just old enough to be confirmed a shintei. Her head drooped, neck broken, and he tossed her body onto the floor.

"Not a single challenge among them," the man said lightly. "And such a *mess* they made." He flicked a wrist and blood spattered a bench near the wall.

"Enough!" Haruto roared. He threw his torch aside and stalked into the room toward the man. He heard the others arrive behind him, heard Kira gasp at the carnage.

"Hmmm?" The onryo glanced past Haruto. "More of you?" He sighed. "I'm bored with killing you. You can go." He flicked a lazy hand toward the temple doors at the far end of the hall. Despite being three times the height of a grown man, the doors were hanging askew, battered from their hinges.

"I name you, harionago," Haruto said. The harionago were a vicious type of yokai formed when a person was drowned, often while by bound by rope or vines or kelp. Usually they wandered the roads between towns and villages, fooling people with their beauty and punishing those who tried to show them kindness. They were vicious, but far from the most dangerous of spirits. But this one had become an onryo somehow, and his power had grown. For him to kill so many shintei... Haruto had never faced a yokai so strong. He stepped forward over the dismembered corpse of a fellow shintei.

"Oh?" A smile spread across the onryo's blood-spattered face. "You must be the onmyoji Xifeng scurried away from. I've never met one before. Tell me--" his smile changed to a vicious grin and a lustful intensity crept into his voice "--will you provide me a challenge? Will you give me what these weaklings could not? I hope so."

Haruto took another step forward. "Harionago..."

"Please," the onryo said with a simpering smile. "Call me Shin. We're about to become very intimate."

"In Omoretsu's name I will destroy you."

Haruto heard Yanmei and Kira shuffle up behind him. "Stay back. This onryo is more dangerous than you know."

"Hmmm?" The onryo fixed his gaze on Kira. "Is that one of my sisters? You're on the wrong side, little girl."

Kira stepped in front of Haruto and looked around at the bodies. "Looks to me like I'm on the right side. The good side."

The harionago chuckled. "Good and evil are human concepts. You are beyond them." He extended his hand toward her. "Come with me and the Master will open your eyes to the truth."

Kira glanced back at Yanmei. The old woman shook her head. The girl looked back at the harionago and shouted, "No chance!"

"Oh well. One more corpse for the pile, I suppose." The harionago stepped forward, spread his arms wide, and raised his chin to look up at the ceiling. "Come. I'll give you the first shot for free."

Kira started forward, but Haruto grabbed her shoulder and pulled her back. He heard glass cracking. A mirrored dagger flashed in her hand and she poked it into his chest. She blinked, gasped, and pulled the dagger away. "Not good. Sorry. Sorry. Sorry."

"I said stay back," Haruto snapped. This onryo was too dangerous. The evidence was all around them. He alone was safe. He alone was immortal.

He drew his katana from its saya and held it before him. "Shiki." The spirit scrabbled out from inside his kimono and leapt into the blade, turning it crimson. Haruto gripped her with both hands. "There is still one shintei left in Sky Hollow who will fight you, onryo. For those you have murdered and the suffering you have caused, in Omoretsu's name I will kill you!" He rushed the harionago.

Chapter 20

Haruto darted in while the onryo was still facing the ceiling. He brought Shiki up in a two-handed slash that should have cut the man in two. The onryo twisted away at the last moment, Shiki's blade just kissing the skin of his chest, drawing a thin line of beading crimson. Haruto stepped back and brought Shiki up into a guard position. Then he circled, stepping over bodies and around broken benches. The onryo smiled at him, hair floating about his head, and dabbed at the cut on his chest. The wound was already closing, but the harionago raised his fingers to his lips and sucked the blood off them.

"You're slow," the onryo said. "I gave you a free strike and you wasted it with such a lazy attack. My turn!" He rushed Haruto. Two of his braids, each tipped with a vicious barb of blood-stained metal, darted at Haruto's face. Haruto parried the first braid with the back edge of his blade, then he stepped back and brought Shiki down in a strike that hit the other braid in a shower of sparks. He felt a tremor pass through Shiki and up his arm and leapt back again. Shiki should have cut straight through the onryo's hair, but the braid just pulled back with all the others floating about his head.

"Slow and weak." The smile slipped from the onryo's face. "So much for the challenge I hoped for. Here, let me make things easy for you. I won't even use my hands." He clasped both hands behind his back.

Haruto was never one to pass on such an offer. Overconfidence was so often the downfall of the arrogant. He leapt forward, feinting to the left. Five braids of hair darted from behind the onryo's at his face and chest. Haruto slid to the right and slashed Shiki at the harionago's side. One braid whipped back and punctured his shoulder in a blaze of pain, but Shiki's blade also caught flesh. There was a slight tug, and then she was through.

Haruto let out his breath and stood. The onryo's overconfidence had been all he needed.

The onryo chuckled and sent a dozen barbed braids at Haruto's head. Haruto flung himself sideways, rolled across a headless body and collided with an overturned bench. He put his back against it and jumped up, Shiki at the ready. The onryo was bleeding from large gash just below his ribcage on his left side, but it didn't stop him or even slow him down. With his hands still behind his back, he ran at Haruto, crossing the distance between them in two easy strides. Haruto flung himself backwards and rolled over the bench to put it between them.

The onryo lurched left and right, leading with his head, the barbed braids darting out and slashing at Haruto. Haruto blocked and parried, and for a few seconds his life became a desperate blur. The onryo hurdled the bench and beat him back, braids hissing through the air and snapping in Haruto's face. Haruto parried one braid, only to find two more shooting at him from the other side. He gave ground again, and his back hit stone, one of the temple pillars. He spun around it, and four barbed braids slammed into the rock, tearing away chunks of stone.

The onryo laughed again from the other side of the pillar. "Xifeng must be weak indeed if she needed to run from you."

Haruto backed up another couple of steps, almost tripping over a severed arm, and took a moment to compose himself. The onryo was still waiting on the other side of the pillar, out of sight. Haruto knew he wouldn't win a defensive struggle. The onryo had too many braids and each one seemed able to move and attack independently. He needed to finish the fight with one decisive strike. It was going to hurt. He shuffled back another step and held Shiki before him in defensive stance. The floor behind him was clear. He needed that space. He also needed the onryo to come to him.

"What's the matter, harionago? Scared?" Haruto put as much

venom into the bait as possible. "After all your bluster, you hide behind a pillar?"

"Hide? Me?" the onryo laughed. "Never. I'm just enjoying the moment." He slid to the side, arms still clasped behind his back, hair writhing like a tangle of eels. Then he rushed at Haruto, cackling madly.

Haruto stood his ground, Shiki held ready, and the onryo was on him. Half a dozen braids thrust towards him. He slashed left and right, parrying them away. One caught him, a trail of fire blazing down his arm. He leapt back out of reach and crouched, holding Shiki horizontal by his shoulder, ready to thrust. The onryo pounced, and Haruto rushed in to meet him, driving Shiki into his gut even as a dozen barbed braids pierced Haruto's arms, chest and neck.

Haruto clenched his teeth so hard he thought they might crumble. The pain burned through his body like boiling oil in his veins. But it was just what he expected. "I have you now, yokai," he said, spitting blood into the rubble at his feet. He shifted his grip on Shiki and started dragging her up, her blade slicing through the onryo's chest, gutting him like a fish.

The onryo grunted in pain. His hands shot out, one closing around Haruto's hands, stopping him from moving the blade, the other around his neck. His hands seemed huge. The onryo seemed massive, as if he had grown as they fought. His skin was tight, stretched unnaturally over his face. His muscles bulged, threatening to split his skin. "Do you really?" He grinned wide as a toad.

Haruto tried to move, but the onryo crushed his hands against Shiki's hilt and slowly pushed it away, drawing the blade out of his chest. The wound closed almost before the blade was even out. All the onryo's wounds had closed. He was healing even faster than Haruto.

"I think it's I who has you," the onryo said, chuckling. He tightened his grip around Haruto's neck, choking him, and lifted him from the floor. The onryo definitely had grown. He was taller, bulky when before he had been lithe.

Haruto forced a grin. He tried to shift Shiki but the onryo still had hold of his hands. Past the choking grip on his throat, he rasped, "I made... you... use... your hands."

The smile slipped from the onryo's face, and a look of pure malice settled there. "Die!" A dozen braids darted out and tore into Haruto's chest and arms.

Kira watched in horror as the harionago tossed Haruto's limp body across the temple. The onmyoji landed with a wet thud on a pile of corpses. Shin had grown during the fight, swelling. He was at least eight feet tall, massive across the shoulders. His smile had gone, and a look of utter boredom lodged on his stretched, brutish features. Kira couldn't take it. She couldn't just stand by and let Shin kill them. She stepped forward and flicked two mirrored daggers into her hands.

"What are you doing?" Guang whispered.

"Stopping him," Kira said through teeth clenched so tight her jaw ached.

Guang scoffed. "Haruto is only getting started. Stay out of the way."

Even as Kira watched, Haruto moved. Slowly at first, he rolled onto his chest and then pushed up onto one knee. He stood unsteadily, using Shiki as a crutch. When he finally got to his feet, he swayed. His face was pale and covered in blood, but his wounds were gone.

"That's another kimono he's wrecked," Guang said with a sigh.

Shin's mouth hung agape as he stared at Haruto. "Shouldn't you be dead?"

"What?" Haruto spat a mouthful of blood against a nearby bench. "You're not the only one who heals fast." He raised Shiki in both hands, launched himself at the harionago, striking at his head.

Shin staggered back, hair writhing, and blocked Haruto's spirited blade. The onmyoji thrust again, quickly cutting a gash across the Shin's chest, but the wound closed just as swiftly, and the onryo whipped a half dozen sharp braids at Haruto's face. Haruto dodged rather than parried, rolling across scattered limbs and bodies and bouncing back to his feet. They seemed equally matched. Both healed almost as soon as they were injured. Both moved with blinding speed and struck with enough force to shatter stone. And then Shin started laughing.

The onryo was growing again, so tall he towered over Haruto, his shoulders grew wider across than Haruto was tall. His eyes blazed with fury, and his lips spread into a leering ruby grin. He flung two braids at Haruto's eyes, and when Haruto moved to parry, punched the onmyoji in the face, sending him flying back into a pillar, the force of the collision cracking the stone. Blood sprayed from Haruto's lips as he slid down the pillar.

Shin rushed forward swinging another punch, and Haruto barely dove out of the way. Shin's punch shattered the pillar, spraying rock out across the strewn bodies and the temple floor. Haruto tried to limp away from the onryo, but Shin was on him immediately. They traded blows, hair and sword meeting in an explosion of sparks.

"He's going to lose," Kira said with a certainty.

"Oh, don't count out the old man out yet."

Kira glanced at Guang, but the old poet did not look nearly as confident as he sounded. Perhaps his old eyes couldn't keep up with the furious action. But Yanmei must see it. She was a warrior regardless of her grey hair. Kira looked over the shoulder at her. "He's slowing down.".

Yanmei met her gaze but said nothing.

"Haruto is tiring," Kira explained. "Shin gets faster and stronger as he grows. Haruto can't win."

Yanmei nodded.

"We have to help."

Guang cleared his throat loudly. "Haruto said to stay back. He can handle it. I've seen him take..."

Kira ignored him, still staring at Yanmei. "You said being good is about helping others. Even if they don't think they need it. Being good is lending a hand when someone is in trouble. He can't win, not alone."

Yanmei smiled, reached over her shoulder and drew her naginata. "You're right," she said. "So let's help him."

Kira felt a flutter in her chest. "Yes!" She jumped and clapped her hands, but Yanmei gave her a stern look. "Sorry. Serious time. I can be serious." She wiped the smile from her face and frowned instead.

Haruto slashed his crimson blade across Shin's thigh, and the huge onryo went down on one knee. The onmyoji shifted his feet to deliver a killing blow, but Shin sent three braids knifing into a broken bench. With a flick of his head, he hurled it through the air. Haruto threw himself down on the floor; the bench sailed over him and crashed into the wall. Yanmei leapt over Haruto, naginata already spinning in her hands. Kira darted past his side.

Kira threw the first of her daggers, and Shin caught it in his huge fist. He glanced at it for only a moment, and Kira showed him Haruto leaping at him from behind in the reflection. The onryo turned, fooled by the illusion, and Yanmei slashed her blade through his hand, severing three fingers. He roared in pain, shaking the walls of the temple and floor beneath Kira's feet. Yanmei spun around and swung the flower-shaped pommel of her naginata hard against Shin's shin, shattering the bone. The onryo stumbled forward, and Kira planted a new knife in his chest then leapt away from his snatching, bloody hands.

"What are you doing?" Haruto said as he struggled to his feet, bleeding from half a dozen slow-healing cuts.

"Helping," Kira said, blocking a braid snaking for her face. Her mirrored dagger shattered in her hand, and the braid whipped about and cut a bloody line across her cheek that burned like fire. She danced back and cursed herself. She needed to be faster. She couldn't hope to match strength with Shin, and her daggers were brittle and useless on the defence.

"Yes. Yes!" Shin said stepping toward Yanmei. "More of you. All of you." He swung his head, laughing, five braids lashing out at Yanmei's face. She retreated, spinning her naginata in a frantic defence.

Kira flicked a new dagger into her hand and flung it at Shin. It stuck in his thigh, and he quickly pulled it out with his free hand, still stepping toward Yanmei. "You dropped this." He laughed and hurled it back at Kira.

Haruto lurched in front of her and swung Shiki at the shimmering dagger, shattering it in mid air, a spray of shards sparkling in the lantern light. "I don't have time to protect you," Haruto snapped at her. He turned and sprinted at Shin. The onryo whipped ten barbed braids at him. Haruto ducked, sliding beneath them.

Yanmei and Haruto had Shin flanked, yet they were struggling. He moved too fast and his floating braids blocked their blows and lashed at them all at once. Yanmei was already breathing hard, struggling to keep up. She wasn't using her fire, for which Kira was happy, but she was already slowing down. Shin laughed as he looked to one side at Yanmei and at the onmyoji on the other. Meanwhile, Kira circled around him and slashed at the backs of his ankles, parting skin and tendon. The giant harionago collapsed to his knees. Haruto lunged at him, letting one braid pierce his arm and another his leg, dodging three more, and thrust Shiki deep into his chest. Kira backed away from Shin and Haruto, and saw the lantern on the wall flicker and then send a torrent of flames into Yanmei's whirling blade. She spun about and slashed a horizontal strike at Shin's neck. Shin's hair drew up around his head and shoulders like a kabuto helm, but Yanmei's fiery blade cut across them, severing two and setting three more ablaze while Haruto twisted Shiki deeper into the onryo's chest. Shin fell forward, smashed both hands on the floor, shattering the rock and releasing a wave of force that sent Yanmei and Haruto tumbling away and Kira staggering back to the wall. He reached up and tugged the three burning braids out of his head. Laughing at what should have been agony.

Kira regained her balance quickly and leapt onto Shin's back. She stabbed her knives into both sides of his neck, then backflipped off him, but a braid wrapped around her trailing leg. Shin whipped his head forward. Kira was torn out of the air. She smashed down on the shattered stone in front of Shin. Pain seared through her back and neck, and her vision flashed white. She would have screamed but all the air was driven out of her. Shin gave her no time to recover. He took a single step forward and kicked her in the chest, sending her sailing across the temple.

Kira sailed through the air and crashed down amidst the bodies and broken benches. Yanmei's chest tightened at the sight. She knew the girl was tough, tougher than she looked, but that kick was powerful enough to kill a horse.

Yanmei struggled back to her feet, already swinging her naginata at the harionago. It was a wild attack, driven by frustration and fear for Kira, but the onryo stepped away from her to dodge the strike. He didn't seem willing to risk his hair against her flaming blade. It wasn't much of a weakness, but even the mightiest tree fell to a hundred axes. If she cut off enough of his braids, he would no longer be able to defend against Haruto and his spirit blade.

Yanmei spun about and thrust her naginata. The onryo chuckled, a throaty smug noise, and stepped aside. He snatched at a broken bench, grabbed it by one of its three remaining legs and swung it at her like a club. Yanmei tried to leap over it, but her body betrayed her; one of her knees buckled, and the bench smashed into her side, bursting into kindling and launching her across the temple.

She hit the ground twenty paces away and rolled to a stop. An intense stabbing pain was growing in her chest like knives piercing closer and closer to her heart. She couldn't breathe. The fire, her fire started to hurt, burning her up from inside. She let it go out, smothered it. The Sage had said this would happen. The more she used her technique, the more it would hurt her until she couldn't use it without the pain and burning seeping into her heart. And there would be no coming back from that. Her own fire would kill her. She had been close. Too close. For Kira's sake, she couldn't use her technique again.

She pushed up onto her knees. The pain in her chest

throbbed, and she clutched at it with one hand, the other still wrapped around the shaft of her naginata. She searched for Kira and found Guang helping the girl to her feet. She was bleeding from a dozen scrapes about her face and one eye was swollen shut, blood leaking down into it from her scalp. Her kimono was a ripped mess, but she looked determined and staggered forwards, limping. Pride swelled in Yanmei's chest. That was her girl, not willing to give up even when she could barely stand. Even when they had no chance of winning.

"Are you alright?" Kira asked, limping toward her.

Yanmei nodded, not able to speak past the clutching pain in her chest.

Haruto crashed to the ground a few paces away, smashing through one of the wooden benches. He jumped back to his feet, shouting defiantly, and then staggered as one of his legs gave way beneath him. His left arm was hanging limp by his side, glistening white bone protruding from the skin just below his elbow. The flesh was already trying to knit itself back together. Yanmei watched the bone snap itself back into place. Haruto hissed in pain and collapsed back onto a chunk of smashed pillar.

Across the temple, Shin laughed, his hair twirling around his head. Despite everything they had done to him, there wasn't a scratch on him. All their pain and sacrifice meant nothing in the face of his regeneration.

Kira helped Yanmei up, and they limped over to Haruto. The harionago started rummaging around in the debris, looking for something.

"That fire of yours would be helpful," Haruto said. He shot them a weary smile.

Yanmei shook her head. "I can't," she rasped. Her throat was raw and her voice grated against it. Kira stared at her, a fierce frown creasing her brow. Yanmei met her gaze evenly.

"We need to distract him then," Haruto said. "He's protecting his head and neck, and that hair of his is as tough as steel. Shiki can't cut through it. If we can get him to let his guard down for a moment, maybe I can finish this in one strike."

"Hmm, this one will do," Shin said, his voice seeming too small for his swollen size. He picked up a chunk of stone pillar twice as big as a man and flung it at them.

Yanmei lurched forward, colliding with Kira and pushing them both out of the way. The stone sailed past them and crashed to the ground, breaking apart and crushing the corpses of the shintei beneath it. Kira clambered to her feet and tried to pull Yanmei up, but her legs just wouldn't hold her. Yanmei sunk back to the floor and shook her head. "I can't..." She panted, trying to catch her breath. "I just..."

"It's alright," Kira said. She caught Yanmei's gaze and gave her a nod. "I can do this." She turned away and muttered again, "I can do this."

Haruto was up and closing on Shin slowly. The onryo picked up a smaller chunk of pillar and launched it at the onmyoji. Haruto swayed to the side, but the stone clipped him on the shoulder and knocked him down.

"Oh, this is more like it," Shin said, grinning. "Don't stop now. I'm just getting started."

"Be ready," Kira called to Haruto as she limped away from Yanmei, mirrored daggers flashing in her hands.

Guang crept over to Yanmei and slipped a shoulder under her arm, grunting as he helped her up. "Come on, you old bandit," he told her. "Best get out of the way and let the youngsters handle it from here." He chuckled, no doubt considering that Kira and Haruto were each older than both of them put together.

Kira and Haruto edged toward Shin, keeping far enough apart that he couldn't target them both with one strike.

"Just the two of you now, is it?" the onryo asked. "So disappointing." He laughed. "I'll just kill the old hag later then."

"Shut up!" Kira screamed. "Just... shut up!"

Shin threw his head back and laughed. Kira did not.

She threw both daggers at his face at once. Her aim was true, but Shin's hair writhed and coiled around his head quicker than a viper. The daggers hit his braids and shattered into sparkling shards in front of his face, each one flaring bright as the sun as Kira used her technique. Shin screamed. He reached up to cover his eyes as he staggered back.

Haruto dashed forward and leapt, swinging Shiki around in a shimmering arc at the onryo's neck. Shin staggered to one knee and roared. His braids shot out in every direction, a halo of barbed death. Three braids hit Haruto, piercing his chest and stomach and arm, and skewering him to a stop before he reached the onryo. He cried out in pain. Shin screamed again and flailed about, swinging his head from side to side and flinging Haruto away.

Yanmei saw Kira flick two more daggers into her hands and approach the onryo as silent as a stalking cat. Then she leapt at him, daggers pulled back and ready to strike. Shin pulled one hand away from one of his eyes and spotted her. His face broke into a wide grin. He shot a massive hand out and caught her by the throat in mid air. Yanmei watched helpless as her girl choked. Kira jammed her daggers into Shin's arm, and then again and then again, each time with less force. The wounds closed almost as soon as they opened. Then Kira stopped struggling, and her hands fell limp to her sides.

Yanmei pulled away from Guang but didn't have the strength to stand. She collapsed, unable to do anything but watch as the life was choked out of her girl, her daughter in all but blood. She could do nothing.

Crow swept into the temple and marvelled at the violence. Benches strewn about, corpses and pieces of stone pillar littering the floor. Shin was in his element, creating a mess he would soon lament.

Two elders hunched on the floor near the wall: a man who looked unhurt and a woman who looked to be standing on the precipice of death and sporting a pronounced lean over the edge. They would be so easy to snuff out. Her smoke was snaking across the floor toward them before Crow realised it. The sight of such carnage woke something in her, a primal need to join in, to wreak her own vengeance upon the living. With some effort, she reined the smoke in before it reached the old couple. She was not some mindless spirit pulled this way and that by a lust for blood. She was more than that. Better than that. Besides, they were Shin's prey, and he would not appreciate her help.

Crow gathered her smoke back inside her robe and swept up the wall to cling to the ceiling, content to watch the last moments of the battle from a good vantage.

Shin had been enjoying himself. He was grinning like a statue of Champa, and had grown to a monstrous size, easily twice that of a normal man. His strength and speed were unreal. He whipped his hair about his head seeking a new target, but he had a small bald patch where some of his braids had been pulled out. He had not come through the battle entirely unscathed. He held a young woman, one hand wrapped around her throat, slowly choking the life out of her.

The old woman shrieked, "No!" and pushed the old man away. She took a step forward and drew back her arm to throw her naginata like a spear. Shin noticed and swung his own arm about, holding the girl in front of him like a shield. The old woman faltered, the weapon fell from her grasp, and she collapsed to the stone floor.

This was how Shin always liked to fight. He didn't just want to win. He wanted to break his opponents, to crush them utterly and scatter their will to fight like petals before a hurricane. Crow had little enough respect for most of her brethren: Xifeng was disgusting; Zen was a lecherous pig; and Shin... Shin was a sadistic bastard. But as the Master always said, you can't choose your family.

Crow stared at the dying girl, and noticed something odd about her. She was an onryo, a little sister. Xifeng had said something about a new little sister travelling with an onmyoji. If Shin was battling a yokai hunter, it was no wonder he was so worked up. But which one was it? It couldn't be the girl, and the two elders looked far too frail to attempt cleansing a spirit.

A wooden bench shifted and man rose unsteadily from behind it. He was tall and muscled, his kimono ripped in a hundred places, exposing a chest covered in little wounds. Shin had clearly already got his braids on the man, puncturing him many times. Yet, the man stood. Hurt but unbeaten. Unbroken. His hair was long and loose about his shoulders and his face a snarl of rage. In one hand he held a katana with a blade as red as blood. The onmyoji.

"Drop her!" the onmyoji shouted.

"Hmm?" Shin's warped face bent into a smile. He waved the girl in front of him, her limp body flailing bonelessly in his grip. "This one?" He shook her like a rag doll. "Make me."

She was still alive. Her fingers twitched with the last spasms of it. She was on the verge of suffocation, yet clinging stubbornly to life and consciousness. The new little sister was strong. But she was also stupid if she had chosen to pick a fight with Shin. Still, the Master would want her alive. Crow let the thinnest wisp of smoke drift down and curl through Shin's writhing mass of braids to his ear. "Put her down, Shin," Crow whispered through the smoke.

Shin stiffened and glanced around for her. The grin slipped from his face and his lip curled in disgust. "Fine," he said. "This one. The other three are mine." He tossed the girl aside and she hit the floor hard, rolling to a stop, and lay there.

The temple shook a little. Not much, but just enough to tell Crow her job was done. The blood of the shintei she had fed to that Cochtan engine had worked its way through the mechanisms, greasing the cogs, powering the infernal device. The door was opening. The prison was unlocked.

The temple shook again, more violently this time and the onmyoji stumbled, catching himself on the edge of a bench. "Time to end this, harionago," he shouted.

Crow felt something. Her smoke shifted on its own. Bubbling, moulding, forming. She didn't like the feeling. "Kill him," she whispered down her smoke into Shin's ear. "Kill him now, Shin."

"Hmmm?" Shin said, the smile returning to his face. "So even the Master's little favourite is not above a bit of lust." He laughed. "She wants you dead, onmyoji. And so do I!" Shin launched himself at the man. The onmyoji rolled underneath an enormous fist and slashed out with his katana, opening a wound along Shin's thigh that healed immediately. A barbed braid shot out and pierced the onmyoji's shoulder and he fell away howling. He pulled the braid out and stumbled back, waving his sword about to block another darting braid.

Shin grabbed a chunk of stone from the floor, swung about and slammed it through the onmyoji's guard. The rock broke apart against the man's forehead and sent him careening away in a shower of rubble and sprawling on the floor. Shin leapt into the air with a grace that belied his size and landed over the onmyoji, the stone floor shattering beneath him. A dozen braids shot out and pinned the onmyoji's arms to the stone. The man screamed in agony and tried to pull free, but could not. Shin bent over him, eyes gleaming with menace.

The temple shook again. Not just the temple, Crow realised. The whole fortress trembled. The entire mountain rumbled. From the warren deep below them, something roared.

"Do you hear that, onmyoji? Do you feel it?" Shin laughed. "We've already won. It's free. The prison is open." Shin reached out a huge hand, wrapped it around the onmyoji's sword hand and squeezed. The man screamed as Shin crushed his hand to a mangled lump of torn flesh and broken bone.

The waking titan roared again, shaking the temple. Bits of rock fell from the temple ceiling, crashing to the floor. Crow felt rock dust crumbling through her smoke. The prison might be open, but it felt like all of Sky Hollow was collapsing in on itself. The two elders had retrieved the young onryo and were pulling her away towards the wall. She was struggling against them though, still trying to fight. Crow respected that from her new little sister. The will to fight was strong in all the onryo.

The wall behind the shrine to the goddess Natsuko glowed orange, then red, then white. The rock turned molten and sloughed away, setting fire to the shrine and the dais it sat upon. Then the dragon crashed through the molten rock into the temple.

It was massive. Its face a snarling tiger's as tall as five men, with a mane of dancing flames. Glowing orange scales, each one as large as Crow ran down its undulating body. It slithered its way through the rock, roaring, paying no heed to everyone still in the temple. Flames spat out towards the great doors at the far end of the chamber, and the dragon flew toward them. Its body was so long, it just seemed to keep coming. Its arms and hands were small, stunted things. It was a creature of the sky. Flames rained from its body, setting benches and mats alight and spilling liquid fire across the floor. It crashed its head through the temple doors, only then did its tail finally appear through the hole behind the dais. The tail was a shrieking eagle, beak wide, spitting fire. Crow watched it pass, transfixed by the scale of the creature.

"Glorious," Shin said, as the dragon's beaked tail whipped about, crashing through a pillar and sending a shower of burning stone over the two elders and the little sister.

Just as the dragon's tail was passing through the temple doors, the onmyoji hissed, "Now, Shiki!" His sword leapt from his mangled hand, spun about, and landed in his other one. He tore free of Shin's braids in a spray of blood and gore. Shin turned just as the onmyoji leapt past him, his red-bladed katana slicing out in a shimmering arc.

The onmyoji landed a few feet beyond Shin and stood there a moment, his back turned, one arm a ruin of torn, mangled flesh, the other even worse. Shin's eyes went impossibly wide a moment, then his head slipped from his body and tumbled to the floor, blood gushing from his neck like a fountain. His huge body collapsed to the stone floor with a thud. The onmyoji toppled over a moment later.

Chapter 21

Guang left Yanmei and Kira holding each other up and rushed over to Haruto. He gave the onryo a wide berth, just in case the monster somehow lurched back to life. After everything Guang had seen in the past few days, he wouldn't bet against it. But neither the onryo's head nor body moved saved for pulsing blood out onto the temple floor. Guang clambered over broken stone and burning benches to get to his friend's side, his gut churning at what he might find.

Haruto knelt motionless. One arm hung limp by his side, bloody and torn, splinters of bone poking through the skin. The other pressed against his chest. Shiki was in her spirit form, the little ball of black fluff with eyes, and was cavorting in front of Haruto, squeaking in alarm.

"Old man," Guang said as he stopped in front of Haruto. "Don't you dare die on me." He lifted Haruto's head and found a weak smile waiting for him.

"Fooled you," Haruto said. Shiki laughed and waved a hairy little limb at Guang. He aimed a kick at the little spirit, and she tumbled away from it, rolling on the ground and squeaking with laughter.

"That's not funny!" Guang felt a smile creep unbidden to his lips. It wasn't funny, but he was also glad his friend was alive. He'd never seen Haruto's immortality tested so sorely before. He sat down in front of him and shook his head. "You did it, old man. You killed the onion."

Haruto's face soured. "It wasn't him. This onryo didn't kill Tian."

"Oh." Guang felt guilt and grief mingle inside him. He was disappointed his son wasn't yet avenged, that was true. But far more than that, he knew Haruto wouldn't stop, couldn't stop until Tian's burden was eased. How long did he have before Tian was thrown out of heaven and into Haruto's body? There would be more onryo to fight, and they had barely survived this one despite the old man's immortality.

"I think the jorogumo I met in Minazuri killed Tian," Haruto said. He looked up and met Guang's eyes. "We'll find her. I promise." He groaned and slumped forwards. Guang caught him and eased him down to the floor. "But first I need to rest a little."

Guang watched Haruto's wounds slowly heal. Bone snapping itself back into position and flesh re-knitting. He knew it hurt. He'd seen it time and again, and Haruto bore it all. Immortality might have its benefits, but immunity to pain was not one of them. With effort, he gripped Haruto under the arms and pulled him away from the dead onryo. The ground was a mess of broken stone, strewn bodies, and rock scorched black. Haruto groaned as Guang propped him up against the temple wall, far away from the wreckage.

"Cabbage," Guang muttered. "You don't know what pain is, old man. Just you wait until you wake one night needing to piss for the third time and find you've slipped something in your back and you can't stand up. That's pain."

Haruto chuckled but didn't open his eyes.

"What was that giant tiger-headed thing?" Kira asked as she and Yanmei limped toward them. She sounded more subdued than usual.

"A dragon?" Guang asked.

Haruto gave a slight nod.

"Never seen one myself," Guang continued. "Before now, I suppose. I thought the Century Blade had killed the last one. I know the story. It's quite an epic tale, swords raining from the sky, thunder and lightning and..."

"And if there's one thing you should have learned by now," Haruto said, cracking open an eye to stare at him. "It's that most stories are only half true."

"So Sky Hollow was a prison for a dragon?" Yanmei asked.

"Not while I was here," Haruto said, nodding over Guang's shoulder. "Ask them."

Guang turned to see several men and women emerging from dark corridors. Only twenty out of the hundreds who had called the place home. All that was left of the shintei.

By the following morning, Haruto had recovered enough to help clean up Sky Hollow. He was grateful for his immortality. He couldn't stand the thought of lying around for another day waiting to heal. He needed to move, to be doing something. Too long spent idle at the mercy of his own thoughts was not good for his sanity.

There was much to do and not enough people to do it. Of the shintei, only twenty had survived, and six of them were not likely to make it through winter, such was the severity of their injuries. Those with injuries deemed not too severe were given time and rest. Most chose to return to work sooner rather than later. There was rubble to be moved, bodies to excavate and lay to rest, names of the fallen to be recorded. Their families would want to know.

Just two shintei masters were left. One had yet to regain consciousness and seemed unlikely to survive. The other was woman named Misaki, who had fought Shin out on the plateau and lost an arm in the battle. The healer, a gruff old man who smoked a pipe so furiously the bowl glowed like molten rock, had closed the wound, but Misaki was struggling to make herself useful, crippled as she was. Nevertheless, she was the eldest and most senior surviving shintei, and Haruto went to her for answers. He needed to know about the dragon and why the onryo had freed it.

Three days after the attack he found time to approach Misaki. She spent most of her time in the ruined temple, so swathed in bandages she creaked like an ancient tree every time she moved. Her greying hair stuck up at a chaos of angles, and her haori didn't quite sit right without her left arm.

"Thank you for all your help," the shintei master said without looking up from her praying. They had cleared away much of the rubble from the temple. The shrine to Natsuko had been destroyed by the dragon's passage, but they had replaced it with a blessing: possessions of those who had been killed, a monument to all of their missed opportunities. It was just the sort of thing the gods would love, heedless of the pain that had made it possible.

Haruto knelt next to her and bowed his head to the makeshift shrine. "It's the least I could do." It was painful to see Sky Hollow in such a sorry state. He had a lot of fond memories of the place though most of them were now half-remembered, eroded by time's eternal waterfall.

"Huh," Misaki grunted. "The least you could do is leave. The least you could have done was let that monster kill us all. Instead you fought and killed him, saved what few of us remain. And now you help us recover." She was wrapped in so many bandages she had to turn her body to glance at him. "What you do now is far from the least you could do, Master Onmyoji." They fell into silence for a while. Haruto remembered praying in the temple next to his brothers and sisters of the shintei. How many times had he fallen asleep during prayer only to wake when master Zuko rapped him on the back of the head with that hateful little stick of his?

"Ask your questions," Misaki said eventually. "Only one of us isn't getting any older."

He tucked his hands into the sleeves of his new kimono. This one was bright yellow with dark lines in the pattern of clouds. "You had a dragon imprisoned here. Sekiryu, if I'm not mistaken."

"You are not," Misaki said. "Her imprisonment here has been the most closely guarded secret of Sky Hollow for as long as any of us have been alive." She glanced at Haruto once more, dark eyes shrewd and piercing. "As long as *most* of us have been alive."

"But why?" Haruto asked. Dragons had once been a regular, if not common sight back in his younger days. To see one winding its way through the sky was considered a sign of good luck, and people made wishes whenever they saw one. Though, now that he thought about it, not all dragons were good luck. Some were considered bad luck. Some were destroyers.

"How much do you know of dragons?" the shintei master asked him.

Haruto shrugged. "As much as anyone, I suppose."

Misaki chuckled and shook her head. "Which is a way of saying *nothing*. There are just seven dragons. They may vary in shape and size, but all call the sky home and the elements their play things. And they have a power structure, just as we humans do. Did you know that? No, of course not. As I said, you know nothing."

Haruto had to concede the point. "I assume you're about to teach me?"

"You're damned right," Misaki said with a lop-sided smile. "Never too old to learn. Back when they were free, the dragons would clash in the sky from time to time, forming tangles and writhing against each other. When they met, the earth shook and rain fell like arrows. Floods swept whole villages away, and lush forests burst into flames. For as the dragons fought, so too did the elements. But the outcome was always clear. Orochi, the eight-headed serpent, would win. He was their king, you see, the greatest of them all. They might debate, but he always had the final say. Eighty years ago, Orochi ordered the dragons to destroy us."

"Us?"

Misaki nodded slowly. "All of us. Orochi gave the order to destroy humanity."

Haruto thought back. He'd been alive a long time. He remembered the dragons flying across the sky, the awe of seeing them. And yes, there was a time when that awe turned to terror, when villages and towns vanished, when rumours of dragon attacks were rife. He'd ignored it. He had been so consumed with serving Omoretsu, he'd let himself get detached from humanity. It wasn't until he met Guang, until the poet started following him, that Haruto really rejoined humanity. Before then... he'd been a ghost.

"Why?" Haruto asked. "Why did Orochi order the dragons to attack humanity?"

Misaki gave him that lop-sided grin again. Haruto saw a bulge move underneath her bandages as she tried to move an arm that simply wasn't there anymore. "There are two stories here, Master Onmyoji," Misaki said. "One is the story of Orochi, of his rage and his vengeance. The other is the story of the Century Blade and the impossible task he set himself. Which would you like to hear first?"

"Tell me of Orochi," Haruto said without hesitation. He needed to understand what had made the dragons turn on the humans. He needed to know what his failure to stop the onryo had just set free into the world.

Misaki nodded as if pleased. "Did you know the dragons can take human form? They are kami, the greatest of spirits and shifting to other forms is just one of their many techniques. Orochi had a favourite spot in Hosa, a glade hidden in the Forest of Bamboo. No human had ever set foot on its emerald grass, for the spirits that infested that forest turned them away or stole their souls. The other dragons knew to avoid it. It was Orochi's little paradise. He liked to curl around a rocky outcropping and watch the waterfall trickle down its many levels to settle in the little lake. Birds, ever the kin of dragons, gathered by the water to drink and hunt insects. Some would even venture close, stepping onto Orochi's great coils. The Eeko'Ai, the spirits of portent would play in the glade, skimming the waters and chasing each other's tails. It was a place of peace, and Orochi would retreat there and sleep for years at a time. When he was curled around that rock, no one would even realise he was there.

"But one day, a human came to his glade." Misaki shifted again and scratched at her bandaged chest with her remaining hand. "A man somehow made it through the Forest of Bamboo, past all the spirits and their tricks and traps. No one special, no prince or lord, he was just a man who had been in love and had his heart broken. His name was Yamasachi, and he had wandered into the Forest of Bamboo hoping the spirits would take him, hoping they would end his life and ease his suffering. Yet, by some miracle, the spirits of the forest let him pass. He came upon Orochi's glade and found the same measure of peace the dragon coveted.

"Orochi sensed the man's presence and opened his eyes. Still clinging to the rock, he was all but invisible. To Yamasachi, he looked like just another part of the glade. Orochi watched the interloper sit by the lake, watched the Eeko'Ai swarm around him, watched Yamasachi strip naked and bathe in the crystal waters of the glade. Orochi found himself curious rather than wrathful. He wanted to know why the spirits had let this human into his glade. He wanted to know what had happened that the man had such a melancholy aura. So Orochi took his human form and sat on the edge of the little lake watching Yamasachi bathe.

"When Yamasachi turned and saw Orochi watching, he startled. The human snatched up a floating branch and held it before him as a weapon. Orochi laughed. He had nothing to fear from this human; he had nothing to fear from any mortal. He bade Yamasachi sit with him and the two men sat in the glade, on the shore of the lake and talked. And talked. And talked. A friendship grew between them. Orochi found the simplicity of the human refreshing, and the dragon's passion became a fire unlike anything he had experienced before. They spent months together in that glade, and as their friendship deepened, it grew into something more. Orochi and Yamasachi fell in love. And in that glade, Orochi's secret little paradise, they married."

Misaki sighed and closed her eyes. "But if there is one thing this world has taught us, it is that peace never lasts. Four years, they spent together in that glade. Four years of peaceful bliss. But the other dragons were gathering once more and Orochi was needed. For the first time in four years, he took his dragon form and rose to join his brethren in their tangle in the sky. For the first time, Yamasachi saw what his love truly was.

"Yamasachi fled the glade in horror, his love's true form was a terrible betrayal of everything they had shared, of the love they had nurtured. Once more he had let himself love, and once more his heart had been broken. He left the Forest of Bamboo and found the nearest town. In fear and in shame, he told everyone who would listen of the glade in the forest and the monster who made it its home. He blamed all the perils of the forest on the creature and claimed he knew how to stop them. He raised an army on those lies and marched it into the Forest of Bamboo. Having been to the glade before, he was able to find it again. Orochi was gone, still meeting with the other dragons, so Yamasachi and his army destroyed the glade. They cut down trees, took picks to the rocks, slaughtered birds with their arrows, and polluted the waters with oil. In his wroth, Yamasachi paid Orochi back for his betrayal ten times over.

"When Orochi returned, he took to his human form and ran into his glade, eager to reunite with his love. He found his glade ruined. Yamasachi and his army waited in the forest, and on his command they rushed into the glade and attacked. Orochi was furious and resumed his dragon form. He laid waste to Yamasachi's army and painted his ruined glade in blood. When he was done, only Yamasachi remained. For despite it all, Orochi loved Yamasachi too much to kill him.

"Orochi took to the skies, and though they had just met, called upon his brethren. None could refuse his call, for he was the eight-headed king of dragons. They tangled there in the sky above the Forest of Bamboo, above the ruin of his secret glade, and of his heart, and Orochi dominated them all. The other dragons argued against his demand for vengeance, but in the end his will was iron. He gave them all just one order. Destroy them all."

Misaki sighed as she came to the end of the story. "And that is why the dragons are imprisoned. Orochi commanded the dragons to wreak such devastation. And if Orochi is free, he will undoubtedly do so again. "

Haruto considered the story. It seemed to explain why the two remaining dragons, Cormar and Zennyo, were peaceful, and also where the five others went. Everyone knew the story of the

Century Blade's fight against Messimere, but all the stories said he slew the dragon. What if that was a lie? "How were they imprisoned?"

Misaki chuckled. "Ah, that is another story altogether. That is the story of the Century Blade and his Abenjazu."

Chapter 22

Kira sat in front of the pyre, watching the flames gorging themselves on wood and flesh. The ground was too frozen and rocky to bury the dead, and there were many bodies to be given back to the stars. She helped wherever they needed her. This was one of the few moments of peace she had been able to snatch, but her mind was drawn back to the conflict. To her part in the fight against Shin. For all her onryo strength and despite her technique, she was helpless against the harionago. He had beaten her so easily. And not just her, but Yanmei too. Kira needed to get stronger if she was going to fight, and there would be more fights ahead as long as they stayed with Haruto. The onmyoji had set himself against the other onryo, and now that he knew they were freeing the dragons he would hunt them no matter where they went.

"You've healed well," Yanmei said as she sat down next to Kira and extended her hands toward the flames. It was true, despite the injuries Shin had given her, Kira was all but healed, another benefit of being an onryo. Another reminder that she was not entirely human.

"You haven't," Kira said. Yanmei was still limping and was panting even as she sat down.

Yanmei nodded sadly. "What do you want to do, Kira?" she asked eventually. "Haruto and Guang will leave soon to chase the onryo. You heard him, he believes they mean to free Orochi, which would be nothing but bad for us all. We were supposed to be searching for the Fourth Sage Under Heaven. I know my mind, but what do you want to do?"

Kira didn't hesitate. She didn't need to. "I want to go with them. To help them. The onryo are my..." Siblings? Brethren?

Enemies? "They killed everyone at Heiwa and hundreds here. We have to stop them." She glanced at Yanmei to see if it was the right thing to say. It sounded right. It sounded good. Those who killed innocent people were bad, and fighting against them was good. That was what Yanmei had once said. Besides, they did not even know where to start their search for the Fourth Sage. At least this way they would do something.

Yanmei smiled and pulled Kira into a hug. "I am so proud of you." There were tears in her eyes, but Kira couldn't understand why. She leaned into Yanmei and melted into her embrace.

"But you're not strong enough to fight," Yanmei said eventually, her voice firm as iron. She let go of Kira and stood. "So get up."

Kira stood quickly. She knew this side of Yanmei; it was the side she had shown at Heiwa. She had given Kira no special treatment in class or in hand-to-hand combat training against the other students. Kira had been stronger than the other students, but strength was only part of the fight. How many times had Gyatso ducked Kira's strike and flipped her onto her back? How many times had he caught her punch, twisted her arm, and kneed her in the gut? Kira had lost count. And each time Yanmei had snapped, *Stand up. Again.* This was sensei Yanmei, and Kira would not get special treatment from her.

"You have to get stronger. You have the potential to be as powerful as Shin was, maybe more so. To start with, I want to teach you a new technique."

Kira jumped and clapped her hands. She loved learning new techniques. The Sage had said she was a natural, and he knew what he was talking about. He knew more techniques than anyone else in the world. But despite praising her, he had only taught her the most simple of techniques, like walking on snow and creating her qi daggers. Kira followed Yanmei away from the pyre, to the open square on the plateau in front of Sky Hollow. The walk was excruciating. She wanted to know what sort of technique Yanmei was going to teach her. She wanted to try it now.

"Alright." Yanmei stopped and turned. Kira was still

bobbing up and down. "Calm down. You need focus to learn."

"Mhm." Kira nodded and forced herself to stop moving. She felt nervous energy building inside her and struggled to control it. "Ready. Ready to learn, sensei."

Yanmei chuckled and shook her head. "I'm not a sensei here, Kira." The wind blew through the square, carrying with it a few embers from the pyre and the scent of death. The embers snuffed out as soon as they hit the icy ground.

"A long time ago, a good friend of mine tried to teach me his technique." Yanmei raised a hand and stroked at the battered remains of the scale mail she wore over her chest. "I never got the hang of it. I think it requires a certain duality of nature, and I have never had that. But you do, Kira. Nevertheless, I learned the theory, and I hope to pass it on to you. I think that would make him happy." Yanmei was silent for a moment, and when she looked up and met Kira's eyes, she smiled. "He called it stepping through the world."

Crow watched her little sister from the shadows. She clung to the remains of the fortress wall, close to the top, hidden by the shadow of the cave roof. The fortress wall was now a wreckage of melted stone and chunks of rock, brought low by the dragon's passage. So much for the impregnable fortress of the shintei.

The girl was training, trying to master some new technique the old woman was teaching her. It did not seem to be going well. Now and then Crow would hear a sound like shattering glass, and her new little sister would collapse, shards of sparkling mirror falling all around her. But she didn't quit. No sooner had the shards of mirror vanished than she was on her feet and trying again.

Just beyond the buildings towards the edge of the plateau, a pyre burned and Shin's body burned with it. He had been a sadistic bastard, and antagonistic as well. He'd never failed to sneer at Crow for the trails of soot she left behind. But he had been family. The Master had made them all family. Crow grieved for the loss and considered taking vengeance. The onmyoji and his companions were not yet recovered, and they did not know she was there. It would be easy to pick them off one by one. But the girl was not one of them, she was an onryo. And the onmyoji was special too, though she wasn't sure how. Crow waited and watched.

A blind raven let out a shrill caw from above. Crow would have smiled if she had a face. The Master was summoning her. She dislodged from the wall and fell to the ground, then she breezed through the abandoned buildings to find somewhere far enough away there was no chance of being overheard. All the surviving shintei were cloistered up inside the fortress. The buildings on the plateau beyond were all but deserted. She found a suitable house and dashed inside, pulling the door closed behind her and making certain all the windows were shuttered. Then she settled down in front of the hearth and filled the empty fireplace with her smoke.

The Master's face appeared in the smoke above the hearth. He was ugly and wrinkled, his hooked nose dominating his features, and his eyes were sharp and swirling like cyclones. Even written only in the dark lines of her sooty smoke, he was clearly frowning at her.

"Master," Crow said, dipping her hood to mimic a bow.

"Is Sekiryu free?" the Master asked. He was never one for idle chatter. Driven, to the point of madness.

"Yes. But Shin is dead."

"What?" the Master snapped.

Xifeng's laughter echoed from the hearth. Her face appeared in the smoke next to the Master's. "Serves him right," she cooed. Crow's smoke could not quite replicate Xifeng's fangs chittering behind her lips. Her maw spun like a blizzard.

"Quiet," the Master said. Xifeng's grinning visage drifted away. "How did he die?"

"The onmyoji Xifeng met in Minazuri followed us here to Sky Hollow. He is immortal, Master."

Silence greeted the revelation.

"He has our new little sister with him," Crow continued. "I

believe she is an ungaikyo. She follows him. She too fought against Shin."

"And survived," the Master mused, his ancient voice crackling.

Xifeng's swirling face appeared again. "Zen has freed Messimere. The dragons are returning." She giggled and held a hand in front of her mouth.

"And how many cities did Zen burn down to free Messimere?" Crow asked.

Xifeng laughed. "Only the one. He must be growing soft."

Crow might have winced if she could. Zen never held back; he revelled in the flames and the slaughter and the pain he inflicted. "You should not have sent him alone, Master. Zen is too destructive. He--"

"Is predictable," the Master said. "Shin was not. He needed someone to guide him, but Zen will never waver from my cause."

"But he will burn everything in his way."

"Yes. And this immortal onmyoji must be dealt with. He cannot be allowed to catch us yet. We have new information about Orochi's whereabouts. The final prison may soon be ours, but we cannot have an onmyoji chasing us. Especially not one strong enough to kill Shin."

"But he is immortal, Master. I saw Shin deal him wounds that would have killed any man. How can we stop him?"

"There are ways to deal with immortals," the Master said. A smile spread across his gnarled face. "Lead him to the capital. We will arrange a welcome for him."

"How?"

"Reveal yourself to him," the Master said. "He will chase you."

Crow lowered her hood again. "What about our new little sister?"

"She will come to us too," the Master said. "I should like to meet this little sister of ours. Perhaps she won't be so quick to follow our enemies if she knows the truth."

Chapter 23

Five days after Shin unleashed the dragon Sekiryu upon the world, Haruto left Sky Hollow behind for the second time in his life. He had to admit, both times he had left it in far worse shape than it had been when he arrived. Guang, Yanmei, and Kira followed him as he knew they would. Sometimes, he wondered which god he had insulted that made people cling to him so tightly. Once, he had tried to push them away, but Guang had put a stop to that. The man was like a rash that Haruto had been trying to get rid of so long he'd given up and let it hang around, quoting bad poetry and mooching off his earnings.

The surviving shintei of Sky Hollow had given them fresh supplies and requested they visit the town of Gushon to the east. The people of Gushon would want to know what had happened, and they would send help. As the sun cleared the horizon, Haruto set out down the mountain via the main pass. The wind was lighter on this side of the mountain, but the snowfall heavier. It drifted down in fat, lazy flakes and quickly coated everything. Haruto remembered the trek all too well. He had made it a hundred times, often carrying a pack filled with rocks as part of his shintei endurance training.

Guang was in good spirits despite the snow. He laughed and joked and cursed the name of various vegetables whenever he tripped and got a face full of snow. He had taken no part in the fight against Shin, but Haruto could not fault him for it. Haruto knew the vows Guang had taken and the reasons for them. He would not pressure his friend to even consider breaking those vows. Except his fourth vow, that one he would happily coax the old poet into tearing up.

Kira was more subdued since the battle. Haruto suspected

she realised she was no match for the other onryo. She wanted to fight, to help, and he respected that, but she would only get in the way. Shin had almost killed her and had done so with ease. Now and then Haruto caught the girl concentrating, focusing on a point in the near distance. Then a sound like glass shattering echoed around them, and shining shards of mirror fell from her. Whatever she was trying to do, she was failing. Guang seemed able to raise her spirits some, and she always laughed at his jokes, no matter how awful they were.

Haruto was most concerned about Yanmei. She struggled to keep up, though she didn't complain. She had been hurt in the battle against Shin, and she had neither Haruto's immortality nor Kira's youth and spiritual vigour to help her recover. Her wounds would take longer to heal, if they ever did. Yet she forged on with a rare determination and offered words of encouragement and advice to Kira whenever the girl failed at her endeavour.

They slept in tents that the shintei had provided them that first night. They were sturdy enough to withstand the strong winds and quickly warmed with a couple of bodies in them. Though Haruto struggled to sleep with Guang's bone-rattling snoring. In the end he admitted it was not his friend's honking that kept him awake. He never slept much anyway. Not for hundreds of years now. He got up and took over the watch from Yanmei, letting her get some rest.

By mid-morning the next day, the sky had cleared a little and the sun shone down through patchy gaps in the clouds. Haruto led them onto a ridge and pointed down into the valley below. Gushon spread out like spilled oil, staining the world around it with trails of dark smoke, and even from the distance, its raw stink itched in his nose. The snow was thinner down there, and the coal fires that burned in the town beat back much of the cold, making the settlement even more of a blight on the landscape.

"Is that where we're going?" Kira asked excitedly. "It's so big. I didn't realise towns could get so big. How many people live there?"

Haruto shrugged. "Thousands. Maybe tens of thousands. It's grown a lot since I last saw it."

"*The contrast of smoke and snow*," Guang said. "*Ever at odds, ever the same. Yet all masks are made to be removed.*"

Haruto sighed.

"Think you can do better, old man?"

Haruto rolled his eyes. "*Smoke is grey, snow is white. Same but different. What's beneath?*"

Guang stared at him in horror for a moment then shook his head. "You might want to leave..."

"The poetry to you," Haruto said. "Yeah."

"That is a lot of smoke," Yanmei said. "Is the town burning?"

"It's a mining town," Haruto said. He turned back to the trail and started moving again. With luck, they would reach Gushon by the following day. Though he had to admit luck was rarely on his side. "They supply half of Ipia with coal, and also burn it constantly to keep the worst of the winter away. See all the dark patches? Some are coal piles, others are ashes. The snow tries to reclaim it over time, but..."

"That's what I said," Guang grumbled. "You people have no poetry in your souls."

Kira skipped along beside the old poet. "*A light so dark. A flame so cold. Ashes blown like petals on the wind. Through labours of love we mend our hearts, but what's done is done is done.*"

"Oh." Guang beamed at Kira. "Perhaps we have a young poet here after all."

"She's better than you," Haruto said. Guang had many skills, but poetry was not one of them. Not that Haruto could claim to be the best judge.

"Radish!" Guang cursed. "How did you come up with that, Kira?"

Kira glanced at Haruto and shrugged, obviously mimicking him. "I think I heard it somewhere once. Maybe... Nope, can't remember. *Radish* is new. What are your other vows?"

Yanmei cleared her throat. "Vows are a private matter, Kira. It's not polite to ask after them."

Guang chuckled. "No, it's fine." He pulled his pack around, untangling it from Haruto's ritual staffs, and fished out a small scroll of paper. He held it tight for a moment, then unrolled it to show Kira. "My fourth vow: to never curse."

Kira stared at the vow for a moment. Haruto didn't need to look to see what it said. It was written in Guang's own hand, signed by him in blood and qi, and witnessed by a priest of Champa, the god of laughter. "What are your other vows?" she asked.

"I took four vows. Each one given freely along with a part of myself to show my commitment to change and to leaving my past behind. The first is never to hold a weapon again. No swords or axes or spears. Even knives."

"Never even hold one?" Kira asked.

Guang nodded.

"Why? Doesn't that make other things harder? What about chopping food? That uses a knife. Shaving?"

Guang scratched at his scraggly mess of beard. "All very good points."

Kira pursed her lips and skipped along beside Guang. "Why not just have the vow say you can't use a weapon to hurt someone?"

"Because he's an old fool," Haruto said.

Guang harrumphed. "Less of the old from you." He turned his attention to Kira. "It's a choice. A commitment to show my determination."

"Is that why you always slurp your food from a bowl?" Kira asked.

Guang nodded. "I don't mind so much. Quickest way to eat anyway. And as a bandit, you learn to eat quickly before someone else eats it for you."

"What happens if you break it?" Kira flicked her wrist and a mirrored dagger appeared in her hand. She tossed it to Guang, and he jumped away from it. The dagger landed in the snow. Then it shattered into a hundred twinkling shards.

"Kira!" Yanmei shouted.

The girl froze, her eyes wide. "Sorry. That was bad, wasn't it? Was it bad?" She looked at Guang, then at Yanmei. Haruto realised she wasn't just apologising, she was asking for an answer. She truly didn't know what she had done wrong.

"Yes," Yanmei said calmly. "Guang has made a choice. It's wrong to force him to hold a weapon if he has chosen not to. It's wrong to force him to do anything he doesn't want to. He's a friend and deserves respect."

"You hear that, old man?" Guang said. "Deserves respect!"

Haruto shrugged.

Kira bowed. "I'm very sorry, Guang. Please forgive me."

Guang just chuckled. "Pah, no harm done. You couldn't have forced me to hold it anyway. I'm the only one who can break my vows. No one else can break them for me. So there's nothing to forgive."

Kira kept her head low.

"Uh, you're forgiven," Guang said.

At that, she leapt up with a clap and gave the old poet a hug. "So what are your other vows?" she asked as they started walking again.

"Never to use my old technique," Guang said. "And never to kill."

"Hmmm." Kira skipped along beside Guang and rubbed at her chin the same way the poet did when he was thinking, though she didn't have the beard to scratch. She seemed to enjoy copying people. "So because of that vow, you *can't* use your technique?"

Guang shook his head. "Not even if I wanted to. Which I don't. That old technique brought nothing but pain and death. It's best left forgotten."

Kira turned to Yanmei. "Can you take the same vow?"

Yanmei smiled. "It's not that simple, Kira. Vows, like oaths, are not something to take lightly. You have to believe in them, heart and soul. Blood Dancer--"

Guang growled.

"Sorry," Yanmei said. "Guang's vows show his commitment to change. They are unique to him and special because he believes in them."

Kira frowned and balled her hands into fists. "But your technique is killing you. Why wouldn't you believe in such a vow if it will save your life?"

Yanmei said nothing for a while. Haruto was quickly realising she was not the type of woman to speak without thinking. She was deliberate in all things. "My technique damages me, yes," she said eventually. "But that is the price that I must pay." She stumbled in the snow and used her naginata to steady herself. "The truth is, Kira, Guang and I have done things that can never be forgiven. We each atone in our own way. He atones by abstinence, vowing to be better, sealing away the part of himself that caused such hurt. I atone by suffering for my actions. The pain caused by my technique is a constant reminder of what I have done. It is a constant reminder to be better."

"So do I need to atone too?" Kira asked. "I caused people pain. When I was trapped in the mirror, I was a yokai. I--"

"No!" Yanmei snapped. "Kira, you were a terrible yokai. I know this, because you were still a yokai when I found you. If you had killed anyone while you were trapped in the mirror, you would have been free already. But you didn't. You just scared a few people. *I* set you free. *I* killed to set you free. You have nothing to atone for."

"But you could stop scaring me with those reflections constantly," Guang said, but the old poet was smiling.

Kira sighed. "Being good is confusing."

Haruto laughed. "You have no idea."

Gushon might have been larger now than it was a hundred years ago, but other than that it was just as Haruto remembered. Which was to say it was as busy as a brothel on a holiday and smelled about as pleasant. The stench of industry hung thick in the air, a stark contrast to the chilly, fresh air of Sky Hollow. Fires burned and smoke billowed. Everywhere Haruto looked, carts laden with stone and coal, and men covered in rock dust trudging behind them, bustled to and fro. He wondered how deep the tunnels were by now in the never-ending search for more coal.

Groups of soldiers stood about, watching over the workers as they laboured from the mines to the city. The soldiers all carried spears and clubs, and each wore a wooden token dangling from their left wrists to prove they were in service of a local lord. Back when Haruto had known the place well, there were three noble families who claimed ownership of certain mines and land. They were constantly at odds and fights regularly broke out in the streets. Sky Hollow had sent shintei down to help police the town and keep order, but he did not know if that was still common practice now. The soldiers eyed the newcomers warily, but none made a move to accost them. Most were far too busy staring at other groups of soldiers wearing different wooden tokens, like cocks squawking over the same hen.

Shiki climbed out from inside Haruto's kimono and sat on his shoulder, staring with eyes almost as wide as Kira's. The little spirit had seen large towns before, but she was always fascinated by places where thousands of humans gathered. Most spirits were solitary creatures, but Shiki whistled and chittered a constant stream, describing everything around her as if Haruto couldn't see it for himself.

Snow still fell, but barely settled before it melted. The houses in Gushon were too warm, and the roads too well trodden.

"We should find a tavern," Guang said. "Put that imperial seal of yours to work."

"You mean put me to work?"

"One of us has to earn a living, old man. My skill lies in words, which I hand out for free. O*h, for a summer morn of which too bright. A sky so crisp even the heavens might deli--*."

"Enough!" Haruto said quickly. "I'll find some work. Just... no more poetry, please."

Kira nudged Guang in the arm. "I liked it. It was pretty."

"See," Guang said and stuck his tongue out at Haruto.

Haruto stopped to ask an old woman for directions, while

Shiki and Kira knelt and appeared to strike up a conversation with the old woman's little black cat. Yanmei had to drag Kira away from the tiny beast. They soon found a suitable inn. By early afternoon they were standing outside a luxurious establishment that Haruto was far from certain he could afford. Before they entered, Guang pulled him onto the porch and cleared his throat.

"Ladies and gentlemen," Guang said loudly, his voice carrying well enough for the people in the street to turn their faces toward him. "It is my pleasure to inform you all that there is an onmyoji in town." He bowed and gestured to Haruto. "Willing to work for those willing to pay." Most of those passing by ignored him; a few even scoffed. And two or three dashed away. Haruto knew then it wouldn't be long before someone found him.

They moved inside, found a table and ordered food and drink. The smell of cooking meat and stewing vegetables made Haruto's stomach rumble like a rockslide and when the food arrived he fell upon it like a starving tiger. It was the warmest and heartiest meal any of them had eaten in weeks. No sooner had they finished than the first employer found them. He was a small man with a pinched face, a servant's kimono, and a pungent aroma of lotus flower perfume. He stopped by the table and bowed low. "Master Onmyoji?"

"How can I help?" Haruto asked.

The pinched-faced servant straightened. "I work for Lord Hishonima. He has heard of you and wishes to contract your services to extirpate a meddlesome yokai from his property."

"He's heard of you." Guang winked at Haruto.

"Of course," the pinch-faced servant said. "The prowess of Master Haruto is well known." Lies and compliments ever went hand in hand.

"What about the eloquence of his companion, Master Guang?"

The servant blinked and after a pregnant pause said, "Uh... of course."

Kira giggled and Shiki, clinging to Haruto's shoulder, quickly joined in. Whether the spirit knew what she was laughing at was another matter.

"What is the nature of Lord Hishonima's problem?" Haruto asked.

"Lord Hishonima owns several mines on the southern side of the city," the gaunt servant said quickly. "Of late, one of his mines has become haunted. It is significantly hampering attempts to extract coal. Many of his employees are going hungry as they cannot currently work."

To Haruto's surprise, Yanmei replied, "Did it not cross his mind to keep paying them?" she said quietly, cradling her tea cup. "It's not their fault they can't work the mines."

"Yes," the servant said, bowing his head once more. "Unfortunately, Lord Hishonima has suffered many such setbacks over the past year and cannot currently afford to pay those who do not work." The man looked nervous, glancing about as though expecting someone. "He suspects there has been--" he lowered his voice "--sabotage."

"Sabotage?" Guang asked, rubbing his hands together. "This is getting interesting."

The servant opened his mouth to speak, but the tavern door banged open. The servant winced, lowering his head as if suspecting a blow, which did not take long to fall. The man who entered was richly dressed in a red hakama and matching haori. He had a katana belted as his waist with a golden sash and carried a little wooden club in one hand. As soon as he spotted the servant, he barged over to the table and clubbed him about the shoulder.

"Get out of here, wretch." He smacked the servant again, and the pinch-faced man yelped and cowered. The richly dressed newcomer pushed the servant towards the door, extending a foot and tripping him. The servant's head hit a table on his way to the floor. Not stopping there, the newcomer kicked the servant savagely in the ribs.

Kira jumped to her feet, daggers in hands, but Yanmei dragged her back down to the table.

"I thought it was wrong to beat people weaker than you?"

Kira said through gritted teeth.

"It is," Yanmei said.

"Shouldn't we stop him?"

"Yes."

"Um..." Kira plopped down on her seat, her daggers shattering, showering the floor in mirrored shards. "I don't understand."

"We don't know the circumstances," Yanmei said. "You cannot fight every battle, and what is right and wrong is determined by law as often as by morality."

Kira groaned, slumped over and rested her head against the table. Shiki leapt from Haruto's shoulder, waddled over to the girl, and gently patted her head with a spindly black paw.

After the man had thrown the servant from the tavern, he returned to their table. He was portly and baby-faced, but not fat. His cheeks were red from beating the servant. He took a moment to smooth down his haori and then another to tug his hair into position. By the way his hair moved all at once, it appeared to be a wig.

"You're the onmyoji?" the wig asked. "Do you have an imperial seal?"

Haruto blinked. He couldn't tear his eyes from the man's wig. It sat slightly askew on his head and looked like a cat had curled up there and died. Wherever Haruto went, there were always people like this. Men, usually lords, who thought themselves divinely important to the world. They were almost always wrong. Haruto pointed towards his seal hanging above the bar, still staring at the wig.

The man peered at the seal. "How do I know it's real?"

"Because impersonating an onmyoji is a crime in Ipia," Haruto said. "Punishable by icing. Which is an extremely unpleasant way to die."

The wig grunted. "I'm Lord Yoshinata. Don't listen to a word Hishonima's snivelling swine said to you. He's the one who's sabotaging *my* mines."

"Oh, it's this again," Guang said. He pulled out his paper and ink pot.

"I assume you also have a haunted mine then?" Haruto asked. Shiki scrabbled up his arm and perched on his shoulder. The little spirit was also staring at the wig. She whistled in Haruto's ear and he glanced at her. "Don't you dare."

The wig looked from Haruto to Shiki and back again. "You're damned straight. My men can't swing a pick without that monster marching out of the darkness and beating one of them to death. Then the others just turn tail and run instead of fighting back. Even the soldiers I send in turn up dead or gibbering fools. It's a yokai, is what it is. A damned yokai. Get in there and deal with it."

"What does it look like?" Haruto said.

"What? What does that matter? Wears a straw cape, I think."

Haruto nodded vaguely towards Guang. "Sounds like a namahage." Shiki leaned forward on his shoulder, grinning at the wig.

Guang whistled. "Tough. Expensive to deal with."

"A namahage?" Kira asked, her head still resting on the table. "That sounds exciting."

Guang smiled at her. "I have a tale or two to tell. How about the namahage of Tsin Province? Just forty years ago..."

Kira looked up eagerly.

"Enough!" Lord Yoshinata snapped, his wig shifting slightly left, eliciting a delighted squeak from Shiki. "Will you deal with the spirit or is that seal of yours fake after all?"

"Dangerous to interrupt a poet," Guang said sulkily. "He might just immortalise you in words."

Lord Yoshinata sneered down at him. "I might just separate your head from your body."

Haruto stood slowly and eased himself between the two men. If anyone was going to have their head separated from their body, it might as well be him. At least then it could be reattached later. Although, he had to admit he'd never been decapitated and was not completely certain he'd survive it. He looked down at Lord Yoshinata, trying to meet the man's eyes instead of the hairy thing on his head. "My poetic friend here was just trying to point out that namahage are especially dangerous yokai. In my line of work, dangerous and expensive go hand in hand." Shiki cooed and leaned forward towards the wig, reaching for it with her hairy little arms.

"The cost does not matter," Lord Yoshinata snapped. His wig flopped down in front of his eyes, and he quickly slapped it back on top of his head. Shiki squealed and jumped up and down, lost her footing and tumbled from Haruto's shoulder onto the tavern floor.

Haruto shrugged. "Might as well get this done now," he said and started towards the door.

"I'll stay here," Guang said, pouring himself another cup of wine. "In case anyone else comes by with tales of devilish yokai."

Yanmei nodded. "I'll stay too."

"Can I go?" Kira asked. She was already on her feet and looking at Yanmei. The woman nodded, and Kira clapped her hands and ran to join Haruto. He sighed, noting that she hadn't asked for his permission.

Haruto glanced at Kira's beaming face. "Stay close and do what I say. These yokai might not be as strong as Shin, but they also won't play with their prey like he did. If they can, they will kill you."

As Haruto pushed open the door, he heard Lord Yoshinata cry out. A moment later, the man's wig scurried past him on the floor and out into the street, squeaking with delight.

Chapter 24

The city was a place of wonder to Kira. So many people, so many sights, smells and sounds.

They passed through a square with tables set up; on each table was a game board and dozens of little stone figures. Some tables had people sitting around them, taking turns moving the pieces. Kira did not know what sort of game they were playing, but it looked fascinating. They passed an open studio where an artist was painting a portrait of a tragically thin man wearing bulky ceramic armour. Dozens of paintings hung on the studio walls, each one with a small price tag at the bottom. Many of the paintings were luxurious green landscapes or blue skies with clouds forming into intricate patterns. Kira stopped to stare at them, wondering if those landscapes were real and where she might find such beauty.

"Keep up," Haruto said, and Kira leapt to follow him.

"There's so much to see," she said, staring at some soldiers on one side of the street staring at some other soldiers across the way. They seemed rather tense, she thought.

Haruto shrugged as he often did. "You get used to it."

Kira tried to copy his shrug again, but failed to capture the gesture. Haruto did it with such ease. She always felt stiff and ungainly.

Shiki was a comforting weight on Kira's shoulder and looked about with unabashed curiosity, big bright eyes staring out from the dishevelled wig. She smelled like mint for some reason, or Kira supposed the wig she was possessing smelled like mint. The little spirit attracted quite a few stares and even a few whispered prayers. Kira felt like defending her. She had an odd kinship with the little spirit. People whispering that she was a harbinger of ill luck was unfair. But Haruto seemed to ignore them all, and Kira thought it best to take his lead.

They were going the wrong way, she realised. They were walking towards the setting sun. "I thought Lord Yoshinaka's mine was north?"

"It is," Haruto said without looking at her.

"But we're heading west."

Haruto shrugged again. Kira tried it, but it was still off, something in the shoulders. She'd have to keep trying. Shiki laughed at her, and Kira flicked a finger at the spirit. Shiki opened her mouth and bit the finger playfully. Kira giggled at the wig savaging her finger.

"That's because we're going to Hishonima's mine," Haruto said.

"Oh." Kira nodded and sped up a little to walk next to Haruto. The streets were full of people. Some pulled carts or carried baskets; others pulled children or stopped to chat. Some rushed about in a determined direction; others sauntered from shop to shop. But all of them gave Haruto a wide berth. "So you've picked a side?"

"Onmyoji don't take sides in such matters," Haruto said. "Well, we're not supposed to. I don't, at least. The other onmyoji are-- not always so discerning. I'll deal with the yokai in both mines. I'm just dealing with Hishonima's first."

"Why?"

Haruto glanced at her, frowning. "Because Hishonima's servant didn't threaten to chop my friend's head off."

They found the pinch-faced servant waiting outside the mine with a few soldiers. He was bruised and had a red welt bulging from his forehead, but he bowed and promised both his thanks and his lord's payment for the service. He offered to send the soldiers in with them, but Haruto only laughed and told them to stay outside. The soldiers didn't look like they wanted to go anyway.

The mine was dark, and not a single lantern had been lit to guide the way. The tunnel extended far ahead of them. It was wide enough for five people to walk abreast but only just tall enough for Haruto to stand up straight. A guide rope ran along the wall, threaded through metal hoops hammered into the rock. Kira shivered, though not from the cold. She had a creepy feeling about the mine. It was oppressive. The gloom seemed to close in on her like wolves around wounded prey. Her back itched as though someone were staring at her, but when she turned around, there was nothing but darkness behind her.

"You don't have to come with me," Haruto said. "But I do need Shiki."

Kira felt another shiver pass through her, starting at her neck and shaking down to her toes. "I'm fine. I just... something feels strange."

Haruto shrugged, and then he shivered too. "It's a haunted mine. I'd be worried if it felt normal. Let's find out what we're dealing with. Shiki, some light, please."

The little spirit popped out from the wig and leapt from Kira's shoulder onto Haruto's, leaving the clump hair on Kira's shoulder. Then she breathed in deep, inflating and glowing as bright orange as any sky lantern. Kira flicked the dispossessed wig from her shoulder. It fell to the rocky floor with a puff of dust. She stared at it for a moment, then turned away. She heard a scuttling noise and turned back. The wig was gone even though Shiki had stopped possessing it. Kira shivered again, there was definitely something in the mine.

Kira whined and ran to catch up with Haruto.

"What?" he asked.

"The wig." Kira pointed behind her. "It's gone."

"Good."

"But it ran off on its own."

Haruto stopped and glanced behind them, then at Shiki. The little spirit, glowing bright and orange, let out a trembling whistle. Kira thought she heard the wig, or whatever had taken it, scurrying about in the gloom, but whenever she turned to look for it, there was nothing but darkness and rock all around. Haruto shook his head and started walking deeper into the mine. Kira hurried to catch up again and hugged his arm.

They followed the guide rope deeper into the mine. The tunnel occasionally forked, but they stayed with the rope. At least it would lead them back out again. It would be all too easy to get lost down there. If Shiki's light went out and they were stuck in the dark, they might never find their way out. When Kira thought about that, the rock walls closed in her again, and she began to hear herself breathe. She hugged Haruto's arm a little tighter.

"Is it normal for two yokai to appear at the same time?" Kira asked. The quiet was making the mine even creepier. She needed some noise, even if it was the sound of her own voice.

Haruto shrugged. "It's becoming more common than you might think. Over the past decade, so many lost things are returning to the world. Spirits, lost techniques, imprisoned dragons. These days more and more yokai are turning up. I used to go from town to town looking for work. Now--" he sighed "--now everywhere I go people are clamouring for my services. The onmyoji, the other onmyoji that is, don't tend to travel much these days. Much easier to find themselves a rich patron to leach off."

The tunnel split in two and they followed the rope down to the right. Kira thought she heard scrabbling claws behind them and turned, half expecting to see the wig somehow grown large enough to devour her. But if there was anything, it was beyond the range of Shiki's light. "Man-eating wigs," she whispered.

"Huh?"

Kira shook her head. "Do you really think the mine owners put yokai in each other's mines?" Kira asked.

"I have long since stopped being surprised at what greed will drive men to, and to what lengths they will go to hide their crimes." He sounded angry, and Kira thought that should make her angry too. "Using spirits in such a way is unforgivable. No one asks to become a yokai – you should know that. It is inflicted upon a person, a curse that turns them into monsters."

Kira looked down at her hands and wondered if he meant her. She was not truly a yokai anymore though; she was something else. Did that still make her a monster?

"Yokai aren't evil," Haruto continued. "Evil isn't something a person is, it's a choice a person makes. Yokai are creatures of instinct. It is their nature to seek vengeance. It is why they exist. They are not evil, but anyone who chooses to use them to commit atrocities is evil. Because that is the choice they have made."

"What about the onryo?" Kira asked quietly.

"Full of questions, aren't you," Haruto said. He tried to tug his arm free, but she felt she needed the contact so clung tighter. "You onryo are different. You are still human enough to make the same choices anyone makes. You don't get to blame your nature or instinct. What you do and what you are is your choice, and the consequences are yours to bear. Shin chose to be evil, to slaughter innocent people at Sky Hollow and probably elsewhere as well."

Kira didn't know if that was true or not. It sounded right, but she couldn't deny she felt a thrill when she scared people with her reflections. Was that her true nature? Was it her ungaikyo side clawing its way up to take control of her? She shivered, heard glass cracking, felt an itch travel down her arm. She looked down to see a crack snaking its way up her hand, as though her skin were a breaking mirror. She quickly pulled the sleeve of her kimono over her hand.

"But what if--"

"Quiet!" Haruto said sharply. He stopped and cocked his head. "Do you hear that?"

A faint noise echoed up from the depths of the mine, but now that Kira listened for it, it was undeniable. Someone was crying. Trapped in the dark and sobbing.

They hurried deeper into the mine. A heavy musty scent hung in the air, mixing with an acrid stench and growing stronger as they went deeper. Kira gagged and held a sleeve over her mouth and nose. If Haruto was put off by the smell, he didn't show it. Shiki, however, whistled out complaint after complaint, not that the little spirit even had a nose.

The sobbing grew louder, reverberating around them until suddenly it was almost deafening, one voice, two, twenty, all mingled together in a cacophony of anguish. Fragments of memories assaulted Kira: people screaming, terrified and begging for release; people staring into her mirror and seeing their own faces decay before them; monsters rearing up to tear them limb from limb. The faces of the people she had tormented as a yokai were trapped in the walls around her, screaming at her all over again. Those screams had been music to her ears once. They had been her song. The one she had been singing when... when...

Glass cracked, a cold itch crept up her chest, prickled her neck.

"Kira!" Haruto grabbed her shoulder and shook her. She shattered, shards of mirror falling all around her. She was crouched down, hugging her knees against her chest, though she didn't remember how she got there. The wailing had subsided. The faces in the rock were shadows... of course, they were. She slowly stood.

"I don't like it here," she said, feeling a tremor in her voice.

Haruto nodded. "You're not supposed to. Whatever we're dealing with, it's trying to scare us." He glanced around. There was still a faint cry coming from somewhere, its words hidden, muffled as if spoken through a thick blanket.

"You don't seem scared," Kira said as she shuffled along behind him. She didn't want to let him get too far ahead, lest the ghosts of her past came calling again.

He shrugged. "Two hundred years of experience has taught me that most yokai who use fear do so because it is all they have. Think about your time in the mirror." She really didn't want to remember it. Fuzzy images that faded like dreams and even that was too much. "You tried to scare people to death, but you couldn't actually reach out of the mirror. You were trapped. Besides, I'm immortal. I'm far more worried about what might happen to you down here than to me."

"What if the yokai collapses the mine and traps us underground? Will you just live forever, trapped in the dark with no one for company, and no light, and no way out."

Haruto stopped walking. "When you put it like that..."

A pealing sob ripped through the stale air of mine, bounding off the stone walls and resounding back even louder, way too loud to be her imagination. It was real, and it was coming from the left where the tunnel split in two once again. The rope, however, led to the right. They left the guide rope behind and struck out into the unknown. The wailing grew louder still, the words between the sobs more distinct. A man was repeating something over and over again.

Kira tried to cover her ears, but the wailing was too much, too loud, too saddening. They could hear the man's words by then. "Help me. Get it off. Help!" Kira felt tears blurring her eyes and wiped them away on her sleeve.

They continued on. Haruto striding faster, Kira hurrying to keep up. The sobs grew louder, echoing all around.

Shiki's light shone on a bend in the tunnel. "Around this corner," Haruto said. "Stay close."

Kira closed the gap between them and clung to Haruto's arm once more. He didn't try to shake her loose. When they turned the corner, Shiki's light shone on a man sitting against the stone wall. He was barely skin and bones, and his clothes were ripped and stained with rock dust. His mouth was covered in little sores; his hair a wild, wiry tangle. He was crouched in a corner where the tunnel turned sharply. One leg was stretched out before him, the ankle twisted at an unnatural angle. The other was drawn up against his chest, and he was clutching it with both hands, fingernails clawing at his pants and the bloody skin beneath. He put his hand over his brow to shade Shiki's light and let out a pitiful whine.

"Poor wretch," Haruto said. "Stuck down here when the others fled, no doubt. Tormented by whatever yokai has taken up residence here." He sighed. "At the very least we need to get him out of here."

Kira noticed bones on the ground nearby. Bits of decaying, ragged flesh still clung to some of them. "How long has the mine been closed?"

Haruto shrugged as he knelt down next to the man. "A couple of weeks."

"What's he been eating to stay alive?" she asked.

Haruto looked back at her, then at the bones. He shook his head sadly. The man just starting sobbing again.

"We have nothing to splint your leg, so you're going to have to limp out of here with us," Haruto told the man, extending his hand toward him.

"Get it off me," the man said, heaving heavy breaths. "Please get it off me." He looked up at them then, his eyes wide with fear. "It's on you too."

Kira spun around, trying to catch whatever was clinging to her. But there was nothing there. Nothing on her. Nothing on Haruto. Nothing on any of them.

Haruto grumbled. "Do I have a hand print on my back?"

Kira looked. "A little one. Like a small chalk hand print."

"Well, at least I know what we're dealing with."

"Get it off get it off get it off," the man wailed.

"It's not real," Haruto said. "It's a buruburu. They cling to people and try to scare them, conjuring up their past."

Kira looked over her shoulder and then the other one. There didn't appear to be anything clinging to her. "Is it on me right now?"

Haruto nodded lazily. "It's on all of us. Probably tagged us the moment we entered the mine."

Kira tried to smile. She also tried to ignore the small dark-haired girl sitting at edge of Shiki's light because she was fairly certain it was herself. Who she used to be. The girl looked up at her and started singing, blood dripping from toothless gums.

She felt herself shattering, cracks forming along her surface. The song brought back memories. Vague images, feelings. Her mother standing behind her, combing her hair. Only it wasn't her mother; it was a man, a skinless ghoul with greed in his eyes and bony fingers like knives. "No." The word fell from her lips as a whisper and glass shattered all around, twinkling shards falling to the ground, the ghoul's face reflected in each one. "Get it off me. Get it off me. Get it off me!"

"Shiki," Haruto said. The little spirit leapt into his sword, illuminating the cave in its red light. "Hold still, Kira." He darted forward and stabbed Shiki at her. The glowing blade passed over her shoulder, and something leapt from her back. It giggled, a child's titter, and vanished into the darkness. The illusions it had conjured went with it. Kira's younger self and her song were gone. The mirrored shards all around her now reflected only the crimson light of Shiki's blade.

Haruto shifted his grip on Shiki and swung it around behind his back. A small boy leapt from him and scampered into the shadows. "And one more." He stabbed Shiki at the sobbing man's injured leg. The boy appeared for a moment and ran into the darkness of the tunnel.

Kira was panting, cold sweat running down her temples and the small of her back. "Was that really what I used to do?"

Haruto looked at her. In the red glow of Shiki's light, he looked angry. "In a way. The buruburu latch onto people and draw out their deepest fears. I'm guessing your deepest fear is being what you once were, trapped in the mirror, tormenting people. Gave you a taste of your own medicine, huh?"

Kira felt tears running down her cheeks and stifled a whimper.

"Sorry," Haruto said quickly. "I didn't mean..." He sighed and turned away.

Kira tried to swallow down the lump in her throat. Her skin prickled annoyingly, but she refused to scratch it. That girl wasn't her anymore. It had never been her. Not really. It was something else, something forced upon her. Wasn't it? She wouldn't let herself be that again. She would be good. She clutched her hands into fists and wished Yanmei was there with them.

"Let's deal with you then," Haruto said, addressing the darkness. "By Omoretsu's will, I name you buruburu."

A little boy's high-pitched laugh echoed around them, and then he stepped out of the darkness. He was small, young, his face dirty with coal dust. He wore ragged trousers and a shirt to match. A peasant, probably a miner's son once. His hair was cut like a bowl around his head, and his toothy smile was full of malice.

"Looks like you found me," he said cheerily. "Oh well."

Kira felt anger clutch her heart. She flicked her wrists, and mirrored daggers formed in her hands. Then she sprinted at the boy. He didn't even try to move. Kira raised her daggers and drove them down at the boy's neck...

The daggers crashed against Shiki's blade as Haruto blocked Kira's strike. They wrestled there for a moment, her daggers caught on the spirit blade, and Haruto grunted from the strain. Cracks spread along her daggers, and they shattered, hundreds of mirrored shards falling to the stone floor of the tunnel. Kira leapt back out of striking distance and flicked new daggers into her hands. But Haruto didn't follow up. He lowered Shiki and stared at Kira.

"Why?" Kira growled.

Haruto loosened his grip on Shiki, and the little spirit popped free of the blade, floated into the air, and inflated into a ball of light again. She blinked at Kira twice and then flipped upside-down. Despite herself, Kira chuckled.

"I already told you, Kira," Haruto said. "Yokai aren't evil. They are simply expressing their nature. Some must be killed. Others can be dealt with more peacefully." Haruto turned to look at the buruburu. "If I can give them a peaceful end, then I will. Every time. They've already suffered enough. You should understand that."

Her daggers shattered, and she didn't form new ones. He was doing the right thing. The good thing. That was what Yanmei would want. It was what Kira wanted.

"Besides," Haruto continued. "If we kill him, he'll only return to heaven unbound to any shinigami. I don't have my ritual staffs at the moment, as the wood staff is still broken..."

Kira felt heat rush to her cheeks.

Haruto crouched down in front of the boy. "I can't take your burden. I'm already carrying another's."

The boy tilted his head to the side. "It's no burden." He grinned. "See the fun we're having." He gestured at the gibbering man. "He didn't find me even once. I'm too good at hiding."

Haruto smiled. "That simple, huh? Go hide then. We'll count to a hundred and come and find you."

The buruburu giggled. "You'll never find me. I'm too good at hiding." He turned and sprinted off into the darkness, boyish laughter echoing behind him.

Haruto stood, stretched, and started counting.

Chapter 25

They needed some new supplies and with Haruto absent chasing down some yokai, it was the perfect opportunity to find the old man a new pipe. Guang usually liked to do the shopping on his own, but the moment he'd announced he was going, Yanmei stood and said she'd go with him. He didn't mind. He was just happy she'd finally stopped calling him Blood Dancer.

Gushon was a thriving town and the streets were busy. Guang walked slowly, keeping out of the way as best he could, and browsing any shops he came across. Yanmei paced behind him, her head bent and gaze distant. He knew the look. Whatever she had to say, she'd get round to it in her own time.

Guang stopped in front of little stall and eyed the brushes the merchant was selling. He'd need a new brush soon enough. He kept his own wrapped in oiled leather, but after a while the bristles lost their flexibility and the ink no longer spread evenly. Unfortunately, the stall only had cheaper brushes and he wanted something that would last. He shook his head at the vendor and they moved on.

"I've never met an onmyoji before," Yanmei said as they stepped around a puddle on the ground that smelled like it might have once been inside a horse. "Haruto is-- not what I expected."

"Hah!" Guang barked. "You can say that again. He's a right old pain in the turnip." He chuckled. "And he's not much like the other onmyoji."

"You've met others then?" Yanmei asked. "I must admit, when the Fifth Sage told me they would one day come to Heiwa for Kira, I didn't entirely believe him. I thought the onmyoji more a myth."

Guang stepped onto a porch of a wood carvers and glanced

inside, wondering if they had any pipes. "I've met a couple since I've been by Haruto's side," he said. "There was, uh, Sima. Young woman, held herself like a princess. She had a real haughty air about her. We didn't get on. Her companion spirit was a great wolf with white fur and six red eyes. Every time it growled, Shiki hid. We met her in Ban Ping and she told us, quite firmly, to get the cabbage out of her city."

"Her city?" Yanmei asked.

"That's what she said. Apparently she lives there. The monks of Ban Ping pay her to stay and if any spirits pop up, she gives them a quick cleanse." Guang pulled open the door to the wood carvers and stepped inside. Yanmei followed him. "It's a well-paying job, by the looks of it. Sima was decked out in all sorts of finery and jewellery. Made the old man look like a pauper. Which, I guess, he is." He nodded to the shop owner, then spotted some pipes and shuffled over to browse.

"You said spirits," Yanmei said. "Not yokai. Haruto seems to make a significant distinction."

Guang nodded. "Not many do, but the old man holds to the old ways."

"What old ways?"

Guang picked up a long-stemmed pipe with a small brass bowl. It was plain with no ornamentation; serviceable. Considering the rate Haruto lost them, that was probably the best sort of thing for him. Guang put the pipe down and looked at another.

"To hear the old man tell it," Guang said. "Things were different before the Century Blade killed the dragons. Or imprisoned them, I suppose. The onmyoji were an order of occultists who considered it their duty, sworn by the shinigami, to find yokai and move them on. Send them to heaven. They had a village where they trained and called home, and those who wanted to leave went out on pilgrimage to see their duty done. It was all very honourable."

Yanmei gestured at a pipe with a large wooden bowl and carvings of waves all around it. "What happened?"

Guang shook his head. "The emperor of Ipia made it imperial law that onmyoji must be paid for every yokai they cleanse," he said. "Worked just fine for a while. Until the Century Blade killed the dragons. With them gone, there wasn't enough kami to protect the spirits. People started asking the onmyoji to get rid of harmless spirits as well as yokai, and the onmyoji thought *why not as long we get paid*."

He looked at the final pipe, an ugly grey thing made from a twisted bough. Nothing caught his eye. "According to the old man, it was the beginning of the end. The onmyoji got greedy. They stopped making any distinction between spirits and yokai. As long as people were willing to pay, the onmyoji would cleanse anything. You saw it in Minazuri, the magistrate didn't care one drop about the difference, she just wanted all the spirits gone. It even became popular among the wealthy to hire an onmyoji on retainer. That's when the Ipian imperial law of paying onmyoji spread to the other nations. It was the only way to get them to leave Ipia and deal with yokai elsewhere." Guang shook his head sadly. "He calls it the Great Spirit Purge."

"I've never heard of it," Yanmei said.

"No one has," Guang agreed. "The onmyoji wanted it that way. They left their little village haven and spread out across the four nations, cleansing every spirit they could find and got rich and fat off it all. The old practices died out. The onmyoji started taking apprentices instead of training pilgrims. Before long, there weren't enough spirits in the world to support the number of onmyoji looking to make it rich off the job. By then most of the onmyoji were rich enough they didn't care anymore."

"But not Haruto?" Yanmei asked.

Guang chuckled. "The old man is just about the last one who sticks to the old ways. The onmyoji got greedy and were so desperate to get rich, they made themselves almost obsolete. Now there's only a few of them left. The old man still wanders about looking for yokai to send on their way. Most of the rest are settled where the money is, like Sima getting fat off the monks of Ban Ping."

Yanmei sighed. "That's sad," she said. "I think Kira would have liked it if there were more spirits in the world."

Guang glanced at her and then away. "You might yet get that wish. The old man isn't lying when he says the lost things are returning. We've been busier in the last few years than I ever thought possible." He spotted a small mirror with a polished red wood handle and looked into the reflection. He almost expected to see something horrible behind him, but Kira wasn't about. He tapped the surface of the mirror and imagined seeing a little girl trapped within. The shop owner cleared her throat.

"How did you get Kira out of the mirror?" Guang asked. "You said you killed someone?"

Yanmei nodded. "An assassin. A friend of mine had Kira's mirror and she came to me for protection. The assassin wanted the mirror; some sort of favour for a god, I believe. He attacked." She winced at the memory. "We fought. When I finally killed him, he was looking into the mirror. Then he was dead and Kira was there. She remembered her name, but that was it. I wasn't sure what she was at the time. A young girl or a yokai, or something else. So I took her to Heiwa. I guessed if anyone would know what to do with her, it would be the Fifth Sage Under Heaven."

Guang nodded and scratched at his beard. "Sure. But why did you raise her? By the sounds of it, you spent more time with her than any of the other students at Heiwa."

Yanmei was silent for a few seconds, frowning. Then she shook her head. "Kira attached herself to me. I... I couldn't push her away."

Guang laughed. "They make us better, you know. If you let them. Children." He shook his head and started for the door. "Come on. We've got some supplies to pick up before heading back to the inn."

Haruto and Kira spent a good few hours searching for the buruburu. He really was quite good at hiding and the mine was labyrinthine. Eventually, they found him crouching inside a little hollow dug out of the wall. They might have missed him but for the little giggle he let out as Shiki cavorted past him, glowing bright as a lantern. No sooner had they found the boy than he simply faded away, leaving an echo of a childish giggle behind. If only all yokai were so simple to put to rest.

He and Kira returned to the poor fellow who had been trapped down in the dark and carried him out of the mine.

Lord Hishonima's pinch-faced servant was waiting for them at the entrance to the mine. Night had fallen and the servant and his soldiers were crouching around a small brazier full of burning coal. After bowing many times and thanking Haruto, he pulled out a purse and counted out sixty lien. Far from a fortune, but more than enough to keep them going for a while. After that, Haruto turned north and started walking.

"To the other mine then?" Kira asked. The girl had recovered from her panic and much of her good cheer had returned. "The one owned by Lord Arsehole?"

Haruto laughed. Miners were going about their business, preparing to re-enter the mine, but most seemed to be winding down for the night. The sun was setting and even the poorest peasants had to go home eventually. Soldiers still loitered about on the streets though, generally frowning and staring down other soldiers. It was an uneasy peace, but then Haruto had never met an easy peace. Most were nothing more than polite lulls while one side worked up the courage to get stabbed again.

"Those daggers of yours," Haruto said as they walked. "You form them from your qi, don't you?"

"Mhm. The Fifth Sage taught me the technique back at Heiwa. He said I wasn't very good at it, though, and I should keep practising."

"He was right," Haruto said. "Your daggers are too brittle. They break too easily."

"But when they shatter, I can use the reflections."

Haruto moved aside to let a man leading a donkey pass them on the street. Shiki leapt at the beast, but he caught the little spirit out of the air and sat her on his shoulder. A possessed donkey was the last thing Haruto needed. She stuck her tongue out at him.

"They need to be strong enough to block a strike if you are to use them as weapons as well," he said. "They are your qi. You can strengthen them to stand against a sword blow. You can also choose to shatter them at will. Practice and concentration are key."

Kira frowned and nodded. She flicked her wrist and stared at the dagger in her hand. Haruto couldn't help but be impressed. Forming weapons from qi was no easy technique and required a lot of energy. Kira appeared to make dozens of them without tiring. She was also strong enough to use her qi to bolster her strength and speed. In most people it would be inefficient and draining, but Kira appeared to be a forge fire that never went out.

"Talk to Guang about it sometime," Haruto continued. "He might give you some pointers. Believe it or not, the old fool is something of an expert on matters of qi."

Night had well and truly fallen by the time they reached the northern mines. A gaggle of Lord Yoshinata's soldiers were standing around a small fire, looking about as happy as a duck on a spit. The biggest of them, a brutish man with an overhanging forehead, stalked forward as soon as he saw them, twisting a wooden cudgel in his huge fist.

"You shoulda been here hours ago," the brute said slowly, as though his tongue were too big for his mouth.

Haruto shrugged. "You should have brushed your teeth before opening your mouth. We all deal with the unfortunate consequences. This mine, is it?"

The brute growled and stalked back to the fire. He pulled a torch from a barrel and lit it on the flames. "You'll need this. It's dark in there."

"We'll be fine," Haruto said. "Shiki." The little spirit clambered lazily out of his kimono, yawned, squeaked a complaint, and inflated into the ball of light once more, floating before them like a toad-shaped ember on the wind.

"Ahhh!" the brute said, backing away and waving his torch at Shiki. The little spirit drifted around slowly to face him and blinked at him a few times.

Haruto shook his head. "I can see you would be a lot of use in there. Feel free to stay out here. We'll deal with your yokai problem."

Kira laughed as she followed Haruto to the mine. "So brave," she said. Haruto saw her flick her wrist, and the brute squealed in alarm as she flashed a reflection at him. "Sorry," she blurted. "That was bad, wasn't it?"

Haruto only shrugged in reply. He was in no position to judge right from wrong.

Yoshinata's mine was much the same as Hishonima's. Wide and squat with a rope hanging from hooks hammered into the wall. Lanterns hung on the outside, but the gloom quickly swallowed all light. Lord Wig had described a spirit in a straw cloak, and Haruto knew of only one such yokai: the namahage. They were disciplinary spirits, formed from ritual punishment taken too far. A man beaten to death for not working hard enough was a common cause, and in a place like Gushon with Yoshinata as a master, it seemed likely.

Haruto and Kira weren't more than two hundred paces into the mine when they heard drums. A regular boom that echoed off the tunnel walls into a painful rolling thunder. Kira drew close to Haruto. She already had daggers in hand. Suddenly, the drums stopped, and the namahage stepped out of the darkness. It wore a straw cloak that hung from its shoulders down past its knees and wooden sandals that clacked on the stone floor. Its face was a hideous mask, a dramatic mimicry of an oni. It had red skin, huge angry eyes, and tusks protruding from its upper and lower jaws. In one hand it held a chokuto with a straight blade and a single edge. In its other hand was a wooden club, just like those the soldiers in Gushon carried. The namahage didn't hide like the buruburu, that was not its way. This yokai was here to inflict the punishment that had created it, to serve its lust for vengeance by delivering its pain onto others.

The namahage stopped just inside Shiki's light and waited, a looming spectre of discipline taken too far.

"Well, you wanted a fight," Haruto said, patting Kira on the back. "Have at it."

"What?" Kira squeaked. "I thought you were putting them to rest peacefully?"

Haruto shrugged. "This is a namahage. There's no putting it to rest, nor taking its burden. I don't have my ritual staffs so I can't trap it. All we can do is kill it."

"Won't it just reform elsewhere?"

"Eventually," Haruto agreed. "But it's the best we can do for now. So go. Kill it."

"You're not going to help?"

Haruto shook his head and leaned against the tunnel wall. He wanted to see what Kira was capable of. If she couldn't beat a namahage there seemed little hope she'd ever be able to help against the onryo.

Kira stared at him in confusion for a few moments, then a smile lit her face. "Fine. It's about time you took me seriously." She faced the namahage and ducked into a ready crouch. This was what Heiwa had taught her, and Haruto suspected she had learned the basics only. Her crouch indicated she was going to rush the yokai, attempt to overcome it with speed. It was too obvious.

Kira sprinted forward, just as Haruto had suspected. She closed on the namahage fast and struck with both daggers. But the yokai saw the attack coming and blocked with its sword. Its club shot out and jabbed Kira in the stomach, staggering her. The namahage kicked out, grunting and putting all its weight behind the blow. Kira tumbled away, clutching at her stomach as she rolled to her feet.

"Sloppy," Haruto said. Shiki whistled an agreement. Kira glared at them both, and the namahage charged her.

Kira flicked new daggers into her hands just in time to use one to block the chokuto slicing at her chest. The namahage swung its club down, shattering her other dagger and clipping her leg. Kira limped backwards, flicking a new dagger into her hand and wincing from the pain. The yokai pressed her, giving her no time to recover. It feinted with its sword, drawing Kira's attention to the more dangerous weapon, then thumped her on the shoulder with its club.

She leapt away, clutching at her arm, wincing and breathing hard. The namahage backed away to the limits of Shiki's light once more. It stopped and waited. It was also breathing heavy, and Haruto noticed sweat dripping from under its mask. He pushed away from the wall and placed a hand on the hilt of his katana.

"Stay back," Kira snapped at him. "You said you weren't going to help, so stay out of it." New daggers in her hands gleamed in Shiki's light.

Haruto moved his hand from his sword and leaned against the wall once more. "Go on then. Do you want a hint?"

"No!" She smiled at him. "I've got this."

"Hmph," the namahage grunted.

Kira approached slowly this time. When she reached striking distance, she feinted right, then leapt left. The namahage made to block, but Kira stepped back, raising her daggers above her head. The yokai flailed at something only it could see, and Kira struck with both hands. The namahage bashed one dagger aside, but the other made it through his guard, pierced its straw cloak, and gashed its side. The yokai grunted and staggered back a few steps. Blood dripped from the tip of Kira's dagger. It hadn't gone deep, but it had struck home. The namahage crouched, holding its side and panting.

They clashed again, Kira slashing low with one dagger and stabbing the other at the namahage's chest. The namahage kicked Kira's low hand away, swept her other dagger aside with its chokuto, then smacked the girl round the head with its club. Kira staggered away. Blood ran down her forehead and dripped from her nose over her lip. She shook her head, blinking furiously, and brought her daggers up in a guard in front of her. The namahage waited, chest heaving, and watched her. Kira glanced at Haruto and he shrugged at her.

Kira looked back to the namahage and darted at it. She

threw one of her daggers at it, and immediately flicked another dagger into her hand. The namahage stepped back, swatting the dagger from the air with its club. The dagger shattered into twinkling shards and the namahage grunted in surprise, swiping at the shards with his chokuto. Then Kira was on the spirit. She stabbed one dagger into its side, but the blade caught in the straw cape. She abandoned it and kicked the namahage in the crotch. It went down on one knee, crying out, and Kira leapt and brought her other dagger down on its mask. The blade skittered off the red painted wood, and slipped to the side, biting down into the namahage's shoulder. The namahage cried out again and pushed Kira away, rolling to the side at the same time. It stood unsteadily and straightened its mask, taking a couple of steps back toward the shadows. Kira raced into the trap, charging in and thrusting with both her daggers. The namahage dropped to its knees and slashed at her stomach. Kira barely brushed aside the club with one dagger and stabbed the other down at the yokai's neck. Haruto sprung from the wall with a burst of qi infused speed and stepped into the fray. He caught the namahage's sword in one hand and Kira's wrist in the other.

"That's enough!" He pushed them apart.

Kira glared at him savagely. She was breathing hard. "You said you'd stay out of it."

The namahage scoffed. He too was panting, and blood was dripping down onto his sandals from his wounded side.

"I did," Haruto said. "Except for two things. First, I'm not sure you can win this fight, Kira. You have the strength and speed advantage. But he has you beat handily in combat skill."

"Hah!" the namahage barked.

Haruto turned toward him. "Which leads me to my next point. I don't know who you are, but you are no yokai. You can take the mask off now."

The imposter grunted and hesitated a moment, then pushed the mask up onto his head. He had a wide smirk plastered on his sweaty face and his cheeks were bright red. "How did you know?"

Haruto shrugged. "It was obvious. Namahage are near mindless spirits of ritual discipline. They don't sweat and they don't talk. They don't even grunt. My guess is Hishonima sent you here to scare off Yoshinata's workers."

The man said nothing, but his grip tightened on his sword.

Haruto turned and started back towards the exit. "Ditch the costume and sneak out when the miners return, or I'll tell the soldiers what you really are."

Kira fell in beside him, wiping her bleeding forehead with her sleeve. "You're not going to tell Lord Yoshinata the yokai was a fake?"

Haruto shook his head slowly. "Nope. Far better he thinks it was a real yokai."

"So you get paid?"

Haruto shrugged. He didn't care about the lien, not really. "You have seen the way Gushon is. Soldiers on every street, glaring at each other. It wouldn't take much to get them fighting. If Yoshinata learns the truth, that's exactly what will happen. And who do you think will suffer most? Yes, some soldiers will die, but the people of Gushon will get caught up in it, and many will be killed or wounded. Meanwhile, the two lords will sit and watch from the comfort of their compounds." He'd seen it all before so many times. Warring lords rarely cared for the people they ruined.

Haruto collected their pay from the soldiers outside the mine. Workers headed into the dark tunnel before the soldier had even counted out the lien.

It was a clear night, thousands of stars twinkling down at them from the bruised sky. Though the air was cold and the smell of smoke still hung about the city, Haruto felt oddly peaceful. Kira paced along beside him as they walked back towards the inn. She was tense, silent, pursing her lips and sighing. When they stepped up onto the porch of the inn, she finally asked.

"You really think I would have lost?"

Haruto didn't even need to consider it. "Yes. You didn't have the skill to beat him. At least, not without sacrificing yourself."

Kira drew in a deep breath, then bowed her head. "Will you train me? Please." When Haruto didn't answer, she looked up at him, her face the picture of innocence. "Please please please."

Haruto shrugged. "On one condition."

Kira shrugged back at him. "Anything."

"Stop trying to copy me. It's creepy." He pushed open the door to the inn.

Chapter 26

The night held no mysteries for Crow. She was as comfortable in the dark as she was in the light. Perhaps even more so. She was more difficult to see in the dark. It was the reason she wore a white robe. It stood out. It made people take notice. With a dark robe, she'd vanish into the night. No one would see her. She would be invisible. Forgotten. Crow did not want to be forgotten.

She drifted over the rooftops and perched on top of a sandal maker's shop next to the inn. Her little sister was in there somewhere. The onmyoji was too. Crow had been watching him from a distance. There was something strange about him, something beyond his apparent immortality. When she was close to him, her smoke shifted almost on its own. That had never happened before, and she wanted to know why. She needed to know why.

She flew across the street, landing on the roof of a noodle shop without a sound. She barely even disturbed the snow on the roof, save for painting it grey with her soot. A man on the street below looked up and startled. He saw her and whispered something to the woman next to him, and they both fled. Crow knew she should follow them and kill them before he told others. Shin would have killed them. The Master would have killed them. But what was the point? They were insignificant amongst the masses. Nobody they'd tell mattered. Only the onmyoji mattered. Besides, the man on the street had seen her. He would tell people about her. She would not be forgotten.

From her perch across the street, she peered into the front window of the tavern. It was the dead of night, mere hours before daybreak. Most everyone was asleep. As she stared through the window, she felt her smoke stir. He was in there. She extended a wisp of curling vapour across the street toward the window. It crashed against the glass and something travelled back along it. A thrill of energy. Excitement. Her smoke shifted within her robe and took on a new form. Or... was it an old form? She remembered... something, a part of who she was. She needed a mirror. She needed to see her face. Crow needed to see who she was.

Something moved in the room, and Crow wrenched her attention back to the window. The onmyoji was awake. She watched him through the glass, her smoky tentacle pushing at the window, trying to seep through a gap. Through her smoke, she saw he had such long, dark hair. Soft features made gaunt by unrest. Days of stubble peppering his chin and cheeks. And his eyes were so dark.

The onmyoji snapped his gaze toward the window. Crow pulled back her smoke, but it was too late. The onmyoji was on his feet. He pulled the window open, climbed onto the ledge, and leapt across the street towards her. Crow flew backwards, her robe rippling, smoke trailing. Could she fight him? This man who had killed Shin? This immortal hunter of her kind? Crow zipped across to the next rooftop, touching it and gliding to the far end. The onmyoji followed, leaping across the gap. His feet sank in the snow, but it didn't slow him.

"Shiki," he said, drawing his katana. A little black ball of fuzzy hair, his companion spirit, scrabbled out from inside his kimono. It rubbed at its eyes with short, hairy limbs. Then it leapt into the sword, turning the blade crimson.

Crow flew across to the next building. She had to escape, but he was so fast. She dropped to the street and zipped between buildings. She'd lose him in the alleyways. A black cat startled at her passing and hissed at her, but she was already past it and gone. She slipped through the labyrinthine alleys, counting on the maze to help her lose the onmyoji.

A clump of snow fell from the rooftop ahead of her, and she looked up. The onmyoji stood there, silhouetted by the moon. Crow slowed to a stop, then floated up onto the building next to her. The onmyoji leapt across onto the same rooftop and stopped. Crow felt her smoke stirring more energetically than before. It was reacting to him. She was reacting to him. Was it fear? She was an onryo. One of the most powerful spirits on earth. No creature save for a kami could match her. She would not let this man scare her. She forced a dozen tentacles of smoke out from below her robe. They boiled around her, ready to strike. The onmyoji just stared at her with those pitch black eyes.

"By Omoretsu's will," he said. "I name you enenra."

Crow floated backwards. No one had called her that since... she couldn't remember. Not since she'd become an onryo. They were no longer bound by the yokai names. She was not an enenra anymore. She was an onryo. She was Crow. The smoke beneath her hood shifted, and she felt a mouth forming. She could even move its lips. Fear hammered at her. She had no blood to pound through her ears, no heart to thunder in her chest. But her smoke writhed with it, and all her instincts told her to run.

No, that wouldn't work. If she ran, the onmyoji would catch her. She had no choice but to fight. She might be forced to use her full strength, regardless of how the city and its people would suffer.

Haruto hesitated. Shin had been a monster. It had taken all of them and the distraction of a dragon to finish him. If all onryo were as powerful, he might only get one chance to kill this one. The enenra were yokai of smoke. They had no true form, but they gathered around a core, and that would likely be at the heart of its robe. If he pierced that core with Shiki, it should kill the enenra.

He dashed across the rooftop and swept Shiki upwards at the smoke-filled robe. The enenra drifted away from the strike, and shot two tentacles of smoke at him. He ducked the first, and brought Shiki down on the second, slashing through the smoke, severing its connection to the yokai. The enenra recoiled, floating back and holding up the severed tentacle before her hood. That was something, at least. He could cut parts of the yokai away. More smoke gathered, forming a new limb in place of the severed one. He needed to keep up the pressure, slice off bits of the yokai faster than it regenerated.

He followed the yokai across the rooftop, swinging Shiki in a blur of red steel, slicing off tendrils as they reached for him. The enenra hissed and drifted backwards to edge of the roof, then breezed across to the next one. Haruto followed, leaping the gap and landing beside the yokai. His feet slipped in the snow, and he fell to one knee just as a spear of smoke passed over his head, missing by a hair's breadth. He pushed off his back foot and unleashed an upward slice to cut the yokai in half, but the enenra hissed at him and soared away, sacrificing wisps of smoke to his blade, trying unsuccessfully to get around his defence.

The yokai flew across to the adjacent rooftop, and Haruto leapt after it. He landed in a crouch and darted inside its writhing tangle of smoke, slashed Shiki across its midsection. The red blade cut through smoke and robe, opening a gash in the fabric. Smoke billowed out. The yokai cried out and backed away. Haruto's leg collapsed beneath him. A smoky blade had pierced his thigh like a spear. He cut it away and the smoke drifted apart. The wounded flesh of his leg began knitting itself back together.

The enenra retreated to the far end of the rooftop. Dark smoke billowed around it, staining the snow a greasy grey. But its white robe wasn't stained. The smoke did not cling to it but was contained by it. Haruto smiled as he stood, testing his weight on his injured leg. "The robe's your core, isn't it?" he said. "I thought it would be something inside you, something in the smoke, but it's the robe. Without it, you're nothing."

"What are you?" the enenra asked. It was a woman's voice. Familiar. Smoke writhed around her, and the robe rose on a nest of thrashing serpents. Haruto glimpsed a smoky chin and lips in the darkness of the hood.

The enenra shrieked and thrust out a dozen spears. Haruto dashed forward as fast as he could. He felt the tentacles close in around him, gashing his arms and legs, but he was inside her guard. He stabbed Shiki into the enenra's hood.

The smoke stopped moving. A dozen bladed tentacles, all

pointed at him like sharpened steel waiting to strike. The enenra leaned away from Shiki's blade. Her hood tore open and fell away. Haruto stared at the past.

"Izumi?" he said. He straightened up to look at her. Her face was written in smoke, but it was still her. It was Izumi. Her eyes darted about, panicked; her mouth moved but made no sound. A curl of smoky hair fell against her forehead.

The tentacles stabbed into Haruto, piercing his chest and lungs. He twitched and writhed, unable to make sense of all the pain. Then the smoke tore him in half and threw him from the rooftop.

Haruto landed on snow. At least his torso did. He wasn't sure where his legs were. He stared up at the rooftop, the enenra staring down at him, silhouetted by the moon. Izumi staring down at the ruin she had made of him.

"If you wish to stop us, onmyoji," she said, her voice cold and distant as the stars, "come to the imperial city." Then she was gone, a wisp of smoke trailing behind her.

Shiki popped out of the sword and into the little black ball of fuzz. She squeaked and nuzzled Haruto's neck, wrapping her little arms around his chin. He couldn't feel her. He was so cold. The pain was distant, his body too wrecked to feel it.

"That--" Haruto coughed blood over his chin "--did not go well."

Chapter 27

Guang poured himself a cup of tea and let it steam as he considered the blank page before him. His brush was inked and poised. Now all he needed were words.

"*All over mountains deep. The sky sheds tears of fire. No hope but that is lost. The returned will reap their war.*" He tugged at his scraggle of beard and put the brush down without writing a word. Then he picked up his cup and blew the steam from the surface of his tea. "It's missing something... everything, really." He was alone in the common room save for the owner busying himself near the kitchen. The peace put Guang in a literary mood.

A screen door at the other end of the inn slid open and Yanmei and Kira walked into the common room, looking refreshed and clean. No doubt they had taken the opportunity to experience the inn's baths. Guang scratched at an itch over his shoulder and considered perhaps he should do the same. The two women spotted him, and Kira broke into a grin. She ran over to the table while Yanmei followed at a sedate walk. Despite the early hour, and that they must have been up for a while already, they both looked well rested. Then again, Kira was still young. She probably never knew real exhaustion.

"That's a very empty page," Yanmei said, lowering herself to sit next to him. She took the teapot and poured two more steaming cups.

"I'm trying to pen an epic poem about the return of dragons."

"In invisible ink?"

"Mhm." Guang nodded. "Still in the planning stages. *Through stone and fire, the serpent erupts*." He frowned. Starting was always the hardest part.

Kira grinned at him. She was wearing new clothes, forgoing her previous kimono for thick brown travelling trousers and a winter coat with a fur-lined hood. She almost looked like a young version of Yanmei. Guang was about to comment when the inn owner appeared behind him. He turned to ask for some food, but there was no one there. When he turned back, he found Kira giggling, a mirrored dagger in hand.

"Well, at least you didn't scare me this time." Guang smiled at the girl. "That was your most convincing yet. I didn't even know I'd looked in the reflection until I saw there was no one behind me."

"I'm getting better," Kira said. "Before, I could only make shadowy monsters, forms without real... uh... form. But I'm realising that's only the beginning."

"You should have applied yourself better at Heiwa," Yanmei said. "Think of all the Sage could have taught you."

Kira groaned. "Heiwa was so boring. But Guang could teach me." She grinned, her eyes twinkling.

"What?" Guang startled and almost dropped his cup of tea.

"Haruto said you were a qi master. He said my daggers are brittle, and you might teach me to strengthen them."

"Cabbage!" Guang swore. "The old man should keep stuff to himself."

"Can you then?" Kira asked. "Teach me?" She seemed so earnest and eager to learn.

Guang glanced at Yanmei. She was sipping her tea despite the steam still rising from it. She caught his eye and nodded.

"Alright," Guang said, grateful to having a reason to put down his brush. Failure was always much easier with a good excuse. "We'll start slow. Those daggers of yours are formed from your qi, correct?"

"Uh-huh!" Kira nodded.

"Hand me one. Hilt first, please."

Kira flicked her wrist, and a dagger appeared in her hand. She spun it around and held it out to him, a smile tugging at her lips. Guang took it cautiously, half expecting it to explode into a thousand mirrored shards as soon as he touched it. When it didn't, he placed it on the table, out of Kira's reach.

"Now, can you still feel it?"

"Huh?" Kira said. "Feel it? No. It's over by you."

Yanmei laughed, but Kira only frowned.

"I don't mean with your hands, girl," Guang said. "Carrots. Save me from the ignorance of youth. You made the dagger with your qi. It is a part of you and remains so even when you aren't holding it. No matter where it or you might be, as long as it exists, a thread of qi will connect it to you." Kira looked about. "Not a real thread. Radish, girl, you can't see it."

"Then how am I supposed to feel it?"

"With your... spirit," Guang said, throwing up his hands. "With your qi."

"I have to feel for my qi with my qi?"

"Yes."

"What if I can't feel my qi?"

Guang groaned and looked at Yanmei.

The old woman nodded back at him. "She's always been this way. Only the Sage had enough patience to teach her techniques and even he said she tested his limits."

Kira sulked. "He told me I was a natural."

Yanmei smiled. "He was also a firm believer that children learned better through praise than criticism. The carrot rath--"

Kira sniggered and looked at Guang. He grinned and winked back.

Yanmei sighed. "Carrot is not a swear, Kira. You are very gifted, but just like now you have never had the ability to focus. Stop trying to do what you think Guang wants. Instead, try to learn what he is teaching you."

Kira frowned, groaned, and rested her head on the table. After a few seconds, she sat bolt upright, slapped her face with both hands and nodded. "Feel the qi?"

"It's inside of you," Guang said. "Always inside of you. Some people feel it as a raging fire, others as an icy stream. Some people feel it as well dug deep inside themselves, and others as inconsistent wind. No one else can tell you how it should feel. You have to find it inside yourself, a source of power unique to you. Once you have that, follow the thread that leads to the dagger."

Kira frowned and scrunched her face. Guang guessed she was looking inside herself, but she just looked constipated. He left her to it and picked up his brush once more, determined to start his epic.

"*Of all things lost*," he said, "*there are some that should stay... lost*?" He shook his head and groaned.

The door to the inn opened and a blast of cold air blew in. The owner of the tavern looked up from cleaning a table and gasped. Haruto stood in the doorway, his kimono a torn and bloody mess, the top half missing, the bottom half hanging around his legs and so soaked in blood it looked a filthy purple. His chest and waist were bloodstained too, and his skin was the pale of curdled milk. He trembled as he staggered over to them. Shiki popped onto the table and gave a low, wavering squeak. Guang couldn't understand what the spirit was saying, but it didn't sound like 'good morning'.

Yanmei jumped to her feet, wincing at some pain, and helped Haruto. "Are you alright?"

Haruto attempted to shrug, but he was trembling so violently it looked like he was having a fit. "I'm fine. I just need some rest and... is that tea?"

As Yanmei helped Haruto sit at the table, Guang poured a fresh cup of tea and waved to the owner for more. "You look like you lost a fight with the Dire Bear, old man."

Haruto cracked a half smile, but it was swept away by the twinge of pain that crossed his face. "If only. Yaurong isn't as tough as the stories make out. Not since he lost his paw, anyway." He sipped at the tea and took a moment to close his eyes and relax a little. He was pale from blood loss and seemed to be in a lot of pain. But his immortality kept him alive through wounds that would kill anyone else.

"I've got it!" Kira shouted. "I can feel it."

"Already?" Guang asked. It was far faster than he expected. Most people took weeks of meditation and training to feel their qi.

The girl nodded eagerly, grinning and running a hand through her messy mop of hair.

"Well," Guang said. "What does it feel like?"

"Like a song humming through me. Many voices and melodies coming together to create wonderful music."

"Huh," Guang grunted. "Well, that's a first. Now try to feel for the thread connecting you to the dagger." He gave the dagger a spin on the table and turned his attention back to Haruto. "What happened?"

"I found her." Haruto opened his eyes and stared at him. "Or she found me." He shook his head. "I found Izumi."

"Melon!"

Haruto flashed him a tired smile. "That's not a vegetable."

"Izumi? You're sure? And she did that to you?"

Haruto nodded. "Tore me in half. It took a few hours to put myself back together." He laughed, but it was more of a wheeze. "I think I scared the town physician into early retirement." What little smile he'd been able to force faded then. "She's one of the onryo."

Guang felt a tightness in his chest as he considered the possibility. "Not the jorogumo."

Haruto shook his head. "No. An enenra." They both fell silent. Guang heard Kira humming a tune under her breath. The girl was so bent on her task, she seemed oblivious to everything else.

"Who's Izumi?" Yanmei asked.

Haruto held up his hands and looked at Guang, but Guang shook his head and grumbled, "Oh no. This is *your* tale to tell. I'm staying out of it."

Haruto glared at him a moment, then turned his attention to Yanmei. "Izumi is my wife. Was my wife, I guess."

Guang felt a tap on his wrist and found Kira smiling at him. "I can feel the thread," she whispered.

"Really?" Guang shook his head. The girl really was a natural. Either that or she was lying. "Next step is to tell it to stop being. Or in your case, tell it to shatter."

Kira stared hard at the dagger. "Shatter!" she hissed.

Guang sighed. "Not like that. It's dagger – it can't hear you. Just tell it to shatter."

"How?"

"Through the thread."

"That doesn't make any sense."

Guang grinned. "Failing already? And I thought you were supposed to be good at this."

She stuck her tongue out at him and went back to staring at the dagger.

"You remember the story about Nightsong?" Haruto continued, recapturing Yanmei's attention. "Well, my story doesn't end there. I told you that Toshinaka couldn't let it go. He believed I had slighted him somehow." Haruto scoffed. "He was a monster. While I was recovering in the imperial palace, he went to my home and set fire to it. My wife, Izumi, was still inside as it burned. She tried to hide from it, crawled into the only stone part of the building, the bathhouse." He sighed and shook his head. "When they got the fire under control, they found her dead, huddled in the corner of the bathhouse, suffocated from the smoke." Tears rolled down Haruto's cheeks. Guang reached out and gave his friend's hand a squeeze.

"You'd think I'd be used to the pain by now, wouldn't you?" Haruto said. Then he leaned forward and buried his head in his hands. Guang decided to take over after all.

After his brutal defeat at the hands of Toshinaka, Nightsong was borne home on the emperor's own palanquin. He was exhausted, injured and barely able to stand. What he returned to took the last of the fight out of him. His home was a charred ruin. His wife was dead. Though the fires had not reached her, the smoke had. She died painfully, terrified and alone. I know it is not pleasant to hear, but you need to know what happened to her to understand what happened later.

Nightsong's status as Ipia's greatest warrior was dashed. The favour of the emperor and his court vanished like mist in sunshine. Izumi was the emperor's cousin, and the emperor blamed Nightsong for her death, claiming he should have been strong enough to stop it. And Nightsong blamed himself, though it was Toshinaka's hand that lit the torch. Nightsong agreed with the emperor. If he had only understood Toshinaka's hatred better, perhaps he might have prevented it. He could not fathom that Toshinaka's ill will was born of mere jealousy and not of any slight Nightsong had visited upon him.

For years, Nightsong wallowed in depression. He took no oaths and neglected those he already had. The shintei disavowed him, and his name became a parable for all those who might rest on their laurels. The order never again wanted anyone to follow in his footsteps. He wandered Ipia from tavern to tavern, drinking his life away. Once he had been a hero, unable to walk down a street without turning heads. People had flocked to him, begging for his favour and believing just the sight of him was good luck. His celebrity was unprecedented, and also unrivalled until the Century Blade's rise to fame a hundred years later. But all that was gone. Almost no one recognised him, and any who did looked the other way, unwilling to risk his ill luck rubbing off on them. Nightsong sold everything of value to him. His jewellery, his shoes, his pipe. He even sold his sword, completing his disgrace, for there is no more valuable possession to a shintei than their sword. He had nothing to hold on to and nowhere to go but the grave.

Then one day an opportunity presented itself. He wandered into a tavern and demanded a drink only to realise he had nothing but the clothes on his back, and even they were but filthy rags most beggars would forgo. The tavern owner offered him a way out of his debt. The village had a ghost, a creature haunting a few ruined buildings that had burned down after a lightning strike a few moons back. Several villagers had died. Now, the workers couldn't get close to clear the ruins out. Every time they tried, the ghost would appear in a flurry of screams and soot. One worker had already been dragged into the ruins by the ghost and never seen again. Of course Nightsong knew he would have no chance against a yokai, but he was past caring. A part of him hoped the spirit would end his suffering. He longed for rest. For peace. For an end to his torment.

He entered the ruins and searched for the ghost. It did not take long to find. The spirit rose from the rubble in a flurry of ash and soot. A malformed thing of smoke bubbling like tar, faces formed in its smoky mass, screamed, then were dashed away to be replaced. Its wail promised pain and death, and Nightsong stepped into its fatal embrace. But the yokai withdrew from him, and in that moment, Nightsong recognised the ghost, recognised the face that bubbled up and stared at him. It was Izumi, his wife. Her features were warped into a misshapen monster and written in smoke, but it was her.

Nightsong collapsed to his knees amidst the cold ashes. Now his fall was complete. His wife was dead and reborn a vengeful spirit seeking only the death of others. It was in that moment of utter defeat and anguish that Nightsong found a new purpose. Not revenge for all Toshinaka had taken from him. Not atonement for the ills he had done. Not restitution of all he had lost. The new purpose he found was to save his wife from eternal torment. The yokai fled him. Perhaps it was the last vestige of the humanity she had once known.

Nightsong left that village with a new resolve. He would find the legendary onmyoji and learn their techniques, for only they knew how to put yokai to rest. Then, he had to find his wife once more and give her the peace Toshinaka had so cruelly taken from her.

But the ways of the onmyoji are...

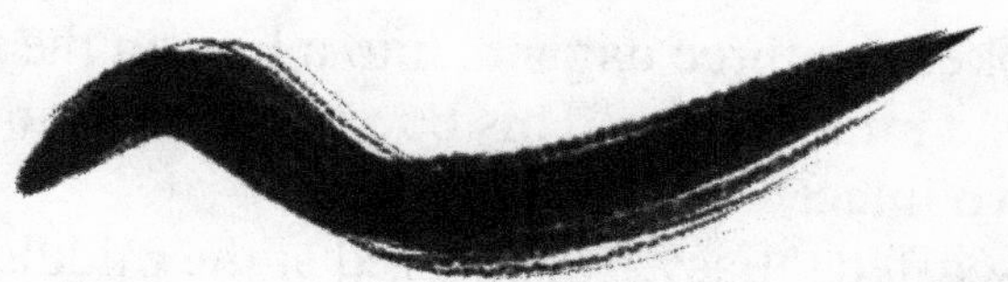

"That's enough," Haruto snapped, his head still in his hands.

Guang stopped. It was a shame, he was just getting to the good part, but he understood why Haruto wouldn't want it told.

"I'm sorry," Yanmei said. She reached out and gripped Haruto's wrist. Such a slight contact, but it brought a smile to his face, albeit a sad one. "We live in a world of people passing their pain to others. It shouldn't be that way."

The dagger in front of Guang shattered, showering him with glass. He shifted away from the cascading shards, but they faded to nothing. Kira giggled and clapped her hands in excitement. Then she glanced at Haruto and the smile vanished. "Sorry."

Haruto shook his head. "No. A two-hundred-year-old grievance should not take precedent over the joy of the moment. Well done... I think?"

Kira nodded eagerly. Guang suspected the Fifth Sage Under Heaven didn't know how right he was about the girl. When she focused, she progressed at a remarkable rate. Still, if she wanted to learn how to control her qi and techniques, she was only at the beginning, though it was a promising start.

"Now create three daggers," Guang said. She flicked her wrists and handed him the daggers, smiling as he took them.

"Are you holding weapons, Guang?" Haruto asked.

Guang dropped the daggers on the table. "Cabbage!" Heart pounding, he pulled his satchel open and fished inside for his first vow, pulled it out and unrolled the scroll, desperate to see if it was still intact. It was, still signed in blood and qi and witnessed by a god. Guang rolled the scroll up, hugged it against his chest, then slid it into his satchel. Then he poked one of the glass daggers with a trembling finger. "Well, isn't that a queer thing?" He didn't like the idea of touching them. It felt like cheating on his vow.

He poked the three daggers into a line on the table and pointed at the middle one. "This one. Shatter this one, but leave the other two intact."

Kira scoffed. "Easy." She stared at the middle dagger and all three of them shattered, again showering Guang in glass that disappeared before it hit him.

"Three more daggers and try again," Guang said. Kira created three more daggers and tried to hand them to him. He stared at them like they were hissing snakes and then gestured for her to place them on the table. He wasn't sure why he could touch the weapons, but he was certain he didn't want to. His apprehension went deeper than his vows. They were only a representation of his commitment. He chose never to hold a weapon again because he chose to be a better person than he was. "This time the left one only." He turned his attention back to Haruto. "You're certain it was her? Izumi?"

Haruto glanced at him out of the corner of his eye and nodded. "I remember my wife, Guang."

"It's been a couple of hundred years, old man."

"It was her," Haruto said and sighed, lowering his head into his hands again. "Maybe she didn't recognise me."

"Maybe she did?" Guang said.

Haruto seemed to think about that for a moment, then he nodded sadly.

They were all silent for a while, except Kira, who was humming to herself.

"She told me to find her in the imperial city if I want to stop the onryo," Haruto said.

"Pah!" Guang grunted. "That's a trap."

"Yup," Haruto said, raising his head to stare him.

"You're going to walk right into it, aren't you?"

"Yup."

"Doesn't seem like a smart move to me."

Haruto shrugged. "It's Izumi. I have to go. I have to..." He paused for a moment. "You wouldn't have left Tian as a spirit, mindlessly bent on vengeance."

"She isn't a mindless spirit," Kira said, staring at the daggers, brows furrowed in intense concentration. "You said she's an onryo now." She glanced at Haruto. "She's not mindless."

"I didn't mean it like that," Haruto said.

"Then you shouldn't have said it like that."

They fell into an awkward silence, and Guang poured himself another cup of tea.

At last Haruto said, "I'm still going. Trap or not. The onryo must be stopped before they find and free Orochi. This is the best chance we have of finding them. Maybe I can talk to her and convince her to give up. Or..." He paused and looked around at them and shook his head. "It's Izumi. I have to try."

"Alright then," Guang said, forcing some cheer into his voice. "The Imperial City of Kodachi it is. It's what, two weeks away? Let's try not to get involved in politics while we're there. I hear the empress is as welcoming as a dagger up the onion."

All three daggers shattered, glass shards spilling across the table before fading from existence. "Cabbage!" Kira cursed.

Chapter 28

They left Gushon the next morning and ventured north towards Kodachi. The road was long, but it was mostly downhill. With the mountains at their backs, they hiked down into the valleys of Ipia, where the trees still grew green despite the harsh winter. The snow became rare and rarer still until it was nothing but a memory stirred by the white-capped peaks in the distance. Kira marvelled at the change and even took off her fur coat to enjoy the warmth.

Heiwa had been her entire life. All she had ever known were frigid places, blanketed in snow all year round. To see the world beyond the mountains and ice was a wonder. She had never known so many colours existed in nature. Emerald trees and ruby flowers, azure lakes and fields of yellow that Yanmei told her were hakusai. A riot of iridescence that took her breath away.

The people they passed on the road, and there were many, were friendly, and they spent many an evening in the company of others and even in their homes. Haruto proved himself to be quite the cook, making wonderful meals out of few ingredients. And Guang was a gifted storyteller who never failed to capture the attention of their temporary companions. Kira tried to entertain people with tricks, illusions seen in reflections. They were not so welcome, and more than once Yanmei criticised her for scaring people, which Kira didn't understand. They were pleased enough to listen to Guang's ghost stories, some of which were terrifying. But the moment she wove an illusion to give them a fright, they panicked and screamed. People made so little sense.

Her training continued. In the mornings, before Guang and Yanmei rose from their pallets, Haruto took Kira aside and trained her to fight.

"You already know the basics, that much is obvious," he said one morning after a brief sparring session in which Kira became intimately acquainted with the stony ground. "But you only know the one way to fight, and it doesn't utilise your strengths. You know what innate techniques are?"

They were standing in a small grassy clearing to the side of the road. Mountains rose to the east, and to the west was nothing but endless fields of snow-dusted earth. "Everyone who can access their qi can strengthen their body and bolster their speed through innate techniques," Kira said. It was one of the few things she remembered from classes at Heiwa, one of the few times she had paid attention to what the teachers were saying. "From the peasant pulling a cart to the warrior fighting off a hundred soldiers on the battlefield. But I've never been good at it."

Haruto laughed at that. "You are both right and wrong. Would it surprise you to know you are stronger than me?"

Kira shook her head. "But whenever we fight, you push me away."

"Because I use innate technique in bursts."

Kira gasped. It seemed obvious now. "That's how you move so fast!"

Haruto nodded, smiling. Shiki, sitting on his shoulder, slapped a hairy little arm to her face and squeaked. "What do you mean you didn't know?" he asked the spirit.

Shiki whistled and stuck her tongue out at him.

Haruto shook his head and turned back to Kira. "You may not know how to use innate technique in bursts, but you are using it, Kira. All the time. Try turning it off."

"I... um..." She concentrated, but it was like focusing on just one dagger. She didn't understand how. "I can't?"

"Exactly!" Haruto said. "You are using it all the time. It makes you that bit stronger and faster all the time. And it is strengthening your qi all the time."

"Huh?"

Haruto sank down onto the grass and motioned for Kira to sit next to him. Shiki jumped into her lap and curled up. "Think of qi as a well," Haruto said.

"Guang said that some people see it as a well, but everyone sees their qi differently. Mine is more like a song."

"For this example, it's a well. It is only so deep and can only contain so much water. Whenever you use it, you are taking water out of the well and draining it. Given time, it will refill. But every time you use your qi, you are also digging the well a little deeper, which allows it to hold more water. You, Kira, never stop using your qi and never stop digging the well. It has given you extraordinary reserves." He shook his head. "I've only ever met one person who had as deep a well as you, and he was a giant of a man who never stopped eating." He shrugged. "Or talking about himself."

Shiki whistled.

"Yes," Haruto said. "He did try to eat you once."

Kira stared at her hands. She didn't feel particularly strong or fast. She just felt... normal. "So I need to learn to use it in bursts instead?"

Haruto shook his head. "Not instead. As well. Once you've got that figured out, I can teach you how to fight."

"You said I already know the basics."

"And if all you want to do is knock a few heads in a tavern brawl, the basics are fine. You only know how to fight as if your opponent is stronger than you. That's fine when you come up against a monster like Shin. His raw strength outmatched us all. But when you fight a weaker opponent, like me, you need to know how to capitalise on your greater strength. A large part of combat is figuring out what your opponent is capable of and using the style best suited to countering it."

For two hours each morning, Haruto trained Kira both to use innate technique and to fight. More often than not, she found herself tired and sore before the others even rose from sleep. The training didn't seem to bother Haruto at all though, and Kira had to admit she hadn't seen him sleep. He always looked tired, dark bags pillowing his eyes like distant storm clouds. But there was nothing she could do to help him.

During the days they walked north and west towards the imperial city. Guang spent the time teaching her to better understand the techniques she already knew. Kira had still not been able to isolate only one mirrored dagger. The threads connecting her to them were there like melodies she could almost hear, strings of a koto plucked and left to resonate. One of the little games Guang played was taking a dagger and hiding it on his person somewhere. Kira then had to follow the thread and say where he had secreted it away. Then he hid two, and she had to find both. Then he hid three, and she had to find a specific dagger. Every new type of training was a game, and Kira loved playing them. At Heiwa, all of her learning had been dry and boring. Hours spent in a class room while Aknar Sensei lectured at them about history or politics, or Kang Sensei about technique theory. Days wasted running laps around the academy grounds or standing on one leg in a blizzard. It had all been so dull. Except for the combat training.

Up until a few years ago, Yanmei had taught most of the combat training at Heiwa. She was tall and strong, indomitable and full of energy. Then she began tiring quickly, unable to keep up with some of the older students. She handed over the duty to Kang Sensei. He was a hard taskmaster, running all the students through hour after hour of kata before letting them get to the real fun: sparring. Kira loved sparring. It felt like freedom; the rest of her time at Heiwa was a structured prison.

Unfortunately, Kang Sensei didn't like her and made no attempts to hide it. When she lost, he called her sloppy and undisciplined. When she won, he accused her of using her yokai techniques to cheat. Kang chose the matches, and for the last year he only pitted her against Gyatso. Even without technique or qi, the Cochtan boy was a terror of fists, feet, and agonising holds. No one had ever beaten Gyatso, and most never even landed a hit on him. Kira counted herself among that number despite many painful attempts.

She had gone to Gyatso once after one of the many beatings he'd given her. She asked him to help her, to teach her to fight like he did. She thought they should have kinship of a sort. Like her, Gyatso was an outcast at Heiwa, a Cochtan in Ipia. He had no techniques, no qi, and the other students shunned him, though out of fear rather than disgust. He refused her. Not because she was a yokai, but because she was weak and he stood to gain nothing from training with someone weaker than himself.

Kira wondered if Gyatso had survived Heiwa's destruction, if any of the others made it out. She hoped so. Even though most of them avoided her as though they might catch the yokai from her, she hoped they had survived, but it seemed unlikely.

As fun as the games Guang taught her were, he had yet to tell her how to strengthen her daggers so they were less brittle and able to withstand an attack. It was frustrating, but more so because she couldn't get the hang of it. At first she had thought it would be easy, shattering her daggers was as simple as a thought now. But isolating them was a different matter altogether.

"You're thinking about it all wrong, girl," Guang said one morning as they walked. They were passing through a small town, keeping to the side of the road so carts could pass them unhindered. A man leading a tired old buffalo took off his sugegase and grinned at them, showing an enormous gap in his teeth where one had fallen out. Kira smiled back at him, and Guang poked her in the ribs. "And it's causing you to get all muddled up there." He poked the same finger at Kira's head, and she considered biting it off. She'd already created so many daggers that day, she'd lost count. Isolating them when Guang hid them was impossible. Though she had made them all shatter once. He had hidden one of them down his trousers, and he danced around like a ningyo with its strings yanked when it shattered. But Yanmei had scolded her for the prank.

"Please, explain it to me, oh wise qi master," Kira said as she dodged the finger she had decided not to bite.

"Hmph," Guang said loftily. "With that attitude, I don't think I will. Figure it out yourself."

That was what Kira had been trying to do for days, but it wasn't working. She sighed and hurried to catch up with Guang, stopping in front of him and dropping into a low, polite bow. "I'm sorry. Please help me."

The old qi master smiled at her. "You're thinking of all your daggers as one. The same thing. Think of it like this tiny village here of, um... I have no idea what they call this place. Hey, old man, what is this village called?"

"Uhhhh..." Haruto finished with a shrug.

"Very helpful," Guang said.

Kira was about ready to kick both of them if Guang didn't get to the point soon.

"Well, think about this tiny village of Uhhhh," he said. "What if I asked you to find a specific person here in Uhhhh?"

Kira shrugged, but somehow failed to do it like Haruto again. She wondered if her back was hunched enough. "Which person?"

"A specific person."

"Who?"

"One of the villagers of Uhhhh."

Kira screwed her eyes shut and forced herself to breathe to stop from screaming.

Guang chuckled. "Alright. You can't do it. But what if I asked you to find Sora, a young Ipian woman wearing a dark brown kimono and carrying a basket of washing?"

Kira looked around as they walked and found the woman Guang was looking for. "Sora!" she said, pointing. She ran over and grabbed Sora by the arm. The woman squeaked in alarm.

Guang hurried over and pulled Kira off the woman. Then he bowed and apologised for the mix up. The woman rushed away, glancing back at them and grimacing.

"Was that not Sora?" Kira asked.

Guang sighed and started walking again, a few steps behind Haruto and Yanmei. "I don't think that was her name, no. But that's not really the point. When I asked you to find a person, you couldn't. But when I asked you to find a woman in a brown kimono, carrying a basket, you found her right away. Your daggers are the same."

"Ohhhh." Kira nodded. "I can't pick out a specific dagger because they're all the same. They're identical. So if I make each one different, I'll be able to tell them apart?"

"It's a start," Guang said. "Make them different, give them names, whatever works. Until your perception of them grows stronger, you need to use a crutch to tell them apart."

He was right, as insufferable as that was. After that lesson, Kira made each dagger distinct. She also named them all, but Guang didn't need to know that. When Guang told her to shatter the middle dagger, she would know he meant Momo. It was a simple thing to follow Momo's specific thread and give a command only to her. Kira still wasn't sure how being able to isolate her daggers would help her strengthen them, but at least she felt like she was making some progress.

In the evenings, most of Kira's time was spent learning the new technique from Yanmei, one an old friend of hers had mastered and tried to teach her. Progress was slow, even slower than it was with Haruto and Guang. Kira suspected this was because Yanmei herself did not understand the technique. She had never used it, though she admitted she had tried many times. Yanmei claimed it was important that Kira have a new technique with which to defend herself, but Kira sensed there was more to it than that, something special about the technique itself and about passing it on. It didn't matter. Kira was just happy to spend time with Yanmei.

Yanmei had always been there for her. From the moment Kira first awoke on a field scorched black by her technique. Kira's memories of her eighty years in the mirror faded quickly, but she knew she was a yokai. And she knew that for her to be alive again, someone else must have died. A life for a life. Yanmei claimed it was a bad person, an assassin sent to kill a friend, but it didn't matter. Kira always knew her life belonged to someone else. Never really hers, just something she had stolen. Yanmei had taken Kira to Heiwa, kept them warm on the road with her technique. She listened to Kira's unabashed wonder at exploring the world outside the confines of her mirror. Yanmei had been comfort and home and safety all rolled into one. She had always been those things to Kira.

Even at Heiwa, surrounded by other students, Yanmei had always been the constant in Kira's life whenever she needed a hug or a shoulder to cry on. If Kira took things too far, Yanmei stopped her before someone got hurt. Being a good person was hard for anyone, it required tough choices. Kira often couldn't see the good path, but it was always clear to Yanmei. She was Kira's guiding light.

Kira couldn't remember what it was like to have a mother, but some other students at Heiwa said a mother was comforting yet strict, loving and encouraging, always there and always on your side. As far as Kira was concerned, that described Yanmei perfectly. Kira had never said it, not to Yanmei or to anyone, but in private and in her own mind, Kira thought of Yanmei as her mother.

"Choose a point," Yanmei said. They were standing at the foot of a small hillock, an area already cleared for a campfire just off the road. They'd chosen to stop there because the little hill cut the frigid breeze and drifting snow.

"There," Yanmei continued, pointing to a lone tree, stripped of leaves but stubbornly clinging to the hillock regardless of winter. "Extend a thread of qi toward it, then pour yourself through the thread and step into the new space." She frowned at her own explanation, as though it didn't quite sound right.

Kira tried. She wasn't sure how to extend a thread of qi, nor how to pour herself into it, but she tried. "And I should just vanish and appear by the tree?"

Yanmei looked melancholic. "My friend used to leave an image of himself behind somehow. It blew away like petals on a breeze." She smiled, but it was the kind of smile that made Kira less happy instead of more.

"That's pretty," Kira said. She liked the idea of petals scattering on a breeze, all soft edges and gentle curves. She was all hard edges, jagged lines. Shattered mirrors.

Yanmei smiled a little better this time and nodded. "It was."

They continued for hours, long past nightfall, until the tree was only visible in the muted hues of moonlight. Kira could not fathom how to *step through the world*, but she kept trying. She needed to learn the technique. Not to protect herself, but to protect Yanmei. Her fiery technique was hurting her. The Sage had said it had already cut twenty years from Yanmei's life, but she kept using it. She used it to protect Kira. Yanmei wouldn't stop hurting herself to protect her. Kira had to learn this new technique to protect Yanmei, so Yanmei wouldn't hurt herself anymore. And maybe eventually, they'd find the Fourth Sage and beg for help. Perhaps the Sage might know how to reverse the damage Yanmei had already done.

But it was another night of failure. Kira blamed herself. Despite the failure, she crawled onto her pallet that night feeling a new determination. Yes, she had failed to learn the technique. But she was committed, had purpose. They were almost at Kodachi, where they would find the onryo, Haruto's wife, and stop the plan to free Orochi. Then Kira would drag Yanmei to the Fourth Sage, whether she liked it or not.

Chapter 29

Kira had thought Minazuri was big. She had thought Gushon was huge. When Kodachi erupted into view, dominating the horizon, she realised just how wrong she had been. The imperial city was a sprawling behemoth. There were people everywhere, even before they hit the city limits. Some were carting goods, others on their way to local farms to work the fields. Here and there, a few soldiers in lacquered ceramic armour lounged about watching people pass. Their armour was a deep green with red trim and had a coiled dragon upon the breastplate. Guang leaned in when he saw Kira staring and told her they were the Emerald Legion, Empress Ise Ryoko's standing army. Given that Ipia was a in a state of civil war with the two branches of the imperial family vying for control over the entire empire, there was no road or avenue into the city that wasn't heavily guarded.

The smoke of industry rose from the city from a thousand chimneys, its stench wafting out to greet them even as the first of the buildings clawed its way from the dirt. Kira had no names for half the fragrances that assaulted her nose, but between cooking food, coal-fed fires, tanning leathers, and human and animal waste, it made the destruction of Heiwa smell like a florist. Kira hadn't realised so many people could exist in one place. They packed the roads, shuffling to and fro. Some bumped into others as they pushed their carts, while others threaded through the masses with amazing agility. She watched them all wide-eyed and unblinking.

There were roadside attractions too. Carts where men and women cooked food to serve to passersby, stalls selling artifacts the hawker claimed were infused with the qi of heroes. Kira stopped to peruse one of the stalls, wondering at the assortment of trinkets on display. Yanmei pulled her away and warned her not to stop. It was far too easy to get lost amidst the crowded streets.

The clamour of cart wheels, bellowing vendors, snorting pigs, and pounding feet was deafening and exciting; it battered Kira's senses. They passed through a bustling market with stalls crammed one against the other and men and women shouting over each other to advertise their wares.

"Fresh ramen, hot off the stove," shouted a woman with chubby red cheeks and a sizzling pan in hand.

A giant of a man with a neck like an overfilled barrel shouted, "Spices, spices. Rare and exotic. Hosan, Nash, and beyond."

A thin man with a hooked nose stood behind a cart, waving clay bottles at passersby. "We at Tsin Xao's House of Refreshment offer only the highest quality wines."

"Come try your mind at this game of wits. Prove you're smarter than the monkey." Kira turned her head. She had never seen a monkey before. She threaded through the crowd until she found a little table and a smiling old man with wispy hair and a single gold tooth standing out amidst the yellow ones. In his lap sat a little brown, furry beast with long limbs, a head that seemed too large for its body, and a curling tail that never stopped twisting, turning, winding, and waving. It made small chattering noises as though it were always talking although in a language only it understood. On the table was an array of mah-jongg tiles. A wiry man with horseshoe of black hair sat down in front of the old man and his monkey and slapped a couple of lien on the table.

"Mix them up. Mix them up," the old vendor said while the monkey chattered along. "Keep them face down. That's right, give them a real mix. Don't let the monkey keep track."

Kira realised Guang was standing at her side. The old poet leaned in and lowered his voice. "Never trust these games, girl. For two reasons. First, the monkey will always win."

The man with the horseshoe hair nodded. He was finished mixing up the tiles.

"Now then," said the man with the monkey. "Think of a

pair. Any pair of tiles. Tell the monkey which pair to find. If he fails, you get double the lien you put in."

The man with the horseshoe hair laughed. "White Lotus."

"White Lotus, it is. White Lotus," the man said. "Monkey, find me the White Lotus tiles."

The monkey chattered and craned its head around to look up at its owner.

"Go on then," the man said. The monkey chattered. "No, don't look at me. Find me the White Lotus tiles." The monkey chattered again. "White. Lotus. *Whiiiite. Looootus*."

"Quite the show, isn't it," Guang whispered. His hand shot out, and he caught a young boy by the wrist. Kira realised the boy had been reaching towards Guang's pack. "Nothing for you here, lad. Keep on moving and I'll keep on saying nothing to the guard." The boy pulled his wrist free and scurried away into the crowd.

Guang leaned in again. "The second reason is that it's not really about the game at all."

The man was still talking to his monkey, trying to get the little beast to pick some tiles.

"If he doesn't pick, do I win?" asked the man with the horseshoe hair.

The monkey twisted about to stare at the tiles and grabbed two quick as a flash. Then he held them up triumphantly above his head and cavorted about in his owner's lap.

"White Lotus, it is. White Lotus. There you have it." The owner pocketed the lien while the monkey clapped the tiles together, grinning like a toad.

It was far from the only distraction in the market, but Guang moved them along. They found Yanmei and Haruto waiting for them at edge of the market. From there, the city proper started, and the buildings rose above them in two and three stories. Heiwa Academy had been enormous before it burned down, so buildings with multiple floors were not new to Kira, but the sheer thousands of them – homes, workshops, a host of shrines and temples – almost overwhelmed her. Pagodas rose so tall they hid the sky.

Lazy rivers flowed through the city in a deep canals. Men and women poled boats up and down the water, some with passengers and others with crates and barrels. Here and there, wooden bridges leapt across the rivers. Each bridge had a small shrine on either side of it, dedicated to Toshama the God of Lakes and Rivers.

The Imperial Palace, Castle Dachi, rose above the rest of the city, surrounded by waterways and ringed by walls. Upon each corner of its great stone walls sat a massive guard house with multiple floors, windows slits for archers, and hanging awnings to catch arrows loosed against them. The very top of the palace, so many floors above, peaked out over the wall. The walls gleamed a painted white, the awnings of the pagoda a deep green.

Yanmei shook her head as they passed the palace and claimed it was unassailable. Haruto snorted and doubled his pace. He was grimacing and Kira guessed it was because he alone of all of them had been inside the castle. He was Nightsong, once favoured by the Ipian Emperor; he hadn't just been in the palace, he had lived there. Kira wanted to see inside.

Guang claimed Empress Ise Ryoko was a vain woman. Kira wondered if that meant she kept a lot of mirrors around. Perhaps if she found a suitable mirror at a vendor's stall, she could spy on the palace and get a glimpse of the inside. Divination was not a simple technique, but the Fifth Sage Under Heaven had taught her the basics back at Heiwa. Kira had never quite made it work, but she hadn't tried since Guang's lessons on mastering qi.

Haruto hurried them on, and soon they came to a small inn in what Guang claimed was a seedier part of the city. There was a sign above the door proudly displaying its name: *Shitataru Baketsu.* Haruto smiled as they approached the place and told them an old friend of his had opened this inn a long time ago. Kira wondered what it was like when everyone you once knew was now dead. Then again, she could make a similar claim – all her family and friends were all long dead, but she didn't remember any of them.

They rented two rooms and ordered hot food and baths. Kira

almost shattered in excitement. She hadn't bathed since Gushon, weeks ago, and worried she smelled worse than a donkey's rear end. She wanted clean clothes too, a nice new kimono that wasn't stiff with sweat. Her hair was getting longer than she liked as well, almost touching her shoulders, and she wondered if Yanmei would cut it like she used to, or if she should just hack it off herself.

"Izumi is here somewhere," Haruto said once they had eaten and were all feeling a little more themselves again. Kira had demolished two full bowls of steaming noodle soup, complete with eggs, pork, and a host of vegetables she hadn't even stopped to consider.

"And the rest of the onryo?" Guang asked. "Including Tian's murderer, maybe?"

"Maybe," Haruto said. He pushed a cup of wine about the table, staring into the surface of the pale liquid. Kira played with the reflections and made him see bats flitting about the rafters, but Haruto didn't bite. So she worked on Guang and startled him with shadowy cleaver-wielding figure. The old qi master jumped as he twisted about to face a monster that didn't even exist.

"You got me good there, girl," he said with a chuckle. "Certainly got the blood pumping." Kira grinned at him.

"So we stay here for the night," Yanmei said. "And then what? In the morning we ask about for smoky demons and imprisoned dragons?"

Haruto shrugged. "A good night's sleep will do you all good." Kira noticed he did not include himself in that. "In the morning I intend to find a temple to bless my ritual staffs. Then I'll hang my seal above the bar and we won't need to ask about yokai. Everyone will want to tell us every ghost story and spooky rumour they've ever heard."

Guang chuckled. "Half of being an onmyoji is learning to tell the truth-tellers from the fools and liars."

"That's why I hire you," Haruto said. He sipped from his wine cup. "To listen to all the crap while I do the actual work."

"I thought I was the pack mule?"

"That too," Haruto winked at his friend. "You have to earn your living somehow. Sure as the stars shine, you aren't doing it with your poetry."

"Cabbage! You wound me, old man. Just for that..." Guang struggled to his feet and coughed loudly to catch the attention of some other patrons. "Who would like to hear the story of the dreaded tengu, the Herald of Bones?"

Kira was the first to raise her hand.

It all started over a century ago, when the Nash horse lords banded together under their supreme leader, the Vhargan, and attacked Hosa. It was a time of strife in the world. Brother fought against sister. Empires clashed. Ipia stood divided, and while the Ise and Ido families tore the empire apart for the Serpent Throne, the Cochtan Empire used its infernal machines to test their border with Hosa. And all the while, the Nash waited in the shadows of their sun-scorched desert land.

The Vhargan was a giant by the name of Ochmaa. A smart woman. She pulled the horse lords together and wrapped them in steel ropes of promise and threat, gathering a mighty horde under her banner. If Ochmaa had used it as a spear to drive into the heart of Hosa, she might have broken the back of the Ten Kingdoms there and then. But Ochmaa was savvy. She realised the truth. Hosa was a low hanging fruit that appeared ripe for the plucking. Its forces were distracted elsewhere; its southern borders all but undefended. But it was a poisoned apple, and if Nash consumed it, everything Ochmaa had built would wither and die. She knew the people of Nash could not govern Hosa: the land was too large and unsuited for the nomadic lifestyle of her people. They would grow fat and lazy in the luxury of the Hosan kingdoms. But she had brought the horse lords together with the promise of wealth and conquest. And the God of War was whispering in Ochmaa's ear, urging her to battle.

Or so she thought.

Ochmaa led her mighty host into Hosa. The river Sera, greatest and most furious of all rivers, stood before them, a natural barrier between Hosa and Nash. There was but one safe place to cross. The Bridge of Peace they called it then, though now it is more commonly called the Bridge of Blood. A host of Hosan soldiers were stationed on the mighty bridge, and Ochmaa knew that a mere one thousand soldiers could hold it against ten thousand, such were its defences. But the Nash are a resourceful people. They built rafts in secret, cutting down the nearby forest and scattering the spirits who lived there. They constructed thousands of rafts and used them to build a temporary bridge across the calmest stretch of the river. There, they crossed into enemy territory. Hosa was under attack and didn't even know it.

Ochmaa rode out with her horde and crushed the nearby towns and villages. It was a bloody slaughter, and bare few Hosans survived to tell a tale of screaming hordes and horses with fangs like tigers'. There was some resistance, small garrisons and wandering heroes, but none could stand against the numbers Ochmaa had at her command nor against Ochmaa herself, who fought with whip and blade and a savagery that stunned even her own generals.

But the Nash did not occupy the towns. They sacked them and took the goods and horses back across the bridge of rafts. In their wake, they left devastation.

Dark things gather at such places of ruin. Vengeful spirits and carrion eaters. Demons drawn by the ill humours of a land soaked in blood. One such figure was seen at the site of every attack the Nash visited upon Hosa. A gigantic man with a feathered cloak and a straw tengai over his head. His eyes swirled with the darkness of his soul, and his aura was so foul it incapacitated even the strongest of heroes. Worse yet, he was seen before the slaughters took place. Survivors said they saw the man wandering the streets hours before attacks, spotted him watching the slaughter with savage glee from the top of a nearby tree, his feathered cloak visible in the light of the moon. But this was no man. This was a tengu. A demon most vile. A herald of dark times.

The Hosans came to call this tengu the Herald of Bones. For that is what his presence brought upon them. Bones and grief. Nobody wanted to be next to see the tengu. Men jumped at shadows. Women screamed at the sound of a raven's call. Children made games and rhymes of his coming.

Walk softly, my friend, the Herald has come.
Run now, quick don't fear the sun.
In shadows he thrives he waits he watches.
In thunder he comes, flee to the torches.

For a full year, Ochmaa and her horde terrorised the Hosans. They burned dozens of towns to the ground and slaughtered countless people. The Hosans tried to fight back, but they were caught between two wars. On one side, the Nash raided their lands. On the other, the Cochtans attacked with their fire and machines. But one Hosan general had a plan, and while the Nash rode out to the assault another village, he and his forces crept in behind them and set fire to the Nash's rafts. That night, the Sera burned. When Ochmaa returned to find her bridge into her own country destroyed, she was furious. Her rage was boundless, and even her friends cowered from her.

The next day, the Herald of Bones was seen standing atop the highest stone of the garrison that watched over the Bridge of Peace. Ochmaa's entire host descended upon the garrison. The battle was the bloodiest in a decade.

Ochmaa was victorious, but many of her people died. Her own horse, a stallion she had raised from birth, was killed by a spear. Some say that was what took the fight out of her.

Ochmaa wanted no more of it. She ordered her horde back across the bridge. Her war against Hosa had run its crimson course.

If only it had ended there...

The Herald of Bones stood in the middle of the bridge. He

had come to Ochmaa. She rode out to meet him in the centre of the Bridge of Peace, her force of horse lords a thousand strong at her back. Rumours of this tengu had reached the Nash, and she was not fool enough to disrespect such a spirit.

The Herald of Bones ordered her three times to return to Hosa and finish what she had started: First he promised her wealth and power. Then he threatened her person. And last, he threatened a terrible plague upon the horses the Nash cared so deeply for. This last Ochmaa could not stand. Insult one of the Nash, you invite retribution. Threaten their horses, you invite destruction.

With a roar, she struck at the tengu. Behind her, her loyal horde charged forward across the bridge. The Herald of Bones was a yokai, yes, but she was Ochmaa, a giant, strongest of all the Nash, fearsome and proud Vhargan of the horse lords. It was not enough. Her attack fell short, faltered. Then Ochmaa turned and charged her own people.

Not a single Nash horse lord made it across the Bridge of Peace that day. Ochmaa was but the first to fall. A thousand warriors. A thousand horses. Beneath the Herald of Bones' maddening gaze, they turned on each other. And when the Hosan relief force reached the bridge, they found every stone stained blood red. You can see it even now. The blood has washed away, but the stain of that atrocity remains.

The audience in the tavern was captivated by Guang's story. The owner, a foreigner with pale skin and large, round eyes, even brought them a couple of bottles of wine on the house. Guang did not receive an applause. It was the Ipian way, but he could tell they appreciated the tale. He still preferred Hosan audiences, which were occasionally raucous enough to call down the attention of the gods.

"I've seen him," one man said. He was thin with hairy jowls that looked like he had once been fat. "The Herald of Bones. Big man. Wears a feather cloak and one of those tengai hat things."

"Ha!" Guang shouted. It was not an uncommon response to that story. But then tengai hats were not uncommon either. "Pray to the gods and the stars that you didn't, my friend. Where the Herald of Bones walks, battle and death follow." With that, he sat back down at the table and cocked an eyebrow at Haruto. "Well, old man? Still think my poems are worthless?" He tapped the free wine they had received and then poured himself a cup.

Haruto shrugged. "It wasn't a poem. Nor did you write it. I think it was She Donglu who first came up with that story."

Guang gave his old friend a good glaring.

"*Dour onmyoji.*
Enthusiastic critic.
How empty his soul."

Haruto laughed. "That one wasn't bad."

"I liked the story," Kira said. "It was exciting." She was playing with her daggers again. She had four of them on the table in front of her, each one distinct. She picked one up, grinning at the reflection. "I call you Momo," she said. "Momo." She pressed the flat of the blade against her forehead. "Momo."

They talked for a while after that, shared a few stories and jokes. Guang kept an eye on Haruto. His friend was trying to hide it, but he knew the old man well enough to see the anxiety in his smile and hear it in his voice. Izumi was in the imperial city somewhere, and Haruto would not rest until he found her.

Chapter 30

Guang slept. The old poet always rolled onto his side during the night, and his snores were thunderous enough to warrant lightning. Yanmei and Kira were in their own room, and Haruto hoped they too were deep in sleep. They needed the rest. They all needed it. The pace he'd set from Gushon had been gruelling. But they'd made it to Kodachi in good time.

Haruto couldn't sleep. He never could, but tonight was different. He sat cross-legged in the middle of their room and meditated. Well, it was a more a restless waiting than a meditation. He was waiting for Izumi. Shiki curled up in his lap, her eyes closed, snoring like a purring cat.

He felt Izumi's presence even before she slid open the window with a smoky wisp. He opened his eyes and walked to the window, and she drew back the smoke, leaving a small patch of soot on the wooden frame. Shiki gave an annoyed, sleepy growl and climbed inside his kimono, settling back down against his chest. Izumi was standing on the street below. She wore the same white robe with gold patterning, its hood up and obscuring her face, black stitches repairing the slices he'd cut out of it. Dark smoke swirled from inside the robe and stained the ground black.

Haruto threw open the window fully and leapt down onto the street, landing with barely a sound. "Izumi," he said as he stood up.

She turned and fled not on feet but flying close to the ground, smoke billowing out behind her. Haruto sighed and gave chase but struggled to keep up. She twisted in mid-air and changed direction. Haruto slid to a stop and then sprinted after her. He almost called out her name, but what would be the point. She knew he was there. She was leading him somewhere.

Probably a trap. Haruto didn't care. It was Izumi.

Even in the dead of night, there were people in street. Kodachi was a city, and cities never slept. Some startled at the passing of a yokai and onmyoji, others hurried away lest they draw unwanted attention. Haruto ignored them all. Izumi was all that mattered.

Eventually, she slowed and drifted to a stop. Haruto stopped a dozen paces away. He wanted to get closer, but was afraid to spook her; last time that happened he found himself separated from his legs. She lured him into a narrow, empty street. Lanterns bathed them in a soft yellow light. The buildings looming over them were dark, and everything was silent. Haruto waited for Izumi to make the first move.

Izumi turned slowly towards him. There was nothing but darkness inside her hood, but Haruto knew she was staring at him. She raised a sleeve and the smoke that extended out of it formed into a hand. She lifted it to her hood and stared at it, turning it this way and that, flexing the fingers, as if it was something unexpected. Then she pulled back her hood. And it was her. Her face written in grey smoke. The softness of her cheeks, the curve of her lips, the little scar on her forehead from when she banged it on a cupboard. Even the same curl of hair that always worked free of bun or braid. It was her, exactly as he remembered her. She touched a smoky hand against her cheek, traced fingers over her nose and mouth and eyes.

Haruto took a couple of steps forward. "Izumi," he said, unable to keep the hope from his voice.

Her hand dropped away from her face, and she looked up at him. Her lips went tight, and she reached up and pulled her hood back over her head.

Suddenly, Haruto heard a commotion, shuffling footsteps at both ends of the street. Men and women in ceramic armour poured in from side streets. Doors banged open and more soldiers rushed out. They surged past Izumi and surrounded Haruto. A dozen of them. Two dozen. Three. Their armour was black, a golden serpent embossed upon the pauldrons. The Serpent Guard,

Empress Ise Ryoko's elite soldiers. Haruto knew of their prowess. He might struggle to fight just one, but couldn't hope to fight so many. They levelled spears at him, pulled swords from scabbards. Haruto found himself ringed by steel and armour with no way out.

"Shiki, vanish," he whispered. The little spirit gave a tremulous whistle from inside his kimono, then disappeared. She was still nearby; he could feel her, watching him, but invisible.

"Come quietly, Master Onmyoji," said one of the Serpent Guard, a large man with the scars on his face and a sword in hand. "Empress Ise wants a word."

Haruto laid a hand on his katana. A ripple of tension passed through the mass of soldiers arrayed against him. Beyond them, he caught sight of Izumi floating in the street, her hood pointed his way. Even if he did fight the Serpent Guard, even if his immortality carried him through the battle, more would come. An endless legion of soldiers. And Izumi. She had already proved she was strong enough to take him alone.

With a shrug, Haruto pulled his katana from his belt and dropped it on the ground.

A lot could be said of the Empress Ise Ryoko. She was a vain woman obsessed with her own image. Her ability to keep the Ipian Empire running despite constant undermining by her distant cousin Emperor Ido Tanaka was nothing short of awe-inspiring. She was not born to the throne but seized it after the assassin the Ticking Clock murdered her two brothers, her husband, her mother, and five of her nephews all in one night. She held on to the Serpent Throne by executing her surviving brother the same morning the assassinations were discovered. She was a doting mother and an expert instructor in both martial combat and statecraft. Some people called her the Fake Empress, while others considered her as close to divinity as a human could be. One thing no one could say about her was that she was lazy.

The sun had barely kissed the horizon good morning when she swept out of her rooms already dressed in luxurious red robes for a long day at court. Crow breezed after her, leaving a dark soot stain on the carpet behind her. Empress Ise Ryoko glanced back with a raised eyebrow at the mess, but said nothing. She didn't need to. Half a dozen servants leapt to clean up after Crow's passage.

"You have him?" Empress Ise Ryoko asked.

"Yes, Empress," Crow said. She hated the formality, but the Master had instructed her to be polite. It did not matter that Crow could easily kill the Empress. They were to defer to her and act like subservient sycophants. For now at least. "Your plan worked perfectly." Crow might have snarled, had she a face to. It was not the Empress Ise Ryoko's plan at all. It was the Master's plan, though he had ceded the credit for it.

They passed a large mirror in the hallway, and the Empress flicked her gaze at it for just a moment and then strode on. Crow floated after her, trailing a smoky vine across the shining surface as she passed. Another of the hustling servants rushed forward with a cloth and set to cleaning the mirror to a blinding shine once more. The Empress Ise Ryoko checked herself in every mirror as though something might have changed in the dozen strides since the last. She was a picture of immaculate beauty. Her dress was long and sweeping and somehow refused to wrinkle. Her hair was pinned high on her head in an artful display, like a halo framing her face, and not a single strand out of place. Her face was decorated in myriad powders without a hint of a crack or smudge. Pinked cheeks and ruby lips gave her a look of healthy colour. The Empress Ise Ryoko had taken the costume they had forced her to wear while her brother sat the throne, and turned it into a symbol of power. Now all the ladies of Ipia wished to dress and look like the Empress. And the men could not take their eyes off her. Crow respected what the Empress had made of it, but that didn't mean she liked her.

The Empress Ise Ryoko paused at a crossroad in the halls of the palace. Plush carpets and spotless walls stretched in every direction. "I wish to see this immortal onmyoji."

"I am not sure that's a good idea," Crow said. There was

something strange about the palace. Something... familiar. It itched at her like an ant crawling across her face. Only she didn't have a face and couldn't even remember what something crawling across it might feel like. She realised everything had gone ominously quiet. The servants had pulled back from her. Three of the Serpent Guard, who had been shadowing them from a distance, stepped closer.

The Empress Ise Ryoko stared over her shoulder, and one eyebrow arched upwards as graceful as a katana. "I will decide which ideas are good, creature." She said the words so softly yet with a menace that drained all colour and warmth from the people around them.

Crow bowed as politely as possible without arms or feet or head. It was really just a dipping of her robe, but it seemed to have the desired effect. The Empress waved for her to take the lead. Crow's smoke boiled as she surged past the Empress. She wanted nothing so much as to turn about and choke the Empress on her smoke. The Serpent Guard would be powerless to stop her. Their blades meant nothing to her. But the Master would be unhappy. For whatever reason, he believed they needed her on their side.

The Empress Ise Ryoko sighed at the soot stains Crow left on the carpets, but strode forwards regardless of the mess it made of her slippers.

They left the carpets behind when they entered the dungeon. Cold grey stone seemed to be the standard décor, and the sound of dripping water was as present as the sobs of prisoners in their cells. Crow heard rumours that no fewer than three of Emperor Ido Tanaka's sons were afforded permanent residence somewhere down in the damp dark. Apparently, the rebellious emperor still had plenty more to throw at his enemies yet.

Two more Serpent Guard stood ready outside the onmyoji's cell. They snapped to rigid attention even before the Empress stormed into view. The door was opened without hesitation, and the Empress Ise Ryoko stopped in the doorway, staring in.

The onmyoji was chained to the wall, kneeling with his arms

pulled out to his sides, manacles snapped around each wrist, pinning him like a dead insect on display. He looked uncomfortable, but far from beaten. His blue kimono had fallen down over one shoulder, making him look only slightly dishevelled.

"Izumi," the onmyoji said. He didn't even spare the Empress Ise Ryoko a glance. Crow winced. Though she knew her hood hid the expression. A smile tugged at her lips as she realised she again had lips with which to wince and smile.

The Empress glanced at Crow and then back at the onmyoji. "You know each other."

"Yes," the onmyoji rasped.

"No," Crow said.

The Empress paused to consider. Then she stepped inside the cell. The two Serpent Guard hurried in after her. Crow was far from certain the woman needed such ardent protection. There was an air of capability about her that spoke of power that went beyond her station. Crow floated in after them and waited by the wall. She didn't like the way the onmyoji stared at her as though there were no one else in the cell.

"You are truly immortal?" the Empress Ise Ryoko asked.

The onmyoji looked lazily at the Empress and shook his head slowly. "Nope."

The Empress Ise Ryoko looked at Crow.

"I assure you, he is. Last time we met I separated his legs from his body. And yet..." She gestured a smoky hand towards the onmyoji, then she waggled her fingers just because she had fingers.

The Empress held out a slender hand. "Sword," she snapped, and a Serpent Guard drew his blade and placed the hilt in her hand. The Empress leaned forward and gently pressed the sword against the onmyoji's face. He groaned. With a flick of her wrist, the Empress cut a thin slice along his cheek then flicked the blood drops from the blade onto the wall and held the sword out for the Serpent Guard to retrieve.

The onmyoji winced in pain as a couple of drops of blood

ran down his cheek and dripped from his chin. They all watched the wound close. The blood was the only evidence it had existed.

"Fascinating," the Empress Ise Ryoko said. "You must tell me how you came by this technique."

The onmyoji sighed and let his head dangle, his chin resting on his chest. "You wouldn't like the price of it."

"You will tell me the secret," the Empress Ise Ryoko said with the weight of certain conviction. "My interrogators are quite proficient at their work. Everyone tells me precisely what I want to know, eventually. And I suppose with you they don't need to hold back. They can experiment. Pull you apart piece by piece to see just how you work."

"Sounds wonderful," the onmyoji said, but Crow heard a slight tremor in his voice.

"You need only keep him here until the Master's plan is complete," Crow said. There was no need for torture.

The Empress scoffed gracefully. "Yes, but while we have him here, we may as well see what he knows." She paused, and the slightest crinkle of a frown crossed her face. "If he can heal as you say, what is to stop him from gnawing off his own arm to escape?"

Crow imagined the pain of such a thing would be sufficient deterrent. But perhaps there were other methods, too. She snatched the sword from the Serpent Guard's hand, rushed forward, and drove the blade into the onmyoji's chest. He screamed and his head shot up. He stared into Crow's hood even as she pushed the blade into him.

Crow flew backwards and felt the wall against her back. She was breathing hard. She was breathing. It made no sense. She didn't need to breathe. She couldn't breathe. Yet her chest rose and fell as though she were. Her smoke boiled and rushed like a heartbeat gone wild, smoke lashing the ground and spreading out to the corners of the cell. She struggled to master herself, to regain control.

"I see," the Empress Ise Ryoko said coldly. "He cannot heal while the blade is still in him." She turned to her Serpent Guard.

"Put a dozen swords in his chest. Make certain at least one goes through his heart. That should keep him idle until I am ready to deal with him further." She strode from the cell, snapping at Crow to follow.

The onmyoji screamed as the Serpent Guard drove another sword into his chest.

Crow fled the cell, but not only to catch up with the Empress; she needed to get away from the onmyoji and his agony. And her own. The further she got from him, the less distinct she became. Her face and hands swirled into formlessness once more. Her control returned even as her form faded. It was for the best. It was comfortable.

"We must discuss my end of the bargain," the Empress Ise Ryoko said as she walked. "I will reunite my empire and you will help me."

They had already dispatched Xifeng to remove the head of Emperor Ido Tanaka, but it was not Crow's place to discuss that. The onmyoji screamed again, and Crow wished the Empress would walk faster. Worse, though, was when the screams stopped.

Chapter 31

Guang grumbled. Yanmei realised it was the noise he made when he had something to say. "There's something I've been wanting to ask you," he said.

Yanmei glanced at the old bandit. He was frowning, eyes fixed on the street below him. It was late afternoon, and they were out searching for supplies they needed to restock: new clothes, food, paper and ink. Haruto was nowhere to be found, but Guang insisted that was not abnormal. The onmyoji often went off on his own when he needed to speak to his shinigami. Kira danced ahead of them, fascinated by the city and its people, by the shops and the shrines. Everything fascinated her. It was the pure wonder of a child, something that had always been denied her.

"Go ahead," Yanmei said as they walked. It was a pleasant morning, despite the chill in the air, and she felt more peaceful than she had since... well, since Heiwa.

"You were a tutor at the academy," Guang said, "along with Tian. Did you know him well?"

"Well enough," Yanmei said. They had been friends. They had disagreed over many things, but there was mutual respect between them.

Guang grumbled again. "What was he like? I, uh... I didn't really know him. He wouldn't speak to me. The last time I saw him was fifteen years or more ago, and we argued. He was smart enough to walk away before one of us did something that couldn't be taken back."

Ahead, Kira stopped to stare into a blacksmith's workshop. The clang of hammer and anvil rang out across the street. A few passersby glanced at Kira as though she were simple, and Yanmei felt the urge to run to her, pull her away from them.

"You have to understand, Guang," Yanmei said. "Life isn't easy for the children of bandits. There's a lot of... grief. The things we're made to see. The things we're made to do."

"I didn't make him do anything," Guang said quickly. "I kept him apart from it all. Separate. It wasn't like you and Flaming Fist. And your brother. I didn't keep him with the war band."

Yanmei let him talk himself into silence. She'd long ago learned there was no point arguing against excuses. Her silence acknowledged them for what they were. "He knew what you were and what you did?" she asked when he was done.

Guang nodded.

"Then you made him an accomplice as surely as if you put a blade in his hand and told him to kill." It was a harsh thing to say, she knew. But it was also the truth. She knew that better than anyone. "He was your son, and he loved you. I know that much for sure. There were times he wished he didn't, but he loved you.

"We children of bandits make excuses for our parents when we're young. We have to because we don't know how else to exist. They're our parents and they're supposed to love us and we're supposed to love them. So we make excuses. We reason away the things we know they do. We make excuses for them, even when they won't make those excuses for themselves. Even when they don't think they need to. That is what you did to Tian. You made him an accomplice of conscience, if not action. He shouldered that burden for you, and that is why you lost him."

Yanmei realised Guang was crying. The old bandit wiped at his eyes as he walked.

Ahead, Kira rushed from one side of the street to the other and sniffed at a restaurant serving grilled fish. She darted inside the building and a few moments later walked out with a fish skewered on a stick. Yanmei heard a shout from within the restaurant and hurried to intervene. It took a couple of lien, far more than the kushiage was worth, and a dozen apologies before the chef agreed not to call the city guard. Kira didn't seem to realise she had done anything wrong. It wasn't the first time this had happened. She'd been in trouble more than once at Heiwa for taking things that didn't belong to her. It had taken quite a bit of explaining that things belonged to people and it wasn't right to take them. Issues of morality were ever a struggle.

"I did it again, didn't I?" Kira said after Yanmei had paid for the fish. "Sorry. I didn't mean to. I know it's wrong, I just forgot. I'm sorry." She looked so crestfallen, her simple joy at the food already forgotten. Yanmei hated taking that from her.

"He was a good man," Yanmei said once they were moving again. "Tian, I mean." She realised she hadn't answered Guang's question, but had used the opportunity to make him feel bad for his past. It wasn't even him she wanted to hurt. It was her own father for all the pain he had visited upon her. But he was fifteen years dead now, and all she was doing was passing on her own sorrow to Guang. "He loved teaching the children. Especially history. I guess he had something of a poetic spirit about him."

"Hah!" Guang grunted. "I guess all those stories I used to tell him made an impact then. I always thought they just bored him to sleep at night."

"Did he--" Yanmei paused, considering whether the question would cause more pain, but she wanted to know. "Did he really come back as a yokai?"

Guang nodded. "Haruto said it was likely the collective pain and anger of all the students and teachers killed at Heiwa focused through Tian. It brought him back, but it wasn't him. Or, it was him, but he was lost in the pain and grief of it all. It warped him into something..." He shook his head.

"It doesn't surprise me it was him," Yanmei said as they crossed the road toward a shop that sold paper supplies. "He really loved the school and the children. Of course he would become the focus for all their grief. I think he would have taken it upon himself had he the choice, as long as it prevented someone else from suffering."

Guang nodded. When they stopped outside the shop, he said, "Haruto is on the case now. He'll kill the onryo that killed Tian and give my son the peace he deserves. He will." Then he stepped into the shop.

Kira waited outside with Yanmei. She'd finished her kushiage and was staying close. She wrapped her arms around Yanmei as they waited. "Sorry."

Yanmei gave her mop of hair an idle stroke. "Was it good fish at least?" she asked.

Kira smiled at that. "It was a bit salty."

"Probably not worth two lien then?"

Kira snorted. "Definitely not worth two. Probably not even worth the apologies. He should have paid me to eat it."

Yanmei laughed along with her.

Further up the street, a man stepped out into the road and waved his fist at something. Yanmei saw a small dog charging between people's legs, darting around folk, yapping and swinging its head wildly, sniffing the air.

"Perhaps you're not the only thief about the streets of Kodachi today," Yanmei said.

Kira shook her head and stepped away from the paper shop. "It's Shiki!" She waved her hands in the air and called to the little spirit, heedless of the commotion she was causing.

Shiki looked at Kira waving, stopped snuffing about, and charged for her. At the last moment, the spirit leapt into the air and popped free of the tanuki. The dog hit the ground in a confused tumble; Shiki hit Kira in the chest and scrabbled halfway into her coat, chittering all the while.

"Slow down," Kira said.

The tanuki growled, yapped, then turned and ran away. Guang wandered out of the shop with an armful of supplies that seemed to consist mostly of paper and a new brush. He took one look at fur ball chirping away in Kira's arms and glanced about the street. His face hardened into a frown. "Where's Haruto?"

"He's been captured," Kira said, still focused on the spirit clinging to her haori. "The Empress has him."

Guang groaned. "Cabbage!"

Shiki wouldn't stop talking. The little spirit was worried, jumping between Kira's shoulders, arms flailing. She told Kira that she hadn't been this far from Haruto since he had first summoned her, and that was a long time, so long that the poor little thing couldn't remember a time before she was bound to her onmyoji.

Kira tried her best to soothe Shiki, to tell the spirit that everything would be alright, but she was in a panic and wouldn't listen, making it quite difficult to pay attention to what Yanmei and Guang were saying. They were walking down the street at speed now towards the imperial palace as though they intended to storm the walls and pull Haruto out by force. Kira liked the idea, but Shiki told her there were thousands of soldiers who had taken Haruto captive. Then again, Kira was far from convinced the spirit could count. Or even knew what numbers were.

The road up to the palace was well guarded. A dozen soldiers stood at the ready on either side. They slowed as they walked discreetly past it. Beyond the guards was a bridge that crossed the waterway. The channel was wide, too wide to jump, and straight after the bridge was the fortress gate and walls. Kira was no expert in laying siege to palaces, but she had a feeling the three of them were unlikely to succeed. She might be able to distract the soldiers guarding the road, but the walls were high and there were even more soldiers inside.

"There has to be a way in," Guang growled at the other side of the road. He turned and strode back the other way, staring at the palace. A thin soldier with a hook nose and overhanging brow took notice. It probably wasn't every day a disgruntled old poet stalked about outside the walls and stared at them with a face like a rock slide in full tumble.

Yanmei grabbed Guang before he crossed the road a third time, and the soldiers began to whisper to one another. She was wearing her jacket with the old, scorched and battered scale armour sewn into it and carrying a naginata, and there was no mistaking her for a warrior, even an old one. "Come on," she hissed, pulling at Guang. "There's no sense getting arrested. That won't help Haruto."

Guang grumbled and let Yanmei lead him away.

They left the palace behind. Shiki kept on chattering, and Kira pushed the little spirit down in her coat to shut her up for a moment. She whistled and nipped at Kira's fingers, but it gave Kira time to think as she hurried to catch up with Yanmei and Guang. "I might have a way to find him," she said. "To see if he's alright at least."

"How?" Guang asked, glaring at her.

Kira faltered and slowed to a stop, unsure why Guang seemed to be angry at her. "I can do divination," she said. It was only mostly a lie. She knew the theory but not much more. "Of a sort. I'll need a mirror, but I can use it... or I *should* be able to use it to see him. If he's near a mirror, I guess." Now she thought about it, the chance of success seemed slim and bordering on ridiculous.

Guang grumbled and stormed off. He pulled aside a few passersby and asked them something. Eventually, a fat woman with a tight bun of hair told him something, and they were walking again. The old qi master led them to a shop far into the city away from the palace. Inside the shop, mirrors were mounted on every wall, stacked three deep in places. The light coming in from the window bounced off every surface and made the shop front bright as a summer day. It was perfect. Kira hadn't felt so at home... ever.

A vague memory flashed through her mind. She was alone, huddled on the floor in complete darkness, a world without boundaries and without meaning. A world of nothing, and she was trapped in it. She had been trapped in it for as long as she could remember with no one but herself for company. Occasionally, people looked in at her, and she would scare them away. Kira didn't know why she scared them away. She heard the icy snap of glass cracking and felt an itching, burning line snaking up her chest. She shook the feeling away. It was no time to dwell on the past.

The owner of the shop, a whip-thin woman with a nasally voice said, "Can I help--" she paused as she looked at the three oddities who had entered her shop "--you?"

Kira was going to need quiet to perform her divination, and she already sensed that this woman would be just the kind to interrupt her. Luckily, Kira was in her element. The thin woman couldn't help but glance at herself in the mirrors, and Kira showed her a gang of red-eyed demons in black ceramic armour behind her, each one carrying a bloody katana. The woman's eyes went wide; she yelped and she bolted out the back door of the shop.

"Huh?" Guang grunted. "What was that about?"

Kira gave her very best Haruto shrug, which still didn't feel quite right, but Yanmei stared at her from beneath furrowed brows. It was the wrong thing to do. She wasn't supposed to scare people for no reason, though this seemed like a perfectly good reason.

"Will any of these work, Kira?" Yanmei asked, turning about to look at all the mirrors.

"Mhm," Kira said, approaching a full-size mirror on an ornate wooden stand. "This one is perfect."

"It's a bit big, girl," Guang said. "There's no chance we're moving that one without a cart."

"Then we best do it here and quickly," Yanmei said. "I imagine it won't be long before the owner works up the courage to return."

"Let's hope she returns alone," Guang said.

"Shhhh!" Kira hissed. She needed quiet, and it was already noisy enough with Shiki squeaking at her. She glanced down at the little spirit hiding in the fold of her haori. "That goes for you too. You want me to find Haruto, don't you?"

Shiki whistled and blinked her big eyes up at her.

"Good. Then shut up!"

Kira exhaled and laid her palm upon the surface of the mirror. They were far away from the palace here, much further than she would have liked. She could feel other mirrors all over the city through this one. It was almost as though all mirrors led to a space that both did and didn't exist, or existed only for her or for those who knew that other place. But even that wasn't quite right. They weren't all connected to a place. They were connected to one another.

"Is it working?" Guang asked.

Kira shot him an angry glare. Then she turned back to the mirror and stared into it. Guang had said the Empress was a vain woman who loved her own reflection. That meant she would have lots of mirrors in the palace. An enormous collection of them all clustered together. They were easy to find, harder to reach. The Sage had taught her this technique back at Heiwa. He'd stared into a cup of tea and saw people and places far away. He said all water is connected, as all water had been one, and it remembered being one, so when you looked into one drop of water, you looked into all water. The real technique was infusing the water with your qi to give it an order, to tell it where you wanted to see. Kira had never managed it, and the Sage had said the technique was beyond her abilities. But she had tried it once with mirrors and connected to that place between them. She let her qi flow through her hand and into the mirror.

Glass cracked, its icy snap long and reverberant. A line of fire itched its way up Kira's neck to her cheek. She saw a girl sitting alone in a dark so complete it was as though light had never existed. She was crying. No, she was singing. The song had no words, but Kira recognised the melody. The girl lifted her head to stare at Kira. She had no eyes; her sockets were black voids.

Kira shattered and recoiled from the mirror, a strangled cry escaping her throat. Glass shards fell all around her, tinkling as they cascaded from her clothes, fading as they hit the floor.

Yanmei was at her side, a steadying hand on her back. "Kira? Are you alright?"

Kira nodded, struggling to find her voice. Her heart raced, and she clutched her hands into fists, digging nails into her palms.

"You don't have to..." Yanmei said.

Kira shook Yanmei's hand off, and shuffled towards the mirror again. She had to do it. She had to find Haruto, and nothing, especially not some vague memory of a past she didn't remember, was going to stop her. She placed a sweaty palm on the mirror again, a smudge of blood smearing the surface from where her nails had bit into her skin. Then she looked into the mirror. No cracks in her skin, no hollow eye sockets of endless void. No one stared back at her but herself. She pushed her qi into the mirror and searched for the mirrors in the palace. And she found them. Hundreds of them, in every room and every hall. She stared through them all. She saw people dressed in lavish costumes, empty corridors, luxurious rooms, a grand hall filled with people and soldiers and a throne carved like a coiled serpent. She cycled through them quickly, so much to look at. But she did not find Haruto.

Kira let out a sigh and shook her head. Once again, she had failed. They were relying on her and she was useless. "I can't find him."

Guang stalked to the other side of the shop, growling like a hungry wolf.

"It's alright," Yanmei said. "You tried."

Kira looked at her, at the compassion in her eyes. "No, it's not. They have Haruto and I'm useless." She pulled her hand from the mirror and heard a thread of qi connecting her to the reflection. It was only there for a moment, a brief note long since struck and echoing, and then it faded almost to silence. But it was there. It was a connection.

"Now what?" Guang snapped.

"Shiki said he was in the palace," said Yanmei. "But I can't see a way for us to get in."

"I'm not leaving him," Guang said. "I can't."

Yanmei only shook her head.

Guang fingered his wispy beard. "Maybe I can get in as a poet, convince them to let me perform for the Empress. Or I could make a paper ladder to scale the walls."

"Every inch of the walls is watched," Yanmei said. "Maybe in an hour or two, when night has fallen, we could find an opening, but..." She sighed.

Kira tried to drown them out. Shiki was squeaking again too. It was too much noise. She pressed her palm against the mirror and struggled to connect to a mirror in the palace. She looked into an ornately decorated room. It appeared to be empty. Kira pulled her hand away and heard the melody of qi again. She held onto it this time, listened to it, straining her ears, and poured her energy across the connection.

Shiki scrambled up onto her shoulder and whistled.

"You have no idea what I'm doing," Kira said.

Shiki whistled again.

"Alright, maybe you do. It might work."

The little spirit's silence was damning.

"I'm going to try it anyway!"

More silence.

"I can get in," Kira said, not letting Shiki convince her otherwise. "I think."

"How?" Guang asked.

Kira looked to Yanmei. "I think I've figured out how to use your friend's technique."

Yanmei frowned. She looked at the mirror, then back at Kira. "It's too dangerous."

Kira bit her lip. "Maybe, but I want to try. Please let me try." She smiled, hoping it would look reassuring.

Yanmei stared at the floor silently for a moment. Then she nodded. "Be careful. Don't take any risks. If it looks dangerous, get out of there. Come back here."

Kira nodded at each of Yanmei's instructions. She plucked Shiki from her shoulder and placed the spirit on the ground. "You can't come with me." Shiki leapt back onto Kira's leg and started scrambling up her trousers. Kira picked her off and placed her on the floor again. "You can't come. I can't take you through." The spirit stared up at her and blinked.

Kira straightened up, and Yanmei wrapped her arms around her. "Be careful," she whispered. "We'll be right here waiting for you to come back. Come back."

Kira nodded and pulled away from Yanmei, then turned to the mirror once more. She drew in a deep breath and focused on the thread of qi still connecting her to the mirror. "I can do this," she said to herself and realised she didn't sound very confident. "I can do this!"

Yanmei watched as Kira took two steps back, then launched into a run and leapt into the mirror. It shattered, shards falling to the floor in a jingling cacophony. She was gone.

"Eh?" Guang grunted as he rushed toward the mirror, carefully stepping around all the shards on the shop floor. He walked around behind the mirror. "Where did she go?"

"Through the mirror," Yanmei said.

The old bandit arched his grey brows at her. "Did you know she could do that?"

Yanmei smiled. "I don't think even she knew until just now."

"Where's she gone?"

"The palace, I hope."

"You hope?" Guang scratched at his chin.

Yanmei didn't think the old bandit understood just how brave Kira was. She had been trapped in a mirror for more than eighty years, and now she was risking it all over again to find Haruto. "If she makes it back, she will need another mirror to emerge from." Yanmei drew in a deep breath and nodded. She wouldn't let herself worry. She'd take a page from Kira's book and be brave. "Looks like I'm staying here for now."

Chapter 32

The mirror shattered behind her and Kira slid to a stop on a plush carpet amidst a shower of tinkling shards. For a moment she just stood there, unsure what to think. Then she leapt into the air and clapped her hands.

"It worked! It worked." A giggle burst from her lips and she clasped a hand over her mouth. "I can't believe it worked." She said between her fingers. She'd been telling herself she could do it, but she half expected to crash into the mirror head first and achieve nothing but a painful bump. But it had worked. She passed through one mirror and out of another. Now she just needed to figure out where she had come out.

She was in a large room. A lady's bedchamber judging by the woman staring at her in mute horror. She was older than Kira and quite pretty in a perfumed sort of way. Her hair was halfway between disarray and architectural construct, and she clutched at the table next to her with a single hand as if it was the only thing keeping her upright. The table was laden with all manner of pots, combs, brushes, and a smaller mirror. She breathed in deep and opened her mouth to scream.

Kira rushed forward past an enormous bed, flicking a dagger into her hand, and pressed the blade to the woman's throat. The woman closed her mouth and stared at her.

"Sorry about this," Kira said. She wasn't sure what to do now that she was here. Should she kill the woman? No, that didn't sound good at all.

Shiki squeaked inside Kira's coat and sprang up onto her shoulder. Kira gasped, and the woman gasped with her. Then the women opened her red lips again.

"Please don't," Kira said, shaking her head. The woman

gulped down the scream. "What are you doing here, Shiki?" Kira asked. "How did you... come through with me?"

The little spirit squeaked.

"Huh," Kira grinned, happier than she cared to admit that she wasn't alone. "That would have been helpful to know. I could have brought someone else through with me." She considered it and shook her head at the idea. "Then again, I need to do this quickly and quietly. Yanmei isn't that quick anymore, and Guang is about as quiet as a rusty wheel. No! I have to do this alone."

Shiki squeaked.

"Well, yes. Alone with you. Now. What should I do about her?"

The fluffy little spirit blinked at the woman on the pointy end of Kira's dagger. Then she narrowed her bright eyes and warbled.

"Ooh, that's a good idea." Kira said. She turned her attention back to the woman. "Sorry about this again. Do you happen to know where the dungeon is?"

"Um," the woman opened her mouth slowly and whispered, "In the basement, I imagine?

Kira nodded. "That makes sense." She looked at Shiki perched on her shoulder, and the spirit crossed its little arms and nodded at her. "That would be downstairs?"

The woman pulled an odd face and nodded once.

"Good. Thank you." Kira pulled her dagger away. "Right. Time to find Haruto and get out of here." She turned and strode towards the door. And then it occurred to her. She couldn't just let the woman stay here. "The moment I'm gone you'll find the nearest guard and tell them about me, won't you?" she asked, her voice as cold as the grave.

"What?" the woman said in a quivering whisper. "No. No I won't."

Kira sighed and looked at the woman. "Yes, you will." She pulled back her arm to throw her dagger, but Shiki squeaked urgently, jumped up and down in an angry dance on Kira's shoulder, and pointed at the woman.

"Oh, stars! You're right. Of course you are. Killing her would be wrong. Yanmei would be furious." The woman was waiting wide-eyed, frozen and clinging to her vanity. "Sorry again." Kira stepped forward, flipping the dagger around in her hand, and struck the woman across the head with its hilt. The dagger shattered, and the woman collapsed with a thud, blood leaking from the side of her head.

"Oh no no no no no," Kira said as Shiki leapt from her shoulder to inspect the woman. "Is she dead? I didn't mean to kill you. I'm sorry."

Shiki whistled.

Kira let out a sigh of relief. "Breathing is good, right?"

Shiki shrugged, much like Haruto. Then she trumpeted.

"So what if you're a spirit? That doesn't mean you can't tell if breathing is a good sign. Besides, I'm a spirit too, so how would I know?"

Shiki squeaked.

"I'm half spirit."

Another squeak.

"Well, if I'm not at least part spirit, then how can I understand you?"

Shiki was silent for a few seconds. They stared at each other. Then Shiki clambered up Kira's leg. Kira picked her up and plopped her on her shoulder. "Alright. I can do this."

Shiki whistled.

"Okay, *we* can do this. Next step, basement."

Shiki sighed, then fluted.

"A disguise? That's a brilliant idea, Shiki." Kira pulled open the giant wardrobe next to the bed. Three dozen kimonos in various shapes, styles, and colours hung inside. "Uhhh..." She stared at them for a few seconds, overwhelmed. Then she pulled out a resplendent azure kimono with a white triangle pattern. It was so light she barely felt it, and the fabric was soft as a cloud. "It's beautiful."

Shiki cooed and reached out an arm to caress the fabric.

"Too fancy?"

Shiki rubbed beneath her mouth, just like Guang rubbed his wispy beard, and squeaked.

"You're right. Something more plain." Kira browsed through the kimonos until she found a serviceable brown hakama with subtle grey clouds stitched into it. She picked out a matching haori. They were clothes more suited to travel than court, plain enough that they wouldn't draw attention, and tough enough that they wouldn't rip at the slightest movement. She stripped out of her coat and trousers and wrapped and belted the kimono around her.

Then she slid the door of the bedroom open, wincing at the noise. The palace was an odd design. Wooden walls and doors, but they slid open just like the paper screens used in much of Ipia. She poked her head out into the corridor and looked both ways. There didn't appear to be anyone about. She stepped out and closed the door behind her. The hallway was short and turned sharply after a couple of dozen paces.

"I guess we need to find some stairs down," Kira whispered. "Does that sound right?"

Shiki trilled.

"You are no help."

Kira stalked down the corridor, taking long exaggerated steps and realising abruptly that she probably looked quite suspicious and might blend in better if she didn't walk like a crane. Would anyone she encountered even realise she didn't belong? She might pass for a servant if they didn't look too closely. She was still considering the possibility when she rounded the corner and found a couple of guards heading her way. They were both men, tall and dressed in the green ceramic armour of the Emerald Legion. Kira pressed herself against the wall and bowed as they passed. One of them, a man with bulbous nose, barely spared her a glance. The other had pitted cheeks and a failing attempt at a beard. He looked her up and down and then stopped and peered at the spirit on her shoulder.

"What is that on your shoulder?" the guard sneered, as though the act of talking to Kira might be enough to contract some sort of disease.

Kira swallowed. She could form a couple of daggers and strike, but even if she won, then she would have a couple of bodies to clean up. And Yanmei would probably disapprove. Was killing people wrong even when they may be dangerous? It was all far too confusing. "Um. This is Shiki. She's a cat."

"Meow," Shiki said in the least convincing cat impression Kira had ever heard.

"A cat?" said the bulbous-nosed guard. "What's wrong with it?"

"It's deformed," Kira said with a friendly smile. "You know how these lords and ladies like their oddities."

The bulbous-nosed guardsman nodded at that. "The prince keeps frogs." He sighed. "Frogs! Slimy little things. I stepped on one once, and it exploded. Goo everywhere."

"It doesn't look like a cat," said the guard with pitted cheeks.

Bulb-nose shook his head. "And that smoke demon at the Empress' side doesn't look like a person, but we're told not to think about it."

"Quiet!" hissed Pit-cheeks. They continued down the corridor, Kira and Shiki already forgotten. "You can't go saying things like that. You can't criticise the Empress out in the open." They disappeared around the corner, and Kira breathed a long exhale.

"Meow," Shiki said again.

Kira rolled her eyes. "You were not a convincing cat at all. Can't you go invisible?"

Shiki whistled and rolled her eyes.

"What do you mean you don't want to?"

The little spirit crossed her arms and turned away from Kira. They moved on and found a stairway leading down. There was no way to tell if it led to the basement or not, but as long as it went down, Kira considered it progress.

Guang paced around the mirror shop. Yanmei's stoic silence made his frustration and unease worse. She knelt on the floor while they waited for Kira to return like an annoying, slightly judgemental statue. It was probably her way of coping with the situation. Many people used meditation as a salve for their anxiety. Not Guang though. He'd never been good at meditation. He preferred to move, to waste some energy. Even in his advancing years, the idea of sitting still when his world was one step from collapsing around him, made him want to scream.

Night fell like a blanket over the city. Street lamps were lit and the bustle of people going about their business continued. Guang lit a lantern inside the shop and hunted about for a stove and kettle. Tea would help calm him down. Tea always helped. He couldn't shake the feeling that something had gone wrong. That he would never see Haruto again.

Unable to find a stove or kettle, Guang gave up and made another circuit of the shop. He realised the owner hadn't come back. Kira gave the woman a good scare, but not enough that she would just abandon her livelihood. He stalked over to the mirror for the fourth time since Kira had disappeared into it. The frame was still intact, but the glass littered the floor in a thousand reflective shards.

"Never seen anything like it," Guang said, staring at the mirror. "That girl is a wonder."

Yanmei chuckled. "She's growing up so fast. It feels like she has matured more in the past few weeks than in the last decade in Heiwa."

Guang grumbled as he searched for the words. "She's a fast learner and no doubt. I've rarely met anyone who picked up qi training so quick."

"The other teachers at Heiwa called her slow. They said there was something wrong with her, that she lacked the focus the other children had. I wanted to believe otherwise, but it was always such a struggle to teach her anything. She never concentrated, never grasped the basics for long enough to learn. Even the Sage despaired. What few techniques he taught her, she never mastered. He said she got bored too quickly or frustrated too easily and moved on before she actually learned anything."

Yanmei fell silent for a few seconds, then frowned at Guang. "You make everything into a game with her. Every lesson a challenge, a game to be won. It seems to work."

Guang scratched at his beard, pulling through a tangle. "It's how I was taught. Worked far better than lessons and such. I never sat still long enough when I was young. Reading books or listening to teachers ramble about history or politics or whatever was so dull. It wasn't until old Jezo One Eye took me under his wing that I learned anything. These days, I figure everyone is different. We think differently, feel differently. Perhaps we learn differently too. Some of us can focus on books and words and learn like that, others do better when it's a challenge, when it's fun."

"Thank you for teaching her. It's good to see her happy and learning, instead of bored and frustrated. It's good to know I was right about her."

Guang grumbled again as he considered whether to say anything. Yanmei's eyebrows arched, and she inclined her head toward him. "I hope you don't mind me saying this," Guang said. "But I think you made a mistake with that girl. Don't get me wrong, you raised her well, but you sheltered her, protected her. It's obvious. You spent years making sure she had no responsibilities."

"I thought it best to shield her from it, give her time to come to terms with what she is. I wanted to protect her from the world."

Guang shook his head. "That's where you went wrong. You didn't shield her, you stifled her. Some people... I think Kira is the type of girl who needs some responsibility to focus her. You say she's grown up more in the past few weeks than the last ten years, then perhaps it's because she doesn't have the choice not to anymore. That's not always a bad thing. It's all fine and well giving someone room to grow, but sometimes you need to give them a reason to grow."

Yanmei stared at Guang in silence for a while. He scratched at his beard again, uncomfortable under such scrutiny. At last she said, "I think my father was wrong about you. He called you a stupid, rabid beast for murdering his son, but you're not. And you're far wiser than I thought you'd be."

Guang chuckled. "Thank you, I think. Backhanded compliments are always welcome. And about your brother..."

"It's alright. He deserved to die."

"Maybe. But I didn't kill him." There was a loud noise outside, footsteps pounding up the walkway. Guang edged to the door and cracked it open. "Oh, cabbage!"

"What is it?" Yanmei was already getting up, using her naginata as a crutch and struggling to straighten her back.

Guang pulled the door closed. "It's our cue to leave. The woman is back, and she brought soldiers with her. Lots of soldiers."

Yanmei rolled her shoulders and stretched her neck until it popped. "I'm not going anywhere. I'm waiting right here until Kira comes back." She strode to the door and grabbed the handle. Then she paused there, handle in one hand, naginata in the other. "She needs a mirror to come back through."

Guang wondered if Yanmei was waiting for him to give her another option. But he didn't have one. They had no chance of making it out of there carrying a mirror big enough for Kira to come through. He didn't even know if the girl could find them if they moved. He didn't understand the technique she had used and did not know its limitations. Nor could he help Yanmei. His vows prevented him from wielding a weapon or taking a life. He had no better option to give her than run. And he knew beyond a shadow of a doubt she would not even consider that. So he gave her the only thing he could think of. "Good luck."

Yanmei let out a deep, steady breath, then pulled open the door and stepped out onto the street. A dozen soldiers waited for her.

Chapter 33

Kira searched for hours. At least it felt like hours. She'd never been good at keeping track of time. Night fell. She caught glimpses of the dark sky through windows. The problem was that the palace was huge, a titan of wood and stone that made Heiwa Academy look like a garden shed, and every corridor looked like the last. Also, now and then she'd hear the tramp of boots and had to duck into the nearest room to hide from passing soldiers. The patrols were infrequent, but she knew she was running out of time. When morning rolled around, the palace would come alive, and there would be no sneaking about then. Someone was bound to realise she didn't belong.

She was waiting in another dark room for the soldiers to pass. There was a man in the bed, tangled up in the sheets and snoring almost as loud as Guang. Kira crept towards the full-sized mirror in front of the wardrobe and pressed her palm against it. Every room in the palace had mirrors, some large and some small. Some corridors had them too. Hundreds of mirrors that Kira could peer through, but none of them could really help her. The place she needed to go was the one place without mirrors. But maybe that was helpful in its own right. She just needed to change the way she was looking at it. Instead of searching for mirrors in the dungeon, she needed to search for somewhere in the palace that didn't have any mirrors.

It was difficult to concentrate with the man's snoring tearing through both the quiet and her calm. Kira considered slitting his throat, but that would be bad. She had to remind herself of that every time he filled the room with his noise. She searched the mirror on the wardrobe for several minutes, peering through a hundred different mirrors until she found one that looked out onto a corridor to the right of which she could just make out some steps leading down. She tried to find a mirror directly below the spot, but there were none. It had to be the dungeon. She was just about to jump through the mirror when she saw four soldiers in the corridor too, to the left of the mirror, dressed in their green ceramic armour and carrying spears. She needed to distract them somehow.

Kira slipped out of the snoring man's bedroom and rushed down the corridor, and then another corridor. After several turns and a close encounter with a drunken man swaying all over the place, she found the hallway she was looking for, but when she walked past it, the four soldiers were still there. Two were leaning against one wall, both with their helms off and smoking pipes. The other two were playing some sort of game, making hand signals to each other. Regardless of what they were doing, they were in her way.

She slipped into the first room she found to formulate a plan. It was small, smelled of vinegar, and was packed with mops and buckets and cloths. She couldn't fail here. She knew she had to get past the guards somehow. Guang and Yanmei would be so disappointed if she returned to them now without Haruto. She had to prove that she was capable of doing this on her own... somehow.

Shiki squeaked.

"I can't fight four of them at once." She paused to consider it, then shook her head. "What if one got away?"

Another squeak.

"I don't know how." She couldn't turn invisible, but maybe she could do the next best thing. She plucked an apron from a hook, slipped it over her head, and picked up a wooden bucket and a mop. At the last moment, she remembered Shiki sitting on her shoulder. "Vanish." The little spirit grumbled, somehow sounding exactly like Guang. "Either vanish or get in the bucket." Shiki stared down into the bucket for a moment, looked up at Kira and whistled, then she leapt down into the bucket with a splash. Kira pulled open the door and strode towards the guards.

The four guards, three men and one woman, were still playing their hand signal game, but they stopped when they saw her approach. Kira kept her eyes down. Servants always did that. They acted meek and nodded a lot. Shiki stared at her from the sloshing muck in the bucket.

"What's this?" asked a soldier with an oiled moustache.

"Cleaning the cells," Kira said.

The woman grunted. "What happened to Chimiko?"

Kira almost panicked. She guessed Chimiko was the usual maid. "She, uh, fell. Broke her wrist."

The other two soldiers chuckled as if a girl hurting herself was a matter of humour.

"Go on then," said the woman.

Kira nodded just like a servant should and hurried past.

"Wait," said the man with the oiled moustache. "I should go with you. There're dangerous prisoners down there. You'll need protection."

"Cabbage!" Kira whispered.

"What's that?" the oiled moustache asked.

"Uh," Kira smiled at him. "Just repeating my shopping list. I need cabbage for the, uh, mistress. Her meal, I mean."

The oiled moustache frowned and kept walking. Kira looked down into the bucket. Two bright eyes peered back at her. Just the sight of Shiki gave her courage. She waited for the soldier to pass her and lead her towards the dungeon.

The steps led down into an oppressive murk. The stone walls were damp and cold. There was a strange feeling about the place, an air of suffering that seemed to seep from everywhere all at once.

"You wouldn't believe some of the monsters we've had locked up down here," the oiled moustache told her as they walked. "Many of them never see daylight again. Sometimes you can still hear their screams. Can you believe that?" He looked over his shoulder, stroking his moustache, and grinned at Kira. "Long dead, but their spirits still haunt the place. Common folk call them yokai. Do you know what that means?"

"Never heard of them," Kira said, keeping her voice flat. At the bottom of the stairs, the dungeon opened out into a wide hallway with a couple of low burning lanterns and doors to either side. The smell of unwashed bodies made Kira's nose wrinkle.

"Ghosts," the moustache said, winking at her. "Terrifying things that wail and stalk the lonesome. But don't worry. I'm here to protect you."

Kira rolled her eyes and glanced down at Shiki in the bucket. "Are we far enough away, do you think?" she whispered. "Please say we are."

Shiki popped her head up from the water and warbled.

"Huh?" the soldier said. He turned around, and Kira swung the bucket into his face. Wood splintered and stinking water splashed the wall. The soldier collapsed against the stone wall, dazed but stubbornly peering at her through one half-open eye. Shiki clung to his pauldron and slapped an arm in his face. Kira punched him in his breastplate so hard it cracked. The guard's eyes rolled back in his head, and he slumped to the floor. Shiki rode him to the ground, then raised her spindly arms in victory despite having done none of the work.

Kira shook the pain out of her knuckles. It had been foolish to punch him like that, but the alternative had been stabbing him. Yanmei would want her to do this as peacefully as possible.

"Alright, now where's Haruto?"

Shiki scrabbled up her apron, sat on her shoulder and shook like a dog, spraying smelly water over Kira's face.

"You are horrible," Kira said, flicking a finger at the little spirit.

Shiki batted the finger away, whistled and made a show of looking left, then right. Then she shrugged.

"You don't know?"

Shiki squeaked.

Kira sighed. "Horrible *and* useless."

Each cell had an iron key hanging on a hook beside its door, and each door had a small slider about eye level to look inside the cell. Kira worked methodically, peering into each one. Most were empty. Some contained unmoving forms and smells that convinced her the occupants had been left to rot. She hoped they had not treated Haruto so poorly. But then, he was immortal, so what could they do to him? She hoped the answer was nothing.

After finding nothing, or at least nothing alive, in more than a dozen cells, she came to a door with a thin line of light seeping from its slider. She slid it back and peered inside. The cell was well lit by couple of flickering candles. There was a small cot wedged into the corner, a desk piled high with books, and chair with a man sitting in it reading. He looked remarkably clean for a prisoner, but he was not Haruto. Kira started to close the slider.

"Hello?" the man said. He had a pleasant voice. Kira glanced through the hatch again to find the man staring at her from his seat. "Who are you?"

Kira considered closing the hatch and moving on, but he might shout after her. She couldn't have that. "I'm a servant," she mumbled.

The man drew in a deep breath, narrowed his eyes, and shook his head. He was slim and elegant, with long dark hair tied into a tail, and light brown eyes. He stood and she saw he was wearing court robes. She thought all prisoners would wear rags, but this one was bedecked in finery and living in relative comfort.

"You're not a servant, nor are you from Kodachi," the man said as he strode toward the door, scratching at the artful stubble on his chin. "Your accent is all wrong, and you have a spirit sitting on your shoulder. Who are you?"

Kira stepped back from the hatch as the man bent a little and pressed his eye to it to peer out at her. "I'm looking for a friend, " she told him.

"In a dungeon?" the man asked, arching his eyebrows.

"He's an... interesting friend. He'd be new. Only arrived today."

"Ahh, the onmyoji," the man said, easing back slightly from the opening. "That explains the spirit."

"You know about him?"

"I listen." The man rolled his eyes. "There's not much else to do." He poked a hand out of the little hatch and pointed a finger. "He's down that way somewhere. I believe he's guarded, which must make him quite interesting indeed, considering they don't even guard me."

"Thank you," Kira said, turning to go.

"Wait! The key to my door is just there," the man blurted. "I'll give you whatever you want. Riches, land. A position in court. My eternal gratitude, of course."

Kira turned back to the door. "How would you have any of those things? You're a prisoner."

"I'm a *royal* prisoner." The man grinned at her through the hatch. "Prince Ido Katsuo. " He pushed his hand through the hatch and pointed it at Kira.

"Why would a prince be in a dungeon?" Kira looked at his hand. It was clean and soft, but she did not know why he was pointing it at her. She was getting distracted. She needed to find Haruto.

"Well, I may have snuck into the palace and tried to kill Auntie Ryoko. Evidently, I underestimated her. And now I am here." He wiggled his fingers, then pulled his hand back inside the cell.

"You're an assassin?" Kira asked.

The man paused and his smile drooped. "I like to think of myself more as an economical problem solver."

Kira turned to go.

"Wait! You won't just be saving me. I have brothers here too, at least two of them. You'll be preserving the Ido line. You'll have an entire royal family in your debt. Think of all you could ask for. And all you have to do, is hand me that key." He stuffed his hand out again and pointed towards the key hanging by the door.

Kira gave the man one of Haruto's shrugs, though it was far from perfect. "All I want is my friend." She hurried away, but slowed as she thought about what the man had said, about what was right, about what Yanmei would do. Kira turned around and walked back to the door. The prince was already back at his desk.

"You're the Empress' enemy?" Kira asked.

"I probably wouldn't have tried to kill her otherwise."

"So if I let you out, it would cause trouble for her?" Kira mused. The Empress was working with the onryo. She had captured Haruto. She was not a good person, so causing her trouble must be a good thing.

Shiki squeaked, but Kira shushed the spirit.

"Here," Kira said. She took the iron key from the hook and shoved it through the hatch. "Free yourself." She turned and hurried away to find Haruto.

Now that she knew Haruto was being guarded, it was easy to find his cell. It was the only one with guards sitting outside. There were two of them sitting at a little table: One was a big man whose armour barely seemed to constrain his chest. The other was a woman with long, raven hair. They were rolling dice and not paying much attention to anything else. Unluckily for them, Kira's patience had run out.

She flicked a dagger into her hand and held it up in front of her face. "Momo." She threw it towards the guards and ordered it to shatter as it reached them. It showered the guards and the table with mirrored shards. Kira couldn't do much with such small reflections, but she made the two soldiers see a blindingly bright flash. They both leaned back in their chairs, rubbing their eyes and grumbling. Kira flicked her other wrist and ran at them.

The big soldier had just reached his feet when Kira slid past him on her knees, slashing at his ankles with a dagger she named Luna. He howled and collapsed to his knees. The woman with the raven hair reached for her sword, but Kira punched her wrist, grabbed her by the rim of her breastplate and flipped her over her shoulder into the wall. Then she kicked the woman's head, shattering her ceramic helmet, and knocking her unconscious.

The big man clambered to his feet, using the table for support. The wound to his ankle wasn't deep, but it was slowing him down. He pulled his sword from his saya, but Kira plucked a chair from the table and smashed it over his head in a shower of sticks and splinters. The soldier swayed for a moment, then slumped facedown on the table, scattering the dice. He lay there not moving.

Kira stared down at her hands for a moment. She had defeated the guards so easily. Perhaps Haruto was right about her. She was stronger than she realised.

Shiki squeaked and waved her arms frantically.

"Right! Sorry." Kira snatched the key from the wall and unlocked the door.

There was neither bed nor desk nor even candles in Haruto's cell, nothing save Haruto sitting chained to the wall, a dozen swords piercing his chest. His hair hung loose about his lolling head, trailing on the floor. His kimono was in tatters. Blood ran in crimson rivers down the cracks in the stone and pooled on the floor. He didn't appear to be breathing.

"No no no," Kira said, rushing toward him. "Haruto? Haruto, can you hear me?" She lifted his head, and though his eyes were open, they were glassy and vacant. His flesh was cool to the touch. She turned to Shiki. "What do I do?" The little spirit stood at the doorway, eyes wide in her dark face. She didn't even squeak.

Kira fretted, clenched her teeth, balled her fists, trying to decide what she should do. Then she grabbed a sword embedded in Haruto's chest and jerked it free. It took more effort than she expected, as if the flesh were holding on to the steel, refusing to let it go. She threw the sword into the corner of the cell. A trickle of dark blood ran from the wound, but Haruto did not move.

Shiki whined from the doorway. Kira just looked at the spirit. She didn't know what to say.

She turned back to Haruto and pulled another sword from his chest. It was driven deep, a fatal strike for a mortal. But he was immortal, wasn't he? She threw the sword away and reached for another. Tears streamed down her face, but she pulled sword after sword from Haruto's chest until there were none left. He slumped in his chains, still not moving.

Kira knelt next to Haruto and grabbed a chain pinning him to the wall. She wrenched on it, yanked it, but no matter how strong she might be, the metal proved to be stronger. She picked up a sword from the pile she'd made and swung it at the chains. Metal sparked against metal with a noise like a flock of angry crows, but the chains still held. She hit it again and again and on the third strike the blade snapped, but the chain held. Kira plucked another of the bloody swords from the ground and pointed it at Shiki. "In you go," she said.

The little spirit stared, shook her entire body, and squeaked.

"No, it won't hurt. You'll be fine." Kira said. "I've seen you cut through things much harder than this. You can do it."

The little spirit plodded forward on leaden limbs and climbed up Kira's apron, clinging to her arm. She whistled a dour note and leapt into the blade.

Pain seared through Kira's arm, across her chest, and down her back with such ferocity she screamed and fell to her knees. She could barely move. It burned through her limbs and scattered her thoughts. She clamped her jaw to stop herself from screaming and heard a different sound, a tremulous low whistle.

"I'm sorry Shiki, but we have to do this."

Squinting through tears, Kira forced herself to stand and gripped the sword in both hands. The pain intensified, racing up her arms and crashing through her back with such blinding savagery she thought she would pass out. She took a deep breath, dropped into a wide stance and swung Shiki at the chain connected to Haruto's left wrist. Crimson blade met black iron and sliced through it, leaving both severed edges of the chain hissing and smoking. Haruto slumped forward, one arm still attached to the wall. Kira staggered across his legs, squinting past tears. She raised Shiki and screamed as she swung the sword down at the second chain. Haruto fell forward, face against the stone floor, and didn't move.

Shiki leaped out the blade onto the floor with a thud. Kira's legs gave out, and she collapsed. She threw the sword away and stared at her hands. Red welts covered her palms, some weeping blood. The pain all over was like a monster she couldn't escape. She felt like if she closed her eyes, it would swallow her and never let her go. But she didn't have time for it.

Shiki chittered as she crawled over to Haruto and nuzzled against his neck, but there were no words to the sounds this time. Only sadness. Kira crawled towards them on hands and knees, but she had no idea what to do now. No idea how to revive Haruto. She looked from the fallen onmyoji to the spirit and back again.

"I'm sorry," she whispered. "I don't know what to do."

"Ow," Haruto said, his voice as quiet as a butterfly's wings.

Shiki jumped up and flailed her little arms at Haruto's face.

Kira shuffled forward and helped Haruto roll onto his back. He stared up at the ceiling and groaned. "If a shinigami ever offers you immortality..." he paused and licked his dry lips "...tell them to bugger off."

Kira giggled. She knew it wasn't funny, but she couldn't help it. She was so glad he was alive. She began to cry again, but not from the pain. She fell forward and wrapped her arms around Haruto.

"Still wounded," Haruto grunted.

"Sorry!" Kira pulled back. "Can you walk? We need to get you out of here."

Haruto groaned. "Help me up."

Kira took hold of his arm, helped pull him to his feet, and put the arm over her shoulders. He was heavier than she expected. His feet dragged along the floor, one step, two... then he pitched forward. Kira would have dropped him, but she flung out her free hand and steadied them on the doorway. Shiki was sitting on his shoulder, hairy arms wrapped around his neck. She chattered to him about everything that had happened since he was captured and how scared she had been. Kira nodded along.

Haruto grunted and arched his brow as they walked past the unconscious guards outside his cell, but he said nothing about it as Kira lead them back they she had come.

"Through a mirror?" Haruto asked as Shiki got to that part of the story.

Kira grinned at him. "How do you think I'm getting you out?"

Chapter 34

Haruto stumbled on the first step up out of the dungeon, and his legs collapsed beneath him. He pulled Kira down with him, and they both hit the steps hard. Every wound he'd ever taken hurt. He'd been stabbed, burned, torn apart... and that was just in the past couple of weeks. So many deaths and none of them had stuck. This was the first time he'd been left with steel inside of him. It almost felt as though his body had tried to heal around the swords, to incorporate them into his flesh, and now that they were gone, something was missing.

He lay on the steps, panting and hurting and wishing it would stop. He was dehydrated, had lost too much blood. Sweat trickled down his back and he shivered from the chills. He wanted to round up everyone who had ever said his immortality was a blessing, and laugh in their faces. "Give me a moment," he wheezed, struggling to catch his breath.

Kira looked up the stairs, then at Haruto. She shifted anxiously from foot to foot. Then she looked down at her blistered hands. "Why did it hurt?" she said. "When I held Shiki, it hurt. It..." She held up her hands to show him the red sores. Shiki squeaked and nodded.

Lost in his own pain, it took Haruto a moment to realize she was talking to him. "Shiki was a gift from my patron shinigami," he said. He closed his eyes and found the darkness comforting. "All onmyoji are required to summon a Shikigami, but Omoretsu sent her to me." He reached across his body and patted Shiki on the head. "She might look cute and fluffy in this form, but when she possesses a weapon, she takes on her true purpose, a spirit blade. Her purpose is to kill yokai. And you, Kira, are a yokai. It hurt because she exists to kill you. You should not have been able to wield her at all without destroying the both of you. Please do not do it again."

Shiki squeaked and patted Haruto's head with a little arm.

"Sorry, it... was the only thing I could think of." Kira breathed a long sigh. "Come on." She grabbed Haruto's arm and pulled him up again. He groaned and sagged against her, unable to stand. She grunted but took his weight on her shoulders again. They continued up the stairs.

Haruto had to concentrate hard on each step, and even then they seemed to swim about his vision. His feet were clumsy, uncoordinated things that refused to do what he told them to, and his strength was all but gone. "You... shouldn't have come for me," he said softly.

"You shouldn't have got yourself captured," Kira said. "But I'm here now and we've just a little more to go. Now be quiet."

They reached the top of the steps and a long, wide corridor lay ahead of them. Near the far end, three soldiers lounged at a small table. They didn't appear to be paying much attention, but they were in the way, and Haruto was in no condition to fight them.

"We're only going as far as the mirror," Kira whispered, pointing to a large mirror hanging on the wall about halfway between them and the soldiers.

"Why?"

"Because I'm going to take us through it," Kira said. "Just keep quiet, and when I jump into the mirror, you jump too."

They crept along the wall towards the mirror. All the guards needed to do was turn their heads, and they would be discovered. There was nowhere for them to hide. Haruto concentrated on his feet, trying to make his steps sure and quiet. Bloody footprints stretched out behind him, a trail so obvious a blind man could follow.

When they reached the mirror, Kira pulled them to a stop. She frowned, stared at her reflection for a few seconds, and placed her palm against its shining surface. Shiki gave a reassuring little squeak, but Haruto wasn't comfortable at the idea of travelling through a mirror. Then Kira's grip on him tightened, and she rushed forward. She jumped into the mirror, and he jumped too.

The mirror shattered into a hundred thousand glittering shards. Haruto hit the wall and fell back among the shards on the floor in a painful, bloody heap. The soldiers shouted. He knew he needed to stand up, to meet them on his feet. Kira was gone, vanished through the mirror just like she said. He needed to fight or they would put him back in his cell. He didn't think he could take being run through again.

The guards rushed toward him. "Shiki?"

The little spirit squeaked once and scrabbled up his chest onto his shoulder. She inflated into a ball of light, one soldier, a woman with a jutting chin, slowed and stared at her wide-eyed. Haruto stooped and picked up a large shard of mirror. Then he looked up at the soldiers running at him and felt his legs tremble.

The first spear took him in the sternum.

Yanmei was a hurricane. The soldiers surrounded her; she let them. They thought they had her trapped. She moved so fluidly her years seemed to fall away from her, twisting and thrusting her naginata. The butt of the polearm, a sculpted blooming lotus flower, connected with a flat-nosed soldier's breastplate, cracking it and sending him sprawling. The others closed on her. Yanmei pulled back her weapon, ducked a spear strike, and kicked the giant soldier's legs out from under him. She spun away and swung her naginata around smashing the soldier's head and leaving him limp on the floor.

Two more soldiers approached her, stabbing with their spears. Yanmei batted them both away with her naginata and dashed between them, sweeping the legs out from under the bigger one with the flat of her blade. Then she pivoted and smashed the flower into the smaller soldier's groin.

Guang winced at the sight and the sound of the smack and then at the soldier's whimper as he clutched himself. It was hard not to feel for the poor man having his grapes crushed like that.

The unfortunate fellow dropped to his knees, still clutching at himself, then toppled sideways. Yanmei was already moving, spinning away from another spear that whispered by her ear.

Three more soldiers fell one by one as Yanmei gusted through them, smashing their helms and cracking their armour. She was a terror, a whirling hellion of crushing blows and the promise of pain. Yet she was going to lose. Guang saw it as surely as if inked on the page. She wasn't killing anyone, wasn't even maiming them. She was only using the flat of her blade and the pommel. She shattered armour and broke bones, but most of the wounds she dealt were not incapacitating. She was carefully not killing anyone, and it was going to cost her life.

Yet, as Guang watched Yanmei fight, he realised something else. She wasn't slowing down. She was breathing hard, snarling, but she was speeding up. Her strikes were hitting harder and harder. The soldier with the crushed nuts clambered to his feet and crept close to her, then he clutched his face with his hand and staggered back from the heat. Yanmei shimmered with it.

The captain of the guard had yet to join the fight. He was a young man with a dark scrub of hair beneath his helmet and a scar over his right eye. His armour was black instead of green, and a red cloak hung from his shoulders. A Serpent Guard, one of the Empress' most elite soldiers. Guang watched the man turn to the tall woman at his side and give an order. The woman ran off into the city, no doubt to fetch reinforcements. Then the captain drew his two swords and swept into the battle.

Yanmei met the Serpent Guard in a blur of strikes that left Guang dizzy. The Serpent Guard captain flowed through forms, whipping his swords at Yanmei in a flurry. Yanmei gave ground, stepping back again and again, her naginata spinning in her hands, blocking every blow. Then she spun around, her naginata blade just a breath from the ground, whipping up eddies of dust as she whirled up and slammed down on the captain's crossed swords. The captain took the full force of Yanmei's strike on his blades. The blow should have mangled his steel, pulverised his flesh, and shattered his bones. But the captain took the attack with a loud grunt and the ground beneath him cracked, fissures running out from him in every direction. Guang recognised a technique when he saw it. This Serpent Guard had a way of deflecting energy, which meant no amount of raw power would break his defence.

The Serpent Guard captain recovered faster than Yanmei expected and rushed inside her guard. He swung a sword across her chest. The scales on her coat took much of the force from the blow, but the sword still found some flesh between them. Drops of steaming blood spattered the ground. Yanmei staggered back a step, but the captain pressed forward. He thrust one sword, and Yanmei batted it away with her naginata. But his other blade seemed to come out of nowhere, an upward strike at Yanmei's groin. Somehow Yanmei twisted her naginata to block it just enough to step back out of range, but the sword cut through the shaft of her polearm, snapping it in half. The captain pivoted and kicked Yanmei in the chest, sending her flying into the outer wall of the mirror shop. She collapsed in a groaning heap.

Guang pulled open the door and stepped outside. The Serpent Guard captain glanced at him, eyes narrowed, then back at Yanmei as she struggled to stand. He had three more soldiers behind him, not that he seemed to need them. Two old bandits were apparently no match for his youthful vigour or his powerful technique.

"Surrender," the Serpent Guard captain said, his voice high and chiding. "You will not receive another chance."

"That'll be one way inside the palace, I suppose," Guang said, holding out a hand to Yanmei. He winced at the heat of her grip. It was like holding a torch by the burning end.

"I'm not going anywhere while Kira is missing," Yanmei said. "She needs a mirror to come back to."

Guang grumbled. He had expected nothing else. And besides, he didn't like the idea of surrendering to a man less than half his age. He cleared his throat. "I'm afraid surrender is not an option, though I appreciate the offer. Very magnanimous of you."

If the captain was put out at all by the idea of killing them, he didn't show it. He stepped forward, swords ready and soldiers at his back.

Guang heard glass shattering inside the shop. He grinned and turned around. Kira wasn't there, but the lantern he had lit earlier was smashed, the fire flaring up the far wall of the shop. The trail of flames rushed through the wooden building, burned through the door like paper, and whooshed into Yanmei's hands.

The Serpent Guard captain took a step back, a frown on his scarred face. Yanmei stepped into the space he left, her fists ablaze, her sleeves burned to embers. Guang hadn't noticed it before, but as she stood there now, she looked a lot like her father. If nothing else, she had inherited Flaming Fist's flaming fists. But it was more than that. They had the same granite jaw and eyes like pools of oil just waiting to be lit.

Yanmei darted at the captain, quicker than she had been before. Her bloodline technique fuelling her innate technique allowing her to move faster. She thrust a fiery jab at the at the captain so fast Guang barely even saw it. The captain slashed back with both swords, left then right in an *X*, but Yanmei spun away, then lunged in and slammed a blazing fist against his breastplate, shattering it and igniting the tunic beneath. He collapsed to the ground and rolled around to quash the flames. Yanmei stood over him a second. Then she raised a knee and stomped down on his thigh. Guang heard a loud crack. The soldier screamed and crawled away dragging the broken leg. A snarling guardswoman stepped up in his place and thrust a spear at Yanmei's face. Yanmei swayed around it, grabbed the shaft. Her hand burned through it as if it were an old scroll. She grabbed the blade end, darted forward and jabbed the spear tip deep into the woman's shoulder. The woman shrieked, dropped the half spear shaft, and Yanmei kicked her in the chest, sending her sprawling backwards onto the street. The other soldier standing in the street yelped, turned, and ran.

That left the Serpent Guard captain. He limped at Yanmei warily. Guang could hardly believe he could stand. Fires spread up Yanmei's arms from her fingertips to her elbows. She took a wide stance so her coat wouldn't go up in flames. The grimace on her face told Guang she was in pain. Kira had been right: Yanmei's technique was killing her.

Yanmei rushed the captain. He flailed his swords at her, but she brushed them aside and punched him in his chest, cracking his ceramic armour. He cried out, staggering and spitting blood, and Yanmei grabbed his blades. Her flames flared higher and hotter. The Serpent Guard screamed and let go of the swords. He stared at her for a moment, then he turned and limped away. Yanmei threw the swords to the ground. They were twisted, smoking things, melted and bent. She watched the captain go. Then her flames guttered out, and she collapsed to her knees.

Guang rushed to her. She was trembling. Her hands were black and red, covered in weeping sores and charred skin. She clutched them to her chest and wheezed in a breath. Her eyes were wild, darting about and unfocused.

"Can you stand?" Guang asked.

Yanmei looked up at him, and he saw fear in her eyes. She'd given her all and won the fight, but the cost was so high. Too high.

"We have to go," he said and hauled her to her feet heedless of her scorching heat. People were already gathering in the street. So many eyes watching them. "We've made quite the scene."

"Not--" Yanmei winced at some pain "--until Kira..."

Guang glanced at the mirror shop. The shop front was ablaze, and by the looks of it, the interior was a furnace of charred wood, falling beams, and floating embers. Guang ventured to the burning doorway, hoping to grab a mirror and take it with them, but the heat was too intense. He backed away and took Yanmei by the arm again. "That's not happening." He tried to pull her away. She fought him, pulled free, and approached the shop. She couldn't get close unless she used her technique again. Guang knew it would finish her if she tried. He grabbed her arm again and pulled her away. "You can't help Kira if you're dead and we can't stay here. The building is going to collapse, and the captain will be back with reinforcements soon. We have to go. Now!"

Yanmei stared at the mirror shop a moment longer, then nodded and deflated, shrinking in on herself. Guang led her away.

"Kira will find us," Guang said, hoping it was true. "Somehow." They fled through the streets, Guang half carrying Yanmei, the sound of people rushing to fight the fire fading away behind them.

Chapter 35

Spear protruding from his chest, Haruto growled through the pain as a pig-nosed soldier pushed him back. He slammed his hand down on the soldier's spear, snapping the haft in half. Then he lurched forward, collapsing against the soldier and driving the shard of mirror into the man's thigh. Pig Nose howled in pain and Haruto grabbed the side of his face and slammed his head against the stone wall. The soldier collapsed, unconscious but not dead, and Haruto fell to the floor a moment later, struggling to draw breath.

Haruto looked up just in time to see the soldier with the jutting chin rush at him, her face twisted in rage. Haruto rose to his knees, pulled the spearhead from his chest and flung it at her. It bounced harmlessly off her ceramic armour. She raised her sword to chop down at him... then her eyes went distant. She teetered and dropped her sword on the floor, reached up and touched the back of her head. Her fingers came away dripping with blood. She toppled sideways and slumped lifeless against the wall.

Haruto grabbed the woman's sword from the carpet and staggered upright. He swayed on his feet and leaned against the wall for support. His vision blurred, but he was able to see the fuzzy outline of the man approaching him. He was not wearing armour. As Haruto's vision focused, he saw the newcomer was wearing court robes, and the soldier Haruto thought was coming for him was lying motionless at his feet. The courtly fellow was cleaning blood from his hands on a small strip of cloth.

"You must be Haruto," the man said. He had a lofty accent to go right along with his robes. "Kira told me all about you. Well, I suppose she told me nothing about you really, but I got the gist. Nice to meet you."

Shiki crawled up onto Haruto's shoulder and squeaked.

"A prince?" Haruto said.

The man bowed far lower than anyone of his station should. "Ido Katsuo," he said. "Last son of Emperor Ido Tanaka."

"That would make you the heir," Haruto said, still pointing his stolen sword at the man.

Ido Katsuo made a show of considering that. "Yes, I suppose it would."

"A valuable prisoner then."

"I was," Ido Katsuo said. "Until Kira freed me. I was hoping for a way to repay the favour, and I think helping you escape might be just the thing. Say, where did she go? She seemed to disappear into that mirror."

Haruto shrugged. He was wondering the same thing himself, but there was no help for it. He couldn't wait around and hope Kira reappeared. He needed to get out of the palace. "You watched that? Where from?"

"The shadows," Ido Katsuo said, waving his hand vaguely upward. "I was wondering how to sneak past the guards, but then you appeared and caused a wonderful distraction."

Haruto glanced at the corpses. "Doesn't look like you needed a distraction."

Ido Katsuo shook his head. "Oh no, I couldn't have done this without you. I'm not one for--" he made a few sloppy punches at the air "--martial combat and all that. Much more of a stick-them-while-their-back-is-turned kind of person."

Haruto groaned. "You're an assassin."

"I prefer to call myself an econom--"

"I don't care," Haruto said with a shrug. He let the sword fall from his fingers, thudding on carpet, and then started forward, limping past the bodies and the prince.

The prince fell in beside him. "I know a way out. I snuck in to kill old Auntie Ryoko, after all. I wasn't going to do that without an escape route. This way." He paused at the end of the corridor and glanced both ways. Then he turned left and continued walking.

Haruto watched the prince go for a few seconds. Shiki squeaked in his ear.

"I don't trust him either," Haruto whispered. "But he's the best chance we have of getting out of here. Besides, Kira trusted him enough to set him free."

Shiki squeaked again, and Haruto had to agree. "Let's leave the discussion of her judgment for another time."

The mirror shattered behind Kira, and the heat hit her like she'd stuck her face in a fire pit, searing her skin and stealing her breath. Flames burned the walls around her, so hot it felt like her skin was melting. The smoke was thick and dark, and she fell to coughing immediately. The roar of the fire was deafening as it consumed everything. Charred beams fell from the ceiling. Flat slabs of burning wood and red-hot ceramic tiles fell in from the roof. Mirrors tumbled from the wall, their glass shattering from the heat; their ornate frames charred and flaming.

Haruto didn't make it through. She'd left him behind, trapped in the palace. She needed to get back to him, but the mirror shop was burning, and the only thing that could have caused it was Yanmei.

Kira tried to draw in a breath to shout for Yanmei, but the smoke was too thick and set her to coughing uncontrollably again. She collapsed onto her hands and knees. The floor was hot as a forge, covered in mirrored shards that burned her palms. Another beam cracked somewhere above and showered Kira with embers. She smelled her hair sizzling and patted blindly at her head to put it out. Another mirror shattered from the heat. She didn't know what else to do, so she screamed.

She had to get out. She had to run. The door to the street was completely blocked by burning ceiling beams and a section of flaming wall. No way through it. She spotted one mirror left leaning against the shop counter, the frame already catching fire. It was small, only half her size, and she had no idea where it led, but it was all she had. Flames licked at her feet as she launched herself forward and dove into the mirror.

Yanmei limped along, using Guang's shoulder for support. The old bandit didn't seem to mind, or at least he put a brave face on it. She was in agony. Her hands were blackened claws, seared by her own flames. The cut across her midsection was shallow but stung like a bee's nest every time she moved. And the cold was an oppressive burden that weighed upon her, threatening to crush her. How long had it been since she'd truly felt the cold? She couldn't even remember. Her technique had always kept her warm. Even in Heiwa, with the winters at their harshest and the snow piled up around them, she was a furnace that beat back the cold. But no more.

The Fifth Sage Under Heaven had told Yanmei that her technique was eating away at her remaining years. Some people lived more than a hundred years with the right application of qi and fitness. But Yanmei expected to live half that. It was something she accepted, or at least so she thought. Not anymore. Now that her time was almost up, she didn't want to go. She didn't want to leave Kira. She had never wanted children of her own, couldn't risk passing on her father's infernal technique to a new generation. Ending Flaming Fist's technique and his legacy was the perfect revenge for everything he had done to her. But Kira had been the child Yanmei thought she had never wanted, and she would not leave her alone in the world.

So Yanmei locked down her technique with a savage intensity, promised herself to never use it again, never again allow the fires to burn inside. Even if it meant her burns would never heal and she would feel cold to the end of her days, she would keep her technique dormant. She would spend all her remaining time with Kira. Assuming the girl found her way out of the mirror again. But that was out of Yanmei's hands. All she could do was wait and hope.

"Here we are," Guang said as he stopped and pulled them both to the side of the road. They were at the city outskirts, outside the wall at the edge of the shanty town that had sprung up along the roadside. It looked familiar. After a moment, Yanmei realised it was the same road on which they had entered Kodachi. "If Haruto and Kira make it out, he'll bring her here. Best place to meet with lost friends, back along the road already travelled."

Guang helped Yanmei sit on a large rock on the side of the road and then frowned at her. She shivered and stared back into the city. The fire she had started burned, an orange smudge above the walls, dark smoke rising to obscure the stars. She hadn't meant to start a fire. Guang fished in his satchel, pulled out a thin, patchy blanket, and draped it over Yanmei's shoulders.

"You're shivering," he said.

"It's cold." She could barely hear her own voice.

The old bandit paced back and forth and then looked back at Yanmei. "You're blocking your qi from flowing."

Yanmei nodded and forced a smile at him, though she couldn't hold it long. "It's the only way to stop my technique. It's part of me, always has been. I don't know any other way to stop it."

"Then we need to bandage your hands because they won't heal without your qi."

Yanmei held up her hands and stared at them. "I couldn't escape him," she said, tears stinging her eyes, hopelessness flooding her chest like ice water. "Even after everything, I became my father's daughter." He had murdered so many people with his technique, with his flaming fists. He terrorised his way across half of Hosa to build his legend. She had inherited his fire, but she never wanted his legacy. Even when she was young and desperate to earn his approval, she had followed in his footsteps. She had killed people for him and hated herself for it. And now she had fully become Flaming Fist.

How could she face Kira again? She'd told her girl she would not use her technique, but her actions made the promise a lie. She buried her face in her ruined hands and wept.

Guang sighed and squatted before her, his knees popping like burning bamboo. Gently, he pulled her hands away from her face to look at them. His touch was agony, but she bore it.

The old bandit shook his head and sighed. "You think you're just like your father because you set your fists on fire? Let me tell you how your brother died, Yanmei."

"My father said you murdered him."

Guang chuckled bitterly. "Well, your father was a carrot-faced liar, so best not trust everything he said." He sat back on the ground and stretched out his legs. "We didn't like each other much, your father and I. We even fought a couple of times, but we respected each other. Well, one day I rode out to loot a village, only to find it had already been raided. Your brother Daizen and his crew had hit it, murdered everyone, and were drinking themselves stupid on the wine they found, dancing around a campfire, and bragging about the slaughter, surrounded by the bodies of folk they killed."

"You were known for slaughtering people too." Yanmei wasn't sure why she said it. She had no love for her brother, no desire to protect his memory.

"I was." Guang scratched at his beard. "But not like this. My boys and I rode into the village and killed your brother's men, gave Daizen a good beating, and told him to run back to his father. A sign of respect between bandits, I thought. Your brother didn't like the idea of running back to Flaming Fist with his tail between his legs, so he grabbed his sword and came at me. I was a bit more spry in those days. I gave him another beating for good luck and told him to run." Guang fell silent then, staring towards the orange smudge of fires in the distance.

"Rather than run away, your brother screamed at me, said he was Flaming Fist's son and would prove it. Idiot boy doused himself in wine, grabbed a log from the fire, and set himself a blaze. He screamed like nothing I ever heard before, and we watched him burn. I didn't kill your dumb onion of a brother. He killed himself."

Guang groaned as he got back to his feet. "My point is, I knew your father. Flaming Fist wasn't known for mercy or restraint. I'm pretty sure he'd have killed everyone in that city; soldiers, civilians, me. He'd have burned them all, and he wouldn't have felt a drop of remorse for it. I knew your brother too. Daizen didn't have your father's technique, but he did have your father's evil."

He drew in a breath and looked up to meet Yanmei's gaze. "And now I know you. You're nothing like either of them. You've got your father's technique, sure, but you're not him. I was with you back there, and by my count you killed no one. You could have. The stars know you could have. But you didn't. You went out of your way to avoid killing them. You're not your father, Yanmei. And you do not carry the burden of his legacy."

He was right. Yanmei hoped he was right.

Guang looked at her hands again and grumbled. "Not sure what else to do but wrap them," he said. "You're going to have to let some of your qi flow or..."

"I can't," Yanmei said.

Guang scratched his beard again. "We'll do what we can then." He chuckled. "I suppose that's all a couple of old bandits like us can ever do."

Chapter 36

Crow swept into the throne room. The Empress Ise Ryoko was sitting on the Serpent Throne. It was shaped like a coiled snake, its rearing its head poised above her, and carved from obsidian. It dwarfed her, but then it did not appear to have been designed for a human occupant. Or perhaps it was designed to dwarf anyone who sat it, a lesson about power. The Empress sat with a straight back, conversing with an adviser whose beard was so long he probably had to throw it over his shoulder to avoid peeing on it.

Soldiers stood along the walls of the throne room, the Serpent Guard in their black armour. Even though they were Crow's allies, they were an intimidating sight. Several mirrors hung on the walls around the vast room, and the Empress Ise Ryoko glanced into one to admire herself.

All eyes in the room watched Crow approach the Serpent Throne. The bearded adviser stepped back from the Empress and bowed to her. No doubt most people who came before the Empress bowed or knelt before her. But Crow had no waist with which to bow and no knees to bend, and she was done playing at subservience to the woman, so she simply floated to a stop, smoke billowing from beneath her robe and staining the stone black.

"It's time to fulfil your end of the bargain, Empress Ise Ryoko," Crow said. "My master has instructed me to collect."

The Empress tapped her fingers on the arms of throne, nails scraping the scales of the obsidian serpent. "And where is he? Your master."

Crow ignored the question. "Emperor Ido Tanaka is dead," she announced. Xifeng had just sent word through Crow's smoke.

The Emperor was dead along with the entire Ido family save for those already in the Empress' dungeon. If her sister was to be believed, it had been quite the massacre and the blood stains might never be scrubbed out. Xifeng always delighted in pain and slaughter. Without the Master's disapproving restraint, Xifeng had likely gorged herself on the bloody remains. The thought made Crow uneasy.

"Truly?" the Empress Ise Ryoko asked.

"Now nothing but your own ability prevents you from uniting Ipia," Crow said. "Fulfil your end of the deal. Tell me where the final prison is? Where is Orochi buried?"

The mirror on the wall to Crow's left shattered, and a figure tumbled from it onto the floor amidst the sparkling shards. A young woman with a soot-stained face, messy hair still smoking. It was Crow's new little sister. All eyes watch her stagger to her feet, pull off her burning apron, and throw it aside. Then the girl looked up at them.

Kira's skin ached from the fading heat, and the acrid stench of burning hair was stuck in her nose. An enormous hall stretched out before her with dozens of people, mostly Serpent Guard in black armour, all around. At one end was a raised dais with a throne in the shape of a serpent on it. It didn't take a leap of logic to realise the woman sitting on the throne was the Empress of Ipia. And the smoky figure standing before her was one of the onryo.

"Shit!" Kira hissed. There was another large mirror on the far wall, just fifty paces away. Kira leapt into a sprint while everyone stared at her bewildered. She made it halfway before a flutter of white robes and smoke flew past her and crashed into the mirror, shattering it.

Kira slowed to a stop in the middle of the throne room. Nobody else moved. The soldiers seemed to be waiting for orders. The Empress stared at her with an amused smile. The smile faded and one perfectly sculpted eyebrow rose. "Take her."

The Serpent Guard drew their weapons and closed in on her

from all sides. Kira spun around, looking for an exit. There was another large mirror in the hall, close to the giant doors. But even as she watched, the smoky onryo zipped across and shattered the mirror with a single blow. She turned and stared at Kira, smoke billowing beneath her, her hood an abyss of utter darkness.

There were windows high up on two walls, far too high to climb to, but maybe she could reach them if she used the technique Yanmei had been trying to teach her. One of the windows had a raven sitting on the ledge, head bobbing about, and Kira concentrated as the guards closed their circle around her. She tried to extend a thread of qi up to the windows and then throw herself along it. She shattered, showering mirrored shards on the floor, and failed. The soldiers closed around her, some with spears pointed her way and others with swords held ready to strike. The Empress' elite, the Serpent Guard, Guang had called them. Kira couldn't hope to fight so many of them. But she had no other way out.

A burly soldier with fish lips reached toward her, iron manacles in hand. Kira pushed his arms aside with one hand and flicked a dagger into her other hand. She punched it into his side once, twice, slipping the blade between the soft seam of his breastplate and backplate. He cried out and staggered away, clutching his side, blood gushing over his fingers.

A guard thrust a spear at Kira's face, and she swayed away from it, turning so it swept past her nose. A snarling guard with a sword attacked from the other side. Kira ducked into a spin, lunged at the woman, and deflected her attack with a dagger, which shattered in her hand. Kira flicked another dagger into her other hand, spun, and slashed the woman's neck, cutting through leather and flesh. The woman collapsed, spurting blood. Kira dashed toward a giant, bearded Serpent Guard. She vaulted over two quick spear thrusts at her chest from guards closing in at her sides, grabbed hold of the giant's spear, and jerked him toward her. Then she punched him in his breastplate, cracking it, and kicked the broken ceramic plate into a hundred jagged pieces, sending the giant tumbling away.

Kira heard an icy snap like glass cracking, felt her skin start to crawl. It started in her chest and spread up her neck and across her face, over her nose. She glanced down into her mirrored dagger and saw something staring back at her. A dark hollow eye socket, like a black void. She tore her gaze from her reflection and looked at the guards.

Twenty of them circled her, and more waited behind them. She flicked a new dagger into her hand. "Momo," she whispered to it and then flung it toward the Empress. The woman stepped nimbly to the side and caught the dagger between two slender fingers. Five soldiers broke off the attack to rush to their Empress, but the woman only stared at the dagger in her hand, a smile on her painted lips.

"Shatter," Kira said. Momo shattered in the Empress' hands, showering her face with razor sharp shards and glass dust. She screamed and clutched her left eye. The soldiers huddled around her, shielding her from view. But the rest of the Serpent Guard closed on Kira. Too many of them.

Kira charged the nearest soldier, an old man with a long face, and flung a new dagger at him. He batted it aside with his sword and slashed at her. Kira leapt up, flipped over the blade, and kicked the soldier in his cleft chin. Even as she landed, a guard thrust a spear at her chest. Kira slipped to the side just in time, the point of the spear cutting through the cloth of her stolen kimono. She brought an elbow down on the shaft, snapping it, then lunged forward, planted two palms on the soldier's breastplate and pushed. He flew away from her, slammed against the wall, and collapsed to the floor.

The remaining soldiers were long done with underestimating her now. They began attacking in twos and threes from two sides at once. Kira ducked, dodged, and jumped their thrusting and swinging blades. She flicked new daggers into her hands and threw them at two soldiers in front of her. They shattered against the ceramic armour of one tall woman, but one young soldier went down with a hilt jutting from his eye. Kira sprinted into the opening, spinning between two guards, and deflected a spear blade from one into the other's arm. She kicked the legs out from beneath the spear wielder and hammered her clenched hands down on his back, smashing him to the ground hard enough to crack the stone.

"Kill her!" the Empress screeched over the clamour of battle. The eight remaining Serpent Guards rushed at Kira, a thicket of spears stabbing at her, and she backed away.

Kira heard glass snapping. Cracks formed along her arms, her teeth felt like jagged razors. She was breathing hard, sweat dripping down her face, and a stinging rib told her she'd picked up a wound she didn't remember taking. She was flagging and she knew it. But Haruto had told her she had unfathomable qi reserves; she had to use them through innate techniques, strengthen the body, bursts of speed.

She growled and crouched, tried to focus her qi into her legs. A Serpent Guard with a twitching eye stepped into her, katana held ready. Kira closed on him faster than she thought possible, grabbed his breast plate just below his neck and pulled him down. His legs buckled and she smashed him against the floor, shattering his ceramic armour and the stone floor beneath him. The twitchy-eyed soldier coughed blood over his chin and lay still.

Two more of the guard had circled her, thrust spears at her from opposite directions. Kira spun, grabbed hold of both shafts at once and snapped both with a twist of her wrists. She jumped inside the guard of the screaming woman to her left and shoved her crashing into the two Serpent Guard behind her.

Three soldiers remained. They were hesitating, glancing at each other, scared. Kira stepped toward them, and her leg collapsed beneath her. She glanced down to find a broken spear head sticking out of her thigh, blood leaking into her kimono. She roared and tore it from her leg, threw it away. Her leg trembled as she stood, but it held her as she stepped forward, flicking new daggers into her hands. The three Serpent Guard backed away from her and huddled together, whispering to one another. Kira screamed at them. No words. No thought. Just a howl of and pain and anger. She saw herself in their wide eyes, her skin pale as an Ume petal, eye sockets black and hollow, craggy mirrored teeth jutting from her gums.

She heard a flutter of wings and something heavy hit the floor behind Kira. Terror seized her, racing her heart, dragging on her limbs. But she couldn't give up. She had to keep fighting. She had no other options.

She spun around and thrust both her daggers at the newcomer. Her eyes met his and she shattered. Glass shards fell all around her, and her will to fight fell away with them. A giant stood before her, cloaked in motley feathers, a bamboo tengai on his head. She saw only his eyes, swirling with a riot of colours. Fear crushed her to dust and scattered her to the wind.

"Let's just take these away, shall we?" the giant said. He had a gravelly voice, hard but not unkind. He gently reached out, plucked Kira's daggers from her hands, and dropped them to the floor. She didn't fight back. Couldn't fight back. She was so scared she couldn't even run. And she recognised him from Guang's story. The Herald of Bones.

Kira's knees buckled and she collapsed to the floor, tears rolling down her cheeks. She wanted to move. To get up and attack the tengu, or run from him, or anything. But she couldn't. She glimpsed herself in a mirrored shard on the floor. The cracks in her skin were gone, her eyes returned to normal, her teeth were just teeth. A sound like distant music filled her head and she tried to shake it away. She looked up again to find the Herald of Bones standing over her, his swirling eyes pinning her to the floor. "What's happening to me?" she asked.

"Kill her!" the Empress screeched again, sounding as if she were far away across a valley or a mountain range.

Kira couldn't tear her eyes from the tengu, from the iridescent madness of his gaze.

"No," the Herald of Bones said softly. "I think not, Empress. This is our little sister. I've been wanting to speak to you for some time. We have much to discuss, you and I." He squatted next to her, his feathers spreading out across the cracked floor. His hands were gnarled like knotted wood, each finger ending in a black talon. "Would you like to know the truth, Kira Mirai? About what is happening to you. Would you like to know what you are? Who you are?" His eyes widened, the colours intensifying. "And what you are capable of?"

Chapter 37

True to his word, Prince Ido Katsuo knew a way out of the palace. He slid a large painting of a long-dead emperor aside, revealing steps that led down into the darkness, so many steps Haruto thought he was descending into the grave. Or maybe just passing through it on his way to life once again, which seemed far more fitting for him. Shiki lit the way, a floating, furry ball of orange luminescence hustling along happily in front of them, her constant whistles and squeaks echoing around the tunnel. Prince Ido Katsuo talked the entire time. He never seemed to run out of things to say even in the face of Haruto's stony silence.

Eventually the steps levelled off and Haruto guessed they must be passing underneath the maze-like waterways that criss-crossed throughout Kodachi.

"How did you know about this secret tunnel?" Haruto asked.

"Oh, I found it when I was a child, playing in the palace. Entirely by accident, I assure you." The prince glanced over his shoulder with a cheeky smile. "My father and Auntie Ryoko were not always at odds, you know. They were quite friendly for a time, when the rest of the Ise family was still alive. I used to spend my winters here in Kodachi, getting to know my cousins, exploring the palace, staying warm. It's bitterly chilly back home in Temboku. But all that went up in smoke when an assassin snuck into Kodachi and murdered Uncle Ise Jinn and all the others. Terrible tragedy.

"Don't give me that look, Master Onmyoji. I'm well aware of the irony. But you must understand, though it is true I was planning, and indeed attempted to sneak into the palace and kill Auntie Ryoko, I had no intention of killing little Cousin Ryo. I quite like the little bruiser. I hoped he might see the death of his mother as an excellent incentive to hand the Serpent Throne over to my father."

Haruto shrugged.

"I can see you judging me, Master Onmyoji. But honestly, this is just the way things are done in the royal family. It's nothing personal against the Ises." He laughed. "Politics in Ipia are most often discussed over the edge of a knife!" He sighed. "Better to be holding it than sheathing it."

They came across another stairway, this one leading up. Haruto felt his body healing, his strength returning, his immortality repairing him. He'd need food and water soon, but for now at least he could walk without a limp. He climbed the steps in silence while Prince Ido Katsuo tried to dazzle him with a story about courtly intrigue.

Water ran down the rocky sides of the tunnel wall, leaving dazzling, colourful streaks in Shiki's light. Without warning, the tunnel ended in a slab of solid stone. The prince apologised and informed Haruto they were about to get a bit wet. Then he pressed his back against the stone slab and pushed. Water rushed over him as he opened the tunnel door and splashed his way up and out. Haruto followed up the steps to find himself standing in a shallow koi pond. The tunnel exit was in the middle of a small, but richly cultivated estate, which appeared to be on the outskirts of Kodachi. The prince assured Haruto that he owned the estate, though not in his own name of course.

They stopped there for only an hour, just long enough for the ancient servant who tended the grounds to cook up some rice and fish. Haruto ate like a gaki, and those poor yokai were formed from people who starved to death. The prince fetched him a new kimono, white with blue trim and a red pattern of stampeding horses stitched into it. It was of far better quality than he was used to wearing.

When Haruto thanked him and started to leave, Ido Katsuo laughed and joined him.

"I can't let you go," the prince said. "Not before I've had a chance to see Kira again. I must thank her for freeing me, and you are the best chance of my meeting her again, Master Onmyoji. I'm afraid you are stuck with me for now."

"Wonderful," Haruto said. Shiki squeaked, and he chuckled.

"What?" Ido Katsuo said. "What did the spirit say?"

Haruto shrugged. "You don't want to know."

"I assure you, I do."

"That's a shame." Haruto had no wish to be followed about by the prince, but he could see no peaceful way of chasing the man away.

They skirted the city. They both knew their absence would be discovered soon, if it hadn't already. They also knew the Empress would not rest until she found her wayward onmyoji and prince. Kodachi would soon crawl with Emerald Legion soldiers like flies on a corpse. They needed to be away and soon, but Haruto would not leave without the others. He needed to find Guang and Yanmei, and hopefully Kira.

He knew where to find Guang at least. When separated, it was best to go back to a time when you weren't. A simple lesson, but one well worth learning. Haruto's injuries had all but healed by the time he saw two old figures sitting by the side of the road. He sighed with relief and doubled his pace. Guang saw him coming, grinned and leapt to his feet. And then they were together again. Haruto wrapped his arms around the old poet and hugged him tightly. Guang returned the embrace, but he was trembling. Haruto couldn't tell if he was laughing or crying.

"I had a bad feeling, old man," Guang choked out. "Thought I'd lost you this time."

Haruto sighed as they separated. "It'll take more than a few swords to put me down for good." He tried to laugh, but it died on his lips. "Felt close though this time."

"Izumi?" Guang asked.

Haruto shrugged. "It was her. She..." He shook his head. "It's her."

"Where's Kira?" Yanmei asked. She looked older somehow, huddled beneath a blanket, her hands and arms swathed in bandages. She was quivering, but her eyes were still sharp.

"An excellent question," said the prince, politely waiting at the roadside.

"Who's the fop?" Guang said.

Haruto told them about his escape from the palace, of Kira's disappearance through the mirror, and his meeting with the prince. Yanmei was silent throughout, but Haruto saw her staring back towards the city.

"She couldn't have gone back to the mirror shop," Yanmei said. "It's... I... burned it down."

"There are plenty of other mirrors," Guang said. He gave her shoulder a squeeze. "She'll find her way out. Stronger than we give her credit for, that one."

Yanmei pulled her blanket a little closer and closed her eyes.

"We shouldn't stay here," the prince said. "I mean, they're sure to come looking for me. Us. Better to be on the move."

Haruto agreed. The Empress would soon have every soldier in western Ipia searching for them.

"We can't leave," Yanmei said. "Kira wouldn't leave you. She didn't. She risked everything to get you out."

Ido Katsuo sighed. "We don't even know if she's alive. We can't just sit--" Yanmei glared at him and he rubbed his hands together. "Then again. I'm new here and probably shouldn't get a say. Whatever you choose, I'm right behind you, Master Onmyoji."

"Shiki," Haruto said. She was sitting beside Guang and pawing at his legs while he soundly ignored her. "Can you find Kira?"

Shiki squeaked.

"Please try," Haruto said. "We'll wait here as long as we can."

Shiki let out an admonishing warble.

Haruto coughed and glanced at the others. "I won't get captured again, I promise."

Another squeak.

"It *is* Izumi," Haruto said, "but she doesn't remember." He shook his head. "I won't get captured again. Next time I see her... I intend to fight her."

Shiki narrowed her eyes and chirped.

"Yes. I promise. Now please, go find Kira."

The little spirit popped out of existence.

Haruto found a spot on the grass next to Yanmei and sat down. The sky was lightening and morning threatened to erupt onto the horizon. People were beginning to move about on the road, some into the city, some leaving. Two old men, an old woman, and a noble were an odd bunch to see sitting at the side of the road. Soon they would have no choice but to run or fight. It was no choice at all. They couldn't win against such staggering odds. And Yanmei was no longer herself. He was used to the air being warmer around her, but now she was cold. It was all his fault. If he hadn't chased after Izumi and got himself captured...

Haruto sighed and lay back on the cold ground to stare up at the fading stars. The constellation Rymer, the keeper of time, hung above him in the pink sky. If there was any truth to the stars at all, Rymer had long ago forgotten about Haruto. Guang always said that immortality was a generous reward for merely hunting yokai, but he had it backwards. Immortality wasn't the reward. It was the price Haruto had to pay.

Kira drifted through the waking city in a daze. She barely noticed the people swarming the streets about their daily duties, nor the sounds of the place rising to a shrill cacophony around her, nor the smell of fresh food, nor any of it. All the wonder had been rubbed away, leaving nothing behind but the truth. The city was a seething mass of humans, who didn't even realise what they were or how easy they had it. The people of Kodachi were sheltered, secure in their worship of gods and stars, and ignorant of the wider world and the pain it held. She envied them. As all yokai did the living.

She still didn't understand what had happened. The Herald of Bones hadn't attacked her. He protected her. When the Empress struggled through her soldiers, one hand pressed against her ruined face, blood pouring from her left eye, she had screamed at them all to kill Kira. But the Herald of Bones stopped them with a mere glance. He'd protected her, called her 'little sister'. All onryo were family. Family Kira never had.

Her feet scuffed the uneven stone of the road and she tripped. She stood up and continued, heedless of the people staring at her and the men who tried to talk to her. They were just humans, brief things. Ephemeral. Their lives meant so little.

She thought back to the throne room, the tengu had held out a wrinkled, black-taloned hand to her. He was gentle. He'd pulled her to her feet and led her from the throne room. The smoky woman had followed. Haruto had called the woman Izumi, but she'd said her name was Crow. The Herald of Bones had led them to a kitchen; the servants fled from him. The tengu had pulled a kettle from a nearby cupboard and set it on the stove, then sprinkled tea leaves into the water. It had all seemed so mundane. Hardly the actions of a nefarious spirit who had slaughtered thousands of warriors on the Bridge of Blood.

Kira knelt before the table in silence, and Crow drifted down to join her. "It's good to finally meet you, little sister," the woman said. She had a strange voice, soft and indistinct. Kira peered into her dark hood and saw no face, only swirling smoke written in shades of grey.

The Herald of Bones approached the table with the teakettle and three cups. He poured each of them a cup, then sat and took off his tengai. Kira expected to see a grotesque monster underneath, but he had a gentle face. His nose was hooked and a little too large for his other features, his skin was wrinkled beyond even the Sage's, and his eyes were shifting colours that twisted and danced in a way that made Kira feel sick. But he smiled at her and didn't seem quite so dangerous.

"They have tried to make you something you are not, Kira," the Herald of Bones said. "They want you to be human, and I can see it in you even now, your desire to fit the mould. You crave their acceptance. You don't wish to scare them with your true self, but you cannot deny yourself without hurting yourself. You are not human. You're better than human. You are an onryo, one of us, our new little sister."

Someone bumped into Kira, jostling her from her reverie. She staggered into another passerby who snapped something at her. She didn't even hear the words, but the anger and intent were clear in his voice. Kira flicked a dagger into her hand and held it up to the man's face. She showed him fear in his reflection. A vision of his face decaying, flesh melting from his bones, eyes turning to jelly and sloughing from his skull. He collapsed onto the road and curled into a ball, weeping. Kira left him there. One more human making insignificant noise, unnoticed among the rest of them. They were so easy to manipulate. So easy to kill. The Herald of Bones was right.

"They fear you," he had said before taking a sip of tea. "What you are and what you are capable of. That is why they have done this to you, forced you into their image, their moral codes. Dressed you up in a form they can stomach."

Kira shook her head and tried to argue, but the words had died on her tongue as the Herald of Bones laid the truth bare.

"You were at Heiwa," he said, raising his cup to his lips.

Crow did not drink, but she held the cup in her smoky grip as though it were comforting. Kira glanced down at her own cup and wrapped her fingers around it, mimicking Crow as best she could.

"Did the tutors ever recognise your strength?" the tengu asked. "Acknowledge how different you were from the other children?"

Kira shook her head again at that. "They didn't want to treat me as special. They wanted me to fit in with the others."

"But you didn't fit in," the Herald of Bones said. "You are not, nor ever were one of the other children. They just wanted to control you. To stop you from realising your potential. They wanted you to be weak like them, to deny your true self."

Kira had opened her mouth to argue – she still didn't know what she might have said – but the Herald of Bones forged on.

"Did they ever let you use your technique?" he had asked then, his voice soothing as a crackling fire. "You're an ungaikyo. Did they ever let you use your reflections? Or did they punish you for it whenever you did?"

He was right. Kira remembered all the times they had

reprimanded her for using her technique, for scaring the other children. Even during sparring, they allowed the other children to use their techniques, but Kira was only allowed to use her martial skill and whatever little technique the Sage had chosen to teach her. Whenever she used the mirrors, the reflections, they decided the match against her. Even Yanmei snapped at her when she used her technique. Her entire life at Heiwa had been a punishment for what she was. But it wasn't fair. It wasn't her fault she wasn't human. The tengu was right.

A horse whinnied and Kira startled, looked up to meet its eyes. Its rider was tugging on its reins, but the beast was backing away. Away from Kira. Suddenly, it lurched sideways, knocking over another man, and leapt forward, running past Kira. The sun was already in mid morning and the city was busy, but she didn't recognise this part of Kodachi. She didn't know where she was. Nor where she was going. She wasn't even sure she cared.

"I'm told you met Shin," the Herald of Bones had said between sips of tea. "Don't worry, I don't blame you for his murder. It was the onmyoji. But you met your brother before his death. You fought him. You experienced his strength. All of us onryo are capable of such power, Kira. Me, Crow. You. Without the humans holding you back, you are capable of more than you could imagine. You have more power than they can stomach."

"You'd teach me?" Kira asked him. She had been curious. She still was.

"Of course," the Herald of Bones said. "Just as I taught Crow here. But I am *not* the Fifth Sage Under Heaven or the teachers at Heiwa. I will *not* force you to do anything. It's your choice, Kira. I will teach you if you wish. Regardless of whether you stay and join our family, I will teach you. You deserve so much more than the humans have given you, so much more than they have allowed you."

"You will still be our little sister, even if you do not stay with us," Crow said, and Kira realised they would not keep her there against her will. "Nothing can change that. We are, and always will be, family."

A thought had occurred to Kira then, and she asked before her courage failed her. "Why are you trying to free the dragons?"

The Herald of Bones' wrinkled face had stiffened. His deep frown made him seem more the monster of legend. "Because the dragons are also kin. And what was done to them is unforgivable. They are kami, the greatest of the spirits. But like all spirits, they did not fit in the humans' vision of the world. They are powerful enough to resist the conformity with which the humans wish to suffocate us. Do you even know why the humans hunted down the dragons?"

Kira thought back to the story Haruto had told them then. "Because Orochi ordered the dragons to destroy humanity."

Crow's smoke seemed to writhe at Kira's words. The Herald of Bones' face twisted into a snarl. "And where did you hear that little story? A human, no doubt. I'll wager they made Orochi seem a monster and Yamasachi a hero. It's a lie."

Kira hadn't thought Haruto's story painted either the dragons or humans in a good light. They were both cruel in the end, heaping misery on those they claimed to love.

"It's true that Yamasachi and Orochi were lovers," the Herald of Bones continued. "But the story you have heard muddles the intent. Yamasachi was never anything but a trickster and a murderer. Seeking fame and glory, he convinced the Ten Kings of Hosa to give him a crown in exchange for the head of Orochi. Yamasachi snuck into the forest of bamboo and found the dragon's hidden grove. Orochi's love of humans was well known, and Yamasachi seduced the dragon into revealing himself. He played the part of infatuated lover to convince Orochi of his devotion, to persuade Orochi to lower his guard. Then he struck while Orochi was sleeping, a dagger to the heart."

Still thinking about the death of Orochi, Kira stopped outside a building and looked up at the sign: *Shitataru Baketsu.* She was outside the inn again, listening to the human noise from inside. Someone bumped her shoulder and grumbled something about her being a stupid girl. She turned away from the inn and started walking again. She didn't belong there.

"But Orochi didn't die?" she had asked.

"Of course not," Crow said. Her soft, indistinct voice was comforting. "Orochi is a kami, a noble spirit. No mortal weapon can kill him. In this mortal world, the kami are immortal."

"Yet Yamasachi did not know this." The Herald of Bones had picked up the story again. "And his hand was played. His true nature revealed. But though nothing of Yamasachi was real, everything of Orochi was. His love was genuine. He was betrayed, furious and confused. He took to the sky and ordered Yamasachi to leave the grove and never return, or he would show no mercy. Then he flew away to stay his wrath.

"Yamasachi did not give up though. He poisoned the waters of the grove, hoping to kill Orochi when the dragon returned. But the grove withered and died around him as it soaked up the poison, and Yamasachi realised he had to flee before Orochi returned. And flee he did." The Herald of Bones had fallen silent then, sipping on his tea as he glared into the cup.

"When Orochi returned," Crow said, "his fury rekindled at the callousness of humanity. Yamasachi had destroyed something beautiful. He had proved to Orochi that humanity was a force of destruction. So Orochi summoned his kin, the other dragons, and begged them to help him. But he did not order them to destroy humanity. He asked them to help him find Yamasachi and bring the human to justice."

The Herald of Bones dragged a talon across the table top, carving a jagged furrow into the wood. "Before Yamasachi went into hiding, he sought a villain to help save him. A warrior without equal. Hosa's greatest *hero*," the Herald of Bones spat the last word as an insult. "He begged the Century Blade to protect him from the wrath of Orochi. To protect *humanity* from the rage of dragons."

The Herald of Bones had stepped away to brew a fresh pot of tea then. Kira looked down at her cup, at her reflection in the greenish water. She wasn't sure who to believe. The onryo didn't seem to be lying any more than Haruto did, and they didn't seem like a danger to her. They felt... like family, more welcoming and comforting than the teachers and students of Heiwa had ever been.

"The Century Blade accepted Yamasachi's request," the Herald of Bones said when he had returned to the table. "And though he could not kill the dragons, he could do something much worse to them. He travelled the four empires in search of help. From Cochtan, he recruited the Ticking Clock, a skilled assassin with an unsurpassed knowledge of engines. The Ticking Clock would construct prisons powerful enough to contain the strength of a kami and hold the dragons.

"From Ipia, he recruited a young sage. Still an initiate at the time, but rumoured to be the only one strong enough to replace the ageing Fifth Sage Under Heaven, the most powerful of the Sages. The young man already knew more techniques than any other person alive, and among those was the technique to bind powerful spirits and diffuse their power.

"From Nash, the Century Blade recruited the Gilded Crone, a woman with a reputation of slaying gods, whose technique turned anything she held into a deadly weapon, a perfect companion for a fight against dragons.

"And from the Seafolk, he recruited a rogue god, an immortal who had been stranded in Nash since his own people were last beaten back into the sea."

The Herald of Bones poured himself another cup of tea. "No more powerful group had ever been assembled before. The greatest warrior from each of the four empires with a foreign god by their side. They bent all their strength, all their techniques, all their martial skill to the purpose of imprisoning the dragons. They fought all over Hosa, all over Nash and Cochtan, all over Ipia. Seven dragons, there were, and one by one they fell to the Century Blade and his group of villains. Alas, when Orochi came before them, they fought the greatest of all battles. Tooth and claw against steel. Orochi's five elemental breaths against mortal techniques."

The tengu had paused then. Kira saw the pain on his face. This was not just some old poet's tale, not to him. It was real, an atrocity committed against his kin and kind. Against Kira's kin too. She was a spirit. That made her a distant relative to the dragons, she supposed.

"Orochi proved himself superior to the humans on that battlefield. Not even the Century Blade could wound him," the Herald of Bones had continued. "The Ticking Clock fell first, ripped in half by Orochi's ferocious jaws. The Sage would have been next if not for the Gilded Crone's shielding him with her own body." The Herald of Bones sighed. "But Orochi was arrogant, and it was his downfall. He thought to mock his attackers and took human form to finish them. It was a trap. It was as the Century Blade had planned, and Orochi walked into it unknowingly. Proof that power and wisdom do not always go hand in hand.

"The Sage used an ancient technique to bind him into his human form so Orochi could not escape. The Century Blade and the Gilded Crone renewed their assault, pressing Orochi back. And the moment Orochi stepped into the prison the Ticking Clock had built, his fate was sealed. The Ticking Clock was not entirely human; it took more than tearing him to pieces to stop him. They sacrificed the Seafolk god's immortality to secure the locks, and they sealed Orochi in his prison. And there he remains."

"We are not releasing the dragons to destroy humanity, Kira," Crow said. "We want to right the wrong that was done to them. We are trying to set them free to roam the skies as they used to. The world lost something when the dragons were sealed away. It was the start of the Great Spirit Purge, and both heaven and earth were diminished by it. Both remain unbalanced by it."

A woman screamed and Kira looked up from her daze to see the woman running down the street, shouting about a monster. Kira glanced at the mirror shop. It was all ash and charred timbers. Fire had consumed it entirely and spread to two nearby buildings as well. But that was not what made the woman flee. In front of the shop were two mirrors that must have been salvaged from the flames. Kira stared into one at her reflection between the smudges of ash and mud. A yokai stared back at her. It was her, but changed. Her skin was pale as rice, her hair as dark as ink. Her eyes were gaping voids that sucked in the light, and her leering mouth was full of serrated mirror teeth. It was the ungaikyo. It was her. She turned from the mirror and fled.

She had no destination. The people and streets of Kodachi passed by in a blur. But she knew it was pointless. She couldn't flee the ungaikyo anymore than she could run away from herself.

Something hit Kira in the chest. She stumbled and fell hard on the cobbled street. The thing scrabbled at her, and she rolled to one knee, clutched its scruff in one hand and held a dagger to it with the other. It barked, and Kira realised it was just a little tanuki. Shiki popped out of the dog, and it scurried away, barking and whimpering. Shiki leapt at Kira. Kira shattered her dagger and hugged Shiki tight against her chest. The spirit squealed and nuzzled her face. Then Kira shattered, mirrored shards falling all around her, tinkling on the stone street. She felt hot tears stinging her eyes, but a laugh bubbled up from her chest.

"Where did you come from?" Kira asked. People moved around her in the street, some staring, others grumbling. Kira ignored them all.

Shiki squeaked and chirped and flailed her arms in the air.

"Well, where are they?" Kira asked.

Shiki squeaked again.

Kira's gut churned and her legs felt weak again. She had to go back to them, had to see them again. She had to find out if the onryo had told her the truth.

"You're free to go," the Herald of Bones had said after he had finished his story. "You can return to your friends. We won't stop you or follow you. I ask just two things of you, Kira: First, know that you are family. You are our youngest sister, the newest member of our family, and your family will never lie to you. Second, when you return to your friends, ask them how you died. It's important for onryo to know how they died, to understand who they truly are." His face tightened again. "Ask them how you died. And know this – they will lie to you."

Chapter 38

The Empress Ise Ryoko summoned them to the throne room. Crow did not appreciate being summoned. The Master got away with it because he was family and because of what he had done for them. But to be summoned by a human who thought she was better than them was galling.

The Master strode ahead of her, his feathery cloak rustling behind him. He had his tengai on again, obscuring everything but his eyes, and servants and soldiers alike shrank from him in the palace corridors. He pushed open the throne room doors and strode in. Crow floated behind him, trailing dark smoke across floor and walls, leaving soot marks behind. It was a petty vengeance, but she took comfort in it.

"It'sh about time you got here," a voice slurred at them. Crow saw her brother Zen leaning against the wall. Squat and half bald, with a singed, ratty tunic that never seemed to cover his pot belly. Zen was Crow's least favourite family member. "Thish *woman* has been quite unwelcoming." He flashed a toothy smile and a thin trail of flames leaked from the sides of his mouth like drool, struck the floor and sizzled.

"How dare you," the Empress Ise Ryoko snarled. She had been out of sorts ever since their new little sister scarred her face and ruined one eye. Nevertheless, she was on her throne again, straight-backed and looking very regal despite the swathe of bandages on the left side of her face. A trickle of blood escaped from beneath the bandages and ran down her chin.

"I dare much more than you realishe, Queeny." Flames dripped from Zen's lips. "It'sh good you're pretty, or I'd have burned off the other shide of your face by now." Flames flew from his lips like spittle.

The master waved a taloned hand at him. "Enough, brother. We have come to collect on our bargain, Empress. Where is Orochi?"

The Empress grimaced. Crow noticed there were twice as many Serpent Guard in the throne room than the last time she was there. Kira had taught them a healthy dose of fear and respect. Soldiers had been rushing through the palace and smashing mirrors all day. For a woman who had been so vain, the Empress now feared her every reflection. Crow would have smiled if she had a face.

"You have not completed your side of the bargain yet, tengu," the Empress said. "You were to kill every member of the Ido family. One still lives."

The Master turned to Crow.

"Xifeng said she killed them all," Crow said. "Even the children." Knowing Xifeng, she took great care with the children. She always said they were the most succulent.

The Master turned his swirling gaze back at the Empress and spread his taloned hands. "If my sister says she killed them all, they are dead."

"Ido Katsuo lives," the Empress hissed. "Your onmyoji, who I was holding here by *your* request, helped him escape."

Crow felt her smoke seething inside her robe and tried to calm it. She had not known the onmyoji had escaped. He was a danger to them and to the plan. She wondered if Kira had helped him too.

Zen snorted fire from his nose. "It'sh not our job to keep watch on your prisoners. Accuse ush of incompetence again, and I'll teach you shome respect."

Crow knew what Zen meant. He was a lecherous creature, and those he showered his attentions on rarely survived the experience. Now that Crow thought about it, death was a small mercy considering the things he did to them.

The Empress Ise Ryoko glared at the Master, but he said nothing to stop Zen this time.

"You think those toy sholdiers will keep me from you,

Queeny?" Zen gestured at the guards lined up along the walls. "I'll burn them to cinders. Then I'll tear that robe off you and melt your bones to that overgrown rock you call a throne..."

"Enough!" Crow barked. Her smoke was boiling around her, convulsing and lashing the air.

Zen leered at her. "Oh, little shister, are you jealous? If only there was shomething to you, think of the fun we could have." He flicked a forked tongue at her.

Crow snarled. "You are the only reason I'm glad I don't have a body, *brother*. At least I never have to smell your acrid stench."

"Ha!" Zen slapped his exposed belly. "You could never shmell me over yourself, *sister*. Two centuries without getting any – no wonder you leave a trail everywhere you go."

Brother or not, Crow hated him. He was a hideous boil on the world, and heaven and earth would be better off without him. She rose on a pillar of smoke, towering over him, tentacles lashing. Zen grinned. Fire dripped from his teeth, from his nose, even from his eyes. His veins flushed orange along his arms, and his pot belly glowed like a furnace. He was strong, perhaps too strong for her, but Crow didn't care. She would suffocate him in her smoke, tear his limbs from his disgusting snot of a body, and wipe his foul stain--

"Stop it. Both of you," the Master said quietly but resonant with the threat of an executioner's axe.

Zen glanced at the Master and chuckled. Then he blew a fiery kiss at Crow and quieted his flames. "Not worth the effort anyway."

Crow stifled her wrath. It was so unfair that an ugly pustule like Zen knew who he was and how he had died, but Crow did not. He was the youngest of them, a yokai for just thirty years and an onryo for only half that, but he was so terribly powerful. Yokai who had died by suicide were often very strong, and Zen had done just that. He killed himself, only to be reborn a kiyo, a serpent yokai of fire and scales and vicious jealousy. Zen had been a repugnant little shit in life and was even more revolting in death. Crow resented that he remembered his death though she could not. After all, hadn't the Master just told Kira that onryo must know how they had died to truly understand themselves?

Crow sank back down to the floor, her pillar of smoke dissipating. She pulled her soot back inside her robe and brooded.

"I'm sorry, Empress," the Master said. "Family members have a habit of squabbling. But then you would know that better than I."

The Empress Ise Ryoko quirked her right eyebrow. Crow wondered if she still had a left eyebrow beneath the bandages, or had Kira's mirror shards ruined that just as they had the eye? "Our deal was that you would wipe out the last of the Ido family so I may reunite Ipia. One of them still lives."

The Master's tengai bobbed as he nodded. "We will correct this matter out of good faith. Zen, can you track this wayward prince?"

Zen flicked out his forked tongue, tasting the air. "Of course I can. I can track anyone."

"Then do so," the Master said. "Hunt down Prince Ido Katsuo and kill him." He turned his attention back to the Empress. "As for you, no more delays. Tell us where Orochi is, or I will find your son, wherever you have hidden him, and skin him alive as you watch. I will raze this palace and this city to the ground and leave you Empress of ashes and grief. Do. Not. Doubt."

It was no idle threat. Crow had seen the Master do worse.

The Empress clenched her jaw and nodded. For all the soldiers between them, for all the power she wielded, the truth was obvious: he was a tengu, and the history books were littered with the deaths of those who had tried to defy such yokai.

Chapter 39

By mid-morning, Yanmei's gut had knotted into a tensely wound ball. She wasn't alone; they were all anxious. Kira had not returned, and worry was as clear on Haruto and Guang's faces as it was on hers. The prince seemed less concerned about Kira, and more concerned that someone might recognise him. He pulled his hood up to hide his face and danced from foot to foot, glancing nervously at everyone who passed. The city was in something of an uproar. Those who were leaving told of soldiers at all the gates, checking everyone who passed. Emerald Legion were searching homes and shops and warehouses. The Serpent Guard had locked down the palace, and hundreds were patrolling the walls. Yanmei knew it would only be a matter of time before the search expanded outside the city walls. They would have no choice but to run or fight, but she was determined not to leave without Kira.

It was reaching midday, the sky a grey blanket that suited Yanmei's mood, when Shiki ran across the road and leapt into Haruto's lap. The little spirit was gibbering, jumping up and down and waving her hairy little arms about. Haruto listened for a moment, then looked up. Yanmei followed his gaze.

Kira trudged down the street toward them. Yanmei struggled to her feet, her body aching and her limbs scorched, and lurched toward the girl. When they met at the edge of the road, Yanmei wrapped her arms around Kira and pulled her close. Tears sprang to her eyes, and she let them fall onto Kira's shoulder.

"I was so worried," Yanmei said.

"Mhm," Kira grunted into Yanmei's chest. The girl felt stiff in her arms.

Yanmei pulled away and looked at Kira. She was staring at

the ground, frowning. Her hair was messier than usual, and her face and kimono were crusty with dried blood. But it was the darkness around her eyes, as though someone had gone overboard with dark makeup, that worried Yanmei. Yanmei reached out and rubbed Kira's cheek with a bandaged thumb, but the darkness didn't rub away.

Yanmei took another step back, staring at Kira, unsure of what to say. Guang rushed between them, scooped up the girl into a bear hug and spun her around. "Never doubted you for a moment, girl," he said, lowering her to the ground. "Although your disappearing into the mirror was quite the trick."

Kira nodded. "I couldn't have done it without you." Her voice seemed flat, devoid of emotion. "You taught me how to extend threads of qi. To make anchors to use the technique."

Guang puffed out his chest and nodded at Haruto. "Hear that, old man? She couldn't have done it without me. That means, I saved *you* this time." He chuckled. "By proxy."

Haruto smiled. "Thank you, Kira. You got me out."

Kira just nodded. Yanmei wondered where her smile had gone.

"Wonderful," the prince said with a single clap of his hands. "Nice to meet you again, Kira. Thanks for saving me too. Can we go now? The sooner we're away, the less likely we are to lose our heads."

Kira frowned at the prince. "What happened to your brothers?"

"Hmm?" Prince Ido Katsuo said. "Oh, of course. I went to get them out too." He tucked his hands inside the sleeves of his court robes. "I was too late, I'm afraid. Auntie Ryoko had already done away with them."

Kira bowed her head. "I'm sorry. I shouldn't have hesitated."

"No no no. I was likely just a day from the chopping block myself. Don't be sorry. Be happy. I'm alive." He grinned. "So. All happy. All ready. Good. Let's go." He glanced down the road toward the city gates. There were soldiers gathered, stopping all those trying to leave.

Yanmei hated to oblige the babbling prince, but he was right. They needed to be gone, even though they had nowhere to go.

The prince led them west, chatting away about how warm a welcome they would receive in western Ipia once his father heard of his survival. He promised banquets and balls and parades and a host of other things none of them wanted.

All Yanmei wanted was to know what was wrong with Kira. "What happened?" she asked her as the afternoon sun waned, and the city of Kodachi became nothing more than a blur on the horizon behind them and a host of terrible memories.

When she did not answer Yanmei, Haruto said, "You must have a tale to tell. What happened after you disappeared through the mirror and left me?"

"Sorry," Kira mumbled. "I thought I could take you with me."

Haruto shrugged. "It all worked out. Thanks to this prattling fool."

"I heard that," Prince Ido Katsuo said over his shoulder.

"I ended up in the throne room," Kira said. "The Empress was there with a lot of soldiers." She looked at Haruto. "And Izumi was there, but she calls herself Crow."

Haruto shrugged. "She always did like animals. Birds, lizards, insects. She loved to draw them."

"She wasn't alone, either," Kira said. Her voice had gone soft. "The Herald of Bones was there too." She looked at Guang. "The tengu from your story. He's their leader."

"Cabbage!" Guang barked. "That's all we need. What about the jorogumo? Is she back in Kodachi?"

Kira shook her head. "They said she's in western Ipia."

"Well, at least we're going the right way," Guang growled. "The sooner we find that spider, the sooner Haruto can be free of Tian's burden."

Haruto asked, "How did you escape?"

"I didn't," Kira glanced up at Yanmei, but then away. "They let me go. They said I was family, that I was one of them and..."

There weren't many people on the road further from the city, and those there were paid them little attention. Still, it seemed like a conversation they should have in private, preferably without the prince within earshot. Yanmei had tried to shield Kira from the yokai side of herself since she'd adopted the girl. Now Kira was being confronted by it, by others both like and unlike her. She was on the edge: her dark eyes were proof of that. Yanmei couldn't let her slip all the way over. She couldn't let Kira become the ungaikyo again. She wished they had never met the other onryo, that Heiwa had never been attacked. It had been so much easier to keep Kira safe at the academy.

Yanmei saw something overhead, a line of emerald streaking across the grey sky. "Look, Kira. A dragon."

They all stopped to stare up as the serpent soared through the sky. It was huge even from a distance. Its scales glistened with myriad shades of green, and its horns shone red like blood.

"That's Messimere," Guang said. "One of the dragons the Century Blade imprisoned. Everyone in Hosa knows the story."

"That's at least two dragons the onryo have freed," Haruto said. "We have to stop them before they free Orochi."

Messimere turned toward them, flying lower, growing larger. He was at least as vast as Sekiryu, hundreds of feet long, his body as scaly and sinuous as a snake. He dove still lower. Yanmei could make out individual scales on his belly. Everyone on the road stopped to stare at the dragon passing overhead with a rush of wind that set cloaks flapping and toppled carts. An old man with a walking stick pitched over into a patch of grass. Rain trailed in the dragon's wake, falling from its scales like a monsoon, soaking everything. Messimere roared and then flew over the dark smudge of Kodachi, away from them.

"Isn't he beautiful, Kira," Yanmei said.

Kira was silent. She was not staring after the dragon, but at Yanmei. When Yanmei turned to her, she blurted, "How did I die?" Her voice was cold and small and trembling. Yanmei felt her heart breaking at the sound, at the lie she had to tell. She had to protect her from the pain of the truth.

"It doesn't matter," Yanmei said. She turned from the others and started walking, trying to put some distance between them, striding past the people on the road still staring after the dragon. The horizon stretched out before her like a grey tide, threatening to swallow everything. She couldn't afford to tell Kira the truth.

The five of them trudged along in silence for a while, Shiki clinging to Haruto's shoulder. Even the prince was quiet.

"It does matter!" Kira caught up to Yanmei and walked next to her. "How am I supposed to know who I am if I don't know how I died? It's part of me. It's part of... what made me. I need to know, Yanmei. What am I? Who am I?"

Yanmei glanced at Kira, at the darkness of her eyes. The skin around them so dark. The tengu had poisoned her mind and tried to bring out the yokai. But Yanmei would not let it happen. She would not push her daughter over the edge. "You want to know who you are?" Yanmei said. "You are Kira Mirai. That's it. Not an onryo. Not a yokai. Just Kira. Just my Kira." She raised a hand to pull her close, but Kira stepped away.

The tension made for an uncomfortable evening. Guang had been the one to call a halt to their relentless trek. It was partly for his own sake – his knees felt like they were about to pack up and find a more sedentary owner – and also for Yanmei's. All the colour had drained from her face and her lips were cracked and blackened in places. She trembled beneath her cloak; only her dogged determination kept her going. Just a few days ago, Kira would have been the first to call for a halt given Yanmei's state, but the girl was a dark cloud of brooding sulk. She made Haruto look positively cheerful.

Guang fussed about building a fire while the others set up a little camp. They didn't have much, a few bed rolls and a couple of extra cloaks. It was going to be a chilly night for all of them.

As soon as the fire was burning, Yanmei shuffled close and stared into the flames. She hadn't spoken to Kira since their argument on the road from Kodachi, and neither looked happy about how they had left it. Unfortunately, it was out of Guang's hands. He'd seen this sort of thing enough times to know that someone else sticking their nose in never did any good. One of them would have to bridge the gap at some point, hopefully before the argument festered. That was what had happened to Tian and him. They'd let it fester and what little relationship they had rotted away.

Guang shivered, and not from the cold. Their maudlin mood was spreading and he didn't want to catch it. "So, you're an assassin then, Ido?" he asked to break the uncomfortable silence. He smiled across the flames at the prince who seemed to be trying to find a comfortable spot of ground. They only had four bed rolls and no one had offered him theirs.

The prince cleared his throat. "I like to think of myself as--"

"Definitely an assassin then," Guang said. "Assassins always pretend they do something less murdery."

Haruto sat down by the fire with a bundle of sticks. "What was it Trembling Spear used to call himself?" He fed a stick to the flames. Shiki waddled up after him and threw a tiny stick of her own to the fire. Then she leapt into the blaze, and stared out at them all. Guang always found that unnerving – fire should not have eyes.

He chuckled. "He called himself a 're-locater of life energies'. A fancy way of saying he would happily sneak into people's houses and kill them in their sleep for a few lien."

Ido Katsuo shook his head. "I assure you I am not some common murderer. I trained for many years with the monks of--"

"'Patience, said the monk, you see,'" Guang recited. "'For only patience can set you free. Life will grant your every wish, as long as you fish and you wish for fish. A man once climbed a thousand steps, he met his father there and wept.'"

"'Two birds you had,'" the prince continued, "'kept in a cage. Now both are dead, not flown away.'"

Guang laughed again and nudged Haruto. "He knows the game." Haruto just sighed and poked the fire with a stick. An arm of flame reached out and tore the stick from his grasp. Shiki crackled with laughter. Haruto glared at the spirit and reached for another stick.

"'The eagle flies so very high,'" said Yanmei. "'A mouse with eyes on ground does die.'"

Guang rubbed his hands together. "A third challenger enters the ring."

It was child's game called *The Thousand Lessons of Xiaomai*, a thousand easy rhymes, each with a hidden lesson. The competitors took turns reciting one of the lessons. If a competitor repeated a lesson or couldn't remember one, they were out of the game. The game continued until only one rhymer remained. Children and adults all over Hosa and Nash had been playing it for hundreds of years, though Guang thought there were probably far more than one thousand lessons these days. More importantly, he noticed Kira watching and listening from just beyond the firelight. He wondered if the girl knew the game, or if Heiwa hadn't bothered to teach her.

"'A man once sat beneath a tree, the rain drip dripped upon his knee,'" Guang said. "When thunder struck and the earth did shake, the man departed with much haste."

Everyone paused and looked to Haruto. The onmyoji sighed. "'Uhh... A man smelled salt upon the breeze... How does it go? He found a cliff and glimpsed the seas?"

Guang chuckled. "Close enough, old man."

They continued for a few more rounds. Haruto was the first to fail, followed quickly by Ido Katsuo. Guang and Yanmei duked it out for another couple of rounds before she repeated one. As always, Guang was victorious. But winning also wasn't really the point. Kira crept closer to the fire and sat across from Yanmei. The girl stared into the flames and said nothing despite Shiki pulling faces in the fire trying to make her smile.

They shared out some rations, and Guang told one of the many stories of how Yaurong, the dire bear, lost his paw. In Hosa, you couldn't drop a lien without hearing a new version of the tale, and no one knew which one was the truth anymore. The one Guang liked most was a fun story, or at least it was supposed to be, about heroism and how one of the great kami had been brought low by its own hubris. He told it more to kill time and dispel the awkward silence than anything else. But as he told it, he wondered if perhaps there was another reason it was on his mind.

The story told of a young hero by the name of Iroh and his quest to bring the head of Yaurong before the king of Lau in order to marry the princess. Iroh knew he had no chance of defeating the dire bear and instead tried to reason with him for a single tooth, but the dire bear refused to cooperate with a mortal. Iroh then devised a trap, baited the bear into attacking him, and severed Yaurong's pawn. It was a story about how spirits and humans did not mingle well, and also a reminder that humans could always best spirits with a little ingenuity. Guang personally thought the latter muddled the meaning of the story somewhat, but it presented a question that he thought Kira might know the answer to.

"You spoke to the leader of the onryo?" he asked her.

Kira looked up at him across the fire, her eyes dark, like black smudges drinking in the fire's light. She nodded. "The Herald of Bones."

"So he called himself," Guang said. He was far from certain the Herald of Bones even existed. "Why are the onryo and the Empress working together? It can't simply be to capture this old fool." He poked Haruto with his foot.

"They think she knows where Orochi is."

Ido Katsuo looked up. Apparently, he had been feigning sleep, but now he was wide awake and not trying to hide it.

Haruto asked, "Why would the Empress know where Orochi is imprisoned?"

"Imprisoned?" the prince said. "You mean interred? The king of dragons is dead."

"You can't kill a dragon," Haruto said. "They're kami. As long as they're on earth, they cannot be killed."

"But I've seen the grave," the prince said. "If it truly is Orochi's resting place, then I assure you he is not alive." The prince sat back with a contented sigh and closed his eyes again.

"You've been to Orochi's prison?" Guang asked.

"Grave," the prince said. "Or tomb, I suppose. And yes. My grandfather built a monastery on top of it. I studied there for... oh, about five years, I think."

Haruto sat forward, pinning the prince with an uncharacteristically intense stare. "How did your father know where they keep Orochi?"

"Ahh, that." The prince pulled a face that suggested he was considering lying. "Best kept secret of the imperial family. The Century Blade came to my great great... great--" he shook his head "--one of my grandfathers down the line and told him where the king of dragons was buried and made him promise to guard the site and keep the secret. My grandfather built the monastery and invited a bunch of militant monks to move in to do the job for him. I'm not sure they know what they're guarding, but they know how to guard it. They also have a wonderfully extensive knowledge of shadows and poisons. And wine." He grinned. "So much wine."

Guang thought about it. The Ipian imperial family split into two branches just a few generations ago, certainly after the Century Blade fought the dragons. "That means the Empress Ise Ryoko also knows where Orochi is imprisoned?"

"I imagine so," the prince said.

"Which means the onryo know too," Guang concluded.

Haruto shrugged and leaned back on his sleeping mat. "And now it's a race to the finish line." He opened an eye and stared at the prince. "I assume you can guide us there?"

"Well, yes. But it's not on the way." Ido Katsuo looked around everyone gathered about the fire. "I should really return to my father. I'm the heir now. His sole heir." The silence was damning. "But, I suppose I am being hunted by a bunch of... what did you call them, onryo? It seems to me, there is no safer place than with an esteemed onmyoji like yourself. I will lead you to the king of dragons' grave. And you can see for yourself that he is very much dead?"

Chapter 40

"Up," Haruto said, nudging Kira with his foot. The sky loomed like a cold, grey smudge of ink, but there were still a couple of hours before real daylight.

Kira's eyes flicked open and she glared at him for a moment. There was a new sullenness to her. Not brooding like Yanmei, but sulking. Wallowing was never a good way to wade through misery. But Haruto had learned long ago – very long ago – that nothing swept away worries of the mind quite like exertions of the body.

"Time to train," Haruto said. He wished he hadn't lost his last pipe; it had been far too long since he'd tasted smoke.

"I don't want to," Kira said, rolling over and closing her eyes.

Haruto nudged her again and then again. "I can do this all day," he said. "One thing life as an immortal teaches you is patience. Actually, that was something my shintei training taught me. Second year? No, it was third year. They made us swear an oath of patience. It's one of those unkeepable oaths. You cut off a lock of your hair, swear the oath, and give the lock to your sensei. They put it deep within the stores of Sky Hollow where the rigours of age won't touch it. It becomes an oath that you can never complete, and so the shintei must always strive to do so. Patience in all things."

He nudged her again. "Up. Let's train."

"I don't need to," Kira said. "I fought the Serpent Guard. I would have won if the Herald of Bones hadn't intervened."

"Impressive," Haruto said and nudged her again. "But that means you still lost."

She turned her head and glared at him.

"Scary eyes don't work on me, Kira." He nudged her again. "Up. Training."

"I don't need to," she snarled. "I already know everything you have to teach."

"Do you now?" This time he kicked her, not hard enough to hurt, but certainly enough to get her attention. "Show me."

Kira surged to her feet, and they moved away from the camp. Haruto selected a sturdy-looking stick. It was no substitute for a sword, but he had lost his katana back in Kodachi. Shiki climbed onto his shoulder and hooted in his ear. "I know that, Shiki. I'm not an idiot." The spirit was right, Kira was struggling with something. She was distracted and angry, a dangerous combination.

Haruto sank into a ready stance and held the stick before him in a loose defensive posture. Kira stopped a few paces opposite him and flicked daggers into her hands. Gone were the smiles and enthusiasm of just a few days ago. She stared at him through eyes dark as midnight, her mouth twisted into a grimace.

Haruto let out a loud yawn. "Come on then. Before I fall asleep."

Kira crouched for just a moment and then darted forward so quickly Haruto barely got his stick up in time and deflected the attack. He stepped back, but Kira advanced relentlessly, striking faster and faster. She had learned to use her innate technique to give herself incredible bursts of speed, but was sacrificing her power for it. Haruto parried another couple of thrusts and dashed away with his own burst of speed. Up close, he couldn't keep up with her. Kira's daggers were far better suited to combat at that range, his stick was too long to do anything but defend.

"Good," Haruto said. "You have--"

Kira sprang at him again, whipping both daggers around in a move that would disembowel him. Haruto spun his stick around and deflected both attacks, but his stick snapped from the battering. He staggered away. "That's enough, Kira."

She came at him again. Both daggers flashing.

"Shiki," Haruto said. The spirit leapt into the half stick he held just in time for him to block the strikes aimed at his neck. Kira shattered a dagger against Shiki, flicked another into her hand, and tried to stab under Haruto's guard. He gave ground again, parrying the strike and shattering another dagger. Kira didn't stop. The moment one dagger shattered, she formed another and came on again. Each move was a burst of speed, fuelled by her qi. Each strike was meant to kill.

"Kira stop," Haruto said, leaping to the side. He rolled and came up in time to block another slash. The parry turned them sideways, and he shouldered her hard, sending her stumbling away. He had to fight the instinct to follow up, to take the opening and strike back. His old instincts were on fire.

Kira spun and flung a dagger at Haruto. He tried to bat it out of the air, but it shattered, a thousand shards of mirror reflecting a blinding light at him. Behind the shards came Kira, a new dagger in each hand. She was humming something under her breath, a song. Her eye sockets were pitch black pits of emptiness, the eyes themselves already swallowed by the darkness. Haruto realised this wasn't Kira at all, it was the yokai. The ungaikyo rising to the surface and assuming control. She grinned at him. Her teeth were broken mirrors reflecting images of his death.

"Stop this, Kira!" Haruto growled.

She didn't. The ungaikyo ran forward and drove both daggers at him. Haruto brought Shiki up and shattered them. He kicked Kira in the stomach, forcing her back even as she flicked new daggers into her hands. She crouched again, ready to spring at him. She was singing now, not humming. A nursery rhyme no one had sung for a hundred years.

"Stop, Mirai!" Yanmei shouted.

The yokai faltered, and the song died on her lips. Kira shattered, shards of mirror falling from her on the snowy grass. And just like that the ungaikyo vanished. Kira was back, her eyes clear. Haruto held up his guard until the daggers in Kira's hands shattered. She shook her head violently. "I'm sorry!" she cried. Then she turned and ran.

Haruto stood up from his crouch, and Shiki leapt from the

stick. It fell apart as soon as she left it. The little spirit waddled after Kira. Haruto was starting to think sparring had not been the best idea after all.

Yanmei shuffled over to him. She was hunched, her cloak pulled tight against the cold. Still, she shivered. She stopped next to Haruto and stared after Kira. "That wasn't her," Yanmei said. "That wasn't Kira."

Haruto wasn't so sure about that. Kira was both the girl and the ungaikyo, and right now the two sides of her were at war.

"Can you do something?" Yanmei asked. "Seal the yokai away or something?"

Haruto shrugged. "Me? Nope. You're the one who kept her yokai side from coming out for so long. Right now she's dealing with whatever venom the other onryo put in her head. If anyone is going to help her through it, Yanmei, it's you."

Kira staggered to a halt under the skeletal branches of an old tree and collapsed there, legs splayed out beneath her. She wept. She had tried to kill Haruto. It wasn't just an act of throwing herself into the fight, knowing that he was immortal. She had been trying to kill him. She hadn't cared. If it had been anyone else, someone slower than Haruto, they would be dead. If it had been Yanmei, Kira would have killed her. She gathered her knees up into her arms and sobbed into her kimono.

She felt a soft tugging on her sleeve and opened her eyes. Shiki was staring up at her. The little spirit squeaked once. No words, only comfort. She had a snowflake stuck to her black fuzzy body, and more were falling around them. Winter was refusing to give up its hold on Ipia. Kira moved to sit cross-legged, and Shiki climbed into her lap.

"You were wrong, Shiki," Kira said. "I am half spirit. I found her, my spirit side."

Shiki squeaked and Kira nodded, fresh tears stinging her eyes.

"I think she was trapped in the mirrors. I took you through, but not Haruto. Spirits can travel through the mirrors with me."

She swallowed down the lump in her throat. "I think she... I... I think part of me was still trapped in the mirror, and I brought her out with me. I set her free."

Shiki whistled.

Kira shook her head. "I don't want to be her. I don't want to be..." A sob shook her.

Another squeak.

"But she's stronger than me. She tried to kill Haruto."

Shiki gave that little trembling shrug and then shook with laughter. She was right. The ungaikyo would not go away. It couldn't. They were one.

Kira flicked a dagger into her hand and held it in front of her. She closed her eyes, too scared to look into the mirror. She felt the snow falling on her head and shoulders, chasing the warmth from her skin. She listened to the world waking. Birds chirping, insects singings, the wind a soft whisper carrying human sounds. She was procrastinating, and she knew it. She squeezed her eyes shut tighter, forced the last of her tears down her cheeks, then summoned unreasonable courage, opened her eyes and stared into the mirror.

The ungaikyo stared back at her.

Chapter 41

They walked for three days, heading west. The prince assured them that their welcome in western Ipia would be grand. To Haruto it sounded a lot like the prince was trying to convince himself. Yanmei struggled to keep pace with them, but never complained or asked to stop. She had a tight rein on her qi, locking it down, but the effort made her weak. Her wounds were slow to heal and she was always shivering. Kira shrunk into a sullen lump. Now and then some of her old enthusiasm would bubble up and erupt like a welcome geyser, showering them all in youthful joy even at something as simple as a lone tree defying the grasp of winter and daring to show its colour to the world. But most of the time the girl was quiet, somber. Haruto woke her each morning to train and spar, but she held back, refusing to use her technique. She was afraid of the ungaikyo inside of her.

Guang, at least, seemed in good spirits. The old poet was always ready with a story or a game to pass the time. But the shadow of Tian still hung over him. It hung over both of them.

Tian's anger rumbled inside Haruto like a storm front waiting to break. It made him terse, irritable, and everything and everyone around him grated against his nerves. He clenched his teeth and silently screamed at his friends to *shut up*. They were moving in the right direction, and Haruto had to hope they would get there in time. When he closed his eyes, he saw Tian's ruined face snarling at him. Too much of the yokai Tian had become had seeped back to earth already. Much more and Haruto feared he would lose himself in the rage.

As they climbed higher into the hills again, the snow fell more heavily. It wasn't like up in the mountains though. The snowflakes were fat, ponderous things. In some places the ground was blanketed in white, and in others the cold refused to take hold.

After almost a week, they began running low on food. Fellow travellers had been kind and generous, but it was winter and many people were going hungry.

On the morning of the seventh day, they saw signs of farmland, tilled earth and the telltale green and yellow of winter crops. Men and women drifted about the fields like gaunt ghosts. Most turned away or pulled their jingasas down over their eyes rather than encounter the passing group. There were guards about too. Men wearing mismatched ceramic armour, carrying spears and clubs. Seemingly armed with whatever they'd scrounged together, they looked more like bandits than soldiers. None approached, but all watched Haruto and the others warily as they passed.

The late afternoon sun was sinking below the horizon when they came upon the village. It had no walls and was nestled between a rocky hillock and thinning forest that had seen too many axes. The buildings were ramshackle, bordering on derelict. A few people drifted about, thin and grey, in rags despite the cold winter. A woman carrying a bucket of water from the well spotted them, turned and ran.

Guang nudged the prince in the ribs. "That was your breath, did that?"

"What are you talking about?" Ido Katsuo asked.

Guang leaned away from the prince, waving a hand in front of his face. "Cabbage! Definitely your breath."

"Ah." The prince shook his head. "You're one to talk. You fart in your sleep loud enough to wake the dead and rancid enough to send them clawing their way back underground."

Guang looked about the others for some backup. They all looked away. The old poet laughed and clapped the prince on the back. "Good one."

"Thank you," Ido Katsuo said.

They moved further into the village but found no inn, no shops, and few people. Haruto assumed they must all be out in the fields; nevertheless, the village had a ghostly quality that set him on edge. At the far end, pressed against a cliff face, was an enclosed compound. Its walls, gate, and the large house beyond them was nothing like the decrepit buildings in the rest of the village. Two guards knelt by the gate, rolling dice on the frozen earth, too busy to notice a group of travellers approaching. Haruto cleared his throat and the older guard, his head ringed with wild grey hair, looked up, startled, and scuttled off. A few seconds later, five more patchwork soldiers appeared as reinforcements.

"Remind you of anything?" Guang asked.

"Far too vividly," Yanmei said, her voice trembling like an injured bird crying for aid. "We should be careful here, Haruto. This place smells like banditry."

"Oh wonderful, just what we need," the prince said. "To get caught up in Auntie Ryoko's mismanagement of justice. I said we should head into western Ipia, not the arse end of nowhere Ipia."

There were eyes on them. Not just the guards', but from the nearby hovels as well.

"That's far enough," said one guard, stepping forward. He was young and scarred and wore a cracked breastplate, a helm that was too large for him, and one dirty vambrace. "Turn around, walk away, and don't stop."

"Show them your seal," Guang suggested.

"I was about to," Haruto said, fishing inside his kimono. He pulled out his imperial seal and held it up. "I'm an onmyoji. Sanctioned by the Empress." It was only a slight lie, but he doubted these guards would send a messenger to Kodachi to check.

"No yokai here," said the guard. "Turn around and walk away. The magistrate doesn't want to see you."

"How do you know? You haven't asked him," Ido Katsuo said.

"Don't need to," said the scarred guard. "*She* doesn't want to see you." Two more guards shuffled out of the gate, bringing the count up to eight. It was far from a convincing force, considering they looked like commonplace bandits, but who knew what sort of techniques they might be hiding? Besides, it wasn't Haruto's place to get involved. He dealt with spirits. The affairs of humans were best left to those who thought authority was power.

"You don't have a temple or shrine dedicated to the shinigami, do you?" Haruto asked. He still needed to fix his ritual staffs and the only place to do that was at a shrine dedicated to the reapers.

"No," the scarred guard said flatly. "Leave." A few of his fellows shifted about, reaching for their weapons.

Haruto shrugged, turned, and started walking. He wasn't sure what was happening here, and he didn't want to know. With rationing, their supplies would last another day or two, hopefully long enough to find a more hospitable village. Yanmei hesitated, but even she turned away with the others.

They were almost at the edge of the village when a shout stopped them. Haruto turned to find a young woman running toward them. She was as gaunt as the other villagers, and her blue kimono was old, faded, and ripped.

"Master Onmyoji," the woman said, breathing hard when she reached them. "You said you are an onmyoji. Sealed and all?"

Haruto noticed two guards had followed them from the magistrate's compound and were watching from a distance. He nodded to the woman.

"Please, you have to help me." The woman dropped to her hands and knees and bowed her head so low it touched the snowy path. "Save my daughter."

Haruto glanced at the guards again and sighed. "It's not my place to clash with your magistrate."

The woman looked up and shook her head. "Please, Master Onmyoji!" Haruto could see tears welling in her eyes. "A yokai has my daughter. You have to help her."

The woman led them to one of the larger buildings in the village. It had a hole in the roof that looked as though no one had ever tried to patch it, and the whole thing was sporting a pronounced lean. She babbled as she pulled open the door. A desperate rush of words that Haruto struggled to interpret. Guang and the prince stayed outside to keep an eye on the guards who were keeping an eye on them. Dirt and leaves had blown in through the hole in the roof, and the fireplace was filled with cold ashes that should have been thrown out days ago. On a table next to the stove, there was a bucket filled with water, but green slime clung to the wood around the lip. The smell of mildew was strong in the air. The woman fretted about the mess, finally stopping in front of a door that was barely hanging from its hinges. Beyond it, Haruto saw stairs leading down and heard the faint cry of a voice from below.

"Shiki, some light please," Haruto said. The little spirit scrabbled out of his kimono and yawned. Then she inflated into a ball of glowing light. "Thank you," he said.

"It's down there," the woman whispered. "It's chained up, but it has her. It has my Shiori."

Haruto took a deep breath. He had a bad feeling about the situation. He pulled open the door and started down the steps, Shiki floating ahead of him. It was a cellar dug straight into the ground, most likely used for storing rice in more plentiful times, but the barrels stood empty now. As he reached the bottom of the steps and stooped to avoid banging his head on the packed earth above him, he saw the girl.

She sat on the ground, sobbing, her body swollen to grotesque portions, folds of fat flowing over each other, sagging and pooling on the cold ground. What few rags she was wearing were ripped apart by the expanding mass. An iron manacle was fixed around her wrist, digging into her flesh, which was angrily ballooning around it. The manacle was fixed to a chain and a metal spike driven into the earth. The girl's eyes were pin pricks in her swollen face. She stuffed a handful of dirt into her mouth and chewed with broken teeth. Her hands were bloody from clawing up earth to shove into her mouth. The yokai did not *have* the girl. The girl was a yokai.

The woman descended the steps and pushed past Haruto. "No no no, Shiori. You mustn't eat that."

Haruto grabbed the woman by the arm just as the yokai's

eyes widened and it snatched at her with its free hand. Haruto pulled her away.

"It's alright, Shiori," the woman cried. "It's alright. I know you wouldn't hurt me." She turned on Haruto, tears streaming down her face. "It's not her. It's not my Shiori. It's the yokai. The yokai has her and won't let her go. Shiori is a good girl."

"Mummy," the yokai said, her voice high and tremulous. "I'm hungry."

The woman tried to wrench her arm from Haruto's grip, but he hauled her back and pushed her up the steps. "Kira, take her upstairs please." Kira glanced at the yokai, then grabbed hold of the woman and hauled her up.

"By the stars," Yanmei said as she reached the cellar. "What the..." She pulled her blanket close and hid her nose with one corner.

"It's a nuppeppo," Haruto said. He watched the sobbing yokai scoop up another handful of dirt and shove it into its mouth. "Come on." He turned and started up the stairs.

"Aren't you going to kill it or something?" Yanmei asked.

Haruto shrugged. "Yes. I am going to do 'something'. But I don't know what yet. Not all yokai are violent, and not all should meet a violent end."

Upstairs, the woman was kneeling on the floor next to a small cot, sobbing into her hands. Kira stood next to her, shifting from foot to foot, clearly uncomfortable.

"Guang," Haruto called. The old poet grumbled something about not being a servant and poked his head inside the door of the house. "Go find some firewood. Take the prince."

"Oh yes, *my lord*," Guang said. "Anything else, *my lord*? Perhaps some fresh steamed buns and hot bath?" He chuckled and disappeared back out the door. A moment later, Haruto saw him out the window, pushing the prince ahead of him across the snowy path.

Haruto knelt in front of the woman and gently pulled her hands from her face. Her eyes were raw and puffy. "Can you save her?"

"My name is Haruto," he said with a smile. "What's yours?"

"Sen."

"Sen," Haruto said. "And your daughter is Shiori?"

She nodded. "Please save her."

Haruto gently squeezed the woman's hands. "Sen, Shiori is dead."

Sen's eyes widened and she rocked her head, already making to stand. Haruto gripped her hands more firmly to stop her from running down into the cellar. "No," Sen wailed. "She can't be. It's the yokai. You're supposed to kill the yokai, not my little girl."

"Shiori is dead," Haruto repeated. She had to face the fact and accept it. What would come next would be even harder.

Sen shook her head.

"The yokai doesn't have your daughter, Sen. The yokai *is* your daughter. And the only way someone becomes a yokai is by dying."

Sen's face crumpled and she collapsed onto Haruto, burying her face in his kimono and bawling. She thumped his leg with her bony fists and mewled into his shoulder. It wasn't long before she ran out of energy. The poor woman was half starved and exhausted from worry. Her denial had been all that was holding her up and had allowed the problem to fester.

"She wasn't always like this," Sen said as she pulled away from Haruto. She wiped her eyes and nose with her sleeve. "Shiori was a skinny little girl. Then she started growing, taller and thinner. Even when she wasn't eating, when we had nothing to eat, she still grew. The magistrate came and accused us of stealing food. She chained my little Shiori up. The only reason she didn't do the same to me was because I could still work. We didn't steal any food. We didn't."

"I know," Haruto said. "Your daughter died, Sen. She's become a nuppeppo. It's a type of yokai that... Well, things will get worse yet. But I can help. I can't save her. But I can try to give her peace. Is there a temple or shrine nearby? One dedicated to the shinigami."

Sen drew in a ragged breath and shook her head. "The

closest temple is at the Graveyard of Swords, but that's three or four days' walk from here."

Haruto smiled past his frustration. "I'll think of something. Lie down and get some sleep. Tomorrow, we're going to give your daughter the peace she needs. Together."

Sen's face crumpled again, but she didn't cry this time. She lay down on the floor next to the small cot and closed her eyes. She was asleep within moments. Haruto envied her a little for that. It always surprised him how easily people could fall asleep when someone else took some of their burden.

He stood and motioned for Yanmei and Kira to leave and followed them out of the house. Guang and the prince were returning, each carrying a bunch of sticks.

"All sorted?" Guang asked.

"Not even started," Haruto said. "Go in and get a fire going. Watch the woman. When she wakes, do not let her go down into the cellar."

Guang narrowed his eyes, but nodded. The prince opened his mouth, but Guang shouldered him inside.

Two of the guards from the magistrate's compound were standing by a decrepit building across the path, watching them. They did not look underfed; one of them was fat as a buffalo.

"That little girl starved to death," Haruto said as calmly as he could. "I don't know if it was before or after the magistrate had her chained up. But she starved to death, and I doubt she's the only one."

"I've seen this before," Yanmei said. "The magistrate and her guards are bandits. Some places deal with bandits by giving them land and title instead of the sharp end of a sword. It never works out. Most often they continue to take and take and take, but instead of roaming, they take only from the very people they are supposed to protect." She glared at the guards watching them a moment. "Can you help the girl?"

Haruto leaned against the wall and sank down until he was sitting. He was so tired. A snowflake drifted down toward him, and Shiki leapt at it, snatching it out of the air and gobbling it up.

She danced around victoriously.

"An onmyoji has four ways of dealing with yokai." He closed his eyes and found Tian waiting for him in the darkness, mouth bloody and leering. Haruto quickly opened his eyes again. "We can't just kill the poor girl. A mortal strike will sever the spirit from the body, but it will only release it. Eventually it will find another body to inhabit, in this case another poor soul who starved to death. With my ritual staffs, I could create a barrier that would funnel the spirit back to heaven and into the arms of Omoretsu, my patron shinigami."

"Sorry," Kira said.

Haruto waved a dismissive hand in the air. It still annoyed him, but he doubted the frustration was truly his. It was best just to let it go. She had only been trying to help. "Onmyoji can also take a yokai's burden onto themselves. Then, when the yokai is killed, they skip the shinigami and proceed straight to rebirth. Unfortunately, I already have a burden. I can't take another."

"Tian?" Yanmei asked.

Haruto nodded. "Until that jorogumo is dead..."

"Xifeng," Kira said. "That's her name, the spider lady."

"Until the jorogumo is dead," Haruto repeated. "I cannot take on another yokai's burden. Shiki is a spirit blade, not a mortal weapon. Her cut can kill a yokai and send it back to heaven, but without the ritual staffs, Omoretsu will not collect the soul."

"What does that mean?" Yanmei asked.

Haruto grit his teeth at having to explain everything to them. "It's the job of the shinigami to collect the souls of the dead and direct them to the next life," he said. "But they're not the most willing or energetic of workers. They're spirits themselves, great kami given the unending task by the gods. They see it as a burden, whereas other kami, like the dragons, get to fly about free as a bird and do whatever they damn well please. Mortal spirits gravitate towards the shinigami. If I send a yokai to Omoretsu, he'll do his job. But the shinigami don't roam heaven looking for untethered yokai. Well, not to send them on to the next life at least. They do it only if they want minions to inflict upon the world." He shrugged. "Unless I direct Shiori's spirit to Omoretsu, she will drift about heaven as she is now. She will always be a nuppeppo. She may even find her way back to earth one day and possess another body."

"And the fourth way?" Kira asked.

"You've seen it," Haruto said. "It's much like the third only less violent. Usually. Yokai come back for a reason – an act of vengeance, an unfulfilled desire, a broken oath. Who knows? But there is always a reason. If I can give the nuppeppo what she wants, the spirit will go peacefully."

"Like the boy in the mine? We played hide and seek with him and he just vanished."

Haruto smiled and nodded.

"And that skips the shinigami too?" Yanmei asked. "Straight to the next life?"

"Yes," Haruto said. "Sounds easy, doesn't it? First you have to figure out what sort of yokai you're dealing with, then you have to decide what caused it to become a yokai and how to fulfil its desire or ease its burden." He sighed. "This one, I think is obvious though. The magistrate is hoarding food. Her guards are well fed, fat even. They accused the girl and her mother of stealing, but the girl starved to death chained up in the cellar. My guess, we need to steal some food from the magistrate and give it to Shiori."

"Justice," Yanmei said, "of a sort."

"Or vengeance?" Kira asked. The darkness around her eyes had faded a little, but it was still there. The girl and the yokai struggling against each other for control. "What if what Shiori wants is to see the magistrate's head separated from her neck?"

Yanmei glanced sidelong at the girl.

"It's possible," Haruto conceded. "But unlikely. The nuppeppo are harmless yokai. Mostly harmless. They just eat everything in sight. If left alone, they rarely kill anyone, but their unquenchable appetite becomes a blight upon food stores and such."

"So break into the compound, steal some food, feed the poor girl, and send her spirit to the next life?" Yanmei smiled. "I'll do it."

"Huh?" Haruto tilted his head at her.

"I'll sneak in and steal the food," she said. "Don't give me that look. I'm not as weak and useless as you think. Besides, those guards are watching you, not me. They probably think I'm just some old, frail woman." Haruto wasn't so sure they'd be wrong about that.

"I'll go too," Kira said.

"You will?" Yanmei asked, a smile spreading across her face.

Kira nodded but didn't look at Yanmei.

"Go after dark," Haruto said. He was far happier with the idea of both of them going. In her current condition, Yanmei needed the help. And Kira needed someone to stop the ungaikyo from taking control. "I'll cause a distraction at the main gate."

"How?" Yanmei asked.

Haruto shrugged. "I don't know. I'll juggle or something."

Chapter 42

"Must you pace like that?" Ido Katsuo asked as Kira walked behind him again. He snapped a stick in half and flicked one end into the fireplace.

Guang watched Kira grind her teeth, turn on the spot, and pace back the other way, behind Ido Katsuo again. Shiki shuffled along beside her like a tumbleweed on the wind.

"I must," Kira said testily. "It calms me."

"Well, it has the opposite effect on me," Ido Katsuo said.

"Then it's a good thing I'm not you." Kira turned and paced back the other way.

Ido Katsuo threw his arms in the air, lurched to his feet, and started pacing the opposite way to Kira. In the little hovel, there was not a lot of room to accommodate them, but the two somehow made it work, glaring at each other as they passed, both of them speeding up with every circuit.

Guang had long since learned that it was the waiting that most often picked apart the threads of a plan. As the philosopher Dong Ao said: 'Ask a man to wait a minute and it will seem like an hour. Ask a man to wait an hour and it will seem like a day. Ask ten men to wait a minute and it will be ten seconds'. It seemed somewhat pertinent now as they all waited around in Sen's little shack for night to fall.

Haruto handled it well enough, sinking cross-legged on the floor and meditating, though he kept cracking one eye open to watch Sen. The poor woman inched towards the cellar door. Yanmei, too, was still, but Guang guessed much of that was necessity. Since she'd blocked her qi, she moved slowly, like a true ancient. Kira and Ido Katsuo were balls of nervous energy; they refused to sit still. The constant distractions were making it far too hard for Guang to pen his latest poem. All he had written so far was, *I hate the cold.*

"You know, we never finished the tale of Nightsong," Guang said, interrupting Kira and Ido Katsuo's latest argument and forestalling her knocking the prince on his arse.

Kira turned her dark eyes on Guang, and he almost thought better of it, but they cleared quickly and she smiled. She was growing scarier by the day.

"Do you have to tell the rest of it?" Haruto asked. "It's not... I don't come off well."

Guang leaned over and patted his friend on the knee. "It's alright, old man. We've all met you, so we know how well you don't come off. Besides, it's pertinent." He looked around to find all eyes on him. Even the prince was leaning against the far wall, arms crossed and listening. "This next part of Nightsong's story is all about how and why he chose the path of an onmyoji."

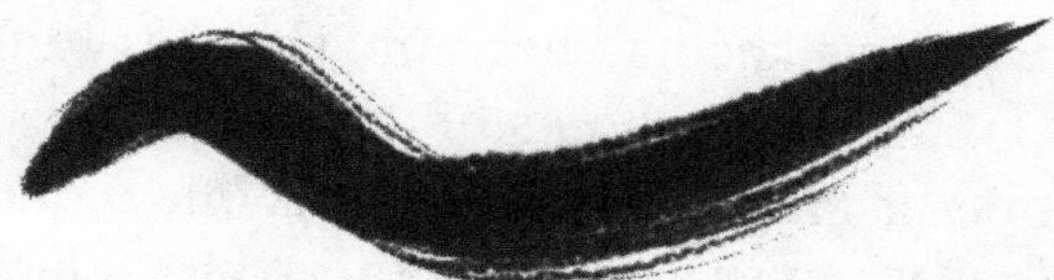

Now, we left our tragic shintei, Nightsong, at the lowest point in his life. After years of renown as the greatest swordsman and hero in Ipia, he was beaten and broken and destitute, his wife, Izumi, murdered. Worse still, he found his wife had risen again as a yokai, a vengeful spirit destined to inflict her pain and misery and anger on the innocent people of Ipia. Seeing Izumi like that was the final straw for Nightsong; it was too much for him to bear. It was bad enough seeing the woman he loved transformed into a monster, but he knew it was much worse for her. Izumi had always been so compassionate, and now she had become a monster, seeking only to harm others. There was nothing Nightsong could do about it. He could neither kill nor save her. Toshinaka's vengeance was complete, and Nightsong was a ruin of a man.

But before Nightsong succumbed to despair, he set himself one last task. For the shintei he had once been, he swore a new oath to Izumi that he would release her from her curse. He knew of an order of well-respected occultists whose jobs it was to hunt down yokai and release their spirits back into heaven. The onmyoji were a secretive lot, their ways as mysterious as their location. But everyone knew they were endorsed by Emperor Ise himself.

Nightsong returned to Kodachi a pauper. The people didn't recognise him. The palace guards didn't recognise him. Even the family he had married into didn't recognise him. He begged and pleaded for an audience with the emperor, and still he was turned away. Bereft of options, Nightsong waited until the emperor left his palace, threw himself before the palanquin and begged for one moment of the emperor's time. Serpent Guard drew their weapons and readied to kill Nightsong, but the emperor stayed their blades. He recognised Nightsong and bade the disgraced shintei to come closer. Nightsong crawled before the emperor, head bowed to the dirt, and apologised for the death of the emperor's favourite cousin, and the thing she had become. He begged the emperor for one final boon: the whereabouts of the onmyoji.

The emperor granted Nightsong his one request with a condition. He was never again to set foot in Kodachi. Never again did the emperor want to hear the name Nightsong. Nightsong bowed his head and agreed. He had already lost everything, and his name meant nothing.

When he reached the onmyojis' forest village, the occultists were not welcoming. They rarely accepted new initiates into their order, and when they did, the newcomers were usually young and strong, not old wandering beggars. Most importantly, they were chosen by a shinigami to serve. They surrounded the wanderer, men and women in grand robes, carrying ritual staffs, with ferocious companion spirits at their sides. They cast him out and told him never to return. Starving and at the end of his will, the wanderer stumbled into the village graveyard to lie down and die.

There were hundreds of shrines in the graveyard, each one dedicated to a shinigami. The wanderer visited them all, praying at each for an end to his miserable existence. The shinigami met him with nothing but silence. That is, until he came to a small shrine in a sorry state of disrepair at the far edge of the graveyard. Its stones were cracked, its doors askew, and the ground around it smelled of urine. You see, among the shinigami, there was one whose name was always met with ridicule, a trickster of a kami upon whom the gods themselves heaped disfavour and the other shinigami shunned. His shrines went untended, his name all but forgotten until the wanderer sat down to pray.

Omoretsu appeared to the wanderer surrounded by spirits. A kindly old man, he seemed, dressed in foul-smelling rags that mimicked the wanderer's own, his feet bare. The wanderer made his case, begged the shinigami's favour. He wished for nothing but to join the onmyoji, find Izumi and give her the peace that had been stolen from her. Omoretsu saw the way the onmyoji looked upon the wanderer and saw an opportunity to sow his mischief. After all, it had been a very long time since he had an onmyoji of his own.

Omoretsu gave the wanderer a task, a simple thing to prove his commitment. He laid a wakizashi in front of the wanderer and bade him take his own life. If he did that, Omoretsu would ensure Izumi had a chance at peace.

The wanderer saw his chance. A peace for Izumi and for himself. He took the blade in hand and steeled himself; then he fell upon the sword, driving it into his chest.

Yet, the wanderer didn't die. Omoretsu had played a trick on the poor fool. The task was a test to prove his commitment. The moment the blade pierced the wanderer's skin, Omoretsu gave his blessing and they struck a deal. The wanderer would train to become an onmyoji. The other onmyoji could no longer deny him now that Omoretsu was his patron. But there was more. The shinigami stripped the wanderer of his mortality, a blessing or a curse, depending on how you view it, to wander the earth serving Omoretsu for as long as the ghost of his wife remained.

And you should know, he wanders the earth still, searching for the yokai his wife has become.

As soon as night fell, Yanmei and Kira snuck away from Sen's home and away from the watchful eyes of the guards. The village was busier now. Farmers slunk back from their fields, wheeling clinking carts along the dirt paths. Women fetched buckets of water from the well, all in near silence, their eyes cast away from the soldiers. The guards – or bandits, as Yanmei knew they were – retreated behind the walls of the magistrate's compound and there was a fair amount of noise coming from beyond the walls.

Ido Katsuo had offered to go in Yanmei's stead, but she didn't trust the prince. There was a duplicity to him she had seen in many others before, and he all but admitted to being an assassin. Besides, she wanted to do this. She needed to prove that she was still useful even without her technique. Her father's legacy had given her much over the years, but it had taken from her even more. She wondered if he had known the cost of using it and if that was why he had used it so sparingly? She had always thought it was because he was weaker than her, but maybe he was just wiser. The thought almost made her laugh. Flaming Fist had been called many things over the years: bandit, murderer, tyrant, father. But she doubted anyone had ever called him wise. Yet when Yanmei was young, she remembered looking up to him and thinking he knew everything. Flaming Fist had an indomitable strength about him, not just a physical strength, but a strength of purpose. So many times Yanmei had watched him ride off to slaughter and pillage, and wished to ride with him. Even knowing what he was and what he did, she had still wanted to be by his side. Even burned and bruised from his abuse, she had still wanted to please him. The draw of family was strong, but just like fire, it could both comfort and burn. Yanmei shook the maudlin thoughts from her head.

They crept around the village, skirting it and heading towards the hillock. Kira was a sullen shade in the dark. All the happy energy had left her, and the girl seemed far more like a yokai than ever before. Yanmei was losing Kira to her other half. She felt the loss even more keenly than that of the fire that had kept her warm all her years.

The climb up the hillock was taxing, and they made the trek in silence. Yanmei's legs burned and Kira strode ahead of her. When they reached the cliff that looked down into the compound, they waited, hunkering down in the gloom until Haruto made his distraction.

"The Herald of Bones said you were holding me back," Kira whispered. Yanmei saw the now familiar darkness haunting her eyes. "He said that you and everyone at Heiwa were trying to make me something I'm not. You were forcing me to be human, to suppress my yokai half."

Yanmei opened her mouth to speak, but Kira barrelled on.

"He said I could be as powerful as Shin, but I have to embrace the ungaikyo and stop letting you hold me back." She drew in a ragged, trembling breath. "I've seen her. Every time I look into a mirror, I see her. The ungaikyo. Me." Kira turned to Yanmei, her eyes shining with tears. "I don't want to be her. I don't want to be the yokai. I want to be good."

Yanmei edged closer and wrapped her arms around Kira, pulling her close. "You don't have to be the yokai."

"But she's waiting for me. I can feel her. She tried to kill Haruto." Kira sniffed. "You're the only one that stops her. Never leave me. Please don't let her come out again."

Yanmei held Kira then, unsure which of them was trembling more. Of course she would stay with Kira. Yanmei would be there... for as long as she could.

Kira stiffened in her arms and pulled away. She wiped her eyes with her sleeve and frowned. "You're cold," she said. "Why are you cold? You're never cold."

Yanmei shook her head, smiled at her daughter, and lied to her. "Just an after effect of using my technique back in Kodachi.

The Sage said something like this might happen. I'm fine."

Kira took her hands and stared at the bandages. "The Sage said your technique was hurting you."

Yanmei pulled her hands away. "He did. And he was right. But I am fine. I just can't use much qi at the moment."

"And your naginata," Kira said. She seemed to be only just noticing the fallout from Kodachi. She had been so distracted by her own struggles with her yokai half that she hadn't noticed everything else.

"I lost it," Yanmei said sadly. "I fought a Serpent Guard. He was stronger than I expected. But you fought many and beat them all." She put a hand on Kira's cheek. "I am so proud of you. You've grown so strong."

Kira shook her head. "I'm not strong. I'm scared."

They heard shouting from inside the compound. Someone was at the gate making a commotion. The distraction was underway; it was time to sneak in and steal some food. She placed a bandaged hand on the back of Kira's neck and pulled her close until their foreheads were touching. "It's alright to be scared. Fear doesn't make you weak, it makes you human." She swallowed the lump in her throat. "Now, we have to move."

They crept closer to the edge and slithered over. With the moon to the north and almost hidden behind a blanket of clouds, they were in shadow, and as long as they kept quiet they were unlikely to be spotted. The climb down wasn't far, only forty feet, but it was taxing. Kira seemed to find it easy enough, her agile fingers digging into every handhold and her qi keeping her strong. Yanmei was not so gifted. Her fingers ached, the nails cracking against the stone. Sweat ran down her head and into her eyes, and her muscles burned. Hand over hand, she went, her feet scrabbling to find purchase in the crumbling rock. Her world shrank down to the cliff face before her and the next agonising hold.

"Jump," Kira hissed.

Yanmei risked a look down. She was only ten feet from the bottom. Kira was standing there below her, motioning her to let go, holding out her arms to catch her. Yanmei already wasn't winning any awards for grace, so she might as well allow herself to be caught. She pushed away from the cliff face and fell, her breath catching as gravity pulled her down.

Kira caught her with a grunt of effort and set her down. Yanmei almost laughed. She remembered carrying Kira around on her shoulders when she was a child and running laps around the academy grounds. The little girl would laugh and demand Yanmei run faster. Eventually, it wasn't enough to be a passenger, and Kira would leap from Yanmei's shoulders and run along beside her, her little legs trying to keep pace, laughing as though she had never had so much fun. A mere decade ago, but it felt like a lifetime. She'd grown up so quickly, and so quickly Yanmei's own body succumbed to the stresses of her technique.

They were standing in a small, lovingly kept garden. Despite the depth of winter, green grass flattened beneath their feet, and Yanmei heard the soft tinkle of running water, a small stream winding through the garden. With a few bonsai trees scattered about, some rocks here and there, and a tiny wooden bridge crossing the stream, it was as though someone had created the garden to mimic a particular bit of scenery in miniature. Two stone plinths sat at the edge of the garden, marking the entrance to the path that led into the compound. Both plinths had candles burning in small sconces, open on all sides but shielded from above. A lot of care and attention had gone into this garden.

Kira picked something up and looked at it, then showed it to Yanmei. It was a wooden carving of a horse, and it was not alone. There were a dozen others in various poses. She dropped the toy and they set off, creeping towards the buildings and hoping Haruto's distraction would last long enough for them to get in and out. Judging by the noise coming from the gates, he had the attention of every guard in the village.

They reached the outer door of the main building, a two-storey mansion that dominated most of the compound. Yanmei slid the door open, and Kira dashed in. Yanmei followed her and slid the door shut behind her. It felt good to be doing this with

Kira, as though the distance that had grown between them was falling away with every moment they spent together.

Yanmei expected the interior to be as ramshackle as the other buildings in the village, but it was far from it. The mansion was clean inside, the walls freshly painted, and the smell of lemons prickled her nose. They were in an antechamber, and to Yanmei's left was an open rack containing enough shoes for a small army. Kira quirked an eyebrow at her in question, but Yanmei motioned her on. They were not there to question the cleanliness of these bandits. Despite that, Yanmei scooped a pair of shoes from the rack and tested their size against her own feet. Then she pulled open the carry sling around her chest, tucked the shoes inside, and followed Kira.

The shouting outside turned into loud laughter, and Yanmei wondered if Guang was out there too, telling jokes perhaps. Another smell wafted over the lemon scent; it was fish cooking. They followed it, creeping past empty rooms, many of which looked as though they housed two or three people judging by the futons. They followed the smell of fish to the left at an intersection of hallways, and heard a grunt of surprise. Just twenty paces away, a sleepy guard was leaning against a wall. He startled at the sight of them and opened his mouth. Kira moved like a striking snake and was on him. She drove a fist into his gut and he doubled over. Then she flicked a dagger into her wrist and went for his neck.

"No!" Yanmei breathed as loudly as she dared.

Kira froze, the mirrored dagger against the man's neck. All trace of sleep left him, and he looked up goggle-eyed at Kira. Yanmei saw Kira look down into the mirror surface of her own dagger and recoil in horror. The weapon shattered in her hand. The guard tried to wrap his thick hands around her throat. Yanmei stepped in and punched him in the jaw. She might be old and unable to use her qi, but she had grown up around bandits and she damned well knew how to throw a punch. Goggly Eyes went down in a heap and didn't get back up. The pain hit Yanmei a moment later. Her hand felt like she had punched a rock.

Yanmei was reaching for the door when she felt a hand grab hers. She glanced back to find Kira looking terrified, one eye socket dark and terrifyingly hollow. She gave Kira's hand a squeeze, but they didn't have time to stop. Kira nodded and then Yanmei let go and slid the door open.

The kitchen was large and open and redolent with the smell of fish and rice and herbs. A young woman in an apron stood over a pot, a leafy twig in her hand. She froze when she saw Yanmei at the door. The woman appeared to be the sole chef, and judging by the variety of foods cooking in the kitchen, she was sorely overworked. Yanmei stared at the woman, held a finger to her lips and entered the kitchen with Kira close behind.

"We don't need much," Yanmei said. "We're not here to feed the entire village, just one child."

The woman was still frozen, the twig in her hand. Her eyes darted to the fireplace and the fish spitted above it. Yanmei nodded to her, and the woman dashed to the fish and turned them to stop them from burning.

"I'm very sorry about this," Yanmei said to the woman. "If they ask, tell them I held a sword to your neck." The woman nodded and went about her work.

Kira reappeared with a sling full of rice, a couple of eggs, and a handful of vegetables. It was enough to feed a small family. Or at the very least, a starving child and her mother. Yanmei smiled at her, and they stole out of the room even more quietly than they'd entered. The climb back up the cliff face was even worse than the descent. Kira managed it with relative ease, but Yanmei struggled with every handhold. She was sweaty and in agony by the time Kira hauled her up and over the edge. She lay there for a minute, panting and listening to the sounds of the night, watching snowflakes fall lazily around her. Her breath burned like fire in her lungs. The compound was coming alive, and that meant they'd discover the man she had knocked out soon enough. They needed to regroup and be ready for the reprisal. If there was one thing Yanmei knew all too well about bandits, it was that they did not allow people to steal from them.

Chapter 43

Sen was awake and fretting. She wanted to see Shiori, to reassure her daughter everything would be alright. The lie would fall on deaf ears – the yokai was already beyond that. There was little left of the girl it had once been. Nothing except a soul that needed shepherding on to the next life. Guang set the fire going and the prince fetched some fresh water from the well. At first, he claimed fetching water was beneath him, but Haruto offered him the job of checking on Shiori instead, and one look at the nuppeppo had been enough to convince the prince that water carrier was a fine occupation.

The distraction had gone well. His demands to see the magistrate were refused, but Shiki drew the attention of almost twenty people outside the compound. She popped from item to item, possessing a broom, a stone, a torch, even a woman's pauldron. That last one had been a stroke of genius and everyone stared as the woman's armour grew eyes and a mouth and produced a sound like a wet fart. Some of the guards laughed; others swore she was an ill omen. All that mattered was that they stayed out of the main building. After that, Haruto retreated to Sen's home to pray to Omoretsu. As usual, without a shrine to draw the shinigami's attention, his prayers went unanswered.

The door slammed open startling Guang, and he spilled boiling water over the floor. Kira was first through and she was smiling like Haruto hadn't seen in days.

"Carrot, girl!" Guang snapped. "Almost scared the hair off my lip."

Kira giggled. "Sorry." She rushed over to him and laid out her stolen goods on the table.

Yanmei was next inside and closed the door behind her. She

was looking both worse and better for the excursion. Colour had returned to her cheeks again, but she was sweating and sank down to her knees. "Here," she said as she pulled her sling over her head and placed a pair of shoes in front of Sen. "I noticed yours are falling apart. I think these should fit you."

Sen stared at the shoes in uncomprehending wonder.

"We don't have long," Yanmei continued. "They'll have discovered the guard by now. I have a feeling we'll be seeing the magistrate after all."

"Master Onmyoji," a woman called from outside. There was a mocking singsong to her words. "Come out, come out, come out. Or I'll burn your house down."

Sen squeaked in alarm.

Ido Katsuo peered between a couple of ill-fitting wall planks. "I believe she may have brought everyone." He turned, looking a little pale. "It looks like a bandit parade out there."

Guang grunted as he added some rice into the water in the pot. "This is going to take a while. It'll be more difficult if the house is on fire."

"I'll go negotiate then," Haruto said with a shrug.

"Sure," Guang said. "If that's what you call stabbing a bunch of folk."

"That's not why I'm..."

Guang just waved a hand dismissively in his direction.

Haruto walked over to the prince. "Stay here and do not let Sen downstairs."

"Babysitting duties?" Ido Katsuo asked. "Wonderful. Far more to my skill set than fighting. I don't have to go down there and look at it again, do I?"

Haruto scowled at the prince, then made for the door. Kira was behind him immediately, and Yanmei stood, groaned, and joined them. "You don't have to come," he said. "I'm not going out there to fight. In case you haven't noticed, they're all armed and we're not."

"You have Shiki," Kira said. The little spirit squeaked and shook like a wet dog.

"Shiki can't be used against mortals," Haruto said. "It's part of the pact when summoning a shikigami. Besides, there's a lot of them out there."

"*You* might not be going out there to fight," said Yanmei. "But that doesn't mean they won't have other ideas. I know these people, Haruto. I was one of them."

"Listen to her, old man," Guang said, not turning from the pot.

Haruto knew arguing would get him nowhere. He shrugged, pulled the door open, and strode out to meet the magistrate.

Guards in patchwork armour crowded the street. Many of them carried torches, and all of them carried weapons and scars that said they weren't afraid to use them. At the head of the group stood a striking woman. She wore a rich red coat over a bleached bone tunic and brown trousers. She was from Nash by the look of her dark skin, and her belly bulged with child. She wore her hair up in high tail that dangled in two thick braids down her back, the traditional Nash fashion for women, and each finger on her left hand ended with a gleaming metal talon.

"Master Onmyoji," the woman set with a slight bow. Her eyes were bright blue like the Seafolk, and she stared at him with an unnerving intensity.

"Magistrate," Haruto said, returning the bow. "I see you've finally come to welcome me to your village."

The magistrate was silent for a few seconds, a smile tugging at her lips. "And these two would be my thieves, I guess. This them, Boko?"

A chubby guard stepped forward and peered at them. "Yup. That's them."

A few of the other guards laughed, and the magistrate grinned at Boko. "You said they were like a couple of tigers. That old lady is peering into an open grave, and the girl is skinny enough to squeeze through my arse cheeks." Another round of laughter and a Boko received a few hard pokes to the ribs.

"Hand over my thieves and my food, Master Onmyoji," the magistrate said. "And you can walk out of my village with your balls still attached."

Haruto glanced over his shoulder at Kira and Yanmei. He hesitated as if debating the offer. "It's tempting. But I'm afraid I have to decline."

The magistrate flexed her talons. "A fight is fine with me," she said, nodding over her shoulder at her minions. "These lot have been getting a bit fat of late."

Haruto held up his hands. "No fight. We don't even have weapons. I don't take part in mortal affairs, magistrate. I'm simply here to deal with a yokai."

"And that involved stealing from me?"

Haruto shrugged. "Yes. Listen, I am not some wandering hero looking to make my name from killing hapless bandits."

"Bandits, are we?" the magistrate said. "I'm in charge of this village, empowered by the Empress herself. I've got a seal around here somewhere. Namika, where's the damned seal."

"I been using it to prop up a chair back at camp," Namika thumbed over his shoulder. The other guards laughed.

"I have one of those too," Haruto shouted over the laughter. He fished inside his kimono and produced the wooden token. "Mine says I'm an imperial onmyoji."

The magistrate peered at the seal in his hands. She stepped toward him and waved for one of her men, an ugly fool with one eyebrow, to hold up his torch. "You really are an onmyoji."

Haruto thought he saw a way to end this peacefully. "Magistrate," he said with another bow. "I am not here to interfere with your village or your rule. But I would like you to come inside and see something."

The magistrate frowned, and a couple of her guards started forward. She held up a hand to stop them. "What do you want me to see?"

"The truth," Haruto said. "And the reason I stole food from you. I promise you I mean you no harm. You can enter and leave at will."

"What are you doing?" Yanmei whispered. "They are bandits, despite what they call themselves, and they are starving the people of this village."

Haruto looked at her and spoke loud enough for everyone to hear. "And if we fight them, they might win. Even if we beat them all, the Empress would only put someone else in charge." He shook his head. "They are here by law, and it is not my place to question mortal laws. My affairs lie only in the spiritual realm. You two can wait out here. We'll be fine." He turned, pushed open the door, and held it for the magistrate.

"If I'm not back out in five minutes, kill everyone," the magistrate said to her troops before stepping inside the house.

Haruto followed her inside and closed the door behind him. Sen looked up and wailed. "You! You did this." She was already crying again. "You killed my daughter."

The magistrate ignored her and sniffed the air, then looked at Guang. "That's my food you're cooking."

Guang winked at her. "There should be some left over if you fancy joining us for dinner."

Haruto stepped past the Magistrate and shooed Ido Katsuo away from the cellar door. "It's down here."

The magistrate narrowed her eyes and flexed her talons again.

"I promise you, magistrate, you are safe down there. I just want to show you why I'm here." With that, he pushed open the door and walked down the steps.

Shiori was just as he had last seen her. Flesh overflowing, eyes little more than pin pricks in a swollen face. Her arms were disappearing into her mass, and she was losing all shape. Soon she would be unrecognisable as anything that had once been human. She scooped up another handful of dirt and shoved it into her mouth.

"Urgh!" The magistrate said as she reached the floor of the cellar. She pinched her nostrils closed and peered at Shiori. "What is that thing?"

"She's the reason I'm here," Haruto said. "And she's your fault."

"What?"

Haruto sighed and crouched next to the yokai. Shiori looked at him. There was pain and pleading in the dark depths of those beady eyes, but it was not a human pleading. It was the insatiable hunger of a nuppeppo. "You had this girl chained up down here."

"She and her mother stole from me!"

"No. They were starving, and you had a little girl chained up down in this cellar and she starved to death." Haruto stood and faced the magistrate. "She became a yokai because you murdered her."

The magistrate lurched forward and clutched Haruto's neck in her taloned grip. Haruto froze. She couldn't kill him, but he knew having his throat ripped out hurt a lot. Shiori began to pant heavily behind him. Could he die if he was eaten? He'd never tried it, nor did he wish to.

"How many times do I have to say it?" Haruto wheezed. "I only deal in the affairs of the spiritual. I'm here to cleanse this yokai. Shiori, a nuppeppo you created. I'm telling you this because she won't be the last."

The magistrate dug her talons deeper into Haruto's throat, and he felt blood running down his neck into his collar. "Killing me won't stop it. The people here are starving. You are starving them. I have no say if that's how you want to run things. I'm not here to depose you." He stopped to gasp in a breath. "But I will tell you, this nuppeppo is only the beginning. More yokai will come, perhaps even ones who aren't as passive. People will die. They will die and turn into yokai. I have seen it time and again. They are drawn to suffering. If you continue starving your people, you'll have a plague of yokai to deal with and no onmyoji to rid you of them." The magistrate eased her grip, and Haruto rubbed his bloody neck. Again, he wished immortality came with an immunity to pain.

"You're serious?" she asked.

"Of course I am!" Haruto snapped. "This poor girl did not deserve her fate. You did this to her, and it was cruel and unfair. If it wasn't, she wouldn't have become a yokai."

The magistrate pursed her lips. "It's been a grim winter."

"And that's an excuse. And I don't care." He shook his head and closed his eyes, only to find Tian grinning at him through sharp, bloody teeth. "My job isn't to prevent yokai being born – it's easing their passing onto the next life however I can. But I am telling you there will be more, drawn by their hatred of you and the suffering you are causing. It's not a threat. It's a warning. You do not want a shichinin rising here."

The magistrate grimaced. "That would be worse than this?" She gestured at the nuppeppo and curled her lip.

"They are the seven spirits of plague. They possess the living and bring disease with them. Everywhere they appear illness and ruin follow. You don't want that."

The magistrate touched a blood-tipped talon to her pointed chin and narrowed her eyes at Haruto. "True. How do I stop it?"

"Feed your people," he said. "Stop murdering them. Be a magistrate, not a bandit. I don't care. I'm going to ease this young girl's passing and then move on. I won't be coming back."

The magistrate paced back and forth in the small cellar, flexing her talons. Shiori watched her, panting and scooping dirt into her mouth. Finally, the magistrate asked, "What if I just kill it? Kill all these things that you say will come?"

"You can't," Haruto said, as calmly as if he was explaining to a child why water will always be wet. "You could kill the body, yes. But the yokai would inhabit another. This nuppeppo was born because of you, and she is here to stay unless an onmyoji cleanses her. They are not choosy about their hosts. A starving old man, a young woman on the verge of death, an unborn child."

The magistrate stopped pacing and glared at him, and Haruto wondered if he had gone too far. "You'll deal with this one? Kill it so it doesn't come back?"

"That's my job."

"And that's why you stole my food?"

Haruto shrugged. "She starved to death, chained up down here accused of stealing from you. The only peaceful way to send her on her way is to fulfil her desire for vengeance. To feed her stolen food." He didn't add that he wasn't completely certain it would do the job because the alternative was killing the magistrate and hoping that satisfied Shiori's vengeance.

The magistrate sneered at Shiori. Then she turned and stormed up the stairs. "Deal with that thing, onmyoji."

Haruto followed the magistrate up the stairs and out of the house. Outside, the atmosphere was tense. The bandits were brandishing their weapons, some even daring to step close to the house. Yanmei stood before them, unarmed and trembling from exhaustion. Kira stood a step behind her, no daggers in her hands.

The magistrate strode past them both without so much as a glance. "Head back," she shouted. "All of you."

"Boss?" asked the one-eyebrowed bandit.

"We're done here," the magistrate said. "The onmyoji has a ghost to kill and then he's leaving and taking the rest of these pathetic peasants with him."

The guards grumbled and sighed and rolled their eyes. They had been looking for a fight, but none of them dared to argue with the magistrate.

"And double everyone's rations," the magistrate said.

There was more grumbling and hissing at that, but the magistrate raked a talon down a complainer's arm, and they all shut up and marched back to their compound, leaving Haruto, Yanmei, and Kira alone outside Sen's house.

Haruto exhaled and felt his legs tremble. "Well, that went better than I had hoped." He forced a smile at Yanmei and Kira.

"They're bandits," Yanmei said. "We should have dealt with them properly."

"What would that achieve?" Haruto asked. "The empress would only send more to take their place, perhaps someone even worse. The people will be fed properly now, and the magistrate knows that if they aren't, more yokai will arise."

"She killed a little girl," Yanmei said through clenched teeth. "For no other reason than to set an example. That sort of evil..."

Haruto stamped a foot on the step and gripped the handle so

hard his knuckles popped. "And killing the magistrate would be murdering another child. It has to stop somewhere. You of all people should understand that." He pulled open the door and stepped inside. It was time to send Shiori on her way.

Kira knelt on the cold earth of the cellar floor, watching the yokai scoop dirt into its mouth and moan pitifully. No one needed to be down there watching the girl, but Kira felt like she should be there. How much really separated them? Kira wondered if she had once been just like Shiori. She remembered so little about her time as a yokai trapped in the mirror. Yanmei saved Kira from that existence. Could Shiori be saved too? Or would that just be condemning her to another form of torture, the life of an onryo, not knowing what she was but knowing that another part of herself was hiding in the shadows, in the reflections, biding its time, waiting for the chance to consume her and become her.

The more Kira thought about that other part of her, the ungaikyo, the more she knew it was trying to take over. She saw it in her reflection now. She felt it beneath the surface when she used her technique. Sometimes, she even felt it clawing up and trying to usurp control. She didn't want to lose control, didn't want to become the yokai again, but she wasn't strong enough to stop it from smothering and supplanting her. Only Yanmei could keep it at bay, could force the ungaikyo back into the reflections.

Shiori shifted, her pink flesh sagging and flowing, spilling onto the ground. She reached for Kira, her beady eyes full of ravenous hunger, but Kira shuffled back away from the yokai's swollen hand. Shiori looked at her and began clawing at the dirt again, digging up handfuls around the stake that held her chains and shovelling them into her mouth.

Kira felt something in her hand and looked down to find a mirrored dagger there. She didn't remember using her technique. She stared into the reflection, and the ungaikyo stared back at her. Its eye sockets, her eye sockets, were yawning pits. Her teeth were broken blades, and she was grinning a smile of malice and victory. The icy sound of glass cracking echoed in the cramped cellar. She felt the cracks forming along her skin, snaking up her chest. She shook her head and ordered the dagger to shatter. It didn't. The ungaikyo stared at her as the cracks in her skin crawled up her neck.

The cellar door opened. Haruto stood there, a steaming bowl in one hand. Kira hid the dagger behind her, pulled up the collar of her kimono to hide the cracks in her skin, and shuffled backwards out of the way. She couldn't let Haruto see her lose control. She needed Yanmei to chase her yokai away.

"You don't need to be here," Haruto said as he descended the stairs.

"Yes, I do," Sen said, following him down.

"Fine. Just stay back. Let me handle it."

"I need to say goodbye to my daughter." Sen slipped past Haruto and stared at Shiori. The yokai shifted, her flesh rolling and pooling in thick slabs, and reached for her mother.

"Stay back!" Haruto shouted.

Yanmei came down the stairs and stood beside Kira. The cellar was cramped with four of them and the yokai, but Kira was glad for the company. She stood and hugged Yanmei tightly.

Shiori sniffed at the air, then focused her beady eyes on the bowl Haruto carried. She flailed her fat hands toward it rabidly, mewling and rattling her taut chain.

Haruto leaned toward Sen. "Say goodbye now. And quickly."

Sen fell to her knees before her daughter and started speaking.

Yanmei shifted a little and stroked Kira's hair. For a moment, it was just like old times. When Kira had first arrived at Heiwa and all the students scared her, she had clung to Yanmei like a bur, wrapped herself in Yanmei's warmth. But Yanmei wasn't warm anymore. She felt cold in Kira's arms. She heard glass crackling again, felt the fissure snaking up her cheek, almost to her eye. She heard singing, distant, but... She almost recognised the song.

"Look at me, Mirai," Yanmei whispered. Kira met her gaze

and realised she was breathing too rapidly, unable to catch her breath. Haruto was watching them over Yanmei's shoulder, his brows deeply furrowed. "Come back to me, Mirai," Yanmei said. She cupped Kira's cracking cheek in her cool hand. "It's not you."

Kira felt the edge of panic fading away, and her breathing slowed. She shattered, glass shards falling all around her on the dirt floor. The cracks in her skin closed, disappeared. The singing had quieted too; she was glad of that. There was something about that song she didn't want to remember.

"It's time, Sen," Haruto said. The woman sniffed and fell silent, whispered words dying on her lips. Haruto knelt in front of Shiori, and the girl flailed her hands at the steaming bowl of rice broth. He placed it on the ground just out of her reach. "This food was stolen from the magistrate," Haruto said. Then he pushed the bowl towards her.

Shiori snatched the bowl and all but fell upon it, her rolls of fat engulfing it as she slurped it up and licked at the bowl.

"Omoretsu," Haruto intoned. "In your name, I act. In your stead, I serve. With your blessings, I bring peace to the dead." He leapt forward and placed a hand on Shiori's head. The yokai growled and flailed at him with her bulbous arms. "I name you, Shiori, daughter of Sen, aggrieved, wronged, murdered. I name you Shiori and send you on your way, your vengeance fulfilled!"

Shiori stopped growling and fell still. A little green wisp of light rose from her, zipped upwards through the ceiling and was gone in a flicker. No one else seemed to notice it. Then Shiori toppled sideways and lay still.

Haruto spent most of the night burying Shiori in the cellar. Guang thought about offering to help, but he hated digging. Kira took a turn with the shovel though. Sen erected a shrine to her daughter and cried herself to sleep at its foot. Eventually, Haruto carried her up to her bed, and they all hunkered down for the night. When morning rolled around, it was time to leave the village behind, but there was one unfortunate matter that always needed seeing to. As the others said their goodbyes to Sen and assembled on the street outside, Guang nudged Haruto in the side.

"I know," Haruto said.

"Has to be done, old man. Imperial rules."

Sen looked at them, confused.

"There's, um..." Haruto coughed and looked at the floor "...the small matter of payment."

Sen frowned. "I don't have any money."

"It's the law," Guang said. "Onmyoji must be paid for their services."

"Oh," Sen said and nodded. She walked over to a somewhat dilapidated dresser and rifled through a drawer. "I have a bracelet. It was Shiori's. My husband gave it to her the day he left to join the army."

Guang stepped out to join the others. It was chilly, but then Ipia always seemed cold. At least it wasn't snowing yet. Yanmei was huddled into an extra blanket in a way that made her seem small, yet still she shivered. Kira was a few steps away, arguing with Ido Katsuo about something, but they were smiling at least.

Haruto stepped out, gave Sen one last bow, and then slid the door closed behind him. "Northwest to the Graveyard of Swords then," he said cheerily. "There's a temple there with a shinigami shrine so I can finally get my ritual staffs blessed."

A few bandits were out about the village, standing guard, but none said anything or ventured too close to them. When they reached the village outskirts, the frigid hills of western Ipia stretching out before them, Guang coughed loudly to get Haruto's attention. "The payment then?"

"Of course," Haruto said, patting at his kimono. "I have it, uh, here somewhere. Huh." He shrugged. "I guess I lost it."

Chapter 44

Three days out from the village, the landscape changed. The relentless hills gave way to gloomy, green forests and frigid rivers with water as clear as the scroll still waiting for Guang's epic poem. Snow continued to fall, but it didn't settle as deeply as it had up on the mountains. Guang was happy to scuff his feet through a few fingers of powder, rather than wade through hip-deep drifts of the stuff. They soon joined a well-travelled road with inns here and there. On the third night, a lively innkeeper informed them that they had officially entered western Ipia. Ido Katsuo beamed at the knowledge and was relentless the following day.

"Why aren't we heading west?" the prince asked.

"Because we're heading north," Haruto said.

"Right, right," Ido Katsuo said. "The Graveyard of Swords. An uncompromisingly depressing place. You know there are plenty of temples in my father's cities. I believe Kanyo is just a little south of here, a day at most, and it has more temples than Yanmei here has bags under her eyes. Ow!" Kira thumped him hard in the arm.

It was a bright morning, though still overcast. Fat white flakes drifted down and the frozen ground crunched underfoot. Guang blew into his hands and rubbed them together. Haruto strode ahead of them, Shiki sat on his shoulder and pointed ahead animatedly as if she were leading them. Kira and Ido Katsuo walked behind, still arguing. Guang glanced at Yanmei, and she gave him a knowing smile.

"Why are you still here?" Kira asked the prince playfully. "If you want to go to Konya--"

"Kanyo," the prince corrected her.

"Then go! No one is keeping you here." The two of them had been at it for days. Everything seemed to spark an argument between them, and they didn't agree on anything.

"My dear, Kira, that simply isn't true," Ido Katsuo said. "*You* keep me here. I am entranced by your beauty; the darkness of your eyes, the way your hair sticks up here and there, defying convention."

"Urgh!" Kira rolled her eyes. She didn't try to scare him away though, Guang noticed. She had scared none of them with her reflections for days. He struggled to remember the last time he had even seen her with a dagger in hand.

"I don't have a choice," Ido Katsuo said. "Auntie Ryoko doesn't like me much."

"Because you tried to kill her."

"So did you," the prince said. "And you got far closer than I."

Kira ran a hand through her messy hair. "I wasn't trying to kill her, I was trying to distract the Serpent Guard."

"By maiming the empress?"

Kira opened her mouth to reply, but closed it and trudged on.

"Well, I know Auntie Ryoko likes to hold grudges, and I don't think she'll be terribly pleased that I escaped." The prince sighed and threw up his hands. "She will send someone after me, and you know as well as I that she is working with the onryo. So I can only assume I have at least one of them after me, and what safer place to be than here with a master of the spiritual, uh, stuff. So, you see, I cannot leave. I am stuck to Haruto until such time as he delivers me to my father."

"Haruto wants no part in this discussion," Haruto grumbled from up front without turning around.

"In that case," Ido Katsuo said. "My dear Kira, I fall back to being captivated by your beauty."

"How about a story?" Guang asked to forestall Kira clawing the prince's eyes out.

"Please!" Yanmei said with a grateful smile.

"I have just the one," Guang said. "This is the tale called The King of Rock and Sky and his Paper Army."

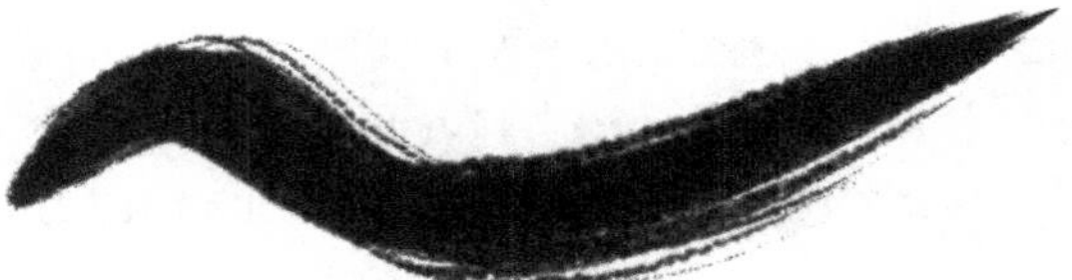

Long ago, before the nation of Hosa united into the ten kingdoms, there was a man called Jun-lu who lived in what we now call Shin province. It's a rugged land, full of mountains and cliffs, rocky plateaus and crumbling trails. Not much grows in Shin save weeds and goats and, of course, people as hardy as the goats. As harsh as life in Shin was, those who lived there had nowhere else to go. To the west lies Sun Valley protected by the wushu masters. To the north, over the Endless Mountains, is Cochtan, and no one from Hosa would willingly live there. South of Shin lies the province of Qing, rich and bountiful, with green fields and boundless forests, and armies to protect its lands.

Jun-lu was a farmer, growing weeds in his field of stolen dirt. Every year, he trekked the broken trails to Qing province, stole a cart full of earth, and hauled it back up to his home. It was hard work, dangerous work, but he did it to give his wife and daughter, whom he loved so much, a life.

But he wanted to give them so much more. He wanted them to know more than stolen dirt and chewy weeds, more than stringy goat meat and backbreaking labour. He wanted to give them freedom from the endless toil.

Luckily for Jun-lu, a travelling merchant sold him just what he needed: a scroll said to contain a powerful technique that, in the right hands, could give the bearer untold power and wealth. Jun-lu traded his life's savings for the scroll, gambling everything he had ever squirrelled away for his daughter's prosperity. The scroll taught him to infuse paper with qi and bring it to life. A useful technique, for sure. With the stroke of a brush, a strip of paper became a rake, a plough, a ladder, or even a sword. Useful, but hardly enough to secure Jun-lu the prosperity he desired. But Jun-lu had a dream and the will to see it through. He experimented relentlessly, dedicating every spare moment to learning and mastering the technique. He took on extra work, anything his neighbours needed, to earn money for supplies. Eventually, he made the breakthrough that would change the face of Hosa forever. He created a paper man. The first was a small homunculus, the size of a child, but it moved and followed simple instructions. It worked tirelessly, requiring neither food nor rest. It was agile and strong enough to perform the labour of two men.

Jun-lu's neighbours soon saw what he was doing and asked for their own paper workers. He was happy to oblige, for a price of course. But still Jun-lu wasn't content. He wanted more for his wife and daughter. He wanted to give them a life away from the rugged confines of Shin's mountains. And so he went to the people of Shin and called a great council of farmers and soldiers and magistrates. He showed them what he could do, and he laid out his plan. They agreed unanimously and provided him with all the paper and all the ink he needed. Jun-lu spent every waking moment of every day and night creating his paper people. In his fervour, he neglected his small farm and even the family he was striving so hard to support. He missed the day his daughter lost her first tooth, missed too the anniversary of his marriage. He even missed the birth of his second child, a son, and also that son's death at the whims of illness.

Jun-lu missed so much, but in his fervour he created a paper army. At first, just a few soldiers, then hundreds, then thousands. After years of work, the paper army swelled to ten thousand strong. The people of Shin hid them in cellars, in caves, as statues in their homes. The paper soldiers needed no food or rest, they would stand dormant until Jun-lu commanded them otherwise.

But his army had a weakness. They were, after all, just paper and ink. If the ink was smudged, the soldier would collapse. They needed to protect the paper. The people of Shin had one resource in abundance. Goats. Well, actually they had two resources in abundance, goats and rock. They also had the skill to work the rock. Two more years went by as the people of Shin fashioned armoured chest plates and helms from rock. They were far too heavy for people, but the paper army cared nothing for the weight and each possessed the strength of several men.

Finally, eight years after Jun-lu purchased the scroll, his army was ready to march. Each of the ten thousand paper soldiers was armoured in rock and armed with a bamboo spear. They marched out of the caves, out of the cellars, out the homes and descended upon neighbouring Qing like a paper plague, ten thousand soldiers marching in perfect unison. No blade could stop them, no arrow kill them. The armies of Qing fell before the paper horde, their soldiers slaughtered, their heroes crushed beneath paper feet.

With Qing province conquered, the people of Shin turned to Jun-lu and gave him a crown of stone. They named him the King of Rock and Sky. Finally, he had his green and fertile lands, a place for his wife and daughter to live happy and healthy away from the weed farms and stone mines and braying goats.

Jun-lu should have spent more time with his family, whom he had all but ignored for almost eight years, but his success was never enough. Conquerors will always find reasons to continue their conquest. Qing province was rich, after all, but Wu, to the east, had excellent vineyards. Ganxi, to the south, had thriving silver mines, and Xihai, to the west, was famous for raising mighty buffalo. Jun-lu told himself he was surrounded by enemies who would take what he had won for his family, by people who would not hesitate to conquer him just as he had conquered Qing. So he struck first.

Jun-lu marched his paper soldiers all over Hosa from Wu to Long, challenging everyone who stood against him. The Hosan have never been a people to go quietly, and they fought back. But none could hope to best the paper army. One by one the other provinces fell until the King of Rock and Sky had conquered all Hosa, the first to ever manage it, long long long before the Emperor of Ten Kings.

But the story doesn't end there. As we all know, Hosa soon fell apart again into the disparate, warring states. You see, although the armies of Hosa fell to the paper soldiers, it had taken several years to complete the conquest. In that time, Jun-lu's daughter, Wei-lu, had grown into a woman. She had a husband, a man of Qing, and they had a son. They lived in Qing, but she longed to return to Shin, to take her son to see her homeland and show him the wonder of the rocky plateaus, the majesty of the goats who climbed sheer cliffs above thousand-foot drops. When Jun-lu pulled most of his army back to Qing, Wei-lu thought it would be over. She hoped they would all go back to their lives and their true home. But the King of Rock and Sky was still not content. He had his sights set further afield. He was already meeting with his war councillors and drawing up plans to invade Nash.

Wei-lu hated the idea of more bloodshed and the power hungry monster her father had become. And she knew the paper soldiers' greatest weakness. As a child, she had sat by her father's side as he learned the technique. With their rock armour, the soldiers were all but indomitable, but they were still paper. And paper burns. Wei-lu strode into the great hall where her father kept his paper army dormant. Only the people he trusted most were allowed in, and the soldiers on guard let her in without question. She lit her torch and ran along the ranks of soldiers, setting fire to them. The paper army went up in a conflagration that burned for ten nights and could be seen by the gods all the way across Hosa on Long Mountain. Wei-lu did not escape the fires. She burned with the paper army she hated so much.

The King of Rock and Sky, distraught at the death of his daughter, was inconsolable. Already, the other provinces were rising in rebellion. He sent his councillors away and refused to see his wife. In his grief, he donned a suit of rock armour his paper soldiers had worn, and marched into the Lake of Mists. Jun-lu was never seen again. But now and again a trail of black ink washes the shore of the Lake of Mists.

Yanmei had a feeling she'd heard the story before, or perhaps read it. She had spent some time at the Standing Stones of Hosa, where the nation's history was recorded going back hundreds of years. Yanmei loved sneaking away to the Stones, not to learn about history, but to escape the attentions of her father and brother. They cared not for history, so they assumed she wouldn't either, and never thought to look for her there. When her brother's viciousness turned too violent, or she couldn't take the burns her father inflicted on her anymore, she ran to the Standing Stones and hid there and read about the history of Hosa and its Ten Kingdoms. It seemed like a lifetime ago now, or perhaps like someone else's life, as though it were just another story she had been told.

"Don't you have any Ipian stories?" Ido Katsuo asked.

"Of course I do," Guang said.

"Well, tell some of those then. I mean, we are in Ipia. I am an Ipian prince. You'll never secure the patronage of a great Ipian lord if all you tell is Hosan stories. I wouldn't hire you."

Guang sighed.

"I liked it," Kira said. "Was it real?"

Guang scratched at his beard. "Doesn't matter. They're our stories, our peoples' stories."

"*Your* people's stories," Ido Katsuo said.

Guang shook his head at the prince. "Our peoples' stories. All of our peoples'. Ipian, Hosan, Nash, Cochtan. It might surprise you how many stories we share. And perhaps even more surprising that the lessons hiding in the stories are the same ones told time and time again."

Guang dropped back to walk alongside Kira. "It doesn't matter if they actually happened hundreds or even thousands of years ago. They have passed into lore, and there are stories and people like me to tell them."

"Terrible poets?" Ido Katsuo said.

"Certainly," Guang said. "Countless stories and countless terrible poets like me who continue to pass them down through the generations. Whether they really happened no longer matters. They have become real by becoming history." He fished around in his satchel for a few moments and pulled out a small scrap of paper about the size of his hand, and then a chip of charcoal. "Maybe it was never anything but a fanciful tragedy to explain how one man raised an army to conquer Hosa, and impart upon the listener the perils of power." He drew a couple of lines on the paper. "Or maybe it's all true and is still told today because it's a good way to teach a person that if they desire all they see, they'll never appreciate what they have." He drew a hasty circle and connected the two lines and the circle with a wavy line. The piece of paper curled and folded itself until a little paper person was standing on Guang's palm. He plucked the little man up by his head and stood him in Kira's hand.

Kira grinned at the paper man, then poked at him. He fell over. "Does he move?" she asked.

Guang shook his head. "If I knew how to do that, do you think I'd be a broke poet following around an old fool of an onmyoji?"

"I heard that," Haruto said from in front.

"Good," Guang replied loudly. "Saves me repeating myself."

The road bent to the right around a rocky butte a hundred feet high that seemed to have torn itself free of the flat land around it to stand isolated. As soon as they rounded the butte, they saw the Graveyard of Swords. It was impossible to miss, thousands of swords thrust into the ground and standing there cold and silent, hilts up to the sky. Some had wide blades, others slim; some were rusted while others still shined with a sparkling edge. In some areas, the swords were clustered, almost grouped together, and in other places they were sparse, single blades standing alone. Some were thrust into the ground perfectly erect, while others leaned one way or another. Between the swords were small shrines dedicated to the gods. They were made of wood and others of stone. They looked like tiny houses, but when their doors were pulled open, there was nothing but a statue of the god inside. Many had offerings laid out before them, covered with a dusting of snow. At the far end of the graveyard stood a grand temple, a pagoda ten storeys high, its wooden walls painted white and orange, its eaves a deep green. It looked remarkably well maintained for a temple in the middle of nowhere.

They passed underneath the torii gate and stopped at the first sword near the path. Yanmei hung back behind the others. It was lonely dao with a wide blade and a rusted ring hanging from its hilt. "That is an impressive sight," Guang breathed, staring at the temple. "Do you suppose anyone lives there?"

"A dozen priests, last time I checked," Ido Katsuo said. "Don't tell me you know nothing of the Graveyard of Swords, O keeper of stories."

Guang glared at the prince out of the corner of his eye. "Stop being so obnoxious, boy. You're ruining the moment."

Ido Katsuo snorted and approached the rusty dao. He poked it with a finger and set the sword wobbling, shedding its crust of snow. "They say every blade of any renown finds its way here. The priests of the temple dedicate themselves to learning the story behind each sword."

Yanmei swept her gaze across the snowy field. Thousands, maybe tens of thousands of swords stretched as far as she could see across the snowy plain. One person could never hope to learn the history of every blade. She stepped past the first sword still wobbling in the ground and found a slim silver-bladed jia with a just a hint of green in the metal. Strange letters were etched all along the blade. Beyond that, she saw a long-bladed katana with an ornate tsuba showing a hawk swooping down on a serpent. Next to the katana was a type of sword she had never seen before, its blade nearly a foot wide and thick as her thumb, made of dark metal with a single edge and no hand guard. It looked as much cleaver as sword, and she couldn't imagine how strong someone would have to be to wield it. There were no names on any of the swords. She brushed away the snow at the foot of one katana, finding only frozen earth beneath it. Tens of thousands of unnamed swords. If she looked hard enough, she wondered, might she find a pair of hooked swords that had once belonged to a renowned bandit. It was a fanciful dream.

"How do they get here?" Yanmei asked. "You said every sword of renown ends up here. How?"

Ido Katsuo approached a thin-bladed wakizashi and plucked it from the earth. Yanmei held her breath, half expecting a vengeful god to appear and strike the prince down for his audacity, but the graveyard remained still and silent. The prince held the sword up, inspecting its edge; then he tutted, dropped the sword, and walked away. "I don't know. Priests probably go around collecting them or something. It's probably all shit anyway. Just a bunch of old swords collected and half buried to get people to come and pray and donate lien."

Kira picked up the wakizashi and thrust it back into the cold earth. "You should be more respectful."

"Why?" Ido Katsuo asked. "It's just a bunch of old swords."

Kira shook her head. "There's more here. There's..."

"Spirits," Haruto said, finishing Kira's thought. Shiki whistled from his shoulder and clapped her little black paws. "Restless spirits, but not vengeful. Try not to disturb them too much."

"You think they're dangerous?" Yanmei asked.

Haruto considered it for a moment, frowning, then shook his head. "No. They just don't deserve disrespect. Hand me my ritual staffs, pack mule."

"Lazy onion," Guang grumbled. "It's about time you started carrying them yourself again. All this extra weight is making my back ache."

Haruto collected the staffs and turned towards the temple. It was at the far end of the graveyard, a fair hike away. He waited. Shiki whistled.

"I hate it too," Haruto said. "Omoretsu is never pleasant company." He glanced at Shiki on his shoulder, and the little spirit visibly trembled. Then he looked at Kira. "Try not to get into any trouble while I'm gone." With that, he set off towards the temple.

Chapter 45

Haruto picked his way through the swords, careful not to disturb any of them. Now and then he saw a flash of colour or movement from the corner of his eye, but when he turned to look, there was nothing there. Spirits stalked the graveyard, but they seemed harmless. Shiki danced from one shoulder to the other, growing more and more anxious as they approached the temple. Omoretsu had gifted her to him, but that didn't mean she had to like the shinigami any more than a person had to like their emperor. The truth was the shinigami terrified Shiki, and for good reason.

He saw a few other people roaming between the standing swords. A fat priest with a ludicrously tall hat was walking a circuit, trailing incense from a smoking brazier. A young Nash woman in riding leathers knelt in front of a curved sabre, two long two braids down her back. Perhaps there was less mystical about the graveyard than the prince claimed. It seemed just place where the dead could be remembered and mourned, even when there was no body to bury.

A flight of steps led up to the temple doors, and Haruto sprang up them. He pushed open the wooden doors without so much as a creak and shuffled in, caked snow falling from his kimono onto the polished wood floor. He was in a small antechamber with dozens of little stone alcoves for boots or sandals set into the walls. In front of him was a closed paper screen door, but he saw shadows moving about on the other side. Haruto looked down at his own sandals. They were falling apart: one of the straps on the left one had frayed away entirely, and the right one had a hole in the bottom through which snow seeped and soaked his socks. He really detested having soggy feet.

Shiki fluted quietly.

"I know," Haruto said as he bent to remove his sandals and slotted them into one of the empty alcoves. "I'll get new ones next time I need a new kimono."

Shiki whistled a low note.

"Don't you start!"

Haruto slid open the paper screen to find a cavernous hall on the other side. A woman in priest's robes was sweeping the polished wood floor. At the far end of the hall stood a colossal statue of Natsuko, the goddess of lost things, depicted as a young, smiling child in a kimono. A scattering of stuff lay at the foot of the statue, among them a single shoe, a toy horse, a spoon. Offerings to Natsuko were always bizarre. The walls of the great hall were lined with paper doors, mostly closed, but Haruto spied a small room open to his left, an empty shrine standing above a prayer mat. At both sides of Natsuko's statue, winding staircases led around it, presumably to the next floor.

Haruto approached the priest and they exchanged bows. "Do you have a shrine to the shinigami here?" he asked.

The priest looked at him and gasped, her wide eyes flicking to Shiki sitting on his shoulder. She nodded vigorously, then pointed upwards.

"The floor above?" Haruto asked.

The woman nodded again. Haruto knew it wasn't uncommon for priests to take vows as Guang had taken, but a vow of silence seemed almost as foolish as his friend's vow not to swear. Nevertheless, he supposed the point of a vow was to show your commitment to a cause by giving up something you loved or were good at. The sacrifice had to be something that mattered. He bowed and thanked the priest, then started up the stairs to floor above.

When he reached the second floor and didn't find the shinigami's shrine, Haruto had to ask another priest where to find it. This priest wasn't silent, but the old man spoke little. He chewed on his wet lip and stared narrow-eyed at Haruto. Then he brusquely shooed him towards an open door and told him to be quick. Haruto guessed the man's dour greeting was probably Shiki's fault. People often reacted to the spirit with either awe or suspicion. The priest apparently chose the latter. Haruto ground his teeth at the foolishness of people.

The prayer room was cramped, barely more than a cupboard. The prayer mat was plush and red and easy on the knees, and the shrine was a small weathered stone statue of a withered old barefoot man squatting behind its wooden doors. A candle flickered at the foot of the statue casting dancing shadows all over the walls. Haruto laid his staffs out before the shrine. Shiki let out a cooing whistle, leapt from his shoulders and settled into his lap, trembling.

"I don't know what you're so nervous about," Haruto said. "It's me he's going to be angry with."

Haruto took the shinigami statue in both hands. "Omoretsu," he whispered to the stone and then placed it back inside the shrine.

The room darkened, and the candle flame shrank as if it were as scared as Shiki. Haruto heard a footstep behind him and felt a presence looming over his shoulder. The acrid scent of burnt juniper filled the little room. When Omoretsu spoke, his voice was the crackle of paper thrown into a fire. "You broke one of my staffs."

Haruto tried to fight the crawling sensation creeping across his skin. He failed and shivered. There was something wrong about being close to a shinigami. The reapers did not belong on earth, and the ground withered and died around them. Even the pungent air fell still and stagnant.

"It wasn't me. It was..." Haruto shrugged, swallowed down his frustration. "It doesn't matter. I need you to make them whole again."

Omoretsu plodded across the room and stood before his own shrine, staring down at himself in miniature. He was an ugly spirit. Wrinkled beyond ancient, sagging skin, a stoop-shouldered slouch that made his belly stick out. His clothes were ratty, little more than rags, and his head seemed too large for his body.

"Come here, my little shikigami," Omoretsu said, holding out a gnarled hand, its fingernails cracked and yellow.

Shiki whistled and clutched Haruto's kimono.

Omoretsu stared at the spirit and cracked a yellow-and-brown toothy grin behind his scabbed lips. "Now."

Shiki whistled again, but she couldn't fight Omoretsu's commands any more than Haruto could. They both belonged to the shinigami. Shiki leapt from Haruto's shoulder like a puppet with its strings being yanked and landed on Omoretsu's arm. She waddled up to sit on his shoulder, and the shinigami turned around and collapsed cross-legged in front of Haruto. His eyes were the darkest brown Haruto had ever seen and glinted with mischief. All the shinigami were mischievous spirits, which was why the lord of heaven had decreed they couldn't wear shoes. Haruto was sure he was missing a part of that tale, but he supposed it wasn't important.

"That burden you carry weighs heavily, does it not?" Omoretsu asked. "The yokai is a strong one, restless and eager to return. He searches heaven for a way back, but doesn't yet realise he need do nothing. I can see the thread connecting you – it grows more taught every day." Omoretsu reached out a gnarled hand and plucked at something above Haruto's head. Haruto felt a sudden rage flood his veins, the need to enact violence, to hurt someone. He clenched his teeth and breathed deeply until it faded. Omoretsu laughed at him.

"Are you going to fix the staffs or not?" Haruto asked.

"Always so terse," the shinigami said, waving a hand over the staffs and renewing the elements within them. It took the shinigami no effort at all. "It is done." Omoretsu stood, joints cracking though he showed no pain. He reached up a gnarled hand and scratched Shiki's head. The little spirit trembled in revulsion. "What happened to the onryo you were tracking? You didn't send any my way."

Haruto waved a hand at the ritual staffs. "I killed one of them, the others are trying to free Orochi from his prison."

Omoretsu dropped into a crouch in front of Haruto and

stared into his eyes. Shiki gave a tremulous whistle and shrank into a small, quivering furball on his shoulder. "You must stop them. Orochi cannot be freed."

Haruto considered for a moment. He agreed with Omoretsu, but he wagered it was for different reasons. If Orochi was free, he would no doubt resume his vengeance upon humanity, and tens of thousands would die. But Omoretsu was a shinigami, a lord of death, he did not care if hundreds of thousands died. Something else was at stake, something he was missing. "Might not be as easy as you make it seem," Haruto said. "The leader of the onryo is a tengu."

Omoretsu snarled. "Demons! What is she up to?"

Haruto was confused. The Herald of Bones was a male tengu. "She?" he asked. "Who?"

Omoretsu glanced at him but did not answer. He plucked Shiki from his shoulder and tossed her into Haruto's lap. "Your companion spirit can kill demons as well as yokai," the shinigami grumbled. "Use her, but be careful around the tengu. Demons are not spirits. They are not bound by the same rules."

Haruto had heard of demons, of course, but only as abstract threats. Most often as a way to keep young shintei honest. *Fulfil your oaths or the gods will curse you and you'll become a demon.* He'd certainly never fought a demon before. The thought of it filled him with dread. "What is this about, Omoretsu? What aren't you telling me?"

The shinigami scoffed. "Much and more, little human. Tengu are demons. They serve the overlords of hell, whether they realise it or not. Demons exist to cause chaos and strife wherever they tread. This creature you hunt will stop at nothing to throw the balance of heaven and earth into turmoil." He stalked past Haruto and disappeared. "Stop the onryo. Stop the tengu. Kill them all. But whatever you do, do not let them free Orochi." His voice faded and the atmosphere in the little room lightened. Haruto glanced over his shoulder to find he was alone once more. He sighed and leaned back until he was lying on the floor, staring up at the cobwebs in the corners of the ceiling.

Shiki waddled up his chest and climbed inside his kimono. She was trembling. Kill the onryo, kill the tengu, stop them from freeing Orochi. It had been his goal all along, he supposed, but now it went further than just trying to ease Tian's burden. It was a command from his patron shinigami, the only command Omoretsu had ever given him. A command to kill the onryo. A command to kill Izumi.

He could neither ignore it nor defy it.

Swords stuck out of the ground like teeth on a hairbrush; Kira followed Yanmei through them. Yanmei was so frail these days, as if cutting herself off from her qi had allowed the rigours of age to rush in and devour what was left of her ebbing vitality. Kira stepped around a long double-edged sword, careful not to touch any part of it, and saw Yanmei stop and kneel in front of a shrine to the god of war. They were running out of time. They needed to find The Fourth Sage Under Heaven soon so he could heal Yanmei.

Not long ago, Yanmei had radiated vigour and burned with healthy energy. The mandate of Heiwa had been to teach the students how to use their techniques and respect the power they earned, but that didn't mean the teachers didn't occasionally show off their own skills. Every year they held a tournament, and every sensei except the Sage took part. Kira never had many friends at Heiwa, so she sat alone and watched the duels. Master Kang was always the most brutal, beating down his opponents – and his friends – with quick, efficient strikes. Master Aknar, the foreign sensei, one of the light-haired, blue-eyed Seafolk always went down in the first round. Master Ogawa liked to dazzle the students with flashy techniques but ultimately lost whenever the fight moved toward physical combat. The range and depth of power on display had always been wonderful to watch.

Yanmei won three years in a row. For those three years, no one stood against her combination of fire and martial skill. And then she had started to fade, her fires dimming, her burns refusing to heal. Most of the other students didn't notice, thinking the other teachers were improving, but Kira knew the truth and she had begged Yanmei to see the Sage about it. A year later, Yanmei was almost unrecognisable as the radiant forge of power she had been. Her skin wrinkled, her back stooped, her fires guttered out. The Sage said her technique was hurting her. She closed off her qi, but doing so left her weak. Her technique was in her blood, a part of her qi, inseparable from her and also killing her.

Guang and the prince were also strolling through the swords. Guang stopped to inspect a blade and smiled fondly as if remembering it, though Kira noticed he did not touch it, nor any of them. Katsuo, on the other hand, made a point of poking every blade, setting them wobbling as though it were a game.

Kira approached Yanmei, the thin carpet of snow crunching beneath her feet. "We should go," she said quickly before her resolve shattered.

"We will," Yanmei said, still kneeling and bowing before the shrine to the god of war. "As soon as Haruto is finished."

"I mean, *we* should go. We need to find the Fourth Sage Under Heaven so he can heal you."

Yanmei straightened up from her bow, wincing at cracking noises in her back. She turned a smile on Kira and gestured to the snowy ground beside her. Kira didn't want to wait. She didn't want to sit and pray. She had too much energy for that. Nevertheless, she approached the shrine, sank down to her knees next to Yanmei, and paid her respects to the god of war. When she straightened up, she found Yanmei's arm draped across her shoulders, pulling her into a hug and wrapping them both in her threadbare blanket.

"I think she'd be pleased to see us here together," Yanmei said, nodding towards the shrine.

Kira sighed and leaned into Yanmei. She wanted to cry, to scream at the unfairness of the world. But that would not help. "We need to find the Fourth Sage."

"I know." Yanmei's voice was as thin as ancient paper. "Perhaps our talkative prince might know the Sage's whereabouts." She smiled at Kira. "It can't hurt to ask."

Kira all but jumped with joy. She liked Guang and Haruto, and would happily follow them all the way to Orochi's tomb if things were different. But if they could find the Fourth Sage and heal Yanmei, that had to come first. A little voice in her head whispered that it would also take her far away from the onryo and maybe her own struggles as well.

"Katsuo," Kira called, looking around for the prince. He was standing next to Guang, staring south towards the entrance to the graveyard. Kira squinted to see what they were looking at. A cloud of white mist was rising from the ground, a dark figure at its centre. A knot of dread formed in Kira's gut like she had eaten something foul. She heard glass cracking.

Yanmei grunted as she rose unsteadily to her feet. She pulled her cloak tight around her shoulders and stepped up next to Kira. "What is that? I can't make it out."

Kira felt close to shattering, but held on to herself. "It's one of my brothers," she said, knowing without a doubt it was true and hating the tremble in her voice. "It's one of the onryo."

Katsuo glanced over his shoulder at Kira, his dark eyes darting, searching. "Shouldn't we, uh, fetch the onmyoji?"

Guang shook his head. "Lad, the old man is in there talking to a shinigami. You do *not* want to interrupt."

"Well, I suppose it's good we have our very own scary ghost person," Katsuo said. "Have at him, Kira."

Kira shook her head and looked about for help, knowing she was unlikely to find any. Katsuo obviously didn't intend to fight, and Guang's vows prevented him from holding a weapon. Yanmei was in no condition, and Haruto was still in the temple. She closed her eyes and saw an image of herself staring back, but her eyes were dark and her teeth glinted like mirrors. The ungaikyo was there, waiting to devour her and take control. The melody of the ungaikyo's song drifted from somewhere, as faint as a whisper in a hurricane. She was glad she couldn't hear the words. She didn't want to know.

She opened her eyes and stared at her approaching brother. She saw him clearly now. His head was bald save for a horseshoe of onyx hair as dark as Yanmei's had once been. He walked on platformed wooden sandals, and his trousers were ragged at the shins and held up by an old rope belt. His bleached bone tunic was stained and full of holes, and his pot belly bulged out beneath it. Steam misted around him, and the snow melted beneath his every step.

Yanmei gasped and she staggered back a step. "It can't be."

The onryo stopped a few paces away and spat onto the snow, which melted instantly. He squatted down on his haunches and stared up at them, his jaw working as though he was chewing on something. "Which of you ish Prinshe Ido Katsuo?" he said, flames dripping from his lips.

Guang and Katsuo glanced at each other, then the prince pointed at Guang. "He is."

"What?" Guang snapped, rounding on Katsuo. "You little carrot! Do I look like a prince?"

The onryo glanced at the two men as he chewed. "I'll jusht kill you both to be shure."

"Uh, a little help, Kira," Katsuo said, taking a step back.

The onryo tilted his head and stared at Kira a moment. Then a buck-toothed grin split his lips. "Ah, sho you're my new little sishter." He looked her up and down in a way that make Kira feel like beetles were crawling all over her skin. "I think the Mashter overestimated you. You're not ready yet."

"Who are you?" Kira asked, her voice trembling a little.

The onryo smirked. "What? Don't tell me that damned Crow didn't even mention me." A forked tongue licked out over his lips. "The name's Zen."

Katsuo coughed. "Why don't I just let you two catch up. Siblings and all that." He took another step back so he was standing just in front of Kira.

"Funny you should mention that." A string of molten drool slipped from the onryo's lips and fell steaming to the ground. He looked at Kira again. "You know he killed hish brothers? Murdered them in their cells in the empressh' palace."

Kira looked at Katsuo. "You said the empress killed them."

Katsuo backed up another step and held up his hands to ward off the accusations. "I distinctly said they died in their cells."

"You murdered them?"

"No... well... uh... I prefer to think of it as an aggressive campaign for an overdue promotion."

Zen chuckled. "I reshpect that."

"Enough to let me go?" Katsuo asked.

The onryo shook his head slowly, a grin on his peeling lips.

"You know I'm the heir to the Ipian throne?" Katsuo said. "Very powerful. Very rich." He tried to smile, but it looked as fake as an oni mask. "I'll pay you to let me go."

Zen threw his head back and barked a belly-shaking laugh. "You don't know, do you? Oh, that's jusht preshious. And I get to be the one that tellsh you. Shorry, princey prince, but you can't be heir of a thing that doesn't exist. My sisther, Xifeng, killed your father and the rest of them. You're the lasht Ido, princey prince. The last loosh end."

"What? My father is--"

"Dead." Zen grinned. "Oh, that's the face I was hoping for. I love it when deshpair creeps in. Weshtern Ipia has already shurrendered to the Easht. No one even knows you're shtill alive. Which ish funny because you won't be for long."

"That's not funny!" Katsuo shouted.

"No?" Zen said. "Guessh it depends on your point of view." He put his hands on his knees and grunted as he pushed back up to standing. "Time to get thish over with." He stretched his neck to one side and then to the other and leaned backwards until his back popped. "Don't get in the way, little sishter." Then he lunged at them.

Chapter 46

Yanmei stared in horror at the squat onryo. It couldn't be him. He was dead. Her brother was dead.

Daizen ambled forward and closed on the prince.

"Help!" Ido Katsuo shouted.

Daizen's outstretched hand ignited in black flames. It seemed in death, he had found the technique he had always coveted in life. He reached for the prince, but Kira flicked a dagger into her hand and stabbed it into Daizen's palm. She held Daizen there, gripping the dagger in both hands, his flames licking over its mirrored surface, his blood sizzling on the ground between them. Yanmei saw Kira's eyes darken, disappear in the hollow void of her eye sockets. Her daughter began to shatter as the ungaikyo emerged.

Kira screamed, "No!" The dagger shattered in her hands, and she staggered back and fell to her knees in the snow. "No no no no no no no." Cracks inched along her skin, like jagged, snaking vines.

Daizen stared down at Kira and sneered. "I was wrong. You are closher than I thought. Give in, child. Let my little sishter come out and play." He kicked her, and she fell over on the snowy ground. She didn't get up.

Ido Katsuo snatched a long-bladed dao from the ground next to him, and dashed forward to stand between Kira and the onryo. His hands were trembling.

"What are you trying to do with that twig, princey prince?" Flaming spittle dribbled from the onryo's mouth. He beckoned the prince with his flaming hand. "Come on. Get over here and face your fate like a man. If you do, I promishe I'll kill you shlowly."

"How is that an incentive?" Ido Katsuo whined.

Daizen's black flames spread up his hand to his elbow. "Becaushe if you fight me, I'll make it shlower. I'll melt every bit of shkin from your bones and--"

Ido Katsuo roared and leapt at the onryo, swinging his dao. Daizen slipped to the side, ducked the prince's blade, and stepped back. The prince lurched from one attack to the next, chopping his sword down at Daizen's head. The onryo laughed, reached up quick as a serpent, and caught the blade in one burning-black hand. He licked his forked tongue over his lips again, and the flames flared around his hand and the blade. The prince's dao glowed a fierce red and the metal bent. He cried out, dropped the blade, and jumped back, snatching up another sword. He threw the sword at Daizen, but the onryo stepped calmly to the side and the blade passed him by harmlessly. "Really, boy?"

Ido Katsuo ripped another sword from the earth, a long jia with black lettering along its silver blade. He screamed again and charged the onryo.

Yanmei rushed to Kira's side. The girl was breathing too quickly, muttering to herself. Cracks ran along her hands and face like a shattered mirror. One of her eye sockets was darker than night, a hollow void. The other eye was wide and panicked. She was barely holding herself together. Barely holding the ungaikyo at bay.

"Why won't you die?" Ido Katsuo screamed as he thrust his sword at Daizen.

The onryo caught the blade in his flaming hand again. "That's my line, boy." The metal went limp in his flaming grip, and Ido Katsuo dropped the sword, twisted away again, and grabbed another weapon.

Yanmei crouched down in front of Kira. "Look at me, Mirai. Look at me!" She gripped Kira's chin and raised her head until her one remaining eye met Yanmei's gaze. "There you are. Still clinging on. You are a tough young woman. You can beat this." She smiled and wiped a tear from Kira's remaining eye. "My little Mirai. You are going to be so strong." She stood, swallowed the lump in her throat, and stepped around her daughter toward the onryo. "Daizen, that's enough!"

The onryo stopped chasing the prince and peered at Yanmei. "Who the... Wait, Meimei? Ish that you?"

Yanmei shuffled over to Guang, put a hand on his shoulder and fixed him with a stare. "Don't let her interfere. Whatever happens."

Guang frowned. "What are you..."

Yanmei walked toward Daizen before the poet could stop her. She felt the heat from the onryo's black flames chasing away the chill in her bones.

"You got old, Meimei," Daizen snarled, burning spittle spraying from his lips.

"You died, Daizen."

He chuckled. "I did."

Yanmei stepped forward again and embraced the onryo's heat. "You killed yourself. Burned yourself alive because you couldn't face the truth." She saw the smile fall from Daizen's face. "Father's infernal technique skipped you, brother. You were never strong enough to wield it."

"Besht thing that ever happened to me, Meimei. Father'sh technique was worthless. Pah! Look at me now, Meimei. Look at me now!" He screamed the last and held his arms out to his sides. His black flames roared to life, enveloping him. The snow around him melted and the air shimmered with heat. He bellowed a mighty laugh. "I am shtronger than father ever was. Shtronger than you ever were, you shelf righteous bitch!" He glared at her, and she could feel his burning hatred. "All thoshe times you pranced about the camp like you owned the place. The way you looked down on ush, even father, for what we did. All thoshe times you snuck up on me and grabbed me, burning me to show off that you had what should have been mine!"

Yanmei felt her anger pounding like a monster bashing at a door to be let in. "Did you ever think I wasn't trying to burn you, Daizen? Did you even consider I was a little girl who wanted the comfort of her older brother, the one other person in the world who knew what I was going through, who knew what father did to me! To us!" Anger Yanmei had thought long forgotten boiled up to the surface, and she wasn't strong enough to stop it.

"*I* should have been father'sh heir!" Daizen roared. "You took that from me, Meimei. You took everything from me. Mother, my flamesh. You even took father from me. Then you acted like you didn't want it. Like you were too good for it."

"I didn't want it, Daizen," Yanmei shouted at her brother. "I wanted none of it."

Daizen sneered, licked his cracked lips. He pointed a flaming finger at Yanmei. "Well, I finally found my own flamesh, Meimei. And they're hotter than father'sh ever were. Hotter than yours! Here, let me show you, Meimei. I will burn all of you to ash!"

Yanmei knew then there was no reasoning with her brother. He was a creature of jealousy and spite long before he died. She knew this meeting could only end one way. She glanced over her shoulder at Kira one last time, still huddled on the ground, struggling against her own yokai. Kira would win her battle. But only if she had the chance. Only if Yanmei gave her the chance.

Yanmei shrugged the blanket and cloak from her shoulders and let them fall to the snow. The cold made her shiver, but not for long. Yanmei loosed her qi, and it roared to life inside her, burning through her veins. Her technique came alive like a forest fire, but it felt so good to be warm again.

"Burn!" Daizen screamed, thrusting his flaming hand forward. A plume of black fire rushed toward Yanmei. She didn't duck, dodge, or step aside. She let his flames engulf her, and she fed them with her qi, turning them a brilliant, blazing orange. The ground scorched around her, the air blistered with her heat. Her skin smoked and sizzled in the flames, and she knew she didn't have long before her technique consumed her. It hurt like nothing she had known before, but it felt so right.

"Yanmei, no!" Kira screamed. "Get off me, Guang!"

Yanmei walked toward Daizen, and the fires grew around her, a glorious firestorm burning brighter than ever before. "I will not let you hurt them, Daizen. Now, let us see which of us burns hotter!"

Yanmei reached for Daizen. The onryo's black flames flared higher as his hands met hers. Their fires exploded together in a torrent of heat that evaporated the snow around them and scorched the dead grass beneath it. The air popped from the blaze, and swords melted into silvery puddles of molten slag. Yanmei poured everything she had into her technique, opening herself completely and letting her qi feed it like she never had before. Her clothes burned away and her skin charred, cracked, and blistered.

Guang struggled to watch the war of flames as Kira wriggled in his arms, elbowed him in the gut, bashed her head against his chin, stamped on his foot, screamed at him to let her go. But he wouldn't. Guang knew how useless he was, but at least he could do this. At least he could honour Yanmei's wish and stop Kira from running into the fire. Holding her back hurt, but it was something he could do.

The two fires twisted together, growing higher and hotter. Yanmei's orange and the onryo's black mixing, pushing at each other, scorching the ground around them. A leather wrapped hilt a few paces away burst into flames and incinerated. All the swords around the two blazing combatants glowed as if new from the forge.

Guang squinted at the two forms in the centre of the blaze. Their hands locked together, the fires bursting around them. The black fire was growing stronger, engulfing Yanmei's orange. Even ten paces away, the heat was too much to bear, and Guang dragged Kira a few steps back. She grew weaker and sagged in his arms, sobbing. The prince stood behind him, silent for once, watching Yanmei throw everything she had into the battle to save him. It wasn't enough. Yanmei was losing.

Guang heard footsteps crunching in the snow behind him, and Haruto slid to a stop next to him, holding a hand up to shield his face from the heat. His staffs were in a sling on his back. Shiki clung to his shoulder, whistling falteringly. "What's going on?"

Haruto asked.

"Yanmei is fighting an onryo," Guang growled, his arms wrapped around Kira.

Kira stopped struggling and stared up at Haruto. "Can you do something?" she asked. "Please."

Haruto looked from Kira to the two fires raging against each other. He crept towards them until the sleeve of his kimono burst into flames; then he backed away, slapping the fire, and shaking his head. Kira sagged and Guang let her go. She slumped to the ground on her knees and stared at the contest of flames. Over the roar of the fire, they heard Yanmei scream.

Daizen roared with laughter in his bonfire of black fire. "Is this all you have, Meimei?" he shouted, flaming spittle flying from his lips into Yanmei's face. "Is the limit of your righteous blaze? You are nothing."

Yanmei's legs weakened. She staggered and fell to a knee. Daizen's fire was too hot. Her skin burned and pealed away, her blood boiled in her veins. She screamed and surged back to her feet, pushing back with her own inferno.

"You were right, Daizen," she shouted. "You should have been father's heir. You and he were always alike." She found his face through the flames and saw him shudder at the sight of her. "He only ever used his fires to destroy. I will use my flames to protect those I love!"

Guang watched the flames grappled like two monsters, the black on the verge of swallowing the orange; then the orange flame brightened to yellow, and the black shrunk back. Yanmei's screaming grew louder. The ground around them cracked and a stone shrine to Yanmei's left burst apart into glowing red rubble. Guang staggered back another step, dragging Kira by the collar of her kimono. Yanmei's yellow flames turned a dazzling white so radiant Guang couldn't see anything of the two figures struggling within the fire. He tried to shade his eyes with his hand, but the light was blinding. The two monsters battled, one as white as the midday sun, the other black as tar. Then Yanmei's flames turned blue as the sky, beating back the darkness, swallowing it bit by bit. Daizen screamed as Yanmei's blue fires grew higher, hotter, blackening the earth, melting the swords around them to bubbling slag. Daizen stopped screaming, and his black fires began to billow thick black smoke and dwindle. At last, Yanmei's blue fire completely consumed Daizen's black.

Yanmei's flames burned for a few more seconds and then gutted out, leaving behind only a shimmer of heat. She stood there, naked, blistered and charred like the corpses at Heiwa. Her left arm was a blackened, weeping stump. Her right hand was clutching her brother's neck until he collapsed and crumbled to ash and dust. When the last charred embers of the onryo had fallen through Yanmei's fingers, she toppled sideways.

Chapter 47

Kira stared at the pile of ash that had been Daizen, at Yanmei lying naked and motionless on the ground, her body a charred ruin. The earth sizzled beneath her; the air above her wavered and danced. Kira felt herself starting to shatter again, heard the mirror cracking, and the sight from her right eye went dark. She ran to Yanmei and knelt beside her. Even though the flames were gone, the heat coming off her body burned Kira's skin as the cracks snaked their way across her arms and the ungaikyo fought to shatter her and take control.

"Yanmei," Kira said, struggling to force the words past the tightness in her throat. She touched Yanmei's shoulder, gasped in pain, and pulled a burnt finger away. But Yanmei's eyelids fluttered. Kira didn't care about the heat or the pain or the ungaikyo trying to claw its way out of her. She didn't care about any of it because Yanmei was all that mattered. She grabbed Yanmei's shoulders, hands burning, and pulled her up to sitting. Yanmei's hair was scorched, falling barely to her neck, the ends sizzling like guttering candle wicks. "Yanmei," Kira said again. She put a hand on the side of Yanmei's cheek to keep her head from lolling. The blackened skin cracked and oozed beneath her touch.

Yanmei's eyelids fluttered again and slowly opened. One of her eyes was blood red, the other cloudy as a stormy sky. She was limp in Kira's arms, her breath rattling in her chest, bleeding from a hundred different sores. Her left arm was gone below the elbow. There was no mistaking it. Yanmei was dying, and Kira was powerless to stop it. She couldn't save her mother.

"I'm sorry," Kira whispered as tears gushed from her left eye. She couldn't feel the right side of her face at all. The ungaikyo already had that part of her.

Yanmei looked up at her, and she smiled through charred lips. "Nothing... to be... sorry for."

"You weren't supposed to use your technique." Kira cried. "We were supposed to find the Sage to heal you. It's all my fault. I wasn't strong enough to protect you."

"No time... for that now," Yanmei said. She raised her left arm toward Kira's face, stared at the charred stump for a moment. Then she coughed blood onto her chin and chest. She looked at Kira again, raised her right hand and cupped Kira's cheek. Kira didn't even feel the touch. That side of her belonged to the ungaikyo. "Come back... to me... Mirai," Yanmei rasped, and Kira shattered, shards of mirror falling on the scorched earth around her. The ungaikyo fled from Yanmei's voice, and Kira saw out of both eyes again, her vision blurred by fresh tears.

"There... you are," Yanmei smiled, but it quickly creased to a grimace of pain. She coughed again, weaker than before, and more blood dripped from her lips. "I have... to tell you something, Mirai. You have to know... how you died."

Kira shook her head. "I don't care!"

Yanmei sucked in a rattling breath. "I was wrong... to hide it from you. Trauma is a monster, Mirai. One you can... never be rid of. You can't ignore it. Can't hide from it. If you try... it will catch you. You have... to deal with it. You have to face it. The yokai is inside of you, part of you. You can't hide from it... or lock it up. You must accept it... Deal with it... Learn to live with it. Or one day... it will consume you." She smiled but her teeth were slick with blood. "But you are my Mirai. You have the strength to conquer it.

"Your uncle murdered you, Mirai. What he felt for you... was wrong. He killed you... rather than face... his own demons." A bloody tear ran down from her red eye. "I am so sorry for hiding that from you."

Kira felt the ungaikyo stirring inside her, a new crack splitting her chest. She heard the faraway melody, the words lost in the drifting snow. "I don't care!" she shouted. "You can't leave me, Yanmei. I don't know how to be good without you. Please don't go!"

Yanmei drew another ragged breath. "Yes... you do," she said. "You've always... been good. The best thing... I ever did with... my life... was you." Her hand fell away from Kira's cheek, and she stared up at the grey sky with vacant eyes.

Haruto, Guang, and the prince watched Kira say goodbye to Yanmei. Haruto wished he had gotten back sooner, but he knew it would have been pointless. Only Yanmei had the strength to deal with that onryo. No one else could have withstood the flames, and no one else had the strength to match him. Shiki trumpeted a soft note from Haruto's shoulder, and he glanced at the little spirit. She looked sad and she was trembling, her black fuzz shaking. He nodded at her. "Go." She leapt from his shoulder and waddled a few steps toward Kira, then paused as the sound of rock crumbling turned their heads.

A woman emerged from the cracked shrine of the god of war. She wore patchwork robes, an old bamboo sugegasa, and a featureless white mask that covered her entire face. She brushed rock dust from her shoulders, patted down her robes and sighed loudly. She glanced at Haruto and the others, then walked over to Kira and Yanmei and stood over them.

Kira looked up at the robed figure and her face crumpled. "Can you save her? Please. She saved you."

The woman put a hand on Kira's shoulder. Then she stepped around the girl and squatted in front of Yanmei. She mumbled something, but Haruto couldn't make it out. Yanmei's lips moved briefly. The robed figure turned her head and stared at Haruto. He could see nothing behind the mask, even her eyes were sheltered. Shiki whistled and hid behind Haruto's legs.

The woman turned back to Yanmei, grasped her remaining hand and pulled her to her feet. Then she stepped back, allowing Yanmei to stand on her own, swaying but upright.

Haruto watched the woman pull a blanket from nowhere and drape it over Yanmei's shoulders. Then she took Yanmei's charred hand once more and led her back to the god of war's ruined shrine. She wrapped her arms around Yanmei, pulled her into an embrace, and they knelt side by side, the woman still holding Yanmei's hand. Then they both went still, all colour draining from them until they were both grey, lifeless stone.

"What just happened?" Ido Katsuo asked.

Guang took a couple of steps toward the shrine and peered at it. "Did the god of war just appear and take Yanmei to heaven?"

Haruto nodded, mute in his own amazement.

"Does that happen?" Guang said. "Have you ever seen anything like it?"

Haruto shook his head. "Not in three hundred years."

"Huh," Guang grunted. "It's going to make one turnip of a poem!"

"Does this not alarm anyone?" the prince asked. "How is no one alarmed at all of this?"

Haruto ignored the prince and walked to where Kira knelt on the scorched earth, staring down at her own hands. He squatted in front of her and patting her knee. "Are you..." He tried to think of the right word, failed. "Alright?"

Kira raised her head to look at him, her eyes red, tears still streaming down her face. She opened her mouth, but no words came out. Then she flung herself at him, wrapped her arms around him, and sobbed into his kimono.

Chapter 48

Haruto didn't know what to do with Kira sobbing into his kimono and trembling. Guang hovered a few paces away for a while, but eventually turned and walked away. The prince was even less help and seemed to have settled on pretending the whole thing wasn't happening. Meanwhile, Haruto had a young woman in his arms, grieving over the loss of her mother, and no words he knew of would do anything to make any of it better. Yanmei was gone. And they were all worse for it. No matter how many times he suffered through it, losing someone always hurt so much worse than any blade.

He held her in silence until the sobbing quieted and the trembling eased, and at last, she pulled away and wiped her nose on her sleeve. Her eyes were red and puffy. Shiki slid from Haruto's shoulder, whistling quietly, and climbed into Kira's lap. Kira hugged the little spirit. That was good. Shiki would be far more of a comfort than him. When he had lost Izumi all those years ago, he had been inconsolable. His grief lasted years and drove him to destitution. These days, he usually left his friends before they died. It was simpler that way.

Kira hugged Shiki in her lap and stared at Haruto like she was waiting for him to say something. "She... uh... no one else..." He sighed. "The god of war, eh?"

Kira nodded.

"Quite a send off."

Kira drew in a hitched breath. Haruto heard glass shatter, and a crack appeared on her cheek. She quickly covered it with her hand. "It's my fault," she whispered. "It's all my fault. I couldn't fight him, so Yanmei died." She stared at him, face red and eyes wet. "She's dead because of--"

"Stop it!" Haruto's tone was far harsher than he intended, but he would not allow the girl to blame herself. "It is not your fault, Kira, and saying so does nothing but cheapen her memory. Yanmei didn't die because of you. She sacrificed herself to save you, to save all of us. She did it because she knew that none of us could fight that onryo, and we would die if we tried. She fought him, knowing what it would cost her, because no one else could.

"You want to blame someone, you point it where it damned well belongs. Blame the bastard who attacked us, and the demon who ordered him to do it. *You* are not to blame. The onryo are. The Herald of Bones is. But you are not."

Haruto nodded and sighed. Kira still stared at him as though she expected more. "And, uh, that's it," he said. "I've run out of inspirational speeches. Your turn. Say something. Please."

Shiki whistled.

Kira shook her head and breathed a laugh. She was exhausted too, barely able to sit upright. Grief did that to a person, robbed them of their energy as well as their will. She opened her mouth to say something, but closed it again. Haruto heard the crunch of a mirror cracking, and Kira clutched her chest. She shooed Shiki off her lap and got unsteadily to her feet, still clutching her chest with one hand and covering her cheek with the other. Haruto saw the spidery black veins of a crack around the edges of her fingers, creeping towards her eye. She swayed, looking like she might faint, then she drew a deep breath and straightened up. "I'm going to go pray," she said. She turned and started walking, stopped after a few paces, and glanced over her shoulder at him. "Thank you." Then she hurried away.

Haruto watched her go. He expected her to stop at the shrine to the god of war, to pray before what was now a statue of Yanmei. Instead, she glanced at it briefly, and ran towards the temple.

"Do you think she'll be alright?" Ido Katsuo asked. The sun was waning, its hazy glow muted by the white blanket of clouds. Haruto doubted the priests would let them stay at the temple overnight, but he would wait until Kira was ready, until they were all ready.

"Maybe," Haruto said with a shrug. "She's struggling with a lot right now, and losing Yanmei is only part of it." Haruto had to admit Kira wasn't the only one who would miss the old woman. There was something warm and supportive about her, and now that she was gone, Haruto missed her calming presence.

"Hard to imagine what she's going through," Guang said. The old poet fished inside his satchel and pulled out his inkpot, stared into it and grimaced. "If I lost you, old man, I... well, it'd be like losing my favourite brush. You know, the frayed one that can't ink a straight line and for some reason smells of rotten egg."

"How did you two meet?" Ido Katsuo asked as he wobbled another sword. "An immortal onmyoji and wastrel of a poet seem odd bedfellows."

Guang chuckled as he approached the stone statues of Yanmei and the god of war. "The old man here saved my life."

Haruto shrugged. "I've not been able to get rid of him since. He follows me like a broke shadow." Shiki whistled.

"What did she say?" Guang asked. He brushed away some snow in front of the shrine and knelt.

"She suggested I try harder."

"Cheeky spirit." Guang scratched his chin, placed the inkpot on the ground before him and pulled a small scroll of paper from his satchel.

Ido Katsuo settled down on his haunches next to Guang and cleared his throat.

"What?" Guang asked.

"Don't give me that," Ido Katsuo said. "You quite clearly love telling your stories, so tell it." The prince nodded toward the temple. "Distract me." Haruto thought maybe he was more worried about Kira than he was letting on.

The old poet sighed and rolled up the paper. "It was in a tavern, I don't remember the name, somewhere up north near the Hosan-Ipian border. I was... not in a good place. My wife had just died and, well, we might not have had the happiest few years, but

I loved her. Her funeral was the last time I saw my son, and he told me in no uncertain terms that he never wished to see me again. Got his wish, I suppose. Anyhow, I was drunk and some fool with a neck as wide as a horse decided to start a fight."

Haruto scoffed. "You forget I was there, Guang," he said. "You started the fight. You recited a poem about how ugly his mother was and then called him a carrot-sucking, ignorant onion."

Guang grinned and nodded. "Aye, I did. And he was. He didn't appreciate my poem one bit."

"It was a little crude."

"So was the subject," Guang said, and they both laughed. "The lad with the big neck swung a punch at me. The old man stepped in and took it for me, right in the face. Then Fat Neck got a bit irate and punched him a few more times." He shook his head and looked at Haruto. "You just stood there, weathered the beating, and refused to back down. That really annoyed Fat Neck, so he pulled a knife and stabbed the old man in the chest. Haruto just sighed, pulled the knife out and handed it right back to him. He sat back down pretty quick after that."

"You didn't fight back?" Ido Katsuo asked Haruto.

Haruto shrugged. "What would have been the point? I punch him, he punches me. Maybe others get involved. Senseless violence. And before long, someone who couldn't survive it gets a knife stuck in them. I'm willing to suffer a bit of pain if it saves others from worse."

"After Fat Neck sat back down," Guang continued, "the old man pulled me aside and said, '*People like you don't stay dead. There's too much pain and grief around you, and too much left undone. And I'm too tired and drunk to hunt you down.*'"

Haruto smiled. "You remember that?"

"Every word," Guang said, scratching at his beard. "You saved my life that night, old man. In more ways than one."

"So you decided to repay me by following me around and leeching off me for fifteen years?" Haruto grinned.

"Cabbage, old man, if you save someone's life you better be prepared to take responsibility." He winked at Haruto. "Now let me get back to my poem, both of you. It's the least I can do for her." Guang unrolled his scroll again, dipped his brush in the inkpot and paused, staring at the blank paper. He and Yanmei hadn't been close, as far as Haruto was aware, but there had been an odd kinship between them. Two old bandits trying to put some good back into the world. Haruto left him to it.

Prince Ido Katsuo stood and paced between the swords, setting them swaying with a touch, then he walked to the temple steps and sat down, hugging his coat close.

Guang hadn't told the whole story of how he and Haruto had met, but that was because he didn't know the whole story. He didn't know that he saved Haruto that night as surely as Haruto had saved him. For years before they met, Haruto had been drifting, as untethered as the yokai he hunted. Over the centuries, Haruto had seen so many of his friends killed or grow old and die, it had become too painful to take. He'd decided it was easier to be alone. If he didn't get close to anyone, he wouldn't suffer the pain of seeing them die while he carried on living, unchanging. Guang hadn't let him be alone. The poet latched onto him and refused to let go. The old poet didn't know it, but he had pulled Haruto back from an abyss far worse than death.

Shiki trumpeted softly from the frozen ground and stared at Haruto. He'd been lost in maudlin thoughts and hadn't been listening.

"What's that?"

She climbed up his leg, nestled in the folds of his kimono and whistled again.

"Good point." He needed a new sword before they met any more onryo, and it just so happened he was in a graveyard full of swords. He turned towards the setting sun and started walking, inspecting each weapon he passed. There were a lot of Hosan dao and jian, plenty of Nash sabres, a few Ipian wakizashi and nagamaki, and even some swords he had never seen before and couldn't name. Some of those were long with two edges and ornate cross guards. He'd heard the Seafolk used all manner of swords, axes, and clubs, but he'd never been far enough east in

Nash to see the raiders or their weapons. It didn't matter anyway, he needed a sword he knew how to use. He needed a good katana, perfectly balanced with a fine edge.

Many of the swords were old, and the rigours of time and neglect had made them brittle and useless. Some had chipped blades, proving they had seen battle. He found one sword with countless fractures running through the steel, as though the blade had once been broken and reforged. He came across a pair of katana, one a glorious silver blade, undoubtedly the work of the great sword maker Mifune. It was planted in the earth, crossed with its partner, a sword with a blade as black as onyx and no tsuba to guard the hand. They were both fine blades, but he only needed one and it felt wrong to separate them. Eventually, he spotted a katana that seemed to suit him. The edge needed a date with a whetstone, and the metal needed a polish, but it had an elongated grip and was the right size for him. Its square tsuba was formed from two dozen flowing prongs that reminded him of crashing waves.

"What do you think?" Haruto asked Shiki. The little spirit needed to be as happy with the sword as he was. He plucked the blade from the snow-covered earth and held it up. Shiki crept down his arm and stepped carefully onto the blade as if testing water to see how cold it was. She took one step, then another, and then sank into the sword. The blade glowed crimson. Haruto tried a couple of practice swings, then settled into a crouch holding the sword by his side. He stepped forward, drawing and cutting in one movement. Shiki blew an appreciative trumpet.

"Excellent," Haruto said. "We'll take it." Shiki leapt out of the blade and scrambled up on his shoulder. "I'll need to work on the edge a bit and have a new saya made at some point." He tucked the sword down through his belt. It felt good to have a weapon. Made him feel like he could fight back if they were attacked again. After all, no one was going to defend them now. With Yanmei dead, Guang's vows preventing him from fighting, Kira unable to use her technique without losing herself to the yokai, and the prince... well, Haruto was certain Ido Katsuo was useless as a blind goat. More onryo would come, and if they were with a tengu, there would be hell to pay.

Omoretsu had said the tengu were not yokai. They were demons, created by divine curses to summon war and death wherever they went. And they served the kings and queens of hell.

Shiki whistled from his shoulder.

"You're right," Haruto said. "I need to figure it out quickly. We can't allow the onryo to free Orochi. He'll lay waste to everything he can, and we no longer have the Century Blade around to stop him."

Another whistle.

"Yeah," Haruto agreed. "And that." He didn't want to know what Omoretsu might do to them if they failed.

Chapter 49

Kira pulled open the temple door, tripped over the step, and stumbled into the welcoming chamber. She felt another icy crack creeping along her back. She was too close to shattering, too close to letting the yokai in her break free. There were stone alcoves for shoes along the walls near the entrance. She didn't have time. She pulled open the door to the inner temple and staggered through, clutching her chest. It didn't usually hurt. The ungaikyo had never caused her so much pain. Something was different this time. The pain was like talons ripping her stomach, tearing her spirit apart from the inside. Or maybe tearing its way out.

A fat priest with one eyebrow stopped halfway across the temple floor, his socks squeaking on the polished wood. He looked at her feet and shook his head. "You can't wear shoes he..." the words died on his lips when he looked at her face. His hand shot to his mouth. The cracks were visible to others now. Kira stared at him out of one eye, and the ungaikyo stared out the other.

"I need a room," Kira said. A crackling fracture snaked up the side of her neck. She was struggling to hold on to herself, to keep the last bits of herself together.

"W-wh-which g-god do you w-wish to pray to?" the priest stammered, gaping at her.

"An empty room," Kira barked, staring at the floor, at the polished dark grain of the wood, the drops of water where snow melted from her shoes, a beetle crawling towards the priest's foot. The details helped ground her.

The priest raised a hand, long sleeve draping from it, and pointed to an open door. The room beyond was just large enough to pace in. It had a prayer mat on the floor and an empty wooden shrine at the far end. It would do. Kira limped towards it. Her legs throbbed, her arms stung, her chest felt like it might explode. Every bit of her was agony; she was breaking apart. "Do not enter," she said without turning to look at the priest. "No matter what you hear, do not let anyone enter."

He mumbled something she ignored.

Kira stepped into the room and slammed the paper door shut behind her. She hoped the priest would listen, would keep everyone at bay. She didn't want to hurt him or anyone, but she couldn't be sure what would happen. She wasn't even sure *she* would ever leave the room. Kira took a deep breath, an attempt to calm herself that failed utterly. Her skin prickled and she felt an energy inside that both demanded action and made her feel exhausted all at once. She stalked over to the empty shrine and kicked it aside. It toppled and fell, snapping the eaves off and unhinging one door. A crack formed along her right hand, inching across her fingers. She was running out of time. The ungaikyo was clawing up from within her.

She flicked a shard of mirror into her hand – not a dagger, just a shard – and looked down into the reflection. Her yokai stared back through the dark hollow voids of her eye sockets. It grinned, craggy mirrored teeth like broken knives. She placed the shard on the floor, leaning it against the wall, then she flicked another shard into her hand. It was a different shape, but it fit against the other. She slotted it into position, its broken edges matching perfectly with the first shard. In a daze, she created another, and another, and another, and assembled them together. Piece by shattered piece, she built a mirror as tall and wide as she was. As she slotted the last piece into position, all the cracks vanished and the mirror became whole and unbroken. The ungaikyo watched her from the other side of that mirror.

Kira looked down at her hands, the fractures were gone. She felt her face; it was smooth and her again. Even the pain inside faded to a dull, throbbing ache. Finally, she looked into the mirror. Her ungaikyo stared back at her, its head cocked to the side. It was her. The same ragged kimono, the same messy mop of hair sticking up in bizarre angles, the same freckles dotting her nose and cheeks, the same red and blistered hands from getting too close to Yanmei's heat. It was her, but it was also not. The ungaikyo's skin was paler, an unhealthy pallor like curdled milk. Her eye sockets were gaping gateways to nothing. Her teeth were jagged shards just like those Kira had built the mirror from.

Kira shivered and hugged herself. The ungaikyo did not; it just stared at her through the mirror. It was the first time she had seen her yokai in its entirety. Every time before, she had seen only glimpses in reflections out of the corner of her eye, so brief she almost thought it her imagination. But this was no dream and no trick of the light. This was who she really was. What she was. Or at least, what she had been, trapped in a mirror for more than eighty years. "Murdered by my uncle," Kira whispered. Had he made her into this spirit of mirrors and vengeance, or had it been her own rage at the unfairness of it?

The ungaikyo's lips moved, but Kira heard no sound.

"Can you hear me?" she asked the mirror.

The ungaikyo grinned, its lips still moving. It was singing, she knew it with a certainty. She almost heard the song, almost remembered it. She found her own lips moving in time to the yokai's as it sang its song, and she crept closer to the mirror. The words. She heard the words and she knew that if she heard the song, if she remembered the song, she would remember everything else too. Was that what Yanmei had meant when she said she had to accept her trauma and deal with it? How could she do that if she didn't remember it? Kira pressed her hand against the mirror and she heard it! The song, the words. A children's rhyme her mother had taught to her. "Come the spring the ice will thaw. New life blooms, watch the ground."

A pale hand shot out of the mirror and grabbed Kira's wrist. She startled and squeaked in alarm, tried to pull away, but she was off balance. The hand jerked her towards the mirror. Her sandals scuffed the floor as she tried to brace herself. Her elbow disappeared into the mirror, passing through its surface like it was water. The ungaikyo grinned mirrored shards of teeth at her from the other side and pulled harder.

"Let me go!" Kira screamed. Her face was a hand's breadth from surface of the mirror. She heard the song like the roar of a waterfall. *Summer sun will light the way. Longest days but mind the storms.* She braced her other hand against the mirror and pushed, wedged one foot against the toppled shrine and the other at the base of the mirror and heaved backward. Her elbow slowly emerged from the mirror, then her forearm, then her wrist with the ungaikyo's hand still clutching it. "I don't want to go in there," she cried. "Let me go!"

The ungaikyo snapped her other hand around Kira's other wrist and pulled it into the shining surface. Kira had only a moment to scream before she was dragged into the mirror.

Autumn brings the colours out. Fallen leaves all around. Kira recognised her own voice, but she wasn't singing. She stood, swaying on her feet, complete darkness all around her. She was standing on nothing but a dark abyss. She looked up, nothing there; spun around, nothing anywhere. Nothing but darkness, a black void. And the same children's rhyme echoed through it, her voice, her words. *Winter brings the snow and ice. Cloudy skies and starless nights.*

She knew the song, had thought it would bring back the memories, but it didn't. She clapped her hands over her ears, but the song only grew louder. *Come the spring the ice will thaw. New life blooms, watch the ground.* She spun about again, looking for something, anything to focus on, to anchor her. The darkness made her dizzy. She saw herself, her arms and legs and chest as though she were standing in light, but there was nothing. Nothing. *NOTHING!*

Kira collapsed to her knees, squeezed her eyes shut. *Summer sun will light the way. Longest days but mind the storms...* "Autumn brings the colours out. Fallen leaves all around." She clasped a hand over her mouth. She had sung the words. She hadn't meant to, but she had, and she had seen something. A room, sunflowers and clouds on its paper walls, a messy futon and ruffled blanket, dolls in the corner. She remembered that room. It had been hers.

Tears rolled down her cheeks as she sang through hitched breaths. "Winter brings the snow and ice. Cloudy skies and starless nights." She was kneeling in front of a dressing table in her nightclothes, her kimono in a heap on the floor. She was staring into her little dressing mirror, brushing her hair and singing the song her mother had taught her. "Come the spring the ice will thaw. New life blooms, watch the ground." Her bedroom door was open and someone was standing there, watching her. Her uncle. He was tall and broad with a long nose, a scattering of stubble on his pitted chin, and a horseshoe of salt and pepper hair around his head. He looked angry. She watched him in the mirror and couldn't understand why he looked so angry. He was Uncle Yoshio. He brought sweet buns or toys whenever he visited. She wanted him to stop frowning at her. She wanted to make him happy, so she smiled at him in the mirror.

Kira's voice faltered on the words and she rocked back and forth, struggling to draw a breath. She knew what would come next. She knew, and she didn't want to see it. She didn't want to feel it. "Summer sun will light the way. Longest days but mind the storms." In the mirror, she watched Uncle Yoshio step into her room. He was crying. Why was he crying? She heard the whisper of steel as he pulled his blade from its wooden saya. Pain erupted in her back and blood spattered the mirror in front of her. In the reflection, she saw the tip of a wakizashi poking out of her chest. She looked up at Uncle Yoshio's crying face in the mirror. And then nothing.

The song stopped. Kira heard nothing but silence in the dark. She wiped tears from her eyes and found the ungaikyo, herself, standing before her. Kira climbed slowly to her feet and stood to face her other half. "You've been trapped here all this time, haven't you?" Kira asked her. "Listening to the song, seeing our death over and over again." The ungaikyo stared at her with those empty, black eyes. "I'm so sorry. I didn't know."

Her other half grinned, each shining mirrored tooth

reflecting Kira back at herself.

"Is this how it is for all the onryo?" Kira asked herself. "Is this why they are... how they are?"

The ungaikyo turned away from her and started walking. Kira saw something in the darkness ahead of her, a shining surface, a small room with a toppled shrine on the floor. The ungaikyo was walking towards it. She glanced over her shoulder at Kira. "Your prison now. Not mine." The words came from Kira's mouth, but they were not hers. They were the ungaikyo's, and she knew beyond doubt that her other half meant to escape and leave Kira here in this mirror prison.

Kira lurched into a run, stumbling in the darkness, unsure how to run on nothing. The ungaikyo stepped one foot out of the mirror into the real world. Kira leapt, grabbed the ungaikyo's trailing arm and hauled her back. For a moment, both of them were half in the real world and half inside the mirror. Voices inside the temple rushed in her ears, loud after the silence of the dark. The voices came from outside the little room; she saw figures silhouetted against the paper door. Then she was back inside the mirror, dragging the ungaikyo with her. Her other half flailed at her, slapped her across her face, clawed her arms. They fell back, sprawling in the darkness. The ungaikyo snarled at her, mirrored teeth snapping, eye sockets filled with the darkness of the eternal void. Kira kicked her in the face, rolled to her feet, and leapt into the mirror. She got her arms out into the temple and grabbed at the wall even as the ungaikyo clutched her feet and pulled her back. Kira pushed forward, out of the mirror and back into the real world. She kicked back ferociously, catching her other half in the jaw. The ungaikyo let go Kira's leg, and Kira tumbled onto the prayer mat in the little temple room.

Kira sat there, panting, sweating, heart thumping in her ears. She looked over her shoulder at the mirror. The ungaikyo stared at her from the other side, one hand pressed against the surface, trapped. While Kira was out in the world, the ungaikyo was confined to the mirror. Kira shivered, jumped to her feet, and strode towards the door. When she reached the door, hand hovering over the handle, she stopped. She heard people on the other side. Voices, concerned or arguing, she wasn't sure. They didn't matter though – the voices weren't what stopped her from pulling the door open and leaving. Yanmei stopped her. Yanmei's dying wish.

Kira turned back to the mirror. The ungaikyo was still there, staring out at her. Kira crept back towards it. "You're me," she breathed. Her other half cocked its head, moved its lips, saying something Kira couldn't hear. "And I'm you," Kira told it. "I won't let you have me, but I won't lock you away either. You don't deserve that. You've suffered enough. We've both suffered enough." She held out a hand to the mirror. "Come with me. Be with me." She smiled at herself. "Please."

The ungaikyo flung a hand out and clutched Kira's wrist, and Kira clutched her back. She took the ungaikyo's other hand as well and stepped back, dragging her other half out of the mirror with her, first her arms, then her head, then her shoulders. But something was holding the ungaikyo back. Kira growled and pulled harder. The yokai's chest emerged from the mirror, then her hips. At last, Kira threw herself backwards, and they both collapsed onto the floor of the temple. The mirror shattered, raining shards all around them.

Kira sat up and looked around for the ungaikyo. She was gone. Kira was alone. The door was still closed and she was alone. She flicked a dagger into her hand and looked down at herself in its mirrored blade. It was just her. No hollow eye sockets, no mirrored teeth or pale skin. It was just her.

She stood, careful not to cut herself on the shards of mirror. They hadn't disappeared, she realised. Usually, her mirrors disappeared after they shattered, but this one was still there, albeit in pieces. She tried listening for the ungaikyo's song, but all she heard were the voices on the other side of the door.

"Winter brings the snow and ice," Kira said tentatively, waiting to see if anything happened. A memory floated to the surface of her mind, a woman standing over her, gently stroking her hair, singing to her. Singing that song. She had raven hair tied up in a bun, freckles over her nose and cheeks. A loving smile. It was her mother. She remembered her mother... and more. She was running through a bamboo forest with her friends Kameyo and Hikaru. Hikaru tripped and skinned her knee. Then she was standing under a parasol, snow drifting all around, watching her father crack the ice on the pond to feed the koi. She remembered it all. Her life, her death, her years trapped in the mirror, her only hope of freedom scaring someone else into taking their own life. She remembered everything. It hurt. The good, the bad, the memories of child and monster. She remembered it all, and it hurt so much she couldn't breathe. She couldn't stand to be there anymore, in such a small room filled with the broken shards of her.

Kira pulled the door open to find four priests waiting on the other side, the fat man with one eyebrow at their head. She felt heat rush to her cheeks as they stared at her. "Sorry about the mess," she said, gesturing to the broken shrine and shattered mirror. "And the shoes. And everything else." She smiled at them. "Sorry." Then she darted around them and ran for the temple door.

Chapter 50

Haruto saw the temple door open and Kira step out. She glanced up at the sky, then started walking. A temple priest appeared in the doorway a few seconds later, staring after the girl. Judging by the look on the priest's face, Haruto and the others definitely wouldn't be staying at the temple tonight. Haruto sighed and went back to honing the edge of his new katana. He was kneeling just half a dozen paces away from the shrine and the statues of Yanmei and the god of war, where Guang was sitting, his paper forgotten in his hands, his eyes closed and a soft snore misting before him, icing up his beard. He'd fallen asleep a few minutes ago, and Haruto didn't have the heart to wake him. The prince was pacing, but when he saw Kira, intercepted her on her way to the shrine.

"It's about time," Ido Katsuo said. "I... uh... I was..." He coughed and looked away. "We should go before any more onryo come after me."

Kira smiled at the prince. Haruto noticed something calmer about her now. The cracks in her skin had vanished, and she no longer seemed on the edge of panic. "No one else is coming, Katsuo."

"How can you know that?" the prince asked indignantly.

Kira stopped in front of the shrine and placed a hand on Guang's shoulder. The old poet flinched, snorted, and set to coughing. Then she turned to Ido Katsuo. "Because the other onryo trusted Daizen to do the job. Just like they trusted him to free Messimere." She knelt down beside Guang and bowed her head to the statues before the shrine.

Ido Katsuo wrung his hands together. "Was Daizen telling the truth?" he asked quietly. He suddenly seemed younger, his aristocratic mask slipping away to reveal a young man barely out of childhood. "Is my father dead?" Kira didn't answer him, and the prince took it as confirmation. He staggered away, weaving in between the standing swords and absently setting them to wobbling.

Kira bowed her head before the statue of her mother.

"I've been trying to write a poem to honour her," Guang whispered to her. Haruto saw him gently nudge her with his shoulder. "Every hero deserves a poem."

"Is it better than your usual ear sores?" Kira asked with a grin.

"Ungrateful little leek! My words are as rich as honey and smooth as silk. People have paid me handsomely to tell my tales."

Kira laughed. "I don't have any money, but I would like to hear her poem if you would like to tell it."

Guang coughed and wiped a sleeve across his eyes. "Just this once then." He shuffled the paper in his hands and stared down at it, frowning. "It's a work in a progress, you understand. Not finished. And I'm not sure I have the skill to do her justice. Maybe we should find a real poet to pay her tribute."

Kira reached out and took Guang's hand. "It could be the worst poem ever made, but it would mean more coming from you than someone she never met."

Guang nodded. "You almost sound like her, girl." He drew in a deep breath and looked down at his paper again.

"Born of fire, untamed by the flames. Before gods and heroes, roaring in the face of monsters, is where you'll find the Last Bloom of Summer."

Kira wiped a sleeve across her face. "I love it," she said sniffling. "Yanmei would love it too." Guang put an arm across her shoulders and hugged her then.

Shiki whistled low and soft. The little spirit was standing next to the statues, staring at Guang and Kira. "I'm sure she won't mind," Haruto said. Shiki waddled over and leapt into Kira's lap, and the girl wrapped her arms around the spirit.

Haruto gave them a few minutes, then he stood, tucked his

new sword into his belt, and approached the shrine. Guang looked up at him and grimaced. "Mind giving me a hand, old man. I'm not sure I can stand without help." Haruto took him under one shoulder and hauled him to his feet. His knees popped and his back cracked, and he moaned. He almost overbalanced and had to hang on to Haruto's arm to stop from toppling. "Ooooh cabbage!" he cursed. "Never get old. And if you, by some unlucky circumstance, find yourself grey and wrinkled, never kneel in the snow for several hours."

"Stop complaining and walk it off," Haruto said with a shrug.

"I'll walk you off a cliff, you old lettuce." Guang grumbled as he limped about in a circle.

"What about you?" Haruto asked Kira. "Have you frozen to the spot too?"

Kira leapt from her knees to her feet like a grasshopper. "No." She smiled at him and wiped unshed tears from her eyes.

"Are you ready to go?"

Kira turned to the shrine once more and looked down at the stone statue that had been Yanmei. In death, she seemed to have regained some of the composure her technique had stolen from her. Even all but naked apart from a cloak, her hair short and frayed, and one arm burned to a stump, Yanmei's statue looked regal, powerful.

Kira stared down at it and frowned. "When does it stop hurting?"

"Never," Haruto said. "It never stops hurting. But that's how you know they meant something. The pain is a reminder of the good times, not the bad."

Kira put her hand on Yanmei's head and closed her eyes. Then she turned, opened her eyes and walked away. "I'm ready."

Haruto caught up to her. "You seem different," he said. Shiki leapt from his shoulder to hers and cooed, stroking her cheek with a little arm.

"I am different," she said.

"Do you know what that means?"

She glanced at him and shrugged. "Not yet."

"Me either."

Guang spotted them walking away and limped to catch up. The prince was waiting ahead of them, pacing back and forth, mumbling something to himself. They had only an hour or two of sunlight left, so Haruto decided they would head back south to the inn for the night, and set off towards Orochi's grave in the morning.

"I realised something about the onryo," Kira said as they walked. "Daizen told me I wasn't ready yet, that I had to let his sister come out and play. I didn't understand then, but I think I do now. I'm not like them, the other onryo."

"I could have told you that, girl," Guang said.

"But I could have been like them," Kira said. She looked at Haruto. "You said an onryo is a yokai who has regained some of their humanity. In my case, Yanmei killed an assassin while he was looking into my mirror. She set me free by putting him in my place. At that moment, I stopped being a yokai, but I wasn't human either."

"You became a little of both," Haruto said. "An onryo."

Kira flicked a mirrored dagger into her hand and stared into the reflection. She no longer flinched from what she saw there, and her eyes didn't darken. "Is that how it happened for the others as well? Daizen and Shin and Crow?"

Haruto shrugged. "I don't know. Izumi became an enenra yokai when she suffocated to death in the fire Toshinaka set. Daizen, from what Guang said of him, was probably a kiyo yokai. They're born of jealous rage, often when someone kills themselves rather than move on from unrequited love. But kiyo manifest as a type of serpent with the body of a snake, but the legs, arms, and head of a person."

"When Daizen became an onryo, he regained his human form," Kira said. "But that wasn't the end of it. The onryo are half human and half yokai, but..." She sighed and shook her head. "It's not that simple. We become two halves in one body, but not united. I think the other onryo are what happens when the yokai half breaks the human half and takes over. They change and become less human. That was what Daizen meant when he said I had to let his little sister come out and play, and it's what the Herald of Bones meant when he said Yanmei and the others at Heiwa Academy were holding me back."

Guang hobbled up on the other side of her. "But you haven't been broken by the yokai?"

"No," Kira shook her head, her hair falling in front of her face. "I'm different because I had Yanmei. I had someone who wasn't willing to let the yokai take me. The others didn't have that. I think the Herald of Bones sought them out and tipped them in the other direction, made the yokai half win." She tucked her hair back behind her ears and then looked at Haruto. "Crow isn't Izumi anymore. That half of her is gone, I think. I felt it in the temple when I was struggling against my yokai. If it took me, there wouldn't be any coming back. I would be gone and it would be all that was left. I'm sorry."

Haruto knew it for the truth, but it still felt like a blade to the gut. He had failed Izumi three times now. First by not stopping Toshinaka, then again by not finding her as a yokai, by not sending her on her way so Omoretsu could claim her soul. And he had failed her again when she became an onryo. Perhaps if he had been there for her, like Yanmei was for Kira, maybe she could have been brought back like Kira. Instead, the Herald of Bones found her and made her a monster. He felt a weight settle on his shoulders. Now he had to fail her once more and kill her. He wouldn't let the turmoil show; the others didn't need to share his pain, and so he just shrugged and kept walking, though his feet felt a little heavier and each step a little harder.

"So there's three of them left, these onryo?" Guang asked. "The Herald of Bones, Izumi..."

"Crow," Kira said.

Guang grunted unhappily. "Crow. And the jorogumo who killed Tian."

Haruto shook his head. "There's only two onryo left." It was time they knew the full extent of what they were up against. "The

Herald of Bones is a tengu, a demon, an entirely different level of bad than a yokai." Shiki trumpeted her agreement.

Ido Katsuo skipped up beside them. "But you can kill it... him... it, right? I mean, we have an onmyoji and a--" he gestured at Kira "--whatever you are now."

"I'm different," Kira said, smiling at him.

"Well, there we go," the prince said happily. "An onmyoji and a Kira. We can't lose."

Silence settled upon them. Haruto heard the wind howling far away and looked up to see the clouds speeding past. A storm was coming, a last blizzard before winter gave way to spring.

The prince slowed to a stop and sighed, then cleared his throat. Haruto and the others stopped and turned around to face him. Ido Katsuo rubbed the back of his neck with one hand and opened his mouth to speak, then closed it again.

"Out with it, lad," Guang said.

Ido Katsuo grimaced. "Look... it's about... about what that fiery, ugly bastard said back there... about me and my brothers."

"That you killed them?" Guang asked. Haruto shot him a look, but the poet held up his hands. "What? Just establishing the context."

"Yeah, that," the prince said. He seemed to be staring at Kira. "I just want you to know, I didn't kill them. My eldest brother, Aki, uh, Akihiko, was already dead in his cell. I went to free him, just like I said I was going to do, but..." He shook his head. "Auntie Ryoko, she... What she left of him was barely recognisable." He swallowed hard. "My other brother, Nori, he attacked me. I opened his door and he flew at me with a knife. He attacked me and... well, I suppose I did kill him. It was self defence, I promise."

Guang grumbled. "Why are you telling us this, lad? I don't care. Haruto, do you care?"

Haruto shrugged.

"Kira, do you care?"

Kira grinned. "About what? I wasn't listening."

"See, lad," Guang said. The old poet ambled over to the

prince and draped an arm over his shoulder. "Nobody cares."

Prince Ido Katsuo laughed and sagged a little, relieved. "You are a strange group."

"I have a question," Kira said. "Why did you lie about it? When Daizen claimed you killed them, why did you say you did it?"

"This is Ipia," the prince said, as if that was all the answer she needed. Kira continued to stare at him, waiting. "Killing relatives and stepping over their bodies to reach the throne is just how things are done here. I mean, if you aren't willing to stab a few siblings in the back for the crown, you obviously don't really want it."

Kira frowned. "Seems like a stupid system to me."

"I agree," the prince said, clapping his hands and leaping forward to walk ahead of them. He turned around to face them, walking backwards. "So we should change it! After you've killed all the onryo and all that, uh, stuff, you can help me retake my throne." The prince paused while the others just stared at him. "What? I'm one of you, part of the group. We help each other out."

Kira scratched at her chin just like Guang often did. "I must have missed your help."

The prince danced ahead again and held his hand over his heart. "You wound me, Kira. Have you forgotten already how I fetched water and stopped that old lady from going down into the cellar?"

"He's right," Guang said. "That was mightily heroic of him."

They passed through the torii at the edge of the Graveyard of Swords, and Kira stopped and stared back. They couldn't see the shrine nor Yanmei's statue anymore, but Haruto guessed that didn't matter. He waited for her until she was ready. Guang and the prince kept walking, arguing about which of them was more heroic.

"You were right," Kira said after a few moments, "when you said the Herald of Bones is to blame." She turned to look at Haruto then, and her eyes had gone dark, but it looked different from before. The skin around them was black, but her eyes were clear. "I'm going to kill him for what he did to Yanmei, and for what he's done to all the other onryo."

"Justice?" Haruto said.

Kira shook her head, turned and walked past him. "Not justice. I am not justice. I am a spirit of vengeance."

Chapter 51

The tavern was busy by the time they arrived. It was full of travellers, merchants trading between eastern and western Ipia, priests on pilgrimage from one temple or another, a giant of a fellow with a loud voice and booming laugh who claimed he was a wandering hero looking for work. The tavern owner seemed surprised when Kira, Haruto, Guang, and Katsuo pushed through the door out of the snowy darkness. Apparently, people rarely stayed at the inn for two nights. He didn't remark about Yanmei's absence, though she had chatted to him only the night before. It seemed wrong to Kira that Yanmei should be so easily forgotten.

She settled down at a Hosan style table with chairs, and Guang sank down opposite her, groaning and rubbing at his knees. Haruto went to secure rooms and food, and Katsuo took his leave to visit the outhouse. Kira found the loudness and warmth of the tavern oddly comforting and aggravating at the same time. The world continued on, heedless of what it had just lost.

"She wouldn't want you to sulk," Guang said. He leaned back in his chair and yawned, stretching out his legs beneath the table.

"I wasn't sulking," Kira said sulkily.

"Really?" Guang scratched his chin. "Because I spied a dragon eyeing up your bottom lip for a landing."

She glared at him. "Maybe I was sulking a little, but I think I've figured something out. Here." She flicked a mirrored dagger into her hand and tossed it across the table. Guang fumbled at it, caught it, then dropped it on the table as if it burned. Kira half expected to hear Yanmei tell her to stop and smiled at the thought. "Sorry."

"Was there a point?" Guang asked. "Other than the one you just tried to stab me with, I mean."

Kira grinned and nodded. "Look at the blade."

Guang frowned at her, possibly expecting another dagger to come flying at him as soon as he looked down. "It's chipped!" he said. "There's a little nick taken out of this edge." He poked at it. "But the dagger isn't cracked."

"I call it Momo," Kira said. She flicked another dagger into her hand and placed it on the table. "I call this one Blair."

Guang looked down at the new dagger. "The blade is a little shorter," he said after a moment of scrutiny. "And the hilt is thinner."

Kira flicked another dagger into her hand and placed it beside the other two. "This one is Hayate."

Guang spotted the difference immediately. "This one's blade is a slightly different shape, wider and flatter."

Kira grinned. "Pick one."

Guang stared at her. "Okay... Blair."

Kira whispered the name of her dagger and ordered it to shatter. Blair cracked apart and a hundred mirrored shards spilled across the table.

"Momo," Guang said. Kira ordered Momo to break, and the dagger burst into shards, mixing with Blair's. Guang nodded. "Figured it out then?"

"You were right," Kira said. She flicked a new version of Momo into her hand and held it up, staring at the notch chipped out of the blade. "I needed a way to focus on individual daggers, and to do that they need to be different, distinct." She placed Momo on the table beside Hayate, then flicked a new Blair into her hand and placed that beside them. Then she flicked another dagger into her hand. "This one is Pabu," she said. "It has a ring instead of a pommel." She placed Pabu on the table. "This is Maru, one of its edges is jagged. This is Jiji, it has a single edge and a bigger pommel. I call this one Luna. It has a hole running down the length of the blade. And this one is Heen, it has a hook on the pommel." She looked down at her collection of daggers.

Eight of them, all unique so she could keep track of them. "I've tried to make more, but I can't. For some reason, I can't create a ninth without one of the others shattering."

"Very impressive," Guang said, looking up as Haruto sat down at the table.

The onmyoji brushed aside some mirrored shards, not even seeming surprised they were there, and set a couple of clay bottles on the table; then he pulled five cups from the folds of his kimono. Shiki leapt down onto the table, shuffled through the shards to Momo, and grabbed the dagger, struggling to pick it up in her spindly arms. She held it aloft, teetered a moment, then steadied herself and trumpeted in victory.

"Truly a dangerous sight," Katsuo said as he sat down at the table opposite Haruto and stared at the knife-wielding spirit. Kira wove an illusion of a charging bear in the reflection on the blade, and the prince flinched and spun about, scraping his chair on the wooden floor.

Guang chuckled. "I must be getting wiser," he said. "You didn't fool me that time."

Katsuo turned back to the table. "That wasn't funny."

"I disagree, lad," Guang said.

"Not surprising. You're very disagreeable."

Haruto poured five cups of wine and slid one in front of each of them, leaving the fifth in the centre of the table. Shiki dropped the dagger and picked up the cup. Haruto raised his cup and paused holding it before him. "To Yanmei. All she did for us, and the memories she left behind." They all drank to that, Shiki noisily slurping at her cup. Kira winced at the taste, hoping they did not expect her to drink any more of it.

"How far is it to this monastery from here, Ido?" Haruto asked.

"Eight or nine days," Katsuo said. He reached for the bottle and poured himself another cup. "Assuming our old poet here can keep up."

"I'll be just fine, lad."

"Are you sure?" Katsuo grinned and poured the old poet

another cup of wine.

Kira turned her cup over before they roped her into their contest. Shiki, on the other hand, pushed her cup into the fray and happily slurped down another, her fur turning pink at the edges. Haruto did not join in. He sat at the far end of the table, brooding. Kira saw his jaw writhing, and he scratched at the table with his fingernail, digging small gouges in the wood and flicking the scrapings away. His eyes were like flint. She reached out and touched his hand, and he flinched and shot her a hostile gaze.

"Are you alright?" she asked.

Haruto's face curdled like he was in pain. "You remember everything now?

Kira nodded quickly.

"How you died?"

Kira remembered it all too well. It was fresh and painful in her mind. If she dwelled on it, she could almost feel the blade in her back, could almost see her uncle's tear-streaked face. She nodded again, more slowly this time.

Haruto sighed and ran a hand down his face. "Do you still want vengeance? On your uncle, I mean."

Kira had to think about that. Search deep inside for an answer. In the silence she left, she heard Guang and Katsuo and Shiki laughing and slurping down wine. "No," she said. It felt like a lie. "Yes. Maybe. I don't forgive him. I won't. I can't. He killed me. I trusted him and..." She had to stop for a moment and breathe past the pain. "I don't think I'll ever *not* hate him. Part of me wants to pity him, but he doesn't deserve it. He deserves nothing but hate. But he's dead and I'm... not, I guess. That's a type of vengeance. I outlived him even though he murdered me. That's vengeance." She nodded and ran a trembling hand through her hair. It was difficult speaking about it and she wished Yanmei were there to comfort her.

Haruto was silent for a while, staring hard at the table, digging fingernails into the wood.

"What's wrong?" Kira asked him.

Haruto glanced at her then away, as though he couldn't bear

to meet her gaze. "Tian wants vengeance still. The need is..." He barked out a humourless laugh. "Very strong. I can feel his anger drawing him back from heaven. I see him when I close my eyes. Eight days is a long time," he said, and Kira thought he looked scared. "I just hope it's not too long."

Chapter 52

The monastery stretched high above them in four tiers built into the cliffside. Crow looked up. It would have strained her neck if she had a neck. The top tier was shrouded by the blizzard that raged around them. The cliffside provided them some shelter, but the wind was an angry, hateful animal snarling at them. Crow hated wind like that, it tugged at her essence and blew her apart. She had once been scattered so completely by a gale that it took her three days to pull enough of her smoke back together to think again. That was before the Master found her and gave her the robe to contain herself.

The Master stood with her at the foot of the cliff, his tengai resting on his shoulders, covering everything but his mesmerising eyes. Neither cold nor wind ever seemed to bother him. His feathers kept him warm, and no breeze nor gust or gale could hope to overpower him. His was a fiercer storm than anything nature could muster.

The first tier of the monastery, sloped roofs of pagodas painted red and heaped with snow, was only fifty feet above them. A frozen stream cascaded from the plateau, clinging to the rock in a pillar of icicles. A pink petal drifted down from one of the tiers, caught in the eddying wind and whipped about. Fools often planted sakura trees to ward off evil spirits, not that it ever did them any good. The genuine marvel was that the monks living at the monastery had somehow coaxed the trees to bloom in the middle of winter.

"Where is your sister?" the Master asked. Xifeng was supposed to meet them here at the base of the monastery. They were to climb together, a united front against the militant monks who guarded Orochi's prison. According to Empress Ise Ryoko, the monks trained for decades to fend off all trespassers from both the mortal and spiritual realms.

"Should we wait for Zen?" Crow asked.

The Master turned slightly and regarded her with his churning eyes. Most people found his gaze unnerving, but not Crow. There was something comforting about it. It quieted her mind and let her think clearly. It was an anchor to cling to even amid the most violent storms. When she looked into his eyes, she saw the path he trod and knew it was right.

"Your brother isn't coming," the Master said in a voice like iced steel. "The onmyoji killed him."

Even with the Master's calming gaze, Crow felt her smoke begin the writhe. It couldn't be true. Zen had the strongest technique of all of them. They each had their strengths. Shin's physical prowess, his ability to regenerate almost any wound combined with his indomitable strength, and his prehensile braids were a marvel. Yet the onmyoji had killed him. Zen's flames were beyond heat and reason, and when he got going, not even the Master could approach him. How could anyone, even an onmyoji, have killed him? What was this immortal monster that hunted them? Xifeng was a creature of shadows and venom who struck without warning; perhaps if she got her fangs into the onmyoji, she could kill him. Crow's body gave her an advantage over most opponents: she had no fixed form, nothing to damage, and she felt no pain. But that was not entirely true. The onmyoji had cut her with his spirit blade. He had carved away a piece of her and it had hurt. If he could hurt her, cut her, then he could kill her. Crow started to feel something new. It was fear, and she didn't like it.

The Master was still watching her, eyes a changing miasma of colours. "Are you afraid, Little Sister?" he asked.

Smoke billowed from beneath Crow's robe. A reflex she thought she had rid herself of long ago. Back when she was just a yokai, she... she... The memory slipped away even as she reached for it. "This creature that hunts us--"

"Man," the Master said. "Just a man."

Crow felt her smoke churning. "He killed Shin and now

Zen. He cannot be *just* a man."

"And you fear him for that?" the Master asked. He pushed back Crow's hood as if to reveal her face, though she had none. "Oh Little Sister, you still don't realise it. You are stronger than all your siblings. Shin's physical strength was useless against your formless power. Zen's flames could never have burned you. Even Xifeng's venom is nothing to you, for you have no blood to poison. You are the strongest of all the onryo. I knew it from the moment I rescued you. I saw what no one else had within your murky depths. Power unrivalled."

He had rescued her, found her fraying and alone, coming apart piece by piece and unable to stop herself. Crow did not know how she had become onryo nor who she was or had been. All she had known was the hazy madness of formlessness. The Master's gaze had calmed her, and he taught her to coalesce, to hold on to her smoke around a core. He gave her the robe, her anchor and saved her from dissolving into a distant memory of soot on the wind. The Master was another wind, but he did not tear Crow apart; he guided her along the path he trod. He gave her purpose.

A cherry blossom petal drifted down on the swirling wind, and Crow caught it with a smoky hand. She smiled as she realised she had fingers again. She rubbed the petal, staining it black. Then she realised the Master was watching her again, his maelstrom eyes narrowed behind his tengai. Crow crushed the petal in her smoky fist and let the remnants fall to the snowy ground. Then she drew her hands back inside her robe to hide them.

"We cannot wait for your sister any longer," the Master said. He turned and strode towards the cliffside.

There were steps carved into the rock, leading up to the first plateau, and the Master started up them two at a time. Crow followed, floating up the steps on a plume of sooty smoke. She trailed a hand along the cliff face as they climbed, fingers searching out the dimples and cracks. She could almost feel them beneath her touch. She could almost feel again. She didn't remember what it was like to feel, but she must have known once.

Something white and sticky tried to cling to her fingers, but it found no purchase on her smoke. She knew what it was, though. Spider web. Silk as strong as steel. She looked up and saw three gleaming black eyes staring down at her. Crouched above them, nestled in a gap in the cliff face, was Xifeng. Her obese body bulged against her kimono. Her hair was spiky and oily black, and her face was a nightmare. Her right eye was a shining orb, but her left was an ugly scar of greening, puckered flesh. Two new spider eyes had burst through the skin above and below the ruined eye. Xifeng smiled wide, clicking and rubbing her fangs together behind her lips.

"Master," Crow said. He stopped and looked up at Xifeng crouched above them in a net of webbing.

"You're late," Xifeng said, her voice sounded like a thousand spiny legs scraping against each other. "I'm so hungry I almost started without you."

"The monks?" the Master asked.

"Have no idea we're coming," Xifeng said. She tittered, holding a sleeved human hand across her mouth. "They will be such easy prey."

"They won't be easy. They have trained to fight people like us," Crow said.

"They will soon learn just how lacking their training has been," the Master said.

Xifeng laughed again. She started pulling at her hair, running her fingers through it. She pulled out a lock and stared at it a moment, then she screeched and dropped it as though it might bite her. "I have waited long enough." Her segmented legs scraped along the rock. "I want to kill them."

The Master turned his gaze upon her. "Then go, Little Sister. Wreak your havoc, lay your traps. But do not eat anyone. Crow and I will proceed to the prison."

Xifeng pouted. "Why not? I'm hungry"

"The onmyoji will be here soon," the Master continued. "And you need to be at your strongest, Little Sister, not curled up sleeping off a belly full of flesh. Once you have thinned his allies, then you may choose one to devour."

Xifeng clapped her human hands together, then turned and scuttled up the cliffside. Crow watched her go. Even Xifeng remembered who she had once been. Crow had been there the day the Master found Xifeng, a new born onryo still trying to come to terms with what she was. She had built a vast lair of webbing in a temple – she always loved to defile temples – and was feeding off the priests she had cocooned. The Master strode into the lair with no regard for the alarm webs he was tripping, and Crow floated behind him. Then Xifeng had attacked. She was shapely then, beautiful even, with brown eyes that glistened with tears. She tried to bite the Master, but his feathery cloak was hard as steel and he threw her off easily. With a blast of air and razor feathers, the Master hacked Xifeng's lair and broke her spirit. She cowered before him, begged him for mercy, her spider legs stabbing at the air, still weaving her web. The Master had strode through the trap, snapping webbing that no blade could cut, and knelt before Xifeng.

He talked to her, his voice calm and caring. He knew Xifeng somehow. He told her who she had once been. Xifeng, the midwife of Ban Ping. Every family of wealth wanted Xifeng to help deliver their children, and nothing gave her greater pleasure than helping bring new life into the world. But Xifeng had a secret: no matter how many times she and her husband tried, they could not conceive. Year after year, her husband grew angrier, blaming Xifeng for being barren. In public, they hid behind smiles and kisses and held hands, but in private her husband shouted and threatened and Xifeng grew small with fear.

Frightened for her life and blaming herself for not being able to give her husband a child, Xifeng stole away in the dead of night. She knew her husband would give chase, for as much as it pained him not to have children, the shame of a runaway wife would be even greater. So Xifeng hid in barns, in bathhouses, and eventually in the cold cellar of an abandoned house. Her husband tracked her. She heard him stalking in the house above her, searching for her, calling her name. Xifeng found a loose floorboard, pried it out, and crawled into the space below it. Then she pulled the floorboard down on top of her and waited, silent save for the clipped sound of her panicked breathing. Her husband shone a lantern into the cellar, light spilling through the tiny gaps in the floorboards, but he didn't see her. Even when he stopped above her, standing on the very floorboard she hid beneath, he didn't see her.

As Xifeng stared up through the gap, watching her husband search, she felt a sharp pain on the back of her neck. She clenched her teeth to stop from crying out. The skin at the back of her neck felt like it was burning. She couldn't move save to push up the floorboard, which would reveal her to her husband. Agony crept through her veins, her arms began to stiffen, but she refused to cry out. Eventually he left, cursing his way up the stairs and out of the house. Xifeng tried to move, but she couldn't. Her arms were like stone, and her legs like wood. She was breathing too fast, then she was breathing too slow. And then she wasn't breathing at all. She died there, trapped beneath the cellar floor, alone and afraid.

When the Master had told Xifeng her own story, the story of her death, Crow saw a change settle upon the onryo. Her beautiful brown eyes darkened to the shiny black of a spider's orbs, and she smiled two big black hooked fangs hanging from furry brown chelicerae behind her lips.

Crow had always been jealous of Xifeng. The Master had given her a gift by telling her who she had been and how she had died. He had looked into her eyes and saw her past, and he gave it to her. But he never did that for Crow. He said onryo needed to know how they had died to understand what they were truly capable of, yet he refused to tell Crow about her death.

"Come," the Master said, snapping Crow out of her self-pitying reverie.

Crow frowned, felt smoky brows pulling together in the darkness of her hood. "Will we not need some of the monks, Master?" she asked. "Sekiryu's prison in Sky Hollow was

Cochtan made. It required blood to open."

The Master grunted and stared back down the steps. "Orochi's prison will not be so easy to open. We will need a key."

"A key?" Crow asked.

The Master nodded. "We have but to wait, Little Sister. It's coming to us."

Chapter 53

The blizzard hit like a tsunami a few days ago, and since then the world had been nothing but a swirling chaos of whites and greys and Guang's complaints. Even Haruto was cold. It was an Ipian winter like none in living memory, and Haruto had lived a long, long time.

The prince led them on though, claiming he could find the monastery with his eyes closed and his nose blocked. He seemed in good cheer, or at least he was putting on a pleasant face for a man who had just learned that his entire family had been slaughtered. Perhaps he was choosing to look at it as an opportunity, to be the last heir of western Ipia, the last Ido. It was a fool's dream, which suited the prince like a saddle on a horse. The west had surrendered, and the generations' long war was over. The Ise family had won with the help of the onryo. All of Ipia belonged to Empress Ise Ryoko now. Considering she had recently imprisoned both Haruto and Ido Katsuo, and Kira had ruined one of her eyes, a vengeful empress was not high on Haruto's list of recent proud accomplishments.

"Cabbage, Ido," Guang shouted over the howling wind. "You said we were close. That we'd reach the monastery today." The old poet stared up into the teeth of the blizzard. "I can't even tell what time it is." He pulled his new coat tighter. The prince had purchased them all new wolf-fur coats in Kuriyetsu town a few days back.

"It's an hour past midday," the prince shouted back. "And we are almost there."

"How can you tell?" Guang said.

"Instinct, my good man," the prince said. "I, uh, have a nose for these things." He pulled a Cochtan time piece from his coat pocket and checked it. "Like I said, just past midday!"

Kira strode across the surface of the snow in silence. She wasn't the carefree girl she had been when they first met, but neither was she on the verge of shattering and releasing a dangerous yokai armed with terrifying reflections. Yanmei's death had changed her. It had changed them all. Or maybe it was because they were getting closer to the monastery, to Orochi's grave, and to the last of the onryo.

Haruto felt a fierce urgency. Tian's burden was a weight on his soul, an anger clutching so hard at his heart it hurt to breathe, plucking at his nerves and making him irritable. The snow, Guang's constant complaining, the prince's blustering, it all flayed Haruto's patience to bloody ruin, and he ground his teeth to stop from lashing out. Izumi was close too, and Haruto needed to see her again. He needed to know for certain that she was gone, that Crow was all that was left.

A snowball hit him in the side of the face, and he staggered and cursed. Kira was crouching on the snow a few feet away, giggling. Shiki on her shoulder, sharing in the laughter. Haruto exhaled very slowly and reconsidered his opinion: perhaps there was still some of the carefree girl left after all.

"Sorry," Kira said, pointing at Shiki. "She made me do it." Shiki warbled and pointed at Kira. Haruto had a feeling the attack had been a collaboration. He scooped up a handful of snow and flung it at the two of them. Kira laughed as she leapt nimbly out of the way.

"See, I told you we were almost there," Ido Katsuo shouted. "And you didn't believe me."

"I never said I didn't believe you," Guang shouted back. "Just that your idea of soon wasn't soon enough."

The cliff face appeared like a dark stain in the gusting blizzard. As they slogged closer, the snow subsided, and the shelter of the cliff turned the howling wind into a distant roar. Haruto brushed ice off his eyebrows and stared up. Just as the prince had told them, there were four tiers of plateaus above them. The steps ahead were carved into the rock, a man-made crevice leading up. On the first plateau was where the monks lived, houses and kitchens and baths and store houses. The second was where they trained, five separate dojos and an open square for sparring. The third plateau was where the monks prayed and was filled with temples, shrines, and incense. The fourth tier, though, well, the prince claimed he had never made it to the fourth tier despite many years at the monastery. It was well-guarded, day and night, and only the elder monks were allowed up there. That was where Haruto guessed Orochi's prison would be found.

They all stopped to stare up at the cliffs and warm themselves in the shelter from the blizzard. "Well, I guess we made it here first," Guang said. "Given the wreckage the other dragon left of Sky Hollow, it seems no great kami has been unleashed here yet."

"Will the monks attack us?" Haruto asked Ido Katsuo.

"Oh no," the prince said. "Not with me here vouching for you. I, uh, hope. I suppose it's possible. They really don't like outsiders. And, to be honest, they're not very friendly to me." He stepped ahead of them and turned around, holding up his hands in a gesture of supplication. "I suppose I should lay my cards on the table. They, uh, kicked me out of the order and told me never to return on pain of death."

Guang rolled his eyes. "What a surprise."

"My thoughts exactly, Grumpy," Ido Katsuo said. "They accused me of trying to steal their secrets or something."

Kira cocked her head to the side. "Were you?"

"That's not the point," Ido Katsuo said. "I just thought you should know that they might not be happy to see me... or you... or anyone."

Shiki whistled, and Kira giggled.

"What?" Ido Katsuo asked. "What did she say?"

Haruto started forward, patting the prince on the shoulder and shaking his head. Then he continued towards the stairs leading up to the first plateau. Shiki was right, the prince was nothing but trouble, but he guessed the same was true of all of them.

"What did she say?" the prince repeated. "You can't just laugh and walk away. Guang?"

"Beats me, lad," Guang said. "Never have been able to understand a thing the little fur ball says. I'm half convinced it's all a bunch of lettuce and Haruto just pretends he understands her."

Kira approached the frozen waterfall cascading down from the first plateau. It was just icicles now, a waterfall caught in mid flow. It was glistening and beautiful despite the grey sky and the snow pelting them all. She snapped off an icicle to stare at it. Then she looked up, following the path of the water. "I think the onryo beat us here," she said. She tossed the icicle to Haruto, and he held it up to look at it. There was a drop of crimson frozen at its tip. "It's fresh," Kira continued. "Still flowing up at the top, I think."

"If they're already up there, we can't have long before they free Orochi, old man," Guang said.

"We best hurry then," Haruto said. "I'll lead. The rest of you get behind me. Keep alert and keep up." He leapt up the first two steps, almost slipping on a patch of black ice. "Shiki, with me." The spirit leapt from Kira's shoulder, waddled across the ground and clambered up his leg. "Let's move!"

Guang clambered up the steps after Haruto, one hand on the crevice wall for support. It was a struggle on his thighs, a terror on his back, and the thought of climbing three more tiers was daunting. If he never saw another set of steps, his knees would be much happier. They ached and more than once he felt a sharp pain in his left knee that convinced him it was about to collapse and send him tumbling back down to the ground arse over head.

Haruto glided up the steps, one hand on his new katana, Shiki chattering on his shoulder, waving an arm around like she was conducting an orchestra. The prince was behind Guang and oddly silent. That's what worried Guang most. Ido Katsuo had proved quite difficult to shut up, but now he was completely silent. Kira came last. The girl was different since Yanmei's death. She seemed pensive, more mature, but that wasn't what impressed Guang. Before, the girl had seemed flighty at best and downright unstable at worst. Now, there was a dependability about her. Guang trusted her at his back. There was no one else he'd rather have guarding it.

Guang's hand on the wall touched something sticky. It clung to his fingers and he wiped it on his trousers to get rid of it. Between the cold and the climb and all the people in Ipia trying to kill them, Guang just wanted to flee back to Hosa and spend a few months in a nice warm tavern, telling stories for drinks. A nice little dream, but he thought it far more likely he'd end up filling a cold, unmarked grave somewhere in the depths of Ipia.

Haruto stopped at the top of the steps, and Guang saw his hand tighten on the hilt of his katana. "She's here," he growled through clenched teeth. When Guang reached the top of the steps a few moments later, his heartbeat quickened. The plateau was a huge, sprawling, mess of buildings. Some were low to the ground, a single floor; others were sky-high pagodas. Thin alleys passed between the buildings in what Guang guessed quickly accumulated into a maze. Snow drifted down in fat, lazy flakes, settling on rooftops and sliding off to the ground below. But what really churned Guang's gut were the glistening silk webs. draped in thick coils and spun in intricate patterns between the buildings. Tian's murderer was waiting for them.

Guang thrust a hand inside his satchel to grip his vows. To remind him. Four rolls of paper, each signed and sealed with his qi. He would not wield a weapon. He would not use his old technique. He would not kill. And he would not swear. The thundering of blood in his ears quieted a little, and he felt a measure of calm return to him. The vows reminded him of who he had been, but more so of who he was now. This was not his fight. Haruto would do what needed to be done. He would avenge Tian and put his soul at peace.

"Spiders," Ido Katsuo quavered. "Wonderful."

"You don't like spiders?" Kira asked.

"Horrible things," Ido Katsuo said. "All legs and eyes and furry fangs. And why do they always come scuttling at you instead of running away? Don't they realise I'm bigger than them?"

Kira shouldered him aside as she topped the plateau. "If it makes you feel better, this spider is bigger than you."

"Gah! How is that supposed to make me feel better?"

Laughter echoed out from the gloomy alleyways before them. Guang felt the skin on his arms and neck prickling.

"I love when my prey comes to me," said a woman's voice, accompanied by clicking and chittering. "Come find me, little flies."

Guang noticed Haruto's hand was trembling over his katana. Shiki stroked a hairy arm across his cheek and whistled. He turned wide eyes her way, and she scurried down into his kimono and hid. "Old man?" Guang said, realising it was Tian's anger rattling the onmyoji. So close to Tian's murderer, the rage was consuming him. Or was it Tian reaching down from heaven?

Ido Katsuo cleared his throat. "The steps up to the next tier are at the far end of this plateau. I'm afraid the only way across is through the alleys. I used to have them memorised, but uh... well, that was a long time ago."

Haruto drew his katana and strode into a narrow passage between a pagoda and a squat building that looked like a barracks. He sliced apart the webbing that stretched across it. The strands fell away in thick clumps, and Haruto had to tug on his katana to extricate it from the sticky mess. "Keep up," he hissed as he continued through tangled gossamer. Guang hurried after him and heard the others following behind, the prince complaining to Kira about how creepy it was.

The atmosphere in the alleyways was dank and oppressive. The moaning wind was oddly muted, and no snowflakes fell around them, but it was dark and cold and the snowfall from the roofs crunched underfoot. Haruto slashed through the web across the alley, but many more strands hung down from the eaves, and when they stuck to Guang's coat, they didn't like to let go. More than once he tugged his shoulder free of threads so fine they were all but invisible. The first alleyway ended at the sheer wall of a tall building and split off left and right. Haruto sliced to the left and kept walking, Guang and the others following. The alleyway curved around another building and then split again into three directions. Haruto chose the leftmost and kept going without hesitation or even checking if the others were still behind him. The furore that drove him on worried Guang. At the next junction, Haruto turned to right, slicing and hacking at the webbing as if it were an oncoming army. His katana caught on the sticky threads and he wrenched it to the side so hard the blade struck the stone of a building wall with a shower of sparks. Haruto barely seemed to notice.

A shadow passed overhead, and a laugh like a thousand bells ringing out of rhythm vibrated the sticky web. Haruto swung his sword up, and Guang had to stagger back to dodge the wildly swung blade. He bumped into Ido Katsuo who stumbled into a draping web against the wall. Haruto crouched, preparing to jump up to the eaves and roof above, but Guang rushed forward and put a hand on his friend's shoulder to stop him.

"Look, old man," Guang told him quietly, "I want this monster dead as much as you do, but you can't just run off. We can't split up. That's what she wants."

More mocking laughter drifted down around them. "Cowardly little fly, come face me."

"A little help, please," Ido Katsuo said, trembling. "I'm stuck. I'm stuck! Help help help! Don't leave me!" Guang turned to see the lad was still fixed to the wall, his back and one arm covered in silken threads. Kira flicked a mirrored dagger into her hand and sawed the threads holding the prince in place. He struggled, despite her attempts to stop him, and by the time she freed him he was breathing too fast, his eyes wild like a panicked beast. He started quickly back the way they'd come, but Kira caught him by the arm. She put a hand on his cheek and looked him in the eye. Guang had seen Yanmei do the same thing to Kira once, and now the girl was using the trick on someone else. "It's alright," she said. "You're safe. You're alright."

Ido Katsuo blinked and shook his head vigorously. "Sorry," he said. "I, uh, really don't like spiders. Or their webs. Or being caught in their webs. I'm starting to wish you'd never let me out of my cell."

Kira nodded. "Me too. But then you'd be dead, and Guang would be complaining instead."

"I don't complain. I grumble," Guang said. "There's a difference."

"Enough!" Haruto snapped. He was still standing at the intersection, staring down the alley to the right. "Move. Now." He disappeared down the alleyway.

"Keep up, kids," Guang said, hurrying after him. He turned the corner and saw the old man's back swing left down another turn in the maze. Guang shuffled on and turned left. The wall of a building rose in front of him, and he skidded to a halt in the snow to stop from running into it. Another alley shot off to his right, and he saw Haruto hacking at a web stretching across the far end. Guang ran after him, ignoring his aching knees. "Slow down, old man," he said sharply. "This is Tian's anger, not yours. Don't let it control you."

"You think I don't know that?" Haruto snapped, turning on Guang, a snarl on his face. He struggled to control his breathing. "I've been holding Tian's burden too long, Guang. *Your* son has been in heaven too long." He shook his head and pinched the bridge of his nose. "If I don't send him to Omoretsu soon, he'll start seeping back to earth. Mortal souls can't remain in heaven for this long. My being this close to the jorogumo is drawing him back."

Guang grabbed Haruto's shoulder. "You think I don't want her dead too? For his salvation and my own vengeance? Let's find this spider and squash the onion!"

Haruto blinked and looked up. "Where are the others?"

Chapter 54

"We're lost, aren't we?" Katsuo whined.

They reached the end of another alleyway, a stone wall in front of them, a dead end. Kira sighed and looked back the way they had come. The alley was long, dingy, and littered with snow-dusted crates. They had passed two narrow alleys, one on each side. She had thought maybe if they just kept going straight, they would eventually find their way out. She had been wrong. She cursed whoever had designed this monastery.

"Yes," she said, pushing past Katsuo. She started walking back the way they'd come. "We are definitely lost. Haruto and Guang are probably lost too. And the biggest problem is we're not lost together."

"That's, uh, not very comforting, you know," Katsuo said from close behind her.

"You'd prefer I lie?"

The prince seemed to think about that a moment. "Yes. I think I'd much prefer a nice, cosy lie right now."

Kira stopped at an intersection and cocked her head, listening. She heard a voice cry out from somewhere. "Well tough," she said, still straining to hear. "We're lost. But it sure would've been helpful if someone had memorised these alleys." That shut the prince up for a moment. Kira decided the voices weren't coming from this alleyway and hurried to the next. She glanced up at the rooftops. The webs were thicker there, a grey latticework piled with snow. They might climb to the rooftops and find the way forward, but climbing across the roofs would quickly get them tangled in web.

Kira stopped at the mouth of the next alley and listened. She heard a voice again, louder this time. She didn't recognise it. It sparked a memory of her time in the mirror. A young woman had found her mirror in an antique parlour. She was beautiful, with long dark hair, soft skin, and brown eyes full of smiles and laughter. Kira had shown her terror, had made her watch her own reflection carve bloody wounds into her face with a knife, stabbing needles into her own tongue. The woman dropped the mirror, screaming, and ran from the parlour. And Kira had been alone once more. She shook her head to free herself of the memory. Now that she remembered, they snuck up on her and pounced, triggered by sights or smells or noises. It was distracting.

"Quick," she said and took off, trusting Katsuo would follow her. She ran, slashing her dagger at the silk threads that dangled from the roofs and eaves. Her dagger caught on the webbing, and she tried to jerk it out but it became more tangled. She left it there and flicked a new dagger into her hand. The alley ended in a small square where five alleys met. Against one wall, an old man with no hair and dark veins snaking across his face and a younger woman with a cleft chin, were stuck to the wood in thick swathes of web. The woman was impotently thrashing about, muttering to herself as she tried to struggle free. The man was deathly still. Kira was certain the dark veins were creeping up his cheek toward his eye.

The woman noticed Kira and Katsuo. "Help me!" she yelled. "Quick, before the spider comes back. Get me out of here."

Kira ran to the woman and started sawing at the webbing with her little dagger. It was tough going – the silk was strong and thick as rope. The woman begged her to work faster. Katsuo approached the man and poked his face with a finger. He didn't so much as stir. "What's wrong with him?" the prince asked.

"The spider bit him," the woman with the cleft chin said. "We thought we could beat them. They trained us to fight monsters like them, but... we were wrong. That thing is deadly. We have to get out of here."

Kira sawed away enough web to pull one of the woman's arms from the swathe of thick thread. She handed her the dagger.

"Keep going on that side. I'll cut a hole for your other arm." She flicked another dagger into her hand and started cutting, sweating despite the cold.

"I think he's still alive," Katsuo said. He had leaned in close enough to grab the man's chin. The man's eyes shot open, he drew in a breath, and shrieked. Katsuo staggered back, hands over his ears.

The woman with the cleft chin grimaced and sawed at her cocoon. "Kill him. I've already seen one friend die from it. There's no saving him. He's already dead, and his screaming will bring the spider back."

Kira glanced at the screaming man, watched the dark veins worming up his cheek. Then his eye turned black and popped like a crushed grape, blood and black gore oozing down his face. Kira threw her dagger to Katsuo and flicked another into her hand to keep working on the woman's cocoon. "Do it!"

"Sorry about this," Katsuo shouted to the screaming man. He held the dagger in his hand, trembling in front of the man's face. "Oh bugger it." He switched grip, raised his hand, and plunged the knife down hard on the man's head. The blade sank deep into his skull and the man fell blessedly silent, his limp body still hanging in the web.

"Oh dear," a huffy voice said from above. Kira spun about, dagger ready. Crouched on the eave above them was the jorogumo Xifeng. Her plump body rested easily on the webs, and her spidery legs curled over her shoulders, plucking at the strands of silk. She had two fresh eyes above and below the one Kira had put out, and they stared down at her, big black orbs reflecting the grey sky above. "I love it when they scream."

"I won't die like him!" the woman yelled. Before Kira could stop her, she stabbed Kira's mirrored dagger into her own neck. Blood sprayed onto the silken cocoon and the snow beneath their feet. She gagged and thrashed and finally collapsed halfway to the ground before she stuck there, dangling in the web, dead.

Katsuo tugged on the dagger in the man's skull, cursing and wrenching the corpse's head from side to side. The dagger didn't budge. He gave up and hurried to stand behind Kira. She flicked another dagger into her hand, silently naming this one Pabu, and pressed it into his grip.

Xifeng slipped through the webbing at her feet easily, despite her bulk, and dropped to the ground in a crouch. Her segmented legs tapped at the air like they couldn't bear to stay still for a moment. Her eyes, three orbs erupting through the pallid skin of her face, shifted about from Kira to Katsuo and back again. "Which of you--"

Kira didn't let the spider finish. She whipped a dagger at Xifeng's eyes. The dagger caught in something just a hand's span from those shiny black orbs and dangled there, swinging from its hilt. Xifeng reached a spidery leg over her shoulder and poked at the blade. "This won't go like last time, Little Sister," Xifeng hissed. She pinned the dagger with a chitinous leg from the other side, and in one sharp motion, shattered it between them, a thousand glittering shards bursting into the webs and sparkling there like stars. Kira caught the reflections of the shards and showed Xifeng flames surrounding her, Daizen standing in the mouth of an alleyway, but Xifeng ignored them all. She grinned and clicked her fangs like she was tutting at Kira. "Your childish light tricks won't work on me, Little Sister. I see more than you know."

Kira backed up a step, pushing Katsuo behind her. "I really, really hate spiders," he whispered.

Xifeng stood from her crouch and wobbled a little on her human feet. Her spider legs couldn't do everything at once, and she only had four of them. That meant she couldn't weave her web and scuttle about at the same time. It was a weakness, but Kira wasn't sure how to exploit it. Xifeng waddled another couple of steps toward Kira and stopped. Her spider legs tugged at the mat of webbing above. "I don't have to kill you, Little Sister," she said, cocking her head to the side. "I want to, for what you did to my eye. But all I have to do is stop you from reaching the prison before our siblings do their work. Maybe I'll spin you a cocoon." She clapped her human hands together. "Yes, that's a wonderful idea. I'll spin you a cocoon and you can watch your friend die slowly. I wonder how he tastes."

Kira slowly turned her head and whispered, "Run." Katsuo bolted. She had expected him to argue a little at least. She spun about and sprinted after him.

Behind her, Xifeng laughed. "Oh yes, do run. Hunting you is so much fun."

Haruto stopped hacking at a stretch of webbing and wiped a sheen of sweat from his forehead. "Do you hear that?" he asked.

Guang stopped fishing in his satchel and squinted into space. "Nope."

"I thought I heard screaming, but it's gone now."

The old poet paced. There wasn't much space to do it in the narrow alley, but he made a good show of it at least. "You think it's Kira and the prince?"

"Kira doesn't strike me as the type to scream," Haruto said, hacking at another length of webbing. He'd need to sharpen his sword soon at this rate.

"And the prince?"

Haruto considered that for a moment. "Let's hope it's not them."

"That's just hoping someone else is in danger, though."

Haruto turned on his friend and shook his head. They were wandering blind, hunted by an onryo through a maze covered in spider webs. He couldn't save everyone, especially not a bunch of monks who wanted him as dead as the onryo did. He knew the frustration wasn't his. Tian's feelings were leaking into him. He'd held the man's burden for too long. Tian was drawing closer to him, trying to possess him, and immortality or not, he would not survive that.

"What about fire?" Guang said. He settled down to kneeling on the ground, groaning at some pain, fished in his satchel, and pulled out a little scrap of paper and his flint. "Are you ready, Shiki?"

The little spirit poked its head out of Haruto's kimono, her coarse fur scratching at his chest. She stared up at him, and he nodded, so she leapt onto the ground and waddled closer to Guang, peering curiously at the paper in his hand.

"I'm going to strike a spark and set the paper on fire," Guang explained slowly. "You possess the flame, and we'll burn these carroting webs."

Shiki whistled.

"What did she say, old man?"

"She wants to know why you're speaking so slowly," Haruto answered through clenched teeth.

Guang sighed. "Turnip spirit!" He struck the flint and a spark leapt onto the paper. A few more strikes and it started to crinkle, burn and blacken. Shiki leapt into the flames with pop. The flames grew hotter and turned orange as Shiki eagerly devoured the scrap of paper. Bright eyes stared at Guang out of the flames. "That's always so unnerving."

Shiki crackled.

"She wants to know now what?" Haruto asked.

"Burn the webs," Guang said, pointing at the webbing hanging in sheets across the alley.

Shiki streaked into the air, trailing sparks and plunged into the webbing with a joyous trill. The webs trembled, but they didn't burn. Shiki's eyes narrowed and her flames flared in every direction. Still the webs didn't burn.

Haruto sighed. "So much for that idea."

"Well, at least I *had* an idea, old man."

Haruto bit back a retort and ground his teeth instead. "Out of the way, Shiki."

The little spirit seemed to tremble in the webbing. Her flames shrank and spluttered. She crackled like a damp sparkler.

"What now?" Guang asked.

"She's stuck," Haruto said.

"Stuck? How can fire stick to a web?"

Haruto slumped. Anger always made him so damned tired. Shiki thrashed about in the web, caught like a fly. Her crackles grew louder and more insistent. "Just leave the damned fire,

Shiki!"

Shiki went still, eyes wide. Then she popped out of the fire and leapt to Haruto, her spindly arms catching his kimono, and scurried up onto his shoulder. The fire guttered out, leaving only a small black smudge on the tangle of silken threads.

Haruto turned to Guang. "Any other bright ideas?"

The old poet groaned as he pushed back to his feet, stumbled a step and finally got his balance. He placed a hand against the wall to steady himself and rubbed at his knees. "Cabbage this cold!"

"You always complain about the damned cold," Haruto said.

Guang thumped the wall with his fist. "We're in Ipia," he growled. "It's always cold!" He thumped the wall a second time, and his frown slackened. He thumped it a third time. "Hey, old man, the walls are made of wood."

"So what?"

"Might be easier to break through the wall than cut through the web?"

Haruto opened his mouth to reply, and then shut it again. He stormed over to the wall and kicked once, twice, a third time. A board splintered and snapped inward. He pulled both sides of the broken plank off and threw them into the alleyway. Then he pulled off another board to make the hole big enough for them to pass through and stuck his head through it. Inside was a small room with a wooden cot and straw mattress, and a chest of drawers. The floor was clean, other than the wooden splinters from the broken plank, and there was a half-burned candle on the chest. The place was someone's home, but they had seen no sign of the monks. Haruto turned sideways, steadied his ritual staffs with a hand on the heads, and eased himself through the gap into the room.

"Not all of us are as scrawny as you, old man," Guang said.

Haruto sighed and kicked another board loose. Guang dodged it as it swung toward his sore knees.

"Sorry," Haruto grumbled. Guang grumbled something back at him, but Haruto refused to listen.

Haruto passed through to a second room in the little house. A cupboard stood in one corner, its door half open, several robes hanging inside it. The only other things in the room were a low table on a plush, green rug. The monks lived sparsely by the looks of it, or perhaps these homes were only for sleeping and nothing else. He pulled open the front door to another alleyway. Webbing stretched across the rooftops, but the end of the alleyway itself looked clear. All they had to do was keep the cliff on their right and keep heading forward.

Haruto led them on. Whenever they found themselves blocked, they broke through the wooden buildings. Eventually, they reached the far side of the plateau and the stairs leading up to the second tier.

"You think the other two will figure this out?" Guang asked.

Haruto shrugged. He had a feeling the jorogumo was playing games with them, delaying them. Izumi and the Herald of Bones were likely already at Orochi's grave, and that meant they were running out of time.

A shadow passed overhead, and Kira whipped a dagger up at it. It tangled in the thick webbing and she heard Xifeng laugh. "Same old tricks. Such a weak little sister."

Katsuo turned right the end of the alleyway and slid to a halt so suddenly Kira almost bumped into him. The way ahead was blocked by a thick span of glistening white threads. The corpse of a man hung encased in the sticky silk, his head hanging, his face dripping dark ooze. Katsuo turned around and charged back in the direction they'd come, bumping Kira aside and almost knocking her over. Kira slipped on a patch of ice and braced herself with a hand on the ground, skinning her palm. She ignored the stinging pain, lurched back upright, and sprinted after the fleeing prince. She had seen the panicked bestial look in his eyes as he passed her. She knew that look far too well. He was lost to the fear now. She had caused it in others time and time again during her time in the mirror, scaring people past the point of reason. She shook off the memories and shouted at the prince as she ran. "Katsuo!"

He didn't even glance back at her, just turned right at an intersection and kept running.

Xifeng leapt overhead again, a passing shadow that set her webs trembling. "You're going the wrong way, little sister."

Kira had already realised that. Above the webbing, she saw the cliff face on her left. That meant they were running back toward the stairs down.

"How will you stop, big brother," Xifeng sneered, "if you can't even reach him?"

"Oh shut up!"

Katsuo turned left and disappeared. Kira followed. Pampered prince or not, he ran fast. He was already at the far end of the alleyway. "Katsuo stop! She's herding us." If he even heard her, he gave no sign. He turned left again. Kira followed him and slid to a stop as she came to another small square where several alleyways intersected. Two people were cocooned against a wall: a man with a mirrored dagger in his skull and a woman whose throat was cut. Xifeng had herded them in a circle.

"We have to..." Kira started and then realised she was alone. Katsuo was nowhere in sight. One after another, she peered down the alleyways leading away from the square, but saw no sign of him. Two sets of footsteps in the snow led down one way, but one of them was hers. He was gone, vanished, and Kira was alone with the onryo.

Something thudded heavily on the alley floor behind Kira. "Oh dear," said Xifeng in a sickly sweet voice. "He left you. Poor little sister. So alone."

Kira turned to face the spider. Xifeng stood with her hands clasped before her mouth. She might have looked innocent if not for the hideous eyes and the hairy segmented legs plucking the air, sharp as spears and nimble as a whip.

"They'll leave you, you know. You are not like them. They won't be able to stand you, won't understand what you've become." She waddled forward a step, two long legs tugging at the webbing above her. "They'll push you away, call you hurtful names." She laughed, a discordant cackle like an out of tune guzheng. "They'll call you ugly, a monster, evil. Think themselves better than you." When the onryo took another ponderous step forward, Kira saw something shift behind her, one of her daggers glinting from the shadows of a pagoda wall, moving towards her. Pabu, the dagger she had given to Katsuo. "They can never understand what you have become," Xifeng continued. "And they will try to kill you, Little Sister. They will try to kill you and you will have to eat them. It is the way. And they are quite delicious."

Kira had to stop herself from staring at the shining dagger behind Xifeng. She had to buy time for Katsuo, had to hope he would summon some courage and strike the onryo from behind. "But not you," Kira said. "You wouldn't kill me. You and the other onryo understand me, right?"

"We do," Xifeng said, nodding her head and creeping closer. Her spider legs were almost close enough to stab at Kira. "We're the only ones who can."

"So I should join you?"

Xifeng giggled, opening her mouth enough for Kira to see her rasping, furry chelicerae and her black fangs. "Ah, Little Sister, that would have been nice, wouldn't it? But you think I would let you go after you stabbed your pathetic little knife into my eye?" She roared and lurched at Kira. Kira grabbed Xifeng's human hands, felt a sharp pain in her thigh as a spider leg stabbed into her. Xifeng twisted Kira's wrists, forced her to her knees. She was too strong. Kira could barely hold her clutching hands away from her throat. Xifeng poised her spider legs over Kira's head. "I think I'll start by stabbing one of *your* eyes," she said as the tip of her spidery leg traced a thin cut up Kira's cheek and hovered over her eye.

Kira saw the dagger flash behind the onryo and Xifeng shrieked, flailing her spider legs. The onryo reared up on her human legs, spun around and slammed into Katsuo. One flailing spider leg caught Kira in the face and sent her tumbling away in the dusting of snow and smashing into a wall. She shook away the dizziness and the spots in her vision.

Xifeng had the prince pinned on the ground of the alley, her human hands on his shoulders. She stabbed him in the thigh with a spider leg and he screamed as blood spattered the snow. Then she leaned her head down and bit him on the neck.

Kira felt the world close in on her as she stared at the fat spider straddling Katsuo, pressing him to the ground, sinking her fangs into his flesh. She saw her dagger glinting in Xifeng's back, between where the onryo's right two spider legs grew from her human flesh. It was her dagger. She had created it. She had a connection to it. She had named it Pabu. And then the world came rushing back in and Kira was standing right behind Xifeng, her hand wrapped around the hilt. She heard something shatter behind her, an image of herself she had left behind, but had no time to figure it out. She twisted the dagger in Xifeng's back and tore it out in a spray of black gore. Xifeng screamed again, pulled her fangs from Katsuo's neck, and whipped around to face Kira. Kira jabbed the dagger deep into the spider's right eye.

Xifeng screeched and staggered back. One of her spider legs caught Kira in the shoulder and sent her stumbling, but she kept her feet and backed away. Xifeng flailed her legs in the air, clawed her face with her hands, Kira's dagger, Pabu, still sticking out of her eye. With a single thought, Kira shattered the dagger. A thousand glass shards filled the oozing wound and carved up Xifeng's face. The spider stumbled, screaming, blood spraying the snow. She reached her spider legs up, latched on to the webbing above them, and hauled herself up on the roof of the pagoda and out of sight, her howls fading into the distance.

Kira bent over, hands on her thighs, panting, pounding heart drowning out all other sound. Her cheek stung from the cut, and she felt blood dripping down her cheek and off her chin. She pressed the sleeve of her kimono against the wound to slow the bleeding and ran to Katsuo. He was lying in the snow, writhing on the ground, arms and legs spasming. Kira slid to her knees beside him, clutched his hand as he thrashed and tried to hold him still. His eyes whirled in their sockets. He clutched her hand so hard she felt her bones grinding, and pounded the ground with his other fist. Dark veins spread out from the wound in his neck, spread up his chin and down his arm to his hand. He clenched his jaw so hard Kira heard his teeth cracking; then he opened his mouth and screamed. She held his hand, not knowing what else to do. She could not save him or prevent Xifeng's venom from spreading through his veins. She was helpless. Tears blurred her vision and she held his hand, watching the venom eat him alive.

The dark veins spread to his lips and the colour drained from them. He stopped screaming and coughed ink-black blood over his chin. His wide-eyed gaze seemed to meet hers for a moment and he nodded to her; then another spasm took him and he screamed again, blood spraying out of his mouth. Kira wrenched her hand from his and flicked a dagger into it. She held it over his chest, blinked away tears, and tried to meet his gaze once more, but he was too far gone. Then she leaned down, pushing her weight against the dagger and drove it down into his heart.

Katsuo's short, frantic breaths eased. And finally, his face went slack, and she felt his body go still beneath her.

Kira let go of the dagger and gripped his hand in hers again. She knelt by his side, numb and raw all at once. She wanted to rage, to run, to scream and fight. The onryo who claimed to be family had taken another friend from her. First Yanmei and now Katsuo. She would make her family pay. They all had to die.

Kira wiped her eyes and stood slowly, still staring down at the prince. Some part of her hoped he would sit up, that it would all be a joke. She shook her head at her foolishness. He was gone and he wasn't coming back. She didn't have time to bury or burn his body. No prayers she could offer him would mean a damn. All she could give Katsuo now was vengeance.

Chapter 55

Guang was so pleased to leave the first tier behind that he all but leapt up the steps toward the second despite the stabbing pain in his knees. Between the maze of alleyways, the mass of webs, and the mocking laughter of the spider, he'd suffered gut wounds that were a more pleasant experience. They'd waited at the bottom of the steps for a while, staring out over the buildings of the first plateau. Homes, workshops, and warehouses all crammed together with barely space for a breath between them. They saw no sign of Kira or the prince. The occasional shout or scream drifted from somewhere, but it echoed strangely like a wolf's howl in a valley. Haruto saw the spider's shadow scurry across the rooftops a few times, but there was no way for them to reach her and she always disappeared back into the maze. They couldn't wait any longer. If the jorogumo was here, then the Herald of Bones was too, and that meant they had to stop him from freeing the dragon. They had no time to waste with the jorogumo's distractions.

"She'll catch up," Haruto said, turning and storming up the steps two at a time. Guang wasn't certain if he meant Kira or the jorogumo, but he hurried after his friend all the same.

The air at the second plateau was even colder than below. In the alleyways it had been icy, but up here the chill bit at Guang's face. His breath puffed out in a freezing mist that clung to his beard, and the cold clawed through his coat and tunic, icing along his skin and frosting up his spine.

The second plateau was much smaller than the first, but it was covered in large patches of rippling black feathers. Guang and Haruto stood at one end of an open square packed with footprints in the snow, surrounded by five large buildings that Ido

Katsuo had told them were dojos for the monks to train in martial arts, each one with a different symbol carved into the wood above the door. Guang peered at the closest mound of twitching darkness and saw a raven raise its head from the squirming mass, a bloody gibbet in its beak. The bird had no eyes, only scratched scars where they should have been.

"Well, that's grim," Guang said. His stomach turned at the sight. There had to be thousands of the birds, clustered in groups around mounds of corpses.

"They're here," Haruto growled. The savage intensity in his voice startled Guang, and before he knew what he was doing, he'd sidestepped away from his old friend.

As they started forward, a dark, bulbous shape to their right scurried up the cliff face from the first tier. The jorogumo was just a hundred paces away. She staggered forward, clutching her face; then she sniffed the air and turned to look at them. Her right eye was a fleshy mound of oozing gore and twinkling shards of glass.

"You die here!" Haruto roared, drawing his katana and striding forward.

The jorogumo scuttled back, cackling. "Not yet, onmyoji," she said. "I need to thin your number a bit more first." With that, she leapt into the air, dragging on a line of silk, and soared over the dojo rooftops towards the cliff side on their left, then scurried up and disappeared over the edge onto the third tier. Haruto growled and continued on, wading through the ankle deep snow, his katana still clutched in his fist. Guang hurried after him.

As one, the ravens all screamed and launched into the air, taking flight in a dizzying thrashing of black wings. Guang paled at the sight they left behind. Hundreds of corpses were scattered about the square in bloody heaps. In some places the bodies were three or four deep, in others sole corpses lay in red splotches on the white snow.

"What do you think she meant by thinning our number a bit more?" Guang asked.

Haruto glanced over his shoulder, his teeth bared in a snarl.

He shook his head, turned back around and kept walking.

One of the dojo doors rattled in the breeze, and Haruto and Guang stopped and stared at it. Haruto's breath hissed through clenched teeth, his brow furrowed in an angry snarl. Guang worried about him. The old man had been carrying Tian's burden for too long. If Haruto didn't kill the spider soon, the spirit of Guang's son would come screaming back from heaven and corrupt his friend, and he'd lose them both.

"Look at the weapons," Haruto said, gesturing to the corpses strewn around them.

Guang glanced about again and cursed himself a fool for having missed it. Some of the bodies were dismembered, arms, legs, heads all scattered about. Others were run through by spear or sword, or beaten to death by fist or mace. But one thing was clear, the jorogumo had not killed these monks, they had murdered each other.

"The Herald of Bones did this," Guang said. "Caused them to turn on each other. That's what he does in all the stories. Causes madness, incites war. Tuns brother against brother and all that."

Haruto nodded slowly. Shiki whistled. One of the dojo doors slid open and Haruto snapped his head around. A hulking woman in a monk's robe stood there, filling the doorway. She held a spear in each hand and a bloody symbol was carved into the flesh of her forehead. The same symbol hung carved into a wooden sign above the dojo doorway. She stepped out of the doorway, and a dozen monks rushed out behind her, all armed, all with the same symbol carved into their scabbed and bleeding foreheads.

Another dojo door opened and more armed and branded monks streamed forth, these with a different symbol carved into the foreheads. They waved their weapons, shouted challenges, and spit insults at the monks of the other dojo. Then a third dojo door opened, and a fourth, and the last. Hundreds of monks charged out into the courtyard, screamed their hatred to the stars.

"Get behind me!" Haruto snarled, stepping in front of

Guang. The first monk to reach them was a skinny old man, blood streaming from his forehead down the sides of his nose. He swung his Nash sabre wildly at them. Haruto stepped aside from the blow and sliced the man from groin to neck with his katana. The man fell to the ground, writhing and bleeding out in the snow.

"Did you see his eyes?" Guang asked.

Haruto didn't answer. The hulking woman with two spears was on him. Her eyes twitched, darting about like a bird's. She screamed and stabbed at Haruto. He dodged the thrust and darted in, but she rammed the shaft her other spear into his shoulder and knocked him to the ground. Haruto grunted and tried to roll away, but the giant woman plunged a spear through his shoulder and pinned him to the ground. She raised her other spear and stabbed it down into Haruto's chest. He groaned and coughed blood on his kimono. The woman stepped away, raised her meaty fists in the air and roared a wordless victory cry. Haruto grit his teeth, pulled the spear from his shoulder, and sat up. The hulking woman stared down at him, cocked her head, and booted Haruto in the face, knocking him back down.

The woman raised her hands again, but her victory roar was cut short when a spear tip jutted from her throat in a gout of blood. She staggered, reaching up for the spear haft, then toppled over, spewing blood onto the snow.

Haruto pulled the spear from his chest, and Guang helped him to his feet. He scooped his katana, and they both watched a battle taking place in the small square. There were no battle lines to the furious melee, no orders being given, no sense in it at all. Monks attacked monks in a chaotic free-for-all. Guang watched a bearded monk with a wood-chopping axe cut down a woman with a naginata and a different symbol carved into her head. Then a fat monk ran through the bearded monk with a spear. In some places the combat was furious, bloody, and quick. In others, the monks traded blows, gaining no ground. Guang and Haruto stood at the edge of it all, while Haruto's wounds healed. Unfortunately, Guang noticed that the stairs to the third tier were right in the thick of the fighting. Either they had to wait for the monks to kill each other, and hope the Herald of Bones took his sweet time resurrecting Orochi, or they had to wade into the combat and try to make it through.

"Another delay tactic," Haruto said. "I am done being delayed. Either keep up or run away and hide." He strode forward, katana in hand, straight into the melee.

Haruto sliced the arm off a lanky monk before most of them even realised he was there. It flopped to the trampled snow, and the man who'd recently been attached to it wailed and careened away, blood spurting from his shoulder stump. Haruto slipped around a spear thrust, snapped the haft with an elbow strike, stabbed his katana into the woman's neck, jerked it back out with a twist and strode on through the melee. Guang followed.

An elderly monk leapt in front of Haruto, dagger in hand. Haruto stumbled on the severed leg of a corpse and took a slash across the chest that would have killed another man. Haruto caught the old monk's wrist, twisted until bones snapped, then gutted the man with his katana. The old monk fell away, clutching at his steaming intestines. Guang followed Haruto closely, grimacing at the slaughter and the stench of blood and viscera.

Guang wasn't just bewildered by the monks killing each other in their strange battle frenzy, he was astounded by Haruto's part in it. The old man was always so careful about saving people, not harming them. To see him wilfully taking part in such slaughter... it wasn't him. It couldn't be. It had to be Tian, but even that was a betrayal of his son's spirit. Tian had hated senseless slaughter; that was why Guang and the boy had fallen out all those years ago. To see his friend and his son's spirit twisted like this was like rusty daggers stabbing into Guang's heart.

A woman with blood streaming down her face backed into Guang and sent him stumbling. She spun about, dao raised and ready to cut him in half. Guang brushed the falling sword aside with one hand and pushed the woman in the chest with the other. She toppled backwards, tripped over a headless torso and fell.

Haruto turned and jumped on her, and drove his katana blade through her chest. "Don't fall behind!" he growled, and strode back into the melee towards the stairs.

Guang wanted to shout at his friend, to tell him he didn't have to kill the woman, but now was not the time. She would have likely died anyway. All because the Herald of Bones and whatever hypnotic technique he possessed had driven the monks mad. A tengu, a demon drawn to war, to creating chaos and death, he was probably feeding off it as well, growing stronger as the men and women of the monastery murdered one another.

Haruto took another spear thrust to the gut. He grabbed the haft and turned his body, pulling the spear wielder off balance and dragging her close, slashed and cut two wide gashes in the monk's chest and she fell away, dead before she hit the ground. Guang ducked a katana slicing at his head, brushed aside a thrust with his palm. The monk roared and leapt at him. Haruto thrust his katana over Guang's shoulder and stabbed the monk in the eye. The monk stumbled, clutching at the bloody socket, and fell to a knee. Haruto danced around Guang and kicked the monk over. Then he pushed Guang to the stairway. "Move, you old fool!"

Guang stubbed his toe on the first step, howled in pain and hissed the name of every vegetable he'd ever eaten. Haruto whipped blood from his katana and marched up the steps two at a time. Guang looked back at the monks fighting, killing each other. As horrific as it was, he knew it was only the beginning. Unless they stopped the Herald of Bones, this slaughter would be nothing compared to the carnage Orochi would wreak.

Chapter 56

Haruto's anger was a weight on his shoulders, pressing him down into a tight little ball begging to explode. He took each step a little faster until he was struggling not to run. Guang laboured up the steps behind him, huffing and puffing and groaning. Guang's veiled bellyaching tugged at Haruto's nerves; he had to clench his teeth to stop from snapping at his old friend. The damned monk skirmish was nothing but a delay, preventing him from reaching the jorogumo, from taking his revenge. He'd see her dead, dismembered, carved up, her head on a spike. Then he would turn his attention to the Herald of Bones and see just how much it takes to kill a tengu.

Shiki let out a tremulous whistle from his shoulder and he glared at her. "Quiet!" he snapped. The little spirit flinched, almost fell from his shoulder.

At the top of the steps, he stopped for a moment to survey the third plateau. It was mostly empty, flat ground covered in ankle-deep snow. At the far end, a large temple loomed, casting a long grey shadow on the snow-white plain. The door to the temple was hanging off its hinges, and an elderly monk lay dead on the portico. In the centre of the plateau stood a huge, solitary sakura tree that the monks had somehow coaxed into bloom despite the frigid weather. A fool's attempt to warn off evil spirits. Clusters of pink petals clung to its branches, and many more had blown away and scattered on the snowy ground. Thick coils of silken web hung down from the tree's branches. Haruto saw movement within the cradle of blossoms. He gripped his sword so tightly his hands trembled.

The jorogumo slid slowly down a thick strand of web and plopped onto the snowy ground, squatting on her human legs, her spidery ones plucking at the air. Dark gore ran from the mound of mangled flesh that had been her right eye, and her two left eyes, above and below the first puckered scar, were dark and unfathomable.

Haruto stepped toward the onryo, foot sinking into the snow, hand hovering over the hilt of his katana, and felt Guang's hand on his shoulder. The poet shook his head and pointed to another set of winding steps carved into the rock, leading up to the fourth and final plateau. To Orochi's prison.

"She's nothing but a distraction, old man," Guang said. "Trying to delay us so her master can free the dragon."

"Then I best finish her quickly," Haruto growled, clenching his jaw so tight his muscles ached.

"She's a creature of traps," Guang said. "Think about it. You're fighting on her ground. She's had time to prepare. You have to go. Now."

"I can't leave her behind us," Haruto said. "She'll strike at our backs." He stretched his neck, trying to relive the coiled tension.

"I know..."

Something glinted in the failing light to their left. A dagger thrown from the plateau below. It soared up, hung in the air for just a moment; then Kira appeared, holding the knife in her hand. She dropped onto the snowy plateau and teetered on the edge of the cliff before lurching forward away from the drop.

The jorogumo hissed at her.

"Impressive entrance, girl," Guang said.

Kira stalked toward them, frowning, her eyes red and puffy. A wound on her cheek looked almost like a brush stroke, red ink running and dripping from her chin. "I finally figured out the technique Yanmei was trying to teach me. She called it stepping through the world."

"Where's the prince?" Guang asked.

The skin around Kira's eyes darkened, but there was no shattering noise. She turned to glare at the jorogumo. "She killed him," Kira said, her voice thin and quiet.

The jorogumo laughed and crept behind the trunk of the sakura tree. "Did the last of the Ido family die screaming? Or did *you* put him out of his misery, sister?"

Kira growled and flung her dagger at the onryo. It caught in a tangle of nearly invisible silken threads draping from the tree. Kira flicked another dagger into her hand. Haruto nodded at her. "You go left, I'll go right. We strike together and give her nowhere to run."

Kira pursed her lips. The darkness around her eyes was almost black, but her eyes themselves were clear. "Her venom is deadly. Don't get bitten."

Guang sighed. "Enough!" He gestured to the steps leading up to the fourth plateau. "You two go. Stop them freeing Orochi. This fight is mine." He barked a humourless laugh. "As it always should have been."

Haruto stared at the snowy ground, shaking his head. "Guang--"

"Haven't you figured it out yet, old man?" Guang snapped, glaring at him. "You can't protect us all the time. You can't fight everyone else's battles for them all the time. Your cabbaged immortality won't see you through every fight, and you cannot use it as an excuse to coddle us. This fetid onion is my fight. Tian was my son. Mine! I spent a lifetime failing him. I won't fail him now. If I have done nothing else for him, I will help his spirit rest. No matter the cost."

"Your vows..."

"Don't you dare doubt my resolve," Guang roared. "Not you, old man. Of everyone, not you."

Haruto held his friend's gaze, saw the determination there. It wasn't anger or hatred that drove Guang; it was compassion. But it couldn't be enough, not against an onryo. Shiki trumpeted a low note, and Haruto knew he was beaten. When Shiki and Guang agreed on something, he had to admit they were probably right.

"What did she say?" Guang asked.

Haruto put a hand on Guang's shoulder. "She said don't you dare die!"

Guang smiled sadly. "I'm not planning on it, you little radish."

Haruto patted Guang's shoulder, then walked away towards the steps to the fourth plateau. Kira followed him but stopped in front of Guang. "She killed Katsuo."

Guang grunted. "I'll make sure he doesn't have a reason to come back."

Kira nodded and wrapped her arms around the old poet. He hugged her back, and then she pulled away and hurried after Haruto.

"Oh no," the jorogumo whined. "Don't go, onmyoji. I want my meal to be a challenge."

Haruto paused and glared at the spider. "You have no idea who you are facing here." He forced his anger into a tight smile. "Fighting me would have been getting off easy." With that, he continued toward the steps. He hoped he wasn't wrong, that he wasn't leaving his friend to die a gruesome death, but he had to trust Guang. He had to believe the old poet knew what he was doing for his son. Besides, Haruto had his own battle to fight. He started up the last stone stairway, Kira just a couple of paces behind him.

Guang watched Haruto and Kira ascend the steps to the fourth plateau, keeping an eye on the jorogumo. She didn't move. She crouched behind the sakura tree, one human hand on its trunk, her spidery legs waving in the air, weaving her silken web. She had laid traps for him on the plateau, she must have. He needed to be careful.

When Haruto and Kira were out of sight, he relaxed a little. He could do what needed to be done and not worry about what his friends would see. He walked toward the cherry tree, feet crunching in the snow, pulled his satchel around, and reached inside it.

"I thought you'd be in more of a rush, yokai," Guang said, his hand brushing the rolled papers of his vows. He flinched away from them as if they burned. They were usually so comforting, but now... he had carried them for so long, both the paper scrolls and the true burden of them on his spirit.

The spider cocked her head and stared at him with her two inhuman eyes. "You think I was here to stop you?" She laughed, scraping furrows down the tree bark with her sharp fingernails. "Foolish fly. My job was only to thin the herd. The onmyoji was never my prey to devour."

Guang stopped and glanced at the steps to the fourth plateau. If the spider was telling the truth, then the Herald of Bones knew they were coming. It was a trap. One they hadn't merely walked into, but had run into head first. He had to warn Haruto.

"Are you thinking of running now, little fly?" the jorogumo said, shifting completely out of sight behind the tree trunk. "Up and up and up the steps to warn your friends. Do you think you'll make it? It's a long way to go with your back turned."

Guang knew he'd never make it. With his stiff knees, it would be slow going. The spider would scuttle up the cliff face and pick him off with ease. No, his best bet was to fight her here. To beat her and stop her from joining the assault against Haruto and Kira.

Guang continued his slow march toward the sakura tree. The snow was ankle deep, dotted with pink blossoms. She had all the advantages. This was her lair. He reached inside his satchel once again, pulled out a scroll of paper and held it up, just a few paces from the tree. Between the cherry blossoms and the draping webs, he couldn't see the jorogumo, but he was certain she saw him.

"Do you know what this is?" Guang asked. Silence greeted him. He unfurled the scroll and looked down at the words written on it, at the signature in his own blood. "It's my first vow," Guang continued. "I took this vow and three others many years ago. They are my promise to be a better person. For the sake and love of my son, I promised not to be the monster I once was." He stared accusingly at the tree. The onryo was there somewhere. "Well, you murdered my son!" he roared. "Because of you, he came back as a yokai and because of you he cannot move on. How can I hope to be a better person if I allow him to linger full of hatred and spite? He was never like that. I was that person, but not him. I gave it up for him. For my son... For Tian, I will give up everything again!" He exhaled slowly, steadying himself for what he had to do. "I will become the monster one last time."

The spider laughed from somewhere behind the sakura tree or among the tangled sheets of webbing across its branches. "He died in such pain, your son. I remember that little fly. How he screamed. How his blood tasted like sweet plums. I wonder if yours will taste the same."

Guang ground his teeth and took his vow in both hands. "My first vow. Never again to bear arms." He tore the scroll in two. His vows were not just promises, they were locks, each one a prison for his qi, a physical barrier as surely as a spiritual one. That qi returned to him now in a rush that chased away his cold, his exhaustion and the aches of age. Snow and petals rose around him, twirling and twisting in the eddies of his energy. He felt younger, stronger, and he felt rage rushing through his blood like a flooding river.

The spider swung slowly down from the tree and plopped to the ground on her human feet. Her spidery legs weaving together a hundred silky threads. "Is that it, fly? I expected more."

Guang reached into his satchel again and pulled out a strip of paper and his ink pot. He dipped the brush in the ink, then slashed a single word across the paper: *dao.* The paper twisted and folded and wrapped around itself; it became a sword, slightly curved, a single edge sharp as a paper cut. He shoved the ink pot back inside his satchel and gripped the dao hilt in both hands. It was so like the sword he had carried when he was young. It felt good to hold a weapon again. It felt right. And he hated that rightness.

Guang fixed the spider with glare and advanced towards her. "This is for you, Tian."

Chapter 57

Guang lurched into a run, swinging his sword in a poor imitation of the old forms he once knew. He was rusty, and it showed with every movement and every twinge and pang that shot through his aching joints. He shouted a battle cry that would once have inspired him and the bandits that followed him, but even that sounded old and gravelly. A few paces before the tree, his trailing foot snagged on something and he fell forward on hands and knees. Something wrenched his foot upwards, and he cried out. The spider giggled, still crouching by the tree trunk, tugging on a thread of silk with her human hands. She hoisted Guang up by his leg into the morass of sticky strands. He swiped his paper dao up and around, its edge as sharp as any steel, cut through the silk, and dropped back to the snow-padded ground. The jorogumo pounced at him on her human legs.

Guang surged back to his feet, swinging his dao, whipping a plume of powdery snow into the spider's face. He slashed at her, but she raised a spider leg, blocking the strike with a clang like metal against porcelain; she shoved his blade away and stabbed him in the thigh with a single spider leg. Pain shot through Guang and he stumbled back, slashing his sword left and right at her bladed feet.

It was a poor match no matter how he looked at it. She was stronger than him and faster too. He was sluggish, the old forms all bumps and angles instead of smooth, speedy strikes. She had four serrated feet on long segmented legs and a mouthful of black fangs he didn't even want to think about. What he wouldn't do for his old ceramic armour; even battered and dented and blood-stained as it was, it would be better than standing here in his ragged trousers and cloak.

The jorogumo tugged a silk thread with her spider leg, and Guang's paper sword jerked to the side. He twisted the blade until the edge bit through the web, but the jorogumo was already on him. She stabbed a foot at him, cutting a hole in his coat. He brought his sword up to parry another, but it skidded off his blade and struck him in the head, knocking him back and slicing his forehead. Blood spilled down his face into his eyes and mouth, and he cried out. He spat the metallic taste from his lips, blocked another spidery leg and pressed his weight on it with his paper blade. The jorogumo's spider leg bent under his dao, and she staggered back until she caught her own footing and thrust two more spider legs at him. He tried to leap away, but she jabbed a foot into his thigh just above his knee that sent blood sheeting down his leg into his trousers.

Guang collapsed onto one knee and the spider leapt at him, three legs stabbing. He rolled in the snow, leaving a bloody print behind, and rose slashing with his paper sword. The blade bit deep into the jorogumo's human hand, slicing flesh and crushing bone. She screamed, scuttled away cradling her arm, and backed behind the tree. Her sobbing was sweet music to Guang's ears and he chuckled as he climbed back to his feet, knees popping, using his sword as a crutch.

"It's all starting to come back to me," Guang said through panting breaths. When had he gotten so out of shape? He rolled his shoulders and leaned into a couple of a leg stretches. He was dripping blood onto the snow beneath him. If he didn't finish her soon, the jorogumo could just wait until he collapsed. She was still hiding behind the sakura tree, crying in pain and cradling her mangled human hand. "What's the matter, you ugly onion, can't heal yourself like your friend Shin? Well, I guess we know who the weakest of the onryo is."

The tree shook and a cascade of pink petals and snow floated down around Guang. He stepped back and raised his sword. The spider stopped sobbing, but he didn't see her anywhere. Then she dropped from the branches and landed behind him, two spider legs stabbing at him. He parried one, but the other sunk deep into his side. He screamed and slashed down with his blade, trying to sever her leg, but the edge hit the armoured spider leg and thudded to a halt. The jorogumo lurched forward, stabbing all her spider legs at him. Guang twisted away, the spider leg in his side ripping away in a spurt of blood, ducked under her other legs and swung his sword up at her fat belly. The paper sword stopped dead, its bladed edge inches from her flesh. He tugged on the hilt, but it didn't budge. It was wrapped in a cocoon of glistening web. She jerked a silken strand with her remaining human hand, and his sword flew from his grasp and skidded across the snow. Then she pounced on him.

A spidery leg punched into his shoulder. He tried to scream, but her hands closed around his face and she ground his head into the base of the tree trunk. From the corner of his eye, he saw her mouth opening and her gleaming black fangs twitching behind her lips. Guang put his left hand up to block her, and she sank her fangs into his arm.

The pain was so intense he couldn't even scream. He was done. He couldn't move from beneath her, and her venom was deadly. He had failed, and Tian and Haruto would suffer because of it.

The jorogumo shifted, pulled her fangs from his flesh, and backed away. Guang groaned as he rolled to his feet, feeling every bit his exhausted, creaky old self. He stood unsteadily, swaying, agony paralysing his arm. He pulled back the sleeve of his coat and saw black veins spreading out from the two puncture wounds, snaking over the back of his hand.

The onryo giggled. "Scream, little fly. Scream and scream and scream until you die!"

The fourth plateau was the smallest yet. At the top of the steps was a little more than a ledge. A wooden shack stood at the far end, nestled in between the cliff wall on one side, and a sheer the drop on the other. A great double door hung ajar at a large cave mouth that led into the rock of the cliff. The snow was thick there, almost knee deep, and a set of tracks led from the stairs to the door, a black trail of soot beside them, grey beneath a dusting of fresh snow. The tengu and Izumi were already inside. Haruto had to hurry.

Kira pulled her coat a little tighter and edged around Haruto, heading for the door. The wind was gusting at this level, snow whipping down from the top of the cliff a hundred feet above, blowing into their faces. They followed the Herald of Bones' tracks to the cave mouth, Kira walking on top of the snow, Haruto slogging through it. The doors were carved with an intricate relief, a story written in pictures of the Century Blade and his band of heroes defeating the king of dragons. Perhaps there was a message there, a clue how to accomplish an impossible feat, but they had no time to study it and Haruto couldn't focus on the pictures, not when his enemies were so close. Kira slipped through the gap in the door and Haruto followed.

After the howling wind and dizzying blizzard outside, it was almost peaceful in the cave. The solid stone all around muted the wind, and a pleasant warmth hung in the air like a kitchen a few hours after the last oven had gone out. The cave was enormous, five times as tall as Haruto and wide enough for six carts to roll abreast. Sconces in the walls were fixed with iron lanterns burning away to illuminate the space. Haruto smelled blood on the air and saw dark shadows on the floor further in. More monks defending the prison, he guessed. Kira glanced at him and he shrugged. "Stay close," he whispered.

They walked side by side, tense and ready. Haruto held his katana in a loose one-handed grip. Shiki rode on his shoulder, chattering away at him in endless breathy whistles. She always nattered at him when she was scared, and she was terrified. He didn't answer her, but he was secretly grateful for the little spirit's chatter. It bolstered his own courage.

The first body they came across was blackened by soot stains around his face. His eyes were wide and his neck raked bloody by his own hands. It was Izumi's dirty work. She had suffocated the man in smoke, just as she herself had suffocated all those centuries ago. This was the true curse of the onryo and all yokai – they forever perpetuated their own pain in others. Haruto glanced at Kira.

He heard breathing on the air, deep and slow and so loud it had to come from a giant. Kira heard it too and tugged on Haruto's sleeve. "Have they already done it?" she whispered. "Is Orochi free?"

Haruto considered that. When the onryo had freed Sekiryu, the dragon had burst out of Sky Hollow, tearing apart rock, stone, and anyone who stood in his way. Surely Orochi's freedom would come with even greater ruin. Haruto shrugged. "Only one way to find out." They crept deeper into the shadowy cave.

The cave soon opened up into an even greater cavern that stretched into the darkness and beyond. Its floor, walls, and ceiling were roughhewn stone straight from the cliff. Pillars ringed with torches stretched from floor to ceiling, and the entire hall was festooned with long red banners hanging down from the roof high above, almost trailing on the floor. Corpses of monks were scattered everywhere. This was the place. Many of the monks looked like they had hacked each other to pieces; others appeared to have been torn apart or lay in patches of dark soot, and the stench of blood filled the air. To their left, at the far end of the cavern, in a gap between the hanging banners, was a great circular relief carved in a language Haruto didn't recognise. A giant stone statue of a dragon stood at either side of the relief, and below it sat a man in a feathered cloak, wearing a tengai over his head. Finally, Haruto would meet this Herald of Bones.

"It's about time you showed up," the Herald of Bones said. He didn't move, but beneath that bamboo bucket over his head, he might have been staring straight at them.

Haruto cast about, trying to spot Izumi, but there was no trace of her. Then again, she could be anywhere, hidden behind one of the hanging banners. He tapped Kira on the shoulder and pointed to the right of the Herald of Bones. She nodded and slipped away around hanging red cloth. Haruto nodded at Shiki. The little spirit shrugged. He nodded at her again and held up his katana. She leapt into the sword, turning the blade crimson.

"I must applaud you, Little Sister," the Herald of Bones continued, his tengai turning. Kira froze mid-stride as though pinned in place, staring at the tengu. "You held up your end of the agreement and delivered the onmyoji as promised."

"What?" Kira said. "I... I didn't..." She shook her head and looked at Haruto. "No. It wasn't me. It's a lie..." Haruto slipped around a banner with golden thread stitched into it, and looked at Kira, then back to the tengu.

The Herald of Bones shifted and stood, a gigantic man, tall and broad as a bear. His cloak was a myriad of shifting black that confused the eye. His hands were thin and wrinkled, and each finger ended in a dark talon. And beneath his tengai were eyes that swirled with more colours than Haruto could name. Just looking into those eyes, Haruto felt a bloodlust kindling within him, the need to rush in and lose himself in the brutality of combat. He glanced again at Kira and felt an urge to strike her down before she turned on him. Of course she was working against him. One of the onryo. His enemy.

"She is rather convincing, isn't she," said the tengu. He spread his arms wide, and Haruto saw a black, serrated katana dangling from his hip. "I've been waiting a long time for this, Nightsong."

He knew Haruto's name, his old name. How could he...

"I didn't know, Haruto," Kira cried, walking toward him, brushing aside a hanging banner and setting it spinning. "He's lying."

"Shut up!" Haruto shouted. Fury thrummed in his ears. Kira had betrayed him. She'd been one of the onryo all along, spying on them and leading them along. But that couldn't be right. Yanmei had died to protect them, to protect Kira. Kira would never work with the monster who murdered her mother. Would she?

"You have no friends here, Nightsong," the Herald of Bones said, his eyes boring into Haruto, blue then green then yellow then gold. A maddening whirlpool that sucked him down and drowned him. "No allies. No hope. You have already failed. You have always failed. It is who you are, who you have always been. A failure."

The tengu's words screamed in his head. Ugly, indomitable truth laid bare. The anger bubbling inside of him was consuming him. It wasn't his, but he couldn't separate himself from it. Shiki whistled, but he couldn't understand what she was saying. Kira was walking towards him, holding her hands up, ready to stab him in the back. She was talking too. They were all talking, a cacophony of words that meant nothing. Haruto closed his eyes, trying to hide from the hypnotic madness in the tengu's eyes, trying to clear his head, but Tian waited for him in the darkness, deformed face snarling and demanding vengeance.

Haruto opened his eyes again. Kira stood before him, reaching out to him. She could flick a dagger into her hand in an instant. Haruto staggered back a step, raised his katana and swung at her neck.

Chapter 58

Guang grunted, pulled his satchel round and fished inside it once more. His sword was lying in the snow, soggy and limp with his blood. "You know," he said, grimacing, agony pumping through his veins. "I wasn't always a poet. I used to be a bandit and had quite the reputation for being far too good at it too." His bitten arm spasmed, his fingers twitching. He pulled out another scroll. "This is my fourth vow, never to use my technique again." He tore the scroll in half and let the pieces float to the ground. A rush of qi flooded through him, the river threatening to burst its banks. He felt his blood stir, his old technique locked away for so long, begging to be used again.

The jorogumo crouched by the tree, ready to spring. "You used your technique to make the sword."

Guang forced a laugh through the pain. "I used *a* technique, you stupid onion!" He placed his right hand over the bite on his arm and concentrated on the venom pumping through him. "Back then," he said through gritted teeth as he pulled the venomous blood out of his arm, "I was known as Blood Dancer." He dragged the last of the infected blood from his arm and used his technique to form it into a solid, crimson spear. "I'll give you one guess what my technique was." He steadied himself and launched the blood spear at the jorogumo.

The spider screamed and threw herself sideways. The spear sailed past her and hit the ground, breaking apart and splattering across the snow. Guang drew more blood from his body, streaming into his hands from a dozen cuts, and fused it into a crimson dao. Then he used his technique to seal his wounds, forcing the blood to clot and scab. When it was done, he stood there holding the dao and panting from the effort. It had once been so easy to manipulate his blood like that, but now it seemed like the stuff resisted him. Age or disuse had slowed him.

Guang spun the blood sword in his hand, reminding himself of the feel of it. It came flooding back as surely as any addiction, the weight of it, the balance, a reassuring extension of his self. The heady rush of his technique flowed through his veins, pulsing with his heart. The power of his qi, always so strong, but never constant. Kira's qi might be a raging river, ever flowing, but Guang's had always been like a flash flood that wiped away everything in its path and then receded, leaving behind only destruction and ruin.

The onryo cowered behind the tree, watching him through her inhuman eyes, spidery legs scraping against each other hungrily. Her four weapons to his one was a problem. Guang decided he needed to do something about that.

He launched into a run, knees aching but his qi keeping them from buckling. The jorogumo yelped and grasped for a strand of web above, but Guang dashed in and struck with his blood dao. It clanged off her segmented leg. He spun and slashed again, but this one, too, glanced off her chitinous armour. She raised her lower legs and jabbed at him, but Guang danced away, twirling through the snow, blood leaking from his blade. He darted in again and thrust his dao at her bulging belly, blocked by an armoured leg; he feinted, spun right and slashed at her throat. Again, the blood blade skittered off her armoured leg, leaving nothing but a trail of Guang's blood splattered on her hairy exoskeleton. Guang spun away again, putting the tree trunk between them. Blood dripped from his sword, leaving a trail in the snow. He really was out of practice; he could barely keep his blade together.

The spider poked a leg up into the branches, and a cherry blossom drifted down in front of Guang. He leapt back, whirling his sword and cutting away the silken threads that dangled down toward him. He was starting to understand how she worked, preferring tricks and traps to straight combat, always trying to immobilise her enemy.

He danced around the tree toward her, sword trailing a bloody line in the snow. He swiped the blade upwards, but she leapt back. He followed, spinning the blade, and struck again from the right. She blocked the slash. He spun left, thrust at her belly. The blood blade slid down the armour of her leg, caught in a joint, and she hissed and scuttled behind the tree again.

Guang thrust his sword to the side of the tree, the spider lurched away from it; he twisted on his heel to the other side of the tree and swung his sword up in a bloody arc. The spider slashed a leg down and blocked it, and Guang stepped inside her reach, jabbed the sword at the joint of her leg. She swung another leg and stuck him in the shoulder. Pain exploded through his left arm, but the blood sword bit into her leg joint and severed the spider leg. The jorogumo screamed and staggered back, curling her legs around her, the stump of the severed spider leg twitching. Guang stumbled and caught himself on the tree, leaving a bloody hand print on the grey bark. He was panting, cold, dizzy from blood loss, but there was no time for it. He shook the white spots from his vision just in time to see the spider jump at him, snarling. She pounced on him with all her weight, slamming him against the tree trunk and grabbed his throat in her human hands, one whole and one mangled. She squeezed his neck and stabbed him with all her spider legs, piercing his arms, legs and chest. Blinding pain exploded through him. Blood seeped from his wounds despite his technique and qi trying to stem the flow. He couldn't breathe through the hands crushing his neck.

He couldn't remember falling, but he was on his knees in the snow, the back of his head pressed against the rough bark of the sakura tree. The onryo stabbed a leg at his face, missed and sliced off part of his ear. He couldn't breathe, didn't care. Would not die like this. He would not die without avenging his son. Without freeing Haruto from Tian's burden.

Guang grabbed the spider's throat in one hand, her bulbous flesh soft and moist in his grip, planted a foot in the snow, and surged to his feet, lifting the spider off the ground even as she stabbed him with her spider legs in the chest, side, and back. Then he drove his blood sword straight through the jorogumo's belly. Black gore splattered the snow behind her, and she screamed. Her spider legs convulsed in a frenzy of flexing and curling. She released his neck and grasped at the blade in her gut with her human hands. Guang threw her away, leaving his sword jutting from her abdomen. She rolled in the snow and scrabbled away from him.

Guang turned away from the jorogumo and limped past the sakura tree, trailing blood behind him. He reached a bloody hand into his satchel for his third vow. His left leg buckled and he fell to one knee, grunting from the pain. Behind him, the jorogumo stopped screaming, and he heard the crunch of footsteps in the snow. He glanced over his shoulder as she extended blood-slick claws at him.

He turned to her and shouted, "Blood Thicket!" All the blood he had leaked across the snow sprung up into a dense thicket of needle-like bloody thorns, piercing the onryo's chest, belly and human legs, skewering her in place. Guang forced a grim smile. "You're not the only one who can set traps, yokai."

The jorogumo shrieked and writhed, thorns scratching her skin, gashing her flesh, dripping black ooze on the snow, but she didn't die. She couldn't die, at least not by his hands. "I'm sorry," she screeched. "It hurts, it hurts! Please, let me go! Please, don't kill me! You'll never see me again."

Guang found the scroll he was looking for and pulled it from his satchel. He stared at it a moment, then unfurled it, leaving bloody fingerprints all over it. "This is my third vow," he said. "My most important vow. I shall never again willingly take another's life." He exhaled slowly, trying to steady his trembling hands. "For Tian!" He tore the vow in two in his blood-smeared grip.

New strength pulsed through him, more qi returning to him, crashing through him, the river bursting its banks and sweeping everything before it away. The snow shifted around him, blown in circles by the energy he was now so unused to containing. He rose to his feet and extended his hand. Blood flowed from his wounds, twisting through the air and coalescing into a new sword, a new blood dao. He gripped the sword in both hands, and with a single stroke, he sliced the jorogumo's head from her shoulders. Her body slumped in the thorny grasp of his thicket of bloody needles, and her severed head rolled in the snow. Black spider eyes stared lifelessly up into the branches of the sakura tree.

Guang dropped his dao and stumbled, caught himself on the tree trunk and sank down to his knees beside the severed head. The raging flood subsided, the river running to a bare trickle. He was so tired. So cold. He'd lost too much blood, and could barely use his technique to scab his wounds. He was covered in them, slashed and stabbed in a hundred different places, but none of that mattered. He had done it. He had killed the monster that had murdered his son. Tian was free to move on now, his soul no longer bound to heaven or earth. He could be reborn, not as a yokai, but as a human once more.

Guang stared up at the patches of sky between the branches of pink blossoms. "It's done, son. I'm sorry it took so long. I'm so sorry."

A cherry blossom floated down and he watched it drift in the winter breeze. Behind it, in the snowy distance, were the steps to the fourth plateau. Somewhere up there, Haruto and Kira were walking into a trap. He had to warn them, to help them. He tried to stand, but his legs didn't move. He didn't have the energy. His qi had surged through him like a tempest and it had drained just as quickly, leaving him cold and tired and old.

"Get up, you old fool," he chided himself. It would be so much easier just to close his eyes and rest for a bit, just a few minutes, until he was strong enough to stand again. Everything was dark, he realised. His eyes were closed, but he didn't remember closing them. His face was stiff, wet and crusted with scabs. A rivulet of blood trickled from a cut on his eyebrow down his cheek. Every bit of him hurt. He summoned his last drops of will and strength, and forced his eyes open.

Snow fell across the plateau, heavier than before. The sakura tree sheltered him from the worst of it, but it was a whirling, dense blizzard. He could just about make out the stone stairway in the cliff through the drifting white vortex. It seemed so far away.

"Maybe..." he sighed and leaned back against the tree trunk. "Maybe after I rest. Just for a bit." He closed his eyes.

Haruto felt Tian vanish, blown away like a breath on the wind. All the scorn and venom, the lust for vengeance, went with him, leaving Haruto raw and trembling. He pulled the blade to a stop a mere finger from Kira's neck. She didn't try to block it or dodge away – she stood there, looking up into his eyes, a whisper away from death.

"It wasn't me, Haruto," Kira said. "I would never do that to you."

Haruto let out a shuddering breath and pulled his katana away from her neck. Tian was gone. He felt like he'd been drowning, water enveloping him, choking him and muting the world, crushing him. But it was gone now. He'd broken the surface and he could finally breathe again. Weeks of drowning, now he was on land once more.

Kira stared at him, eyes wide and earnest. He smiled at her and turned to face the tengu, looked into the monstrous swirling eyes, but the hypnotic technique could no longer move him.

"Your spider is dead, Herald of Bones," Haruto said.

"I'm not joining you!" Kira shouted, standing beside Haruto.

Haruto grinned. "Looks like you're running out of minions."

The Herald of Bones was silent for a few seconds. Beneath his tengai, Haruto saw his swirling eyes staring at him and then at Kira. He sighed. "Well, that's a shame. Crow."

Haruto heard a rustle of fabric behind them and glanced over his shoulder. A white robe in a plume of smoke dropped, twisting around one of the hanging banners to land on the stone floor in front of the cavern entrance. Within the depths of the robe's hood, Haruto saw the faint outline of a sharp nose and pointed chin. Smoke billowed beneath her, tendrils crawling across the ground like snakes slithering towards them.

"Can you beat Crow?" Kira asked.

"What?"

Kira turned to him. Her eyes were bright in sockets gone dark as coal. "I need you to deal with Crow."

Haruto glanced from the Herald of Bones to Izumi drifting closer between the swaying banners. They were being flanked and couldn't hope to take them both on at the same time. "You mean to fight the Herald of Bones alone?"

Kira nodded fiercely. "I told you back at the Graveyard of Swords," she said, her voice trembling. "The Herald of Bones sent Daizen to kill Yanmei. So I am going to kill the Herald of Bones."

"You can't face him alone – he's a tengu."

Kira's eyes sparkled like embers. "Watch me." She turned to the Herald of Bones, stepped forward and whipped a mirrored dagger at him.

The tengu swayed to the side nonchalantly, and the dagger flew past him. "You'll have to try harder..."

"Momo," she whispered. Kira shattered and jangled to the ground in a million shining mirror shards. The Herald of Bones grunted and staggered forward. Kira stood behind him, already flicking another dagger into her hand.

Chapter 59

The onmyoji turned away from the Master and the new little sister. The girl had chosen the wrong path, the human path. The Master would kill her. It was a shame, but it wasn't Crow's concern. Her job was to stop the onmyoji from getting away, to capture him so they could use him to free the dragon. They were so close to fulfilling the Master's wishes, to destroying the mortals who had murdered them all and persecuted them. At last, it was time for the onryo, the yokai, and all the spirits to take back their place on earth.

The onmyoji shrugged and smiled at Crow... then he sprinted at her. Crow raised a cluster of smoky limbs, but the onmyoji dodged her, twisted around one of the streaming banners, and headed for the exit. It was a trick. She wouldn't let him confuse her. Crow whipped around, lashed out a tentacle, and snagged the onmyoji's foot, pulling him to a stop. He cried out, crashed to the ground, snagging in one of the banners and ripping it from the roof to float down around him. Crow dragged him back on the end of her tentacle. A scrape along his cheek was bleeding, but it was already healing, his flesh re-knitting itself.

"Why are you doing this, Izumi?" the onmyoji asked. He stood up and wriggled his foot from her smoky grasp.

"That's not my name!" Crow hissed. She thrust a spear of smoke at him and he leapt to the side, slicing through her smoke with his crimson blade and stepping behind one of the banners. A jolt of pain raced through Crow. She screamed and staggered towards him. Why was it she could only feel pain around this onmyoji? She held her severed smoke up and stared at it. It wasn't regenerating. The tentacle was just gone. The work of his spirit blade. She hated him. Hated him for hurting her, hated him for setting himself against them, hated him for somehow revealing who she was. She hated him for making her feel something again.

The onmyoji stepped past a hanging banner, watching her, both hands on his crimson sword, then passed behind another of the streaming red cloths. "What have you done to me?" she snarled, waving the severed limb at him. Then she surged toward him on a plume of rising smoke, tearing the banner aside to get at him. "What have you done?"

The onmyoji backed away slowly, holding his crimson sword before him. "I don't understand this any better than you do, Izumi."

"My name is Crow!" She stabbed at him, three smoky blades at once. He rolled away, swivelled his sword around, and severed another of her limbs. She howled in pain. Then she lashed a whip of smoke around his arm and stabbed another into his side like a knife. The onmyoji grunted and glared at her, grimacing. Then he twirled his sword about, severed the whip around his arm, and in the same stroke plunged his crimson blade into the knife in his side. Crow hissed and pulled back from him. The pain was... pain, excruciating, but she always had more smoke. She was limitless. And yet, each time he cut a piece of her away, she felt like a part of herself was lost.

The onmyoji bounded away from her. She ran after him. Ran. On legs. She had legs! She pushed aside her shock then stabbed out with a smoky spear, piercing his back and spraying blood out in front of his chest. It should have killed him instantly, but the onmyoji merely cried out and tried to keep running. Crow dragged him back, lifting him from the ground and shaking him, twisting her smoke inside him, trying to pull his insides out. The onmyoji twisted somehow, shifted the grip on his sword and cut away the spear from his back. He dropped to the ground on his feet, standing atop one of the fallen banners. He turned to face her. The wound in his chest was already healing, but he was panting, clutching it with one hand and dragging his sword at his side with the other. Still, he was staring at her with a look that almost seemed like pity. "Stop looking at me like that."

"Your name was Izumi," the onmyoji said, his voice like needles in her ears. He shifted his sword into his other hand and pulled a staff from the harness on his back. A new weapon, but she wouldn't give him time to use it. She flew at him again, ten smoky whips flailing. Even if he cut half of them, she still had enough to tear him apart. He leapt back, batted away one with his staff, then plunged the metal stick down into the rock and left it standing there.

The onmyoji drew another staff from his harness. "You were born in Kodachi."

Crow screamed.

Kira stepped back, leaving Momo jutting from the tengu's back, and flicked a new dagger, Blair, into her hand. She threw it left to clatter on the ground behind the Herald of Bones. He spun about to face her, wrenching Momo from his back and clutching it in his taloned hand. Kira ordered Momo to shatter, showering the Herald of Bones in mirrored shards, and flicked a new dagger, Jiji, to her right hand and dropped it.

"Blair," she whispered and stepped through the world, leaving an image of herself behind. The Herald of Bones slashed a taloned hand at the image of her, and it shattered into a thousand twinkling shards. Kira reappeared behind the tengu, clutching the hilt of the Blair and buried the dagger in the back of his thigh. "Jiji," she whispered and stepped through the world again, appearing behind the tengu again even as he spun about and shattered another likeness of her.

Kira flicked another dagger into her hand, Luna, tossed it up over the tengu's head, and darted in to stab him, but he twisted about and kicked her in the chest. Jiji fell from Kira's hand as she hit the ground. She flipped back to her feet, wincing from the pain in her ribs.

"Blair," she whispered and stepped through the world again. The image she left behind lingered for a moment then shattered, but it was long enough to distract the Herald. She appeared behind him again, ripped Blair from his thigh and plunged it through his feathery cloak under his arm, aiming for his heart. The Herald of Bones roared in pain and flung an elbow, catching Kira in the face and sending her stumbling back. He pulled the dagger from his side and tossed it on the stone floor of the cavern.

"You had a chance to be one of us, Kira," the Herald of Bones said as he lurched toward her. He slashed a taloned hand at her face. Kira turned away, but his claws dragged along her shoulder, tearing through coat, kimono and flesh in a torrent of pain. "You could have been a sister instead of an enemy!"

"Blair," Kira whispered. She appeared gripping the hilt of the knife the tengu had discarded and hurled the dagger at the Herald as he shattered the image she had left behind. The dagger sank into the back of his shoulder. Kira flicked another knife, Pabu, into one hand, and another, Maru, into the other. She let both fall to the floor. "Jiji." Kira reappeared in front of the tengu, standing amidst the fallen shards of her image. He was reaching for the dagger in his shoulder, and Kira thrust Jiji up into his stomach. He swept a taloned hand at her head, but she was gone again. She reappeared wrenching Blair from his shoulder and leapt away from him, tossing the dagger up and over his head. She landed on her feet and staggered back a couple of steps. Guang might have claimed she had a lot of qi, but she was beginning to tire. This new technique was draining her. She needed to finish the tengu before she exhausted her reserves.

The Herald of Bones turned, glancing at her discarded daggers. He chuckled. "It's a cute trick, Kira, but that's all it is."

Kira flicked Hayate and Heen into her hands, dropped them, and flicked two more daggers, another Momo and Luna, into her hands. She was panting, and sweat was beginning to drip into her eyes. Her arms trembled. She skidded Momo across the stone floor and kept Luna in hand. The trap was set, now all she needed was the Herald of Bones to step into it.

Kira met his kaleidoscope gaze and saw death. Her death, Haruto's death. The deaths of thousands, millions of mortals sacrificed to a dragon's rage and a tengu's war. She saw the truth that he had been hiding from them all, even his own allies. This wasn't about freeing a fellow spirit from its prison, not for him. It was his task, his orders from those he served in hell. He was to bring utter ruin to the world. Unbalance the delicate scales of heaven and earth.

Kira felt talons around her neck, wrenching her from the ground, crushing her throat, piercing her skin. He had shown her the vision in his hypnotic gaze to distract her. And she'd fallen for it. She couldn't breathe, couldn't run. Caught in his grip, unable to speak, she couldn't even use her technique.

The Herald of Bones squeezed her neck tighter, her final breath a burning brand in her chest. Kira thought her neck was about to snap, felt her eyes bulging, her face getting numb. He pulled her close until his swirling gaze swallowed her. "How disappointing you were."

Kira couldn't breathe. Her vision dimmed at the edges. She scrabbled at his hand, but her fingers were weak. Even the pain in her neck began to feel distant. She was losing consciousness. She was losing. She gaped, trying to breathe. In desperation, she kicked up at the Herald of Bones' face... and missed, barely catching his tengai and knocking it off his head. He stared at her scornfully, wrinkled face and hooked nose. The face of a demon.

Haruto batted away a smoky spear with his fourth staff and drove it in the rock behind him. "You used to love watching insects," he shouted at her as he drew the Wood staff from its harness. "There was an ants' nest in one of our fields and you wouldn't let the workers dig it out because you loved to sit and watch the ants rushing about their business, carrying leaves and larvae and dead bugs to the nest on their tiny backs. You had drawings of them all over our house."

Izumi screamed again and flailed at him, but her smoke was thinning, drifting. He ducked a churning grey blade and thrust the staff at her, striking her robe and toppling her off balance. Then he stepped back and drove the staff in the ground, completing the barrier... not around Izumi, but around himself. "I name you Iso Izumi," he shouted.

She surged at him, dozens of smoky tentacles streaming out of her robes and surrounding him. They slammed against the barrier of his staffs and rebounded back at her. Then she threw herself at him, struck the barrier and bounced off, smoke diffusing along it. She shrieked and swept into the barrier again, but the impact merely spread smoke around the cavern. She screamed, "That's not my name. That's not my name!" And threw her tentacles at the barrier.

Haruto stood behind the shield, smoke dispersing around him. It had protected him well, but it couldn't last. Already a small finger of smoke had needled in around the water staff like a creeping vine crawling across the ground to snatch at him.

Shiki trumpeted from the crimson blade. Haruto held the sword up and looked at it. "Yes, she's strong," he said.

Shiki whistled again.

"I know. Whatever it is in that robe... It's still her. Still Izumi. I can't..."

Another whistle and Haruto sighed. He didn't want to do it, but he had made a deal with Omoretsu all those centuries ago. Immortality to hunt down the ghost of his wife and offer her the peace that had been stolen from her.

Izumi continued to batter at his barrier. Most of her smoke bounced off, but enough drifted through to tickle at Haruto's skin, dry his throat, and waft up his nose. He didn't have long before the barrier failed completely. He glanced past her. In his battle with the yokai that had been Izumi, he had forgotten Kira. Through a gap in the hanging banners, he saw the Herald of Bones had Kira by the neck, her feet off the ground, and he was squeezing the life from her. Kira kicked weakly at his face and missed, knocking the tengu's hat off, and went limp in his grasp. Haruto stared at the tengu's face, the hooked nose, the pointed chin. He recognised the man, and he knew all once that the brutal fury that burned inside him was not Tian's.

"TOSHINAKA!"

The tengu's head snapped to the side as he stared at Haruto.

His grip loosened just a little. Kira sucked in a wheezing breath. "Momo," she whispered. She felt the dagger pull her from the tengu's grip and reappeared holding it in her trembling hand. The image she left behind shattered in the tengu's grasp. She staggered a couple of paces and collapsed to her knees against a stone pillar, gasping for air.

Haruto had shouted something. The Herald of Bones was standing in the middle of her discarded daggers, right where she wanted him. She took a deep breath and whipped Momo at him. The dagger sank deep into his side just above his hip. He grabbed for it, no doubt expecting Kira to appear holding it, but she told it to shatter, and it sprayed the Herald with glass shards. She flicked a new Momo into her hand, tossed it up into the air above the Herald of Bones, and whispered its name. She appeared above him, gripping the dagger. He shot up a hand and raked her leg with his talons.

From above him, she saw all her daggers and heard the humming melodies of qi connecting herself to them. She poured herself into all seven of them at once. For one moment, she was in seven places, each a reflection of her thrusting the dagger into the Herald of Bones. Seven deadly strikes delivered as one, parting skin, piercing flesh, rending organs. The tengu grunted and collapsed to a knee, blood spraying from his mouth.

Kira couldn't tell which of her was real. She froze in seven overlapping images, then she shattered into a million glass shards until only she remained. She stood in front of the kneeling tengu, flicked another Momo dagger into her hand, and stabbed it into his throat. Blood gushed over her hand. She shifted her grip and ripped the dagger across his neck.

The Herald of Bones roared and shot back to his feet, his cloak billowing out like wings. A howling wind whipped up from nowhere and buffeted Kira backwards. She tumbled through a hanging banner and hit the stone ground, collided heavily into a pillar. Bright spots danced in her vision as she squinted at the Herald of Bones. She realised then that the cloak he wore wasn't just a coat of feathers; it was his wings. He spread them wide like a vulture springing from its perch.

"I've had enough of this," the Herald of Bones spat, blood spurting from the wound in his neck and down his chest. "Die!" He swept his wings at Kira. She curled into a ball, shielding her face as a dozen razor feathers flew at her, burying themselves in her arms and legs and the stone pillar behind her.

Haruto watched Kira curl into a ball just as Toshinaka's razor feathers hit her, tearing bloody gashes in her arms and legs, sinking into flesh. He had to help her somehow, but he couldn't with Izumi trying to kill him. Her smoke was gaining form, streams coiling into grasping hands and tearing at the invisible barrier. She pushed a hand through a gap, grabbed at his kimono, and he slashed it with Shiki. Izumi screamed as the smokey hand dissipated. Shiki whistled. She was right. There was no other way to stop Toshinaka and save Kira. He had to kill Izumi.

Shiki whistled again, and Haruto saw Kira uncurling on the floor. She put a bloody hand on the stone and slowly pushed herself back to her feet, swaying as she stood. Her eyes were darker than before; her pupils had vanished so nothing but white showed surrounded by darkness. "You killed Yanmei!" Kira screamed at Toshinaka.

"Who?" Toshinaka said.

"You sent Daizen after us," Kira continued, her voice shattering on each word. "You killed Yanmei. And I will avenge her." She drew in a deep breath then screamed, "I swear I will kill you!" She shattered. Toshinaka's feathers fell to the floor amidst a million mirrored shards. Then she was behind him, thrusting her dagger at his back. Toshinaka turned, staggered back a few steps, drew his jagged, black sword, and blocked Kira's mirrored blade. They stood there for a moment, growling at each other, both bleeding from countless injuries.

A smoky hand closed around Haruto's neck. He turned away from Kira and Toshinaka, and slashed at the hand. He had to trust Kira. If she could just keep Toshinaka busy, maybe he had a little longer. Maybe Izumi didn't have to die just yet.

"Do you know how you died, Crow?" Haruto shouted into the tempest of smoke battering his barrier.

"I was murdered," she spat at him.

Haruto nodded. "Do you know *who* murdered you?"

She said nothing, still scraping her tentacles along the faltering barrier, trying to find a way in.

"Your name was once Iso Izumi. You were the emperor's cousin. You loved art and insects and thought me a better man than I was." Haruto ground his teeth and wiped tears on his sleeve. He had thought his grief over Izumi so long gone he couldn't even remember how it felt, but here she was and that same heart-rending ache came flooding back. "Toshinaka Heiru murdered you to hurt me. He left me wounded but alive and burned down our home with you in it for no other reason than he hated me."

Crow watched him, her smoke settling, drawing back inside her robe. She had the same crinkle between her eyes when she frowned. He remembered it so well. He used to tease her that it would develop into wrinkles as she aged. She hated that and slapped him whenever he said it, but it always brought a smile to her face. But that face was gone, and all that remained was a memory of it written in churning smoke.

"The creature you follow," Haruto spat. "The thing you call 'master' is not an onryo. He is a tengu, a demon, and he was once called Toshinaka Heiru." Haruto pointed to Kira and Toshinaka clashing with dagger and sword.

"*He* murdered you, Crow. You say you want vengeance against the mortal who murdered you, well there he is. He may not be mortal anymore, but *there he is!* You've been travelling with him, helping him, killing for him." Haruto stepped towards her, and Shiki trumpeted high and loud. He ignored her and stepped out of his barrier. Crow stared at him, tentacles snaking along the floor toward him, closing in on him from below and above. Haruto held Shiki ready in one hand. He could dart forward, bury the spirit blade in her body. He could end it, but he didn't. Instead, he walked past her, ignoring the smoky veins writhing about his feet. They didn't grab him. Crow didn't move. She was frozen, that unforgettable frown crinkling her nose.

Haruto walked slowly towards Toshinaka. The Herald of Bones raised his arms and the wind stirred around him, circling him, plucking half a dozen of his fallen feathers from the ground and spinning them around him. Kira whipped a dagger at him, but the winds caught it and spun it around with his swirling feathers. Kira staggered back. Blood dripped from her fingers, ran in rivulets down her face from a cut over her eye. She healed faster than a mortal, but not fast enough.

"Toshinaka," Haruto called as he stalked toward them. The Herald of Bones turned to stare at him, an ugly grin on his gnarled face. "It's about time we finally end this."

Chapter 60

Kira staggered and almost collapsed. She saw a razor-feather sticking out of her leg. The pain hit a moment later and she screamed, ripped the feather out and threw it away. Another feather whipped out of the tengu's circling winds toward her. She leapt to the side and it stabbed into the rocky floor just behind her. He wasn't even looking at her anymore; his entire attention was focused on Haruto. After everything Kira had done, all the wounds she had given him, she still wasn't strong enough to beat him. She wasn't even strong enough to warrant his attention. She had sworn to avenge Yanmei, but it was beyond her. The Herald of Bones was too strong, too skilled, and he had figured out her technique. And now he was done with her. He ignored her to face a stronger challenge. Kira spat blood on the stone floor and glanced back at Crow. Haruto had left the smoky onryo frozen in place somehow, smoke drifting aimlessly about her, soot staining the ground.

Haruto walked up to the Herald of Bones and faced him, gripping Shiki's hilt. "Which god did you anger to suffer this curse, Toshinaka?"

The Herald of Bones chuckled. "All of them." The swirling wind around him intensified, tugging at his wings and loosing another few feathers. The banners in the cavern were twisting, swaying, pulling and knotting in the winds. Some were ripped from the roof and fell to the ground, others whipped about in a red frenzy of cloth. "Not all of us are given everything we want, Nightsong. Not all of us are handed the world on a platter simply for being born under the right star. You coasted through your privileged life while I had to sacrifice for everything I ever wanted. You can never know how much I have suffered to become--"

"Still the same tired story, Toshinaka," Haruto said, shaking his head. "You always blamed me for everything I had. Always blamed me for everything you went through. You blamed me for your life, and I never even knew who you were. And somehow that's my fault?"

A slow, ugly smile crept across the Herald of Bones' gnarled face. "You knew who I was once I beat you. Once I took everything from you."

"That I did," Haruto said. Then he lunged, thrusting Shiki at the tengu's heart. Toshinaka blocked the blade with his jagged, black sword, sending a shower of sparks flying into the tornado whirring around him. Feathers swirling in Toshinaka's winds thudded into Haruto's arm and leg, but he ignored them and slashed Shiki upwards at the tengu's crotch. Toshinaka blocked the crimson blade again and stepped back. Haruto pursued him with a flurry of strikes, but the Herald of Bones swatted them away with his blade. The wind whipped at Haruto's kimono, pulled his hair loose from his braid, but he kept pressing the giant tengu. He cut at Toshinaka's head, blocked, stepped sideways and thrust at his leg, blocked, spun and slashed a one handed chop at his body, blocked again. Toshinaka was panting and grimacing and giving ground. Haruto stepped out of the circling winds and pulled the razor-feathers from his arm. His wounds knit themselves back together. Kira noticed a few notches in Shiki's red blade.

The Herald of Bones snarled. "Though immortality was given to you, Nightsong. *I* was not so fortunate. I had to sacrifice everything I was to claim it for myself."

Haruto pulled a feather from his leg and wiped the blood on his kimono. "You did this to yourself? How many of your oaths did you break?"

"All of them!" Toshinaka roared. "Every oath I ever made I broke willingly. No matter who I had to kill, no matter what I had to do, I did it. I committed such atrocities that even the gods took notice of me." He smiled that ugly, wrinkled grin again, crinkling his hooked nose. "They afflicted me with a curse befitting my acts as a mortal. Batu himself tore my humanity from me and cast me into hell." He spread his wings wide, feathers fluttering in his swirling winds. "And I clawed my way back out."

Haruto shook his head. "You made yourself into a demon to spite me? What did I ever do to you, Toshinaka? What did I do to earn such hatred, to inspire such a vengeful spirit?"

Toshinaka sneered at Haruto. "You think this is about you? Of course you do." The Herald of Bones lunged at Haruto and slashed his jagged sword down in a blur of black steel. Haruto staggered to the side, and raised Shiki, deflecting the strike a hand's breath from his head. Toshinaka's blade slammed onto the ground, shattering stone. He stepped to the side and smashed the back of his blade into Haruto's ribs, sending him tumbling across the cracked stone. Haruto rolled to his feet, clutching his ribs with one hand. Toshinaka leapt into the air, crossing the distance between them with a single beat of his motley wings, and chopped the jagged blade down from over his head. Haruto rolled out of the way and the black blade shattered the ground, sending shards of rock flying. As the Herald landed beside him, Haruto slashed Shiki at his gut. Kira only saw the sparks flying into the air as the tengu blocked the strike.

Kira watched in awe, frozen. How had she ever hoped to defeat the Herald of Bones? He moved so fast; his strikes powerful enough to break stone. He had been playing with her all along. She never stood a chance. Even after everything she had been through and as strong as she had become, even after training with Haruto, focusing with Guang, and learning Yanmei's technique, she was still too weak to matter.

Toshinaka slashed left then right, using his longer reach and greater strength to batter Haruto about. The onmyoji staggered under each blow, barely blocking with Shiki. Each time the swords clashed Shiki's blade took another deep notch. Haruto faltered in his defence and Toshinaka's sword slashed across his body, slicing through cloth and carving flesh, spraying blood across the floor. Haruto screamed in pain and staggered back again. It was a wound that would have killed a mortal, but Haruto's immortality was already healing him. Toshinaka advanced on him again, raining blow after blow down on Haruto, beating him back towards the dragon statues at the far end of the cavern.

Kira looked back at Crow. The onryo was still frozen in place, smoke drifting from her robe. Kira turned back to the fight. Haruto was down on one knee. Toshinaka slashed his jagged sword through Haruto's sword arm, lopping off his hand at the wrist. Haruto howled as his hand, still clutching Shiki's blade, spun away across the floor. He clutched his bloody stump against his chest. Toshinaka raised his sword to strike a final blow.

Kira flicked a dagger into her hand and flung it whirling into Haruto's chest. He grunted from the pain. Kira whispered the dagger's name and reappeared between the two swordsmen. "Sorry," she said, ripping the dagger from Haruto's chest. She spun around and thrust it into Toshinaka's gut. The tengu stumbled back, clutching at the hilt protruding from his midsection. Kira whispered to the dagger, and it shattered, exploding glass shards through Toshinaka's gut. But it wouldn't be enough to kill him. She didn't know if anything could kill him.

"Thank you," Haruto wheezed as he struggled back to his feet.

Kira flicked a new dagger into each hand and pressed one of them into Haruto's grip. "Take it," she said. "Will your other hand..."

"Already... growing back, but I don't... think I can... beat him."

Kira glanced over her shoulder and smiled. "Me either. Not alone anyway. I guess we'll just have to do it together."

Crow found herself in a bathhouse, oiled wooden floor beneath her, stone walls on three sides and a paper screen on the fourth. Beyond the screen she saw the orange, flickering blur of flames licking at the ceiling, silhouettes of people running, screaming, others swinging swords, blood spraying across the paper shoji. The bathroom itself was mostly empty save for a few buckets filled with shimmering water, a small table stacked with scented oils, and a round, wooden bathing tub in the centre of the room. Crow floated toward the tub. It was empty, recently drained, only a few droplets stubbornly clinging to its wooden sides.

She drifted away from the tub, searched the rest of the room, already knowing what she would find. Who she would find. Curled up on the wooden floor in the corner, sat a woman staring blankly at the paper screen door. She hugged her knees to her chest and was utterly still. Crow peered at her. The woman seemed familiar. The slope of her nose, the dimple in her chin, the shape of her eyes, the messy curls that refused to be bunned or braided. Crow knew the woman, though she had no memory of her. She drifted closer, soot stains trailing behind, and shrunk down to look the woman in the eye. It was her. The woman the onmyoji had called Izumi.

Crow glanced towards the paper screen. The fires still flickered; the chaos still raged. A silhouette streaked past, screamed; blood splashed the paper. Was this how Crow had died? She was supposed to remember – all the onryo were supposed to remember their deaths, but she never could. The Master said it would come in time, and when it did, she would be stronger than all her siblings. But Crow could no more remember her death than her own face. She turned and stared at the woman once more. *Her* face.

Crow tried to mimic the face, to force her smoke into the shape of its features, but nothing happened. She remained featureless, formless, dead smoke, a dark stain, an acrid scent on the wind. Nothing.

The woman shot a hand into Crow's hood. Crow tried to pull away, but the woman held on somehow. Crow felt the pressure of fingers clutching at her. She panicked, flailing her smoky limbs, but the woman ignored them and held on, her depthless, emotionless eyes boring into Crow.

"I won't let you take it back," Crow screamed. "I won't let

you take control!" She was certain that was what the woman would do. Izumi, their human side, had somehow dragged her to this place, and she would consume Crow until there was nothing left of her. Crow didn't want to be nothing again.

Tears streaked down Izumi's face as she stared into Crow's hood. Crow stopped struggling. There was something terribly broken inside this woman. Inside them both. A vase smashed and put back together, but pieces were missing and it could no longer hold water.

"I don't want it," Izumi said, her voice a croaking whisper that Crow knew all too well, the voice of someone whose throat was damaged by inhaling smoke.

Another scream from outside. Crow tried to turn and look, but Izumi held her tight, gripping her smoke in her human hands. "I don't want it," she wheezed, tears streaking from her dead eyes. "I don't want any of it. All the memories. Who I was, what you were, what you've done. I don't want it. Let me go. Please... please, let me die." Izumi's hand fell away from Crow's hood and she collapsed against Crow's robe.

Crow didn't know what to do. This was what the Master had always wanted for her, wasn't it? To remember everything, to know how she died and became a true onryo? She held the woman close in wisps of grey smoke. She felt Izumi pressing against her, leaning into her, disappearing into her. She looked down at her smoky hands, her slender grey fingers, reached up and touched her smoky face, her nose and cheeks and chin, pulled at the curly lock of hair lying across her forehead. Crow smiled.

"Thank you," Izumi rasped from somewhere. Then she was gone, and Crow was all that was left.

Memories tugged at her. Not an incomprehensible rush of them, but small strands she could follow like trails through a forest. The onmyoji, Nightsong, had said she loved watching ants work and a memory floated to her thoughts. It was a glass box with wood panelled edges, a gift from her eldest cousin, the emperor. It must have been outrageously expensive, but her cousin only smiled as his attendants brought it out to her. She was kneeling before him, in the imperial palace in Kodachi. He sat upon the Serpent Throne, smiling at her. He hadn't smiled like that in years, she recalled, not since he took the throne. Not since they played together in the gardens, chasing Eos, the little black kitten that always snuck into the palace. The attendants carried in the glass box on a small palanquin and lowered it before her. It was half full of earth. Hundreds of ants scurried about through the dirt. She watched them through the glass. There was a nest near the bottom, a queen laying eggs while her workers busied about her.

Crow staggered back as the memory faded, and braced herself with a smoky hand against the stone wall. She heard a scream from beyond the paper door and it stirred another memory. A man cowered before her, his hands raised in defence, bloodshot eyes goggling as Crow forced black smoke up his nose, down his throat. He struggled, waving at her smoke, trying to escape, but his attempts were useless. He choked on her and she watched with – she reached for the emotion – not joy, but retribution. Rightness. She did not know the man, she did not know anyone, she was an untethered yokai, drifting from place to place, inflicting her vengeance upon others because... because that's what she did. That was what she was, and it felt right. Crow pulled away from the memory, cringing from the feeling of forcing her smoke down the man's throat. It wasn't right. It wasn't vengeance. Vengeance needed a target, needed to be built upon a wrong visited. The man had done nothing to her, had not known her, yet she had inflicted death upon him. That wasn't vengeance – it was murder and malice and rage.

Crow pulled back her hood and breathed deeply, trying to centre herself. She felt air rushing in to mix with her smoke. She didn't need to breathe, but she sucked in deep lungfuls. She remembered who she was now, her face, her body, but she did not have a body. She was still just smoke. Another thread of memory drifted past her, promising answers and revelations, but she ignored it. Crow was already in a memory, the memory of the day Izumi had died. The day she had died.

Crow floated over to the paper screen door. It was patterned with swirling clouds and butterflies, now streaked with blood. She gripped the edge of the door with a smoky hand and flung it open. A man stood before her, tall and broad, dark hair and darker eyes, blood dripping from his black sword.

Kira stood beside Haruto, both of them clutching a mirrored dagger. The little knives seemed such feeble weapons compared to Toshinaka's black, serrated katana. Haruto's immortality was healing him, but slowly. His sword hand was new bone growing out of ragged flesh, muscle and skin stitching around them, and blood dripped from him in a dozen different cuts and scrapes. Kira was not in much better condition. The Herald of Bones' razor-feathered wings had sliced her arms and face. She was healing, but she was not immortal. The process was slow and she was in pain. She'd like to think the tengu was weakening as well – they had both wounded him several times over – but he still stood tall and moved with incredible speed and strength. The Herald of Bones was neither mortal nor spirit, he was a tengu, a demon. Doubt crept in and sapped Kira's strength.

Toshinaka rushed forwards, beating his black wings at them. Kira lurched in to stab him, but he brushed her dagger aside with his jagged sword and punched her in the face with the butt of its hilt. Kira staggered back, clutching her face. Blood gushed from her nose. A taloned foot hit her in the stomach. She flew backwards, crashed on the floor, and rolled to a stop against a stone pillar. She forced her eyes open and saw the tengu close on Haruto, backhand him across the face, and grab his neck in a taloned hand. Haruto stabbed Kira's dagger into the tengu's chest once, twice, and drew the blade out for a third time. Toshinaka laughed and tossed Haruto back against a stone dragon near the back wall. Haruto grabbed the dragon's leg and pulled himself back to his feet, still clutching Kira's dagger. The stone relief behind him glowed, the letters carved into it bright with a fierce inner fire.

The Herald of Bones flew at Haruto, twirling his sword in

his hands. Haruto raised his dagger, but Kira knew her little knives were useless against the tengu. They needed something else. Kira spotted Haruto's katana on the cracked floor, his severed hand still gripping its hilt. Shiki was waiting by the blade, spinning in anxious circles like a dog chasing its tail. Kira staggered to her feet and limped towards the little spirit. The Herald of Bones had all but forgotten Kira, such was her power against his, and she crossed behind him without notice. She was just a few paces away from the blade when a scream filled the cavern so loudly Kira covered her ears and winced.

As the scream died down, Kira noticed Crow was on the move, rising on a growing tide of smoke, tentacles thrashing beneath her, each as thick as her waist, lashing the air and ripping banners from the ceiling. Crow's white robe bulged with churning smoke, and her hood was thrown back. The face of a woman written in grey-black soot snarled as she floated across the cavern towards them.

Toshinaka turned and stared at the monstrous onryo. Crow pointed a slender smoky finger at him. "You murdered me!"

Toshinaka sighed and rolled his colourful eyes. "Shit!"

Crow surged on a tsunami of smoky tentacles and crashed into the tengu.

Chapter 61

Izumi, or Crow, or whoever she was slammed into Toshinaka, lifted him up on a stampeding cloud of smoke and carried him away. Haruto collapsed to a knee as he watched, his flesh re-knitting, a new hand growing out of the stump.

Crow smashed Toshinaka into a pillar, shattered it to rubble, spilling crumbled stone on the cavern floor. Toshinaka fell covered in dust and blood, and stained with soot. He rolled to his feet, hanging banners whipping around him, and swung his jagged sword up as Crow flew at him again. Her smoke parted around the blade and she hammered into him once more, but Toshinaka held his ground, clinging to the stone floor with taloned feet.

"Murderer!" Crow screamed as she buffeted the tengu with her smoke, slicing gouges from his skin, splattering blood on the fallen banners.

"I made your anchor, Crow," Toshinaka coughed into her seething smoke. "I can destroy it. I can destroy you!" He thrust a clawed hand into the heart of the smoke and ripped Crow's hood from her robe. Crow pulled back, fully unmasked. Haruto saw her features written clearly in the smoke, but her face was twisted into a malicious snarl he had never seen on her in life. Toshinaka grinned, his gnarled skin wrinkling and making him seem ancient, his hooked nose so large he no longer looked human. He dropped Crow's hood. The white fabric caught in the winds cavorting around him and blew away.

Crow screamed again and twisted up over the howling wind, then swooped down at Toshinaka. The tengu snapped his wings up over his head and Crow slammed into his feathers, smoke spilling around them like water poured onto stone. The wind was picking up around Toshinaka now, the breeze turning to a gale focused solely around him, tugging at Crow's smoke, tearing at it. She reached for him, but her smoke whipped away to nothing. Toshinaka snagged a handful of white fabric with his talons and ripped it away.

Crow howled and backed away from Toshinaka. He held the patch of white cloth for only a second then released it into his cyclone. "I will tear your anchor apart piece by piece. You will be as you were before I saved you, nothing but drifting smoke and formless anger."

Crow backed up and fell, landing on a cloud of smoke. She stared at her feet, held her smoky hands before her face. She pulled at the hole in her robe, and through it Haruto saw her knee.

"I don't need your cloth prison anymore, Mas..." Crow paused. "Murderer! I remember who I am and who I was. At last, I remember my face!"

Toshinaka sighed and slumped his shoulders. When he looked up, it was at Haruto. "Why must you ruin everything?" he roared. Toshinaka beat his black wings and soared towards Haruto. Crow flew to meet him, but her smoke caught in his vortex, spinning her around and flinging her out behind him to collide with one of the few remaining banners. Toshinaka ignored her and closed on Haruto.

Haruto raised Kira's mirrored dagger, ready to block Toshinaka's sword, but the tengu didn't stab at him. He grabbed Haruto's neck in his taloned hand and slammed him against the base of the relief on the wall behind him. Haruto wheezed but kept his feet, and Toshinaka ran his jagged sword through Haruto's chest and into the relief behind him.

Agony exploded in Haruto's chest. He looked down at the jagged, black blade jutting from his sternum, dripping with his blood, and coughed gore into Toshinaka's whirling winds. The tengu grinned at him. "I win again, Nightsong."

Kira watched, helpless, as Toshinaka pressed Haruto to the wall at the end of his blade. She glanced across at Crow, but the onryo lay still in the midst of a fallen banner, smoke billowing around her. Shiki whistled shrill and loud, and Kira remembered the little spirit was waiting there, standing over Haruto's katana.

"He can't die," Kira said. "He's immortal."

"Is he?" Toshinaka asked, turning from Haruto and leaving him pinned to the glowing relief. Kira crouched and drew back her hand to hurl a dagger at the tengu, but Toshinaka shouted, "STOP! Nightsong doesn't have to die here. But if either of you come another step closer, I will kill him now."

Kira looked to Crow again, but the onryo still lay unmoving on the banner, smoke pooling around her. Kira didn't know what was happening, but she knew Haruto was in trouble and she needed to save him somehow.

"You do not know how long it took me, Nightsong," Toshinaka said, "to find a way to strip someone of their immortality." He turned and stretched his arms toward the relief, the runes etched into it pulsed and glowed more brightly. Rock dust fell from it, crumbling to the floor. Kira saw dull metal beneath the facade. "The Cochtans are marvellous for creating such a thing."

Haruto laid his newly regrown hand on the sword pinning him to the relief and tugged feebly. It didn't budge. He coughed, painting his chin red. "A Blood Engine?"

"Yes," Toshinaka said, stepping back from the glowing relief. "When the Century Blade defeated the dragons, he had his Cochtan companion, the Ticking Clock, build a Blood Engine to hold each of them, the strongest prisons the world had ever seen. For all except Orochi, they built the engine so mortal blood would be enough to hold the lock in place, but for the king of the dragons, the prison needed to be built of sturdier stuff." Toshinaka chuckled and gestured at some dusty old bones that lay at the feet of one of the dragon statues. "To seal the prison, they used the blood of an immortal, a god of the Seafolk. The engine stripped his immortality from him to lock Orochi here. Only the blood of another immortal can open it and free Orochi." He laughed. "In one monumental victory, I will strip you of your immortality and free the dragon."

Haruto struggled against the blade pinning him to the engine, but he couldn't free himself. His blood dripped down onto the relief, soaking into the metal. Somewhere beyond the walls of the cavern, Kira heard movement, metal grinding and creaking against metal. The door to Orochi's prison unlocking. "Stop this," Haruto coughed. "Orochi will bring ruin to the world."

Again Toshinaka smiled. "Yes. He will bring ruin to *your* world, Nightsong. To the humans. Orochi and the other dragons will destroy this pitiful balance between heaven and earth and pave the way for spirits to reclaim their place here in the mortal world. The lost things are returning. I am but the herald. And you, Nightsong, are merely the key." Haruto slashed Kira's dagger weakly at Toshinaka, but the tengu stepped back out of reach, chuckling.

Shiki whistled.

"Are you sure?" Kira asked the little spirit. Shiki stared at Haruto, bouncing up and down, and chirruped urgently. Kira scooped up Haruto's sword, peeled the fingers of his severed hand from it, and dropped the dead thing to the floor. The blade was chipped, spotted with blood, and dulled from combat. Shiki rolled about, spinning in circles, watching her. Kira looked up and met Haruto's wandering gaze. He smiled.

"What are you grinning at, fool?" Toshinaka snarled. "You've lost." The tengu turned and saw the sword in Kira's hands. "Not one step, Little Sister."

Kira ignored him, looked down at Shiki. The little spirit trembled with fear. "We can do this."

Shiki leapt into the sword; the blade burst into a bright crimson glow. Pain lanced up Kira's arms and through her chest. Shiki screamed in her mind. No one but Haruto could wield her. Haruto raised his hand and dropped her dagger. Kira whispered the dagger's name and stepped through the world, dragging Shiki with her.

Kira reappeared in front of Haruto, dagger in one hand, Shiki in the other. The image she left behind shattered. She spun about, screaming, and swung Shiki at the tengu's neck.

The blade shattered in her grasp, shards of metal exploding across the cavern floor. Shiki fell to the ground, eyes closed, unmoving. Kira stared at the katana hilt in her blistered hands. So close. She had been so close.

The Herald of Bones glared at her, chromatic eyes swirling. Then he swayed and fell forward, hit the floor with a thump, and his head rolled off his shoulders. Kira stared down at him, not quite believing it was true. She had done it. The Herald of Bones was dead. Her stomach lurched and she clasped a hand over her mouth to stop from giggling.

"Shiki!" Kira said. "Are you okay?" She had felt the little spirit break, the strain of being wielded by someone other than Haruto too much for her. She knelt down in the slick blood next to the spirit, and scooped the little black fuzz ball into her arms. Shiki whistled softly, falteringly, but her eyes fluttered open, and Kira hugged her tightly to her chest. "I'm so sorry. I know it hurt. But we did it. We did it. You did it, Shiki!" Kira's hands were blistered and raw from the spirit blade; she could only imagine what it had cost the spirit.

Haruto coughed from behind Kira. "A little help here?"

Kira gently put Shiki back on the stone floor and turned to Haruto. He was impotently trying to pull the jagged sword from his chest. The relief behind him was glowing bright as a campfire now, and the clanging and grinding from the cavern wall was growing louder. Kira grabbed Toshinaka's sword and tugged on it. The blade didn't budge but Haruto winced and blood dripped down his chin.

"Sorry," Kira said, cringing. She gripped the sword hilt with both hands. "I'm really sorry."

"Get on with it," Haruto growled.

Kira put one foot on the wall next to Haruto and pulled with all her might. The sword came loose from Haruto's chest with a grating of stone, a gush of blood, and howl of agony. She tossed the jagged, black blade on the floor and caught Haruto as he slumped forward into her arms. She dragged him away from the glowing relief. Shiki followed, trumpeting quietly. Crow watched from a distance, silent, wispy smoke smoothly cascading on the stone floor. Kira dragged Haruto past Toshinaka's body and helped him kneel on the ground. He clutched at the gaping wound in his chest, trembling and hissing through clenched teeth. He wasn't healing. The wound wasn't closing. Shiki crawled into his lap, staring up at him, and whistled softly.

"You did good, Shiki," Haruto said, patting the spirit with a trembling hand. "You both did."

Kira shuffled about on the spot, unsure what to do, and glanced over at Crow again. The onryo was drifting closer. She wrapped one tendril around Toshinaka's katana and dragged it scraping across the floor.

Shiki fluted. Haruto smiled down at her and shook his head. "I don't think so. The Blood Engine took too much... too much of my immortality." He pulled his hand away from his chest. The wound was still gaping, blood trickling, staining his kimono. "Don't think... I'm coming back from this one."

Shiki gave a mournful cry and buried her face in Haruto's stained kimono.

"Is there anything I can do?" Kira asked. After everything they had been through, she didn't want to lose Haruto. She didn't want to lose anyone ever again.

"Hope," Haruto said. "Hope it didn't take enough of me to free Orochi."

"Fool!" Crow spat.

Haruto lifted his head to look at her. His face was already pale, corpse-like. "Are you... Izumi?"

"Your wife is dead," Crow said. "But I... I remember her."

Haruto frowned and looked to Kira.

Kira shook her head. "She's not like me. The yokai half of her won, but I don't think she's like the other onryo either."

Haruto shrugged and chuckled wearily. "I guess you're both something new then."

The metal clanging from the cavern wall was growing louder. Kira looked over Haruto's shoulder. The relief was collapsing, the metal behind it sliding away. Rock dust showered the ground and whole sections of the wall collapsed away to reveal darkness beyond. "Were we too late?" Kira asked.

Crow tossed Toshinaka's sword to the ground in front of Haruto. "The prison didn't need your life, only your immortality."

Haruto groaned. "Even in death, he still wins." He picked up Toshinaka's sword by the hilt, and used it to push himself to his feet. Blood leaked from the hole in his chest. He trembled, swayed, and Kira jumped to her feet to help him. Together, they watched the last of the relief crumble away.

Chapter 62

Haruto stepped in front of Kira and stumbled towards the yawning hole left by the crumbled relief. He needed to stand on his own feet if they were going to... fight a dragon? Now that he thought about, it seemed like madness. Kira and Crow stood behind him, waiting for Orochi to emerge.

Haruto looked over his shoulder at Crow, Izumi's features written in smoke, but not Izumi. "You're helping us now?"

Crow blinked, her smoky face almost seemed solid enough to touch. "Freeing the dragons was Toshinaka's dream, not mine. The dragon... Orochi will slaughter everyone indiscriminately. It isn't vengeance without a target. That's nothing but murder. I--" She shook her head, smoky hair waving. "--don't want that."

"A bit late to change your mind," Kira said. Crow glared so furiously at her that she took a step back. "Sorry," the girl said.

Haruto shrugged and winced at the pain in his chest. "I'm not sure it matters. Even the Century Blade couldn't kill a dragon. They had to imprison them. So unless you spent the last two centuries secretly training to be a Cochtan Enginseer and learning to build new prisons, we're screwed."

"Don't be stupid, onmyoji," Crow said. "We have something the Century Blade didn't. We have her."

Kira took a step back and held up her hands. "Me?" She looked at Haruto. "I can't kill a dragon."

Crow sighed. "Not you. Her." She waved a smoky hand at Shiki.

Shiki fluted and scrambled behind Haruto's leg, peering out at Crow.

"She's a spirit blade," Crow continued. "I felt her cut through me. Nothing else has ever hurt me like that. If she can kill spirits and demons. She can kill a dragon."

Haruto looked down at Shiki, cowering behind his leg. "What do you think?"

Shiki trumpeted querulously.

"I know you've never killed a dragon before," Haruto said. "No one has. Want to give a try?"

Shiki shook her entire furry body.

"Would you like to tell Omoretsu we failed?"

Shiki narrowed her eyes.

Haruto chuckled. "In you go," he said, holding up Toshinaka's katana. Shiki whistled a low warble, but leapt into the sword. The black blade turned a dark crimson and Haruto felt Shiki shudder through its hilt. She did not like the jagged sword.

Haruto turned back to the gaping tunnel. Orochi was in there somewhere. He clutched a hand to the hole in his chest. It wasn't healing. He wasn't dead, but he felt his immortality peeling away like fraying rope. "I'm not in peak condition here," he said. "You need to protect me so I can get close."

"Worry about your own part," Crow snapped from behind. "I know what I have to do."

Kira giggled nervously. "What are we expecting here, exactly?" she asked, her voice trembling. "The prison door isn't much taller than me, so how big can Orochi be?"

A crack ran up the cavern wall, starting at the prison door and splitting the wall all the way to the ceiling. The cavern shook and rocks and dust cascaded down around them.

"The Century Blade imprisoned Orochi when the dragon was in human form," Haruto said. "I don't think he's in human form anymore."

The cavern wall exploded out towards them, showering them with stone.

A rock the size of a horse tumbled towards Haruto. He tried to stagger away, but he was too weak and slow. Crow flew in front of him, smoke billowing out to shield Haruto. A crush of small stones sunk into her smoky blackness and when the big rock hit, she shouted and pushed it aside. It crashed to the floor a few paces away. Another section of wall hit Kira and she shattered. Haruto hoped she'd used her technique to step away.

A giant shadow moved inside the gaping prison, a long sinuous neck writhing in the dusty gloom. Another joined it and another. The hiss of serpentine scales echoed from the dark depths, and the eight-headed Orochi slithered into view.

A mirrored dagger hit the ground next to Haruto, and Kira appeared, picking it up off the floor and coughing dust. She looked up at the dragon king and whispered, "I think we need a new plan."

Crow shrank back down to her human size, gathering her smoke beneath her. "This is the only plan."

Kira shook her head. "It's a really bad plan."

Haruto stepped past them both, staring up at Orochi. The dragon king was immense and terrifying beyond any of the other dragons, beyond anything he had ever seen before. Eight monstrous, serpentine heads, each as large as a house and topped with half a dozen horns. Serrated teeth glinted from inside his mouths, and slick papillae hung from his jowls like a fleshy moustache. Each of his necks was at least a hundred feet long, scales like armour running along their lengths, and thin, membranous flaps of skin waved about as the dragon's heads moved. His body was twice as long as his necks, and slumped against the rock beneath him, small legs pawed useless at the ground, talons raking through the stone. His tail was even longer still, whipping about, stirring up dust and slamming against the cavern walls. His scales were iridescent, even in the gloom their colours seemed to dance. Haruto saw scars on some of his heads, missing scales and bleeding gouges, healed wounds, evidence of the battle Orochi had fought against the Century Blade over a hundred years ago still showing as though it were yesterday.

Orochi opened his eyes and twisted his heads toward them. Haruto opened his mouth to speak, but the dragon king roared, all eight heads bellowing a single name, so loud Haruto staggered under the weight of sound: *Yamasachi*, Orochi's human husband.

Orochi started thrashing about, shaking the rock with the

force of his body and tail only to realise there wasn't enough space inside the rock prison.

"We have to stop him before he escapes," Haruto said.

Orochi cast a big serpentine eye on Haruto. A head with one broken horn opened his massive jaws and a voice like a hundred strong choir said, "Escape? I am not running from you, human. You are nothing!" Orochi surged from the tunnel of darkness, eight massive heads barrelling towards Haruto.

Crow flew at the dragon king, a blur of smoke crashing into Orochi's lead head, blinding him and stabbing smoky blades into his scales. Orochi hissed and pulled the head back from Crow. She swirled around one of his other necks. A head with only one eye snapped its jaws at Haruto and he lurched aside, slashing Shiki across his giant snout. The one-eyed head screamed and fat drops of blood splattered on the stone floor. Another head with frills along its neck reared above Haruto and swooped down to smash him against the ground. A mirrored dagger whirled through the air and plunged into the dragon's eye. He roared and thrashed, and Kira appeared, clinging to his head, clutching the dagger. She jerked it from Orochi's eye, swung herself up onto his thrashing head and leapt onto another head with a hair-lip, her dagger raised to strike. A third head with elongated fangs coiled around to meet her, and snapped its jaws around her. Kira shattered into a thousand twinkling shards.

Haruto gathered his qi into a burst of speed and whipped Shiki along a shining dragon's neck, splitting scales and spilling blood. The one-eyed head darted at him from his right and he jumped, twisting in mid-air and landing on the approaching neck. He stabbed Shiki down into flesh and held on as Orochi thrashed around, trying to throw him off.

Haruto's chest wound throbbed; the hole was gaping and slick with blood. He knew he should already be dead, only the last throes of his immortality were keeping him going. His vision was already fading. Shiki howled as she slipped off Orochi's head, and the dragon threw Haruto from his neck. Haruto toppled thirty feet and hit the ground hard. His left arm snapped with a loud crack.

Haruto sucked in a breath and rolled to his feet. Crow was flying from the frilled head to another with a crown of horns. Her white robe was torn and flapping, smoke trailed behind her. Kira appeared on top of the one-horned head, plunged a dagger down into Orochi's scales, but the blade shattered and Kira shattered a moment later. She reappeared on the ground, threw another dagger at the creature's eye, then shattered again so fast Haruto lost track of her. He stumbled, almost collapsed, ran at the hair-lipped head as it swept past the tunnel mouth, and slashed at the scales of its throat. Then he rolled away as the head slammed down on the stone floor, trying to crush him. He bounced up and stabbed Shiki's jagged blade deep into the snout and it stuck into bone. Orochi roared, reared up and hoisted Haruto from the ground. He scrambled, pushing away from the hair-lipped head's gnashing teeth, and clambered up onto the snout. The head stopped thrashing, and Orochi focused a narrow-pupiled eye on him. Haruto stared into the eye and saw the reflection of the crowned head rising behind him. Its mouth opened and flames shot up from its throat. Haruto threw himself off the snout as a burst of flame roared from the dragon's mouth, engulfing him. He screamed as he fell, his hair burning, his kimono seared away, his skin blistering in the heat. The ground rushed up at him. He clenched his jaw and readied himself to be splattered on the cavern floor. Smoke curled around him, wrapped him up, slowing his fall, and then dropped him on his arse on the ground.

Crow landed next to him, glanced at his broken arm and blistered skin. "Stop trying to get yourself killed and slay this thing." Then she flew back into the air on a geyser of smoke. The dragon swung its one-horned around and snapped his jaws on her, smoke puffing from the sides of its mouth. The tattered remains of her white robe floated to the ground.

Kira leapt through the air above him, landed on the crowned dragon head and stabbed a dagger down into its snout. The dagger shattered against the scales, and the crowned head twisted and snapped its jaws around Kira. She shattered and reappeared clutching a dagger on the neck of the frilled dragon head. Another head of the dragon, this one with cracked scales around its eyes, slid towards her, slithering along the neck she was standing on. It crashed into her and sent her flying into a pillar, smashing the stone. The frilled head she had been standing on breathed bolts of lightning at her. She screamed, shattered and reappeared on floor below the monster, her mop of hair smoking, another dagger clutched in her hand. She fell to her knees.

It wasn't working. Shiki might cut through his scales, but Orochi's necks were too thick to cut his heads off. They needed a different plan, a better option. And they were out of time. Haruto felt cold, numb, distant. The hole in his chest pulsed with blood and his broken arm wasn't healing. He felt like he was slipping away, dying.

Shiki whistled softly, and he held up the blade to look at her. "We can't win," he said, the weight of truth settling upon him like a tombstone. Shiki trumpeted a short melody, but no amount of false optimism would overcome the king of dragons. They could not beat him. They never stood a chance. Maybe they could still run? He glanced at the cavern entrance. Guang stood there, leaning against the cavern wall, covered in blood, staring open-mouthed at the dragon. Haruto sighed. They couldn't run. There was nowhere to run to. Nowhere safe from Orochi's wrath. If they failed here, tens of thousands of humans would die. And Guang would be the first. Haruto wouldn't allow it. He wouldn't let his friend die.

"One last try, Shiki," Haruto said. Shiki whistled.

Haruto summoned the last of his qi and sprinted toward the dragon king. Orochi's crowned head snaked along the floor and lunged for him. Haruto leapt to the side, then vaulted up on to the dragon's neck. The one-eyed head surged in from Haruto's left; he ducked into a slide, felt the whoosh of air as jaws snapped closed above him, jumped to his feet and onto the charging neck. The one-eyed head thrashed about, but Haruto kept low and trailed his broken arm on the scales for balance. The fanged head to his right bubbled boiling water between its teeth, and Crow exploded out from its mouth, shattering two of its fangs. Her robe was gone, her whole body was surging black smoke. The dragon reeled and pulled its head away. The one-horned head darted in, craggy teeth snapping at Crow, and tore half her body away. She screamed and fell, smoke drifting to the ground. The frilled head swooped in and snapped her up. Haruto stumbled on – he couldn't help her now.

The soles of Haruto's feet were torn and bleeding from the dragon scales. His lungs burned from running and jumping and climbing. The hole in chest throbbed with blood and agony, and his qi was ebbing away. The hair-lipped head swept down at him. He tried to spin away, but its serrated teeth snagged his broken arm and tore it off his shoulder. The neck beneath him bucked, trying to throw him, but Haruto used the momentum to jump onto the head that was chewing his arm. If he could just get to where the necks met the monster's body.

Haruto stumbled down the neck, dragging his feet along the scales, blood leaking from his shoulder stump and the hole in his chest. The cavern was fading around him, light growing so dim. Haruto dangled Shiki at his side, unable to summon the strength to lift her anymore. His breath came in choking, wheezing rattles each more painful than the last. The crowned dragon head rose to his left, its lip curled in an almost human expression of distaste; another head, the broken toothed one, swung to his right. They stopped and seemed to watch him. Haruto stumbled on, one foot barely in front of the other.

The head with the broken tooth opened its great maw. "You're dying, mortal."

"First time... for everything," Haruto said. Shiki whistled a piercing note from the blade, but he ignored her. Stopping wouldn't save him now, it would only condemn the others. It would only condemn all of humanity.

The two heads continued to watch him as the others swung around until all eight of them swayed around him, staring at him. He fell to his hands and knees and crawled the last few feet from the dragon's neck onto his enormous body. The crowned head looming above the broken-toothed one rumbled, "What are you trying to achieve?"

Haruto crawled another ten feet, then stopped. He tried to take a deep breath, coughed and spattered blood on the dragon's iridescent scales. He got up slowly and tottered upright. With his last sliver of strength, he raised Shiki in his one hand.

"No mortal blade can kill me, fool," Orochi's eight heads said in thundering unison.

Shiki whistled tremulously.

Haruto tried to chuckle, but merely coughed more blood over his chin. "Shiki is no mortal blade. She's a spirit blade."

Orochi's scarred, one-eyed head drifted closer, peering at him through its one yellow orb. "It makes no difference, mortal. I cannot be killed."

Haruto stared at the dragon head, wondering when his vision had become so blurry. "Just because it hasn't happened yet... doesn't mean... it can't."

He turned Shiki sideways in his grip and drew in a deep breath, and roared, "QUELL YOUR RAGE, DRAGON!" Then he dropped Shiki clattering on the dragon's back at his bleeding feet, raised a foot and stamped down on the blade. Toshinaka's katana shattered under his heel, and Shiki popped out on Orochi's back, staring up at Haruto and blinking. Haruto slumped. "I don't want to kill you."

He collapsed backwards, sprawling onto his arse on scales scarred by a battle that was ancient history to all but the serpent. "I don't... want to kill... any of you," he said. "The world would be... so much poorer... without... dragons in it."

Orochi's eight heads hovered about him on swaying necks. "Do you believe breaking your little sword will stop me from killing all of you?"

Haruto shrugged and even that seemed far too much effort. "It was more... of a symbolic gesture... really," he said, his voice slurred and distant. Shiki crawled into his lap, coarse black fur nuzzling against his naked skin. He laid a hand on her and peered up at the dragon's heads, trying to focus on each one in turn. Each head was different, individual and unique. Some by way of scars, others by the shape of the horns or the patterns of scales. Each one was glorious and wondrous. "I know your story, Orochi. I know... what Yamasachi did to you, how he betrayed you."

Orochi shuddered, rippling his scales, and his heads variously growled, grumbled and snarled. "Yamasachi will pay," the frilled head said, confirming Haruto's suspicions. "You will all pay. Yamasachi and the fleas who sealed me in this stone prison. You all will die. Humanity will burn."

Haruto exhaled a sigh, had to concentrate to inhale again. "They're all dead, Orochi," he said. "Yamasachi, who betrayed you and destroyed your glade, is dead. Has been... for a hundred years. The Century Blade and... all the others who imprisoned... you, they're all dead. You already have... your vengeance. You outlived them all. They're dead, and you're free."

"Humanity will pay the price for them!" Orochi's eight heads bellowed in unison. "I am not satisfied."

Haruto tried to move his hand, to stroke Shiki, and found he couldn't. The little spirit stared up at him, trembling. "Your satisfaction... means nothing, King of Dragons." He wanted to laugh at the foolishness of it all, but even that was too much effort. He couldn't move at all but to speak. "Everyone... who ever wronged you... is long dead. If you attack humanity now, it will not be vengeance. It will be murder. The murder of innocents." The cavern had gotten so dark that the dragon's swaying heads were just shadowy blurs.

One blur drew closer. "Call it what you will, mortal. I will visit my wrath upon all your kind."

"You'll lose," Haruto said quietly. Something on the air stung his nostrils.

"You said the mortal who imprisoned me is dead."

"The Century Blade is dead, but if you... go to war with humanity, there will be... another Century Blade. The humans will band together... to fight you. Spirits will die... humans will die. Needless deaths. Pointless. They will find a way... to imprison you again. Or another onmyoji... with another spirit blade... will strike you down. Not all of us see spirits like I do. Not all of us... want peace between heaven and earth."

"They cannot kill me," Orochi growled. The head swayed closer to Haruto, so close he felt the heat of the words against this skin. "I am immortal."

Haruto stared at the blurry dragon king. "So am I."

Orochi was silent at that. They both knew he was dying.

Haruto turned his head, searching for the cavern entrance beyond the tunnel prison. He could barely see it anymore, but the grey blur next to the wall had to be Guang. Haruto felt a smile tugging at his lips. "You won, Orochi," he whispered. "They're all dead. You have... your vengeance... If you fight them now... you'll never find it again."

"Find what?" Orochi rumbled.

"Love," Haruto said. "It's easy to become detached... when you live... as long as us.... Despite what Yamasachi did... to you... for a while... he gave you something no immortal... can. He gave you love..." The cavern was so dark now Haruto could no longer see Guang or the entrance. Shiki whistled, but he couldn't see her anymore, couldn't feel her anymore. "If you fight them. If you kill them. You'll never find... that again. All they... will ever give you... is hate."

Chapter 63

The dragon floated, lifting its enormous bulk off the ground. A scarred head with only one eye twisted about and opened its mouth, and for a moment Guang thought it was going to eat Haruto. Instead, it gently picked him up in its jaws and placed him on the rocky ground near the wall of the cavern. Then it turned toward Guang and flew at him. He stumbled away from the cavern entrance. The dragon slowed to a stop and turned all eight heads to stare at him.

A glittering head with a crown of horns opened its mouth. "He is dying."

"Uh..." Guang shook his head. He was feeling a bit fuzzy either from the blood loss or the sight of the massive dragon peering down at him. "C-can you save him? You're a kami. You can do..."

A second head, with a broken tooth, said, "There is nothing to save. His immortality is gone." The heads fell silent, all eight of them swaying, twisting as they watched him.

Guang staggered, caught himself on the cavern wall with a hand. He couldn't let Haruto die. He couldn't face life without his old friend in it. "What if you gave him what's left of my life?" Guang asked. "I know it's not much but..."

The one-eyed head drifted closer to him, so close the stench of serpent musk filled his nostrils. He blinked his one eye, sniffed at him, and said, "Perhaps he was right."

Orochi turned from him and flew out of the cavern, his body scraping the rock as he passed. Guang watched the dragon's tail whip overhead, crashing into a section of wall and sending boulders the size of horses tumbling, then Orochi was gone. Guang stared after it for a moment, then shook himself and limped towards Haruto.

Kira struggled to her feet on a pile of broken pillar stone. Her kimono was singed and bloody. She staggered toward Haruto, limping even worse than Guang. A thin trail of smoke hovered over Haruto as he lay still on the stone floor near the wall of the cavern, but it drifted away as Guang arrived.

Guang dropped to his knees next to his fallen friend, knees popping. Haruto was torn and mangled. His left shoulder was a ragged stump of leaking flesh. He had a hole in his chest big enough for Guang's fist. The right side of his body was a mess of red blisters, charred flesh, and angry skin. His face was pale and ghostly, his lips blue as ancient ice. Shiki trembled, nestled between his right arm and his body, softly fluting over and over again.

"Old man?" Guang asked as he laid a hand on Haruto's chest. His skin was cold and clammy, the blood still wet.

"Guang? Is that you?" Haruto's eyes opened, but they were like white clouds on a winter's day. No iris, no pupil.

"Aye, old man," Guang said. "I'm here." He wiped a sleeve across his eyes. "You ruined another kimono."

Haruto's lips quirked a little at the edge. "You'll have to... buy me a new one."

"Always do."

"You won," Haruto said. "I felt... Tian go. Did you have to... break all... your vows?"

Guang shook his head. "All but one."

"Which one... did you keep?"

Guang chuckled and wiped his eyes again. "Cabbage, old man. Which one do you think?"

Haruto wheezed softly, spattering blood on his blue lips. "I really... hate... that vow."

Guang dug a hand into his satchel. "I got something for you, old man. Picked it up in Kodachi and, well, I was saving it for, uh, now." He pulled out a long pipe, ornately carved from white wood with a depiction of a dragon winding along its stem. He pressed it into Haruto's hand, and curled his fingers around it. "It seemed a fitting way to celebrate." The moment he let go of Haruto's hand, the old man's fingers uncurled.

Haruto was silent for so long, Guang laid a hand on his chest to check he was still breathing. "What... is it?" Haruto asked.

"It's a pipe," Guang said. "I got you a new pipe."

"Thank you." Haruto wheezed again, blood bubbling at the corner of his mouth.

"You're not healing, old man," Guang said. "Why aren't you healing?"

Haruto's eyelids fluttered. "Took it... from me."

Guang glanced over his shoulder at Kira. The girl stood just a few steps behind him, wringing her hands together, chewing on her lip. Guang looked back to Haruto and shook his head. "I don't understand, old man."

Haruto was silent for a few laboured breaths. "Goodbye, Guang. Thank you."

Guang hung his head, shaking tears from his eyes. It couldn't end like this. Haruto couldn't die. He was supposed to be immortal. "No. Thank you. For letting this old fool tag along, for keeping me out of trouble all these years. For everything."

Haruto wheezed and his cloudy white eyes closed. "You helped me... far more than... I ever... helped... you." A breath hissed from his throat and his head fell to the side.

"Old man?" Guang clutched Haruto's hand. "Wake up, old man. Don't leave me, Haruto. You can't... Don't go."

Chapter 64

Guang fell asleep next to Haruto's body, his head resting on his friend's chest, his tears mixing with the blood. Kira wasn't sure what to do. She left him to his grief, crept away and collapsed against a pillar, fighting the urge to scream.

Eventually she stood, wiped her tears away, and busied herself about the cavern, looting supplies from the dead monks underneath the rubble. She found an old wooden bench pushed into a corner of the cavern and smashed it apart, then set a small fire close to Haruto and Guang. The old poet woke and crawled closer to the fire. He said nothing, just lay down, closed his eyes, and drifted back to sleep. Kira collected Haruto's ritual staffs and laid them on top of him, then began picking up rocks and laying them around him. Stone by stone, she built a cairn for Haruto. She'd never been one for praying, barely even knew the names of any gods, but she said a prayer over his grave when it was done, directing it to the only god she thought might listen, the god of war.

She settled down by the fire across from Guang, fed a few more bits of bench to the flames and finally lay down to sleep. Shiki crawled to her then, whistling softly, and snuggled inside Kira's kimono.

When Kira woke the next morning, the fire was ash and embers. Guang was up, standing by Haruto's grave, his head bowed. "Thank you," he said. She stood up next to him, took his hand in hers, and he squeezed it. His eyes were red, and he looked like he'd aged ten years overnight.

After a long while, Guang said, "Time to go." He looked at Haruto's grave one last time, then turned, pulled his satchel over his head, and limped towards the cavern exit. Kira hurried to catch up. She still ached, but most of her wounds had healed. It felt wrong somehow, that she had healed so quickly from the fight that claimed Haruto's life.

Evidence of Orochi's escape was everywhere. The tunnel walls were scraped smooth by his passing and the door leading outside was simply gone, torn from its hinges and flung down the cliff side. It was morning, the sun low and dull behind the puffy grey clouds, but for a wonder it was not snowing. The wooden shack was a ruin, flattened by a brush with a dragon, and there was nothing else on the fourth tier except a floating patch of smoke in the shape of a woman hovering near the edge of the cliff, her smoky face tilted towards the sky.

"You're Izumi?" Guang asked as they waded through the snow towards her.

A ripple passed through Crow's smoke and she glanced over her shoulder at them. "I am Crow. I... was Izumi once."

Guang nodded, though it seemed more to himself than to her. He shuffled right up to the edge of the cliff next to her. "He loved you. Never stopped looking for you, even though he knew what he'd have to do and what it would cost him. He wanted to give you peace."

Crow turned her face back to the sky. "I never asked for any of that," she said sharply.

"Hah! Well, that's life, isn't it? You don't ask for a lot of the stuff it throws at you, but you either look at it like a gift or a curse, and then figure out the rest from there."

Crow's smoke billowed out beneath her, spreading from her legs and staining the snow around them black with soot. "Are you an onmyoji too?" she asked. Kira stepped closer, flicking a dagger into her hand, but Guang chuckled and threw up his hands.

"Not me," he said. "I'm just... Well, I guess I'm just an old poet who tore up his last chance for redemption. And a man who lost his best friend." He sighed. "I hope you find the peace he wanted for you, Izu... sorry, Crow."

Crow frowned at Guang, then turned and leapt off the cliff, a trail of soot falling in her wake. Kira watched her go. She had a feeling she hadn't seen the last of Crow. Whether she liked it or not, they were family, and the bond between onryo went deeper than anything the Herald of Bones had tried to create.

Shiki whistled from inside Kira's kimono and clambered out to perch on her shoulder. She hopped up and down a few times, nuzzled against Kira's cheek, squeaked, leapt to the ground, and then waddled back towards the cavern. Tears stung Kira's eyes.

"What did she say?" Guang asked, staring after the little spirit.

Kira wiped her eyes with her sleeve. "She said goodbye."

"Good riddance, you little carrot!" Guang said, his voice breaking on the words.

Shiki warbled loudly and disappeared into the cavern.

"She said she'll miss you too," Kira said. She'd only known Shiki for a short time, but seeing her leave broke Kira's heart. Yet Shiki was a companion spirit, and with Haruto dead, she no longer had a companion. Kira guessed she'd return to heaven soon enough.

She lurched toward Guang, wrapped her arms around him and hugged him. After a moment, he hugged her back.

They turned away from the cavern and walked down the steps to the third tier. The snow was thinner there. Cherry blossoms and blood splatters covered the ground. Beneath the tree lay Xifeng's body pierced by a thicket of a shining red thorns. The onryo's head lay beneath her bloated body. Guang pointedly did not look that way as they made their way to the next set of steps.

"What do I do now?" Kira asked as they descended to the monastery.

"Hmm?" Guang grunted.

"Heiwa Academy is gone. Yanmei is gone. Haruto... The onryo are defeated." Kira sighed, kicking at the snow. "What do I do?"

Guang sighed, his gaze distant. Then he shivered. "Can you sing?"

Kira nodded. It had been one of her greatest passions when she had been alive, and she remembered that now. Though that was almost a hundred years in the past.

"There's good lien to be made for singers," Guang continued, his voice oddly flat. "Good profession. Goes very well with old poets." He looked at her, smiled, then away.

"But I'm supposed to be a spirit of vengeance."

"Oh? Is that different from a yokai?"

"I don't know."

They limped down to the second plateau in silence. Snow had fallen overnight, turning all the monk's bodies into shadowy white mounds. "Hey," Guang said, "I thought of a title for my masterpiece. *Nightsong, the Hero of Ages*, a three-part epic poem."

Kira shook her head as she navigated the mounds of snow.

"You don't like it?" Guang asked.

"Too generic."

"Hmm," Guang grumbled. "How about *The Onmyoji and the Dragon*?"

Kira shook her head again. "Needs more action. What about *Nightsong Vs the Herald of Bones*?"

Guang chuckled, though it sounded hollow somehow. "We'll come up with something."

"Will Yanmei be in it?" Kira asked.

"Of course! She'll have a starring role in the third act when Nightsong and his heroic, handsome friend take pity on an old woman and her hideously deformed daughter." He laughed again, and Kira joined in.

At the first plateau, the webbing still festooning the buildings brought back all the horrors of the previous day, and Kira huddled deep into her mangled coat. But it was not the cold that made her shiver, she needed to check something. They retraced their steps through the abandoned homes until they came to a small square where several alleyways intersected. Cocooned against a wall were two monks. One, a woman who had cut her own throat, the other a man whose face had been ruined by dark venom crawling through his veins. There was a patch of blood on the snowy ground in the middle of the square. Kira stood over it, chewing her lip, anxiety worming through her chest.

"What is it?" Guang asked.

"He's gone." Grief swelled within her all over again, but she felt something else now, a new determination. "Katsuo is gone."

Guang sighed. "Oh Kira, I'm sorry."

Kira shook her head and stared at Guang. "Haruto once said I could never be an onmyoji. But maybe I can be something else, a spirit who helps other spirits? If I can find yokai, maybe I can help them complete their vengeance. If I can help them move on like you did for Tian, and like Haruto did for Shiori, then maybe that's what a spirit of vengeance is. That's what I can do, what I can be. Someone who seeks vengeance to help others?"

Guang scratched at his beard and nodded. "I don't see why not?" He stepped closer and wrapped an arm around her shoulders, and she leaned into him. "I think Haruto would be proud, and Yanmei too. A spirit who helps other spirits move on. I'm not sure it's ever been a thing before, but you just can't help being unique, can you?" He chuckled.

"And I already have my first mission," Kira said. She hoped Yanmei would be proud. "I can't leave him as a yokai, Guang. I have to help Katsuo move on."

They heard a roar overhead and looked up. Orochi wound across the sky, silhouetted against the grey clouds. Even so high above them, he was enormous. A smaller dragon, orange with only one head, joined him, and they writhed together in a maddening tangle. Then another dragon joined in, and another. Six dragons whirled and streaked in the sky above the monastery, growling and roaring.

Dragons had returned to the mortal realm. Kira doubted things would be the same ever again, but at least Haruto had convinced them not to start a war against humanity. She had to wonder if the humans would be so tolerant.

Epilogue

Shiki stepped out of the cavern and into the snow, soft flakes drifting down and sticking to her coarse hair. She looked left and right, then trumpeted.

"Are they gone?"

Shiki whistled impatiently.

Haruto stepped out of the cavern. The sky was dark and a few fat snowflakes drifted around on a light breeze. High above them, the wind howled over the cliff side, but it didn't reach him so close to the rock. Which was good because his kimono was in tatters, and he was already cold. The wooden shack was a ruin, and Kira and Guang were nowhere to be seen.

"They're gone," Haruto said. His throat felt raw, his voice hoarse. His left arm ached with a sensation he knew far too well. New limbs always ached until they'd settled properly into place. He still had a hole in his chest. The flesh had healed up around it, but the hole straight through him remained. The more he thought about it, the stranger it felt. He'd need to find something to wear soon or people would ask questions. He had to fight the urge to poke his hand through himself out of morbid curiosity.

He'd woken up alone and buried beneath a pile of rocks. Someone, likely Guang or Kira, had laid his ritual staffs on top of him. When he'd finally felt strong enough to dislodge the rocks and sit up, he found Shiki waiting for him. She flung herself into his face and hadn't stopped chatting since. Even now, outside of the cavern again, she was whistling about how excited the others would be when they saw him.

"We don't have to go after them," Haruto said. That quieted her. She glared at him and he shrugged. "Hey, I died. Immortality over. I don't know why I'm alive, but I definitely died. Maybe that's my time served. Maybe I can retire now, find a nice house somewhere, and grow old in peace. Maybe even get a good night's sleep." He couldn't remember the last time he had slept for more than a couple of hours, not for a century at least.

Shiki blasted a sharp trumpet at him and scrambled up his leg. He picked her up by her scruff and deposited her on his shoulder. She narrowed her eyes and stared at him. "Yeah, you're right. I guess we better catch them up." He tucked the stem of the pipe Guang had bought him between his teeth. "Bloody poet could have least left me some leaf."

Haruto turned toward the steps and stopped. Crow floated above a patch of sooty snow in front of him. She folded her arms across her chest and hugged her elbows, just like Izumi used to do.

"I thought you'd have left," Haruto said around the pipe. Shiki whistled a low, quivering note.

"I did," Crow said. "She asked me to come back." The onryo extended a smoky hand and pointed behind Haruto. He turned to find a god leaning against the cliff side, beside the cave entrance. She wore a patchwork robe of myriad colours, an old straw sugegasa and white mask, featureless save for the black void where the eyes should have been and a single crack running down the cheek like a tear.

Haruto shrugged. "I don't suppose you're here to spirit me away to heaven for a bit of peace like you did Yanmei?"

"Peace?" The god of war laughed. Shiki chirped and tried to shuffle across Haruto's shoulder and hide behind his head. "I'm afraid not, onmyoji. You see, there's a war coming and I find myself in need of allies."

"Look elsewhere," Haruto said. "I just died. It's given me a fresh perspective on things. I'm done."

Laughter echoed from the gloom of the cavern entrance. "Done?" an ancient voice rasped. Haruto smelled burnt juniper on the breeze. "Done? You don't really think I'd let you die before you fulfilled your part of our deal, do you, Nightsong? 'Immortality for as long as your wife's spirit still haunts the mortal realm'." A gnarled, stoop-shouldered old man with a face like sloppy porridge stepped out of the cavern. Omoretsu grinned at Haruto and cackled. "As you can see, she still lives. Of a sort." The smile fell from his gnarled face. "And so does Orochi. Which means you owe me, Nightsong. Twice."

Shiki whined. Haruto sighed and shook his head. Perhaps he wouldn't catch up with Kira and Guang after all. "Cabbage!"

Books by Rob J. Hayes

The War Eternal
Along the Razor's Edge
The Lessons Never Learned
From Cold Ashes Risen
Sins of the Mother (coming 2022)
Death's Beating Heart (coming 2022)

The Mortal Techniques novels
Never Die
Pawn's Gambit
Spirits of Vengeance
The Century Blade (short story)

The First Earth Saga
The Heresy Within (The Ties that Bind #1)
The Colour of Vengeance (The Ties that Bind #2)
The Price of Faith (The Ties that Bind #3)
Where Loyalties Lie (Best Laid Plans #1)
The Fifth Empire of Man (Best Laid Plans #2)
City of Kings

It Takes a Thief...
It Takes a Thief to Catch a Sunrise
It Takes a Thief to Start a Fire

Science Fiction
Drones

Printed in the USA
CPSIA information can be obtained
at www.ICGtesting.com
LVHW042140071123
763356LV00034B/461

9 780957 666894